PENGUIN BOOKS

FORCE OF CIRCUMSTANCE

Simone de Beauvoir was born in Paris (above the Café de la Rotonde in Montparnasse) in 1908. Her father was a lawyer of conservative views. She took a degree in philosophy at the Sorbonne in 1929 and was placed second to Jean-Paul Sartre, who became her firm friend. She taught in the *lycées* at Marseilles and Rouen from 1931 to 1937, and from 1938 to 1943 was teaching in Paris. After the war she emerged as one of the leaders of the existentialist movement. Her first novel, *L'Invitée*, was published in 1943, and in an essay, *Pyrrhus et Cinéas*, published in the following year, she developed some of the major themes of existentialism. *Le Sang des autres* appeared in 1945, when she also had a play, *Les Bouches inutiles*, presented at the Théatre des Carrefours. There followed *Tous les hommes sont mortels* and *Pour une morale de l'ambiguité* in 1947. Two years later she published her famous two-volume study of women, *The Second Sex*, and in 1954 won the Prix Goncourt with her novel, *The Mandarins*. Since then she has written *The Long March* (1958), *Memoirs of a Dutiful Daughter* (1959), *Djamila Boupacha* (with Gisèle Halini), *The Prime of Life* (1963), *Force of Circumstance* (1965), *A Very Easy Death* (1966), and *The Woman Destroyed* (1969). Her latest books are *La Vieillesse* (1970), and *All Said and Done* (1974), the fourth volume of her autobiography.

Simone de Beauvoir has travelled widely in Europe and America.

SIMONE DE BEAUVOIR

Force of Circumstance

*

*Translated from the French
by Richard Howard*

PENGUIN BOOKS

Penguin Books Ltd, Harmondsworth, Middlesex, England
Penguin Books Australia Ltd, Ringwood, Victoria, Australia
Penguin Books Canada Ltd, 41 Steelcase Road West, Markham, Ontario, Canada
Penguin Books (N.Z.) Ltd, 182–190 Wairau Road, Auckland 10, New Zealand

—

La Force des choses first published in Paris by Librairie Gallimard 1963
This translation published in Great Britain
by André Deutsch and Weidenfeld & Nicolson 1965
Published in Penguin Books 1968
Reprinted 1975

—

Copyright © Librairie Gallimard, 1963
English translation copyright © G. P. Putnam's Sons, 1964, 1965

—

Made and printed in Great Britain
by Hazell Watson & Viney Ltd,
Aylesbury, Bucks
Set in Monotype Fournier

INTRODUCTION

I HAVE explained why, after *Memoirs of a Dutiful Daughter*, I decided to continue my autobiography. I stopped, breathless, when I had reached the liberation of Paris. I needed to know whether my undertaking was of interest to others. It appears to have been so; yet before resuming, I hesitated once again. Friends, readers, urged me on: 'And then? What happened next? Where are you now? Finish up; you owe us the rest. . . .' But from others as well as from myself there was no lack of objections: 'It's too soon. You don't have a sufficient body of work behind you. . . .' Or else: 'Wait until you can say everything: lacunae, silences, distort the truth.' And also: 'You lack perspective.' And even: 'After all, you reveal more of yourself in your novels.' None of this is untrue; but I have no choice. Serene or sour, the indifference of decrepitude would keep me from grasping my subject: that moment when, hard upon a still-vibrant past, the decline sets in. I wanted my blood to circulate in this narrative; I wanted to fling myself into it, still very much alive – to put myself in question before all questions are silenced. Perhaps it is too soon; but tomorrow it certainly will be too late.

'Everyone knows your story,' I've also been told, 'it's become public property since '44.' But such publicity has been merely one dimension of my private life, and since one of my purposes is to clear up certain misunderstandings, it seems to me worthwhile to tell the whole truth about that life. Involved much more than hitherto with political events, I shall have more to say about them. My narrative, however, will not become more impersonal on that account. If politics is the art of 'foreseeing the present', not being a specialist it is an unforeseen present that I shall discuss: the way in which history has happened to me day by day is an adventure quite as individual as my subjective development.

In the period of which I shall speak, the point was no longer to educate but to fulfil myself; though faces, books, films and encounters mattered to me as a whole, almost none of them was essential to me in itself. When I evoke them, it is often the caprices of memory that control my choice, which does not necessarily imply a value judgement. On the other hand, I shall not linger here over the experiences which I have described elsewhere – my trips to the United States and to China – whereas I shall discuss in detail my visit to Brazil. Of course this will distort the symmetry of my book: so be it. In any case, I make no claim to its being – any more than its predecessor – a *work of art*. The term suggests a statue dying of boredom in some villa garden; it is a collector's term, a consumer's term, not a creator's. I should never think of saying that Rabelais, Montaigne, Saint-Simon or Rousseau produced *works of art*, and it is of little concern to me if such a label is denied to my memoirs. No; not a work of art, but my life with its enthusiasms and disappointments, its convulsions, my life attempting to express itself and not to serve as a pretext for elegance.

This time, too, I shall cut as little as possible. It always amazes me that a memorialist should be criticized for his *longueurs*. If he interests me, I'll read him volume after volume; if he bores me, ten pages is already too much. I do not mention the colour of the sky, the taste of a fruit out of self-indulgence; telling someone else's life, I would note these so-called trivial details in the same abundance, if I knew them. Not only do they allow us to apprehend a period and a person in flesh and blood, but by their non-significance they are the very touch of truth in a true story. They indicate nothing other than themselves, and the only reason to include them is that they were there: that is enough.

Despite my diffidences which also apply to this last volume – it is impossible to tell everything – certain critics have accused me of indiscretion. It is not I who began; I prefer rummaging through my past to leaving the task to others.

It has generally been granted that the previous volumes possess one virtue I had striven for: a sincerity as far from boastfulness as from masochism. I hope I have kept it. For over thirty years I have practised it in my conversations with Sartre, observing myself from day to day with neither shame nor vanity, as I observe the things around me. It is natural to me, not by a special grace, but because of the way in which I consider people, including myself. I believe in our freedom, our responsibility, but whatever their importance, this dimension of our existence eludes description. What can be described is merely our conditioning; I seem to my own eyes an object, a result, without involving the notions of merit or fault in this estimate. If, in the course of time, an action should seem more or less praiseworthy or regrettable, I am much more concerned, in either case, to understand than to judge it. I prefer to fathom rather than to flatter myself, for my love of truth far exceeds my concern for my own image: that love is explained by my own history, and I take no credit for it. In short, because I offer no judgement of myself, I feel no resistance to speaking frankly about my life and myself, at least insofar as I place myself within my own universe. Perhaps my image projected in a different world – that of the psychoanalysts – might disconcert or embarrass me. But so long as it is I who paint my own portrait, nothing daunts me.

My 'impartiality' of course must be understood. A Communist, a Gaullist, would describe these years differently; so would a labourer, a farmer, a colonel, a musician. But my opinions, convictions, perspectives, interests, commitments, are stated; they constitute part of the testimony that I offer on their grounds. I am objective to the degree, in other words, that my objectivity envelops me.

Like its predecessor, this book asks the reader for his collaboration. I present, in order, each moment of my development, and the reader must have the patience not to close the accounts before the end. He is not entitled, for instance, to conclude, as one critic has done, that Sartre likes Guido Reni because he liked him when he was nineteen. Indeed, only malice dictates such blunders, and against malice I do not intend to be on my guard. On the contrary, this book contains everything likely to provoke it, and I should be disappointed if it failed to displease someone. I should also be disappointed if it pleased no one, and that is why I suggest that its truth is not expressed in any one of its pages but only in their totality.

Readers have pointed out many small errors and two or three serious ones in *The Prime of Life*; for all my care, I have certainly made a number of mistakes in this book, too. But I repeat that I have never intentionally distorted the truth.

PART ONE

CHAPTER ONE

We were liberated. In the streets, the children were singing:

Nous ne les reverrons plus,
C'est fini, ils sont foutus.

And I kept saying to myself: It's all over, it's all over. It's all over: everything's beginning. Patrick Walberg, the Leirises' American friend, took us for a jeep ride through the suburbs; it was the first time in years that I'd been out in a car. Once again I wandered after midnight in the mild September air. The bistros closed early, but when we left the terrace of the Rhumerie or the smoky little red inferno of the Montana, we had the sidewalks, the benches, the streets. There were still snipers on the roofs, and my heart would grow heavy when I sensed the vigilant hatred overhead. One night, we heard sirens. An airplane, whose nationality we never discovered, was flying over Paris; V-1s fell on the suburbs and blew houses to bits. Walberg, usually well-informed, said that the Germans were putting the finishing touches to new and even more terrifying secret weapons. Fear returned, and found its place still warm. But joy quickly swept it away. With our friends, talking, drinking, strolling, laughing, night and day we celebrated our deliverance. And all the others who were celebrating too, near or far, became our friends. An orgy of brotherhood! The shadows that had immured France exploded. The tall soldiers, dressed in khaki and chewing their gum, were living proof that you could cross the seas again. They ambled past, and often they stumbled. Singing and whistling, they stumbled along the sidewalks and the subway platforms; stumbling, they danced at night in the bistros and laughed their loud laughs, showing teeth white as children's. Genet, who had no sympathy with the Germans but who detested idylls, declared loudly on the terrace of the Rhumerie that these costumed civilians had no style. Stiff in their black and green carapaces, the occupiers had been something else! For me, these carefree young Americans were freedom incarnate: our own and also the freedom that was about to spread – we had no doubts on this score – throughout the world. Once Hitler and Mussolini had been overthrown and Franco and Salazar driven out, Europe would be cleansed of Fascism for good. Through the C.N.R. charter, France was taking the path of socialism. We believed that the country had been shaken deeply enough to permit a radical remodelling of its structure without new convulsions. *Combat* expressed our hopes by displaying as its motto: 'From Resistance to Revolution.'

This victory was to efface our old defeats, it was ours, and the future it opened up was ours, too. The men now in power had been in the Resistance and, to a greater or lesser extent, we knew them all. We could count many of the important figures in the press and the radio as close friends. Politics had become a family matter, and we expected to have a hand in it. 'Politics is no longer dissociated from individuals,' Camus wrote in *Combat* at the beginning of September, 'it is man's direct address to other men.' We were writers, and that was our job, to address ourselves to other men. Before the war, few intellectuals had tried to understand their epoch; all – or almost all – had failed in the attempt, and the one we had admired the most, Alain, had fallen into disgrace. It was our turn to carry the torch.

I knew then that my destiny was bound to that of all other people; freedom, oppression, the happiness and misery of men was a matter of intimate concern to me. But I have already said that I had no philosophical ambition. Sartre, in *Being and Nothingness*, had sketched a total description of existence whose value depended on his own situation, and he intended to continue this work. He would have to establish his position not only through theoretical speculations, but also by practical choices. Hence he found himself committed to action in a much more radical way than myself. We always discussed his attitudes together, and sometimes I influenced him. But it was through him that these problems, in all their urgency and all their subtlety, presented themselves to me. In this realm, I must talk about him in order to talk about us.

In our youth, we had felt close to the Communist Party insofar as its negativism agreed with our anarchism. We wanted the defeat of capitalism, but not the accession of a socialist society which, we thought, would have deprived us of our liberty. It was in this sense that Sartre wrote in his notebook, on 14 September 1939: 'I am now cured of socialism, if I needed to be cured of it.' Yet in '41, when he was forming a Resistance group, the two words he brought together for its baptism were: socialism and liberty. The war had effected a decisive conversion.

First of all, it had shown him his own historicity; and the shock of this discovery made him realize how much he had been attached to the established order, even while he was condemning it. There is a conservative in every adventurer. To create his image, to project his legend into the future, the adventurer needs a stable society. Utterly dedicated to the adventure of writing, having longed to *be* a great writer, having coveted *la gloire immortelle* since childhood, Sartre had been counting on a posterity that would continue to use the heritage of this century for its own purposes without any break in continuity. At heart, he remained faithful to the same 'aesthetic of opposition' he had believed in at twenty. Relentless in his denunciation of this society's faults, he still had no desire to overthrow it. Suddenly everything fell apart; eternity exploded into a thousand pieces; he found himself drifting aimlessly between a past of illusions and a future of shadows. He defended himself with his morality of *authenticity*: from the point of view of freedom, all situations could be salvaged if one accepted (assumed) them as a project. This solution was still very close to Stoicism, since circumstances often leave us no other way of transcending ourselves than submission. Sartre, who hated all the little deceptions we practise upon ourselves, could not be satisfied for long by disguising his passivity with verbal protest. He realized that, living not in the absolute but in the transitory, he had to renounce *being* and resolve to *do*. This transition was made easier for him by his previous development. As a thinker, a writer, his primary concern had always been to grasp meanings. But after Heidegger and Saint-Exupéry, whom he read in 1940, had convinced him that meanings came into the world only by the activity of man, practice superseded contemplation. He had said to me during the 'phoney war' – he had even written as much in a letter to Brice Parrain – that once peace was restored he would go into politics.

His experience as a prisoner left a profound mark on him. It taught him the meaning of solidarity; far from feeling persecuted, he took great joy in this participation in a communal life. He loathed privileges; his pride compelled him to make his way in the world by his own resources. As merely one cipher among the rest, he took an immense satisfaction in making a success out of all his undertakings, starting from scratch. He made friends, imposed his ideas, organized activities and mobilized the whole camp, at Christmas, to put on and applaud a play he had written against the

Germans, *Bariona*. The difficulties and the warmth of prison *camaraderie* loosened the contradictions in his anti-humanism. Actually, he was in rebellion against bourgeois humanism, which reveres a Nature expressed in man; but if man is still to be created, no task could have impassioned him more. Henceforth, instead of setting individualism in opposition to collectivity, he conceived of them only as linked to each other. He would achieve his freedom not by subjectively accepting the given situation, but by modifying it objectively, by constructing a future in accord with his aspirations. This future, in the very name of the democratic principles to which he was attached, was socialism, from which he had hitherto been diverted only by his fear of losing his individuality; but now he saw it both as humanity's only chance and as a necessary condition of his own fulfilment.

The failure of 'Socialism and Liberty' gave Sartre a lesson in realism; his first serious work came only later, within the F.N. in collaboration with the Communists.

In '41, as I have said,[1] the Communists turned a cold shoulder to the *petit-bourgeois* intellectuals and had started a rumour that Sartre had bought his release by acting as an informer for the Germans. In '43 they wanted unity of action. There was, in fact, a pamphlet, reputedly of Communist origin and printed in the south of France, in which Sartre's name appeared on a blacklist between Châteaubriant and Montherlant; he showed it to Claude Morgan, who exclaimed: 'That's disgraceful!' and they buried the incident. Sartre's relations with the Communist partisans had been perfectly friendly. Now that the Germans were gone, he had every intention of maintaining this accord. Rightist ideologists have explained his alliance with the Communist Party by psychoanalytical jargon; they have imputed it to inferiority or rejection complexes, to repressed aggression, to infantilism and to nostalgia for a church. What nonsense! The masses were behind the Communist Party; socialism could triumph only through the Party. Furthermore Sartre was now aware that his connexion with the proletariat entailed a radical reconsideration of his whole existence. He had always supposed the proletariat to be the universal class. But as long as he believed he could attain the absolute by literary creation, his relation to others (*être pour autrui*) had remained of secondary importance. With his historicity he had discovered his dependence; no more eternity, no more abso-

1. In *The Prime of Life.*

lute. The universality to which, as a bourgeois intellectual, he aspired could now be bestowed on him only by the men who incarnated it on earth. He was already thinking what he later expressed[1]: the true perspective is that of the most disinherited; the hangman can remain ignorant of what he does; the victim experiences his suffering and his death irrecusably; the truth of oppression is the oppressed. It was through the eyes of the exploited that Sartre was to learn what he was. If they rejected him, he would find himself imprisoned in his *petit-bourgeois* individualism.

There were no reservations in our friendship for the U.S.S.R.; the sacrifices of the Russian people had proved that its leaders embodied its true wishes. It was therefore easy, on every level, to cooperate with the Communist Party. Sartre did not contemplate becoming a member. For one thing he was too independent; but above all, there were serious ideological divergences between him and the Marxists. The Marxist dialectic, as he understood it then, suppressed him as an individual; he believed in the phenomenological intuition which affords objects immediately 'in flesh and blood'. Although he adhered to the idea of *praxis*, he had not given up his old, persisting project of writing an *ethics*. He still aspired to *being*; to live morally was, according to him, to attain an absolutely meaningful mode of existence. He did not wish to abandon – and indeed, never has abandoned – the concepts of negativity, of interiority, of existence and of freedom elaborated in *Being and Nothingness*. In opposition to the brand of Marxism professed by the Communist Party, he was determined to preserve man's human dimension. He hoped that the Communists would grant existence to the values of humanism; and he was to try, with the tools they lent him, to tear humanism from the clutches of the bourgeoisie. Apprehending Marxism from the viewpoint of bourgeois culture, he was to place the latter, by an inverse process, in a Marxist perspective. 'Coming from the middle classes, we tried to bridge the gap between the intellectual *petite bourgeoisie* and the Communist intellectuals.'[2] On the political level, he felt that its sympathizers should play a role outside the Communist Party similar to that assumed inside other parties by the Opposition: a role that combined support and criticism.

These pleasant dreams were engendered by the Resistance, which had revealed history to us but had also concealed the class

1. In 1952, in *Les Communistes et la paix*.   2. *Merleau-Ponty vivant*.

struggle. It seemed that all reactionary influences had been politically liquidated along with Nazism; only that fraction of the
bourgeoisie which had cooperated with the Resistance was now
participating in public life and accepted the charter of the C.N.R.
On their side, the Communists supported the government with
'national unanimity'. Thorez came back from the U.S.S.R. and told
the workers it was their duty to revive our industries, to work, to be
patient and to refrain for the time being from all claims. No one spoke
of putting back the clock; reformists and revolutionaries were
taking the same paths into the future. In this atmosphere, all antagonisms became blurred. That Camus was hostile to the Communists
seemed a subjective trait of little importance, since in his struggle to
bring the charter of the C.N.R. into effect he was defending exactly
the same positions they were. Sartre, a Communist sympathizer,
nevertheless approved of *Combat*'s policy enough to write an
editorial for it. Gaullists, Communists, Catholics and Marxists
fraternized. All the newspapers expressed the same ideas. Sartre
gave an interview to *Carrefour*. Mauriac wrote for *Les Lettres
françaises*; we all sang in chorus our hymn of the future.

Soon *Les Lettres françaises* began to grow sectarian. *Action* was
more open-minded; it seemed possible to reach an understanding
with the young men who were running it. Hervé and Courtade
even asked Sartre to join them. He refused because *Action* had attacked Malraux in a way we thought unfair. We were very surprised
when Francis Ponge, who ran the cultural section, told us that a
mountain of articles against Sartre was piling up on his desk. He
published some of them, and Sartre replied with a *Mise au point*
(Definition of Terms). He was blamed for being influenced by
Heidegger: the political position Heidegger had taken did not
retrospectively invalidate all his ideas. Moreover, far from being a
quietism or a nihilism, Existentialism was a definition of man
through action; if it condemned him to anxiety it did so only insofar as it obliged him to accept responsibilities. The hope it denied
him was the idle reliance on anything other than himself; it was an
appeal to man's will. Sartre was convinced that henceforth the
Marxists could no longer consider him an adversary. So many
obstacles had been overcome that none now seemed insuperable.
From others and from ourselves, we hoped for everything.

Those around us shared in this euphoria. First the family and the
old guard of the 'fiestas'. Then there were the younger members

who had joined us. G.-F. Rolland, though he had become a Communist at the age of twenty in the *maquis* and was deeply convinced of the virtues of the Party, tolerated our deviations good-humouredly. Scipion laughed so loudly that we thought he was happy; his specialities were parodies, puns, spoonerisms and picaresque anecdote. Gabriel Astruc, of the great liquid smile, wrote for all the newspapers in strict rotation, and when he wasn't writing he talked – mostly about himself. With touching narcissism, he would make the most naïve and raw admissions about his private life. To be twenty or twenty-five in September of '44 seemed the most fantastic piece of luck: all roads lay open. Journalists, writers, budding film-makers, were all arguing, planning, passionately deciding, as if their future depended on no one but themselves. Their gaiety fortified my own. In their company I was their age, though without relinquishing anything of a maturity so dearly come by that I wasn't far from taking it for wisdom; thus I reconciled – in a fleeting illusion – the contradictory privileges of youth and age. It seemed to me that I knew a great deal and that I could do almost anything.

Soon the exiles began to return. Bianca had spent a year hidden in the Vercors with her parents and her husband; she had married one of her classmates. Raymond Aron had left in 1940 for London where he and André Labarthe had edited a review called *La France libre* which the Gaullists hadn't approved of. Although he wasn't given to effusiveness, when he appeared one morning at the Café de Flore we fell into each other's arms. Albert Palle had reached England somewhat later; parachuted back into France, he had fought in the *maquis*. I found it very moving to see these faces once again; then there were the new ones. Through Camus we met Father Bruckberger, chaplain of the F.F.I., who had just finished making *Les Anges du péché* with Bresson. He had a *bon vivant* act, and would sit white-robed in the Rhumerie, smoking a pipe, drinking punch and talking lustily. Aron took us to lunch with Corniglion-Molinier who had been condemned to death by Vichy; his furniture had been confiscated, and he was camping out in a vast, luxurious but empty apartment on the Avenue Gabriel; attentive and charming, he was full of stories about the French in London. Romain Gary told us stories, too, one evening on the terrace of the Rhumerie. At a cocktail party given by *Les Lettres françaises* I caught a glimpse of Elsa Triolet and Aragon. The Communist writer we enjoyed most of all was Ponge; he talked, as he wrote, in little touches, malicious and slightly self-satisfied. At Versailles, during an evening of festivities that included a play by La Fontaine, under the auspices of Éditions de Minuit, I talked for a while with Lise Deharme. I can no longer recall all the hands I shook, all the smiles I exchanged, but I know how much all this sociability pleased me at the time.

These meetings revealed to me a history that was my own but that I had not known before. Aron described the bombing of London in great detail, the cool-headedness of the English, their endurance; the V-1s, which I had watched going over Neuilly-sous-Clermont, red against the black sky, across the Channel were a raucous whistle, an explosion, corpses. 'When you heard one, you had to throw yourself flat on the sidewalk,' Aron told us. 'Once, as I was getting up, I saw a very old lady who had stayed on her feet. She was looking me up and down. I was so annoyed that I reprimanded her: "Madame, in cases like this one should lie down!"' He lent me his collection of *La France libre*, and now I could decipher the war not from the perspective of Paris but from the point of view of London, from the other side. I had been living in a prison; now the world was restored to me.

A ravaged world. Immediately after the Liberation, the Gestapo's torture chambers were discovered; mass graves were unearthed. Bianca told me about the Vercors; she told me about the weeks her father and her husband had spent hidden in a cave; the newspapers gave us the details of massacres, of the executions of hostages; they published accounts of the annihilation of Warsaw. This brutal revelation of the past thrust me back into horror; one's new delight in life gave way to shame at having survived. Some of us were unable to accept. Jausion,[1] sent to the front as a war correspondent by *Franc-Tireur*, did not come back, and his death was almost certainly not accidental. Victory was a costly commodity. In September, the Allied Air Forces turned Le Havre into a rubbish heap; the dead numbered thousands. The Germans dug themselves into Alsace and around Saint-Nazaire. In November, those huge silent engines of destruction, the V-2s, so much more effective than the

1. His fiancée, as I have said, had been deported. He had been arrested in the Place de la Concorde during the insurrection, then exchanged for a German officer just before the entry of the Allies. He left one novel: *Un Homme marche dans la ville*.

V-1s, began to fall on London: were they the secret weapons Walberg had talked about, or were there others still to come, even more dreadful? Von Runstedt's army overran Holland and created a famine there. In Belgium, German troops regained a little of the ground they had lost and massacred the inhabitants. In a flash, I saw them re-entering Paris in triumph. And one did not dare to think about what was happening in the concentration camps now that the Germans knew they had lost.

Materially, the situation had grown even worse than the year before; transportation was in chaos; there was a shortage of food, coal, gas and electricity. When it got cold, Sartre wore an old, threadbare lumber jacket. One of his prison-camp friends sold me a rabbit coat that kept me warm; but, except for a black suit that I kept for special occasions, I had only the oldest of clothes to put on underneath it, and I continued wearing shoes with wooden soles. Moreover, this didn't matter to me in the least. Ever since I had fallen off my bicycle, I had had a tooth missing; the gap was quite visible, and I didn't even think about having a false one put in: what was the point? In any case, I was old, I was thirty-six; a fact I noted without the slightest bitterness. The flood of events and activities constantly took me out of myself, and I was the least of my worries.

Because of this general poverty, very little was happening in the realm of literature, the arts and the theatre. Nevertheless, the organizers of the Salon d'Automne made it into a great cultural manifestation, a retrospective of pre-war painting. The canvases had been packed away in the corners of studios and in the dealers' cellars because of the Germans, and it was a great event to see them brought out into the light of day. A whole section was devoted to Picasso; we visited him quite often and knew his recent work, but here all his work of the past few years was gathered together. There were beautiful canvases by Braque, Marquet, Matisse, Dufy, Gromaire, Villon, and the astonishing 'Job' of Francis Guber; the surrealists exhibited too: Dominguez, Masson, Miró, Max Ernst. Loyal as ever to the Salon d'Automne, the bourgeoisie arrived in droves, but this time they were not offered their usual fare; in front of the Picassos, they snickered.

There were not many books coming out; I was bored by Aragon's *Aurélien*; and no less by *The Walnut Trees of Altenburg* which had been published in Switzerland a year before and had prompted old Groethuysen to remark: 'Malraux is in full possession of all his weaknesses.' *L'Arbalète* published a collection of texts, mostly translated by Marcel Duhamel, by American authors both unknown – Henry Miller, Horace McCoy, Nathanael West, Damon Runyon, Dorothy Baker – and known – Hemingway, Richard Wright, Thomas Wolfe, Thornton Wilder, Erskine Caldwell, and, of course, Saroyan; it was impossible to open any periodical without coming across his name. There was also an English writer in that number: Peter Cheyney. Several new English writers were being mentioned – Auden, Spender, Graham Greene – but nothing was known about them yet. Someone lent me Hillary's *The Last Enemy*; shot down over the Channel, this young pilot, one of the last of the long-haired Oxonians, described with a slightly discordant laugh the operations and grafts that had restored his eyes, face and hands; by its rejection of all humanism and all heroism, the story managed to transcend the episode that had inspired it. I also read a great quantity of war books – of lesser quality – specially printed in the U.S.A. for export; on their white, red-ruled covers, Liberty brandished her torch. In *A Walk in the Sun*, Harry Brown told the story of a handful of men landing in Italy. In *G.I. Joe*, Ernie Pyle drew the portrait of the American soldier. The Americans adored this 'little man in a tattered uniform who hates war but loves and understands soldiers'.[1] He described the everyday side of war: 'The war of the men who wash their socks in their helmets.'[2]

On stage, *Huis clos* was revived. Dullin put on *Life is a Dream*. The 'Spectacle des Alliés' at the Pigalle was mostly a patriotic ceremony; the plays given were of very slight interest. I went to a private performance of Malraux's film *L'Espoir* which moved me as much as the book. Except for the Capra series *Why We are Fighting* and some old Mack Sennett shorts, the cinema had very little to offer. Patience! There were fantastic stories of the wonders taking place in Hollywood. A twenty-seven-year-old genius named Orson Welles had revolutionized the cinema; he had succeeded in giving the backgrounds of his shots as clear a focus as the foreground, and in his interior shots the ceilings were visible. The technical revolution was so complete, it was said, that we would need special equipment to show the latest American films.

I sent *The Blood of Others* to Gallimard; Sartre gave them *The Age of Reason* and *The Reprieve*. My *Pyrrhus et Cinéas* was

1. Steinbeck.   2. Steinbeck.

published. It was one of the first books to appear after the Liberation; in the general euphoria, and because we had been starved for ideology and literature for four years, this slender essay was very well received. I began to write again. I had all my time to myself because Sartre, who had asked for a leave of absence from the University, was earning money from the cinema and the theatre; we had always pooled our resources, we continued to do so, and I was no longer obliged to worry about food. I have so often advised women to be independent and said that independence begins in the purse, that I feel I must explain this attitude which at the time seemed to speak for itself. My material autonomy was assured, since if the need arose I could always go back to my teaching post;[1] it would have seemed stupid and even criminal to sacrifice precious hours in order to prove to myself day by day that I still had this autonomy. I have never directed my actions according to principles but according to ends; I had plenty to do; writing had become a demanding task. It also guaranteed my moral autonomy; in the solitude of risks taken, of decisions to be made, I made my freedom much more real than by accommodating myself to any money-making routine. For me, my books were a real fulfilment, and as such they freed me from the necessity to affirm myself in any other way. I therefore devoted myself wholly, and without scruples, to *All Men are Mortal*. Every morning I went to the Bibliothèque Mazarine to read historical narratives; it was icily cold there, but the story of Charles the Fifth, the episode of the Anabaptists, took me so far from my own body that I forgot to shiver.

The year before, as I have recounted previously, we had conceived two projects: an encyclopedia and a review. Sartre did not pursue the first one, but he held fast to the second. Because of the paper shortage, the only authorized publications were those that had existed before the war and those that had been founded in the free zone during the Occupation. *Esprit*, *Confluences* and *Poésie 44* were interesting enough, but inadequate to express the age we were living in. We had to find something else. Sartre himself has given an account of his intentions:

If truth is one, I thought, then we should seek it, as Gide said of God, nowhere except everywhere. Every social product and every attitude – from the most intimate to the most public – are allusive embodiments of it. An anecdote reflects a whole epoch as much as a political

1. I had been reinstated at the University, and had taken a leave of absence.

constitution does. We would be hunters of meaning, we would tell the truth about the world and about our lives.[1]

In September, we formed an editorial committee; Camus was too absorbed by *Combat* to be a member; Malraux refused; it was made up of Raymond Aron, Michel Leiris, Merleau-Ponty, Albert Ollivier, Jean Paulhan, Sartre and myself; in those days, none of these names clashed.

We tried to find a title. Leiris, who still retained a taste for scandal from the surrealist days of his youth, proposed a name in that vein: *Grabuge* (Squabble); we didn't use it because, although we certainly wanted to disturb people, we also wanted to be constructive. The title was to convey our positive commitment to the present – so many newspapers had been saying the same things for so many years that there was scarcely anything left to choose between them. We agreed on *Les Temps Modernes*; it was dull, but the reference to the Chaplin film pleased us. (Often, after the magazine had been started, the Argus Agency would send us clippings about the film.) And then, Paulhan pointed out in his mock-serious tone, from which real seriousness was not excluded, it is important to be able to refer to a review by its initials, as in the case of the *N.R.F.*; and *T.M.* had a good ring to it. The second problem was the format of the cover. Picasso designed one which was very handsome but really more suitable for an art magazine than for *Les Temps Modernes*; it was impossible to fit a table of contents into it; its partisans on the committee, however, made it the subject of several quarrels that grew quite violent, though without bitterness. In the end, a Gallimard designer submitted a project that reconciled us all. We were discussing no more than trifles, but already I was beginning to enjoy myself enormously; this community of enterprise seemed to me the highest form of friendship. In January, since Sartre was away on a trip, I went in his name to Soustelle, the Minister of Information at that time, to ask him to allot us a quota of paper. Leiris, who knew Soustelle through the Musée de l'Homme, went with me. Soustelle was very pleasant but the composition of the editorial committee made him shy away slightly. 'Aron? Why Aron?' He complained of his anti-Gaullist attitude. In the end, he made promises which were kept several months later.

As soon as the trains began running again, we went to spend three weeks with Mme Lemaire; sitting in a packed compartment,

1. *Merleau-Ponty vivant.*

we rode from eight in the morning till eight at night; the train didn't take the usual route; we left our luggage at the Lion d'Angers and walked the seventeen kilometres from there to La Pouèze without a stop. This stay, like all the others, was happy and without incident.

Back in Paris, I made it my principal task to get my play *Les Bouches inutiles* performed. Sartre had given a copy to Raymond Rouleau. He told me that I had 'not set my sights high enough'; the concision of the dialogue bordered on aridity. I passed the script on to Vitold; he told me he was quite willing to direct it. Badel, the director of the Vieux-Colombier, agreed to produce. Vitold began to hold auditions and cast some of the parts; I had always intended the part of Clarice for Olga. It was suggested that Douking should do the sets, and I discussed them with him. All this activity meant that I went to dinner several times at Badel's with Sartre. One evening we played Murder, and I was very proud because I was the only detective who discovered the killer. I grew fond of Gaby Sylvia whose beauty and talent left her unsatisfied and who wanted to educate herself: Robert Kanters was tutoring her quite seriously for the *baccalauréat*. But I didn't really feel at ease in this too-luxurious salon where people did not speak my language. Gaby Sylvia wore gowns by Rochas that dazzled one by their cunning simplicity; next to them, my black suit, the artlessly simple dress I had had made in La Pouèze, seemed almost a discourtesy. I was very sociable in those days, but the ritual of society bored me.

'Would you and Sartre like to meet Hemingway?' Lise asked me one evening. 'Of course!' I said. That was the sort of proposal that really pleased me. Though this one didn't surprise me all that much. Lise's principal pastime, since the Liberation, was what she called 'Hunt-the-American'. The Americans were very free with their cigarettes and their rations, and Lise, always famished, had every intention of profiting from their prodigality. Usually alone, though sometimes, in the beginning, with Scipion, she would take a seat on the terrace of the Café de la Paix or along the Champs-Élysées and wait for a G.I. to speak to her; she never lacked admirers. If she found one who seemed both discreet and entertaining, she would accept a drink, a jeep ride, a dinner; in exchange for the promise of a rendezvous, which she generally failed to keep, she would bring back to the hotel tea, Camels, instant coffee and tins of Spam. The game had its risks. Along the boulevards, soldiers would call out: 'Zigzig Blondie'; she would laugh and walk on; if they didn't stop, she would shout insults at them that would make a soldier blush, for her English vocabulary equalled her French in eloquence. One of them, in the Place de l'Opéra, got annoyed; he banged her head against a lamp-post and knocked her out. But she had enjoyable encounters too, sometimes. She had made friends with a happy-go-lucky, blond giant who turned out to be Hemingway's younger brother; he used to show her photos of his wife and children, bring her cartons of food and talk to her about the best-seller he was going to write. 'I know the recipe,' he told her.

That evening, Hemingway, who was a war correspondent, had just arrived in Paris and had arranged for his brother to come and see him at the Ritz where he was staying; the brother had suggested that Lise come with him and bring Sartre and myself along. The room, when we went in, bore no resemblance at all to the idea I had always had of the Ritz; it was large but ugly, with its two brass bedsteads; Hemingway was lying on one of them in pyjamas, his eyes shielded by a green eyeshade; on a table within easy reach stood a respectable quantity of Scotch, some bottles half empty, others entirely so. He heaved himself up, grabbed hold of Sartre and hugged him. 'You're a general!' he said as he squeezed him. 'Me, I'm only a captain; you're a general!' (When he'd been drinking he always pushed modesty a bit too far.) Our conversation, punctuated by numerous glasses of Scotch, continued in this enthusiastic vein; despite his flu, Hemingway was bursting with vitality. Sartre, overcome by sleep, tottered away at about three in the morning; I stayed until dawn.

Bost wanted to become a journalist; Camus read the manuscript of the book he had written during the war about his experiences as an infantry private, *Le Dernier des métiers*; he took an option on it for the series *Espoir* which he was editing for Gallimard and sent Bost to the front as a war correspondent. Whenever you asked Camus for a favour, he would do it so readily that you never hesitated to ask for another; and never in vain. Several of our younger friends also wanted to work for *Combat*; he took them all in. Opening the paper in the morning was almost like opening our mail. Towards the end of November, the United States wanted its war effort to be better known in France and invited a dozen reporters to the States. I've never seen Sartre so elated as the day Camus offered him the job of representing *Combat*. To obtain all the necessary papers, as well as the dollars, he had to go through a labyrinth of red tape. He made his way through the whole thing during a freezing December with a joy marred only by a nagging uncertainty: in those days nothing was ever definite. And, in fact, there were two or three days when it looked as though the project had fallen through; Sartre's dismay then told me how much he wanted to go.

It meant so many things, America! To begin with, everything inaccessible; its jazz, cinema and literature had nourished our youth, but it had always been a great myth to us as well; myths do not allow themselves to be handled. The trip was to be made by plane; it seemed unbelievable that Lindbergh's great exploit should now be within our reach. America was also the country which had sent our deliverance; it was the future on the march; it was abundance, and infinite horizons; it was a crazy magic lantern of legendary images; the mere thought that they could be seen with one's own eyes set one's head whirling. I rejoiced, not only for Sartre's sake, but also for my own, because I knew that one day I was sure to follow him down this new road.

I had hoped that the New Year celebrations would revive the gaiety of the 'fiestas', but on 24 December the German offensive had only just been halted, and the air was full of anxiety. Bost was at the front, Olga was worried; we spent a little while with Camille and Dullin, but it was dreary there; at about one in the morning, we walked with Olga and a few others to Saint-Germain-des-Prés and finished the night at the beautiful Evelyne Carral's; we ate turkey; Mouloudji sang his usual successes and Marcel Duhamel – who had not yet begun editing the *Série noire* – sang some American songs with great charm. We celebrated New Year's Eve with Camus who was living in Gide's apartment on the Rue Vaneau; there was a trapeze there and a piano. Directly after the Liberation, Francine Camus had arrived from Algeria, very blonde, very fresh-looking, and beautiful in her slate-blue suit; but we hadn't met her often, and several of the guests we didn't know at all. Camus pointed one of them out to us, a man who had scarcely spoken a word all evening. 'He's the man I modelled *The Stranger* on,' he said. For us, the gathering lacked intimacy. One young woman forced me into a corner and began accusing me vindictively: 'You don't believe in love!' At about two in the morning, Francine played some Bach. No one drank very much except Sartre; he was convinced that the party was just like old times, and he was soon too elated with alcohol to be able to tell the difference.

He left on 12 January, in a military plane. There was no civilian mail service between the United States and France; the only way I could get news of him was by reading his articles. He began his career as a journalist with a *gaffe* that shook Aron to the core: he described the anti-Gaullism of the American leaders during the war with such satisfaction that he was almost sent straight back to France.

According to an agreement made between Camus and Brisson, some of the articles were supposed to be given to the latter; Sartre sent him his impressions, the notes and reflections written in passing, keeping the pages that had cost him most effort and struggle for *Combat*. Camus, having read a sprightly and entertaining description of American cities in *Le Figaro* the day before, was flabbergasted when he received a careful study of the Tennessee Valley Authority.

Then my chance came. My sister had married Lionel, who was now attached to the French Institute in Lisbon; he was the editor of a Franco-Portuguese review called *Affinidades*. He invited me, on behalf of the Institute, to go to Portugal and give some lectures on the Occupation. I rushed to the offices of the Relations Culturelles and demanded a travel permit. I had to ask an enormous number of people; but they all promised to do what they could, and I was consumed with hope.

At the Vieux Colombier, they began rehearsing the third and fourth scenes of *Les Bouches inutiles*. I was getting material together for *Les Temps Modernes* and making contacts. At the Deux Magots, I met Cyril Connolly, the editor of the English review *Horizon* which had published the work of Resistance writers during the war, among others Aragon's *Crève-Coeur*. He told me about the new English literature and about Koestler, who was living in London. I had enjoyed *Spanish Testament*; on Christmas night, Camus had lent me *Darkness at Noon* and the next night I had read it straight through without stopping; I was pleased to learn that Koestler enjoyed Sartre's books. At lunch, at dinner, I kept meeting old friends again; we went to Chéramy, to the Vieux Paris, to the Armagnac, to the Petit Saint-Benoît; I spent my evenings with one or another at the Montana, the Méphisto or the Deux Magots. Bost took me to lunch once at the Restaurant du Scribe, to which all the war correspondents had *entrée*; it was an American enclave in the heart of Paris: white bread, fresh eggs, jam, sugar, Spam.

I made new friends. Before the war, an unknown woman had sent Sartre a copy of her little book *Tropisms*, which had gone unnoticed and whose quality struck us both; this was Nathalie Sarraute; Sartre had written to her and met her. In '41 she had worked in a Resistance group with Alfred Péron; Sartre had seen her again recently, and I had made her acquaintance. That winter I went out with her a lot. She was the daughter of Russian Jews exiled by the Czarist persecutions at the beginning of the century, and it was to these circumstances, I suppose, that she owed her restless subtlety. Her vision of the world spontaneously accorded with Sartre's own ideas: she was hostile to all essentialism, she did not believe in clearly defined characters or emotions, or, indeed, in any ready-made notions. In the book she was writing at the time, *Portrait of a Man Unknown*, she was determined to recapture, beneath its commonplaces, life's ambiguous truth. She was very reticent and talked mostly about literature, but with passion.

During the autumn, through my companion in a cinema queue on the Champs-Élysées, I met a tall, elegant, blonde woman with a face both brutally ugly and radiantly alive: Violette Leduc. A few days later, at the Flore, she handed me a manuscript. 'Confessions of a woman of the world,' I said to myself. I opened the book: 'My Mother never gave me her hand.' I read the first half of the story without stopping; it fell off suddenly, the end was just padding. I told Violette Leduc this. She scrapped the last chapters and wrote new ones as good as the beginning; not only did she have talent, she knew how to work. I suggested the book to Camus; he accepted it immediately. When *L'Asphyxie* came out, several months later, it did not reach a wide public, but it gained the favour of many discriminating readers and won its author the friendship of Genet and Jouhandeau. Violette Leduc was not, in fact, a *femme du monde* at all; when I knew her, she earned her living by going out to the farms of Normandy, finding meat and butter, and bringing them back in her arms to Paris; she invited me to dinner several times in the black-market restaurants she supplied with food; she was gay and often funny, but she gave the impression that there was something violent and mistrustful lurking beneath her apparent openness; she told me with great pride about her bargaining, her forced marches across the countryside, the village bistros, the trucks, the dark trains; she felt quite naturally on the same footing as the peasants, the truck drivers and the pedlars she dealt with. It was Maurice Sachs, with whom she was very friendly, who had encouraged her to write. She lived in utter solitude. I introduced her to Colette Audry, whom I saw quite often, and also to Nathalie Sarraute; a friendship sprang up between them, but was soon broken off by the clash of their temperaments.

The weeding out of collaborators after the Liberation immediately created divisions among the ex-members of the Resistance; everyone agreed that the way it was done was wrong; but while Mauriac preached forgiveness, the Communists were demanding severity; Camus, in *Combat*, was trying to work out a middle course; Sartre and I shared his point of view: vengeance is useless, but there were certain men who could have no place in the world we were trying to build. Practically speaking, I had little to do with it; I had enrolled in the C.N.E. on principle, but I never so much as showed my face at any of their meetings; I thought that Sartre's presence there made mine superfluous. However, hearing about the decisions of the Committee through Sartre, I quite agreed that its members should not write in reviews and newspapers which accepted material from ex-collaborators. I did not want to hear the voices of people who had consented to the death of millions of Jews and Resistance members; I did not want to find their name in any publication side by side with my own. We had said: 'We shall not forget'; I was not forgetting that.

It was a tremendous shock, therefore, when a few days before Brasillach's trial someone – I can't remember who it was – asked me to sign a document Brasillach's lawyers were sending around: the undersigned declared their solidarity as writers with the defendant, and asked the court's indulgence.[1] In no way, on no level, did I feel the slightest solidarity with Brasillach; how many times I had wept with rage as I read his articles! 'No mercy for the murderers of our country,' he used to write; he had claimed the right 'to point out those who betray us' and had used it freely; under his editorship, the staff of *Je suis partout* denounced people, specified victims, and urged the Vichy Government to enforce the wearing of the yellow star in the Free Zone. They had done more than accept; they had demanded the death of Feldman, Cavaillès,

1. I don't recall the exact wording of the petition, but this was its substance.

Politzer, Bourla, the deportation of Yvonne Picard, Péron, Kaan, Desnos. It was with these friends, dead or alive, that I felt solidarity; if I lifted a finger to help Brasillach, then it would have been their right to spit in my face. There was not even a moment's hesitation on my part, the problem did not even arise. Camus had the same reaction. 'We have nothing to do with those people,' he said to me. 'The judges will decide; it's their business, not ours.'

Nevertheless, I wanted to watch the trial; my signature carried no weight, my refusal was a mere gesture, but even a gesture commits one to a responsibility, and it seemed too easy to evade mine by mere indifference. I managed to get a seat in the press gallery; it was not a pleasant experience. The reporters casually took notes; they drew little pictures in their notebooks; they yawned; the lawyers declaimed; the judges sat; the presiding magistrate presided; it was a play, a ceremony. For the accused it was the moment of truth in which his life and death were weighed in the balance. Confronted by the futile pomp of the assizes, he alone, his fate condensed into this moment, existed in flesh and blood. He faced his accusers calmly, and when the sentence fell he did not flinch. In my eyes, this courage effaced nothing; it is the Fascists who attach more importance to how we die than to our acts. Nor did I accept the way in which time had changed my anger into resignation; resignation cannot bring the dead to life, nor wash their murderers clean. But, like so many others, I was troubled by the apparatus of justice, which by transforming this executioner into a victim, gave his condemnation an appearance of inhumanity. As I came out of the Palais de Justice, I met some Communist friends and told them about my distress. 'You should have stayed at home then,' they replied dryly.

Some days later, Camus confided somewhat sheepishly that, yielding to certain pressures and for reasons that he did not explain very clearly, he had finally signed a petition for a recommendation of clemency. Personally, although on the morning of the execution I could scarcely tear my thoughts away from it, I have never regretted my abstention. People have condemned the weeding out of collaborators for dealing more severely with those who talked approvingly about the Atlantic Wall than with those who built it. To me, it seems utterly unjust that economic collaboration should have been passed over, but not that Hitler's propagandists in this country should have been so severely dealt with. By trade, by vocation, I attach an enormous importance to words. Simone Weil used to demand that anyone who used writing to tell lies to men should be put on trial, and I understand what she meant. There are words as murderous as gas chambers. Jaurès' assassin was armed with words, words drove Salengro to suicide. In the case of Brasillach, there was no question of a mere 'offence of opinion'; his denunciations, his advocacy of murder and genocide constituted a direct collaboration with the Gestapo.

The Germans had lost, but they were desperately hanging on. Famine: they had brought the ancient scourge back to Europe again. Scratching at the earth, gnawing the bark of trees, thousands of the Dutch had struggled in vain against this medieval death. Bost brought back some photos from Holland that Camus showed me. 'We can't publish these!' he said, and he spread out on his desk pictures of children without bodies and without faces: nothing but eyes; huge, mad eyes. The newspapers only released the least ghastly, and even those one could scarcely bear to look at.

On the evening of 27 February, I got into the train for Hendaye, armed with escudos and my travel permit; a scrap of paper with red, white and blue stripes, it had, in my eyes, all the glamour of an old parchment scroll with a thick wax seal. My neighbour was studiously reading a life of Stalin. 'It's very dry,' he said: the whole night, he kept up an exchange of remarks on Bolshevism with two young women; on the whole, he was pro. I finished Peter Cheyney's *Poison Ivy*; I began Graham Greene's *Brighton Rock* and towards dawn I fell asleep. Suddenly the sky was blue: Hendaye. Except for myself and a little old man who was also going to Madrid, the end of the line; to cross a frontier was still a rare privilege. I had not done so for six years, and it was fifteen since I had last said good-bye to Spain. I had to wait an hour in the office of the commanding officer. At last the barrier was raised, I saw once more the customs officers' shiny two-cornered caps. By the side of the road, a woman was selling oranges, bananas and chocolate; my throat gagged with desire and revulsion: all this plenty only a few yards away from us, why was it forbidden? Suddenly all the shortages in France no longer seemed inevitable; I had the impression that someone was imposing a penance on us. Who? And with what right? At customs, they changed my escudos and refused my francs. Carrying my suitcase, I walked the mile and a half between the frontier and Irun, reduced to a heap of ruins by the Civil War. On the train I met the old man again. He told me that the Spaniards who had seen me go by along the road had said: 'She must be poor; she has no stockings!' And it was true that we were poor; no stockings, no oranges, and our money was worthless. On the station platforms I saw young women sauntering, laughing and chatting, their legs in silk stockings; in the towns we passed through I saw shop windows piled high with food. When we stopped, men walked along the platform selling fruit, sweets, ham; the station buffets were crammed with things to eat. I remembered the station at Nantes, where we were all so hungry and so tired, and where we could find nothing to buy but a few crumbling cookies at an exorbitant price. A furious solidarity with the poverty of France raged inside me.

Then I fell asleep; when I awoke, France was far behind; above the plateaux with their velvety covering of frost spread a sky of triumphant blue. Spain. The Escorial, just as it had been fifteen years before; in other days I had gazed at the age-old stones without surprise; now their permanence disconcerted me; the norm, it seemed to me, was the ruined villages and the ramshackle houses in the suburbs of Madrid.

In Madrid, I could not find my past; the same shadowy cafés were there on the Gran Vía, the same smell of hot oil hung over the Plaza Mayor, but my eyes had changed; the abundance that had been invisible before seemed something quite new to me now and dazzling. Silk, wool, leather, food! I walked till I was out of breath, and as I walked I ate; I sat down and ate – raisins, brioches, *gambas*, olives, pastry, fried eggs, milk chocolate; I drank wine and real coffee. In the crowded streets of old Madrid, in the wealthy neighbourhoods, I watched all the passers-by for whom the dramatic history I had just lived through was no more than a rumour. I was stopped short by a display window: superb photographs with captions underneath extolling the heroism of 'the women of Germany during the war', the heroism of the *Volksturm*; it was a German propaganda centre. I stood there, I saw with my own eyes these pictures of heroic crusaders, members of the S.S. A little later, Madrid streamed with light; I mixed with the crowd that flowed indolently up and down the Alcala, just as it used to; here, the thread of time had been mended, but it was not my time, mine had been broken, forever. Suddenly my mind was filled with anguish; one day, in Rouen, another conscience had taken my place in the centre of things; on the Alcala, it was the same shock that harrowed me. Until that moment, the subject of history had been France; now Spain, separate and foreign, was imposing its presence on me with such force that it became the subject instead; France was becoming a misty object on the horizon, and I myself, powerless to affect these places where my body moved, had ceased to exist. There was merely a thick fog of weariness that belonged to no one, dragging itself through the crowd.

Next day I was myself again; but I walked through the Prado like a bored tourist. I was cut off from El Greco, from Goya, from the past, from eternity; my century clung to my feet and hindered my steps; I did not fully return to myself until it had been restored to me, on the bald, battered, cracked hill where the University used to stand. There were people sitting about on this empty lot, children were playing, men were sleeping; all around rose tiers of new apartment houses and factories; in the centre, the remains of houses, stretches of wall, doors that led nowhere; in the wrecked villages of Normandy, I had walked among rubbish heaps that were brand new, but these bricks had the dignity conferred on ruins, since Volney and Horace Vernet, by literature and art; yet their history was engraved in my own life, deep inside me; that, too, was a change. In the old days I walked through a universal time, as though along a road; now it was inside me, a dimension of my experience; at intervals, stretching into the distance, was the inscription: VIVA FRANCO; red and yellow flags fluttered on all the new apartment buildings. *I was wearing a red and yellow scarf and a man had spat after me: 'None of that here!'* I considered the dry plains of Castile stretching out at my feet, and the distant snow-covered mountains, and at last managed to return to reality: 1945, Franco's Spain. There were *falangistas*, policemen and soldiers on every street corner; on the sidewalks, a procession of priests and little children dressed in black went by, carrying crosses. The well-fed bourgeois I passed on the Gran Vía had hoped for a German victory. And the splendour of their avenues was only a façade.

A friend had given me the address of some Spanish people who were anti-Franco. On their advice I went to Tetuán, to Vallecas. Just north of Madrid, I saw, suspended on the hillsides, a district the size of a big town and sordid as a shantytown: hovels with red roofs and rubble walls, filled with naked children, goats and hens; no drains and no water. Young girls passed back and forth, bent beneath the weight of buckets; people walked about barefoot or in slippers, almost naked; occasionally a flock of sheep would cross one of the alleys, raising a cloud of red dust. Vallecas was less rustic, it smelled of factories; but the poverty was the same; the streets were used as garbage dumps; the women washed out their rags on the doorsteps of their huts; they were all dressed in black, their faces so hardened by poverty that they looked almost wicked. A worker earns nine to twelve pesetas per day, I was told; I looked at what things cost, and I understood why nobody in the markets seemed to smile. These people were getting from a quarter to a half pound of bread a day, and a handful of chick-peas, which cost five pesetas a pound on the black market. Eggs and meat were completely beyond the means of people in the suburbs. The big baskets of rolls and fritters I saw women selling on the corners of the main streets were treats only for the rich, like the people I had seen in the railway stations, and they alone profited from the abundance I had envied.

I looked, I listened. I was told how, during the war years, the Falange had collaborated with Germany; the police had been in the hands of the Gestapo; the leaders had attempted to propagate anti-Semitism, but in vain, for the word Jew today awakened no echo among the Spaniards. The people as a whole were growing increasingly impatient under the dictatorship. The week before, three bombs had exploded in the quarters of some *falangistas* and two men had been killed; as a reprisal, Franco had ordered seventeen Communists to be shot; many more were killed without such publicity, and torture was habitual in the prisons. What was keeping the Americans from driving Franco out? I wondered. But I had no doubt that they would decide to do so before long.

In Lisbon, I found my sister and Lionel waiting at the station; in the taxi, walking, standing, sitting, in the street, in the restaurant where we ate, in their apartment, we talked until I was felled by sleep. I described the gaiety of this arrival in *The Mandarins*. Lisbon was like Marseilles, like Athens, like Naples and like Barcelona: a burning city, whipped by the smell of the sea; the past suddenly became alive again in the novelty of its hills and promontories, its soft colours, its white sails.

As in Madrid, the opulence of the stores seemed to me part of another age; I entered it. 'What are those clogs you're wearing?' my sister had asked, staring down at my feet; and immediately took on the job of dressing me. Never in my life had I surrendered to such a debauch; my lecture tour was very well paid, and in one afternoon I assembled a complete wardrobe: three pairs of shoes, a bag, stockings, lingerie, sweaters, dresses, skirts, blouses, a white wool jacket, a fur coat. At the cocktail party given by the French Institute I was dressed in all new clothes. There I met some of Lionel's Portuguese friends, all opposed to the regime; they told me resentfully about Valéry, who had not wanted to see anything in Portugal except the blue sky and the pomegranate trees in bloom. And all that nonsense about the mystery and the melancholy of the Portuguese soul! Out of seven million Portuguese, there are seventy thousand who have enough to eat; the Portuguese are sad because they're hungry.

With my sister and Lionel, I listened to *fados*, I watched a Portuguese bullfight. I walked in the gardens of Cintra, among the camellias and the tree ferns. Despite the 'carless days' and the gas rationing, we made a long tour through the Algarve in a car lent by the French Institute; time had not dulled this pleasure: finding new aspects of the world day after day, from hour to hour. I saw earth the colour of Africa covered with mimosa, bristling with aloes; I saw steep cliffs breasting an ocean calmed by the soft sky, whitewashed villages, baroque churches statelier than the Spanish ones. Often, behind the sober façade with its curving lines, we found what seemed like a magic cave; the walls and the columns were covered with crude paintings, and the confessionals, the pulpit, the altar as well; from the shadows emerged strange objects made of wood, cloth, hair and wax that turned out to be Christs or saints. Along the roads, I passed peasants in sheepskin trousers, with manycoloured blankets thrown over their shoulders; the women wore brilliant dresses; on top of the kerchiefs knotted below their chins they set wide sombreros; many balanced a large jar on their heads, or on one hip. From time to time, I noticed groups of men and women bent over the earth, all hoeing together in the same rhythm; red, blue, yellow and orange, their costumes were dazzling in the sunlight. But I no longer allowed myself to be deceived; there was a word whose weight I was beginning to appreciate: hunger. Under their bright clothes, these people were hungry; they went barefoot, with stony faces, and in the false gaiety of the village I could see the dulled look in the men's eyes; under the terrible weight of the sun, they were consumed by a wild fire of despair. The following week, we took the train for Oporto; at every station the train was invaded by beggars. At night, Oporto glittered; in the morning, it was red and beautiful beneath the warm white mist that rose from the Douro; but it did not take me long to discover the damp filth of the 'unhealthy sectors' teeming with scrofulous children; little girls in rags were digging avidly into the trash cans. Nevertheless, I did not yield to disgust, or to compassion; I drank *vinho verde* and arbutus brandy, I lost myself in the gaiety of my blood and of the sky; we got up early to see the dawn bleach the sea; we watched the harbour lights appear in the evening, as the ocean slowly consumed the glowing sun; I joyfully accepted the beauty of the landscape and the buildings: the flowered slopes of the Minho, Coimbra, Tomar, Batalha, Leiria, Óbidos. But everywhere the poverty was too flagrant to be forgotten for long. At Braga, it was fiesta; there were processions and a fair; I bought scarves, vases, jugs, pottery roosters; I admired the magnificent lyre-horned oxen, paired in carved wooden yokes; but it was impossible to ignore the beggars, the children covered with scabs, the lines of barefoot peasants, the women bent beneath their burdens. At Nazaré, the prettiness of the little harbour, the boats, the costumes did not mask the sadness in the people's eyes. The Portuguese bourgeoisie bore others' poverty with the utmost serenity. To the pale children who asked them for alms, the ladies in their furs would reply impatiently: '*Tenha paciência.*' At V., a little port of the Minho, we dined on a terrace with the consular agent, a Portuguese; some children silently watched us eating; he chased them away; one of them came back, and I gave him five escudos; the Portuguese leaped up. 'That's too much! He'll just go and buy himself candy!'

During the war, Portugal had offered all its sympathy and a certain amount of help to Germany; now that Hitler had been defeated, the government was attempting a *rapprochement* with France, and it was in accord with this policy that the French Institute had been authorized to sponsor my lecture tour. I had been a teacher, so talking in public did not frighten me; but there was a gap that often discouraged me between my audiences and the experiences I was trying to evoke; they came to hear me out of idleness, out of snobbery, and often with ill will, for many of them still held Fascism very close to their hearts. At V., the audience was icy; no one wanted to believe in the prison camps, the executions, the tortures; the consular agent said, as I stood up at the end: 'Well! I must thank you for having told us about all these things. Up till now we have heard nothing about them, nothing whatever,' and he emphasized the last word with an ironic inflection. The Francophiles, on the other hand, turned my reports into epics; I was overcome with shame when I read in one illustrated magazine: 'Simone de Beauvoir reports: "We cooked our potatoes over fires of newspapers; we kept the kerosene to throw at German tanks." ' Paris had suffered both more and less than they imagined; had been both less self-satisfied and less heroic; all the questions they asked me were beside the point.

On the credit side, I was very interested by my talks with the Portuguese anti-Fascists; most of the ones I met were ex-teachers, ex-ministers of state, men of middle age or older; they wore starched collars, bowlers or black derbies, and put their trust in an eternal France and Georges Bidault; but they provided me with a host of documents on the population's standard of living, on the economic organization of the country, on the budget, the unions, the incidence of illiteracy, and also on the police, the prisons and political repression. A young doctor took me into some working-class homes – hovels where the staple diet was stale sardines; he gave me precise figures on the inadequacy of the hospitals, of medical attention and general health measures; although, in fact, one had only to walk through Lisbon and keep one's eyes open to be aware of such things. The people were deliberately kept in a state of filth and ignorance: Fatima was being launched. 'The terrible thing is that Salazar will never fall until Franco does,' these people told me. And they added that the two dictators would find the defeat of the Axis a very minor inconvenience indeed! The English capitalists had considerable interests in Portugal, America was bargaining for air bases in the Azores; Salazar could count on Anglo-American support; that is why it was so necessary to awaken public opinion in France. One ex-minister asked me to take back a letter to Bidault: if Bidault would help him set up a new government, then that government would cede Angola to France. This colonialist scheme would have upset me considerably if I had taken it seriously, but I knew that the letter would end up in the wastepaper basket. I delivered it to the Quai d'Orsay.

I arrived back in Paris at the beginning of April, on a beautiful sunny day. I had brought fifty kilos of food with me: hams, rust-coloured *chorizos*, Algarve cookies sticky with sugar and eggs, tea, coffee, chocolate. Triumphantly I made the rounds of my friends. To the women I gave sweaters and shawls; for Bost, Camus and Vitold I had brought back chequered fishermen's shirts from Nazaré. And I paraded myself in all my new finery. A very elegant woman I did not know came up to me in the Place Saint-Augustin. 'Where did you find those?' she asked me, gesturing towards my new crepe-soled shoes. 'In Lisbon,' I told her, not without pride; it is so difficult not to become vain about one's own good luck. Vitold had some unpleasant news for me; he had quarrelled with Badel, who no longer wanted to produce my play; but we should be able to find another theatre quite easily, he assured me.

I wrote my articles; the one on Madrid appeared in *Combat* Magazine, under my name; the Spanish radio accused me of inventing slanders for money without leaving Paris. *Combat* began printing a series of articles on Portugal which I signed with a pseudonym in order not to compromise my brother-in-law; Camus was in North Africa at the time, and Pascal Pia, who was replacing him, abruptly broke off the series; it was continued in *Volontés*, which was edited by Collinet. I received encouraging letters from a certain number of Portuguese, but the country's propaganda service protested. I returned to work on my novel; now, through the windows of the Bibliothèque Mazarine, I could see leaves and blue sky, and I often read the old stories over for the simple pleasure of reading, without thinking of my hero.

Dullin put on *King Lear*. Camille had made a good adaptation, and also helped Dullin with the staging. The costumes and sets – which I personally liked a lot – were a little aggressive in their extravagance; but the cast was good, with a ravishing Cordelia, Ariane Borg; by turns hateful, pathetic, decrepit, visionary, inhuman and only too human, Dullin had managed to make *Lear* one of his best creations. Yet the critics fell on the production with all the savagery at their command. The public stayed away. For Dullin, this flop was a major disaster; there was talk of taking the direction of the Sarah-Bernhardt Theatre away from him. He asked me to defend his *Lear*. I wrote an article that Ponge got printed in *Action*. I accused the critics of bad faith: they had attacked the production because they did not dare admit they were bored with Shakespeare. My little polemic was more violent than inspired; I had no great hopes for it, and nothing came of it. It merely earned me a few steadfast enemies.

It was spring, the first spring of peace. They were showing Prévert's *Les Enfants du Paradis* in Paris, and at last some American films: *I Married a Witch*, *My Girl Friday* and *The Old Maid* with Bette Davis. I was a little disappointed. Where was the revolution that was convulsing the cinema?

That April sparkled. I sat on the café terraces with friends; I went for walks in the forest of Chantilly with Herbaud, who had come back from London; our quarrel had evaporated of its own accord. On the first of May it snowed, there were only a few stunted slips of lily of the valley to buy on the street corners. But the air was warm again that evening when the great V's stood out against the sky and when all Paris was out in the streets singing and dancing.

Sartre was still in New York, Bost was in Germany. I spent the evening with Olga, Mme Lemaire, Olga Barbezat, Vitold, Chauffard, Mouloudji, Roger Blin, and a few others. We went to the Place de la Concorde together on the métro; we were walking arm in arm, but as soon as we came out onto the square, our little group was broken up; I hung on to Mme Lemaire and Vitold, who kept groaning merrily: 'What an asshole game!' as the surging crowd carried us towards the Place de l'Opéra; the opera house was streaming with red, white and blue lights, flags were snapping and snatches of the 'Marseillaise' floated everywhere; we felt suffocated; one false step and we could have been trampled where we stood. We made our way up towards Montmartre and stopped at the Cabana Cubaine; what a crush! I can still see Mme Lemaire walking over the tables to get to the banquette where I managed to ensconce myself; Olga Barbezat, tears in her eyes, was talking to me about my dear friends. Then we were out in the street again, almost ready to give up. Where could we go? Vitold and Mouloudji suggested the studio of one of their lady friends. We set out; a jeep drew up to the sidewalk and offered us a lift. Two G.I.s and two W.A.C.s went with us to visit Christiane Lainier; the two W.A.C.s sat on a chest of drawers and nodded off, while Mouloudji sang and Blin recited, very well, a poem by Milosz. My recollection of this night is much more confused than my memories of our other, earlier festivities, perhaps because my feelings were so confused. This victory had been won a long way off; we had not awaited it, as we had the Liberation, in a fever of anxiety; it had been foreseen for a long time, and offered no new hopes. It simply marked the end of the war; in a way, this end was like a sort of death; when a man dies, when time stops for him, his life hardens into a single lump in which the years are superimposed and inter-mingled; in much the same way, all the moments of the past were hardening behind me: joy, tears, anger, grief, triumph, horror. The war was over; it remained on our hands like a great, unwanted corpse, and there was no place on earth to bury it.

And what was going to happen now? Malraux assured us that the Third World War had just begun. All the anti-Communists were anticipating disaster. Some optimists, on the other hand, foresaw eternal peace; thanks to technical progress, all nations would soon be united into one indivisible bloc. Personally I didn't think things were as rosy as that, but I didn't think we were going to start fighting again next week, either. One morning in the métro, I noticed some strange uniforms decorated with red stars: Russian soldiers. It was like seeing characters from a fairy tale. Lise, who spoke her native language fluently, tried to talk to them; they asked her sternly what she was doing in France, and her enthusiasm quickly waned.

A short while after V.E. Day, I spent a very happy evening with Camus, Chauffard, Loleh Bellon, Vitold, and a ravishing Portuguese girl named Viola. We left a bar in Montparnasse, which had just closed, and walked down to the Hôtel de la Louisiane; Loleh walked barefoot on the asphalt, saying: 'It's my birthday, I'm twenty.' We bought some bottles and drank them in the round room; the window was open to the warm air of the May night, and the people walking outside called out friendly words to us; for them, too, it was the first spring of peace. Paris was still as intimate as a village; I felt myself linked with all the unknown people who had shared my past, and who were as moved as I was by our deliverance.

Not everything was going so well, however. The material situa-tion was not getting any better. Mendès-France had resigned. The charter of the C.N.R. had remained a dead letter. Camus, on his re-turn from Algeria, described in *Combat* the exploitation of the na-tives, their poverty and their hunger; Europeans there were entitled to two thirds of a pound of bread per day, Mohammedans to only a half pound, and even then they rarely got more than half of that. We heard very little about what had happened at Sétif: on 8 May, during the victory celebrations, *agents provocateurs* – Fascists, according to *Humanité* – had fired on the Mohammedans, who had retaliated; the army had restored order; a hundred or so victims were rumoured. It was not until much later that we learned the enormity of this lie.[1]

Ugly rumours were beginning to circulate about the prison camps liberated by the Americans. At first, bread and jam and sausages had been distributed with complete thoughtlessness. The inmates died like flies; now more care was taken, but the change of diet was still killing off large numbers. The fact that was none of the doctors knew how to treat the particular type of malnutrition found in the concentration camps, it was something entirely new; perhaps the Americans were less to blame than was thought at the time. There were also complaints about the dilatory way in which they were repatriating the internees. There was typhus at Dachau, people were dying there in hundreds; they were dying in all the camps; the French Red Cross had asked permission to enter them, but our allies had refused. This prohibition angered us. Furthermore, we found it intolerable that German prisoners should be well fed while the French population was dying of hunger. Our feelings towards our saviours had grown considerably colder since December.

Those who had been deported returned, and we discovered that we had known nothing. The walls of Paris were covered with photographs of charnel houses. Bost had gone into Dachau a few hours after the Americans; he could find no words to describe what he had seen. Another war correspondent told me for the first time about the death camps: 'And the worst of it,' he ended wildly, 'is that they disgust you.' Soon I saw pictures of them in the newspapers. There were a few short films made by the Americans, reports, eye-witness accounts, both written and oral: the death trains, the 'selections', the gas chambers, the crematoria, the experiments of the Nazi doctors, the daily exterminations. When, fifteen years later, the Eichmann trial and its accompanying spate of films and books revived these already long-distant days, people were overwhelmed, they sobbed and fainted; in '45, we received these revelations in all their immediacy, they concerned our friends, our comrades, our own lives. What horrified me most was the bitter and futile struggle of the doomed to breathe for just one more second; the armoured cars, the men pulling themselves up, already half-asphyxiated, towards the air outside, trampling on corpses, falling back dead; the ones who were slowly dying dragging themselves to work, collapsing, and

1. About eighty Europeans were massacred, after provocation on their part. The army raked the district: forty thousand dead.

being immediately finished off; the refusal to accept, the immense inanity of the refusal, and the last flicker so brutally stamped out; then nothing, not even the night.

Yvonne Picard did not come back; Alfred Péron died in Switzerland, a few days after being evacuated. Pierre Kaan was brought out of Buchenwald on 10 May. 'At least I'll have seen the Germans defeated,' he said; he died on 20 May. There was a rumour that Robert Desnos was on his way back; he died of typhus on 8 June, at Kerenice. Once more, I was ashamed to be alive. I was just as frightened of death as before; but those who do not die, I told myself with disgust, are accepting the unacceptable.

Sartre came back to Paris and told me about his trip. First, his arrival at the Waldorf; his lumber jacket and the clothes of the other journalists caused a sensation. A tailor had been summoned immediately. Then he told me about the cities, the country, the bars, the jazz; he had been shown around America by plane; in the Grand Canyon the pilot had asked every now and then: 'Have I got room? Is the wing clear?' Sartre was a bit stunned by all he had seen. Apart from the economic system, segregation and racism, there were many things in the civilization of the western hemisphere that shocked him – the Americans' conformism, their scale of values, their myths, their optimism, their avoidance of anything tragic; but he had felt a great deal of sympathy for most of the people he had come into contact with; he had been greatly moved by the crowds of New York and felt that the people were worth more than the system. He had been very much struck by Roosevelt's personality during an interview the President had given to the French delegation a few days before his death. He was surprised to learn that certain intellectuals were worried about the rise of Fascism in the country; in various places, in fact, he had been told things that were by no means reassuring. During lunch one day, Ford's director of public relations had cheerfully referred to the coming war with the U.S.S.R. 'But there's no frontier between America and Russia, where will you fight?' one of the Communist journalists asked. 'In Europe,' he replied, quite simply. This remark startled the French members, but they did not take it seriously. The American people did not appear to be at all bellicose. And so Sartre had abandoned himself to the pleasures of travel. He told me about the exiles he had met over there: in New York, Stépha and Fernand who was painting some very beautiful pictures; in Hollywood, Rirette Nizan who was earning a living writing subtitles for French films. He had met Breton, a remarkable man; he had met Léger too, whose style had changed considerably; Sartre liked his new paintings better than the old ones. A few days after his return, a huge black suitcase was dragged up to my room crammed full of clothes and food.

We continued to see lots of people. We enjoyed mixing with *le Tout-Paris* at previews and premières, because the word Resistance, although it had lost its political power, still meant something among the intellectuals; when they found themselves side by side at these events, they were able to affirm their solidarity, and the performances had a value for us as demonstrations. In this atmosphere we saw *Murder in the Cathedral*, very well staged and acted by Vilar at the Vieux-Colombier, but boring. And *The Great Dictator*, which we had awaited so impatiently; almost everyone was disappointed; Hitler wasn't funny any more. René Leibowitz invited us to visit him one afternoon with the Leirises and played twelve-tone music for us on his piano; I didn't understand it at all; but it had been forbidden by the Nazis and Leibowitz had lived in hiding for four years, every moment a miracle. It was at about the same time too, I think, that we went to the opening of the Gipsy in the Latin Quarter, where Mouloudji was making his début as a professional singer.

One evening I went with Sartre and the Leirises to the home of Dora Marr who painted very good pictures. She believed in table turning; we didn't; she suggested we give it a try. We all put our hands on a fairly large round table. Nothing happened, and it soon became rather tiresome. Suddenly the table began to shake, to move, to walk; we ran after it, our hands still joined and pressing down on top of it. The spirit informed us that it was Sartre's grandfather; the table spelled out the word *hell* with little knocks. For nearly an hour, running around the room or whirling around and around, it condemned us all to the everlasting fire and told things about Sartre that only he or I could possibly have known. Dora was exultant; the Leirises and Sartre were so stupefied they could only laugh. When we came out, I told them that it was I who had moved the table. Since I had been so sure it would not move, no one had suspected me.

In June, the Prix de la Pléiade was awarded for the second time. I was invited to take coffee with the members of the jury, who were all assembled at a luncheon at Gallimard's. I don't know who had forced on them the choice of author for the prize, but they all seemed upset. There were a great many people, bright sunlight, champagne, gin and plenty of whisky. Towards the end of the afternoon, sitting on the grass next to Queneau, I had a discussion with him about the 'end of history'. It was a frequent subject of conversation at the time. We had discovered the reality and weight of history, now we were wondering about its meaning. Queneau, who had been initiated into Hegelianism by Kojève, thought that one day all individuals would be reconciled in the triumphant unity of Spirit. 'But what if I have a pain in my foot?' I said. '*We* shall have a pain in your foot,' Queneau replied. We argued for a long time; and the alcohol fumes that were so pleasantly muddling our brains served only to make the dispute more vivacious; we decided to continue the following day and made a date. Queneau offered me a last drink; I knew my limit and declined; he insisted: 'Just one glass of champagne.' All right. He handed it to me, I drank it down and came to lying on a divan, my head burning and my stomach upset. Queneau had filled the glass I had drunk in one gulp with gin. I passed out immediately; it was very late, all the guests had gone home; only Sartre and the Gallimard family were still there; I was very ashamed and Jeanne tried to cheer me up as best she could. I was taken back to my hotel by car and went straight to bed. When I woke up twelve hours later, I was still in a bad way and had completely forgotten my date with Queneau; he hadn't remembered it either.

We drank hard in those days; first because the liquor was there, and also because it helped us find the relief we needed, it was part of the celebration; a strange celebration; close and appalling, the past was haunting us; looking ahead, we were torn between hope and doubt; no serenity was possible; the world opposed all our passions. We had to forget, and then even forget we were forgetting.

My sister and Lionel returned to Paris towards the end of May. During her years away she had done a great deal of work. She exhibited at Galerie Jeanne Castel – compositions inspired by things she had seen in Lisbon Hospital. I went with her to the Louvre, which was just reopening, and saw all the collections again. Sartre went out to the country with his mother, whose husband had died during the winter. I decided to go for a bicycling holiday; since Vitold was taking his holiday at the same time, we rode together for several days, side by side, from Paris to Vichy, along the gorges of the Creuse, then over the plateau of Millevaches and through the Auvergne. We talked about *Les Bouches inutiles*, for which he had a theatre in sight; we discussed possible rewriting and details of staging; Vitold was unhappy in his personal life, and told me about it. It was still difficult to find food and lodging; we had brought some canned American food with us which came in very handy for filling up after meals. We slept in the back of a baker's shop, on café benches, and once we even slept in a charcoal burner's hut, practically in the open air. At Vichy I left Vitold and went up to the Vercors which I wanted to see for myself; it was then that I attended the great funeral feast at Vassieux that I described in *The Mandarins*.[1]

On 7 August – I had just got back to Paris – the A-bomb was dropped on Hiroshima. This meant the end of the war, and a revolting massacre; it heralded the possibility of perpetual peace, and also the possibility of the end of the world. We argued about it endlessly.

We spent a month at La Pouèze; we were there when the second bomb was dropped, when the Russians went into Manchuria and Japan capitulated. Sartre received letters that brought us echoes of the V.J. Day celebrations in America. For us, the victory had been won in May.

For the first time I went abroad again with Sartre: to Bruges, to Antwerp, to Ghent. Things had always exceeded my imagination; now I realized that they also exceeded my memory. I began to taste the pleasure of re-seeing. I had truly left one age of my life behind, and begun another.

CHAPTER TWO

Blood of Others was published in September; its main theme, as I have said, was the paradox of this existence experienced by me as my freedom and by those who came in contact with me as an object. This intention was not apparent to the public; the book was labelled a 'Resistance novel'.

1. There is one point in which that account is inexact. I described it as happening after the A-bomb, whereas in fact it took place a few days before.

Sometimes this misunderstanding irritated me, but I made the best of it, since the book's success far exceeded my expectations. It created much more of a stir than *L'Invitée*; all the critics rated my second novel above my first; editorials expressing deep emotion were written about it in several newspapers. Both orally and by letter I received floods of compliments. Camus, though he liked the book, did not conceal his surprise at this success; as for Aron, he told me straight out, with the frankness of true friendship: 'The fact is, I find this success revolting!' What he disliked, I think, was the approval I was receiving from the middle-of-the-road orthodox intellectuals who had made my book a sort of fad. Writers, journalists, intellectuals, still united by the events of the recent past, we were all inclined to indulge in mutual admiration; and apart from this, my novel was the first to speak quite openly about the Resistance. Nevertheless the reading public was not obeying orders from outside; the praise it showered on me was sincere; it read *Blood of Others* through the same spectacles that I had put on to write it.

Technically, I was under the impression that I had broken new ground; some congratulated me for it, others complained of the 'long tunnel' which opens the book; everyone agreed that the form was original, for the French novel had up till then become largely a matter of respecting the rules. What I find even more surprising is that my narrative was said to be 'bursting with blood and life'. A book is a collective object. Readers contribute as much as the author to its creation; and mine, like myself, were concerned with morality; I had adopted a perspective so natural to them that they took what it showed them for reality itself. Beneath the veneer of abstract concepts and edifying sentences, they perceived the emotion so clumsily buried there; they brought it back to life; it was their own blood and their own life that they were lending to my characters. Then time passed; circumstances changed, and our hearts with them. Together we undid the work we had created together. Today there remains only a book whose defects can be seen at a glance.

It was labelled not only a 'Resistance novel' but also an 'Existentialist novel'. Henceforth this label was to be affixed automatically to any work by Sartre or myself. During a discussion organized during the summer by the Cerf publishing house – in other words, by the Dominicans – Sartre had refused to allow Gabriel Marcel to apply this adjective to him: 'My philosophy is a philosophy of existence; I don't even know what Existentialism is.' I shared his irritation. I had written my novel before I had even encountered the term Existentialist; my inspiration came from my own experience, not from a system. But our protests were vain. In the end, we took the epithet that everyone used for us and used it for our own purposes.

So that, without having planned it, what we launched early that fall turned out to be an 'Existentialist offensive'. In the weeks following the publication of my novel, *The Age of Reason* and *The Reprieve* appeared, as well as the first numbers of *Les Temps Modernes*. Sartre gave a lecture – 'Is Existentialism a Humanism?' – and I gave one at the Club Maintenant on the novel and metaphysics. *Les Bouches inutiles* opened.[1] We were astonished by the furore we caused. Suddenly, in much the same way as one sees the picture in certain films breaking out of its frame and spreading to fill a wider screen, my life overflowed its old boundaries. I was pushed out into the limelight. My own baggage weighed very little, but Sartre was now hurled brutally into the arena of celebrity, and my name was associated with his. A week never passed without the newspapers discussing us. *Combat* printed favourable comments on everything that came from our mouths or our pens. *Terre des hommes*, a weekly started by Pierre Herbart and destined to survive only a few months, devoted numerous friendly or bittersweet columns to us in every number. Gossip about us and about our books appeared everywhere. In the streets, photographers fired away at us, and strangers rushed up to speak to us. At the Flore, people stared at us and whispered. When Sartre gave his lecture, so many people turned up that they couldn't all get into the lecture hall; there was a frenzied crush and some women fainted.

This uproar was partly a result of the 'inflation' that Sartre was denouncing at that very moment;[2] now a second-class power, France was exalting her most characteristic national products with an eye on the export market: *haute couture* and literature. Even the humblest piece of writing was greeted by cries of acclaim, and its

1. 'In the same week, we have listened to a lecture by Sartre, attended the opening of *Les Bouches inutiles* and read the first issue of *Les Temps Modernes*,' wrote one surfeited critic in *Arts*.
2. '*La nationalisation de la littérature*', in *Les Temps Modernes*, November 1945.

author immediately surrounded by an enormous fuss. Other countries were affected by the racket and seemed only too happy to make it even louder. However, if circumstances happened to be so favourable to Sartre it was no accident; there existed, at least at first glance, a remarkable agreement between what he was offering the public and what the public wanted. His *petit-bourgeois* readers had lost their faith too, in perpetual peace, in eternal progress, in unchanging essences; they had discovered History in its most terrible form. They needed an ideology which would include such revelations without forcing them to jettison their old excuses. Existentialism, struggling to reconcile history and morality, authorized them to accept their transitory condition without renouncing a certain absolute, to face horror and absurdity while still retaining their human dignity, to preserve their individuality. It seemed to offer the solution they had dreamed of.

In fact, it did not; and it was for this reason that Sartre's success was always as ambiguous as it was voluminous, bloated by its very ambiguity. People flung themselves avidly on nourishment that they were starved for; they broke their teeth on it and uttered howls that intrigued and attracted others by their violence. Sartre seduced them by maintaining, on the level of the individual, the rights of morality; but the morality he meant was not the same as theirs. His novels presented them with an image of society which they rejected; they accused him of sordid realism, of 'miserabilism'. They were prepared to listen to a few gentle truths about themselves, not to look themselves in the face. When confronted with Marxist dialectic, they clamoured for their freedom; but Sartre went too far. The freedom he offered them implied wearisome responsibilities; it could be turned against their institutions, against their *mores*; it destroyed their security. He invited them to use this freedom in order to ally themselves with the proletariat; they wanted to enter History, but not through that door. Labelled, pigeonholed, the Communist intellectuals worried them much less. In Sartre, the bourgeois recognized themselves without consenting to the self-transcendence he exemplified; he was speaking their language, and using it to tell them things they did not want to hear. They came to him, and came back to him, because he was asking the questions that they were asking themselves; they ran away because his answers shocked them.

A celebrity and a scandal at the same moment, it was not without uneasiness that Sartre accepted a fame which, exceeding all his old ambitions, also contradicted them. Although he had wanted posterity's approval, he had not expected to reach more than a very small public in his lifetime. A new fact, the advent of 'one world', transformed him into an author of world fame; he had imagined that *Nausea* would not be translated for many years; as a result of modern techniques, the rapidity of communications, his works were already appearing in a dozen languages. It was a great shock for a writer reared in the old tradition, who had viewed the solitude of Baudelaire, of Stendhal, of Kafka, as the necessary price of their genius. Far from the circulation of his books being a guarantee of their worth, there were so many mediocre books achieving success that success seemed almost the sign of mediocrity. Compared to Baudelaire's obscurity, the inane glory that had burst upon Sartre had something annoying about it.

And its price was high. He received worldwide and unexpected attention, but saw himself robbed of that of future generations. Eternity had collapsed; the men of tomorrow had become the crabs Franz talks to in *Altona*: impervious, hermetic, radically alien. His books, even if they were read, would not be the ones he had written; his work would not remain. For him this was truly the death of God, who up till then had survived under the mask of words. Sartre owed this total catastrophe to his pride in accepting (assuming) it. He did so in his *Présentation* which opened the first number of *Les Temps Modernes* in October. Literature had shed its sacred character, so be it; henceforth he would posit the absolute in the ephemeral; imprisoned in his own epoch, he would choose that epoch against eternity, consenting to perish entirely along with it. This decision had more than one meaning. As a child, as an adolescent, Sartre's favourite fantasy had always been that of the *poète maudit*, misunderstood by all during his lifetime and struck by fame's lightning only beyond the grave, or perhaps, so he can enjoy it a little, on his deathbed; once more he was counting on the transformation of failure into triumph. His success had now overflowed all expectations, and in winning everything he had lost everything; by accepting that loss, he nourished the secret hope that everything would be restored. 'The rejection of posterity would give me posterity.'[1] Furthermore, at the age of forty, his highest ambitions had already, on one level, been satisfied;

1. Unpublished notes.

however ambiguous that success may have been, he would never exceed it. Repetition bored him; the best thing to do was to change his goals. Detesting passivity, if he preferred writing to actions, it was because he had never conceived of it as contemplation, as dream, as an escape from the self, but as construction. He had discovered, in the Stalag with *Bariona*, under the Occupation with *The Flies*, the vital role writing could play. When he renounced *being* and decided to *do*, to *make*, to *act*, he insisted that henceforth writing would always be a rallying cry, a commitment. This did not imply a contempt for literature but, on the contrary, the intention to restore its true dignity. If literature was in essence divine, then by toying with one's pen one could produce a sacred object; if it was human, then it could be kept from becoming degraded to the status of entertainment only by being identified with man's very existence, without dividing his life into various parts. Commitment [*engagement*], then, is simply the writer's total presence in what he has written.

This is a good example of the way in which Sartre could convince and outrage at the same time: his article provoked impassioned arguments that still continue today. In those troubled days when the world's rumours could violate even the most silent retreats, the public wanted nothing better than to fill the gap that separated journalism from literature, their daily interests from their cultural concerns; they were hungry for knowledge about this changed world they saw around them; they would satisfy this curiosity nobly if art seized upon these living, burning realities no academician had ever approached. But, they did not want to give up eternity. They wanted literature to transport them into those higher spheres where the work of art holds sovereign sway. Sartre respected literature to the point of identifying its destiny with that of humanity; to the public it seemed a sacrilege that he should bring it down from heaven to earth. It was the same in every realm. What he offered his readers enriched but disturbed them; and their resentment exceeded their gratitude.

He left himself wide open to attack by remaining faithful to the rule we had decided on: to react to the situation without assuming a role. He made no change in his habits; he lived in his hotel and in the cafés, he gave no thought to how he dressed, he avoided society; not only was he not married, but we both led such independent lives that it was impossible to think of our relationship as a classic example of 'free love'. All these eccentricities would have been forgiven if only Sartre had taken shelter behind his role as writer. He has never done so; and, in the surprise of his meta-morphosis, it never occurred to him that he should at least take his new status into account. This simplicity earned him many friends. But public opinion was shocked. Ignorant of the real seriousness of a writer's work, the public only forgives him his privileges if he appears to them as the Other, flattering their taste for myths and idols and disarming envy. But the Other is the in-human; the farces of vanity and prestige never suffice to hide the fact that the famous author is a man, a fellow being: he yawns, he eats, he walks – so many proofs that he is an impostor. A writer is hoisted up onto a pedestal only to scrutinize him more closely and conclude that it was a mistake to put him up there in the first place. All the same, as long as he hangs on up there, the distance between himself and the public will blunt the edge of their malice. Sartre wouldn't play the game, he stayed down with the crowd, with everyone, with anyone. Then, determined to identify him as the Other while noticing that he was just like them, people began to denounce him as a barefaced hoaxer. One evening, as we were coming out of the Golfe-Juan, one of the diners who had been eyeing Sartre malevolently all evening said to his wife: 'Well, there you are! He blows his nose. . . .' All these grievances reinforced each other. Insofar as he was unable to conform to bourgeois behaviour, his very simplicity became a weapon that could be used against him. The fact is that there was something suspect about it; it implied democratic convictions too extreme for the élite not to feel its superiorities were being challenged.

The idyl of the autumn of '44 was soon over. Nothing serious had been written about *Being and Nothingness*, but it was already being attacked in reviews, in classes, in lectures, by right-thinking people. On 3 June 1945 *La Croix* had denounced atheist Exis-tentialism as 'a graver danger than eighteenth-century Rationalism or nineteenth-century Positivism'. The extreme Right was be-ginning, though still with some caution, to come out of hiding; in pamphlets, in newspapers, in gossip columns it started a rising flood of calumnies about Sartre. In November 1945 a blue-eyed young man in the Flore asked me to tell him about Sartre; he had to write an article about him in *Samedi-Soir*, a sensational weekly that had just been launched. I refused; he told me he would write the piece anyway, so he might as well get the information from me. I gave in and told him what he wanted to know. Several days later Sartre found a garbage can had been emptied over him: sordid and frivolous, his philosophy was fit for a sick people; morally and physically, his sole delight was filth. We were disconcerted by this display of mud-slinging. But after all, what could you expect, such people would never be able to like us; we would learn to armour ourselves against their insults. When Boutang wondered in public if Sartre were a madman, we were unaffected. Sartre had torn himself away from his class, so the animosity it displayed towards him was natural. The animosity of the Communists, on the other hand, struck him as an injustice.

At their side, in June 1945, he had participated in the C.N.E. sale. ('Monsieur Sartre,' one middle-aged lady had asked him, 'according to you, Hell is other people?' 'Yes . . .' 'Well, myself, I'm Heaven,' she said with a beatific smile.) He imagined that his *Mise au point* had settled all their differences; he was mistaken. In an article that appeared in *Action*, Henri Lefebvre accused Sartre, in a very disagreeable tone, of demonstrating things in *Being and Nothingness* that for a Communist were self-evident; he was blocking the way to any philosophy of history and concealing from his readers all the really important problems. Kanapa contributed an article to the first number of *Les Temps Modernes*. 'Come and see Maublanc with me,' he said to Sartre. 'Garaudy and Mougin want to talk to you about something.' The morning of the interview, Kanapa telephoned in some embarrassment to say that he couldn't come. Sartre went to Maublanc's alone, where Garaudy and Mougin told him off: he was an idealist, he was turning young people away from Marxism; no Communists were writing for *Les Temps Modernes* any more. However, we had no wish to break with them. Politically, that fallacious entity, the Resistance, no longer existed. In December 1945, Malraux mentioned it in the Chamber of Deputies and caused nothing but embarrassment, whereas a year earlier the mere word would have produced an automatic burst of applause. The Resistance had been split in three, and only the Communist Party sustained its revolutionary hopes; the rigid and anachronistic S.F.I.O. had been deserted by the masses. When the country, having voted for a Constituent Assembly with limited powers, proceeded to elections, the result was a triumph for the Communists. Our aims were the same as theirs, and they alone could achieve them. In the conflict between Thorez and De Gaulle, we sided with the former.[1] We continued our dialogue with the Communists. Merleau-Ponty expressed his views in the November number of *Les Temps Modernes*; in December, *Action* replied harshly with an article entitled 'Either-Or', and took the same tone with Beaufret, who had written about Existentialism in *Confluences*. Early in 1946, after Merleau-Ponty had published a paper in *Action* on the nature of the hero in our time, he was informed in *Cahiers d'Action* that 'the Communist is the permanent hero of our time'. Hervé attacked another article by Merleau-Ponty, published in *Les Temps Modernes*, about political realism. Aliquié and Naville debated, though in a more moderate tone, in the March issue of the *Revue internationale*. Since Existentialism's vogue showed no signs of diminishing – the public came in droves to the lecture Beaufret gave on it at the Vieux-Colombier in April – *Action* finally decided to open a symposium: *Must We Burn Kafka?* directed against *littérature noire*; fortunately the question roused many readers to indignation; among the replies there was only a single yes. When we met Courtade, Hervé, Rolland or Claude Roy in private, we always argued with good humour and seemingly on a basis of mutual esteem; which made this public campaign all the more infuriating.

Of course Sartre was still far from having understood the fecundity of the dialectical idea and of Marxist materialism; the works he published that year are proof of that. His study of Baudelaire's *écrits intimes*,[2] written two years earlier, is a phenomenological description; it lacks the psychoanalytical dimension that would have explained Baudelaire on the basis of his body and the facts of his life history. *Anti-Semite and Jew* (*Reflections on the Jewish Question*) shows how the phenomenological method can be enriched and made flexible by constant recourse to the social; but the concrete factual basis necessary to a history of anti-Semitism is not there. The article 'Materialism and Revolution', which

1. Thorez demanded one of the three major ministries for his party; De Gaulle refused; a compromise was reached. But on 22 January 1946 De Gaulle resigned because he disapproved of the Constitution drawn up by a Chamber of Deputies with a Socialist and Communist majority.

2. It was published in book form soon afterwards with a preface by Leiris. Sartre's intention – to understand the moments of a life through the totality of that life – escaped the critics (with the exception of Blanchot), who accused him of misunderstanding the nature of poetry.

appeared in *Les Temps Modernes*, was a direct challenge to orthodox Marxism. Sartre criticized – with arguments less valid than those he would use today, but inspired by the same principles – the idea of a dialectic of nature; he analysed materialism, in its strength and in its weaknesses, as a revolutionary myth. He indicated what status revolution necessarily and effectively grants the idea of freedom. At that point his line of thought stopped short, for he had not determined the freedom situation relation and was even more vacillating about history.

Less profound on certain points, on others more demanding than Marxist doctrine, Sartre's philosophy did not radically contradict it; he was seeking exchanges. The Communists rejected them. It is true that the bourgeois public interpreted Existentialism in such a way as to pervert its meaning; they regarded it – as they regarded the moralism of Camus – as a spare or emergency ideology. The Communists took the same view. Was this sectarianism forced on them by the political situation? The reasons are of little importance here. The fact is that intellectually a dialogue with Sartre was possible and that they chose instead to use for their own purposes the insults invented by the Right: poet of the sewers, philosopher of nothingness and despair. What hurt Sartre was that they thus transformed him into an enemy of the masses. 'Fame, for me, was hatred,' he wrote later in his notes. It was a frustrating experience; with publicity far beyond his expectations, he had begun to exist for others; but as a person hateful and hated. In 1945–6, he still hoped to change this situation; he no longer imagined that it would be easy.

I have often wondered what my position would have been if I had not been associated with Sartre in the way that I was. Close to the Communists certainly, because of my horror of all that they were fighting against; but I loved truth too much not to demand the freedom to seek it as I wished. I would never have become a Party member; since I had less objective importance than Sartre, the difficulties of this attitude would have been reduced, but the attitude itself would have resembled his. I therefore found myself in perfect agreement with him. Only, since it was not me the Communists were blaming, insulting, denouncing, since I was not personally compromised by their hostility, I was tempted to take it lightly. Sartre's tenacity in attempting to disarm it astonished me; sometimes I urged him to strike back. At other times, though, after a chance meeting or after reading something, I would wonder if we shouldn't have jettisoned our scruples as intellectuals and fought in the ranks of the Communist Party. Sartre too went through these periodic oscillations which sometimes coincided with mine and sometimes didn't. We argued a great deal.

I had never believed in the sacred nature of literature. God had died when I was fourteen; nothing had replaced him: the absolute existed only in the negative, like a horizon forever lost to view. I had wanted to become a legend, like Emily Brontë or George Eliot; but I was too firmly convinced that once my eyes had closed nothing would exist to cling very tightly to such dreams. I would perish with the age I lived in, since I was going to die; there are not two ways of dying. I wanted to be widely read in my lifetime, to be esteemed, to be loved. Posterity I didn't give a damn for. Or I almost didn't.

I had grown used to living inside a writer's skin and nowadays scarcely ever caught myself looking at this new character and saying: It's me. But I enjoyed seeing my name in the papers, and for a while the fuss about us and my role as a 'Parisian figure' gave me a good deal of amusement. In many ways, of course, I found it unpleasant. Not that I was over-sensitive; when people called me 'la grande Sartreuse' or 'Notre-Dame de Sartre' I just laughed, but certain looks men gave me left their mark; looks that offered a lewd complicity with the Existentialist, and therefore dissolute, woman they took me for. To provide food for gossip, to titillate curiosity – that I did find repugnant. On the whole, however, I wasn't much affected by malice at the time and I enjoyed my new-found notoriety. It did not astonish me; it seemed to me quite normal that the Liberation should have transformed my life along with the rest of the world. Nor did I exaggerate it: it was very slender compared with Sartre's. I observed this difference without envy, because he meant too much to me for me to be jealous of him, and also because it seemed to me quite justified. I didn't even regret not having deserved more; my first book had only come out two years before, it was not yet time to start adding up scores. The future lay before me, and I had faith in it. Where would it take me? I avoided questioning myself about the value of my work, in the future as in the present. I wanted neither to surround myself with illusions, nor to run the risk of a possibly cruel lucidity.

All things considered, unlike Sartre, I jeopardized myself neither as writer nor in my social reality. I could pride myself on having been less deceived than he by the illusion of being, for I had paid the price of this renunciation during my adolescence; and I could reproach myself with having refused to confront my objective existence; there is no doubt that my scepticism helped me evade the difficulties that Sartre was coming to grips with. This escape was made easier for me by my temperament. I had always taken more pleasure in the immediate than he. I enjoyed all the pleasures of the body, the feel of the weather, walks, friendships, gossip, learning, seeing. And also, far from being saturated by success as he was, I could see no limits to my hopes; I was satisfied but not satiated. Circumstances assured every effort and even the slightest success a resonance that stimulated me further; tasks presented themselves, and also the means of performing them. The present and its near horizons were enough for me.

For some time our review took all my attention. Thanks to Sartre's renown and to the controversy his theory of *engagement* provoked, we had a great many readers; our aim was to reflect an epoch which sought to know itself, and *Les Temps Modernes* had a lasting success. Paulhan, who had edited the *N.R.F.* for many years, gave us the benefit of his experience; he usually made up most of the numbers, and he taught me the technique. Aron, who had acquired a lot of experience with *La France libre*, also gave us technical advice; he followed the progress of *Les Temps Modernes* very closely, trusting, I think, that Sartre would not have the perseverance to find it interesting for long and that he would then take over. He was chiefly concerned with the political section and was very skilful at finding reasons for not publishing articles favourable to Communism. Excellent as an analyst, he was pathetic as a prophet: he announced a Socialist triumph on the eve of an election that was a landslide for the M.R.P. and a defeat for the S.F.I.O. Leiris was in charge of poetry, and our tastes rarely coincided. The committee met often and argued hotly.

I have said what the review meant to Sartre. Everything in this world is a sign that points back to everything: our originality lay in our search for facts that were both banal and revealing. Further, we hoped to influence our contemporaries by our choice of texts and by the orientation of our articles. Besides which, it was very useful to have at hand the means of expressing immediately our impatience, our surprise, our approval. A book takes a long time to write and, in those days, a long time to publish; in a review, it is possible to catch the news on the wing, to address one's friends and refute one's adversaries almost as quickly as in private correspondence. I would read an article that made me angry and say to myself immediately: 'I must answer that!' That's how all the essays I wrote for *Les Temps Modernes* came into being. In this groping, seething period of renascence, there were always new problems presenting themselves, challenges to be taken up, errors to be rectified, misunderstandings to be cleared up, criticisms to be answered. Very few books and reviews were being published; our polemics had the intimacy, the urgency and the warmth of family quarrels.

I wanted very much to see *Les Bouches inutiles* put on. At the preview of *Huis clos* I had been stirred by the thunder of the applause; it was much more immediate, more intoxicating than the scattered echoes wakened by a book. I had been to see Camus' *Caligula* which had left me cold when I read it. Gérard Philipe transformed the play. I wanted my own play to undergo a similarly flattering metamorphosis. And then I yielded once more to illusions: my name on the métro cards would be the name of a playwright, and the playwright would be me. When Vitold suggested a meeting with Serge who ran the Théâtre du Carrefour, I accepted greedily.

Ten years earlier, at Rouen, I had heard about a handsome young man whom everyone had been in love with; he had married the prettiest of my third-year students; his name was Serge: this was the man. Olga knew him; when she saw him again, she exclaimed: 'Serge! It's you!' 'Well, yes,' he said apologetically. He was older, fatter and had lost a lot of hair. He had been divorced and had married again, this time Jacqueline Morane, who wanted to play the part of Catherine. She had stage presence and a lovely voice. Serge decided to produce my play; no sooner had rehearsals begun than he told me he was going to have to stop. He was short of money; could I put my hands on any? It wasn't easy. Because of the paper shortage, books were printed only in editions of five thousand; our normal income was enough to allow us to live comfortably, but with nothing left over. I was just thinking that all was lost when, quite unexpectedly, a fortune fell out of the sky.

Nero[1] had been released from Fresnes early that year, and I had seen him three or four times since then, at the Brasserie Lipp, at the Flore, at the Deux Magots. He would have liked to work in some capacity for *Les Temps Modernes*, but there was nothing we could give him to do. 'In that case, my only salvation is to write,' he said to me; the tameness of the samples he showed me left little hope in that direction. Yet when he told me about one of his latest suicide attempts, he spoke with great artistry: a hundred aspirin tablets swallowed one by one, the slowness, the lugubriousness of this operation, which ended with his throwing up. He had made other attempts with barbiturates. Each time he managed to leave himself an emergency exit, while taking considerable risks all the same. 'It's not a game, it's not an act,' he explained. 'There's a state of indifference you reach with regard to both life and death: you have to give death its chances.'

One October morning, he pushed open the door of the Flore. 'I know you need money,' he said. He must have heard this from Renée, whom I saw from time to time. He put down a bundle of notes on the table in front of me – a hundred thousand francs; it was a lot in those days. 'Don't worry, it's mine. I earned it.' Renée had told me Nero had found a good job, and he was so persuasive with people that I was scarcely even surprised; he was connected with the ministry responsible for reconstructing disaster areas and was in charge of estimates. By financing *Les Bouches inutiles*, he hoped he would be making up to some extent for the nasty trick he had played on Sartre. I took the money straight to Serge.

At seven the following morning, there was a knock on my door: 'Police!' Two cops came into my room and ordered me to go with them to the Quai des Orfèvres; I was accused of receiving stolen goods, and I would have to return the hundred thousand francs. I dressed and ran along the corridor to let Sartre know; he could go and borrow the money from Gallimard. We were intrigued. What new scheme had Nero thought up? And why had he mixed me up in it? In any case I was to blame. The government wasn't going to put a notorious con man in charge of their estimates; my desire to see my play performed had clouded my judgement.

At the Quai des Orfèvres I was seated in a vast room furnished with tables and benches. I had brought some work with me, and

1. cf. *The Prime of Life*.

for three or four hours I wrote. Inspectors came in and out, bringing people accused of various offences and questioning them; baskets of sandwiches were passed around; between interrogations, they ate and chatted. Towards noon, one of them told me to follow him; he took me to the office of a magistrate to whom Sartre had just given the money and who asked us for our autographs. The next day, all the newspapers printed the story. One journalist introduced his piece with the ingenious headline: 'Cruel as his homonym, Nero hands the Existentialists over to the cops.'

Nero gave his explanation. He obtained – he didn't say how – the names of people who had suffered war damages and who were suspected of having made false declarations. Furnished with false papers, he would threaten them with heavy fines and imprisonment, then he would let it be understood that his silence could be bought. To others who had not yet put in their claims, he would suggest that they pad them a bit: a small bribe and he would approve them. Here too, his victims' complicity would assure his impunity, or so he thought; but nevertheless his machinations were brought to light. He had not committed forgery and could only be accused of fraud because he had avoided imitating official papers exactly and had changed the placing of the red, white and blue band running across them. Caught unexpectedly, and under pressure to return the money, he had thought it would seem more honourable to have invested his profits in an artistic venture than to have squandered them, and so he brought me into it; at least, that's how he explained it to me. He was only in prison a short time; I saw him again afterwards, but not often. All the deals he managed to pull off after that were pretty small-time. Now and then he would try to kill himself. One day, he made up his mind to do it properly. He was found in his hotel room, lying on his bed with Renée's photo on his chest, finished off by a massive dose of prussic acid.

Les Bouches inutiles was put on after all. I attended rehearsals; I was so amazed to hear my lines become real voices that it all seemed perfect. Only one thing disappointed me. I had expected it to be staged so that one scene would follow another in a flash; but each one had a separate set. The theatre was poor and didn't have many stage-hands; when Sartre saw a run-through, the slowness of the scene changes worried him, but I was assured that they would be fast enough when the time came. However, on the afternoon of the dress rehearsal, the performance was delayed by infuriating waits, and I grew more uneasy. I had amused myself by playing a harmless enough game; suddenly, there were witnesses, judges, turning it into a public event for which I was responsible; I had invited them, words sprung from my pen were assailing their ears. I was ashamed of my immodesty; at the same time, their view superimposed itself on my own; I could no longer see clearly. At certain lines, too naïvely inspired by Existentialist philosophy, friends winked at each other. I was sitting next to Genet, who is never tactful with his criticisms. 'This isn't what the theatre's about! This isn't theatre at all,' he whispered in my ear. It was agony. However, after the final curtain, I was congratulated and my confidence returned. On opening night, watching through a hole in the curtain as the audience came in, I was anxious but optimistic. Once more my friends were encouraging and it seemed to me that the applause was quite enthusiastic. A play is not inert like a book; something had happened, through me, to a great number of people – director, actors, stage-hands; something good, I thought. I had planned a supper in Gégé's apartment, my guests were all very gay and, with the help of the whisky, I felt quite elated. Jacques Lemarchand took me aside; he deplored all those static scenes, those dead waits; and then, with one or two exceptions, he had found the actors inadequate; the play's qualities didn't come across, whereas its defects came across only too well. Knowing his kindliness, I lost my confidence. What were the less well disposed critics going to say?

The dailies tore me to pieces almost unanimously; it was a pretty harsh disappointment. The weeklies were less hostile; I even found some warm defenders: Philippe Hériat, who devoted two articles to me; the critic of *Lettres françaises*, who talked about Cornelian theatre; and the critic of *Terre des hommes*. *Action* condemned the play's morality but was more or less favourable. Word of mouth was not too bad; the audiences kept coming for several weeks. Then it got cold and the theatre was very badly heated; it was also poorly situated: every now and again the noise of the elevated métro trains drowned out the actors. Receipts began to drop; after fifty performances, the theatre closed. This setback didn't hit me too hard. Without blinding myself to the play's defects, I did think it hadn't really had a fair chance. There were people who liked it; naturally I was more inclined to give their opinions more weight than those of the people who didn't. Above all, there were too many interests beckoning me on to linger over my regrets.

Bost came back from America, where he had been sent as a reporter by *Combat*; he was exultant. Lise had got engaged to a G.I. whom she was getting ready to join in the States; she was eager to get out of France, where there was no future for her and where she was hungry. Sartre was also going back to New York. In January, he had met a young woman there, half-separated from her husband and, despite her brilliant position in the world, not very satisfied with her life; they had been very attracted to each other. When told about my existence she had decided that when he went back to France they should forget each other; his feelings for her were too strong for him to accept this; he had written to her from Paris and she had replied. In order to see her again, he had had himself invited back by some American universities; on 12 December, he embarked on a Liberty ship.

I should have liked to leave Paris. The food situation was still bad; in the little restaurants I frequented I never had enough to eat. I couldn't find anywhere to work; in my room, I was cold; at the Flore, too many people knew me; since we had begun *Les Temps Modernes*, which had its offices at Gallimard's, we had been going a lot to the bar of the Pont-Royal, which was nearby; it was warm and quiet in that gilded basement room, but it was inconvenient trying to write on the casks they used for tables. I had a carbuncle on my leg which incapacitated me for several days. The Alliance Française had invited me to give some lectures in Tunis and Algiers, but this time the Relations Culturelles didn't give me any help in getting there: there was never room for me on either the boats or the planes, which were very infrequent anyway, leaving for Tunis.

I went to the preview of *The Brothers Karamazov*: Vitold was playing Ivan, Dufilho, Smerdiakov, and Maria Casarès was a delicious Grushenka. I saw Camus quite often. One evening, after we had both eaten at the Brasserie Lipp and drunk at the bar of the Pont-Royal until closing time, he bought a bottle of champagne and we emptied it together at the Louisiane, talking till three in the morning. Because I was a woman – and therefore, for he was quite feudal about such things, not quite an equal – he would end up telling me intimate secrets about himself; he gave me bits of his notebooks to read and told me about the difficulties in his private life. There was one theme that preoccupied him, and he often came back to it: some day he must write the truth! The fact is that in his case there was a much greater gap than for many others between his life and his work. When we went out together, drinking, laughing, chatting, late into the night, he was funny, cynical, rather coarse and often very bawdy in his conversation; he would admit his emotions, give way to his impulses; he was capable of sitting down in the snow on the edge of the sidewalk at two in the morning and meditating pathetically about love. 'You have to choose. Love either lasts or it goes up in flames; the tragedy is that it can't last and go up in flames as well.' I liked the 'hungry ardour' with which he abandoned himself to life and pleasure, I liked his enormous consideration for others: when Bost was a war correspondent, every time Camus received a dispatch from him he immediately telephoned Olga. And yet, on the staff of *Combat*, he was accused of being arrogant and peremptory. During serious discussions, he would close up and become very formal, replying to arguments with noble phrases, high-flown sentiments, righteous rages it seemed to give him great satisfaction to produce. Pen in hand, he became a rigid moralist who seemed to have nothing in common with our happy nocturnal companion. He was aware that his public image utterly failed to coincide with the truth of his private self, and this occasionally embarrassed him.

Tired of dragging about Paris, I went skiing in Mégève; I returned to the Chalet Idéal-Sport and was moved to open my eyes in the morning and recapture the white splendour of the high snows, the memories of another age. For those times, today long gone and flattened by the weight of time, like contours of the earth seen from a high-flying plane, still had varying depths then, to the eye of memory; the past, still fresh but already strange, was amazing.

Six years ago [I wrote to Sartre] I wrote you from here and the war was on. It seems much longer ago than six years. I feel in some way out of things, as though in another life; I don't recognize either myself or the world as it was thenany more. And yet there are still memories, the memories I shared with you in that first life. But they have so little connexion with the present that they have a strange, rather painful effect.

I had company; Lefèvre-Pontalis, one of Sartre's ex-pupils who had been a friend of Bourla's, had brought his wife to a little hotel on the slope of Mont d'Arbois; shortly after my arrival, Bost arrived at the Idéal-Sport with Olga and Wanda; the two women only ventured onto the ski slopes now and then, they preferred sunbathing. Salacrou was staying right over my head, Chez Ma Tante. He was a much better skier than all of us, but often came for a drink. Sometimes, in the morning before the ski-lifts had started working, I would go down the deserted slopes to Saint-Gervais, alone in the silence and the cold. But generally I only went out during the afternoon; before lunch I worked at *All Men are Mortal*, surrounded by the vast, glittering landscape of the mountains. Up till then I had always been too strict ever to mix work and play; now I found the combination very pleasant. After the continual agitation of Paris, the calm of the chalet suited me. 'I feel so relaxed with no one looking at me and no one talking to me!' I wrote Sartre. All the same, I was very flattered when the lady who owned the chalet said to Bost: 'But she's very well known, Mlle de Beauvoir; any number of people ask if that's who she is; it's the same as with M. Salacrou.'

Finally I got a message that I had been allotted a seat on a plane leaving from Marignane three days later; I hurried back to Paris, which seemed very dreary. 'Paris is icy, the hotel isn't heated, and there seems to be absolutely nothing to eat. It doesn't get light before nine in the morning and there's no electricity; all the bars close at ten; everyone looks mournful, and the whole thing is intolerably boring and miserable,' I wrote Sartre. I leapt joyfully into the train that was to take me to Pas-des-Lanciers, where a bus picked me up and took me to the airport; it was early in the morning. I was slightly nervous. I had never been in a plane before but how marvellous, I thought, not only that there should still be first times left for me, but that they should be happening!

Alas! Someone had taken my seat, and the next plane didn't leave for three days. I hadn't a cent on me, it was drizzling, they were counting on me in Tunis, and my anger only served to increase my despair. I pleaded, the pilots relented and made a place for me between them in the cockpit; it was a maiden flight far beyond my wildest dreams. To the left, to the right, in front of me, out to infinity shone the Mediterranean Sea, and it seemed to me miraculous to look down on it from so high in the sky. *We used to say to each other: some day, when we're rich, we'll take*

the plane to London; but they say you're ill most of the way, and in
any case you can scarcely see a thing. I soared over the mountains
of Corsica without having had to climb them; I could make out
people, sheep. Then the outline of Sardinia appeared against the
sea's blue, as precise as it was in my childhood atlas. Suddenly
there were stucco houses below, flat roofs, palm trees, camels:
Africa and my first plane landing.

There was no one waiting for me at the airport; so much the
better; this unexpected freedom, this incognito arrival enchanted
me; coming from the grey atmosphere of Paris, the *souks* were as
fresh-looking as the ones in Tetuán, once upon a time.

The next day, the representative of the Alliance Française, M.E.,
took me in hand; his wife looked like Kay Francis. They found me
a room at the Tunisia-Palace; they took me by car to Carthage, to
Hammamet. At Sidi-bou-Saïd we had to walk ten yards to reach
the sea and a magnificent panorama; they had brought Julien Benda
here and he had refused to leave the car. 'I can imagine, I can
imagine . . .' he had said. I hoped I would never become indifferent
to such things.

I certainly wasn't then. The whole time not devoted to my
lectures and to the unavoidable social functions I spent on expeditions. I went alone, to visit the Roman ruins at Dougga. My hosts
were worried; a year earlier, a teacher had been raped and butchered
on this road. For my outing the following day, they suggested I
go to Gramat, quite near Tunis; there was a little hotel, at the sea's
edge, and sun-covered dunes where, after lunch, I lay down with
a book. I dropped off to sleep and, half-dreaming, I thought:
'How odd! There are cats on these dunes.' I opened my eyes:
no cats, but a very dirty old Arab sitting on my stomach; in the
sand next to his basket, a knife. 'Better raped than butchered,' I
said to myself, but I was almost fainting with terror. As I pushed
him off I suggested, extremely volubly, that he might like some
money; he hesitated. I emptied my purse into his hands and ran,
slipping and stumbling out of the dunes as fast as my legs would
carry me; fortunately I had left the greater part of my fortune at
the Tunisia-Palace. I told the woman at the hotel that I had met
an old tramp; she knew him – a petty thief who used his knife for
cutting asparagus. I supposed afterwards that he had attacked me
without much conviction, simply because he felt he oughtn't to
miss an opportunity.

My stay in Tunis was pleasant; the E.s took me to the nicest restaurants. One evening we went to dinner at the house of Bernard Zherfuss, the architect, the brother of one of my friends with whom I had studied at Désir; he was married. I had made some progress in psychology; in spite of their utter discretion, it seemed to me that something intangible passed between him and Mme E. I was to learn a year or two later, that they had each sought a divorce and then married each other.

The E.s regarded French policy in Tunisia as clumsy; they were in favour of a *rapprochement* between the French and Moslem middle classes. At their house I met Tunisian women dressed, made up, groomed and scented just like Parisiennes; they no longer wore veils except in the morning, to go to market; they were eager for their liberty. Among the men, the young ones were on their side; they resented having their fathers choose wives for them who were ignorant and unenlightened. No one had anything to tell me about the Franco-Tunisian situation in general, and I did not question them too closely. The demon of adventure had possessed me again. I was getting ready to explore Tunisia and then go back up to Algiers through the Sahara; the transportation situation was so unreliable that it was a risky undertaking, but that only whetted my appetite.

Sousse, Sfax, the great Roman Circus of El Djem, Kairouan, Djerba – I reached them all without difficulty by train, by bus and by boat. At Djerba, Ulysses had forgotten Penelope and Ithaca: the island was worthy of its legend. It was a cool orchard with a carpet of dappled grass; the glossy crowns of the palms sheltered the delicate blossoming trees; the edges of this garden were lashed by the sea. I was the only guest in the hotel, and the owner spoiled me. She told me that the summer before, one of her boarders, a little English girl, had gone every day to a deserted beach to lie in the sun; one day she came back to lunch, her face all crumpled, and did not touch her food. 'What's the matter?' my hostess asked; the girl burst into tears. Three Arabs, who had been watching her for several days, had raped her, one by one. 'I tried to cheer her up,' the woman said. 'I said to her: Oh! Mademoiselle, when you're travelling . . . Come now, calm yourself; after all, when you're travelling!' But she had insisted on packing her bags the same evening. Obviously rape is no myth around here, I thought; there are many men who live in such extreme poverty that marriage, and therefore a woman, are denied them. Their loins cry out; and then, they're used to the veils, the modesty of Moslem women; a woman stretched out on the sand, half nude, is offering herself, she is a woman there to be taken. After that, to go into the village, where there was a fair the following day, I accepted the services of an escort, a bearded old man whose virtue my hostess had guaranteed.

To continue my journey I had to avail myself of military transport; I stopped at Médenine, where I saw those curious vaulted granaries, stuck one on top of the other, called *gorfa*; the captain promised me that the day after next a truck would take me on to Matmata; then I took another bus on to Tatahouine: this alarming name attracted me. As I got down from the bus, a spahi in ceremonial dress very formally prevailed on me to follow him. He accompanied me as far as a villa, furnished with cushions and carpets, which was the home of the A.I. commander, a bearded Breton with very blue eyes; someone in Médenine had forewarned him of my arrival and he let it be understood that there was no question of my going around alone and on foot while I was in his territory; such behaviour would cast a slur on the good name of France. If I went out it would be under escort and in a jeep. I yielded to his decision. I was seated at a table where he was dining with the other officers of the A.I. and a lady doctor whose husband, also a doctor, was away; I was flabbergasted by the outrageousness of her language and her jokes, which the male members of the party lapped up with scandalized laughter – what a virago! I was given a bedroom adjoining hers; she became quite different. She explained to me that her extreme freedom of speech was a protection against advances and coarseness. She worked very hard; her main task was the treatment of the venereal diseases which infested the population; she had artificially inseminated the wives of the caïd, who was incapable of getting them with child himself. A strange life, which she led at a great pace, though not without finding it wearisome. She told me that the officers of the A.I. never mixed with the officers of the Legion; they formed a small, closed circle of their own. They rode; they went to Gabès from time to time. They were unutterably bored.

No doubt that explained the warmth with which I was received: any diversion was a welcome one. In the morning they took me across landscapes whose glaring nakedness already presaged the desert; at noon they organized a great *méchoui*; we went to look at troglodyte villages hollowed out of cliffs the colour of dawn; the notables invited us into their caves hung with rich rugs, offered us hard-boiled eggs which it would have been offensive to refuse, but which I simply couldn't get down; I made a cache of them in my bag. In the evening, it appeared that the captain had made inquiries about me and I was asked to talk about Existentialism; they had invited the local teacher. I can't remember what I stammered out.

At Médenine, the promised truck was waiting for me. I was the only passenger. The driver must have known the Matmata road before it was damaged in the war. In two or three places bridges had been blown up, but he managed to ford the wadis and eventually got me to that strange village where ten thousand people live under the ground. The market-place was a seething mass; nothing but men, swathed in snowy burnouses, chattering and happy; the dark, blue-eyed women, some young and beautiful, but all sad-looking, were to be found at the bottom of the many shafts which opened onto the caves; I visited one of these dungeons. Down in these dark, smoky caverns I saw crowds of half-naked children, a toothless old woman, two dirty-looking middle-aged women, and a pretty girl covered with jewellery who was weaving a carpet. As I came back up into the light, I passed the master of the house returning from market, resplendently healthy and dazzling in his white burnous. I pitied my sex.

I slept at Gabès; the man who owned the hotel slipped a poem under my door in which he deplored, between courtly compliments, the fact that I was an Existentialist. I was disappointed by the oasis at first; I found myself walking along muddy roads between earth walls, and except for the palms overhead, I couldn't see a thing. Then I managed to slip into the orchards and discovered the gaiety of fountains amid flowering trees. The gardens of Nefta were even more delicate. On one side of the main square there was a charming hotel. In the visitors' book, Gide had written: 'Had I known Nefta, I should have loved it more than Biskra.'[1] Next morning, I sat on the sunny terrace reading Koestler's *Spartacus* while I waited for the truck that was to take me into the heart of the desert. The driver, a Tunisian, made me sit beside him: there was no other woman among his passengers, and no

1. I quote from memory.

[66]

European. Before long, I was surprised to see the road fading out; we were going straight over the dunes. It had been explained to me that in order to drive on sand you have to let some air out of the tyres, and then have the requisite knack; beginners always break down after the first hundred yards. Our driver seemed to be an expert; all the same, every time he hurled the truck towards a dune, I thought: He'll never get to the top. At the top, the truck would pause for an instant at a very precarious angle. It's going to turn over, I thought. Then it would continue down; and we'd begin all over again. The dunes spread in waves as far as the eye could reach in all directions, and I asked myself: 'Why is it so beautiful?' The sand stretching to infinity gave the impression of a smooth, simple world, formed from surface to centre out of a single substance; a delightful play of curves and light breathed, like music, from the serenity of the One.

I walked in the moonlight at El Oued; the earth was hollowed out into vast funnels with gardens buried at the bottom; from a distance, there was something charmingly fantastic about seeing the crowns of the palm trees sprouting straight out of the sand. I spent the day on the crest of a dune; the women from a nearby *douar* climbed up and encircled me; they opened my bag, played with my lipstick, undid my turban, while the children played tag with great shrieks across the sand. I never tired of contemplating the calm monotony of those tall, motionless waves. On a bench in the public square, I was shown the name of Gide, carved with his own hand.

I was delayed at Ouargla for three days. I wanted to go on to Ghardaïa. A date merchant was waiting for a truck that was supposed to take a shipment for him; every morning I crossed the fantastic esplanades thought up by a homosexual colonel – Colonel Carbillet – who had evidently thought he was Lyautey. I would ask the merchant: 'Has the truck arrived?' 'No. But it's sure to be here tomorrow. . . .' I would go back to the hotel, where I was the only guest, and they would feed me camel; I liked sitting on the terrace, moored at the edge of the undulating sands. I had nothing left to read, and all I could find in the village was an old number of *La Bataille*; there were moments when it seemed that time had ceased to exist, and I felt a strange weakness come over me; at those moments I would go out, my sandals in my hand, into the swell of the apricot-coloured dunes, intercepted far away by hard, pink cliffs. Under the palms a veiled woman would pass silently, or an old man with a donkey; it is beautiful to see a human being pass across the motionless face of nature without disturbing it; I would come back towards my hotel and be moved to see my own footprints in the soft sand. After years of living with others, this encounter with myself stirred me so deeply that I believed it to be the dawn of a sort of wisdom. It was only an interim, but for a long time I kept the palm trees, the sands, and their silence in my heart.

They were expecting me in Algiers; I decided to forego Ghardaïa. In the bar of the Grand Hôtel at Touggourt I uneasily rediscovered a civilization I had forgotten: restless, verbose, gluttonous. I left the next day, not by the express that most Europeans take, but – because I wanted to stop off at Biskra for a few hours – by a much earlier, slower train almost exclusively filled with Arabs. All the cars were packed; a cluster of people hung from every footboard; I managed to get up onto a platform where I stood, lashed by gusts of sand. I hadn't had time to get a ticket; I asked the conductor for one. 'A ticket? Do you really want one?' He laughed and shook his head. 'You're a European! You don't have to pay.' I marvelled at this logic: since I had money, he wasn't going to ask me for it. But the natives he treated abominably; the ones who were hanging on to the buffers he knocked off and sent sprawling onto the ground; the train didn't go very fast and they weren't hurt, but they stared despairingly at the desert surrounding them, yelled and shook their fists.

Biskra was less attractive than it is in Gide's books. Constantine, rainy and full of hate, chilled my spirits. In Algiers I was never left on my own and saw nothing but 'sights'. To my eyes, still dazzled by the Sahara, the north seemed dull.

I came back by plane and found Paris deserted. Sartre hadn't returned, Lise had gone, Olga was staying in Normandy with her parents. Bost was travelling in Italy with a group of journalists, Camus was about to go to New York. I worked, I moped a bit. Through Queneau I met Boris Vian. Trained as an engineer, he wrote and played the trumpet; he had been one of the guiding spirits of the *zazou* movement engendered by the war and the Collaboration: since their rich parents spent most of the year in Vichy, these young upper-middle-class boys and girls organized anarchistic parties in the abandoned family apartments; they emptied the wine cellars and broke the furniture, imitating the plundering soldiers; they bought and sold on the black market. Anarchistic, a-political, they reacted against their Pétainist families by flaunting an aggressive anglophilia; they imitated the stiff elegance, the accent, the manners of English snobs. America counted so little for them that they were abashed when Paris was suddenly filled with Americans; however, they had one very strong bond with them: jazz, about which they were fanatical. The Abadie band, in which Vian played, was hired by the 'French Welcome Committee' on the very first day the Americans entered Paris, and was then attached to the Special Service Show. This explains the way the ex-*zazous* dressed for the next three years: American surplus blue jeans and checked shirts. They used to meet on the Avenue Rapp, near the Champs-Élysées, and also at the Champo at the corner of the Rue Champollion, which was a dance hall at the time. A handful of them not only liked jazz but also Kafka, Sartre and American novels; during the war they rummaged through the bookstalls along the Seine and were triumphant if they dug out some forbidden work by Hemingway or Faulkner. To read and talk, they came to Saint-Germain-des-Prés. That's how I met Vian at the bar of the Pont-Royal; a manuscript of his was being read by Gallimard, and Queneau thought highly of it; I had a drink with them and with Astruc; it seemed to me that Vian listened to himself too much and that he was too inclined to cultivate paradoxes for their own sake. He gave a party in March; by the time I arrived, everyone had already had quite a bit to drink; his wife, Michelle, her long, silky blonde hair spread over her shoulders, was smiling beatifically; Astruc was asleep barefoot on the divan; I too drank manfully while we listened to American records. At about two in the morning, Boris offered me a cup of coffee; we sat down in the kitchen and talked on into the dawn: about his novel, about jazz, about literature, about engineering, which was his trade. I no longer found anything affected in that long, pale, smooth face, but instead great kindliness and a sort of stubborn candour. Vian was as vehement about hating what he called '*les affreux*' as he was about liking what he liked. He played the trumpet in spite of the fact that it was bad for his heart. ('If you go on, you'll be dead in ten years,' his doctor had told him.) We talked on and the dawn came too quickly: I valued beyond price these fleeting moments of eternal friendship.

A month later, the first Gallimard cocktail party was given; Astruc went to sleep behind a sofa; when he woke up the room was empty; he tried to feel his way out, stumbled into the dining room, where the Gallimard family had just gathered for dinner, and stuck both his hands in the soup tureen.

One of the people I saw often was Merleau-Ponty, with whom I was working on *Les Temps Modernes*. I had reviewed his thesis on *The Phenomenology of Perception* for the magazine. Our middle-class religious backgrounds created a bond between us, but we reacted to them in different ways. He still retained a nostalgia for a lost paradise; I did not. He liked being with older people and mistrusted the young, whereas I greatly preferred them to their elders. His writing revealed a sense of nuance, and he talked hesitantly; I was for clear-cut opinions. He was interested in the peripheries of thought, in the nebulous fringes of existence rather than in its hard core; with me it was the opposite. I had great respect for his books and essays, but it seemed to me that he didn't understand Sartre's thinking very well. I brought to our discussions a vehemence to which he submitted with a smile.

Towards the middle of March, Olga came back from Normandy; the family doctor, unable to account for her fever and lassitude, had had her X-rayed: both her lungs were infected. The failure of *Les Bouches inutiles* had been a violent setback for her, and her sunbathing at Mégève had not been beneficial. I cabled Bost, who came home immediately. The specialists all contradicted each other. Unless she had a pneumothorax, Olga would die; a pneumothorax was certain death. She must be sent to a sanatorium, above all she must not go to a sanatorium. Finally she was admitted to the Beaujon hospital and was given a pneumothorax. It was all the more heartrending because Dullin was about to revive *The Flies*. The project was abandoned, for neither Dullin nor Sartre wanted anyone else for Electra.

At Mégève, I had finished *All Men are Mortal*, begun in 1943. Back from America, Sartre read the last part of it in the noisy, smoky cellar of the Méphisto, where we were spending most of our evenings at that time.

'How can one consent to not being everything?' Georges Bataille asks in *L'Expérience intérieure*. The phrase had struck me because that had been Françoise's devouring hope in *L'Invitée*:

she had wanted to be everything. I regretted not having shown this illusion and its collapse in a clearer light, and decided to rework that theme. Gnawed by ambition and envy, my new hero was to seek complete identification with the universe and then discover that the world resolves itself into individual liberties, each of which he is unable to attain. While in *Blood of Others* Blomart believes himself responsible for everything, this man would suffer the incapacity to do anything. In this way, his story would be a complement to my first novel and the antithesis of my second. But I didn't want it to resemble them. In 1943 and 1944, I had been obsessed by History, and it was on the historical level that I meant to situate myself; not content with possessing riches and fame, my hero would also seek to influence the course of events. I had the idea of making him immortal; this would make his failure even more shattering. I set out to explore in every direction what it would mean to be immortal. I continued the meditation on death into which I had been drawn by the war; I questioned myself about the meaning of time; it had been brutally revealed to me, and I had realized that it was just as capable as space of dividing me from myself. I gave no answers to the questions I raised. *Blood of Others* had been conceived and constructed abstractly, but around the story of Fosca I let my dreams cluster.

The dominant theme, which reappears perhaps a little too stubbornly throughout the book, is the conflict of the point of view of death, of the absolute, of Sirius, with that of life, of the individual, of the earth; at twenty I was already vacillating, in my private notebooks, from one to the other; I had set them in opposition in *Pyrrhus et Cinéas*; in *L'Invitée* what happens to Françoise is that, whether from wisdom or weariness, she renounces the world of the living and slides into the indifference of death; against the intolerable present, Hélène, in *Blood of Others*, tries to use the infinity of the future as an alibi; this time, too, I was confronting the relative and the absolute through history; but we had gained our victory, the present was all we could desire; it was the future that made us uneasy. We had disdained the grumbling voices which had whispered in August 1944: 'And after?' and also the disaster-mongers who prophesied in 1945: 'The Third World War has just begun.' I didn't imagine that the atom bomb was going to blow up the whole world the next day; nevertheless the meaning of the Allied victory had been compromised, and I wondered:

What is the true substance of our present? Between the nihilism of the false prophets and the giddiness of the good-timers, where should we take our stand?

First of all I involved Fosca in a finite undertaking: the achievement of glory, at Carmona. In order to gain success, he chooses immortality; but this terrible privilege makes him aware of the counter-finalities that corrode and destroy all individual successes; the personal pride embodied by Fosca divides Italy and leaves it defenceless against the King of France, then against the Emperor of Austria. Then Fosca renounces his country and becomes the *éminence grise* of Charles the Fifth; if he could succeed, through the Emperor, in uniting the whole world, then his work would be proof, he thinks, against the challenges of time; but how make the whole world one when each man is unique? Terrified by the massacres and the misery brought about by the search for universal Good, he begins to doubt this Good itself; men reject, even at the price of terrible destruction, like the Anabaptists, that motionless fulfilment which would leave them nothing more to *do*. The universe is nowhere, he realizes: 'There is nothing except men, men forever divided'; he renounces the idea of governing them: 'There is nothing to be done for mankind; their good depends only on themselves. ... They do not want happiness: they want to live. There is nothing one can do for them, there is nothing one can do against them. There is nothing one can do.'

Fosca's unhappy experience covered the end of the Middle Ages and the beginning of the sixteenth century. Stupid wars, a chaotic economy, useless rebellions, futile massacres, population increases unaccompanied by any improvement in the standard of living, everything in this period seemed to me confusion and marking time; I had chosen it for this very reason. The conception of history that emerges from this first part is resolutely pessimistic; I did not by any means consider it as cyclic, but I denied that there was any progress in its course. How could I think that my own epoch was any better than those before it, when it had so multiplied the honours of the past on battlefields, in concentration camps, in bombed cities? The romanticism and the moralism that counterbalance this pessimism also came from the circumstances of that time; our friends who had died in the Resistance, all the members of the Resistance who by their deaths had become our friends – all they had done had been of very little use, even of no use at all;

one had to accept their lives as their own justification; one had to believe in the value of devotion, of ardour, of pride, of hope. I still do believe in those values. But does the separateness of men prevent humanity from undertaking any collective conquest? That is another question.

In any case, I did not say so. The sombre vision proposed in the early part of the novel is challenged in the final chapter. The victories won by the working class since the beginning of the Industrial Revolution were another truth I recognized. In fact, I had no philosophy of history, nor does my novel arrive at one. In the triumphal march that closes his recollections, Fosca sees only the trampling of feet, but he does not hold the key to the enigma. First he had surveyed the world with the eye of a politician fascinated by its forms – city, nation, universe; next, he had given these forms a content – men; but he tried to govern them from outside, almost like a God; when he understands at last that they are free and self-determining, that one can serve but not possess them, he is too exhausted to feel any friendship for them; his defection does not deny History its meaning: it simply shows that the breaks between generations are necessary in order to move ahead. The Communists, following Hegel, speak of Humanity and its future as of some monolithic individuality. I was attacking this illusion by embodying this myth of unity in Fosca; the meanderings, the backslidings, the miseries of History, and its crimes, are too hard to encompass for one consciousness to recall them down through the length of centuries without yielding to despair; fortunately, from father to son, life begins afresh indefinitely. But this perpetual renovation implies also the pain of separation. If the desires that inspired the men of the eighteenth century are realized in the twentieth, the dead have no joy in the harvest; Fosca, swept along in a tumultuous procession, thinks of the woman he had loved a hundred years before: what is happening now, he tells himself, is exactly what she wanted then, it is not at all what she would have wanted now. This discovery completes his defeat. He cannot create a living link between the centuries, since they transcend each other only by forswearing what they have been; if he feels indifferent to the people who live in those centuries, there is nothing to involve Fosca in their projects; if he loves them, he cannot bear the infidelity to which his destiny condemns him.

For Fosca represents the terrible pit of forgetfulness and

betrayal; I had experienced the cruel pain of being unable to grasp in any way the deaths of others; all absences are contradicted by the immutable plenitude of the world. In my second novel, Blomart thinks of a friend killed at the age of twenty: 'Who has he not been?'; about a woman he loved, Fosca wonders: 'Where is she not?' Several times I put into his mouth a phrase that appears once in *The Mandarins* as well: 'The dead were dead, the living lived.' He cannot even toy with the hope that he will *always* remember; for him that word has no meaning. All his dealings with humanity are perverted by this fact; he never reaches the true meaning of friendship or love because the whole basis of our brotherhood is that we all must die: only an ephemeral being is capable of finding the absolute within time. Beauty cannot exist for Fosca, nor any of the living values instituted by human finitude. To look at the world is, for him, to lay it waste, for he sees with the eye of God, whom I rejected at the age of fifteen, the eye of the Being who transcends and levels everything, who knows everything, who can do anything, and turns man into a worm. From everyone he encounters, Fosca steals the world, without reciprocity; he casts them into the agonizing indifference of eternity.

That is Régine's tragedy, which I conceived as a counterpoint to that of Fosca. An immortal being I could endow with the most far-reaching ambitions, but not, since he has no peer, with that emotion of mingled fascination and rancour, human envy; I bestowed it instead on a woman greedy for domination over her fellow men and in revolt against all limitations – the glory of others and her own death. When she meets Fosca, she wants to inhabit his immortal heart; then she will become, she thinks, the Unique. What happens is the opposite; under his gaze, she crumbles; all her enterprises and her virtues conceal merely an absurd effort to exist, identical with the effort of all other men; with terror, she sees her life degraded to the status of a farce;[1] she sinks into madness. She had glimpsed a way to salvation, but lacked the strength to cling to it; she should have held fast to her own mortality. One of the main characters, Armand, meets Fosca face

1. The party scene, where she becomes conscious of the farce, recalls the scene in *L'Invitée* when Elisabeth, receiving the trio, gets the impression that she is taking part in a parody; but her disturbance was only psychological; with Régine, it has a metaphysical dimension.

to face and is not turned to stone because he is committed body and soul to his own epoch. This morality relates to the conclusions of *Pyrrhus et Cinéas*, but it is not driven home in the form of a lesson; rather, it serves as a pretext for an imaginary experience. Some critics, the very ones who are annoyed when a novel *proves* something, blamed this one for not proving anything; which is precisely the reason why, despite the *longueurs*, the repetitions, the excesses, I still feel warmly towards it. Re-reading it, I asked myself: But what was I trying to say? I was trying to say nothing more than the story I invented. The conflict is presented throughout within the narrative itself; an attempt to isolate specific assertions from it would only produce a set of contradictions; no one point of view finally prevails; Fosca's point of view and Armand's are true together. In my earlier essay I had said that the dimension of human enterprise is neither the finite nor the infinite but the indefinite: this word cannot be fixed within any given limits, the best way of approaching it is to explore its possible variations. *All Men are Mortal* is an organized version of such an exploration; its themes are not theses, but points of departure for uncharted wanderings.

Once back from Tunisia, I had begun an essay in which I was tackling the same questions. I had had the idea for it a year earlier. In February 1945 I had given a lecture at Gabriel Marcel's to a group of mainly Catholic students; I had taken with me an ex-pupil of Sartre's, Misrahi, an Existentialist and a Zionist. He belonged to the Stern group; every time Gabriel Marcel attacked me, he would fling himself forward to defend me, vehemently and pertinently: he had made himself thoroughly disliked. When it was over, I had a chat with him upstairs at the Flore; I told him that in my opinion it was possible to base a morality on *Being and Nothingness*, if one converted the vain desire to be into an assumption of existence. 'You must write it!' he told me. During that winter, Camus had asked me, though I can't remember for what collection, for an essay on action; the reception of *Pyrrhus et Cinéas* was an encouragement to return to philosophy. Besides which, when I read Lefebvre, Naville or Mounin, I always wanted to reply. It was partly against them, therefore, that I undertook to write *The Ethics of Ambiguity*.

Of all my books, it is the one that irritates me the most today. The polemical part still seems valid. I was wasting time rebutting absurd objections; but at the time Existentialism was being treated as nihilist philosophy, wilfully pessimistic, frivolous, licentious, despairing and ignoble; some defence had to be made. I commented critically and, to my mind, convincingly, on the delusion of the *one* monolithic humanity used by Communist writers – often without admitting it – in order to evade the difficulties presented by death and failure; I sketched the antinomies of action, man's indefinite transcendence against his demand for regeneration, the future against the present, the collective reality against the interiority of every being; returning to the question of ends and means, a burning one at the time, I demolished certain sophistries. On the role of the intellectual within a government he approves, I raised problems that are still topical today. And I still subscribe to the passage on aestheticism, and to the reconciliation I suggested between the remote impartiality of the work of art and the commitment of the artist. The fact remains that on the whole I went to a great deal of trouble to present inaccurately a problem to which I then offered a solution quite as hollow as the Kantian maxims. My descriptions of the nihilist, the adventurer, the aesthete, obviously influenced by those of Hegel, are even more arbitrary and abstract than his, since they are not even linked together by a historical development; the attitudes I examine are explained by objective conditions; I limited myself to isolating their moral significance to such an extent that my portraits are not situated on any level of reality. I was in error when I thought I could define a morality independent of a social context. I could write a historical novel without having a philosophy of history, but not construct a theory of action.

I had contributed four articles to *Les Temps Modernes* which were afterwards published by Nagel as a book, of which three also deal with morals; so soon after a war which had forced us to re-examine all our ideas, it was natural enough to attempt to re-invent rules and reasons. France was crushed between two blocs, our fate was being decided without us; this state of passivity prevented us from taking practice as our law; I find nothing surprising, therefore, in my concern with moral questions. What I find hard to understand is the idealism that blemishes these essays. In reality, men defined themselves for me by their bodies, their needs, their work; I set no form, no value above the individual of flesh and blood. On my return from Portugal, when I blamed the

English for their complicity with a regime condemned for one thing by its tragically high rate of infant mortality, Herbaud said to me: 'Agreed, it's regrettable that there should be children dying of poverty; but perhaps that isn't too high a price to pay for the miracle of English democracy.' I was revolted. I also quarrelled with Aron, who thought England's higher interests justified the measures she was taking against immigration in Israel: the beauties of English democracy were so much hot air to these hopeless men jammed in the camps or on ships without harbour. But then, why did I take this circuitous route through other values besides need to justify the fundamental importance I assigned to need itself? Why did I write *concrete liberty* instead of *bread*, and subordinate the will to live to a search for the meaning of life? I never brought matters down to saying: People must eat because they are hungry. Yet that was what I thought. In *Oeil pour oeil*, I justified the purges after the Liberation without ever using the one solid argument: these mercenaries, these murderers, these torturers must be killed, not to prove that man is free, but to make sure they don't do it again; for one Brice liquidated, how many lives would have been spared! I was – like Sartre – insufficiently liberated from the ideologies of my class; at the very moment I was rejecting them, I was still using their language to do so. That language has become hateful to me because, as I now know, to look for the reasons why one should not stamp on a man's face is to accept stamping on it.

After his return from America, Sartre talked to me a great deal about M. At present, their attachment was mutual, and they envisaged spending two or three months together every year. So be it: separations held no terror for me. But he evoked the weeks he had spent with her in New York with such gaiety that I grew uneasy; till then I had supposed him to be attracted mainly by the romantic side of this adventure; suddenly I wondered if M. was more important to him than I was; my heart's old armour of optimism fell away; anything could happen to me. In a relationship that has lasted for fifteen years, how much is a matter of mere habit? What concessions does it imply? I knew my answer: not Sartre's. I understood him better than I used to, and for that reason I found him more opaque; there were great differences between us; this did not disturb me, quite the contrary, but him? According to his accounts, M. shared completely all his reactions, his emotions, his irritations, his desires. When they went out together, she always wanted to stop, to go on again, at exactly the same moment he did. Perhaps this indicated a harmony between them at a depth – at the very source of life, at the wellspring where its very rhythm is established – at which Sartre and I did not meet, and perhaps that harmony was more important to him than our understanding. I wanted to free my heart of this uncertainty. It often happens that when a dangerous question is burning our lips we choose a particularly unsuitable moment to ask it. We were just leaving my room to have lunch with the Salacrous when I asked: 'Frankly, who means the most to you, M. or me?' 'M. means an enormous amount to me, but I am with you.' His answer took my breath away. I understood it to mean: 'I am respecting our pact, don't ask more of me than that.' Such a reply put the whole future in question. It was all I could do to shake hands, to smile, to eat; I saw that Sartre was watching me uneasily, I pulled myself together, but I felt that the lunch would never be over. That afternoon, Sartre explained what he had meant: we had always taken actions to be more truthful than words, and that is why, instead of launching into a long explanation, he had invoked the evidence of a simple fact. I believed him.

Shortly after his return, Sartre caught the mumps. He retired to his bed in the round room; a doctor painted his neck and his face with black ointment. At the end of a few days he was able to receive visits from friends. Not all of them came: his illness scared some off. All the same, the room was always crowded and I had difficulty protecting him from bores.

During this time, I kept a diary. Here are some extracts from it; they reveal what my memory cannot revive: the daily dust of my daily life.

30 April 1946

When I went out at five this afternoon, the Carrefour de Buci was swarming with activity; women buying cauliflowers, asparagus, the first strawberries; they were selling slips of lily of the valley in little pots wrapped in silver paper. On the walls, the words YES or NO were scrawled in huge chalk letters.[1] Last year, there was something miraculous about spring, it was the first spring of the

1. They referred to the referendum on the Constitution proposed by the Constituent Assembly and supported by the Communists.

Liberation. This is already a peacetime spring. There is food in the shops, dates for example, and cloth and books; in the streets there are buses and taxis; a great change from May last year.

At *Les Temps Modernes*, I found Merleau-Ponty, Leiris and Ponge. Ponge has left *Action* (for what reason?). He says he finds having to choose between all the objects he'd like to describe perplexing: why not write for twenty years about moss? Or, from the opposite point of view, why not write about everything one encounters as one encounters it, without preference? He has more than two hundred poems still waiting to be finished, and expects to publish them some day in the form of an alphabet with illustrations. Gave Genet's and Laronde's poems to Festy to be printed, and told him I shall definitely not publish my novel in the magazine. Had a drink with Merleau-Ponty and Suzou at the Pont-Royal. Went home. With Sartre, still swathed in Velpeau bandages and wearing a pointed nightcap, I found Lefèvre-Pontalis. Sartre much better; brought him some books and magazines and made his dinner. Went to the Petit Saint-Benoît with Bost and Pontalis; Giacometti came in just as we did and sat with us. He was in better form than ever and told lots of stories. At the end of the meal, a saltcellar got knocked over. Bost picked it up; G. assumed his sorcerer's manner: 'I wondered who would pick it up; and it was you!' 'I wouldn't have picked it up,' said Pontalis. 'They always get picked up,' said G. Then Bost: 'Obviously, they're not meant to be upside down.' Giacometti, appalled: 'Ah! if you had said that in front of Breton, it would have been war!' He talked about the painter Christian Bérard: 'He's so handsome!' 'As handsome as Sartre?' I asked. He replied, very seriously: 'It's different. Sartre has a classical, Apollonian beauty; Bérard is Dionysiac.' Finished the evening at Chéramy's.

This morning, Boubal approached me with a radiant smile. 'If you read in the paper that M. Sartre is at death's door, don't get upset; there was a journalist looking for him, so I said: "He's ill, it may be the end." "What's the matter with him?" "A mysterious disease."'

On the stairs, I ran into B.,[1] who was on his way up to see Sartre; I stopped him; he told me he knew a lot of bores were always trying to see Sartre and he didn't want to bore him, but he had something fascinating to tell him: a friend of his, Patrix, has

1. An ex-pupil of Sartre's, who had become a doctor.

brought off 'a plastic transposition of the viscous'. Apparently it's 'a grandmother, an old grandmother who turns into a candle'.

1 May

Last year it was snowing, I remember. This morning was bright blue. Stayed in. Drank a cup of Nescafé and worked on *The Ethics of Ambiguity*. Sartre better; no more helmet of bandages, no more nightcap; instead, long black sideburns and a beard that looks like vegetation; he's still swollen, with a pimple on his nose. The dirty dishes, old papers, books, pile up day after day in his room; there's no place to put one's feet. He read me some Cocteau poems, very pretty. Outside there was bright sunlight: through the windows, one was very much aware of the street with its lily of the valley sellers and the pedlars selling stockings and rayon panties. I didn't put on stockings or coat to go out. Lilies of the valley everywhere, and all the chestnut trees along the Boulevard Pasteur heavy with white and red flowers, they're even beginning to lose their petals. Had lunch at my mother's; she's reading *Darkness at Noon*. Coming back, in the subway, I saw posters for Dullin's company with no mention of *The Flies*; that gave my heart a pang.

The first posters about the referendum are up on the hoardings: Vote YES, vote NO. All the Noes have been crossed out.

Work. At six in the evening, had a drink with Bost and Rolland at the Bar Vert which is making a clumsy attempt to compete with Chéramy's; beautiful posters, but ugly red tables and aggressively green walls. Youki was there in a pretty black and white check dress; she talked about the Belgian poet she had sent to me at the magazine.'You know,' she said with her usual unawareness, 'my house is the house of poets.'

2 May

Even fairer and warmer than yesterday. Lilies of the valley everywhere; there are more flowers this spring than I can ever remember. Went with Bost to Beaujon. From a long way off you see the hospital, built of brick, with its great red crosses; it's very tall, grand and severe, and reminds me of Drancy. Lots of people in front of the main door, women mostly, dressed in their best clothes; one would think that these visits are a sort of holiday for them; they laugh among themselves in the elevator as it slowly climbs up the eleven floors. The eleventh floor is for chest patients;

young women are on one side of the ward, older ones on the other; there's a single line of beds facing a large balcony with a grille (to prevent suicides, since some of the patients, especially the younger ones, would gladly throw themselves out of the window); there's a wide view of the suburbs, with a German prisoner-of-war camp in the foreground and, beyond that, the whole of Paris. Olga's room is a large, white cube which also opens onto this balcony. She says the view is extraordinarily beautiful in the evening, when all the lights come on. She's looking well today, hair carefully arranged, wearing make-up. She's had a third in-sufflation. She's now been in bed fifteen days and is beginning to get impatient.

In the bus, I read Troyat's *Life of Pushkin*, which I find interesting, and glanced through *Samedi-Soir*. There's a piece about *Arrival and Departure*. 'Koestler brings great pathos to his understanding of the anxieties of our age but is unable to provide us with any means of escaping them.' That's the kind of criticism that really goes far. I've heard at least a hundred discussions of the book; the fairest is what Giacometti said the other day: Roubachev ought to oppose No. 1 in the name of some other objectivity, not merely subjectivity; there should be some explicit issue between them, of a political or technical kind; without it Roubachev is unconvincing.

Work. Went to see Sartre at eight; he was reading *Prête-moi ta plume* by Scipion, who today was awarded the prize for satire given by the newspaper *Le Clou*, and whose picture is all over *Combat*. He's seen Pontalis, who likes Bost's book very much;[1] and Genet, who wanted Sartre to write a letter on his behalf asking the Minister for authorization to visit the reform schools. Bost is looking for a subject for a *Combat* article; I suggested one on the Hôtel Chaplain. He told us a lot about *Combat*, about the passion Pascal Pia was bringing to the task of killing the newspaper and himself with it, about Ollivier, whom everyone loathes and who knows it, about Aron, who's also getting himself disliked by understanding *Combat* so intensely and insisting on saying so. Everyone congratulated Bost on his article about the Pope, and Altmann came up from *Franc-Tireur* to say: 'It's below the belt, but it's damned good.' People were stunned by the conviction with which he called a surplice a bolero and a skullcap a caul. There have been three cancelled subscriptions.

1. *Le Dernier des métiers.*

3 May

A morning of work in my room. In the afternoon, looked through the weeklies with Sartre. There are stories in *Cavalcade* and in *Fontaine* about the fact that we now go to the Pont-Royal instead of the Flore. A fairly friendly article by Wahl on Existentialism occasioned by Merleau-Ponty's lecture. Went over to the magazine. Lots of people there. Vivet introduced me to one of his friends: 'X, who's enormously talented.' I said to him: 'I congratulate you; what do you have for us?' 'Anything.' A pause, then he asked: "What would you like?' 'Anything.' Another pause. 'Well, thank you very much,' he said. 'No, I'm the one to thank you.'

Paulhan has put together a very nice collection of texts: extracts from his own work, from Léautaud and from baroque manuscripts. I went to thank him. In his office, ten people dipping into a box. 'We were looking at photos of all the places Rimbaud visited,' Paulhan told me. 'Would you like to have a look?' But I went to collect some proofs from Festy and then had a drink with the Leirises at the Pont-Royal. Met Roger Stéphane there, and he asked to have his 'Conversation with Malraux' back.

Back at Sartre's we were talking once more about the connexion between lucidity and liberty, and whether our moral system is not really an aristocratic one. Bost dropped in. He told us that there was a great to-do at *Combat* because of the recent articles by Ollivier and Aron championing the No; many of the people on the paper were going to vote Yes; and they wanted to start a campaign urging people to vote Socialist; otherwise *Combat* would become a right-wing paper. It appears that everyone stays on only because of Pia's personal charm, and he's so absorbed by his anti-Communism that he forgets he's supposed to be a leader of the Left.

Had an ice at the Flore while I read *La Médiation chez Hegel*, from which I learned nothing. Adamov was there, Henri Thomas, Marthe Robert, then Giacometti, Tzara and a host of others. I bought some tea at Boubal's and then went home to bed.

4 May

A grey morning, rather cold. Went to the L.s' to get the Malraux interview for Stéphane. It puts Malraux in a very unsympathetic light; he thinks he's Goethe and Dostoyevsky rolled into one, and talks about everyone very maliciously. About Camus: 'Oh please, let's be serious. We're not at the Café de Flore. Let us talk about La Bruyère or Chamfort.' Stéphane says to him (I don't know where he got such an idea): 'Sartre wants to write a big, sordid book about the Resistance.' Malraux replies: 'I shall write one that will not be sordid.' But he defends himself pretty well against the accusation that he's becoming a Fascist. 'When a man has written what I have written, he does not become a Fascist.'

Work. From time to time, automobiles with loudspeakers on them go by the window yelling: 'Vote No!' or 'Vote Yes!' One hears about nothing but the vote. We have no electoral registration card. (We went to the *mairie*, but didn't make a fuss.) Pouillon isn't going to vote, and Bost probably won't either, but we discuss it all the same. Besides, the result is a foregone conclusion; the public opinion poll this week showed a 54 per cent Yes vote.

At half past twelve, Pontalis stopped by the hotel. He had met Genet the day before at Sartre's bedside and asked him: 'Would you like a weed?' Genet looked him up and down. 'Why do you call a cigarette a weed?' And he gave him a long lecture, explaining that culture, as Herriot put it, is what's left when one has forgotten everything, but that that was no excuse for going around pretending one had forgotten everything in order to seem cultured – as if that was Pontalis' main concern! Pontalis brought Sartre a hard-boiled egg and some ham, which he pulled out of his pocket with a somewhat shamefaced air. They had a long conversation; Sartre said we couldn't spend our lives thinking everything the Communist Party does is idiotic and help them at the same time; the best thing is to vote Communist and vote No to the referendum. Pontalis left, very shaken.

Found Pouillon and Bost at the Flore. Pouillon just back from Nuremberg; it's appalling, he says, to see how they all play the game, lawyers and defendants included; he's going to write a piece on it for *T.M.* He says that if he votes it will be No, because as recording secretary he was present at the drawing up of the Constitution and finds it despicable; but he won't vote; he'd have to go out to the country to do it. He justifies himself by saying: 'M. Gay has announced that anyone who doesn't vote is a traitor and a malefactor; given what M. Gay is, one can only respect oneself by not voting.'

To Beaujon with Bost. Olga doesn't seem too impatient.

Leaflets in the hotel corridors: VOTE NO. Back in Sartre's room we decide that people, whether they vote Yes or No, will do so reluctantly. I said: 'I'm keeping out.' 'It's very bad to say that!' Sartre told me. 'But you're not voting yourself.' 'Voting isn't what's important; it's knowing which way you would vote.' I had to laugh, as Giacometti would say.

Ate dinner at the Catalans with Bost; Solange Sicard was there, Grimaud, etc. Bost showed me a very friendly article about him by Vintenon, and Fauchery showered him with bouquets on the radio.

Sunday 5 May

When I've been working very hard, there are sometimes days when I feel like those dabfish which have used all their energy spawning and get washed up onto the rocks, dying and drained. Felt like that this morning. Had bad dreams which left a sort of chill around my heart. Blue sky, blustering wind; the newspaper vendors shouting very loud, some sort of argument going on in the *carrefour*: the referendum. We aren't voting, partly through feck-lessness and laziness, because we haven't got voters' cards, and mainly because we probably would have abstained anyway.

Work. At four, went to see Palle and asked him to make some alterations in his article on Petiot. He was very tanned and handsome and very nice. He hasn't voted either.

Chéramy's in the evening; the radio gave the results of the referendum. To everyone's surprise there seemed to be a preponderance of Noes. A great many abstentions. It's because people are just as uncomfortable about saying Yes as about saying No.

Went home, still feeling this strange anxiety around my heart. There must be people who feel like this most of the time, their skin separating them from the world; it must make a big difference to one's life. This evening everything was somehow tainted with horror: for example, the woman's hand I saw, all the bones showing so clearly, fingering its way through blonde hair; the hair was a plant, with a *root* in the scalp. The word *root* was fascinating and frightening as I fell asleep.

Monday 6 May

Result of the referendum: No by 52 per cent against 48 per cent; 20 per cent of the voters abstained. Ran out to get the papers immediately; no copies of *Humanité* or *Populaire* left; the Right is patting itself on the back, naturally.

Lunch at the Petit Saint-Benoît with Merleau-Ponty, who defended the Communist point of view; that led to Sartre's philosophy, which he thinks has an insufficient feeling for the dense intricacy of reality. This revived the desire to write my essay, but I'm too tired, I don't know why. Sartre is making a miraculous recovery; he shaved and put on a beautiful pair of new blue pyjamas. Genet stopped by and left him the magnificent book Barbezat has printed, *Le Miracle de la rose*, enormous, with huge black letters and red headings.

Went up to my room at four, and was so tired I slept for two whole hours. Then I set to work and suddenly my head was buzzing with ideas. At ten, went down to see Sartre. The room was very dark, with just the little lamp over his head switched on. Genet and Lucien were there. No one knows what's happened to the manuscript of *Pompes funèbres* that was entrusted to Gallimard. Genet says he'll do something terrible if they've lost it.

Tuesday 7 May

Tea, newspapers, work. Sartre began his sketches of America,[1] which rather tire him. Genet stopped by to see me. He's just had a row with the Gallimards about the lost manuscript; he bawled them out and then he added: 'And on top of all that, your employees think they can treat me like a faggot!' Claude Gallimard didn't know where to look. To Beaujon with Bost. They've given Olga a final insufflation, and she'll know tomorrow whether it's taken or not. She had seen some young women in the X-ray room who had just been operated on and had bits of metal sticking out of them, and that has upset her terribly. She finds it hard to take all that bright, white light in her room, and also the windows onto the corridor which allow everyone to look in at her.

At the Flore, Montandon showed me a copy of *Labyrinthe* which contained an announcement about our lectures in Switzerland and some quite good pictures of Sartre and myself. Congratulated Dora Marr on her show, which I visited the day before yesterday. At Gallimard's I passed Chamson on the stairs; he asked after Sartre. 'He's got mumps,' I said. He began to back down the stairs away from me. 'But that's contagious.' 'Very; I'm probably giving it to

1. Which he abandoned.

you this very moment.' He fled. I frightened M., too, when he came in to bring me some rather uninteresting pieces on England. A visit from Ansermet; then one from a young man who wants to do some articles on the cinema, then a young couple who sing completely amoebic songs about their nights of love, then Rirette Nizan. She brought me a letter written by Nizan to his parents when he was seventeen; in it he recounts a conversation with Sartre in which they sat on the stairs and decided they were both supermen; then he elaborates all the moral considerations that follow from this fact. Went home. On the stairs I met a girl who said she was an ex-pupil of mine and then asked me, on behalf of the Gallup Institute, how I saw the future of France. I told her I didn't see it at all, which she seemed to find very profound. With Sartre, looked through the letters and manuscripts I brought back from *T.M.* There were two chapters by Louise Weiss; I made a note of one passage. During the exodus a Frenchwoman meets her ex-lover, Andlau, wearing a German uniform:

Andlau, handsome, intelligent and cynical as ever – why should he have changed? – said with a smile: It seems to me you need a bath. Blanche smells the contempt.

There was also the *Mémoires d'un obscur*, the story of a private who had been a prisoner of war; we'll publish the chapter recounting his life on the farm. Poems, stories, reviews. A young 'Existentialist' of seventeen sends us a poem which begins: 'The empty tends toward the full.'

A visit from Genet and Barbezat. The owner of the Flore gave me another tiny book by Jean Ferry, with a very nice dedication. It's called *Le Tigre mondain* and I like it very much.

8 May

Slight headache, but did quite a lot of work all the same. The second part's giving me trouble, but it's interesting to find out what my own thoughts are.

Sartre got up for the first time. We're going to have a drink at the Rhumerie Martiniquaise and have a talk about the magazine and Sartre's *La Morale*. Spent the evening with Bost in his room. Bost says Aron and Ollivier couldn't care less about the way people have to live, about their exhaustion, their hunger; the problem just doesn't exist for them. He told us that people living in the Hôtel

Chaplain recognized themselves in his *Combat* article, though he signed it Jean Maury, and they're wild with anger. We talked about the Communists again. We'll vote for them; but it seems as impossible as ever to reach any kind of ideological agreement with them. Lengthy vaticinations. The problem of our relationship with them is crucial for us and they won't allow us to resolve it; it's a dead end.

9 May

Am annoyed because as soon as I work for an hour or two I get a headache; yet the work's interesting. In the afternoon, I went out with Sartre; we went up to his mother's and he admired the room that will be his. In the evening at the Flore I caught sight of Limbour and asked him to give me some topical squibs. Zette was there with Leiris. Bost is in a terrible state because the Hôtel Chaplain business is getting worse; some men have been around to *Combat* looking for him so that they can knock his teeth out.

10 May

Vitold came around to see Sartre. Discussion about the possibility of a tour of Italy and of a performance of *Huis clos* in Switzerland; Vitold's hesitating because he has a film to make in June. Lunched with him at the Brasserie Lipp, then went back for Sartre. We sat on the terrace of the Deux Magots; it was a beautiful day. We patched together a copy of *The Victors* so that it could be given to Nagel to be typed. A great fuss at the magazine. Vittorini came to the office with Queneau and Mascolo; he seems very shy and speaks French badly. He expressed his regret that we'd been invited to Italy by Bompiani, who's a reactionary publisher; he said: 'If you'd been invited by *my party*, you'd have been driven around by car; we took Eluard everywhere.' We decided to have an exchange of magazines; we'll see each other in Milan and get an Italian issue ready. There was quite a crowd suddenly; Gaston Gallimard arrived; I had put my nose in his door earlier and then fled, because I'd had to shake hands with Malraux and Roger Martin du Gard: the two of them always carry such a load of high seriousness around with them, and Gaston Gallimard's den seemed to be full of incense. Now he wanted to talk to me about Genet who's written him a very rude letter, after his scene with Claude. He practically apologized to me, and assured me that the manuscript wasn't lost. Had to talk to a lot of people.

The lubricious young couple were there; the man had brought me a story; he asked me in his naïve, singsong voice: 'Will Sartre give me his vote for the Prix de la Pléiade?' I settled some things with Renée Saurel,[1] looking splendid with her wind-blown hair, caught a glimpse of Leiris, and took Nathalie Sarraute's manuscript to Paulhan; he wrote the title and the author's name on it in his beautiful script; by some miracle he was alone. He showed me a lovely little Wols that he'd framed in a box with indirect lighting.

At seven I met Queneau and his wife at the Pont-Royal. Georges Blin was there and took me up on the subject of *Sexualité et existentialisme*. He gave me the best pages of a review by Wahl that's to appear shortly. Wahl's critical approach to *Being and Nothingness* is analytical in a surprising way: 'The first paragraph on page 62 is good, but the tenth line is weak' – that sort of thing. I drank two gin fizzes and was very animated. Our eighth issue is out, and people seem to think it's quite brilliant.

The hotel's been repainted; it gets prettier every day, and now there's a beautiful, brunette chambermaid, an ex-client who's fallen on hard times, and another blonde one who rustles and bustles around all over the place. One might almost think one was in a brothel. The redhead I got on with so well has disappeared.

Saturday 11 May

I seem to be working at half speed; I'm tired; it's so annoying to have obstacles in one's head. Lunch at Lipp with Sartre and Pontalis. Dullin signed his books at Odette Lieutier's. Camille had decorated the bookshop with masks and photos and a lot of beautiful things; Dullin looked very handsome and seemed happy, surrounded by a crowd of admirers. There are a few flags in the streets in honour of V Day; it makes one rather sad.

I'd like to work, but sleep instead, my head bothering me. Went down to see Sartre at six. Nathalie Sarraute was there, hair beautifully waved and wearing a lovely bright blue suit. She explained quite soberly that we act as if we were Kafka's Castle; in our records, each person has a number he doesn't know; we allow so many hours per year to one, so many hours to another, and it's impossible to get an extra hour even by throwing oneself under a bus. We manage to convince her, after endless arguing, that we like her. She admits, moreover, that in her eyes we are pure abstractions, and that she

1. She was the secretary at *Les Temps Modernes* at the time.

doesn't give a damn about our contingent, human individuals. It's still 'a straw man'. She told us about her article on Valéry, which will undoubtedly be very entertaining.

Dined with Bost at the Golfe-Juan. The Gallimards were there with Badel. The one-eyed Salvation Army man with the scar sold Jeanne Gallimard a Bible.

Sunday 12 May

No time for this diary. I scarcely manage to jot down the day's anecdotes. The sky is overcast and the chestnut flowers are beginning to drop.

Worked this morning, after I had gone to the Deux Magots to buy cigarettes and rolls for Sunday breakfast. At noon, I met Pagniez there; he had brought a very amusing article on the history of the Constituent Assembly. Lunch with Sartre at Lipp; Vitold stopped by to discuss plans for Switzerland and Italy. Coffee at the Montana. Work. Felt full of enthusiasm because, at last, my headache had gone. Started over from the very beginning; it's always the most exciting part, doing the second draft and seeing it take shape. At six, a meeting of *T.M.* in Sartre's room. His mother had made some fritters and I brought some cognac I had bought from the manager. Vian was there with his trumpet to keep him company, he was going on to play at the Point Gamma afterwards; that's how he earns his living. His *Chronique du menteur* was too facile, but funny. Paulhan was there, Pontalis, Vivet and his friend, who argued that you couldn't blame Steinbeck for having written *Drop the Bombs*, because his book was a failure. We thought of doing a study of American *engagé* writing: how Steinbeck, Dos Passos, Faulkner allowed themselves to be recruited into providing propaganda for the state. Roger Grenier came too, and, at half past seven, when it was all over, Bost, fresh as a daisy. The next three issues are crammed to bursting point.

Bost stayed with us. He told us Olga had been receiving visits from some of the young girls in the main ward; she had been very struck by the callous way they talked about their illness. When Olga mentioned that she had no 'threads',[1] one girl told her: 'Oh! you'll get threads quick enough. The cutter comes round once a month. As long as he's not here, you won't get any threads; but as soon as he does come back, you'll see, your threads will be down again.' They

1. A colloquial expression for adhesions. – Tr.

told her that men suffer from T.B. much worse than women. Some of the girls lean out over the grille round the balcony, although it's very high and curves inwards at the top. A great deal of flirting goes on between the eleventh floor and the men on the tenth. Often there are shows which everyone attends in pyjamas. The tubercular patients despise the ones who aren't; they judge each other according to the seriousness of their cases and their moral resistance.

13 May

For a long moment, I thought: 'I am imprisoned inside my dream, the way it is in Henry's drawing; I'll never be able to get back into my room.' There was a high fence all around my bed. At last I woke up, but it was already late, almost nine o'clock. I was in very good spirits because I'm not tired any more, and because Sartre is better and we're off to Switzerland on Saturday. Rolland has invited us to Constance. He said: 'We'll be among friends – Hervé and Courtade will be there.' No trace of irony in his voice: written insults don't count.

We had lunch at the Casque with Giacometti.

We're wondering how Breton will be received when he comes back to Paris. Aragon was stunned by the lack of enthusiasm which greeted *Personne ne m'aime*; he thinks it was a Fascist plot.

At the Flore I found three big handsome American books in which we'll choose the Wright texts for the August–September issue.

Work from three to six. Went to the Flore to settle things with Montandon about the Swiss trip. Glimpsed Salacrou with Sophie Desmarets, very beautiful with her red hair. Have come home to bring this diary up to date. I notice as I re-read bits here and there that already it evokes nothing for me. And why should one hope that these words would be different from any others, that they should have the magic power of retaining life within themselves and re-suscitating the past? No. For myself, the last fifteen days are already merely sentences written down, nothing more. The only alternative would be to pay real attention to how one writes things down, and I haven't time.

Dined with Bost in Sartre's room; eggs and corned beef. Bost has been back to the Hôtel Chaplain and resumed diplomatic relations with Jeannette, who's relented slightly. He saw Wright on the terrace of the Flore this morning and Wright laughed in his face; apparently he always laughs, but it's his way of avoiding contact with people. Sartre and Bost took turns in parting their hair in the middle to prove that it makes you look stupid. The main effect was to make them look more feminine, which is odd. Bost talked about the 70,000-word pulp books he used to write two years ago; he would write them in two days for 1,500 francs; one of them was called *Eva was Only Beautiful*. He showed us a letter from a certain Jules Roy congratulating him; and another from a man complaining that the information signs in the *mairie* of the 16th Arrondissement are badly placed; his book is very successful. At eleven, Sartre's eyes began to get inflamed, though not without some encouragement, and we let him go to sleep. Had a drink at Chéramy's, where a mysterious general bought us a second. Bost talked to me about my novel which he finally took around to Gallimard today; he likes the Indian episode very much, but finds the beginning a bit drawn out. Pontalis also thinks it sounds too much like a chronicle.

Home at midnight and spent an hour re-reading and continuing this diary. I'd like to take more trouble over it. Feel very comfortable in bed, nodding slightly between words. I can hear the rain falling gently outside, and footsteps a long way off. Tomorrow I'll work and soon I'll be going to Switzerland. I'm very happy with things as they are. At the moment, I'd really like to have a lot of time for writing.

Tuesday 14 May

Everything grey when I awoke. Thought about all the arrangements I've got to make; hate making arrangements, and hate thinking about making them even more; especially since the more I think the less I actually do about them. Went out for the newspapers. There was a malicious article by someone called Pingaud[1] about Bost's novel; Bost is obviously an Existentialist, this person writes, because he's dedicated his book to the Russian woman at the Café de Flore; and besides, Sartre published a great eulogy of the documentary novel in the first issue of *T.M.*, the same issue in which *Le Dernier des métiers* first appeared. Another unfriendly article by little Clément on Existentialism. Found the manuscript of *Blood of Others* in a cupboard; I'm going to give it to Adamov for the Artaud

1. Bernard Pingaud; he has since become our friend, and is on the board of *Les Temps Modernes*.

benefit sale; it's a lovely manuscript, all dog-eared and covered with cross-outs, and written on different sizes of paper with different inks and even in different scripts. It's so much more alive than a book; it makes you feel it really came from inside you; the memory of certain times when I was writing it still cling to it. Went through *Black Metropolis* to choose some things that might fit into our American issue. Wish I had more time to read.

Made some of my travel arrangements. Worked at the Pont-Royal. Went up to the office of *T.M.* at half past five. Alquié and Pouillon were discussing Communist policy with Sartre.

Aron stopped by for a moment; Paul Morihien came in to collect the *Anti-Semite and Jew* and my four articles from *T.M.* Went back down to the Pont-Royal to see Vian, who had brought me his novel and an American book on jazz from which we'll translate a piece. He told me that there are some very good radio plays in America, a bit naïve but charming, like the one about the little caterpillar who dances to 'Yes sir, that's my baby', or the one about the little boy searching among the stars for his dog that's been run over by a bus, and then at the end you realize that the little boy's been run over too. He's going to write an article about them. His novel[1] is very entertaining, especially the lecture by Jean-Sol Partre, and the murder with the heart extractor. I also like Gouffé's recipe: 'Take a small salami; skin it and ignore its cries.'

Came home at eight with Sartre, who was very tired. The evening was very beautiful just then, the trees still wet, the red and green lights, a few lighted windows, and some of the day still left in the sky.

We ate some ham while going through the booty accumulated at the office. Some short stories, all bad; a very good 'Nuremberg Trial' by Pouillon; a good 'Petiot' by Palle; Ponge's piece, '*Ad Litem*', doesn't amount to much. A visit from Bost. Olga has her threads; she doesn't think they're taking proper care of her at the hospital; she must get out of there. He told us that there had been a riot in an American prison the day before, and five prisoners had been killed, but when he went to ask the U.S. information services about it, the officials angrily denied it.

In a lecture given at the Sorbonne to commemorate the anniversary of Descartes, Thorez has rehabilitated Descartes as a great materialist philosopher.

1. *L'Écume des jours.*

Had to wait two hours at the Swiss Legation. But they passed quickly because I was reading Vian's *L'Écume des jours*, which I like very much, especially the sad story of Chloé who dies with a water lily in her lung; he has created a world entirely his own, which is rare and always moving. The last two pages are electrifying; the dialogue with the Crucifix is the equivalent of the 'No' in Camus' *Cross Purposes*, but less obvious and more convincing. What strikes me most is the truth of the novel, and also its enormous tenderness.

Lunch and coffee with Sartre at Lipp, at the Flore and at Chéramy's. Bought a lovely Blue Guide to Switzerland; it makes me excited and depressed at the same time, because I know there are so many things to see and I won't be able to see them. I'm afraid the trip is going to be rather official. But I look forward to it all the same.

On the stairs, a lanky young man with an umbrella came up to me and asked what Sartre meant by 'essence'. I referred him to *Being and Nothingness*. He told me that he had read it of course, but he didn't want to be superficial and so I really ought to give him a definition in as few words as possible. It was for a newspaper in Strasbourg.

Thursday 16 May

Spring is coming back. On my way to buy some cigarettes, I saw some magnificent bunches of asparagus with the bottoms wrapped in red paper, lying on a green paper in a vegetable stall; they were so pretty. Work. I've rarely taken so much pleasure in writing as I do these days, especially in the afternoon when I come back at half past four into this room that's still thick with smoke from the morning, the paper already covered with green ink lying on the desk; and my cigarette and fountain pen feel so pleasant in my fingers. I can understand Duchamp's saying to Bost, when he asked him if he didn't sometimes regret not painting any more: 'I miss the feeling of the tube of paint in my hand when I squeezed it and the paint smeared across the palette; that was nice.' The physical part of writing is very pleasant. And even inside, I sense things loosening up; perhaps I imagine it. At any rate, I feel lots of things to say. There's also the idea for a novel that began to come to me yesterday, at Chéramy's.

The Kermadec show. Dinner at the Catalans with Sartre and Bost who shamelessly talk about New York in front of me.

17 May

At the Flore with Sartre, at noon, I was introduced to Soupault. I still find it odd when I meet a man I admired from afar when I was twenty, and he turns out to be just a flesh-and-blood person, and getting on in years. Soupault asked me if I'd like to go to America. He promised to get me an invitation in October if I really want to go, and he amuses Sartre because he seems to be a bit concerned about my fragility. Of course I want to go, and I insisted, and I'm bursting to go, and yet at the same time I feel a mild pang at the thought of going away for four months.

This morning, in *Cavalcade*, there was a stupid and venomous article on Sartre by Monnerot. Also accounts of Mounin's article which is supposed to have K.O.'d Sartre; they're not hard to please. In the *Littéraire*, there was an interview with students of the École Normale Supérieure by Paul Guth, in which Sartre was mentioned. And in the middle of an article by Billy on 'literature and metaphysics' there was a drawing of me, very fat and bovine. Lunch at the Golfe-Juan with Pagniez and his wife. Pagniez defended reformism.

At *T.M.* we're setting up the ninth issue. It's astonishing the number of texts we have to choose from these days. People stopped by but didn't stay, and we were able to work in peace. It seems that Nero is out of prison, according to Merleau-Ponty. We had a drink at the Pont-Royal with Leiris, Queneau, their wives and Giacometti. Dinner at the Golfe-Juan with Giacometti and Bost. There was a long discussion about the trial of a gentleman farmer who recently took a gun and shot his gardener, who was his daughter's lover. The girl was sixteen, and the letters she wrote were so obscene they couldn't be read out in court; the gardener was thirty-six and an old offender; the father went with his son to keep watch in the girl's room, and they killed the gardener; the son missed the fellow twice, but the father got him. He's been condemned to only four years in prison, and the son got three years with a suspended sentence. Sartre made Bost laugh until he cried by developing the theory that the crime was a direct consequence of the last elections, that since the Liberation the father had felt surrounded by a revolting world and that this murder expressed the paroxysm of his revolt. Which led

Giacometti to tell the story of Sergeant Bertrand, who was such a gentle, steady fellow, but every night went digging up corpses in cemeteries, cutting them up and nibbling the pieces; they could only punish him for desecration of graves, since neither the mutilation nor the ingestion of corpses had been provided for in the criminal code. He talked about Picasso, whom he had seen the evening before and who had shown him some drawings; it appears that, confronted with each new work, he's like an adolescent who has scarcely begun to discover the resources of art. He says: 'I think I'm beginning to understand something; for the first time I've done some drawings that are really drawings.' And he was delighted when G. said: 'Yes, you're making progress.' We finished the evening at Chéramy's. But, as I agreed with Bost, a diary is useless for this sort of thing; to keep any sort of record of the irresistible conversation between Sartre and Giacometti we needed a tape recorder.

18 May

This evening I leave for Switzerland. For three weeks now I've scarcely left my room and seen almost no one except Sartre and Bost. It was restful and fruitful. This afternoon I'm upstairs at the Flore, near the window; I can see the wet street, the plane tree swaying in the sharp wind; there are a lot of people, and downstairs there's a great hubbub. I don't feel at ease here. Something tells me that I'll never again work here as I used to for so many years.

Bost came to look for me. He had received a short letter from Gide congratulating him on *Le Dernier des métiers*. He also showed me an issue of *La Rue*, a newspaper that's being started by Jules Vallès but won't be out for a while; they're issuing just one number 'to preserve the title'. Prévert is in it, and Nadeau, some of Henry's drawings, and a lament by Queneau on the refrain '*Je suis un pauvre con*'. We went to Beaujon. Olga told us about the patients she's seen. Yesterday, a young woman, mother of three children, went in to have a pneumothorax, they tried it three times in three different places, and three times it didn't work; in the end she fainted from sheer despair and remained unconscious for three-quarters of an hour. A little country girl was brought in, thinking she had only one lung affected; when she said to Dr Benda, who had just looked at her X-ray: 'I've come to have my pneumothorax,' he asked her: 'Which lung?' And that was how she found out that both her lungs were diseased. Olga says the worst part of it is that you gradually grow resigned to it as you lose your vitality.

Took the train for Lausanne. We were alone in the compartment except for a little, dark-haired girl who held her overnight bag pressed against her heart all night long; she slept sitting up. I stretched out and slept quite well. I can remember going to Limousin on the train when I was thirteen or fourteen and spending the whole night with my face at the window, swallowing soot and feeling immeasurably superior to all the grown-ups dozing in the warmth of the compartment. It's things like that that make me realize I've aged. Just for one moment there was a beautiful, bright moon in a sky streaked with clouds; and, in the morning, the mountains in a greyish-pink dawn. That still never fails, the shock of awakening, when I've been asleep for a long time and then suddenly I find I've been transported into an early morning somewhere a long way off. This feeling was strongest in the desert, before Tozeur; and then arriving at Sallanches in winter; and also, I don't quite know why, the wet countryside of Auvergne when I got to Mauriac.

Skira, the publisher who organized this lecture tour, had booked us in a hotel close to the lake in Geneva. From my window, I saw glistening swans and magnificent beds of flowers. Switzerland's opulence left me open-mouthed. 'It's one of the pleasantest and most forgotten things, being able to eat anything you like at any time,' I noted; and again, later: 'What a pleasure it is to be able to have supper after the cinema: it reminds one of before the war!' At the Brasserie du Globe, you could order as much whisky, sherry, port flips, or anything you felt like; there were little cards that said: TOAST AND RUSSIAN CAVIAR. I remembered going through Annemasse in 1943 and the emotion I felt when I saw a signpost that said: GENEVA, 9 KILOMETRES; and the people there said, in voices full of wonder: 'At night, you can see the lights'; I saw the Kursaal with its illuminations, and the flashing of the neon signs. At Lausanne we were taken to a store that sold clothes 'by correspondence and by temperament'; Sartre came away with a suit and a raincoat, and I with a green tussore silk dress and a red, white and blue linen skirt. In Geneva I had already bought some superb leather shoes, suitcases, and a watch with a black dial and green hands.

The three weeks were full of chores: not only the lectures

themselves but book-signing sessions and radio interviews. One morning, we were accompanied by a camera for almost two hours through the somnolent streets of the old town; then there were the dinners, the receptions, the small talk. We got on very well with Skira and his pretty wife; he knew the surrealists, he had published them. 'I was the lion tamer,' he said. Detached almost to the point of absence and yet always disturbed, passionately interested in women, doubtless bursting with complexes for all his air of being a pleasure-seeking egotist, Albert Skira's conversation was cynical and very funny when he managed to relax. We got along well with Montandon, who ran *Labyrinthe*, too; we understood each other, despite his reservations about Existentialism: he belonged to the Labour Party and was a Marxist. 'All the Swiss intellectuals are reactionaries,' he told us. 'During the war, there was an attempt to organize an anti-Nazi demonstration, and we could only find two old professors to take part. That's what persuaded me to become an out-and-out member of a working-class party.' We met a few other people who were interesting and pleasant. But there were also a great many we were forced to see who bored or even repelled us.

Our first meal at the Globe overwhelmed me: 'A magnificent meal, with tournedos, ices and very good Swiss wines; but horribly dreary. B.[1] is loathsome when he talks about the Arab midwives with whom he travelled by truck in Africa; they were encamped away from the others at night, "because they smelled so badly"; they had been converted to Catholicism and protested in the name of their religion: "But we have souls the same as you." We just laughed at them, said B.; he told the story with intolerable complacency, and boasted extravagantly of his anti-Vichyism: "I'm a *Vichyssois*, but not a *Vichyiste*." There was only one interesting moment, when Montandon described Merleau-Ponty's argument with Tzara about *Arrival and Departure*. Tzara insisted that Koestler was a bastard; his proof of this was the fact that, during the war, Koestler had been able to pay for his invalid wife's stay in a sanatorium. At that Merleau-Ponty smashed a glass, saying: "Under these conditions, no discussion is possible." The gesture astonished me, especially since Merleau-Ponty could quite easily have reduced Tzara to a pulp; in any case, it was a healthy reaction. I was relieved when lunch was over. I find this sort of thing even more painful when I am with Sartre. Alone, as in Portugal or Tunis, it's

1. A very high-ranking French official.

bad enough, but when he's there I always think how much we could employ the time together, without the others. . . . '

The day after our arrival, we went for a walk in the environs of Interlaken; when we came back, Sartre received the press. When I came down into the lobby, there were already a lot of people around Sartre: a whole swarm of journalists, mostly old and frightfully proper. We went into the room off the lobby and found ourselves enthroned, side by side, like a Catholic king and his queen; I thought we looked rather ridiculous, especially me. A little old man with a white moustache opened fire; he hadn't read anything about Existentialism, he said, he only knew about it from hearsay: 'But it appears that it is a doctrine which permits everything; isn't that dangerous?' Sartre explained. The atmosphere was clearly hostile. In particular, there was a paunchy gentleman with squinting, wrinkled eyelids who paraded all the disabused, 'realistic' superiority that reactionary idealists tend to have; he questioned Sartre on education: 'Should we respect the child's freedom?' And there was an assumption in the question that the worker is a child. (The questioner turned out to be Gillouin, Pétain's *éminence grise*, as we learned later from the press attaché, who was furious that he had managed to insinuate himself into the conference. The session lasted for more than an hour, with the help of a little vermouth and some cheese and biscuits. A dark-haired girl, with a braid, asked some questions with sympathy; all the others reeked of Fascism or religion, and were resolutely against us without knowing even what we were talking about.

I didn't go to Sartre's first lecture because I was out sight-seeing, but he told me about it. There were 1,100 people; they listened well but didn't clap much; he spoke for two hours. After that he drank four martinis, ate dinner and spent the evening dancing; naturally he didn't remember very much, except that he gave some advice to a very respectable lady from La Chaux-de-Fonds concerning her son's sex life. The lady was terrified he would get some tramp of a girl pregnant. 'Then teach him to withdraw, Madame,' Sartre told her. 'Yes, of course,' she said. 'I'll tell him the advice came from you; it'll have more effect then.'

In Zurich, Sartre gave a lecture, and there was also a performance of *Huis clos* at the theatre.

Wednesday

Skira came to pick us up at the station buffet, dressed in an amazing striped shirt and escorted by two men from the French bookshop, one sedate with dark hair[1] and the other lively and blond; both were very nice; they had made a display in the bookshop window from newspaper cuttings, books and caricatures and photographs of Sartre. *Labyrinthe* had covered the town with posters shouting Sartre's name in huge red letters. Dinner and a lecture. Sartre was greeted with applause on his entrance, and took off his overcoat like a boxer entering the ring; there were about six hundred people, mostly young, who seemed very interested. At six o'clock, the people at the bookstore had managed to send the journalists to meet the wrong train, but by now they'd found their way back and there were at least fifteen at our table, battering Sartre with questions. All this while, the dark-haired man from the bookstore was talking to me in his slow sad voice; he told me he had been a Communist, but then he'd become disgusted by the Party's methods. We talked a bit about Koestler; it's amazing how one always seems to find one's way back to the same conversations. . . .

Thursday

I met Sartre about seven, when he came back from rehearsal; he had terrified everyone by falling into an orchestra pit ten feet deep; there was a tarpaulin stretched over it; he walked on it, the cloth ripped, and he disappeared before their very eyes. 'Good-bye lecture!' said the owner of the bookstore; then a rather dazed-looking face reappeared through the hole. We went to the theatre. Full house. I had a seat in the second row. Sartre spoke very well for twenty minutes about the theatre; everyone seemed pleased. After rather a long wait, the curtain rose. The actors were a bit nervous. Chauffard had the shakes. Balachova was wearing a different wig and dress, an improvement on the old ones. They all fluffed their lines a bit, and the curtain didn't come down at the end; but they acted very well and there was a great deal of applause. We all went to supper in a big *brasserie* decorated with magnificent paintings by Picasso, Chirico, etc. They belonged to someone who was exhibiting his collection there. At midnight we split up. Sartre took Wanda home.[2]

1. This was Harold, who has since become known for his photographic montages.

2. Marie Olivier, the actress.

I left with Chauffard, and we had a gin fizz in a basement café; he was happy because Laffont was publishing his short stories. Didn't want to sleep at all; but they turned us out; after midnight, everything in Zurich closes. Outside, it was raining, and we were about to go our separate ways rather dolefully, when we met the bookstore man trudging along under a big umbrella. He suggested buying a bottle of wine and drinking it in the bookstore. We stayed there until three in the morning, looking at art books, drawings, magazines; Chauffard read aloud some obscene poems, signed Claudinet, which I thought might be by Cocteau;[1] the title of the book on the cover was *Vies*, but inside it was called *Vits*;[2] there was one very lovely one with the refrain: 'If I had only had a couple of francs.'

In Berne, we dined at the embassy; a theologian took me up at great length on nothingness, being, being-in-itself and being-for-itself. In Paris all conversations seemed to become political ones; in Switzerland they become theological. They even pressed Sartre very insistently with questions about the nature of angels. Existentialism had caused a quarrel between Ansermet and René Leibowitz; Ansermet wanted to reach an understanding of all music from the standpoint of Existentialism; but according to Leibowitz, only serial music can be considered in accordance with this philosophy. They had been insulting each other with great vivacity in *Labyrinthe*.

I gave a lecture at Lausanne. A lady came up to me as I was leaving. 'I don't understand. M. Sartre talked so well! He looks so respectable! And yet it seems he writes the most dreadful things! But why, Madame? Why!' I also gave a talk to some students in Geneva. That night and the night after we went out with Skira and Annette, a young woman in whom Giacometti was intensely interested.[3] We both thought her very attractive. To me, she seemed quite like Lise in many ways; she had the same dogged materialism, the same fearlessness, the same avidity; she devoured the world with her eyes; she didn't want to miss anything or anyone; she enjoyed violence and laughed about everything.

At a party in Lausanne, Sartre had met a young man, called Gorz, who knew all his writings like the back of his hand and talked very

1. They are not, I have discovered.
2. The oral pun is on the French words for *life* and *penis*. – Tr.
3. She is now his wife.

knowledgeably about them. In Geneva we saw him again. Taking *Being and Nothingness* as his starting point, he could not see how one choice could justifiably be given preference over another and consequently Sartre's commitment troubled him. 'That's because you're Swiss,' Sartre told him. As a matter of fact, he was an Austrian Jew who had settled in Switzerland since the war.

We saw Fribourg, Neuchâtel, Basel, and their museums. The villages were a bit too scrubbed and polished, but some of them were pretty. We drank white wine in *weinstübe* with spotless floors. We fell in love with the little squares and fountains of Lucerne, its painted houses, its towers and, above all, its two covered wooden bridges decorated with old painted pictures. We climbed up to Selisberg, where Sartre had spent vacations when he was little; he showed me his hotel, his room, with a balcony that stuck out over the lake; the balcony from which Estelle, in *Huis clos*, throws her baby into the water. It rained a lot: I didn't care much for the fat Swiss women, or for the men with their velour hats bristling with edelweiss, or for the accordions and the songs they sang rather badly in chorus; but my mania still had me in its grip, and often I would leave Sartre in one of the towns and go up into the mountains for a few hours or a few days. I persuaded him to go to Zermatt, and we rode in the funicular to the top of the Gonergratt, more than 9,000 feet up; sitting on a bench, our feet in the snow, we gazed for a long time at the Matterhorn, half hidden, like some fearful divinity, in its own private cloud. The next morning, we both felt as though our heads were screwed in a vice: mountain sickness. On the hotel terrace, there were sixty Swiss men, each with a badge in his buttonhole, examining the landscape with a knowledgeable air; they called themselves 'the contemporaries of La Chaux-de-Fonds': contemporary with whom? We caught the train back to Paris. At Vallorbe, one of the customs officers said to Sartre, as he handed back his passport: 'Your books are unobtainable, Monsieur'; and then to me: 'Still riding tandem?'

On his return from America, Sartre had received a letter from a *khâgneux*,[1] Jean Cau, asking help in finding work; he was preparing for the École Normale entrance exams, though this was his first attempt and he hadn't much hope; after the exams his parents would insist that he go back to live with them in the country. Sartre replied

1. Someone who 'crams' *lycée* students for exams.

that he would look around for him. He fell ill, went to Switzerland, and didn't look around. In June, Cau – who had addressed similar requests to other writers without success – came to see him; the academic year was almost over. 'All right,' said Sartre, 'be my secretary.' Cau accepted, Sartre summoned him to the Deux Magots; but his mail had not yet become very voluminous; he didn't really need help with it. I can still see him, from my vantage point at a nearby table where I was working, hunting through his pockets and rooting out two or three meagre envelopes; he explained to Cau what he should write in reply. He confided to me with a sigh that his secretary was in fact using up time instead of saving it. Cau found the situation irritating too; he had wanted employment, not charity. But the situation gradually improved when Sartre moved into the new apartment in the Rue Bonaparte with his mother. In the morning Cau would sit in the room adjoining Sartre's study, answering the telephone, making appointments and keeping the correspondence up to date; it seemed almost as though the organ had created the function. It was time that Sartre put some order into his life; but I wondered with some regret if he wasn't going to lose the liberty so dear to our youth.

The June issue of *Les Temps Modernes* appeared with the rubric: edited by Jean-Paul Sartre. The committee had fallen apart. Ollivier was moving towards the Right; he sympathized with the Gaullist Union which had just come into being. Aron's anti-Communism was becoming more pronounced. At about that time, or a little later, we had lunch at the Golfe-Juan with Aron and Pia, who was also being attracted by Gaullism. Aron said that he had no great affection for either the U.S.A. or the U.S.S.R., but that if there were a war he would be on the side of the West; Sartre replied that he himself had no relish for either Stalinism or America, but that if war broke out he would be found in the ranks of the Communists. 'In short,' concluded Aron, 'we should make different choices between the two evils; but in any case we should both be making the choice over our dead bodies.' We felt he went too far in thus minimizing an antagonism we regarded as fundamental. Pia explained the Gaullist economic theory to us without so much as mentioning the problems of wages, of prices, of the working-class standard of living; I expressed my astonishment. 'Oh! We'll leave all that Social Welfare business to the Jocistes,' he answered contemptuously. In less than two years, the words Right and Left had resumed their old meanings, and the Right was gaining ground; in May the M.R.P. had gained a majority vote.

Genet told me about the *Dame à la licorne* and I went to see the exhibition of French tapestry. *Citizen Kane* was finally shown in Paris: yes, Orson Welles had revolutionized the cinema. For the Prix de la Pléiade, Queneau and Sartre supported Boris Vian, but the jury chose Malraux's candidate, the Abbé Grosjean, instead.

My essay was finished, and I was asking myself: What now? I sat in the Deux Magots and gazed at the blank sheet of paper in front of me. I felt the need to write in my fingertips, and the taste of the words in my throat, but I didn't know where to start, or what. 'How wild you look!' Giacometti said to me at one point. 'It's because I want to write and I don't know what.' 'Write anything.' In fact, I wanted to write about myself. I liked Leiris' *L'Age d'homme*;[1] such sacrificial essays, in which the author strips himself bare without excuses, appealed to me. I let the idea begin to take shape, made a few notes, and talked to Sartre about it. I realized that the first question to come up was: What has it meant to me to be a woman? At first I thought I could dispose of that pretty quickly. I had never had any feeling of inferiority, no one had ever said to me: 'You think that way because you're a woman'; my femininity had never been irksome to me in any way. 'For me,' I said to Sartre, 'you might almost say it just hasn't counted.' 'All the same, you weren't brought up in the same way as a boy would have been; you should look into it further.' I looked, and it was a revelation: this world was a masculine world, my childhood had been nourished by myths forged by men, and I hadn't reacted to them in at all the same way I should have done if I had been a boy. I was so interested in this discovery that I abandoned my project for a personal confession in order to give all my attention to finding out about the condition of woman in its broadest terms. I went to the Bibliothèque Nationale to do some reading, and what I studied were the myths of femininity.

On 2 July, the Americans exploded a new bomb on Bikini. Personally, I was not – and have never been – much affected by the dangers of the atomic bomb; but many people were very alarmed. When Jean Nocher announced during a radio programme that a chain reaction had accidentally been started, that matter was beginning to disintegrate, and that within a few hours we should

1. Published in America as *Manhood* in 1963. – Tr.

all be dead, people believed him. 'I was with my father,' Mouloudji told me. 'We went out for a walk, and we thought, It's the end of the world; we were very, very sad.'

Our publisher, Bompiani, had invited us to Milan, and Mme Marzoli, who ran the big French bookstore in the city, had organized – in collaboration with Vittorini – one or two lectures for us. To see Italy again! The thought drove everything else from my mind. Circumstances were not propitious; Brigua and Tenda had just been assigned to France, and Italy was reproaching her 'Latin sister' bitterly for this 'stab in the back'. Further, Tito was demanding that Trieste be ceded to Yugoslavia, and the French Communist intellectuals had signed a manifesto in support of his claim. Two days before the date fixed for our departure, I happened to be in the bar of the Pont-Royal; I was called to the telephone. It was Mme Marzoli calling me from Milan; she advised me to postpone our trip; the Italians were in no mood to listen to us. She was so insistent that if it had been Sartre on my end of the line, he would certainly have given in to her; I stubbornly refused to. It doesn't matter, we'll just keep quiet, I told her; but we've got a few lire at Bompiani's, we've got visas; we'll come anyway. She tried to dissuade me, but it was so much wasted breath; as I hung up I said: 'See you soon!' I gave Sartre an expurgated account of the incident, for I feared his scruples.

We were welcomed when we arrived in Milan by the staff of the *Politecnico*, edited by Vittorini; our magazines were very similar; the first issues had both appeared at about the same time; a weekly at first, then a monthly, *Politecnico* had published Sartre's manifesto on *littérature engagée*. We had met Vittorini in Paris; I had read his *Conversations in Sicily* in French. He was fanatically attached to his Party. 'If you cut me into eighty pieces, you'd end up with eighty little Communists,' he used to say; yet we felt no barrier between us. From the very first evening, dining to the sound of a violin in the Milanese intellectuals' favourite restaurant, with Vittorini himself and his friends – Vigorelli, Veneziani, Fortini and a few others – we realized that in Italy the Left presented a solid front. We talked late into the night. Vittorini told us about the difficulties the Italian Communists had just encountered. First of all, in the name of Revolutionary Internationalism, they had supported Tito; but the reactions of the rank and file had persuaded them to switch to the patriotic gambit, and now they were singing the same tune as the rest of the country. He told us that Éluard, who was in Italy on a lecture tour, had warmly supported their original policy and given it his endorsement in public; one fine day the newspapers published the French Communist manifesto in favour of Yugoslavia. Éluard's name, of course, was on it; that day he spoke in Venice. He was booed!

We met every day, sometimes under the arcades of the Piazza della Scala, sometimes in the bar of our hotel, thronged with elegant Italian women with pale silver hair, and we talked. It was fascinating to see Fascism and the war through the eyes of our 'Latin brothers'. One of them confessed that, born and brought up under the Fascist regime, he had remained loyal to it for a long time. 'But the night that Mussolini fell I understood!' he told us, with the accents of a triumphant fanatic. These converts despised the exiles who had been cut off from their homeland by their intransigence and found it difficult to regain a footing in reality; the converts saw their past errors, even their compromises as stages on a journey towards their present political maturity. They kept their virtuous zeal in check by a liberal use of irony. 'Now,' they told us, 'there is a population of ninety million in Italy. Forty-five million who were Fascist; forty-five million who weren't.' I remember one of their jokes. An Italian tourist bus was taking some people on a tour of the battlefields; every time they passed through a ruined village a little man, sitting in the back of the bus, started to wring his hands. 'It's my fault! It's my fault!' One of the passengers became so curious he asked: 'Why is it your fault?' 'I'm the only Fascist in the bus.' One man, politically a follower of Stendhal, as zealous then as he was now, but under different colours, told us with a laugh that he had been nicknamed 'the Black and the Red'.

I saw the brick palaces and churches of Milan, but not *The Last Supper*, which was undergoing restoration. Vigorelli drove us around Lake Como; he had a little Romanesque chapel at the water's edge opened for us; it was very beautiful, decorated with frescoes by Masolino. He showed us Dongo, the birthplace of Stendhal's Fabrice, and also the place where Mussolini was arrested and his escort butchered. These flowers were watered with blood, he told us, pointing to the bright flower beds reflected in the blue water. In this passionate landscape, we ate ices as smooth as sin, before going on to stay the night at Vigorelli's villa above the lake.

Bompiani, who belonged to the extreme Nationalist Right, told Sartre once more that a left-wing Frenchman was at that particular moment an enemy twice over: he was both an annexer of Brigua and Tenda and a supporter of Tito. If he opened his mouth in public, Sartre would get himself lynched, and what is more he would deserve to be lynched! Our friends were afraid that the neo-Fascists might start a riot. At the entrance to the courtyard where Sartre spoke, and even upon the platform, they stationed policemen armed with sub-machine guns. The courtyard was full; not a boo, nothing but applause. Another evening, I gave a talk in Mme Marzoli's bookstore without causing the slightest disturbance. All this was very compromising for Bompiani, who had wanted to dissociate himself from us entirely. Reluctantly, he invited us to dinner. He lived in a palace; on the ground floor we stepped into an elevator that brought us directly into a salon upstairs; at table, we were waited on by footmen wearing livery and white silk gloves. Bompiani didn't so much as open his mouth; when coffee was served, he seized a newspaper and buried his face in it. The next day he let it be understood that he wasn't going to provide Sartre with the money he had promised, and which we were counting on to allow us to continue our trip.

Luckily, the publisher Arnaldo Mondadori heard of our difficulties through Vittorini, and his son, Alberto, a magnificent moustachioed pirate with a deep bass voice, came and negotiated with Sartre; it was agreed that henceforth Mondadori would be his sole publisher in Italy, and that on the strength of this agreement Sartre was to receive a substantial advance. Alberto also offered to drive us to Venice and then to Florence. We accepted gladly; we both liked him, and we also liked his wife, Virginia, who was exquisitely beautiful and endowed with that naturalness Stendhal prized so much in Italian women. Her lively young sister came with them, and also an architect friend. As we rode along, they laughed and chatted and hummed; at one point they broke off in confusion when they realized that they had all been singing *Giovinezza* at the tops of their voices. I was astounded, in Venice, to find myself living in the Grand Hotel, in which, in the old days, I never dreamed of setting foot. Restaurants, bars, they knew all the good places; and they also loved Italy, and showed us everything there was to be seen with the gayest erudition. Among so many shining moments, I recall our departure for Florence; dawn was turning into morning as I loaded my baggage into the gondola; I could feel the cool breath of the water and the gentle warmth of the rising sun on my skin. That evening in Florence we prowled for a long time in front of the Signoria; the moonlight reached in under the loggia to caress Cellini's statue, and the architect, too, touched it with emotion. Despite all the deaths, the ruins, the tide of disaster, the beauty was still there.

Mondadori and his wife went back to Venice. We hired a car to go on to Rome; we were lucky enough to run out of petrol at the gates of the city or I might never have known the odour of dusk in the Roman Campagna. We had booked rooms at the Plaza Hotel on the Corso, where all the French officials stayed; I missed the Albergo del Sol.

Sartre gave two lectures; and since, at that time, every French writer was a representative of our national prestige, we were shown every consideration. The French cultural attaché took us by car to see the lake and the castle of Bracciano. Jacques Ibert invited us one evening to the Villa Medici; the park was full of bonfires that scented the night air. The French *chargé d'affaires* gave a dinner for us at the Palazzo Farnese; for the first time in my life I wore an evening dress, not *décolletée* but long and black, that the cultural attaché's wife had lent me. I was nervous about these ceremonial occasions, but their formality was softened by the Italians' natural grace. Carlo Levi appeared without a tie, his unbuttoned collar wide open. A few weeks earlier, Jacques Ibert's son had come into the offices of *Les Temps Modernes* with a book in his hand. 'It's just been published in Italy and it's having an enormous success; I'm translating it,' he told me; it was *Christ Stopped at Eboli*. I read it and we were to publish some long excerpts in November; in it Levi described the life of a village in the south of Italy where he had been forced to live before the war on account of his anti-Fascist beliefs; I had been very taken with the person I could sense behind this account; when he appeared in flesh and blood, I was not disappointed. Doctor, painter, writer, journalist, he belonged to the Action Party, which was the offspring of the 'Justice and Liberty' movement started in France by the Rosselli brothers, who had united the democratic bourgeoisie against Fascism; the Action Party, born in Milan in 1941–2, had made a resistance pact with the Italian Socialist and Communist parties; under Parri, it had led the first Resistance government; it was a small group composed mainly of intellectuals and without contact with the masses; a split had occurred a few months earlier between the Liberals within the party and the Revolutionaries, of whom Levi was one, and whose position was very near that of the Communists.[1] Our position was therefore very similar to his. He talked as charmingly as he wrote. He noticed everything, was amused by everything, and his insatiable curiosity reminded me of Giacometti; even death seemed to him an interesting experiment; he described people or things without ever using general ideas but, in the Italian manner, by the use of brief and well-chosen anecdotes. He lived in an enormous studio on the top floor of a palace; at the foot of the monumental staircase – which the noble owner once used to ascend on horseback – there was a marble finger the size of a man; on the wall beside Carlo Levi's door, we read terrible insults scribbled there by the owner who was vainly trying to get him out, and also Levi's replies. We understood why he had dug his heels in: from his windows giving onto the Piazza Gesù, he looked out over the whole of Rome. Amid the motley accumulation of papers, books and canvases cluttering his apartment, he was carefully preserving some dried-up roses. 'Anywhere else, they would have fallen to bits long ago,' he said. 'My presence is beneficent.' And he believed his influence was quite as decisive on men as it was on flowers. 'I won't have a show this year,' he said. 'I'm going through a period of research. All the young painters would start imitating me, when I'm not sure what I'm doing myself.' Although so convinced of his own importance, he was not the least bit vain about it. He attributed it less to his own merits than to an aura, bestowed upon him in the cradle by some lucky chance and always surrounding him; this atmosphere was a protection against all misfortunes. His optimism amounted practically to a superstition. During the war, he had decided it was pointless to hide and was convinced that a pair of glasses and a moustache were camouflage enough; he was recognizable a hundred yards away; fortunately anti-Semitism never gained a strong hold in Italy. He appreciated all the pleasures of life and displayed towards women an affectionate devotion rarely found in Italians; furthermore he was of a romantic disposition; as

1. The Action Party split in 1947. Some of its members enrolled in the Communist Party, some in the Socialist Party; others, like Levi, although their sympathies were with the Communists, remained independent.

we left him one evening, we watched with surprise as he climbed up a street lamp and climbed in through a window.

Less expansive in manner, more reticent, Silone – whose *Fontamara* I had liked so much in the old days, and more recently *Bread and Wine* – was also a raconteur; I took great pleasure in his stories about his childhood in the Abruzzi and the hard peasants of the village where he was born.

From 1924 to 1930, he had been one of the main figures and then the leader of the Italian Communist Party, which was in exile at the time; he was expelled from it in 1931, for reasons of which we were ignorant.[1] Back in Italy after the war, he joined the Italian Socialist Party. He talked very little about politics. We were merely struck by his scepticism, which at that time we attributed to his situation as an Italian, rather than to his personal position. At the top of the Janiculum, looking at Rome spread out before us, he said pensively: 'How can you expect us to take anything completely seriously! So many centuries superimposed, each one contradicting the rest! Rome has died so many times, and been reborn so many times! It's impossible for an Italian to believe in absolute truth.'[2] With great charm, he described what went on behind the scenes in Vatican politics; he told us about the ambivalent attitude of the Italian people – religious, superstitious, but forced into savage anticlericalism by the insistent presence of the clergy. I felt a great sympathy with his wife, an Irishwoman whose pious childhood had been even more stifling than my own.

Moravia we saw very little of. I sat next to him once at a literary luncheon. We got the impression that the Italian writers didn't get on very well among themselves. Sartre's neighbour whispered in his ear: 'I'm going to ask you out loud who, in your opinion, is our greatest living novelist, and you answer: Vittorini. Then just watch Moravia's face!' Sartre refused. Whenever an absent colleague's name came up, he was disposed of in two sentences: 'Oh! he's not a writer; he's a journalist!' And: 'His tragedy is that he didn't know how to grow up.' Then someone would add: 'He still has the

1. In 1950, there was a long public controversy on the subject between him and Togliatti. It was published in *Les Temps Modernes*. The least one can say is that from 1927 to 1930 Silone, by his own admission, had played a strange double game.

2. This relativism, so dear to right-wingers, was doubtless a way of justifying himself. When the Italian Socialist Party split up shortly after, Silone followed Saragat. Soon after, he had become a wholehearted anti-Communist.

mentality of a child'; or: 'He's an eternal adolescent.' It was as though each of them were throwing back at the others the image of himself he caught in their eyes. We didn't find this malice unpleasant, it seemed to be merely the underside of the acute interest that Italians always have in each other – an improvement, we thought, on our own tepidity.

At the Plaza, we met Scipion who was on his way back from Greece; dining with us one evening in a tavern on Monte Mario, Rome illuminated at our feet, he told us about his fistfight with a monk on Mount Athos who had made an attempt on his virtue; he lamented the Italians' Francophobia: in the course of their embraces, a whore had taken a very dangerous hold on him and cried: 'What about Brigua, what about Tenda!' He cut a very grave figure at the Farnese dinner, in a dress suit lent him by the cultural attaché.

Jeanine Bouissounouse and her husband Louis de Villefosse, the French representative at the Allied Commission, took us in their car to Frascati and Nemi; they introduced us to their Italian friends: Donnini, a Communist and professor of religious history, who had been in exile for a long while; Bandinelli, the Director General of Fine Arts, also a Communist, who had started a peasant cooperative on his property in Tuscany; Guttuso, a Communist painter who invited us to spend an evening in his studio on the Via Margutta. With its layers of terraces, hidden courtyards, staircases and catwalks, this street, inhabited mainly by painters and writers, had become a veritable *maquis* during the Roman Resistance. I visited the Ardeatini quarries, next to the Catacombs. As a reprisal for an attack that had cost the lives of thirty-three Germans, three hundred and thirty Resistance members were machine-gunned here on 24 March 1944. The Germans abandoned the bodies in the quarry and then blocked the entrance by dynamiting the sides; the corpses were not found until three months later. In 1946, the memory of these victims (cooled, a few years later, by marble) was still fresh; the wooden coffins lay in rows along the galleries, flat on the tawny ground, each one marked with a name and two dates; the only ornaments were a few wilting flowers and photos of each victim at his first Communion, at his wedding, as a soldier, in soccer clothes.

The returned exiles with whom we talked in Rome held the recent converts to anti-Fascism in pretty low esteem; we were struck by this conflict between the intransigents – mostly quite old men –

and the realists of the rising generation; these latter seemed to us much better adapted to the new situation than the exiles.[1]

We spent two days in Naples. The city had suffered a great deal. The only hotel which was open was falling to pieces; you could see the sky through gaping holes in the ceilings; the staircase was covered with rubble; the harbour and the district surrounding it was one intricate ruin. In the hot streets the wind raised sandstorms from the dust of the disaster. The museum was closed. On Capri, which had been untouched, I rediscovered my past. We stayed a few more days in Rome, at the Hotel della Città, without meeting anyone.

We were very happy to see Italy again, but even happier to find there the atmosphere we had known, for such a short while, after the Liberation. In France, that unity had been achieved, in opposition to a foreign occupation, on the equivocal basis of nationalism; the Left and the Right were bound to move apart again, once the circumstances that forced them together had disappeared. In Italy, the Nationalists were the Fascists; the coalition which opposed them was unanimous in its desire for freedom and democracy; its coherence was a product of its principles and not of events; for this reason it survived the war; Liberals, Socialists and Communists united against the Right to make sure the new constitution was respected. The sincerity of the republican and democratic positions of the Italian Communist Party was never at any time doubted by its allies. The German-Soviet pact and the uncertainty it caused among the French Communists provided a weapon against them; the record of the Italian Communists' resistance to Fascism remained without a blot; all the anti-Fascists – which is to say, at that time, almost the whole country – paid tribute to their courage.

The situation of the Italian Communist Party was more favourable than that of the French for reasons that dated back many years. In France, the bourgeoisie, having made a success of its Revolution in 1789, went on without hesitation to wage an all-out war against the working class. In Italy, the bourgeoisie rose to the position of a ruling class only in the nineteenth century, after many divisions and crises; in the course of this upward movement it was forced, especially at the beginning of the twentieth century, to accept the

1. There were also men in Italy who were intransigent and realistic at the same time; the anti-Fascists who had fought on the spot, in secret. But we only met these later.

support of the proletariat. This collusion had important cultural consequences. A bourgeois philosopher like Labriola, initially a Hegelian, found the approach to Marxism easy. This widening of bourgeois thought produced a reciprocal effect in the thought of the Marxists. In one brilliant synthesis, Gramsci, a Marxist, was able to use the whole of bourgeois humanist thought for his own purposes. History presented the Italian Communists with still more good luck. After the First World War, the ebb of the European proletariat sent Italy into Fascism and the Italian Communists into hiding; they fought within their own country, which meant they were spared many risks. The French Communist Party, a minority with scarcely any influence in their own country, took internationalism as its primary objective; obedient to the directives of the Comintern, obliged to endorse Stalin's politics *in toto* – including, among other things, the Moscow trials – it came to be viewed as 'the Foreigners' Party', and this unpopularity was the cause of its subsequent rigidity. During the Resistance it earned letters patent for patriotism, and in the elections won more votes than either of the other two parties; still it did not become a party of the masses. France in 1945 had an industrial and stratified society; the interests of the peasants were not the same as those of the workers; and even among the latter there were different layers in conflict. The Communists were recruited mainly from among the salaried workers. Despite the large number of votes they won, the number of Party members continued to be low; to remain strong they needed to make themselves into a bloc without a flaw.

Italy, lacking iron and coal – almost an underdeveloped country – was still in a state of flux; there was no great distance between the workers and the peasants, many of whom – especially in the South – constituted a revolutionary force. Above all, both peasants and workers, deeply marked by the memory of Fascism whose corpse was then still warm, believed that Communism alone was capable of consolidating its defeat. The Italian Communist Party therefore had solid foundations in the population as a whole. Not finding itself cut off or enclosed on any level, it had no tendency to interpret differences of opinion as constituting opposition. In particular it considered the Italian intellectuals, who were all leftist and all sympathizers, as friends and not as adversaries.

Its alliance with the Italian Socialists also contributed to its freedom from the isolation which so beset the French Communists. As a result of the rupture brought about by the Fascists, the Italian Socialist Party under Nenni had been able to renew itself; and it had decided, after so many years of united struggle, to maintain its friendly relations with the Communists. In France, the Socialists had inherited everything from the S.F.I.O., including its anti-Communism. If the French Communist Party regarded all non-Communists as enemies, it was for the good reason that in most cases that is what they were; mistrust, justified by the situation, forbade them to make exceptions.

At the time we did not clearly understand the differences we observed between the Communists in the two countries; but, saddened by the hostility at home, we profited from the friendship of the Italians with a pleasure which, over a period of sixteen years, has never been belied.

I left Sartre in Milan to spend three weeks exploring the Dolomites. My first night alone was spent at Merano; it remains one of my most precious memories. I ate dinner and drank white wine in a courtyard hung with ivy, opposite a copper-faced clock that seemed to watch over me from high up on the wall; it had been a long time since I had contemplated several weeks of mountains and silence stretching ahead of me: unhappiness and dangers that I now knew about added to my joy a dimension of pathos that made my eyes mist over.

Bolzano, its hillsides covered with pale vines, Vitipino, its streets gay as a travelogue – I explored all the Austrian part of Italy. And also, from peak to peak, from one mountain hut to the next, across alps and rocks, I walked. Once more I smelled the grass, heard the noise of pebbles rolling down the screes, experienced again the gasping effort of the long climb, the ecstasy of relief when the haversack slips from the shoulders that lean back against the earth, the early departures under the pale sky, the pleasure of following the curve of the day from dawn to dusk.

One evening, in the heart of the mountains, a long way from any road, in a mountain inn, I asked for a room and dinner; they served me, but without a word, without a smile. On the wall I noticed the photograph of a young man hung with a piece of black crepe. As I rose from the table, the women who ran the place managed to get out one word: '*Tedesca?*' No! I said, I was French. Their faces lighted up. My Italian, they explained, had a German terseness about it. And the son of the house had been killed in the *maquis*.

It was one of my hardest journeys on foot, one of the most beautiful and – as I knew then in my heart – the last.

When I got back to Paris, I learned the details of the 'Existentialist crime' which had kept the newspapers in copy for weeks. B.[1] owned a little house at Gif-sur-Yvette which he used to lend to Francis Vintenon during the week and then go and spend the weekend there himself. One Saturday morning, as he told it to us, he couldn't find the key in the usual hiding place; the door wasn't locked. Francis is still asleep, he thought, and hoping to surprise him with his girl friend, he tiptoed along the hall; there was a very funny smell in the house. 'I went into the bedroom,' he said, 'gave one look at the bed and exclaimed: "A Negro!"' It was Francis, his face blackened, a bullet in his temple, his body half burned up by phosphorus. Someone had seen a man with a beard prowling around the village; B. and his friend the painter Patrix both wore beards; they were questioned; they had had nothing to do with the murder. It seems that Vintenon, who had entered the Resistance movement in 1943, was killed by an ex-collaborator; a name was even mentioned, but the matter was hushed up.

An Italian director wanted to make a film of *Huis clos*. Sartre returned to Rome at the end of September to work on the scenario and discuss it with him; I accompanied him; Lefèvre-Pontalis, whom he had asked to help him, came along with his wife. We set up headquarters at our old favourite, the Minerva Hotel, right in the centre of town. I had never seen Rome in the gentle October light, and I had never been free enough from social obligations and sightseeing to spend quiet days simply working. But now, when I was living there as though the city's beauty were a mere accessory, a delightful familiarity grew up between us; there were still many unexpected ways for me to explore the good things of this world.

Thanks to Soupault, who had got me invitations from a great many American universities, it was definitely decided that I was going to America; the office of the Relations Culturelles had agreed to pay my plane fare over; I was due to go in January. The whole three months beforehand were illuminated by this fact. For me it was a period of feverish activity. The past two years had not stifled my

1. One of Sartre's ex-pupils, who had become a doctor.

happiness; now it was difficult to know what to feed it with. I could not give up the old illusions, yet I had ceased to believe in them. Political decisions were becoming increasingly difficult, and our friendships were being affected by our hesitations in this area.

Despite the imperious counsels of De Gaulle, who had re-entered public life with his knightly, copybook speeches, the French people had accepted the Constitution proposed by the National Assembly. In the November elections, the Communists resumed their position as the leading political party in France. But the M.R.P. remained powerful. The Gaullist Union was growing stronger; we had no thought of moving away from the Communists, despite their continuing enmity (a novel by Kanapa about the Resistance was published in which Sartre was depicted as a conceited blockhead, a coward and almost an *agent provocateur*). In reply to Koestler's *Arrival and Departure* and his more recent book *The Yogi and the Commissar*, Merleau-Ponty wrote a piece in *Les Temps Modernes* called 'The Yogi and the Proletarian'. In it he clarified the meaning of the Moscow trials, especially Bukharin's. The reality of our acts escapes us, he wrote, but it is on that reality that we are judged and not on our intentions; although he is unable to predict exactly what that reality will be, man as politician must assume it at the moment he makes any decision, and he never has the right to wash his hands of it afterwards. In 1936, in a Soviet Russia isolated, threatened, and unable to preserve the Revolution except at the price of a monolithic severity, all opposition assumed the objective aspect of treason. Merleau-Ponty reminded the Russians that, inversely, the traitors were merely those in the opposition. He subordinated morality to history much more resolutely than any Existentialist had ever done. We crossed this Rubicon with him, conscious that moralism – although we were not yet free of it ourselves – was the last bastion of bourgeois idealism. His essay diverged too far from orthodox Marxism to be well received by the Communists. The Right waxed indignant; he was accused of writing an apology for Stalinism.

Camus found our position distasteful. His anti-Communism had already caused dissension between us; in November of '45, as he was driving me home, he had defended De Gaulle against Thorez; as I was leaving him he shouted through the car window: 'At least General de Gaulle cuts a better figure than M. Jacques Duclos!' Such an ill-tempered way of arguing surprised me, coming from him. At present his position was a long way from De Gaulle's, but even further from the Communists. He came back from New York with even less sympathy for the U.S.A. than Sartre had had, but this didn't decrease his hostility towards the U.S.S.R. in the slightest. While he was away, Aron and Ollivier had used *Combat* to support the S.F.I.O. which now drew most of its members from the lower middle classes; Camus did not dissociate himself from them. Shortly after his return, Bost was going to see him in his office and passed Aron on the way out as he was saying in a sarcastic tone: 'Well, I must be off to write my reactionary editorial.' Camus expressed astonishment; Bost made it clear to him what he thought about the paper's current policy. 'If you don't like it, why don't you leave?' Camus asked. 'I'm going to,' said Bost. He broke with *Combat* and Camus was indignant: 'There's gratitude!' However, if Camus stopped writing in *Combat* for a long while, it was because he resented, or so I was told, Aron's increasing influence there. But I think he was also disillusioned with politics in general, which he had entered only because he envisaged it as 'a direct address of man to other men', in other words, from the moral point of view. Sartre took him up on this confusion of ideas one day: '*Combat* is too concerned with moral issues at the expense of political ones.' Camus denied the accusation. Yet the article with which he made his reappearance in the newspaper in November 1946, entitled 'Neither Victims nor Executioners', was still really concerned with ethical considerations. He had no taste for the deliberations and the risks entailed in political thought; he had to be sure of his ideas so that he could be sure of himself. His reaction to the contradictions of the political situation was to detach himself from it, and Sartre's efforts to adjust to them made him impatient. Existentialism irritated him. When he read the first part of my *Ethics of Ambiguity* in *Les Temps Modernes*, he offered a few acid observations; in his eyes, I was sinning against *la clarté française*; we, on our side, found that he sometimes failed to pursue his thought as far as he might, simply in order to live up to this ideal; not through any irresponsibility, but because these were his principles; he was protecting himself. It is hard to depend on others when one has believed oneself to be a sovereign individual. This illusion is common to all bourgeois intellectuals, and we were none of us cured of it too easily. In all of us, our ethical thinking was an attempt to regain that pre-eminence. But Sartre, and myself in his wake, had thrown a great deal of our ballast overboard; yesterday's values had been stripped from us by the existence of the masses – magnanimity, to which we had clung so savagely, and even authenticity. As he searched, Sartre sometimes groped blindly, but always remained open. Camus was keeping himself covered. He had an idea of himself which no task, no revelation, would have made him give up. Our relations remained very cordial; but from time to time a shadow darkened them; these fluctuations were due much more to Camus than to Sartre and myself. He admitted that when he was with us he couldn't help sympathizing with us, but that when he was away from us we angered him.

In October, a tumultuous newcomer burst into our group; Koestler, whose play *Le Bar du Crépuscule* was about to be put on in Paris. Friends of his had assured us that his anti-Stalinism had not forced him over to the Right; he had told an American newspaper that if he had been a Frenchman he would rather live in exile in Patagonia than under De Gaulle's dictatorship.

We met first at the Pont-Royal. He accosted Sartre with pleasing simplicity: 'Hello. I'm Koestler.' He saw him next in the apartment where Sartre had just gone to live with his mother in the Place Saint Germain-des-Prés. In a peremptory tone, softened by an almost feminine smile, he told Sartre: 'You are a better novelist than I am, but not such a good philosopher.' He was in the process of writing a *summa* of philosophy whose main outlines he described to us: he wanted to assure man a margin of freedom without departing from physiological materialism. Taking his inspiration from works which we both knew, he explained to us that the systems governed by the cerebellum, the thalamus and the lower brain overlapped but did not rigidly control each other; between the lower and the upper parts there must be room for a 'bubble' of liberty. It reminded me of *La Contingence des lois de la nature* by Boutroux, and I thought to myself that Koestler was certainly a better novelist than he was a philosopher; he made me want to laugh when he talked about the thalamus, because he pronounced it thalamoose, and I couldn't help thinking of the cakes I used to eat as a child, called *talmousses*. That day we were a bit embarrassed by his self-taught pedantry, by the doctrinaire self-assurance and the scientism he had retained from his rather mediocre Marxist training. This embarrassment persisted. With Camus we never talked about each other's books, whereas Koestler was continually exclaiming every other minute: 'You must read what I wrote about that!' Success had gone to his head; he was vain and full of self-importance. But he was also full of warmth, life and curiosity; the passion with which he argued was unflagging; he was always ready, at any hour of the day or night, to talk about any subject under the sun. He was generous with his time, with himself and also with his money; he had no taste for ostentation, but when one went out with him he always wanted to pay for everything and never counted the cost. He had a naïve pride in the fact that his wife, Mamaine, belonged to an aristocratic English family. She was very blonde, very pretty, with a sharp wit; graceful and fragile, she was already suffering from the lung infection to which she succumbed some ten years later.

During the three or four weeks he spent in Paris, we met Koestler often, usually with Camus; they were very close. Bost went with us once and the conversation degenerated into an argument because Bost defended the politics of the Communist Party. 'You shouldn't have brought him, it was wrong of you,' Koestler told us severely the next day; he disliked young people; he felt excluded from their future, and any exclusion seemed to him a condemnation. Touchy, tormented, greedy for human warmth, but cut off from others by his personal obsessions – 'I have my Furies,' he used to say – Koestler's relations with us were always fluctuating. One evening we had dinner with him, Mamaine, Camus, Francine, and then went on to a little dance hall in the Rue des Gravilliers; then he issued an imperious invitation to the Schéhérézade; normally neither Camus nor myself would ever have set foot in that sort of place. Koestler ordered *zakouski*, vodka, champagne. The following afternoon, Sartre was to give a lecture at the Sorbonne, under the aegis of Unesco, on 'The Writer's Responsibility', and he hadn't yet prepared it. But the alcohol, the gypsy music and above all the heat of our discussions made him lose track of the time. Camus returned to a theme very dear to him: 'If only it were possible to tell the truth'; Koestler grew gloomy as he listened to 'Dark Eyes'; 'It's impossible to be friends if you differ about politics!' he said in an accusing tone. He rehashed his old grudges against Stalin's Russia, accusing Sartre and even Camus of trying to compromise with the Soviets. We didn't take his lugubriousness seriously; we were not aware of the passionate depths of his anti-Communism. While Koestler continued his monologue, Camus said to us: 'What we have in common, you and I, is that for us individuals come first; we prefer the concrete to the abstract, people to doctrines, we place friendship above politics.' We agreed, with an exaltation partly caused by alcohol and the lateness of the hour. Koestler repeated: 'Impossible! Impossible!' And I replied, in a low voice, but clearly: 'It *is* possible; and we are the proof of it at this very moment, since, despite all our dissensions, we are so happy to be together.' Politics had opened abysses between some people and ourselves; but we still thought that nothing separated us from Camus except a few nuances of terminology.

At four in the morning, we went to have something to eat and some more to drink at a bistro in Les Halles. Koestler was very jumpy; whether in irritation or in fun, he threw a crust of bread across the table and hit Mamaine right in the eye; he apologized and sobered up a bit; Sartre kept giggling: 'To think that in a few hours I'm going to give a talk on the writer's responsibility!' and Camus laughed. I was laughing too, but alcohol has always made me much more inclined to weep, and when I found myself alone with Sartre in the streets of Paris at dawn I began to sob over the tragedy of the human condition; as we crossed the Seine, I leaned on the parapet of the bridge. 'I don't see why we don't throw ourselves into the river!' 'All right, then, let's throw ourselves in!' said Sartre, who was finding my tears contagious and had shed a few himself. We got home at about eight in the morning. When I saw Sartre again at four in the afternoon his face was ravaged; he had slept for two or three hours and then stuffed himself full of orthedrine in order to get his lecture prepared. I thought to myself as I went into the packed amphitheatre: 'If they had seen Sartre at six this morning!'

Through Koestler, we met Manès Sperber, whom Koestler considered his master and the most competent psychologist of our age. He had a reticent charm; but he was a rigid Adlerian, a fanatical anti-Communist, and we found his dogmatism repellent. He told us that Malraux had been talking to him about a Russian secret weapon even more terrible than the atomic bomb: suitcases, quite innocent in appearance, containing radioactive dust; members of the fifth column – that is, Communists – would place these on a given day in previously selected spots, and then, after setting a certain mechanism in motion, they would steal away; the inhabitants of Chicago, New York, Pittsburgh, Detroit would die like flies. It was understandable that, faced with such a danger, the Right should advocate a War of Prevention.

About two weeks after our evening with Koestler, Boris Vian and his wife gave a party; there were a great many people there, including Merleau-Ponty. Vian had published several *Chroniques du menteur* in *Les Temps Modernes*, as well as a short story, *Les Fourmis*, and some extracts from *L'Écume des jours*, whose failure he had apparently taken in good humour. That evening, while listening to jazz, we talked a lot about Vernon Sullivan, the author of the novel *I Spit on Your Grave*, which Vian had just translated: there was a rumour going around that Sullivan didn't exist. At about eleven, Camus arrived in a bad temper, having just got back from a trip to the Midi; he attacked Merleau-Ponty on the subject of his article, 'The Yogi and the Proletarian', accused him of justifying the Moscow trials and was appalled that opposition could be made into treason. Merleau-Ponty defended himself, Sartre supported him; Camus shattered, left, slamming the door behind him; Sartre and Bost rushed out and ran after him along the street, but he refused to come back. This quarrel was to last until March 1947.

Why such an outburst? I think that Camus was going through a crisis caused by the feeling that his golden age was drawing to a close. He had known several years of triumph; he was attractive, people liked him. 'People thought I had charm, think of it! Do you know what charm is? It's a way of hearing oneself say yes, without having asked any definite question.'[1] His good luck went to his head; he thought there were no limits to what he could do: 'As success succeeded success, I began to think of myself, though I hesitate to admit it, as *chosen.*' The success of *The Outsider* and the triumph of the Resistance had convinced him that everything he undertook must be crowned with victory. We were with him once at a concert which everyone who was anyone in Paris attended; he was accompanied by a young singer in whom he was interested. 'When I think,' he said to Sartre, 'that we can foist her on this public tomorrow!' He swept the auditorium with a triumphant gesture. Sartre, at his request, wrote the first words of a song: 'Hell is all my habit now.' But that was as far as it went. During lunch with me one day at the Petit Saint-Benoît, shortly after Hiroshima, he told me that in order to prevent an atomic war, he was going to ask all the great scientists in the world to stop their researches. 'Isn't that a bit Utopian?' I objected. He flared up immediately. 'They also said it was Utopian to want to liberate Paris ourselves. To be realistic

1. *The Fall.*

means to dare.' I was used to these haughty fits of temper; afterwards, without openly admitting it, he would compromise. He never mentioned this project to me again. He saw quickly enough that nothing was ever as easy as he had supposed; instead of facing them squarely, he would back down when confronted with obstacles. One day when I was preparing a lecture, he gave me a piece of advice that left me flabbergasted: 'If someone asks you an embarrassing question, answer it with another question.' Students were more than once disappointed by his evasions. He skipped through books instead of reading them; he made up his mind beforehand instead of thinking things out. I mentioned earlier that discretion masked this laziness. He loved the nature he ruled over, but history was a threat to his individuality and he refused to bow before it. It was this very refusal that laid him open to attack; it made him, instead of 'an exemplary reality', into 'the empty affirmation of an ideal', as Sartre wrote in 1952. He fought against this intrusion rather than summon the strength to rid himself of his old dreams. Little by little, rancour began to collect in his heart, against the resistance of his opponents, against systems of philosophy, against the world in general. They seemed to him injustices and therefore wounded him, for he believed in his rights over things and people; he was generous and expected acknowledgement of it; the word that came immediately to his lips when he was contradicted or criticized was ingratitude. Until, later on, he reached the point, overwhelmed though he had once been with success, of hoping 'to die without hatred'.[1]

In November, *The Victors* opened. Sartre had written this play a year before; at the time when the ex-collaborators were beginning to show themselves again, he had wanted to refresh people's memories. He had thought a great deal about torture for four whole years; alone, and among friends, he asked himself: Should I not speak about it too? What would be the best way to handle it? He had also pondered a great deal on the relation between the torturer and his victim. All these thoughts that haunted him he threw into his play. Once more he confronted ethics and *praxis*: Lucie retreats stubbornly into her individualistic pride, while the militant Communist, presented by Sartre as in the right, aims at effectiveness.

Sartre had given the parts to Vitold, Cuny, Vibert, Chauffard and

1. *La Mer au plus près.*

Marie Olivier. Vitold was to direct. But it hadn't been easy finding a producer and a theatre. While Sartre was away in America, I spent countless hours of exasperation looking. The torture scene scared people off. 'Given my position during the war,' said Hébertot, 'I just can't allow myself to put on a play of this sort.' After letting me hope that he would do it at the Théâtre de L'Oeuvre, Beer slunk away too. Finally Simone Berriau, who had just taken on the Théâtre Antoine again, accepted it. Masson did the scenery. To make up a full bill, Sartre spent a few days writing *The Respectful Prostitute*, inspired by a true story that he had read in Pozner's *États désunis*. The tortures in *The Victors* took place almost entirely behind the scenery; seen from the wings they weren't very frightening, and even made us laugh, since the martyr, Vitold, always famished at that hour, would hurl himself on a sandwich as soon as he got off stage and bolt it between shrieks. On opening night I was in the audience, and everything changed. I had experienced before the process by which a game without consequence is transformed into an event; but this time, as the cautious theatre managers had predicted, the fruit of this metamorphosis was a scandal. It even affected me; hearing them with the ears of the other spectators, Vitold's shrieks were almost intolerable. Mme Stève Passeur stood up and shouted, very straight underneath her hat: 'It's a disgrace.' In the orchestra, people even came to blows. Aron's wife left at intermission, having almost fainted, and he followed her. The meaning of this uproar was clear: the bourgeoisie was initiating a reunification, and to awaken such unpleasant memories seemed the height of bad taste. Sartre himself was strongly affected by the anxiety he was causing; the first few nights, when it came time for the torture scene, he would drink whisky to ward it off, and often zigzagged a bit on his way home. The bourgeois critics talked about Grand Guignol, and censured Sartre for reviving old hatreds. A new gutter-press weekly, *France-Dimanche*, sent a reporter to his home who took a photograph as soon as the door was opened and published it as a picture of Sartre's mother: it was someone else. They also published an article even more nauseating than the one in *Samedi-Soir* a year earlier.

Almost simultaneously, at the Marigny, Barrault put on Sala-crou's *Les Nuits de la Colère*, which was also about the Resistance. Technically he had borrowed a great deal from the cinema, and used flashbacks and faces; we were very impressed by the conversations in which Madeleine Renaud and Jean Desailly gradually shifted from neutrality to treason; the 'positive' side of the play came over less well. In the same way, the conversations of the soldiers in *The Victors* came off better than those of their victims. Portraits of heroism are not profitable; for two such clever dramatists as Sartre and Salacrou to have risked the attempt, the ethical trend of that period must have been almost irresistible.[1] A little later, in January of 1947, Mouloudji's play *Quatre femmes* was acted at the Théâtre de la Renaissance; it had been inspired by Lola's detention in prison camp and depicted the daily life of four women prisoners. The play was not successful; the critics repeated irritably that it was time to bury the past.

The Communists, generally speaking, had supported *The Victors*. Yet when Sartre saw Ehrenburg for the first time, at a lunch organized by Sartre's theatrical agent, the publisher Nagel, Ehrenburg reproached him bitterly for having depicted the members of the Resistance as cowards and traitors. Sartre couldn't believe his ears. 'Have you read the play?' Ehrenburg admitted that he had merely skimmed through the first scene or two, but his mind was made up. 'If I got that impression, there must have been some reason for it.' As for *The Respectful Prostitute*, the Communists thought it a pity Sartre had shown his public a Negro trembling with fear and respect, instead of a real fighter. 'That's because my play reflects the present impossibility of solving the colour problem in the U.S.'[2] Sartre replied. But the Communists' conception of what literature should be was very rigidly fixed, and one of their grievances was that he wouldn't comply with it.

What they wanted to see were great, inspiring works: something epic, something optimistic. Sartre did too, but in his own way. He has explained himself on the subject in his unpublished notes. He refused to accept hope as an assumption, 'hope *a priori*'. At that time he saw action as an intermediary idea between a certain ethical system inspired by the Resistance and the realism of *praxis*; the undertaking is not to be based on a calculation of chances; it is itself

1. Public gossip, and Henri Jeanson especially, attributed to Sartre the malicious comment that 'Salacrou does better with his collaborators than with his Resistance members, because he knows them better.' What Sartre said was that Salacrou knew the middle classes better, in general, than the *dinamiteros* of the Resistance.
2. This was in 1946.

the only hope permitted. The writer should not sing of some glorious possible future but depict the world as it is, and thereby arouse the will to change it. The more convincing the picture he presents, the better he will attain this end; even the darkest of works is not pessimistic, once one accepts that it is a rallying cry for freedom, that it exists only as a function of freedom. Thus, *The Respectful Prostitute* provokes the indignation of the spectators, while, on the other hand, Lizzie's efforts to escape from her hoaxed condition suggest the possibility that she may succeed. Moreover, Sartre understood the Communist point of view on this matter: on the level of the masses, hope is one of the elements of action; the struggle is too hard for them to risk entering it unless they believe in their ultimate victory. What he called 'a hard optimism' was suitable only for a public that did not experience reality as a painful daily struggle for life; reflection is necessary, and perspective, and trust, if one is to transcend the critical attitude instead of becoming bogged down in it. When *The Respectful Prostitute* was made into a film, he changed the ending of his own accord: Lizzie perseveres in her attempt to save the innocent Negro. The style of the play, harsh but comic, kept the original dénouement at a distance; in the film it would have appeared true but vile. And then, when one demonstrates to people privileged enough to go to a theatre that there exist today situations that are both appalling and without remedy, one disturbs them, one shakes them up. Well and good; but a film is shown to millions of spectators to whom their own lives are appalling situations without remedy: any defeat is their defeat too; merely adding to their discouragement is a betrayal. Sartre noted, several years later:

The Communists are right. I am not wrong. For people who are tired and crushed, hope is always a necessity. They have only too many occasions for despair. But one must also maintain the possibility of an undertaking embarked upon without illusions.

He did maintain that possibility.[1]

1. In his plays and novels, Sartre is very close to the aesthetic defined with reference to the novel by the younger Lukács. For Lukács, says Goldmann, in an introduction to his early writings (*Les Temps Modernes*, August 1962), 'the hero of the novel is a *problematic* being'; he 'is searching for absolute values in an inauthentic and corrupt mode'. The world of a novel 'cannot possibly include a positive hero, for the simple reason that all the values which govern it are *implicit*, and therefore in relation to those values all the people in the novel have a character that is both positive and negative at the same time'. But as soon as literature is directed to the oppressed and not to the privileged,

I was working on my essay and keeping busy at *Les Temps Modernes*. Every time I opened a manuscript I had a sense of adventure. I read English and American books no one had heard of in France. Every Tuesday I joined the selection committee at Gallimard. There were moments of gaiety, mostly when Paulhan carefully tore a book to pieces and concluded: 'Of course we must publish it.' Once a week, we received in the offices of the magazine people who brought us material and suggestions, or who came to ask our advice. A great deal had been written during the past few years that neither the press nor the publishers as yet had the material resources to print; the tide of testimony was rising. I was always happy when I could tell an author that his work had been accepted; though less so when we were forced to cut: every line seemed essential to the man who had written it. An even more ungrateful task was having to say no. The writer would object, he would prove to you that his article was good, that he was talented. He would leave convinced that he was the victim of some conspiracy. There were young ones who were determined to succeed straight away, at any cost; there were the old ones trying for the last time; misunderstood ones who dreamed of escaping from the humdrum routine of home life; the men and women of every age who needed the money. Many were seeking in all sincerity for a sort of salvation in literature, but most of them wanted to obtain it at a discount, without paying the fair price in work, trouble and care. Generally speaking, they had some very strange ideas about how much you could earn by writing. One young woman entrusted me with the manuscript of a novel in which the heroine was torn between a loathsome middle-class husband and a working-class lover endowed with all the virtues; the heroine wrote down her story, a publisher accepted it, she made a vast amount of money and went off on a cruise with the man she loved. Among other things, I criticized the angelic conception of

---

simply to pose the problem without at least sketching a solution is not enough. In 1955 we discovered Lousin, the great Chinese writer of the later thirties, and were amazed to discover that he had gone through a quarrel with his Communist comrades analogous to Sartre's own: he offered a description of the society around him, in which revolution was for the time being impossible, that was purely critical; he was asked to give some picture of what its future was to be. In the end he consented, yielding to the imperatives of action; but he was of the opinion that from this time on, his works no longer possessed the slightest aesthetic value. Brecht was long suspect in the U.S.S.R. for the same reasons: his weapon is irony, not virtuous sentiments.

the lover. 'I understand how you feel,' she said, 'but you don't know him. He really is like that!' Two years later she wrote me: 'Your criticism was quite right; I was taken in; he was playing a game with me; he wasn't the man I took him for.' Sometimes I laughed; at other times I felt there was something slightly sinister in all these wild and humble ambitions fermenting in our office. Sometimes we came very close to tragedy; often we descended to pure farce. One of our most troublesome visitors was the Abbé Gengenbach, a semi-defrocked surrealist, who insulted his cloth, drank prodigiously, openly carried on liaisons with women, and then periodically shut himself up in a monastery to repent. He used to come and offer us material, often quite sensational, and ask for money; drink tended to make him rather vehement. One day he talked to me about Breton. 'But why does he hate God?' he asked, beginning to weep so copiously that I led him into an empty room. One of our secretaries suddenly dashed through the room as though shot from a gun: an author we had rejected had just slashed his wrists in Lemarchand's office.

In November, I went to Holland on a lecture tour. 'Two years ago I weighed nearly forty pounds more than I do now,' I was informed by the young woman who met me at the station in Amsterdam. Everyone talked about the famine. The parks were stripped bare; all the trees had been chopped down to fill the fireplaces. The old lady who showed me around Rotterdam took me across vast stretches of empty lots: 'This used to be the old residential district; my house stood here.' The entire town had been reduced to rubble. The country was taking a long time to recover; in the shop windows, only 'ersatz' products were displayed; the big department stores were empty; to buy even the smallest article one had to produce a card. I came back to Paris with my pockets full of florins I hadn't managed to spend.

I knew how the Dutch had resisted the Occupation; I felt friendly towards almost everyone I met there. Nevertheless, the official side of the trip was tedious. To give myself up to the beauty of the towns, to the riches in the museums, I needed solitude; people were so kind to me I was never alone for a second. Once or twice I rebelled openly; more often I tried cunning; I went to Haarlem on a morning train and pretended I wasn't returning till the evening; that way I was able to look at the Franz Hals collection without witnesses.

A week later, Sartre joined me; he had been to the opening of *Le Bar du Crépuscule*: a disaster. We looked at Rembrandts and Vermeers together: a little patch of red wall as moving as the yellow wall Proust loved so much. 'Why is it so beautiful?' Sartre wondered; we were riding in a train through moorlands, and I listened to him with a curiosity that fifteen years of familiarity had not blunted. Those painted red bricks were the starting point of the definition of art which he put forward a few weeks later in *What is Literature?*: the reassumption of the world by a freedom.

We spent two days in Utrecht; there we observed the ravages caused by Italian influence reflected in the work of the local artists; vigorous and truthful at first, after a journey to Florence they painted nothing but fashionable trifles. We visited the Psychological Institute run by Van Lennep. He had written to Sartre and conferred with him in Paris; how far does any *projected action* imply an evasion, he wanted to know, and this question touched me deeply: I had always been tempted to regard any occupation as a diversion. Van Lennep put us through a graphology test; he had invented an apparatus that enabled him to measure the pressure, the speed and the rhythm of the subject's strokes as he was writing; after that, our handwriting was projected, many times enlarged, on a screen. The contrasts between them were so glaring that the technicians present were quite upset on our account. We also took some visual tests invented by Van Lennep, and still not widely known. He showed us pictures of a galloping horse, a motorboat, a train and a man walking: which one gave us the most immediate impression of speed? The man, I said, without hesitation; his was the only case in which speed seemed to me consciously experienced. Also without hesitation, Sartre chose the motorboat, because it *tears itself away* from the surface it devours. My answer made him laugh, and I laughed at his, each of us seeing the other's reaction as a naïve self-disclosure.

We returned to Paris. Calder was having a show of his Mobiles which had never been seen before in France. Sartre had met him in America and found great charm in these 'little local celebrations'; he wrote the preface to the catalogue. Tall, potbellied, his big chubby face haloed by thick white hair, Calder seemed to have been created as he was for the express purpose of recalling, amid his airy creations, the heaviness of matter. One of his pastimes was making jewellery; the day of the private viewing he gave me a spiral brooch which I wore for a long while.

We were seeing a great many people and, since 1943, I had not changed my opinion: in the writers and artists whose work I liked, there was always something that awakened my sympathy for them personally. Though I was surprised, all the same, to find that some of them had defects that limited this response: vanity or self-importance. Instead of living in the reciprocity of one's relation with the reader, one turns back towards oneself, one apprehends oneself in the dimension of the Other; that is vanity. In young people I find it almost touching; it is a sign of their ingenuous confidence in others. But this freshness soon evaporates; prolonged, naïveté becomes mere childishness, and confidence servility. Someone who is blissfully vain may be very pleasant company, even though he talks too much about himself, but he is an object of ridicule; he is a dupe; he will take any courtesy at face value. Thwarted, he will retreat into fantasy and provide for himself what he cannot win from others; or he will become bitter, and the aroma of his simmering rancours and revenges will not be pleasant. He cheats, in any case; his complacency is belied by the dependency he submits to; begging for flattery, he abases himself by the very means he uses to boost his self-esteem. Gazing too long and too lovingly at his own image of himself, he ends up its prisoner; he inevitably falls into the self-importance which is the vehemence of vanity.

Each time I recognize it in a colleague, I am aghast. How can anyone destroy himself for the sake of a mask? But I have learned that it is foolish to discount the reality of this problem; the image we present to others is one we must assume; further, if one has abilities it is good to employ them, it is legitimate, if the need arises, to avail oneself of them; a man's truth includes his objective existence and his past, but it is not inevitably limited to such fossilizations. It is in their name that the self-important man denies the perpetual newness of life and becomes in his own eyes the Authority against which all judgement shipwrecks; to the ever-renewed questions that are put to him, instead of trying to think out answers honestly, he looks them up in Holy Writ – in his Work; or else he cites himself as an example, as he once was; by such repetitions, whatever the original brilliance of his successes, he drops behind the rest of the world, and ends up a museum piece.

This sclerosis always involves hypocrisy: if one really does think one's opinions at all worthwhile, why shelter behind one's name, one's reputation, one's past achievements? The self-important man either affects contempt for people or demands their respect. This is because he hasn't the courage to face them as equals; he renounces his freedom because he is afraid of its dangers. This blindness, this deceit, shocks me particularly in writers, whose first virtue – no matter how fantastic their flights – should be a fearless sincerity.

I was in no danger of becoming fascinated with myself, since I had not yet got over the amazement of my good luck. Despite the difficulties of travel, I had already visited many countries, and now I was going to America. If someone awakened my curiosity, in most cases I was able to make his acquaintance. I was a person who received invitations; if I never set foot in any of the *salons*, it was because I had no desire to. To have a good time with people, I need to feel in harmony with them; society women, even the most emancipated ones, were just not my sort; if I had taken part in their rituals, I should have felt bored and guilty. That is why I've never owned an evening dress; I found it repugnant to put on the uniform, not of my sex (I've often worn the sort of clothes that are called very feminine) but of their class. Genet used to complain about the simplicity of my clothes; Simone Berrieau said to me one day: 'You don't dress as well as you should!' In Portugal, I had taken pleasure in buying myself a wardrobe; I appreciate lovely things; but the cult of elegance implies a system of values which is foreign to me. Besides which, money could be used for too many things to exempt me from scruples about squandering it on finery.

Money presented problems for me. I respect it because for most people it is hard to earn; when I realized, during the course of that year, that from now on Sartre would have a lot of it, I was alarmed. It was our duty to use it to the best advantage; but how were we to choose among all those who needed it? Along the little roads around La Pouèze, we discussed our new responsibilities uneasily. In fact, we evaded them. Sartre had never taken money seriously, he loathed counting. He had neither the time nor the inclination to turn himself into a philanthropic institution; besides which, there is something unpleasant about charity when it has been carefully thought out. He gave away most of what he earned, but as chance dictated — to friends, to people he met, to people who wrote and asked. I thought it a pity he should be so feckless about his generosity, and I soothed my uneasiness by spending as little as possible on myself. For my tour of America I needed a dress; I bought one at a little place I knew, it was a knit and, I thought, ravishing, but expensive: 25,000 francs.[1] 'It's my first concession,' I told Sartre, and then burst into tears. My friends laughed at me, but I understand myself. I still imagined — in spite of having demonstrated the opposite in *The Blood of Others* — that there existed a way of not being involved in social injustice, and I thought we were to blame for not trying to find it. In fact, there is no such thing, and in the end I came around to thinking that Sartre's solution was as good as any other. Yet he himself was not satisfied with it, for he found it a burden to be privileged. Our tastes were lower middle class, our style of life continued to be modest. All the same, we did go to restaurants and bars frequented by the wealthy, and we would meet right-wing people in them; it irritated us particularly that we were always running into Louis Vallon. Without ever getting used to our new position, little by little — whether for good or for bad — I grew less hesitant about benefiting from it: it was all so contingent, the way the money came and went! Several times I dragged Sartre with me on expensive trips; I yearned for them so deeply, and they gave me so much, that I never blamed myself on that score. On the whole, the way in which I decided to permit myself certain 'concessions' and refuse others was decidedly arbitrary; but it seems to me impossible to establish any coherent principle of behaviour in this area. I shall come back to this later.

On my return from Holland, I learned that *All Men are Mortal* had just come out. 'My wife likes your last novel very much,' the publisher Nagel told me. 'Many people think it much inferior to your others, as you know; but she likes it very much.' I didn't know. Working on it had been such a pleasure that I had supposed it to be far and away my best. Several of my friends who had read it in manuscript shared this opinion. I had heard (perhaps erroneously) that Queneau had suggested to Gallimard a first printing of 75,000 copies. I had been disconcerted when I learned from Zette that Leiris thought I had used the fantastic too rationally: that's just the reaction of a surrealist, I reassured myself. Nagel's words

1. £30.

caught me quite unprepared, and came as something of a shock. But what he had said was soon confirmed. The critics were by no means kind; Rousseaux went so far as to say that he regretted having written about me favourably in the past, and announced that I would never write anything worthwhile again. Among my intimate friends, the book still had its partisans, and also some outside that circle; but after my previous successes it was an indisputable failure. The judgements of certain critics I was unable to reject, and even less so that of the public; such widespread condemnation must mean that I had more or less failed in my attempt. I regretted it, but without being too upset. I still refused to question myself, to torment myself, and I still kept my trust in the future.

CHAPTER THREE

I WAS not planning to write a book about America, but I wanted to have a good look at it; I knew its literature and, despite my dismaying accent, I spoke English fluently. I had a few friends over there: Stépha, Fernand, Lise. Sartre gave me some addresses. I had dinner with Ellen and Richard Wright, who were getting ready to return to New York before coming back to make their home in Paris.

I went to say good-bye to Olga, who was undergoing treatment at Leysin; she had decided not to stay there very long, boredom was making her lose weight; it was as sinister as Berck; at the end of twenty-four hours I already felt crushed by it. I went back to Paris, and I waited. There were still very few planes making the Atlantic crossing, and that winter was so treacherous they were often forced to turn back in mid-ocean. One evening Sartre finally went with me to the Invalides air terminal and I spent two troubled hours at Orly – the distance, the length of my absence, the magic of America, everything to do with my journey excited and frightened me; and then, suddenly, the plane wasn't going to take off until the following day! I called the Montana and rejoined Sartre and Bost there, but I felt I was nowhere, and all the following day I drifted in limbo. At last I flew away.

In New York I met M. She was about to leave for Paris, where she would remain until my return. She was as charming as Sartre had described her, and she had the prettiest smile in the world.

France was still doing penance, Italy too; Switzerland was insipid. The abundance of luxuries in America bowled me over: the streets, the shop windows, the automobiles, the hairdos and the furs, the bars, the drugstores, the flashing streams of neon, the distances devoured by plane, by car, by train, by Greyhound, the shifting splendour of the landscapes, from the snows of Niagara to the burning deserts of Arizona, and all the different kinds of people with whom I talked through the long nights and days; I scarcely met any but intellectuals; but all the same what a distance from the cottage cheese salads of Vassar to the marijuana I smoked in a room at the Plaza with bohemians from Greenwich Village! One of the fortunate things about this trip was that, although its general plan was determined by my lecture programme, it left enormous room for chance and invention; I have related in detail how I profited from this good luck in *America Day by Day*.

I was prepared to love America. It was the homeland of capitalism, yes, but it had helped save Europe from Fascism; the atomic bomb assured it world leadership and freed it from all fear; books written by certain American liberals had convinced me that a large section of the nation had a clear and serene awareness of its responsibilities. The reality was a great shock to me. There flourished among almost all the intellectuals, even those who claimed to be of the Left, an Americanism worthy of the chauvinism of my father. They approved of all Truman's speeches. Their anti-Communism verged on neurosis; their attitude towards Europe, towards France, was one of arrogant condescension. It was impossible to dislodge them, even for an instant, from their convictions; discussion often seemed to me as futile as with advanced paranoiacs. From Harvard to New Orleans, from Washington to Los Angeles, I heard students, teachers and journalists seriously wondering whether it would not be better to drop their bombs on Moscow before the U.S.S.R. was in a position to fight back. It was explained to me that in order to defend freedom it was becoming necessary to suppress it: the witch-hunt was getting under way.

What I found most disquieting was the inertia of all these people ceaselessly nagged by the wildest propaganda. No one, as far as I know, was talking about the *organization man* yet; but that was whom I described in my reports, in terms scarcely different from those used later by American sociologists; they characterized him above all by his *other-conditioning*; and I was struck by the absence, even among very young boys and girls, of any interior motivation; they were incapable of thinking, of inventing, of imagining, of choosing, of deciding for themselves; this incapacity was expressed by their conformism; in every domain of life they employed only the abstract measure of money, because they were unable to trust to their own judgement. Another of my surprises was the American woman; even if it is true that the spirit of revenge in her has been exasperated to the point of making her a 'praying mantis', she still remains a dependent and relative being; America is a masculine world.[1] These observations, and the importance I granted them, are such that my American experience still remains valid in my eyes today.

All the same, I met a few writers, more or less intimate friends of Richard Wright, with whom I got on very well; they were sincerely pacifist and progressive, and though they were mistrustful of Russia and Stalin, they were free with their criticisms of their own country. And yet they loved so many things about it and taught me to become so attached to it myself that I adopted its history, its literature and its beauties almost as my own. America became still closer to me when I became attached to Nelson Algren towards the end of my stay. Although I related this affair – very approximately – in *The Mandarins*, I return to it now not out of any taste for gossip, but in order to examine more closely a problem that in *The Prime of Life* I took to be too easily resolved: Is there any possible reconciliation between fidelity and freedom? And if so, at what price?

Often preached, rarely practised, complete fidelity is usually experienced by those who impose it on themselves as a mutilation; they console themselves for it by sublimations or by drink. Traditionally, marriage used to allow the man a few 'adventures on the side' without reciprocity; nowadays, many women have become aware of their rights and of the conditions necessary for their happiness: if there is nothing in their own lives to compensate for masculine inconstancy, they will fall a prey to jealousy and boredom. There are many couples who conclude more or less the same

1. Eve Merriam, in an article published in 1960 in *The Nation*, has demonstrated that the American male is crushed, not by the female, but by the Organization.

pact as Sartre and myself: to maintain throughout all deviations from the main path a 'certain fidelity'. 'I have been faithful to thee, Cynara, in my fashion.' Such an undertaking has its risks. It is always possible that one of the partners may prefer a new attachment to the old one, the other partner then considering himself or herself unjustly betrayed; in place of two free persons, a victim and a torturer confront each other.

In certain cases, for one reason or another – children, a common concern, the force of the attachment – the couple is impregnable. If the two allies allow themselves only passing sexual liaisons, then there is no difficulty, but it also means that the freedom they allow themselves is not worthy of the name. Sartre and I have been more ambitious; it has been our wish to experience 'contingent loves'; but there is one question we have deliberately avoided: How would the third person feel about our arrangement? It often happened that the third person accommodated himself to it without difficulty; our union left plenty of room for loving friendships and fleeting affairs. But if the protagonist wanted more, then conflicts would break out. On this point, an unavoidable discretion compromised the exact truthfulness of the picture painted in *The Prime of Life*, for although my understanding with Sartre has lasted for more than thirty years, it has not done so without some losses and upsets in which the 'others' always suffered. This defect in our system manifested itself with particular acuity during the period I am now relating.

'When you get to Chicago, go and see Algren for me,' a young intellectual called Nelly Benson had told me when I was having dinner with her in New York. 'He's an amazing man, and a great friend of mine.' I have given a faithful account of my first meeting with him in *America Day by Day*, our evening in the lower depths of the city and the following afternoon spent in the bars of the Polish district; but I did not mention the complicity that immediately sprang up between us, nor how disappointed we were not to be able to have dinner together: I was obliged to accept an invitation from two French officials. I called him before I left for the railroad station; they had to take the telephone away from me by force. On the train to Los Angeles I read one of his books and thought about him; he lived in a hovel, without a bathroom or refrigerator, alongside an alley full of steaming trash cans and flapping newspapers; this poverty seemed refreshing, after the heavy odour of dollars in the big hotels and the elegant restaurants, which I had found hard to take. 'I'll go back to Chicago,' I said to myself; Algren had asked me to, and I wanted to; but if we found this parting painful already, wouldn't the next one hurt us even more? I asked that question in the letter I sent him. 'Too bad for us if another separation is going to be difficult,' he answered.

The weeks passed; back in New York, friendships grew stronger; one, especially, absorbed a great deal of my time. At the beginning of May, Sartre asked me in one of his letters to postpone my departure because M. was staying another ten days in Paris. Suddenly that made me feel the nostalgia I described Anne as feeling in *The Mandarins*: I'd had enough of being a tourist; I wanted to walk about on the arm of a man who, temporarily, would be mine. I thought first of my New York friend, but he didn't want either to lie to his wife or admit such an affair to her; we decided against it. I called Algren. 'Can you come here?' I asked him. He couldn't; but he would like very much to see me in Chicago. I arranged for him to meet me at the airport.

Our first day together was very much like the one Anne and Lewis spent together in *The Mandarins*; embarrassment, impatience, misunderstanding, fatigue, and finally the intoxication of deep understanding. I stayed in Chicago only three days; I had a great many things to settle in New York; I persuaded Algren to go there with me – it was the first time he'd been in an aeroplane. I went around arranging things, shopping, saying good-bye; at about five in the afternoon I came back to our room and we stayed with each other until the next morning. People would often talk about him to me; they said he was unstable, moody, even neurotic; I liked being the only one who understood him. If he was sometimes blunt and rude, as people claimed, it was certainly only as a defence. For he possessed that rarest of all gifts, which I should call goodness if the word had not been so abused; let me say that he really cared about people. I told him, before I left him, that my life was permanently fixed in Paris; he believed me without at all understanding what I meant. I promised him we should see each other again, but we did not know when or how, and I arrived in Paris in a dreadful state. Sartre was in trouble, too. Before getting on the boat that brought her to France, M. had written him quite frankly: 'I am coming determined to do everything I can to make you ask me to stay.' He hadn't asked her to stay. She wanted to prolong her visit until July. Although she had been very friendly with me in New York, she did not really like me. In order to avoid friction, I went with Sartre to live in a little hotel near Port-Royal on the outskirts of Paris; it was almost the country, there were roses in the garden, cows in the meadows, and I worked outside in the sun. We went for walks along the path Jean Racine used to use, overgrown with grass and punctuated with bad alexandrines. On certain evenings Sartre would go into Paris to meet M. This way of life would have suited me if she had been satisfied with it; but no. The evenings when Sartre stayed out at Saint-Lambert he would receive dramatic telephone calls from her. She could not accept his letting her go away again. But how could he do otherwise? The circumstances were not favourable to compromise solutions. If M. were to make her home in Paris, sacrificing her job, her friendships, everything to which she was accustomed, she would be entitled to expect everything from Sartre; and that was more than he was able to offer. But if he loved her, how could he bear not to see her for months at a time? He listened to her complaints with remorse; he felt that he was to blame. Of course he had warned her there could be no question of his making a life with her. But by saying that he loved her he gave the lie to that warning; for – especially in the eyes of women – love triumphs over every obstacle. M. was not entirely in the wrong. Love's promises express the passion of a moment only; restrictions and reservations are no more binding; in every case, the truth of the present sweeps all pledges imperiously before it. It was natural that M. should think: Things will change. Her mistake was to take for mere verbal precautions what were, with Sartre, less a decision than simply knowledge; and one might conclude that he misled her insofar as it was impossible for him to communicate to her the evidence on which that knowledge was based. Besides which, she, on her side, had not told him that when she began the affair she also rejected its limits. Perhaps he had been thoughtless not to have realized this; his excuse was that, while refusing to alter his relationship with me, he cared for her intensely and wanted to believe that some compromise solution could be found.

Despite the pleasures of the approaching summer, I went through two painful months. At the time, I had swallowed the failure of my last novel, following on that of *Les Bouches inutiles*, with scarcely a murmur; but underneath, it was still depressing me. All progress had stopped; I had become stagnant. My resolution was insufficient to cut myself off completely from America, and I attempted to prolong my trip by writing a book. I had taken no notes; my long letters to Sartre and a few engagements scribbled in a notebook eked out my memory. This report interested me; but like my essay on Woman – abandoned for the time being – it did not give me what I had always demanded of writing up till then: the feeling of risking and at the same time of transcending myself, an almost religious joy. 'I'm just writing a potboiler,' I told Sartre. But in any case the pain and the pleasure of writing would not have been enough to settle the memory of my last few days in America. It wouldn't have been impossible to go back to Chicago, since the question of money was no longer crucial; but wouldn't it be better to give up the whole thing? I asked myself that question with an anxiety that bordered on mental aberration. To calm myself, I began to take orthedrine. For the moment, it allowed me to regain my balance; but I imagine that this expedient was not entirely unconnected with the anxiety attacks I suffered from at the time. Since they were founded in reality, my anxiety could at least have been discreet in its manifestations; but it was in fact accompanied by a physical panic that my greatest fits of despair, even when enhanced by alcohol, had never produced. Possibly the war and the period just after it had undermined my health and predisposed me to these paroxysms. Perhaps, too, these crises were a last revolt before resigning myself to age and the end that follows it; I still wanted to separate the shadow from the light. Suddenly I was becoming a stone, and the steel was splitting it: that is hell.

To celebrate my return I gave a party in the *cave* into which the Lorientais[1] had moved in the Rue de la Montagne-Sainte-Geneviève. Vian, who was tending bar for me, immediately began to serve the most merciless concoctions; many of the guests sank into a stupor; Giacometti went off to sleep. I was careful and kept going till dawn; I forgot my purse when I left, and went back with Sartre in the afternoon to get it. 'And the eye?' the concierge asked us. 'Don't you want the eye?' A friend of Vian's, known as the Major, had put his glass eye on the piano and left it there. A month later, in a *cave* in the Rue Dauphine, a place called the Tabou opened,

1. The group Claude Luter had formed.

where Anne-Marie Cazalis, a young red-haired poetess who had won the Prix Valéry a few years earlier, received the customers; Vian and his orchestra went to work there and it had an enormous and immediate success. People drank and danced and also brawled a great deal, both inside and out front. The neighbourhood declared war on Anne-Marie Cazalis; at night, people threw buckets of water on the customers and even on people just passing by. I didn't go to the Tabou. I didn't see *Gilda*, the film everyone was talking about. I didn't even go to the lecture Sartre gave on Kafka, to raise money for the Ligue Française pour la Palestine Libre.[1] I almost never left Saint-Lambert.

Sartre had kept me in touch with what was happening in his life by letter, and we talked about all the things he had mentioned. He had been to see *The Maids* by Genet, which Jouvet had completely misdirected. He had seen Koestler again, intending to give him his *Anti-Semite and Jew* which had just come out; Koestler had stopped him: 'I've been to Palestine; I've reached the saturation point about the subject. I must warn you that I won't read your book.' Thanks to the intervention of M., who knew Camus, he and Sartre had been reconciled. *The Plague* came out just at that time; here and there, one could still hear the voice that spoke in *The Outsider*. It was Camus' voice and it touched us, but to treat the Occupation as the equivalent of a natural calamity was merely another means of escaping from History and the real problems. Everyone fell in only too easily with the abstract morality expressed by this fable. Shortly after my return, Camus severed his connexion with *Combat*: the newspaper strike had seriously affected its financial stability. The paper was re-financed by Smadja and taken over again by Bourdet, who had founded it but who had happened to be in a concentration camp at the time it had been able to come out of clandestinity. In a sense this change was fortunate. *Combat* once more took up a resolutely left-wing position. But Camus had been so closely associated with it that his departure marked for us the end of an epoch.

The new one was not particularly gay. From the moment I landed, I had been struck by how poor France was. Blum's policy – a price and wage freeze – had been a failure; there was not enough coal or grain, the bread ration had been reduced, it was impossible to eat or dress decently without recourse to the black market, and

1. It was at the time of the *Exodus* affair.

[138]

the workers' wages made this impracticable for them. In order to protest against the lowering of their standard of living, 20,000 workers in the Renault factories had gone on strike on 30 April. The food shortage provoked riots and further strikes – stevedores, gas and electricity workers, railroad workers – which Ramadier blamed on an invisible impresario. I learned the extent of the reprisals exacted by the army from the Malgaches: 80,000 dead.[1] And there was fighting in Indochina.[2] At the time of my departure for America, the newspapers were full of stories about the rebellion in Hanoi. It was only when I got back that I discovered it had been provoked by the shelling of Haiphong: our artillery had killed 6,000 people, men, women and children. Ho Chi-minh had taken to the bush. The government was refusing to negotiate, Coste-Floret asserting there were no longer any military problems in Indochina, while Leclerc was prophesying years of guerrilla warfare.

The Communist Party had declared its opposition to this war. It had protested the arrest of the five Malgache members of Parliament. The Communist ministers supported the Renault strike and left the government. Meanwhile De Gaulle was talking to Bruneval, and in Strasbourg he announced the formation of the R.P.F. The class struggle was coming out into the open, and the odds no longer favoured the proletariat. The bourgeoisie had re-formed its ranks and the present situation was to its advantage.

This break-up of French unity was, in effect, determined to a great extent by the collapse of international solidarity. Only two years had gone by since I had seen newsreels of G.I.s and Russian soldiers dancing together for joy at Torgau on the banks of the Elbe. Now, carried away by its own generosity, the United States was planning to make satellites out of all the countries of Europe, including those in the east. Molotov countered this by rejecting the Marshall Plan. The Cold War had begun. Even on the Left, very few people approved of the Communist refusal; among the

1. In March, they had massacred about 200 European *colons*. The figure of 80,000 was not denied by the government. It was divulged – while the number of victims in the Sétif reprisals remained secret – because the Communists were at present in the opposition.
2. On 6 March 1946 France had recognized the Republic of Vietnam with Ho Chi-minh as its President. But the machinations in Saigon and Bidault's 'firmness' had thwarted these agreements.

intellectuals, Sartre and Merleau-Ponty were almost the only ones who rallied to Thorez's point of view of the 'Western trap'.

However, the bridges between Sartre and the Communists were broken. The Party intellectuals attacked him unmercifully because they were afraid that he would steal their clientele; that his position was so close to theirs only made them consider him as more dangerous than ever. 'You are preventing people from coming to us,' Garaudy told him. And Elsa Triolet: 'You are a philosopher and therefore an anti-Communist.' *Pravda* had spat out insults against Existentialism that were laughable but none the less painful. Lefebvre had 'executed' it in a book praised to the skies by Desanti in *Action*, and by Guy Leclerc in *Les Lettres françaises*. And in *La Pensée*, Mougin's *La Sainte Famille existentialiste* had appeared; also a masterly work of annihilation according to the connoisseurs of the Communist Party. Garaudy, although he described Sartre as a 'gravedigger of literature', nevertheless kept his insults within the limits of decency, but Kanapa in *L'Existentialisme n'est pas un humanisme*, accused us in the crudest language of being Fascists and 'enemies of mankind'. Sartre decided to throw off the restraint he had imposed upon himself until then. He collected signatures – those of Pierre Bost, Fombeure, Schlumberger, Mauriac and Guéhenno among others – for a text protesting against the calumnies heaped on Nizan, and the press had published it. The C.N.E. had replied and Sartre was going to answer them in the July issue of *Les Temps Modernes*. This break was inevitable since, as he wrote in *What is Literature?*, which was published at about that time in *Les Temps Modernes*: 'The policy of Stalin's Communism is incompatible with the honest exercise of a writer's trade.' He took the Communist Party to task for the precedence it gave to scientism, for its oscillations between conservatism and opportunism, and for a utilitarianism which degraded literature to the status of propaganda. Suspect among the bourgeoisie and cut off from the masses, Sartre was condemning himself to a future without a public; from now on he would have merely readers. He accepted this solitude willingly, because it titillated his love of adventure. Nothing could be more despairing than this essay, and nothing more high-spirited. By rejecting him, the Communists were condemning him to political impotence; but since to name is to unmask, and to unmask is to change, Sartre extended his notion of commitment still further and discovered a *praxis* in writing.

Reduced to his *petit-bourgeois* singularity, and rejecting it, he was aware of himself as 'an unhappy consciousness', but had no taste for jeremiads and was confident of being able to find a way of going beyond this state.

I went to a screening of *The Chips are Down*, made by Delannoy from a scenario Sartre had written a long while before. Afterwards we had supper at the Véfour with Bost and Olga, who had come back from Leysin and was much better. Micheline Presle was brimming with beauty and talent; but Pagliero, whom I had so liked in *Rome, Open City* – I had seen it in New York – spoke French with such a bad accent that they had been forced to dub him; the effect was regrettable. And the hero and heroine appeared to be just as dead after their resurrection as before.

In June, the Prix de la Pléiade was awarded (for the last time). The jury's session was a very stormy one, according to Sartre; he succeeded in getting the prize for Genet's plays – *The Maids* and *Deathwatch* – but Lemarchand handed in his resignation. As in preceding years, I was invited to take coffee with the members of the jury. When I went into the dining room, Malraux was speaking and everyone was very quiet; he was talking about *The Plague*. 'The question is,' he said, 'to know whether Richelieu could have written *The Plague*. I say he could. In any case, General de Gaulle *has* written it, it's called *The Edge of the Sword*.' He also said, aggressively: 'It is so that a Camus can write *The Plague* that men like myself have stopped writing.'

Despite its being so late in the season, a theatre in London was putting on *The Respectful Prostitute* and *The Victors*. Nagel passed on an invitation to Sartre from the manager; I should have been delighted about it if only he hadn't come with us; being afraid of aeroplanes, he forced us to make the journey by train, and didn't stop chattering the whole time. In London, he had taken a bizarrely furnished apartment on one side of St James's Square. We revisited the museums and the streets without him. The blitz, V-1s, V-2s – ruins everywhere; overrun with tall hollyhocks, they made vistas and gardens in the heart of this dense city. Once more, after fifteen years of absence, London won our hearts. I was sorry we were there for only four days.

Nagel had organized a press conference for Sartre; he was stupefied when I said I wasn't going to attend it; then his face suddenly lit up. 'Ah!' he said. 'That's very clever of you.' He couldn't imagine that I merely wanted to go for a walk, and assumed that it was part of a scheme on my part, that I intended to wait until the English journalists put themselves out for *me*. In a setting of overpowering ostentation – antique furniture, Old Masters – we saw the great satrap Alexander Korda. We met a lot of theatre people in restaurants and bars. We went to the opening. Laughing, the director said to Sartre: 'You've got a surprise coming. . . .' We had indeed; he had cut one whole scene. During the performance, Rita Hayworth, wearing a short black velvet evening dress and followed by a female companion, made a universally observed entrance – into the auditorium. We had supper with her at the home of a Dutchman. There were only seven or eight people there, and it was a fairly dreary gathering. With her golden shoulders and her magnificent bosom Rita Hayworth was magnificent; but a star without a husband is a sorrier sight than an orphaned child. She spoke charmingly about her past. The Dutchman made some racist observations and she protested. 'But all the same, if you had a daughter, would you let her marry a Negro?' he asked. 'She'd marry whomever she wanted to,' was the reply. The star was certainly no less intelligent than most of the women who don't make their beauty a profession.

Shortly after that, Sartre accompanied M. to Le Havre. She left complaining of the pain he was causing her. She wrote that she would come back either never or for good. In sweltering heat (there had never been such a summer according to the newspapers) we dragged through day after intolerable day in Paris. Pagniez, whom we no longer saw very often but for whom we still had a great deal of affection, told us that his wife was suffering from a blood disease always fatal within two or three years. Sartre was brooding remorsefully. It was a great relief to get into the airplane that took us to Copenhagen. It was cool in that beautiful red and green city. But our first day reminded me of the dark hours when Sartre was followed by lobsters. It was a Sunday, we mingled with the families wading along the sea's edge. Sartre was very quiet, and so was I. I wondered in terror if we had become strangers to one another. Our obsessions melted away little by little during the following days, as we walked among the attractions of the Tivoli and visited the sailors' dives, where we drank *akvavit* late into the night.

In Sweden we disembarked at Helsinborg. After three days

along canals and lakes full of flotillas of logs, we reached Stockholm. I loved the city, all glass and water, and also the slow whiteness of the evenings hesitating on the brink of night.

Some Swedish people whom Sartre knew showed us the old streets and restaurants, a charming old theatre set among the woods and lakes. One night, when they had taken us out into the country, we saw the aurora borealis. Often I felt they were in the way; how could one be open to things when one was being forced to make polite remarks the whole time? This constraint aggravated the tension inside me which had not completely subsided. I had nightmares. I can remember a yellow eye at the back of my head which was being pierced by a long knitting needle. And my anxiety attacks came back. I tried to conjure these crises away with words:

The birds are attacking me – must drive them away; it's such an exhausting struggle, keeping them off, day and night: death, our deaths, solitude, vanity; at night, they swoop down on me; in the morning, they take their time flying away. And if something inside my body weakens, there they are, in the flash of a wing. In the café in Stockholm, there were two colours shrieking at one another: orange and green, their meeting was an agony. A hand took me by my scalp; it pulled, it pulled and my head grew longer and longer as it went on pulling, it was death trying to take me away. Ah! let's put an end to it! I'll pick up a revolver, I'll shoot. I must practise. On rabbits, perhaps, to begin with . . .

Sartre and I continued north, first by train and then by boat, along a string of lakes. We discovered landscapes that were new to us: dwarf forests, earth the colour of amethysts planted with tiny trees red as coral and yellow as gold. They gave me a feeling of childhood and mystery; a troll was bound to pop up at a turn in the path. We did, in fact, see one apparition: a fat woman's extremely white bottom. Two couples were bathing at the foot of a waterfall in nude tranquillity. We left the boat at a peaceful Lapp village; the Lapps were quite short, their faces creased by a fixed smile, and they wore bright blue clothes embroidered in yellow, and sealskin moccasins. The only way a doctor could get there was by the boat we came on, which only called once a week at the most. We stayed several days at Abisko; the hotel was built of wood, and there was a knotted rope in every room so the occupant could climb to safety in case of fire.[1] Around it, there was only the vast forest stretching away on every side, and when I sat there with a book, reindeer would come up to me.

There was no road to Abisko, only the railway; the mailman and the milkman both used the tracks, pedalling up and down on strange vehicles painted bright red. One evening, however, amid all that solitude, the telephone broke the silence; a journalist in Stockholm told Sartre that, because of complaints by neighbours, the police had closed the Tabou for two weeks; did he have any comments? We climbed Mount Njulja and were astonished to find perpetual snow at 4,500 feet and disturbed by the thought that we should never see that spot again; even Sartre, less sensitive than I to the loneliness of things, was moved: that snow-capped landscape of many-coloured stones, where dusk melted into dawn, would go on offering itself when our eyes had deserted it forever. One morning we took the train for Narvik. The town had been shelled to bits; its wretchedness was a striking contrast to Swedish opulence. A good example of history laughing in the face of morality.

On our way back, we stopped to visit an old Swedish prince, a lover of literature and the arts, whom Sartre had already met; he was married to a Frenchwoman; they lived in a pretty house amid peaceful valleys, and were full of wonder at their good fortune. 'We too will have a happy old age!' I said to myself as I sipped a glass of old *akvavit*, aged in little wooden casks; I must have been even more shaken up than I actually recall to have taken refuge in such a far-off, well-behaved dream; but the fact is that it put the finishing touch to my convalescence and I returned to France with my mind completely calm again.

I left again immediately; I had decided to return to Chicago in the middle of September. I had sent a cable to Algren asking him if he agreed; he did. I got on a T.W.A. plane taking some Greek peasants and tradespeople from Athens to America. It was a terrible old crate which flew at a ceiling limit of about six or seven thousand feet, and took twelve hours to get from Shannon to the Azores. I went to sleep during that part of the journey and woke with a start. The plane was turning around; a motor had just given out and we were going back to Shannon. I was scared for the next

1. The hotel was destroyed by fire two years later, in 1949.

five hours without a break; I read science-fiction stories, escaping for the minutes to another planet or into prehistory, only to find myself back over the ocean: if another motor gave out, I would disappear into it. Ah! how I longed for death to come to me disguised, without inflicting its imminence and, above all, its loneliness! Around me, no one turned a hair. But what a sudden explosion of talk as soon as the plane was on the ground! A bus took us a long way away, to the edge of a fjord where there was a mock village that belonged to the airport; everyone had a little house to himself with a peat fire burning in it. I stayed there two days, dragging myself along roads whose signposts and notices bore indecipherable words, I sat on the soft slopes of ash-green meadows laced with low walls of grey stones. In the bar I drank Irish whisky while I read Algren's first novel which told me all about his childhood. I was no longer sure that he existed, or Chicago either, or Paris. We set out again; when the plane landed in the Azores, a tyre burst and I had to wait another eighteen hours in the airport concourse. Then we flew through storms; the plane fell nearly 5,000 feet from cloud to cloud. When we arrived, I ached all over, in body and soul. It seemed as though the customs officials would never finish evaluating the miles of lace that the Greeks were dragging about in their suitcases; when I came out, Algren was not there, and I thought I was never going to find him again.

He had been waiting for me for four days in the house on Wabansia Avenue, and the moment we looked at each other again, I knew I had been right to come back.

It was during these two weeks that I discovered Chicago:[1] the prisons; the police stations and the line-ups, the hospitals, the stockyards, the burlesque houses, the slums with their empty lots and their nettles. I saw very few people. Some of Algren's friends worked in radio and television, though they were finding it pretty hard to keep their jobs; the Communist purge was spreading panic in Hollywood, and all over the United States liberals were being thought of as Reds. The rest were dope addicts, gamblers, whores, thieves, ex-convicts or outlaws; they were all escapees from American conformism; that is why Algren liked to be around them; but they were not particularly friendly. He was

1. In *America Day by Day* I amalgamated this second visit with the first.

writing about them in the novel he was working on at the time. I read a first draft of it, typed on yellow paper and covered with cross-outs. I also read Algren's favourite authors: Vachel Lindsay, Sandburg, Masters, Stephen Benét, all old rebels who had defended America against what she was now becoming. I re-read newspapers and magazines to fill in the gaps in my reportage.

Again Algren asked me to stay with him for good, and I explained that this was impossible. But we parted less sadly than in May, because in the spring I was to return so that we could take a trip together lasting several months, down the Mississippi and then to Guatemala and Mexico.

In July, De Gaulle had called the Communists separatists and the Communist Party 'public enemy Number One'. The French bourgeoisie was already dreaming of preventive war. They were having a fine time reading books by Koestler and Kravchenko, and other works of the sort written by repentant Communists.

I met a certain number of these converts, and they astonished me by the lyric ecstasy of their hatred. None of them proposed an analysis of the U.S.S.R. or offered any constructive criticism; they were content to grind out romantic novelettes. Communism, for them, was a world-wide Blot, a Conspiracy, a Fifth Column, a sort of Ku Klux Klan. The hysteria in their eyes was an accusation of the regime that had put it there; but it was impossible to establish any connexion between their exotic stories and the lies of the Stalinist government. They were almost maniacally suspicious of one another, and each considered those who had left the Party later than himself to be criminals.

There was another category which we found equally unpleasant: the sympathizers at all costs. 'As far as I'm concerned,' said one of them proudly, 'the Communists can give me as many kicks in the ass as they want; they still won't discourage me.' Faced with even the most disturbing facts – at that time, the hanging of Petkov – they simply closed their eyes: 'You have to believe in something, after all.' For us, the U.S.S.R. was the country which embodied socialism, but also one of the two Great Powers hatching a new war; no doubt Russia didn't want it; but she was accepting it as inevitable, preparing for it, and thereby putting the world in danger. A refusal to side with the U.S.S.R. was not a negative attitude, as Sartre had affirmed in *What is Literature?* By eluding the alternative between the two blocs, he was making the decision to invent another way out.

One of his old colleagues, called Bonafé, knew Ramadier well and suggested to him that we should be entrusted with a radio programme to express our views; Sartre accepted. We did not wish to be dependent on the Présidence du Conseil; the *Temps Modernes* hour was attached to the 'literary and dramatic programmes' department. The first week, Sartre – with the help of a group of friends including myself – urged his listeners to reject the Cold War politics of the two blocs. To become part of either one or the other would only aggravate the conflict between them; he declared that peace was possible and censured the editors of *France-Dimanche* for leaving their front-page headline space blank in one of their recent issues because they could not bring themselves to print the words they felt were necessary: 'War before Christmas'.

The day after the triumphant victory of the R.P.F. in the cantonal elections, we used our programme to attack De Gaulle. Following the method used by Pascal in his *Provincial Letters*, we demolished – *we* being Sartre, Bonafé, Merleau-Ponty, Pontalis and myself – the arguments of a pseudo-Gaullist played by Chauffard; all the arguments we put in his mouth were taken from the R.P.F. newspapers, and we had been quite explicit that the character was being played by an actor; we were accused of trickery nevertheless. Bonafé was blamed for being too violent, which unfortunately was true; but in any case we aroused a great deal of indignation; the press gave us the mudslinging of our lives. Bénouville and Torrès insisted that Sartre continue the discussion with them, on the air. He accepted; but they were probably afraid he would settle their hash too easily; leaving Sartre in one of the radio building offices, they got together in another for consultation and, when they came back, said they had thought it over and decided that because Sartre had gone too far they refused to hold a public discussion with him. Aron had accompanied Bénouville, with whom he was in agreement. This attitude brought to a head the quarrel which had been brewing between Sartre and him ever since he began writing for *Figaro* and sympathizing with the R.P.F.

Our discussion of the Communist Party was broadcast two weeks later. Forced out of the government, attacked by the Socialists and hated by the bourgeoisie, the Communists were in a state of isolation scarcely calculated to make them flexible;

nevertheless, Sartre had been officially asked, at Hervé's instigation, to take the initiative in the formation of anti-Fascist 'vigilante committees'. We portioned out our criticisms and reservations in such a way as to make the common struggle possible. But in vain. The programme inspired by Hervé was revoked, and he tore us to pieces. We recorded several other conversations: an interview with Rousset, just back from Germany; a discussion of what the Right called the 'sordid materialism' of the masses. But on 3 December, when Schumann replaced Ramadier, he suppressed our programme immediately.

While Schumann was busy trying to create a 'third force', prices rose 51 per cent and wages only 19 per cent. Ramadier suppressed the coal subsidy; there was an immediate jump of 40 per cent in the price of coal, gas, electricity and transportation. In the mines around Paris and Marseilles, strikes broke out which turned into riots when Schumann attempted to pass an anti-strike law; railroads were sabotaged; the miners fought with the C.R.S. sent by Moch to guarantee 'the freedom to work'. Nevertheless, the unity of the trade unions was broken; the number of strikers fell from three million to one million, F.O. broke away from the C.G.T.; the working class found itself in too weakened a state to be able to prevent the Marshallization of France.

A few Socialists – Marceau-Pivert, Gazier – seeking to constitute an opposition within the S.F.I.O., solicited the support of those men of the Left who did not belong to any party; they would draw up together an appeal in favour of peace and the creation of a neutral and socialist Europe. We met every week at Izard's home: Rousset, Merleau-Ponty, Camus, Breton and a few others. We argued over every word, every comma. In December, the text was finally signed by *Esprit, Les Temps Modernes*, Camus, Bourdet, Rousset, and published in the press. Camus and Breton then brought up the problem of the death penalty; they demanded its abolition as a political measure. Many of us thought on the contrary, that it was only as a political measure that it could be justified. The group dispersed.

There were other points of dissension between Camus and ourselves; politically, at all events, we still had some things in common; he had an aversion for the R.P.F.; he had quarrelled (or was preparing to do so) with Ollivier, who had espoused Gaullism and was writing for *Carrefour*. Camus was less free, less intimate with us than he had once been, but our friendship still subsisted. On the other hand, we broke with Koestler during that winter.

At first he was very friendly towards us. I was working in the Flore one autumn morning; he came in with Mamaine and said: 'Shall we go have a glass of white wine?' I followed them to a neighbouring bistro; as we stood at the counter, he asked: 'We're going to the Jeu de Paume. Would you like to come with us?' 'Why not?' I said. They laughed. 'We appear, you're free; you're always free, it's marvellous.' They were happy to be back in Paris again, and it was pleasant looking at the paintings with them. Koestler examined the large photographs exhibited on the ground floor and squinted slyly. 'You see? All the painters with great handsome heads, all the ones with the faces of geniuses, are quite mediocre. Whereas Cézanne and Van Gogh have little heads, no faces at all . . . like Sartre and me.' I found such childish vanity almost touching. I was a bit more embarrassed when he asked in his knowing tone: 'How many copies did they print of *The Plague*? Eighty thousand? That's not too bad . . .' and he reminded us that *Arrival and Departure* had sold 200,000 copies.

When I saw him again with Sartre, we found him much gloomier and more excitable than the year before. He was worried about the success of his latest book, which had just appeared in London. He was always going to the desk of the Pont-Royal to see if his publisher had sent him any press clippings. The occupation forces had withdrawn from Italy, where preparations were getting under way for the first elections. He was sent to report on them by an English newspaper, and came back convinced that they would be a triumph for the Communists; the French Communist Party would then take heart, seize power, and the whole of Europe would speedily fall into Stalin's hands. Excluded from such a future himself, he intended to forbid it to all his contemporaries; the very mechanisms of thought would be overthrown. He believed in telepathy; it was a means of communication due to develop in a way that would defy all expectations. His 'catastrophism' expressed itself in headaches, fits of lethargy and black moods.

He wanted to repeat our night at the Schéhérézade. We went with him, Mamaine, Camus, Sartre and myself – Francine wasn't there – to another Russian nightclub. He insisted on letting the *maître d'hôtel* know that he was being accorded the honour of waiting on Camus, Sartre and Koestler. In a tone more hostile than the year before, he returned to the theme of 'No friendship without political agreement'. As a joke, Sartre was making love to Mamaine, though so outrageously one could scarcely have said he was being indiscreet, and we were all far too drunk for it to be offensive. Suddenly, Koestler threw a glass at Sartre's head and it smashed against the wall. We brought the evening to a close; Koestler didn't want to go home, and then he found he'd lost his wallet and had to stay behind in the club; Sartre was staggering about on the sidewalk and laughing helplessly when Koestler finally decided to climb back up the stairway on all fours. He wanted to continue his quarrel with Sartre. 'Come on, let's go home!' said Camus, laying a friendly hand on his shoulder; Koestler shrugged the hand off and hit Camus, who then tried to hurl himself on his aggressor; we kept them apart. Leaving Koestler in his wife's hands, we all got into Camus' car; he too was suitably soused in vodka and champagne, and his eyes began to fill with tears: 'He was my friend! And he hit me!' He kept collapsing onto the steering wheel and sending the car into the most terrifying swerves and we would try to haul him up completely sobered by our fear. During the next few days we often went back to that night together; Camus would ask us perplexedly: 'Do you think it's possible to go on drinking like that and still work?' No. And in fact such excesses had become very rare for all three of us; they had had some meaning when we were still refusing to believe that our victory had been stolen from us; now, we knew where we stood.

Koestler was now declaring that the best solution for France at that time, all things considered, was Gaullism. He had several arguments with Sartre. One day, when I happened to be in the bar of the Pont-Royal with Violette Leduc, he came up to me with a member of the R.P.F. in tow. The latter immediately attacked me point-blank: publicly, Sartre was opposing De Gaulle; but the Rassemblement had contacted him, made him offers that would be very worth his while, and, in sum, he had promised to support the movement. I shrugged my shoulders. The Gaullist refused to let the matter rest and I grew heated; Koestler listened to us with a smile on his lips. 'All right! Make a bet on it,' he said. 'I'll be witness to it. Whoever is in the wrong will buy a bottle of champagne.' At that I left. When Sartre challenged him about his attitude, Koestler replied laughingly that one should always be prepared for anything from anyone, and that I had taken the matter too seriously. 'It's just a woman's squabble!' he ended up, unsuccessfully trying to trap Sartre into a male complicity. He left Paris; when he returned shortly afterwards, he ran into us outside the Pont-Royal and asked: 'When are we going to see each other?' Sartre got out his notebook, then changed his mind. 'We haven't got anything to say to each other any more.' 'But we're not going to quarrel over our political opinions!' said Koestler, with an inconsistency that left us temporarily speechless. Sartre put his notebook back in his pocket. 'When people's opinions are so different, how can they even go to a film together?'[1] And that was how things remained between us. A few weeks later, we read two articles in *Carrefour – Où va la France? –* in which Koestler accused the French Communist Party of secretly preparing for civil war. He was hoping for, and predicted, the triumph of Gaullism.

Sartre's enemies continued to add fuel to the flames of the ambiguities that had been created around Existentialism. The Existentialist label had been applied to all our books – even our pre-war ones – and to those of our friends, Mouloudji's among others; also to a certain style of painting and a certain sort of music. Anne-Marie Cazalis had the idea of profiting by this vogue. She belonged, like Vian and a few others, both to the literary world of Saint-Germain-des-Prés and to the subterranean world of jazz. While talking to some journalists, she baptized the clique of which she was the centre, and the young people who prowled between the Tabou and the Pergola, as Existentialists. The press, and particularly *Samedi-Soir*, which had a financial interest in her success, gave the Tabou a tremendous amount of publicity. No week passed that fall of 1947 in which something wasn't printed about the brawls and festivities of its habitués, writers, journalists and politicians. Anne-Marie Cazalis was only too delighted to be photographed and interviewed, and people also began to be interested in her friend, the plump Toutoune, who had become a beautiful young girl with long black hair: Greco. At Agnès Capri's Gaieté-Montparnasse, she had played the part of the farting girl in Vitrac's *Victor ou les enfants au pouvoir*. She wore the new

1. Koestler, when he wrote about this episode, erroneously attributed the initiative for breaking off our relationship to me.

'Existentialist' uniform. The musicians from the various *caves* and their fans had been down to the Côte d'Azur during the summer and brought back the new fashion imported from Capri – itself originally inspired by the Fascist tradition – of black sweaters, black shirts and black pants.

Anne-Marie Cazalis had seemed very pleasant when I had seen her in the Flore at the time she was awarded her prize. She and Astruc were very attached to each other; Bost was quite friendly with her and said she was very intelligent and remarkably cultivated; she was of Protestant upbringing, and the reserve of both her manners and her conversation was in striking contrast to the effect she had made on the tradespeople of the district. However, I had a grudge against her because it was she who had written most of the article in *France-Dimanche* on the 'Sartre Scandal'. While we were out one evening with Herbaud, he said he wanted to go down to the Tabou. The place was so noisy, crowded and smoky, that we could hardly hear each other or even breathe. Nevertheless we sat at the corner of a table with Anne-Marie Cazalis and managed to chat; she proved to be both funny and very sharp-witted, manipulating ellipsis, litotes, and allusion with great dexterity. She defended herself about the 'Sartre Scandal' and ended up: 'In fact, it was Astruc who was to blame.' I was very fond of Astruc and this piece of perfidy flabbergasted me. We let the matter drop, and the conversation came to an end. Every time I have seen Anne-Marie Cazalis since, I have appreciated her sharp-witted charm, but she carried gossip to the point of tactlessness.

Sartre, who loved youth and jazz, was irritated by the attacks on the 'Existentialists'; wandering about, dancing, listening to Vian play the trumpet – where was the harm in that? All the same, they were used to discredit him. What confidence could one have in a philosopher whose teachings inspired orgies? How could one believe in the political sincerity of a 'master thinker' whose disciples lived for nothing more than having a good time? There was even more gossip about him than in 1944–5, but of a far more unpleasant sort; the Resistance press had not been able to weather the storm, and we had seen the return of professional journalism which was prepared to stoop to anything. During a big dinner he gave on his return from America, at the time when he was preparing to take over *France-Soir* again, Lazareff said publicly: 'I'll have Existentialism's scalp.' He wasn't the only one after it. But to demolish

Sartre, they had to talk about him; so much so that the press itself was creating all the publicity it was accusing him of seeking. Between a venomous report of his broadcast on Gaullism and another, equally ill-intentioned, on a debate about him by some theologians, they described a typical evening at the Tabou, of which, according to them, he was one of the pillars.[1] They churned out a thousand unpleasant or ridiculous details about him, all categorically false – for example, the pearl-grey hat, contrasting with the sloppiness of his suits, that he was supposed to have replaced every month out of vanity, during the period when he was teaching. Sartre had never at any time worn a hat. The stares directed at us in public places were already soiled with this dirt, and I no longer enjoyed going out much any more.

We spent the Christmas holidays at La Pouèze. Mme Lemaire thought Sartre's political views extreme, and we suspected her of voting for the M.R.P. She was against free education (scholarships were quite enough), against Social Security (it would be abused), and against union minimum wages (in the name of the freedom to work). But we attached no more importance to her political opinions than she did to ours. We were always happy to see her, both for her own sake and because she was a link with our lost past. Pagniez, as I have said, had moved far away from us. Marco had gone completely out of our lives; at the end of the war, an unhappy love affair, the frustration of his ambitions, his baldness and his obesity had sent him half mad. He used to weep buckets of tears over Sartre, who still visited him devotedly every week. A psychiatrist gave him a series of electric-shock treatments. He stopped weeping but began to hate the people around him. He spread the rumour that Mme Lemaire was a poisoner, and also that I had stolen his library. He still came to see her, but less and less frequently.[2] During this stay, I went on with my essay on Woman. Sartre let his mind wander, then began work on a new play, *Les Mains sales.*

In February, we were invited to Berlin for the opening of *The Flies.* 'Above all,' said Sperber, when we ran into him about that time, 'don't set foot in the Soviet Zone: a car draws up to the sidewalk, a door opens, they pull you in; no one ever sets eyes on you again.'

1. We have been there twice.
2. He died in an automobile accident in Algeria, in 1957.

I felt very uneasy getting on the train to Berlin. The idea of seeing Germans and talking to them was painful. But there it was! I had been taught, once, that to remember is to forget; time passed for everyone, for me as well. As soon as I set foot in Berlin I found my bitterness disarmed. Everything was in ruins; so many cripples and so much poverty! Alexanderplatz, Unter den Linden, everything had been smashed to pieces. Huge stone doorways without doors opened on to kitchen gardens, balconies dangled crookedly across the façades of buildings that were nothing but façades. As Claudine Chonez had written in *Les Temps Modernes*, an umbrella and a sewing machine on top of an operating table here would not have seemed at all out of place; the premises themselves seemed to have no premise any more. To cultivate a derangement of the senses, as Rimbaud suggested, would have been superfluous; reality itself was an insanity. And I walked in flesh and blood through that legendary nightmare: Hitler's Chancellory.

We were living in the French Zone, in the residential quarter where a few villas were still standing. We took our meals at the Cultural Attaché's, in private homes or in clubs. Once, armed with coupons, we tried to eat in an ordinary restaurant; all we got was a bowl of bouillon. We talked to some students; no books, not even in the libraries; nothing to eat, the cold, journeys of one or two hours every day, and an agonizing question: We didn't do anything, is it fair that we have to pay?

The problem of punishment was troubling all the Germans. Some of them – mostly those on the Left – thought they should keep the memory of their errors alive forever; this was the theme of the film *Murderers Among Us* made in the Russian Zone. Others submitted to their present misfortunes with bitterness in their hearts. The censorship prevented them from speaking out; the various publications and the theatres avoided the problem by playing off the different zones against each other: the Americans allowed them to laugh at the Russians, the Russians at the Americans. We went to a revue full of sinister humour, which was a satire on this Occupation.

We were disconcerted by the production of *The Flies*; the play had been staged in an expressionist style in settings reminiscent of Hell. The temple of Apollo looked like the inside of a bunker. I didn't think it was very well acted; however, the audience applauded enthusiastically because the play urged them to rid themselves of their guilt. In his lectures – which I didn't attend, preferring to wander about among the ruins – Sartre repeated that it was better to build a future than to lament over the past.

We had walked into the Soviet sector without even being aware that we had done so, and no car drove up to kidnap us, but two Russians whom we met at the Cultural Attaché's proved to be as cold as ice toward us. At a private screening of *Murderers Among Us*, there was no one to receive us – neither the director, nor the theatre manager. However, Sartre didn't think this was any reason – the contrary in fact – to play along with the Americans who were trying to monopolize him; he agreed to attend only one private dinner given by an American woman who wanted him to meet some German writers. When we were ushered in, we found ourselves in a room with about two hundred other people; we had fallen right into the trap: instead of having dinner, Sartre was obliged to answer questions. Anna Seghers happened to be there, so radiant with her white hair, her intense blue eyes and her smile that she almost reconciled me to the idea of growing old. She didn't agree with Sartre. 'We need to feel guilt, we Germans, right now,' she said emphatically. Sartre was taken aside by a Marxist called Stainiger who had recently described him in an S.E.P. newspaper as being an agent of American capitalism; he replied to this charge and Stainiger more or less accepted his reasoning. As a result of that evening, we were invited to lunch in a Soviet club, and this time the Russians thawed slightly – very slightly. Sartre was placed between a Russian woman and a German woman who asked him to sign one of his books for her; he did so and then turned to his other neighbour feeling slightly embarrassed. 'I expect you find it silly, writing dedications in books. . . .' 'I don't see why,' she said, and tore off a piece of the paper tablecloth; but her husband gave her a meaningful look and she crumpled it up. Germany, by the time we had left, had made a very lugubrious impression on us. We were very far from foreseeing the 'miracle' that was to transform it several months later.

Misrahi, who was a member of the Stern group, had been arrested for possession of arms and immured in the Santé prison. On 15 February Sartre gave evidence on his behalf. Misrahi had the full sympathy of both the court and the public. When Sartre gave it as his opinion that the defendant had been a good student, the judge interrupted him. 'Good? Do you mean excellent?' 'Certainly,' replied Sartre, realizing that he must depart from his usual moderation of tone. Misrahi got off with a 12,000-franc fine. Betty Knout attended the trial.

It was at about this time that Altmann and Rousset had a long debate with Sartre. Of all the people we had met at Izard's, David Rousset was, if not the most interesting, at least the most voluminous. Merleau-Ponty had been in contact with him before the war, when Rousset was a Trotskyite; he described him to us when he got back after being deported: a frail skeleton drifting about in a Japanese bathrobe, he weighed less than 90 pounds. When Merleau-Ponty introduced us to him, Rousset had regained his corpulence; one eye was covered with a black patch, and he had several teeth missing; he had the look of a pirate and the voice of a megaphone. The first thing of his we had read was his essay on '*L'Univers concentrationnaire*', in *La Revue Internationale*, then *Les Jours de notre mort*; I admired the will to live that illuminated all his accounts and stories. Taking his inspiration from the 'appeal' drawn up at Izard's, he was working with Altmann, Jean Rous, Boutbien, Badiou, Rosenthal and several others to start a '*Rassemblement démocratique et révolutionnaire*' that would draw together all the various Socialist forces not aligned with Communism and use them to construct a Europe independent of the two blocs. There were many movements fighting for a united Europe; the 'Estates-General of Europe' was due to be convened in The Hague during May. But the idea of Rousset's group, the R.D.R., was that the union should be formed at the level of basic principles and from a Socialist and neutralist point of view. It was hoped that Sartre would play a part on the executive committee. I was afraid he would simply waste a lot of time in such an enterprise; we had already wasted so much at Izard's! He told me he could scarcely preach commitment and then avoid it when he was offered the chance. The creation of the Kominform and then, on 25 February, the 'coup' in Prague, aggravated both anti-Communism and the general war psychosis. Americans began cancelling trips to Europe. In France, though no one began packing to leave, there was much talk of a Russian invasion. Sartre believed that between a Communist Party aligned with the U.S.S.R. and an S.F.I.O. that had sold out to the bourgeoisie there was still room for action on our part. He therefore signed a manifesto in which he associated himself with Rousset and his comrades and, on 10 March, gave a lecture in which he developed the theme 'War is not inevitable'. On 19 March he called a meeting in the Salle Wagram; an enormous number of people attended, and the movement began to collect adherents. Bourdet didn't become a member, but he supported it in his articles while launching a campaign in *Combat* for peace and European unity. Notwithstanding this support, the R.D.R. still needed a newspaper of its own. Sartre rather expected Altmann to make the *Franc-Tireur* into the mouthpiece of the movement, since, with Rousset, he was one of its founders. He refused to do so; it was necessary to make do with a bi-monthly called *La Gauche R.D.R.* whose first issue appeared in May and was not particularly scintillating: there was a shortage of funds. That was also the reason, according to Rousset, why the R.D.R. was getting off to such a slow start; but he had an infectious confidence in the future. However, in his speech at Compiègne in March, De Gaulle redoubled the violence of his attacks on the Communists; an enormous R.P.F. congress was held at Marseilles in April. The Americans were demanding that Joliot-Curie be dismissed from the Atomic Control Commission. Gasperi carried off the victory in the Italian elections. To oppose such a Right while keeping the necessary distance from Stalinism was not an easy task. Sartre gave an account of his attitude in the *Entretiens* with Rousset, which appeared first in *Les Temps Modernes* and subsequently in book form.

All the reasons he gave for his adherence to the R.D.R. were merely objective ones; but why had he felt the need to enter a movement which (in principle at least) was of such a militant nature? He gave some indications of the answer to this question in some unpublished notes written several years later:

My deepest idea at the time: all one can do is to bear witness to a way of life which is doomed to disappear but which will later be reborn; and perhaps the best works will testify to this way of life in the future and so be a way of permitting its preservation. One vacillates, then, between the adoption of an ideological position and action. But if I advocate an ideological position, immediately people begin urging me into action. *What is Literature?* led me into the R.D.R.

He consented to this shift because he himself had found a new relation, born of the hatred he had provoked: 'Good effects of hatred. To feel oneself hated; an element of culture.' At first, he had been appalled by it; in the very name of bourgeois humanism and the democratic ideal, he was with the masses; and they were against him! But if God does not exist, the judgement of the other is the absolute: 'The hatred of others reveals my objectivity to me.' Whereas before he reacted to the situation in all innocence, without thought for himself, he now knew that it enveloped his reality for others; he was now forced to regain that objectivity, to set it, in other words, in agreement with his inner decision. 'From '47 on, I had a double principle of reference: I also judged my principles in relation to those of others – those of Marxism.' This implies that he could not rest content believing himself to be right subjectively. He refused to tolerate *being* an enemy of the oppressed; he had to transform his relation to them by contributing to the modification of both the internal and the international situation. It was necessary to take part in an action.

Let us suppose that this contradiction of which I am an example (torn between bourgeoisie and proletariat), and which I now know to be characteristic of our time, instead of representing a freedom, a positive content, is merely the expression of a very specific and limited way of life (that of the socialistic bourgeois intellectual). What if it were to disappear without a trace in the future? In short, I fluctuate between this first idea: that my privileged position affords me the means of making a synthesis of formal liberties and material liberties; and this second idea: that my contradictory position affords me no liberty at all! It gives me an unhappy consciousness, and there's an end of it. In the second case, what disappears is my transcendence. I merely reflect my own situation. All my political efforts are directed toward finding a group that will give a meaning to my transcendence, that will prove by its existence (European R.D.R.) that my contradictory position was the true one.

If I am wrong, however, my situation is one of those in which synthesis is impossible. Even my attempt to transcend myself is rendered false. In that case, I must renounce the optimistic idea that one can be a man in any situation. An idea inspired by the Resistance: even under torture one could be a man. But it was not there that the problem lay; it lay in the fact that certain situations are perfectly *liveable* but made intolerably false by objective contradictions.

The R.D.R. for me:

(1) Middle classes and proletariat (I cannot comprehend the non-Communist proletariat choosing the bourgeoisie. It has a different structure).

(2) Europe. Not America, not the U.S.S.R., but the intermediary between them (therefore a bit of both).

[158]

(3) Democratic and material liberties. At bottom, I wanted to resolve the conflict without *transcending* my own situation. ...

The uneasiness that had induced Sartre to enter the R.D.R. also led him to an ideological reconsideration. He worked assiduously for two years confronting dialectic with history and morality with *praxis*, in the hope of reaching a synthesis between *doing* and *being* which would preserve strictly ethical values.

We were working less on the magazine than in the years just past. To all intents and purposes, it was Merleau-Ponty who ran it. People claimed that I was the author of the *Vie d'une prostituée* we published in it; it was certainly beyond my powers to produce that astonishing piece of raw writing. Marie-Thérèse existed, and it was she herself who wrote down these memories in a single spurt, before returning to her old profession as a nurse.

We went out very little now. The day *Paris 1900* was presented there was a general transportation strike, and we went to it in a *fiacre*. Nicole Vedrès had done her work well; she blew the myth of *la belle époque* to bits. Thanks to Gérard Philipe and Micheline Presle, the movie of *Devil in the Flesh* which we saw at a private screening seemed to us not unworthy of Radiguet's novel. Among the new Italian movies, we were already familiar with *Rome, Open City*, *Shoeshine* and *Four Steps in the Clouds*; but *Paisà*, especially the episode in the reeds, filmed by Rossellini, was far and away the best of them all. From America we had *The Grapes of Wrath*. Dullin put on Salacrou's *Archipel Lenoir*. He had been put out of the Sarah-Bernhardt and no longer had a theatre of his own, so it was at the Théâtre Montparnasse that he created the role of the old satyr of a grandfather. We also went to the Marigny to see Barrault's production of *Occupe-toi d'Amélie*. At the Orangerie, we saw the Turner exhibition. From time to time we went to hear a concert. Sartre was beginning to develop a taste for Schönberg and Berg.

He turned his mind to getting *Les Mains sales* put on. The subject of the play had been suggested to him by the assassination of Trotsky. I had known one of Trotsky's ex-secretaries in New York; he told me how the murderer, having managed to get himself hired as Trotsky's secretary, had lived for a long time by his victim's side in a house fanatically well guarded. Sartre had pondered on this dead-end situation; he had imagined a young Communist, born into the middle classes, seeking to erase his origin by an act, but unable to tear himself away from his subjectivity, even at the price of an assassination; in opposition to him he had created a militant politician utterly devoted to his objectives. (Once again, the confrontation of morality and *praxis*.) As he said in his interviews, Sartre had no intention of writing a political play. It became one simply because he had chosen members of the Communist Party as its protagonists. The play didn't seem to me to be anti-Communist. The Communists were presented as the only valid force against the Regent and the bourgeoisie; if a leader, in the interests of the Resistance, of socialism, of the masses, had another leader suppressed, it seemed to me as it did to Sartre that he was exempt from all judgement of a moral order. It was war, he was fighting; this did not mean that the Communist Party was made up of assassins. And then – just as in *The Victors* the arrogant and egocentric Henri is morally dominated by the Greek Communist – so in *Les Mains sales* Sartre's sympathy went to Hoederer. Hugo decides to kill in order to prove that he is capable of doing so, without knowing if Louis is in the right against Hoederer. Afterwards he decides to take credit for this irresponsible act when his comrades order him to keep quiet. He is so fundamentally in the wrong that the play could be put on, during a period of thaw, in a Communist country; which is in fact what happened in Yugoslavia recently. Only, in the Paris of 1948, circumstances were different.

Sartre realized this and knew what to expect. His adherence to the R.D.R. had earned him a new series of attacks. In February, there appeared on the *Pique-Feu* page of *Action* several anonymous and sickening insinuations about our private life. *Les Lettres françaises* printed *Le Génie de six heures*, in which Magnane had sketched a heavily distorted and scarcely recognizable portrait of Sartre which one could only despise. Meanwhile Kanapa was pulling *Situations I* to pieces. Elsa Triolet was writing a book and lecturing in an attempt to instigate a boycott of the filthy writings of Sartre, Camus and Breton; my sister had heard her speak publicly against Sartre in Belgrade with the deepest hatred in her voice. The situation could scarcely have been any worse.

Simone Berriau accepted *Les Mains sales* without hesitation; the parts of Hoederer and Jessica were given to Luguet and Marie Olivier; but who could play Hugo? Names were suggested and discarded. One afternoon, at the Véfour, Berriau suddenly said:

'I know it sounds stupid but – why don't we try Perrier?' We had imagined Hugo as thin and tormented; but anyway, all right, we might as well try it. From the very first rehearsals, Perrier triumphed: he *was* Hugo, just as Vitold had been Garcin in *Huis clos*. The direction was assigned to Valde, and amicably supervised by Cocteau; Bérard came round to give advice about the sets; there was always a smell of ether floating around his beard. I was enchanted by the language of these theatre folk. At first, Luguet gave his militant Communist too much drawing-room comedy. 'You know,' Cocteau told him, 'you're utterly charming, you drip charm; so don't *try* to be charming; on the contrary, try *not* to be charming; if you don't, what you come up with will be quite extra-ordinary, but the character won't come out true.' 'In fact, you think I have no talent,' Luguet answered grumpily. There was one line in the play that irritated him. 'He's vulgar,' Jessica says to Hugo. Sartre explained it: she's lying in order to conceal the inter-est Hoederer arouses in her. 'Oh well! If you suppose the audience will think I'm vulgar, you're within your rights I suppose,' was Luguet's last word.

Sartre wasn't there on opening night. (He was giving a lecture to a Masonic Lodge, certain Masons having assured him that their organization could give serious support to the efforts of the R.D.R.: he saw, he heard, he understood.) All the actors were perfect; the newspapers announced next day that Perrier was a new Guitry. I was in a box with Bost, and people came up and shook our hands. 'Magnificent! Wonderful!' However, the bourgeois critics did not announce their verdict straight off; they waited to see what the Communists would say. The Communists spat it out like tainted meat. 'For thirty pieces of silver and a mess of American pottage, Jean-Paul Sartre has sold out what remained of his honour and probity,' wrote one Russian critic. The bourgeoisie immediately buried Sartre in bouquets. One afternoon, on the terrace of the Rhumerie Martiniquaise, Claude Roy was going by and stopped to shake my hand; he had never stooped to using low methods against Sartre. 'It was really too bad,' I told him, 'that you Com-munists didn't take over *Les Mains sales*.' As a matter of fact, such a recuperation of our losses was inconceivable at that time. The play seemed anti-Communist because the audience was on Hugo's side. Hoederer's murder was taken as an equivalent of the crimes imputed to the Kominform. Above all, the Machiavellian plotting of the leaders in the play and their reversal of policy at the end was a condemnation of the Communist Party in the eyes of its adversaries. Politically, that was the most truthful moment in the play: in Communist Parties everywhere in the world, when an opposition group attempts to introduce a new and correct line of policy, it is liquidated (with or without physical violence); then the leaders take the new policy and use it for their own purposes. In the case of Illyria – inspired by Hungary – the Party's hesitations and its final decision were justified by the circumstances; it was simply that its internal difficulties were exposed to people who were looking at it from outside with animosity. They gave the play a meaning which it did, in fact, have for them. It was for this reason that Sartre refused several times to let it be acted in other countries.

In October, a great many Vichyists had rallied to the R.P.F. and a great many collaborators were getting back up on their perches. Flandin was writing in *L'Aurore*, Montherlant was having *Le Maître de Santiago* put on, and Sacha Guitry was doing his *Diable boiteux*, a transparent apology for the collaboration. Maurras was preparing a lawsuit against Stéphane and Bourdet. Under Mauriac's wing, *La Table ronde* fraternally opened its pages to ex-collaborators and their friends. (Camus made the mistake of writing for the first issue, but then realized his error and didn't repeat it.) A spate of books appeared excusing or justifying the policies of Pétain, a thing which would have been inconceivable two years earlier; in his *Lettre à Mauriac*, Bardèche went so far as to defend *Je suis partout*. Boutang was giving lectures for the greater glory of Maurras. Pétain's name was cheered in meetings, and in April a 'Committee for the Liberation of Pétain' was formed. In certain circles, people talked sarcastically about 'the Resistentialists', and spoke of the Resistance as though it had been a fashion, intended to serve the personal interests of its followers. A counter-purge swept the country; ex-Resistance members were accused of performing summary executions, were arraigned and often condemned.

I was moving somewhat in theatrical circles, because of Sartre, and often heard things that appalled me. It was said that Jean Rigaud, running through a list of well-known people in the audience before he went on, had come across some Jewish names and murmured: 'They must have put them in incubators, not crematoria.' This witticism was retailed with appreciative laughter. At the Véfour, the person sitting next to me, pretending not to be able to read the menu I was holding, asked: 'What's that? Cutlets à la Buchenwald?' I didn't want to make a scene and I said to myself: 'After all, it's only words.' But the fact that people dared say them meant something. Yesterday's profiteers assumed the role of victims and explained how base it was to be on the side of the conquerors. They pitied poor Brinon; they turned Brasillach into a gentle martyr. I rejected all such betrayals; I had my own martyrs. When I thought of them and told myself that so much grief and misery had been in vain, I was filled with distress. Behind us, that great cadaver, the War, was finally decomposing, and the air was sickening with the stench.

Now that rehearsals were finished, there was nothing to keep us in Paris and we went to the south of France. I chose Ramatuelle, where we found a country inn which had rooms with red tile floors; the dining room was a glass enclosure opening onto a garden and then beyond, far off, the sea. In the evening a wood fire glowed on the hearth; every morning, I worked in the sunshine, under the flowering trees. We were the only ones there; it was almost as if it were our own house. We went up to the Saracen towers, and down to Saint-Tropez to have a drink at the harbour or buy Provençal skirts at Vachon's. I worked, and I read Henry du Moulin de Labarthète's memoirs about Vichy and Gide's correspondence with Jammes.

Bost, who had rented a little house at Cabris with Olga, came over and spent two days with us. He was there at lunchtime one day when Simone Berriau, wearing her hooded cape and followed by her husband, Brandel, and Yves Mirande, sprang out of an American car. They had all come from Mauvannes, the property she owned near Hyères. She came into the dining room and trumpeted in her grand manner, with a gesture toward her husband: 'Do you know what this gentleman did to me this morning?' Then she told us. 'All right,' said Mirande, 'but there's no need to tell the servants about it.' We spent a day and a night at Mauvannes; in the morning, when she was alone with me on the terrace, Simone gave me the benefit of confidences so precise, and so abundantly accompanied by winks of complicity, that I wanted the ground to open up and swallow me. She loved to play at matchmaking and found it impossible to conceive that a young actress should refuse to jump into bed with the first millionaire who presented himself. She had great vitality and persistence, but they were exclusively at the service of her own interests. Yet she seemed to be sincerely attached to Mirande, who lived in her house. He was an outmoded embodiment of the *esprit boulevardier* so dear to my father and, despite his age, still obsessed with the fair sex; his conversation was highly spiced but funny; he had a *'fleur bleue'* side to him, and that always sits well on rakes. He told us that in Hollywood he had had a passionate liaison with Greta Garbo; though heartbroken, he had broken it off: 'Because I didn't want to make myself ridiculous,' he said, adding what seemed to me a mysterious comment, coming from his lips: 'And besides, she had vices.' He was charming with Sartre. His witticisms, his laughter and his kindness lightened the burden of many meetings that the presence of Simone Berriau's husband did nothing to enliven.

Sartre was getting very gloomy letters from M.; she had reluctantly agreed to spend four months with him while I was on my trip with Algren. A few days before I was due to leave, she wrote to Sartre saying that she had decided not to see him again, on those conditions. This threw me into a great perplexity. I wanted enormously to be back with Algren, but after all I had only lived with him for three weeks; I didn't really know how much he meant to me: a little, a lot, or even more? The question would have been an idle one if circumstances had decided for me; but suddenly I had a choice: knowing I could have stayed with Sartre, I was leaving myself open to regrets which might turn into a grudge against Algren, or at least into bitterness against myself. I opted for half measures: two months of America instead of four. Algren was expecting me to stay a long time, and I didn't dare announce my new arrangements in black and white; I would talk things over with him when I got there.

This time I took a plane that flew high and fast. It landed me at two in the morning in Iceland, where I drank coffee surrounded by bearded old sea dogs; when we took off again I was dazzled by the landscape: a silvery light on high white mountains at the edge of a smooth sea, against a raspberry-coloured sky. I flew over snow-covered Labrador and landed at La Guardia. My visa gave the purpose of my trip as 'lectures'. 'On what?' the immigration official on duty asked me; when I said philosophy he shuddered. 'What philosophy?' He allowed me five minutes in which to give him a brief account. I said it was impossible. 'Has it got anything to do with politics? Are you a Communist? You wouldn't admit it if you were.' I got the impression that any French person was suspect *a priori*. After having consulted some files he gave me an authorization to stay for three weeks.

I spent the day with Fernand and Stépha; it was raining in torrents and I was in limbo. New York seemed less opulent than the year before because Paris no longer looked so impoverished; except in the very elegant bars, the over-long skirts of the New Look made the women look like scullery maids. The next day, under a scorching sun, New York along the East River seemed like a great Mediterranean port. I looked up some of my friends and went to see *The Respectful Prostitute*: a disaster! Most of the scenes between Lizzie and the Negro had been cut, and they talked in flat voices without even looking at one another. All the same, they had reached their hundredth performance and the house was full.

The day after that, at midnight, I landed in Chicago and spent the next twenty-four hours wondering what I was doing there. Algren took me in the afternoon to visit a gang of junky thieves whom I simply *had* to visit, according to him. I spent two hours in a filthy den, surrounded by strangers talking, too fast for me to follow, to other strangers. There was a forty-year-old woman, an habitual offender drugged to her eyeballs; her ex-husband, with an enormous pallid face, even farther gone than she was, who spent his nights playing drums to earn some money and his days at the wheel of a taxi, driving round the city looking for fixes; also her present lover, wanted by the police for theft and fraud. They all lived together. The woman had a ravishing daughter, respectably married two months ago, who was there visiting. For her sake, the trio made an effort to appear decent. All the same, the ex-husband rushed into the bathroom and gave himself a shot under Algren's nose – they were trying in vain to draw him into their rites. All they really enjoyed was to be with other addicts and chat about syringes, Algren told me. My anxiety was quickly dissipated when I found myself alone with him again. The next day I went with him to see the wife of a thief, also in hiding from the police, who had started to write since he had known Algren; she was waiting in tears for her husband, but she displayed with great pride the book she had written and which he had had typed at his own expense; she was raising two deaf-mute children. Meanwhile we were going about in the rain, shopping and making arrangements. The Guatemalan official who gave me my visa spent an hour explaining how much his country loved France. He was very curt with Algren, especially when Algren stated his nationality: 'American citizen.' 'Citizen of the United States,' the official corrected him. 'We are both Americans.'

After a day of phlegmatic but frantic agitation, we took the morning train for Cincinnati: 700,000 inhabitants; squares, green hills, birds, provincial calm. We ate dinner watching television, which was beginning to appear in all public places. The evening of the following day we embarked on a side-wheeler. It was a holiday in Cincinnati. Airplanes and searchlights were wheeling around the sky, there were bonfires along both banks of the river, and the headlights of the automobiles lit up the great metal bridges; then we slid off into the darkness and silence of the country.

I loved the monotony of the voyage through this wide watery landscape. On deck, in the sun, I translated one of Algren's stories, I read, and we chatted over glasses of Scotch; Algren kept trying to take photographs with a German camera he didn't understand; he was quite satisfied because he had managed to get a tiny noise out of it when he pressed down a catch. In the evening light, I saw the waters of the Ohio mingle with those of the Mississippi. I had dreamed of the Mississippi listening to 'Old Man River', and also while I was writing *All Men are Mortal*. But I could never have imagined the enchantment of its evenings, its moons.

Each day we went ashore for a few hours. Louisville, sinister in the rain; a little town in Kentucky with decrepit bars full of celebrating farmers; Memphis – cotton bales along the docks, cotton factories, cotton brokers' offices; Natchez, one of the oldest towns in the South with 40,000 inhabitants. The landing jetty turned out to be at the very end of the town. A huge man came up and offered to drive us downtown by car. Despite the heaviness of the heat, like most whites he was wearing a stiff collar and a suit. He explained to us that in Natchez the Negroes led an extremely easy life, and took great care to avoid calling them niggers; he only let the word slip out once. We left him at the edge of the Negro quarter. We went out by taxi to look at the old plantations, among others that of Jefferson Davis. We drew up in front of an extravagant, columned house whose construction had been interrupted by the Civil War and which was decaying among giant trees draped with Spanish moss. An old woman made a fuss because Algren wanted to take a photograph. The chauffeur shrugged his shoulders. 'That's the owner's sister; *she's from New York*,' he said with distaste. Here the whites and the blacks understand one another, he explained, because both groups stay in their place. The Negroes are polite. But in California, he said with sudden rage, they don't take off their hats, they say just 'Yes' and 'No', and they talk to the whites! He was nervous, furious at having to serve as a guide to people from the North. That evening we passed Baton Rouge. Behind the lights of the port and the illuminated buildings, the tall furnaces were spitting out flames. The afternoon of the following day we landed at New Orleans.

In the heart of the French Quarter we found an immense room, with a huge electric fan and a wooden balcony overlooking a patio. There were burlesque dancers and young prostitutes wandering around the hotel corridors in housecoats, and the owner, a fat, half-mad Russian woman obstinately decreed that I too was Russian. After a creole dinner and ices *flambés au rhum*, we went out to look for the Napoleon Bar at the Absinthe House, for julep zombies and some good jazz; but it appeared that there was no longer any Negro jazz in the white quarter. Spring was already over; the azaleas were gone and the rains had stopped, the weather was heavy and dry. We spent the day swimming in Lake Pontchartrain. None of Algren's photographs had come out.

Next came Yucatán, with its jungle, its fields of blue aloes, its red flamboyant trees; Mérida, its Spanish churches amid subtropical damp and luxuriance. I have already described our trip to Chichén-Itzá in *The Mandarins*. The ruins of Uxmal were even more beautiful, but to see them one had to catch a bus at six in the morning and we couldn't even find anywhere to have a cup of coffee. Algren, overcome with despair in the presence of these stubborn stones, refused to give them so much as a glance; I explored them all on my own with a far from light heart. These sullen moods were rare; he accepted everything, the beans, the tortillas, the insects, the heat, captivated as I was by the little Indian girls with their long skirts and shiny braids, and exactly the same features we saw on the bas-reliefs in the Mayan temples. I have already described what we liked in Guatemala. But the streets were sad: the women went barefoot, dressed in magnificent, filthy materials; the men trotted along, crushed beneath their heavy burdens. In front of the wooden or mud huts thatched with straw which clustered together to form hamlets were children with swollen bellies and eyes blinded by trachoma. The Indians, sixty-seven per cent of the population, had been free for only twelve years; before 1936, on the pretext that they were repaying debts, they were kept in penal servitude; when we saw them they were living just as they had then, in wretched and hopeless poverty, and it seemed to me that they submitted to it with a stupefied inertia.

Mexico City was a real town where things were happening; we wandered around in the residential quarters and in the districts of dubious reputation. One evening we let ourselves be persuaded into attending a show of 'native dancing' actually organized by an old American con man; it consisted of tourists long past the bloom of youth soulfully applauding as young women in luxurious costumes went through imitations of peasant dances. We walked out after half an hour and by way of revenge ended up in the sleaziest joint in the entire slum area; here enormous taxi-girls were dancing with tiny evil-looking Mexicans, Indians and Spaniards; we were stared at with surprise, and some of them came over to talk to us while we were emptying our glasses of *tequila*. For most Americans, Mexico City is a jungle with an assassin working full time on every street corner. But Algren had been around hundreds of cut-throats in his life without seeing a single throat cut. And in any case, he told me, the incidence of crimes is much lower in Mexico City than it is in New York or Chicago. On Sunday we went to see the bullfights in the giant arenas; out of a dozen, there were three or four really good ones. What annoyed Algren was that each *corrida* constituted a self-terminating event, whereas a boxer's victory opens a fresh cycle of challenges and bouts. On the way out we mingled with the crowd and followed it a long way into the outlying districts; we came back to the centre of town to eat turkey with chocolate sauce, *tamales* which practically burned away one's mouth, and murderous *chili con carne*. At night it rained and in the morning we would walk through big puddles under the mildest of blue skies.

I hadn't yet broached the subject of my departure, not having the heart to do it as soon as I arrived; the following weeks I still couldn't face it. Every day it became more urgent and more difficult. During a long bus journey between Mexico City and Morelia, I announced to Algren with clumsy flippancy that I would have to be back in Paris on 14 July. 'Oh, all right,' he said.

I'm flabbergasted today when I look back and think how I allowed myself to be fooled by his indifference. At Morelia, I found it quite natural that he shouldn't want to get out and walk around; I strolled gaily through the streets and squares of the old Spanish town on my own. Gaily, I visited the market of Pazcuaro where Indians dressed in blue sold blue fabrics. We went across the lake to the island of Janitzio, decorated from top to bottom with fishermen's nets; I bought some embroidered blouses. We walked back from the jetty to the hotel and I began making plans for the next day. Algren stopped me; he'd had enough of Indians and markets, of Mexico, and of travelling. I thought it was just another fit of temper like the one at Uxmal and not of any particular consequence. All the same, it lasted a long time and I began to get uneasy. He walked on in front of me, very fast; when I caught up with him, he wouldn't talk to me. At the hotel I went on plying him with questions: 'What's the matter? Everything was going so well; why are you spoiling everything?' Far from being moved by my distress, which eventually reduced me to tears, he just walked out on me. When he came back we were reconciled, though without explanations; that was enough to restore my equanimity. The next few days I was quite carefree. We saw Cholula with its three hundred churches; at Puebla, whose brothel district reminded me of the Rue Bouterie, the little prostitutes deloused their children on the thresholds of their rooms, all open to the passers-by. Enormous dark green trees shaded the old colonial squares of Cuernavaca. At Taxco, sprawling over hills, in the heart of the silver mines, they sold silver jewellery along the streets; we drank delicious whisky sours on the terrace of a hotel, surrounded by bougainvilleas and overlooking a beautiful baroque church. 'At the end of two days I'd be shooting off a revolver in the streets just to make something happen,' Algren said; Mexico was decidedly getting on his nerves. All right. We took a plane to New York.

In the white-hot streets, women walked about under vast cocktail hats, their bosoms exposed almost down to the nipples and their navels bare; the city had taken on carnival colours, while remaining hard and bustling. I began to pay for my cowardice and my thoughtlessness. Algren didn't talk to me in quite the same way he used to, and every now and then I even felt a stab of hostility from him. One evening I asked him: 'Don't you care for me as much as you did?' 'No,' he said, 'it's not the same any more.' I cried all night, leaning out of the window between the silence of the sky and the city's indifferent noises. We were living in the Brittany on lower Fifth Avenue; we wandered around the Village; I dragged myself along over the hot asphalt; we bought bricks of black raspberry ice-cream and ate them in our room; my throat still burned. We spent painful hours in French restaurants on the East Side, where I dragged him in search of a little respite from the heat, and in the suffocating West Side restaurants which he preferred because they didn't oblige him to wear a jacket and tie. It was my turn to resent him on account of his sullen behaviour. One evening, when we had dined in a tavern in the open air in the middle of Central Park and then went on to listen to jazz at Café Society, he was particularly disagreeable. 'I can leave tomorrow,' I told him; we exchanged a few more words and then suddenly he said to me impulsively: 'I'm ready to marry you this very moment.' I realized I would never be able to harbour rancour in my heart against him for anything ever again; all the wrongs were on my side. I left him on 14 July, uncertain whether I would ever see him again. What a nightmare, that return flight, high over the ocean, plunged into a night without beginning and without end, stuffing myself with sleeping pills, unable to sleep, lost, and utterly dismayed!

If I had the honesty and the intelligence to let Algren know the limits of my stay before going over to see him, things would have worked out better; doubtless he'd have received me with less ardour; but would have had no reason to feel bitter towards me. I've often wondered what part his sudden disappointment actually played in our affair. I think it did nothing more, in fact, than disclose to him a situation he wouldn't have accepted for long in any case. At first sight, it was identical with mine. Even if Sartre hadn't existed, I would never have gone to live permanently in Chicago; or if I had tried to do so, I would certainly not have been able to bear more than one or two years of an exile which would have destroyed both my reasons for writing and the possibility of doing so. On his side, although I often suggested it to him, Algren could never have come to live in Paris, even for six months of the year; to write, he needed to stay rooted in his own country, in his own city, in the world he had created for himself. We had both already shaped our lives, and there could be no question of transplanting them elsewhere. Yet our feelings were, for both of us, far more than a diversion or even an escape; each of us regretted bitterly that the other refused to come and live with him.

But there was one great difference between us. I spoke his native language, I also knew the literature and history of his country pretty well, I read the books he loved and the books he wrote; when I was near him I forgot myself, I entered his world. He knew almost nothing about mine; he had read a few articles I had written, scarcely any more of Sartre's work, and French writers in general held little interest for him. Also, I was far better off in Paris than he was in Chicago; he was a prey to the harsh loneliness of America. Now that I existed, the emptiness around him became indistinguishable from my absence, and he blamed me for it. Our farewells tore at my heart, too; but primarily because Algren let me leave with the uncertainty of ever seeing him again. If he had said firmly: 'Till next year,' I'd have been perfectly content, or almost. I would have had to remain 'schizophrenic' – in the sense Sartre and I gave that word – to imagine that Algren would accommodate himself to that state of things. I often grieved to myself that he didn't make the effort to accept it; but I also know perfectly well that he could never have done so.

Then should I have refused our affair and limited myself to enjoying the fellow feeling I had for Algren? That he had agreed with me in despising such prudence would not suffice to excuse me; what I said earlier about Sartre and M. is valid here. I possessed an incommunicable knowledge of my bond with Sartre; from the very first the dice were loaded; even the most truthful words still betrayed the truth. But in this case as well, the great distance involved forced us into an all-or-nothing situation: one doesn't cross the ocean, one doesn't cut oneself off from one's life for weeks on end, just for fellow feeling; it could only last by turning into a more violent experience. I don't regret that it existed. It brought us more than it tore from us.

Sartre had kept me in touch with what was happening in France; at the end of May he wrote to me:

Some ex-Resistance members from La Charbonnière near Lyon kidnapped Sacha Guitry as he was coming out of one of his eternal self-justification lectures (or as he was going to it, I can't remember which) and forced him to take off his hat in front of a monument to the Resistance members killed in 1944, and then made him clear out.

Paris-Presse paid a million francs[1] for a picture of Sacha (a bit blurred but still fairly striking), head bare, eyes like a frightened rabbit, running a hand over his bald pate. No one talks about anything else.

It was just one episode in the struggle between the ex-Resistance members and the ex-collaborators. The Vichyists won an important victory: on 20 June, at Verdun, De Gaulle paid homage to the 'victor of Verdun', and almost went so far as to forgive Pétain for his politics on the grounds that he was 'swept along under the influence of his age, by the wholesale desertions'.

Sartre, like all the non-Communist Left, put great hope in the break between Tito and the U.S.S.R. If Yugoslavia could refuse to choose between the two blocs, the cause of neutralism would be strengthened. For the moment, the chances of peace were very uncertain. The creation of the new Deutsche Mark by the Americans was obviously a prelude to the setting up of a government in West Germany; the Russians' countermove, the Berlin blockade, had brought international tension to fever pitch. In France and in Italy, this crisis aggravated existing dissensions. I had just got back to Paris, when on 14 July, at about eleven in the morning, a student called Ballante, the son of a Fascist volunteer killed on the Russian front, fired a revolver three times at Togliatti. The Italian proletariat reacted so violently that some thought there would be a revolution.

America Day by Day had just been published by Morihien and had a fair critical success. I resumed my study of the feminine condition. Sartre was reading a lot of political economy and history; he was still filling notebook after notebook with minuscule handwriting in his attempt to work out his system of morality. He had begun a study on Mallarmé.[2] And he was working on *Troubled Sleep*. We were expecting to take a vacation together towards the end of July; unexpectedly, M. telephoned him from New York. She couldn't bear being away from him any longer; she wanted to spend a month with him; she sobbed across the ocean; they were burdensome tears, but nonetheless genuine; he agreed to her request. But during the whole of the month they spent touring the south of France together, he held this piece of capricious coercion against her, he had exchanged his guilt for resentment; it was, for him, a good bargain.

1. £1,000.   2. He wrote several hundred pages of it that he afterwards lost.

I regretted having cut short my stay in the States. I sent a cable to Algren suggesting I return to Chicago. 'No, too much work,' was the answer. I was hurt – work was only an excuse; but I was also relieved: these meetings and partings, these rejections and impulsive offers were getting to be too much for me. For a month I stayed in Paris, working, reading and seeing friends.

At last I set out with Sartre for Algeria; we wanted sun, we loved the Mediterranean; it was a vacation, a pleasure trip; we would go touring, write, talk. One day Camus had said: 'Happiness exists, and it's important; why refuse it? You don't make other people's unhappiness any worse by accepting it; it even helps you to fight for them. Yes,' he had concluded, 'I find it sad the way everyone seems to be ashamed of feeling happy nowadays.' I agreed with him completely, and the first morning I looked out of my room in the Hôtel Saint-Georges at the blue sea with a light heart. But that afternoon we walked around the Casbah, and I realized that tourism, as we had practised it in the old days, was dead and buried; what had been picturesque before no longer seemed so: what we encountered now in those narrow streets was misery and bitterness.

We stayed in Algiers for two weeks, and the owner of the hotel confided to some journalists that he was astonished by Sartre's 'simplicity': when we wanted to go into town on our first day there, we had taken a trolley bus! When Bernstein was working, he asked that all the clocks be stopped; the hotel-keeper seemed disappointed that Sartre hadn't come up with any such demands. I wrote sitting in front of my window; we ate dinner in the garden under the palm trees and drank a heavy wine from Mascara; we followed the roads along the coast in a taxi, we walked among the pines, over the hills. But Camus, now that I thought it over, had put the question badly; we weren't refusing to feel happy, we just couldn't.

No word came from Algren; I sent him a cable to which he didn't reply. I decided to forget him for the time being; I'd had enough of that particular sadness. One morning, I was walking along by the sea at Tipaza, crushing the mint leaves and inhaling the age-old odour of the Mediterranean scrub warmed by the sun, and suddenly I was twenty again: no regrets, no great expectations, simply the earth and the water, and my life. But in the cities I froze: how dismal Cherchell was! We went on with the trip simply out of curiosity; we no longer expected any pleasure from it.

[173]

'Don't go to Kabylia. I always carry a revolver when I can't avoid going,' one of the people staying at the Saint-Georges had told us; other *colons* had agreed in chorus. We booked several days at the Hôtel Transatlantique in Michelet. We walked through some of the villages: huts of beaten earth, stuck one against the other, and sunken alleys so narrow that they gave us the impression of walking along hallways. No fountains. The men were working a long way off in the valley; outside the houses we saw only children and women with kohl-smeared eyes. It was impossible to tell what they were thinking. There was a fair at Michelet. Just men and animals; the air was full of the greasy smell of sheep's wool. I had a strange feeling that evening when I went back up to my room: a pack of cigarettes I had left on a table was missing; I discovered that some sweaters and money that had been inside a closed suitcase had been taken; and someone had vomited on my balcony. I was forced to tell the hotel-keeper that someone had been in my room. 'Was anything stolen?' I said no, but had some difficulty convincing him. That night I locked myself in, and thank goodness I did, because someone turned the doorknob very noisily. In the morning they found a butcher from a nearby village dead drunk and asleep in an unoccupied room. The hotel-keeper hesitated for a while but finally decided against calling the police. There was something sinister about this pitiful and clumsy attempt at theft that made me sick at heart for a long while.

Bost joined us at Bougie. We spent several days together in a deserted palace, on the beach at Djidjelli; all around us there was nothing but sand and sea, and we swam day and night. I wanted to see Ghardaïa which I had missed two years before. I went down in a bus with Sartre as far as Bou Saâda; a taxi took us on to Djelfa, where the people were living not even in caves but in holes. The heat was still scarcely bearable, the buses ran only at night. Once more I was forced to give up the idea of seeing Ghardaïa.

CHAPTER FOUR

I'D HAD enough of living in a hotel, where there was very little protection against journalists and inquisitive people generally. Mouloudji and Lola told me about a furnished room they had lived in in the Rue de la Bûcherie: the tenant who had taken it after them wanted to leave. I moved into it in October; I put red curtains up at the windows and bought some green bronze lamps designed by Giacometti and executed by his brother; I hung on the walls and from the big ceiling beam many of the objects I had brought back from my travels. One of my windows overlooked the Rue de l'Hôtel-Colbert which led down to the banks of the Seine. I could see the river, ivy, trees and Notre-Dame; opposite the other window was a hotel full of North Africans, with a café called Le Café des Amis on the first floor; they were always fighting inside. 'You'll never be bored,' Lola had told me. 'All you have to do is go to the window and look out.' She was right: in the morning, the rag pickers wheeled up perambulators piled high with old newspapers to sell to the junk merchant on the corner; bums of both sexes sat on the stepped sidewalk drinking their litres of red wine, sang, danced, talked to themselves and bickered. Hordes of cats wandered over the roofs. There were two veterinarians on my street; women brought their pets to them. The house, once a private mansion now beginning to come apart at the seams, was full of the sound of barking dogs, the ones in the clinic 'under the patronage of the Duke of Windsor' and my concierge's big black one keeping up a constant exchange that echoed right up to my landing; the daughter of the impresario Betty Stern, who lived opposite me, had four dogs. Everyone knew each other. Mme D., the concierge, a slim, lively little woman who lived with her husband, her tall son and a tall nephew, helped me keep house. Betty, who had been very beautiful, who had known Marlene Dietrich intimately and Max Reinhart very well, often came and talked to me. She had spent a year hiding in the *maquis* during the Occupation. Below me lived a woman who worked as a film editor and who shortly after I moved in gave up her apartment to the Bosts. Finally, upstairs there was a dressmaker I occasionally patronized. Neither the façade nor the staircase were much to look at, but I was very pleased with my new home. We spent most of our evenings there because people were always bothering us in the cafés.

Every week I found in my mailbox an envelope with a Chicago postmark; I found out why I had received letters so rarely from Algren while I was in Algeria: he had written to me in Tunis instead of Ténès. The letter was returned to him; he sent it to me again. It was lucky it got lost, because I would have found it painful reading at the time. While speaking at rallies for Wallace, he had fallen in love with a young woman, he wrote; she was being divorced and he had thought of marrying her; she was in analysis and didn't want to get involved in a relationship of that sort until the analysis was finished; by the time the letter finally reached me in December they had almost stopped seeing each other. But he explained what he felt in detail:

I won't have an affair with this girl, she doesn't really mean anything to me. But that doesn't change the fact that I still want what she represented for me for two or three months: a place of my own to live in, with a woman of my own and perhaps a child of my own. There's nothing extraordinary about wanting such things, in fact it's rather common, it's just that I've never felt like it before. Perhaps it's because I'm getting close to forty. It's different for you. You've got Sartre and a settled way of life, people, and a vital interest in ideas. You live in the heart of the world of French culture, and every day you draw satisfaction from your work and your life. Whereas Chicago is almost as far away from everything as Uxmal. I lead a sterile existence centred exclusively on myself: and I'm not at all happy about it. I'm stuck here, as I told you and as you understood, because my job is to write about this city, and I can only do it here. It's pointless to go over all that again. But it leaves me almost no one to talk to. In other words, I'm caught in my own trap. Without consciously wanting to, I've chosen for myself the life best suited to the sort of writing I'm able to do. Politicians and intellectuals bore me, they seem to be unreal; the people I see a lot of these days are the ones who do seem real to me: whores, junkies, etc. However, my personal life was sacrificed in all this. This girl helped me to see the truth about us more clearly; last year I would have been afraid of spoiling something by not being faithful to you. Now I know that was foolish, because no arms are warm when they're on the other side of the ocean; I know that life is too short and too cold for me to reject all warmth for so many months.

In another letter, he returned to the same subject:

After that wretched Sunday when I began to spoil everything in that restaurant in Central Park, I had that feeling I told you about in my last letter – of wanting something *of my own*. To a great extent it was because of this woman who seemed so near and dear to me for several weeks (it's over now; but nothing has changed). If it hadn't been her it would have been someone else; it didn't mean I had stopped loving you, but you were so far away, it seemed so long before I would see you again. . . . I feel it's a little silly to talk about things we've gone past. But it's just as well, since you can't live in exile in Chicago nor I in Paris, since I'd always have to come back here, to my typewriter and my loneliness, and feel the need of someone close to me, because you're so far away. . . .

There was nothing I could say in reply; he was absolutely right, which didn't make it any easier to bear; I would always have felt a painful regret if our affair had ended then. The happiness of the nights in Chicago, on the Mississippi, in Guatemala, and the sudden botched-up ending would have turned it into no more than a dream. Happily, Algren's letters gradually grew warm again. He told me about his daily life. He sent me newspaper clippings, edifying tracts against alcohol and tobacco, books, chocolate, and two bottles of old whisky concealed in two enormous bags of flour. He also wrote that he would come to Paris in June and was booking his passage on a boat. I grew easy in my mind again, but every now and then I realized with anguish that our relationship was doomed to come to an end, and soon. Forty. Forty-one. Old age was growing inside me. It kept catching my eye from the depths of the mirror. I was paralysed sometimes as I saw it making its way towards me so steadily when nothing inside me was ready for it.

Since the beginning of May, my study on *La Femme et les mythes* had begun appearing in *Les Temps Modernes*. Leiris told me that Lévi-Strauss was criticizing me for certain inaccuracies in the sections on primitive societies. He was just finishing his thesis on *Les Structures de la parenté*, and I asked him to let me read it. I went over to his place several mornings in succession; I sat down at a table and read a typescript of his book; it confirmed my notion of woman as *other*; it showed how the male remains the essential being, even within the matrilineal societies generally termed matriarchal. I continued to go to the Bibliothèque Nationale; it is pleasant and restful to fill one's eyes with words that already exist, instead of having to wrest sentences from the void. At other times I wrote, in my own room in the morning, and at Sartre's in the afternoon. From my table, I would glance over between erasures at the terrace of the Deux Magots and the Place Saint-Germain-des-Prés. The first volume was finished during the fall and I decided to hand it over to Gallimard right away. What should I call it? I thought about it for a long time, with Sartre's help. *Ariane*, *Mélusine*: that sort of title was no good because my work was a rejection of the myths. I thought of *The Other, the Second*: that had already been used. One evening in my room, Sartre, Bost and I spent several hours trying out words. I suggested: *The Other Sex*? No. Bost changed it to *The Second Sex* and when we thought it over that was exactly right. Whereupon I set to work like a beaver on the second volume.

Twice a week I went to a gathering of all the regular contributors to *Les Temps Modernes* in Sartre's office: Merleau-Ponty, Colette Audry, Bost, Cau, Erval, Guyonnet, Jeanson, Lefort, Pontalis, Pouillon, J. H. Roy, Renée Saurel, Stéphane, Todd; a lot of people for such a small room, and it soon filled up with smoke; we drank brandy Sartre's family sent him from Alsace, passed the world in review, and made plans.

In October or November, Gaston Gallimard asked Sartre to have a talk with him. Malraux had been discussed in the July issue of *Les Temps Modernes* in a manner which had displeased him. Merleau-Ponty had quoted an article in *The New York Times* which congratulated Malraux on rallying to Gaullism and thereby remaining faithful to his old Trotskyist position; the indignant reaction of Trotsky's widow was then printed after the quotation.

> Malraux was never a sympathizer of Trotskyism, quite the contrary. . . . Malraux gives the appearance of having broken with Stalinism, but he is still serving his old masters by trying to establish a link between Trotskyism and the reactionaries.

The dossier was completed by a letter from an American revealing that Trotsky had twice asked Malraux to speak out on his behalf, and that on both occasions he had avoided doing so. Merleau-Ponty recalled that before 1939 Malraux had in fact supported Stalin against Trotsky; he reproached him for pretending the contrary now and for likening Gaullism to Trotskyism. Malraux had immediately gone to see Gallimard and threatened him with reprisals if we weren't dropped. Sartre took the matter lightly to the great relief of Gaston Gallimard, who announced in emotional tones to his collaborators: 'Now *he* is a real democrat!' We were taken in by René Julliard. Malraux tried to intimidate his partner, Laffont, who was about to publish De Gaulle's memoirs: it would scarcely please the General to be published by the same house as *Les Temps Modernes*, and he might very well withdraw his manuscript. Nevertheless we moved over to the other side of the Rue de l'Université in December.

Sartre had another setback. The production of *Les Mains sales* in New York was a flop. The script had been sabotaged. Boyer, playing Hoederer, had also balked at the line 'He's vulgar.' He had made Jessica say: 'He looks like a king.' They had stuck in a speech about the assassination of Lincoln and butchered the whole thing. The play came out like an incredible melodrama; Sartre tried to make them take it off and brought a suit against Nagel, who had authorized the whole thing without his permission.

Things in general were still going as badly as ever. The R.P.F. had collapsed, for the good reason that the bourgeoisie no longer needed it; reunited and strong again, they had won an ominous victory over the divided proletariat, which turned out to be the losers in the battle over wages. Despite Marshall Plan aid, despite increased production and an excellent harvest, prices had doubled between the summer of '47 and the fall of '48; the purchasing power of the workers had never been so low. On 4 October, 300,000 miners began a strike which lasted eight weeks. Jules Moch once more set the C.R.S. on them, and two men were killed, 2,000 put into prison, 6,000 fired. The stevedores and the railroad workers also stopped work. In vain. The Socialist dreams of 1944 were truly dead. Every issue on the C.N.R. programme had petered out. The class in power was resolutely colonialist. The verdict on Tananarive was delivered on 5 October: six men condemned to death, including two deputies. In Indochina, the leaders were putting the Bao Dai operation into effect against the Vietminh,[1] though its futility was obvious. *Les Temps Modernes* had been denouncing the imbecility and horror of this war since 1947. We often saw Van Chi, the cultural attaché to the Vietnam delegation – which still existed, paradoxically enough – and he introduced us to its president. Bourdet took part in these discussions.

The Berlin blockade was still going on. In China, Mao Tse-tung was winning a series of smashing victories. Nanking was collapsing; there was some doubt as to whether the United States would intervene. If so, it was thought, it would concentrate its force in the Far East, and if it abandoned Europe even temporarily the Russians would invade; the two Great Powers would then confront each other in Germany and in France. One of the most ardent of the American war-mongers, Forrestal, began to have such horrible

1. On 8 March the Bao-Dai–Auriol agreements were signed.

visions of the Red Army flooding across the whole world and into New York, he let out such howls that they had to lock him up; he threw himself out of the sixteenth storey of the hospital. In France, the Right was scientifically propagating panic; it used two themes which it thundered out either alternately or together: 1. The Soviet regime is cruel and terrible and inevitably entails poverty, famine, dictatorship and murder. 2. Without the help of America, we shall be defenceless; the Red Army will reach Brest in less than a week and we shall be subjected to all the horrors of Occupation. It was in this spirit of planned panic that *Carrefour* – in the same issue in which it triumphantly announced: 'Thomas Dewey, the thirty third President of the United States, will enter the White House with a broom in his hand' – launched an inquiry: 'What would you do if the Red Army occupied France?' The real danger was in fact the Atlantic Pact that Robert Schumann, a partisan of 'Little Europe', was preparing to sign: it would cut the world in two for good and involve France in the war if America should ever launch it.

A great number of pacifist movements were born and developed at that time. The most publicized was that of Gary Davis. This 'little man', as he was then called, took up a stand under the peristyle of the United Nations Building, which was considered international territory and declared in interviews that he was giving up his American citizenship in order to become a 'citizen of the world'. On 22 October a 'council of solidarity' was constituted around him which included Breton, Camus, Mounier and Richard Wright, who had recently come to live in Paris; the day in November when Davis made a scene at the United Nations, Camus gave a press conference in a café during which he defended him; Bourdet reinforced Camus' support with an editorial, and from then on *Combat* devoted a page every month to the 'World Government Movement'. On 3 December there was a rally in the Salle Pleyel during which Camus, Breton, Vercors and Paulhan defended this idea. Camus was hurt that Sartre refused to participate, and announced to us triumphantly that the rally on 9 December at the Vel' d'Hiv' had drawn twenty thousand people. Sartre was in complete agreement with the Communists that the Gary Davis affair was nothing but hot air. We couldn't help laughing when the Right accused Davis of being 'in Moscow's pay'. His idea wasn't new; there had once been a great deal of talk for a whole year about a 'World Federation'. Even his activities weren't parti-cularly astonishing; America is swarming with inspired eccentrics solemnly proclaiming platitudinous slogans. The significant thing was that he should have been taken seriously by European 'left-wing' intellectuals.

A few days after the meeting on 9 December at which Camus had spoken for peace, Van Chi presented him with a petition being circulated by Sartre and Bourdet against the war in Indochina. He didn't sign it: 'I don't want to play the Communists' game.' Camus rarely descended from lofty principles to particular cases. Sartre thought that it was by opposing wars one by one that we could work for world peace.

The R.D.R. wanted to unite all the Socialist forces in Europe behind a definite policy of neutralism. Sartre envisaged it as a group of moderate size, but dynamic enough to affect public opinion and influence events. Rousset wanted mass action. 'There are fifty thousand of us now,' he said in February (five thousand would have been nearer the truth). 'There must be three hundred thous-and of us by October, or we'll have lost.' We felt much less sym-pathetic towards him than we had at first. He was possessed by an ambition that was all the more disquieting for being without any clear aim; his self-confidence covered abysses of uncertainty and ignorance; his admiration of himself was breathtaking. The sound of his own voice intoxicated him; all he had to do was talk in order to believe what he was saying. He conjured up images of the im-mense 'audience' the movement had already reached, without giving a thought to the woeful deficiencies of its organizational aspects: often when people came to a district meeting they would find the door locked and no one would have a key. All Rousset liked were the rallies; at these he could declaim himself into a state of ecstasy. The R.D.R. organized one at the Salle Pleyel at the beginning of December; intellectuals from different countries were invited to talk about peace. Camus took part, as did Rousset, Sartre, Plievier, the author of *Stalingrad*, Carlo Levi, and Richard Wright, whose speech I translated. Many people attended, and there was much applause. Rousset delivered himself of a diatribe against the Communists. A split was beginning to appear within the R.D.R.; the majority wanted to align itself with the social action of the Communist Party; a minority – which included most of those responsible for its conception – on the pretext that the

Communists were treating the movement with hostility, were slipping towards the Right.

Rousset announced that he had found a way of procuring the money the R.D.R. needed: he was going to the United States with Altmann in February; they would contact the C.I.O.[1] We were not aware to what extent the C.I.O. was supporting the government in its struggle against Communism, but we knew that it practised class collaboration, and Sartre didn't approve of this step. The R.D.R. was a European movement; Americans were free, like Richard Wright, to sympathize with it but not to finance it.

The label 'left-wing American' was in any case a very uncertain guarantee; we realized this the afternoon when Wright got together a group of French and American intellectuals in the public rooms of a big hotel. I made the acquaintance of Daniel Guérin and discussed with him the economic aspects of the American colour problem; also that of Antonina Vallentin, the author of excellent biographies of Heine and Mirabeau. Sartre and some others said a few words. The American Louis Fischer, who for several years had been a journalist in Moscow and a Communist, stood up and delivered an attack on the U.S.S.R. He dragged Sartre over into a corner and treated him to an account of the horrors of the Soviet regime. He continued it while we were having dinner at Lipp with the Wrights. His eyes glittering with wild fanaticism, Fischer poured out an unending stream of stories of disappearances, betrayals and liquidations, of which, though they were probably all true, we could grasp neither the meaning nor the general significance. Then he sang the praises of America and its virtues.

Sartre conceived of the R.D.R. as a mediating influence between the advanced wing of the reformist *petite bourgeoisie* and the revolutionary proletariat: those were the circles from which the Communists recruited their members. More clearly than ever Sartre was now an adversary in their eyes. At the Wroclaw Congress, which was intended to seal an alliance between intellectuals throughout the world, Fadeev had referred to him as 'a jackal with a fountain pen' and accused him of 'dragging man down onto all fours'. With the Lysenko affair, Stalinist dogmatism had penetrated even into the realm of science; Aragon, who knew nothing about it, demonstrated in *Europe* that Lysenko was right: Art was no longer

1. The C.I.O. was the farthest to the left of the American trade union groups, and Rousset was playing on this misunderstanding.

free; all Communists were obliged to admire Fougeron's 'The Fishmongers' exhibited at the Salon d'Automne. Lukács, passing through Paris in January, attacked 'the decadent cogito of Existentialism'. In an interview in *Combat*, Sartre replied that Lukács didn't understand the first thing about Marxism. Lukács' retort and Sartre's second reply were printed together in the next issue. Ehrenburg was in Paris in February and explained that Sartre had once inspired him with pity; since *Les Mains sales*, however, he felt nothing but contempt for him. Finally, Kanapa had been put in charge of *La Nouvelle critique*, almost every number of which contained an article attacking Existentialism in general and Sartre in particular.

He was no less harshly treated by the magazine which began appearing in February under the editorship of Claude Mauriac called *Liberté de l'esprit*, and which was dedicated to defending 'Western values'. Its writers included R.P.F. members and ex-collaborators. A newcomer, Roger Nimier, author of a poor little novel called *Les Epées*, called attention to himself in the first issue by writing apropos of the war: 'We shall not wage it with M. Sartre's shoulders nor with M. Camus' lungs (and even less with the beautiful soul of M. Breton).' The allusion to 'M. Camus' lungs' disgusted so many people that Nimier was forced to apologize. In the issues that followed, 'Western values' were conspicuous by their absence, but the anti-Communist crusade was going great guns.

The anti-Soviet campaigners were leaving no stone unturned. In November a White Russian girl named Kosenkina jumped out of the window of the Soviet Consulate in New York. This melodramatic event was given enormous publicity.

In January, the Kravchenko trial opened; he was bringing suit against *Les Lettres françaises* for defamation: the newspaper had revealed that his book *I Chose Freedom* had been fabricated by American government services. I went with Sartre to one of the hearings which was very unexciting; yet this affair, which filled the newspapers for weeks, was of the greatest interest: it was the trial of the U.S.S.R. The anti-Communists, supported by M. Queuille and by Washington, mobilized hordes of witnesses; the Russians on their side sent witnesses from Moscow. No one won. Kravchenko got damages, but they were very much smaller than he had claimed, and he emerged from the trial pretty well discredited.

However, whatever lies he told, however great his venality, and despite the fact that most of the witnesses were as suspect as himself, one truth did emerge from their evidence as a whole: the existence of work camps. Logical, intelligent and confirmed in any case by numerous facts, the account given by Mme Beuber Newmann carried conviction. As soon as the Russo-German pact had been signed, the Russians handed over to Hitler deportees of German origin. They did not execute their prisoners in large numbers, but exploited them in such a way, and ill-treated them to such an extent, that many died. The number of victims was not established, but we began to wonder whether the U.S.S.R. and the People's Democracies deserved to be termed socialist countries. Certainly Cardinal Mindszenty was guilty; how had he been persuaded to admit it? He confessed everything they wanted him to. What was happening in Bulgaria? What was the meaning of Dimitrov's 'rustication'? The Communists were launching a peace offensive in countries all over the world; we began to think the reason must be that it was in their interest to prolong the truce to give themselves time to prepare for war.

Sartre continued to reflect on his split position and to search for a means of surmounting it; he read, and his notebooks were piling up. He was also writing the sequel to *Troubled Sleep*, which was to be called *The Last Chance*. In order to be able to work quietly, we went to the south of France. I picked out an isolated hotel on the Esterel coast; it was built in the shape of a ship, and stood directly over the water; at night, the sound of the waves came into my room, and I felt I was on the high seas. But the solemnity with which the meals were served in the vast, empty dining room took away our appetites. There were very few places to walk to because the mountains rose steeply just behind the hotel. We migrated to a less forbidding place: Le Cagnard, high up in Cagnes. We had pleasant rooms on the top floor; mine opened onto a terrace where we could sit and talk. An agreeable smell of woodsmoke came up from the tiled roofs below, and we could see the sea in the distance. We walked among the trees which were in bloom and visited Saint-Paul-de-Vence, less mundane then than it is now; sometimes we went for an outing in a taxi. Sartre was very gay, but uneasy because M. was thinking of coming to France to live; he was trying to dissuade her.

The first volume of *The Second Sex* was about to appear; I

was finishing the second and wanted to publish some extracts of it in *Les Temps Modernes*. Which ones? The final chapters were suitable, but they didn't exactly convey the basic point of the book. We settled for the chapters I had just finished, on female sexuality.

For some time I had been thinking about a novel. I often let it run through my mind as we drove through the pinewoods or walked through the lavender fields. I began to take notes.

When we got back to Paris after three weeks, the date set for the signing of the Atlantic Treaty – 4 April – was drawing near. Gilson, supported by Beuve-Méry, attacked it in *Le Monde*. In *Combat*, Bourdet suggested the creation of a 'neutral bloc', fully armed, but pledged to the defence not of American bases but of an independent Europe. Also, the Peace Movement created by the Communists held a rally of its 'partisans' in the Salle Pleyel on 20 April under the presidency of Joliot-Curie. The Congress, for which Picasso designed the emblem, his famous dove, ended with a mass demonstration.

Rousset had returned to France, bringing back with him from America a project for 'study courses' devoted to peace which would go into operation ten days after the Pleyel rally. We realized at once that he intended his project as a rejoinder to the Peace Movement. In *Franc-Tireur*, Altmann ran a series of reports on America. An idyl! The regime was not socialist, of course, but it was not capitalist either; it was a trade-union culture. There was not complete equality either, of course; there were even slums – but what comfort! There was a series of anti-Communist trials going on, all right – but people could speak freely in the streets. Whites and blacks fraternized together. And, to sum up, it was the workers who governed the country.[1] As for Rousset, he gave me the most unpleasant impression. He told us what a triumph his tour had been, what banquets had been given for him, what an 'audience' he had succeeded in winning. He came up with a defence for the American union leaders, for Mrs Roosevelt and for American liberalism. He had garnered flattery and a few subsidies, and he had turned his coat. (Unless he was already wearing it that way around before. . . .) I questioned his view on the United States. He pointed an accusing finger at me and said in his most orotund voice: 'It is

1. 'The dignity and defence of labour influence public affairs with all their weight.'

easy, Simone de Beauvoir, in France today, to speak ill of America!'
Among the people he expected to take part in the projected debates, he mentioned Sydney Hook. I had met him in New York;
this ex-Marxist had become a frenzied anti-Communist. Sartre
asked if, instead of holding public debates with foreigners, we might
not convene an internal congress which would include as many
active members from the provinces as possible; Rousset objected
that we lacked funds for that. In which case who was financing the
'Day of Resistance to Dictatorship and War'? And also what
dictatorship in particular was to be resisted? Richard Wright was
being pressed by the American Embassy to take part in the demonstration and told Sartre that he found their insistence suspicious.
Sartre was wondering if he should attend in order to defend his
own point of view against Rousset's or if he should abstain from
attending; for once I gave him a piece of political advice: not to go.
On 30 April Merleau-Ponty, Wright and Sartre sent a collective
message to the Vel' d'Hiv' directed against the policies of the State
Department. Woolly messages from Gary Davis and Mrs Roosevelt were read out. Sydney Hook and a Socialist member of the
Dutch Parliament glorified the virtues of the Marshall Plan as opposed to Stalinist dictatorship; someone contributed a justification
of the atomic bomb; there were disturbances on the floor, and the
platform was taken over by Trotskyites. Sartre organized a meeting
of the Congress of the R.D.R. at his own expense which pronounced its opposition to Rousset. The movement ceased to exist.
At the time, we imagined that Sartre's only mistake had been to
place his faith in Rousset and Altmann who, being more ambitious
and more disturbed, had prevailed over more honest men; the
group was still so limited in extent that small matters of this sort
could still have important consequences, especially when they
concerned the question of personality; the collapse of the association did not prove that it had been doomed to failure from the
start. Soon, Sartre came to think the opposite: 'Splitting up of the
R.D.R. Hard blow. Fresh and definitive apprenticeship to realism.
One cannot create a movement.'[1] To attract the masses had not
been his ambition; but to be satisfied with such a small movement
was mere idealism: if four workers from the R.D.R. had participated in a Communist-organized strike, they would not have been
able to modify its course or its intent.

1. Unpublished notes.

[186]

Circumstances merely appeared to be favourable to the association. It did answer to an abstract need, defined by the objective situation, but not to any real need among the people. Consequently they did not support it.[1]

I enjoyed Queneau's *Saint-Glinglin* very much, his language, his savage humour, his calmly horrific view of existence. I admired – though slightly less than his earlier works – Genet's *Pompes Funèbres*. Plievier's *Stalingrad* was a terrifying document. In America, Dr Kinsey's report on *Sexual Behavior in the American Male* had just come out: a great deal of noise over very little.

After having lived in Vienna and then in Belgrade, my sister and Lionel had come back to Paris. They rented a pretty eighteenth-century house at Louveciennes, a bit dilapidated and flanked by a big garden that had run to seed. We saw a great deal of each other. One evening I went with Olga to hear some jazz at the Rose Rouge in the Rue de la Harpe, run by Mireille Trépel – who had once been at the Flore – and Nico; they had moved to the Rue de Rennes and were living opposite the building where I had spent my adolescence. I heard the Frères Jacques there; they were becoming enormously successful, and deservedly so. At the Théâtre des Champs-Élysées, Boris Kochno put on a new ballet called *La Rencontre*; Cocteau and Bérard asked Sartre to write a text for the programme; we went to a rehearsal; we saw Leslie Caron, in black tights, lending the Sphinx all the mystery of her fifteen years with grave and graceful diligence. She completely conquered the glittering horde of first-nighters. We found the ballets of Katherine Dunham of little interest, though they were the rage of Paris. We abstained from Camus' *L'État de siège*, though not out of lack of friendship. We attended the production of *Les Fourberies de Scapin* at the Marigny: Barrault had chosen to be no more than a purveyor of entertainment.

Sartre was politically very close to Bourdet – who was to write the political column in *Les Temps Modernes* shortly afterwards – and asked me one afternoon to go to a cocktail party Ida was giving. She was a good hostess and there was an enormous number of people – too enormous. All those people, separated by so many things and going around slapping each other on the back, made me very uncomfortable. Altmann, who at the time I took to be a member of the Left, fell into Louis Vallon's arms; and the hands

1. Unpublished notes.

I shook! Van Chi wandered about in the crush, looking as unhappy as myself. To smile at opponents and friends alike is to debase one's commitments to the status of mere opinions, and all intellectuals, whether of the Right or Left, to their common bourgeois condition. It was that condition which was being imposed on me here as my truth, and that was why I was experiencing such a burning sensation of defeat.

At the beginning of June, I put on the white coat I had worn two years ago in Chicago and went to the Gare Saint-Lazare to meet Algren's boat train. How were we going to get on with each other now? We had parted badly; but he was coming. With my eyes I devoured the rails, the train, the flood of passengers. I couldn't find him; the last cars were emptying; they were empty; Algren wasn't there. I waited there a long while; by the time I turned and left there was no one left on the platform; I walked away slowly, glancing back over my shoulder several times – in vain. 'I'll come and look for him when the next train comes in,' I told myself and went home in a taxi. I sat down on my divan and lighted a cigarette, too upset to read. Suddenly I heard an American voice in the street; a man carrying a vast amount of luggage was going into the Café des Amis. He came out again and came over to the door. It was Algren. He had recognized my coat from the train window, but he had got into such a mess with his luggage that he didn't manage to get off the train until long after all the other passengers had left.

He brought me chocolate, whisky, books, photographs and a flowered housecoat. As a G.I. he had spent two days in Paris, at the Grand Hôtel de Chicago, out near Batignolles. He had seen almost nothing. It was odd reminding myself as I walked with him down the Rue Mouffetard: 'This is really the first time he has ever looked at Paris; what do they look like to him, these houses, these shops?' I was anxious; I didn't want to see that sullen face he had sometimes turned on me in New York. He confided to me later that my excessive solicitude during those first days made him uncomfortable. But I soon grew more confident; his face was always radiant.

On foot, in cabs, once in a fiacre, I took him everywhere and he loved it all: the streets, the crowds, the markets. Occasionally little things shocked him. There were no fire escapes down the fronts of the houses, there was no railing along the Canal Saint-Martin: 'So, if there's a fire, you just burn alive? I begin to understand the French. If you burn, you burn! If a child is drowned, it drowns – no interfering with fate!' He thought all the drivers were mad. French cooking and Beaujolais filled him with delight, even though he preferred sausage to foie gras. He particularly liked shopping in the stores nearby; the ceremonial exchange of conversation was a delight to him: '*Bonjour*, Monsieur, how are you today, thank you very much, very well and you, fine weather, nasty weather today, *au revoir*, Monsieur, thank you, Monsieur'; in Chicago, one shops in silence, he told me.

I took him to meet all my friends. With Sartre, conversation was a bit difficult because Sartre doesn't know English and I haven't enough patience to be an interpreter; but they got on well. We talked a bit about Tito and a lot about Mao Tse-tung. China was so little known that it provided matter for all sorts of extravagant notions. People were amazed that Mao Tse-tung should write verses, because they were unaware that every general in his country has a go at the pen. Because they were also literate, these revolutionaries were being endowed with an antique wisdom that combined with Marxism into some mysterious and seductive amalgam. Beautiful, and also true, stories were being told about education in the fields, theatrical performances in the army, and the liberation of women. It was thought that 'the Chinese road to Communism' would be more flexible and more liberal than the Russian way, and that the entire face of the socialist world would be changed by it.

At the Rose Rouge, Bost and Algren swapped infantry reminiscences. Olga seduced Algren utterly by listening to all his stories with eyes wide in astonishment. He knew hundreds, and when he ran out he made them up. The four of us had dinner together in the restaurant on the Eiffel Tower – crammed with Americans. The food and drink were terrible, but the view very beautiful – and he talked for two hours straight about his friends the drug addicts and thieves, till I could no longer tell what was true and what wasn't. Bost didn't believe a word; Olga lapped up everything. I got up a little party at the Vians'; we invited Cazalis, Greco, and Scipion. I took Algren to a cocktail party given by Gallimard in honour of Caldwell. We often went for drinks at the Montana with various people. At first, the 'leftists' of our group, Scipion among others, eyed this American with suspicion. Annoyed by this antagonism, he delighted in giving out with paradoxes and unseemly truths. But when they found out he had voted for Wallace and that his friends were all being forced out of work in radio and television because of their anti-Americanism, and above all when they got to know him better, he was in. He was very fond of Michelle Vian, whom he called Zazou and who very conscientiously interpreted everything for him, even when we all got carried away by the heat of our own conversation. On 14 July, after rushing about in a group to all the neighbourhood street dances, one after the other, we all collapsed in one of the big cafés that didn't close till dawn. Queneau was in top form and from time to time I would turn to Algren and say: 'He just said something very funny!' Algren would reply with a sketchy and rather forced smile, whereupon Michelle sat down beside him and translated everything that was said. He also liked Scipion very much because of his laugh, and thought he had the prettiest nose in the world. At the Library over the Club Saint-Germain he met Guyonnet, who was trying to translate his latest novel and was having difficulty with all the Chicago slang. Guyonnet invited him one morning to go and box with him and Jean Cau. When he met me for lunch on the terrace of the Bouteille d'Or, down by the Seine, he collapsed into his chair exhausted. 'These Frenchmen, they're all crazy!' he said. Following Guyonnet's instructions, he had gone up to a sixth-floor room, and was greeted by a shout of: 'Here's the brave American!' He looked out the window and saw Cau and Guyonnet beckoning him to join them on a terrace to which the only means of access was the gutter leading to the roof. For Algren, who suffers from vertigo, it was a terrifying experience. The terrace was about as big as a pocket handkerchief and had no railing; they were boxing on the edge of a precipice. 'All mad!' Algren repeated, still not quite recovered.

To show him a Parisian crowd, I took him to the celebration on 18 June: the Avenue d'Orléans was being rebaptized 'Avenue du Général Leclerc' in a ceremony presided over by the General's widow. As we were walking along in the crowd under the burning sun a man recognized me: 'You have no right to be here!' He looked at me with murder in his Gaullist eyes. We went together to see the Van Goghs and the Toulouse-Lautrecs at the Jeu de Paume. I took him to the Musée Grévin as well; he was so filled with wonder at the 'palace of mirages' with its endless forests and columns, its stars and lustres, its tricks of light – especially the 'black light' – that he sent all his fellow Americans there whenever they came to Paris. One afternoon, Sartre hired a Slota; with Bost,

Michelle and Scipion we went for a grand tour of the suburbs. We walked around the dog cemetery at Clichy, a little island in the middle of the Seine; at the entrance we were greeted by the statue of a Saint Bernard who saved, as I remember it, ninety-nine people. The inscriptions on the graves declare the superiority of animals over men; they are guarded by plaster spaniels, fox terriers and hounds. Suddenly Algren aimed an angry kick at a poodle, whose head fell off and rolled along the ground. 'But why?' we asked him, laughing. 'I didn't like the way it was looking at me,' he answered. This cult of animals irritated him.

I thought he would enjoy a day at the races at Auteuil, but he couldn't make head or tail of the French betting system or understand the announcements of the results. On the other hand, he was very interested in the boxing matches at the Central. He filled me with confusion because I had managed to acquire a certain amount of respect for human beings since my childhood, whereas he didn't have a shred. He took photographs while the contestants were actually fighting, using flashbulbs and a reflector.

I went with him to the Club Saint-Germain, started a year earlier by Boubal. Vian and Cazalis had migrated there. The New Orleans style was still in vogue at the Tabou, but here it had yielded to bebop. The cellar was packed; a bearded lady smiled from a frame. At the Rose Rouge, I heard the Frères Jacques again in *Les Exercises de style*. Algren liked them, but he liked Mouloudji even more, and also Montand, who was singing at the A.B.C. For the first time in my life I drank champagne at the Lido, because of an act there that Sartre had recommended: a ventriloquist called Winces who used his left hand as a dummy; two boot buttons for eyes, two fingers painted red for the lips; on top he popped a wig and arranged a body underneath; the doll moved its mouth, opened it wide enough to swallow a billiard ball, smoked and stuck out its tongue – a third finger. It was so alive that one really did believe it was talking, and when he took it to pieces it was as though some charming and impertinent little being had died.

Algren wanted to see the Old World. Spain was closed to us; there could be no question of setting foot in Franco's territory. We took a plane to Rome. It was amazing to me to be able to see the city, the sea and vast parched stretches of the Campagna all at the same time. And I was overcome by the strangeness of having been in Paris in the morning and then having lunch in the Piazza Navona!

We walked a lot and saw a great deal. We went up to the Janiculum to have dinner and bowled with Carlo Levi in a little tavern there; we had lunch with Silone and his wife; we saw *Aïda* in the Baths of Caracalla. I liked hearing a plane thrumming in the sky over one of Verdi's great arias. One night, a fiacre took us through a storm along dark streets streaming with water. But there were too many ruins and the city was too quiet for Algren's taste. We took a bus to Naples. We stopped at Cassino; the ruins scorching under the sun seemed as remote as those of Pompeii.

Algren loved Naples; he had known poverty and still brushed elbows with it every day; he didn't feel the slightest bit uncomfortable walking through the overcrowded slum districts. When he began taking photographs I was even more embarrassed than I had been at the Central; actually the people all smiled at his flashes, and the children squabbled over the hot bulbs as they fell to the ground. They greeted him as a friend when he came back to hand around the prints.

He found the Italians charming. When we reached Porto d'Ischia where we wanted to spend a few days, we went into a restaurant; he asked for a glass of milk; there wasn't any; the waiter, who came up to Algren's waist, lectured him: 'But you shouldn't drink milk! You should drink wine, Monsieur; that's the way to get big and strong!' The little port with its dusty oleanders and plumed horses didn't take our fancy. We pushed on as far as Forio; our little hotel, from which we looked straight down into the sea, was completely empty; there was a shady dining room and a terrace; the woman who ran it stuffed us with baked lasagna. Out in the square where we took our coffee, someone pointed out Mussolini's widow. We went for excursions in a carriage. We lounged on the beach for hours on end. In our memories, Ischia remains our paradise. But we were happy at Sorrento too, and at Amalfi and Ravello, and as it turned out Algren was deeply impressed by the ruins of Pompeii.

A plane took us from Rome to Tunis; the *souks* and the Mellah fascinated Algren. I can't remember now how we met Amour Hassine, a chauffeur who was driving his family to Djerba to celebrate the end of Ramadan; for a small sum he took us along with them. The island was in a state of frenzy the evening we arrived; among Moslems all over the world lookouts were keeping a watch out for the moon; if it appeared during the course of the night, they would advise their fellow worshippers of it by telegram and the fast would be over; if not, it would go on for yet another day until the next evening; eating, drinking, dancing, smoking, scouring the sky with their eyes, everyone was killing time at a pitch of tension that did not seem to me to be justified by the prospect of one day's postponement. Sitting at a café table, surrounded by maniacal music and chanting, Algren smoked a narghile with Amour Hassine; the latter confessed to us that he sometimes drank wine during the year and often disobeyed the Koran, but during Ramadan he did not swallow as much as a crumb or smoke a single cigarette between dawn and dusk. 'That, God would never forgive!' he said. The tension and the fatigue of these days of abstinence explained the crowd's impatient frenzy. The moon did not appear. The following night everything was calm because there was no longer any uncertainty: Ramadan was over.

We stayed on the island for three days. In the Jewish village Algren gazed with astonishment at the beautiful women with their dark eyes and their heads wrapped in the traditional black shawls. 'I know women exactly like that in Chicago,' he told me. We visited the synagogue to which Jews come on pilgrimage from all over the world. We spent quite a long time in a grotto that had been made into a tavern; the bottles of beer lay in the water of a little pool, in which the owner would dabble his feet to cool them off. He gave Algren some *kiff* to smoke: 'You'll see; you'll fly away!' All the customers watched and waited. Algren felt a slight shudder that lifted him off the ground, but he came down again almost immediately.

At the house of some cousins of Amour Hassine, we ate vermilion-coloured stew and drank violet syrup. We returned to Tunis with him by way of Médenine and Kairouan. In front of the *gorfa*, Algren stared wide-eyed: 'I just don't know where I am!' Amour Hassine showed us a photograph of himself with a telephone against his ear. 'I was calling Paris!' he told us with great pride. He was also proud to be driving an American, but found it difficult to understand why the American didn't have a car of his own. 'Not everyone's rich over there,' Algren told him. Hassine pondered over that; he noticed that we bought a lot of fritters and cakes and asked: 'Are there eggs in America? And milk? ... Then take me back with you; we'll set up at a crossroads somewhere, we'll make fritters and cakes and we'll be rich.' There were two things he hated: France and Israel. He only expressed his opinions on the former in guarded allusions because of me; but on the subject of the Jews, since Algren didn't even flinch, he poured out his bitterness: 'They've never even had a flag; and now they want a country of their own!'

After Tunis came Algiers, then Fez and Marrakesh; so much light, so many colours and sights, so many wounds; Algren's eyes opened wider and wider. He wanted to have another look at Marseilles where he had waited for his ship back to the States when the war was over. Afterwards Olga and Bost welcomed us to their house at Cabris; the windows overlooked terraces of olive trees with the sea in the distance. The village had scarcely changed since 1941. One evening we hired a car to go and lose a little – a very little – money at the casino in Monte Carlo. In a loft in Antibes, to which the Club du Vieux-Colombier had migrated, we listened to Luter play; Greco sang *Si tu t'imagines* and *La rue des Blancs-Manteaux*. Algren drank a lot; he danced with Olga and then, very gracefully, with a chair.

Back in Paris, the month of September was magnificent. We had never got on better together. Next year I would go to Chicago; I was certain when I said good-bye to him that I would see Algren again. And yet there was something terribly tight around my heart as I accompanied him to Orly. He went through the door to Customs; he disappeared; that in itself seemed so impossible that everything became possible, even or especially that we would never meet again. I went back to Paris by taxi: the red lights on top of the pylons were all omens of some dreadful calamity.

I must have been mistaken. Algren's first letter was brimming over with high spirits. When they landed at Gander, he discovered from a magazine that he had been awarded the National Book Award. Cocktail parties, interviews, radio and television appearances: New York celebrated his return. A friend had driven him back to Chicago. He was very happy about his trip through Europe, very happy to be back home. He wrote:

We drove all Saturday and all Sunday, and it was marvellous to see American trees again, and the big American sky, the great rivers and the plains. It isn't as colourful a country as France; it doesn't captivate you in the same way as the little red roofs you see coming into Paris on the boat train or when you fly over them in the plane from Marseilles. Nor is it awesome like the grey-green light of Marrakesh. It's just huge, warm and friendly, confident and sleepy and taking its time. I was glad to think I belonged to it, and sort of relieved at the thought that wherever I go, this is the country I'll always be able to come back to.

He repeated that he was looking forward to seeing me over there, and my confidence returned.

The first volume of *The Second Sex* was published in June; in May, *Les Temps Modernes* had printed the chapter on 'Woman's Sexual Initiation' and followed it up in the June and July issues with the chapters on 'The Lesbian' and 'Maternity'. In November, Gallimard published the second volume.

I have described how this book was first conceived: almost by chance. Wanting to talk about myself, I became aware that to do so I should first have to describe the condition of woman in general; first I considered the myths that men have forged about her through all their cosmologies, religions, superstitions, ideologies and literature. I tried to establish some order in the picture which at first appeared to me completely incoherent; in every case, man put himself forward as the Subject and considered the woman as an object, as the Other. This assumption could of course be explained by historical circumstances, and Sartre told me I should also give some indication of the physiological groundwork. That was at Ramatuelle; we talked about it for a long time and I hesitated; I hadn't expected to become involved in writing such a vast work. But it was true that my study of the myths would be left hanging in mid-air if people didn't know the reality those myths were intended to mask. I therefore plunged into works of physiology and history. I didn't merely compile; even scientists, of both sexes, are imbued with prejudices in favour of man, so I had to try to dig for the exact truth beneath the surface of their interpretations. From my journey into history I returned with a few ideas that I had never seen expressed anywhere: I linked the history of woman to that of inheritance, because it seemed to me to be a by-product of the economic evolution of the masculine world.

I began to look at women with new eyes and found surprise after surprise lying in wait for me. It is both strange and stimulating to discover suddenly, after forty, an aspect of the world that has been staring you in the face all the time which somehow you have never noticed. One of the misunderstandings created by my book is that people thought I was denying there was any difference between men and women. On the contrary, writing this book made me even more aware of those things that separate them; what I contended was that these dissimilarities are of a cultural and not of a natural order. I undertook to recount systematically, from childhood to old age, how they were created; I examined the possibilities this world offers women, those it denies them, their limits, their good and bad luck, their evasions and their achievements. That was what I put into the second volume: *L'Expérience vécue.*

I spent only two years[1] on this work. I already knew some sociology and psychology. Thanks to my university training, I had the habit of efficient working methods; I knew how to sort books out and strip the meat off them quickly, how to reject those that were merely rehashes of others or pure fantasies; I made a pretty exhaustive inventory of everything that had appeared on the subject in both English and French; it was one that had given rise to an enormous literature but, as is usually the case, only a small number of these studies were important. When it came to the second volume, I also profited from the continual interest that Sartre and I had had for so many years in all sorts of people; my memory provided me with an abundance of material.

The first volume was well received: twenty-two thousand copies were sold in the first week. The second one also sold well, but it shocked people. I was completely taken aback by the fuss it provoked when the extracts from the book appeared in *Les Temps Modernes.* I had completely failed to take into account that 'French bitchiness' Julien Gracq mentioned in an article in which – although he compared me to Poincaré making speeches in cemeteries – he congratulated me on my 'courage'. The word astonished me the first time it was used. 'How courageous you are!' Claudine Chonez told me with an admiration full of pity. 'Courageous?' 'You're going to lose a lot of friends!' Well, I thought to myself, if I lose them they're not friends. In any case, I had written this book just the way I wanted to write it, but there had been no thought of heroism in my mind at any time. The men whom I knew well – Sartre, Bost, Merleau-Ponty, Leiris, Giacometti and the staff of *Les Temps Modernes* – were real democrats on this

1. It was begun in October 1946 and finished in June 1949; but I spent four months of 1947 in America, and *America Day by Day* kept me busy for six months.

point as well as on any other; if I had been writing it for them I would have been in danger of breaking down an open door. In any case I was accused of doing just that; also of inventing, parodying, digressing and ranting. I was accused of so many things: everything! First of all, indecency. The June, July and August issues of *Les Temps Modernes* sold like hot cakes; but they were read, as it were, with averted eyes. One might almost have believed that Freud and psychoanalysis had never existed. What a festival of obscenity on the pretext of flogging me for mine! That good old *esprit gaulois* flowed in torrents. I received – some signed and some anonymous – epigrams, epistles, satires, admonitions, and exhortations addressed to me by, for example, 'some very active members of the First Sex'. Unsatisfied, frigid, priapic, nymphomaniac, lesbian, a hundred times aborted, I was everything, even an unmarried mother. People offered to cure me of my frigidity or to temper my labial appetites; I was promised revelations, in the coarsest terms but in the name of the true, the good and the beautiful, in the name of health and even of poetry, all unworthily trampled underfoot by me. Certainly it is monotonous writing inscriptions on lavatory walls; I could understand that many sexual maniacs might prefer to send their lucubrations to me for a change. But I was a bit surprised at Mauriac! He wrote to one of the contributors to *Les Temps Modernes*: 'Your employer's vagina has no secrets from me,' which shows that in private life he wasn't afraid of words. When he saw them printed, it upset him so much that he began a series in *Le Figaro littéraire* urging the youth of France to condemn pornography in general and my articles in particular. Its success was slight. Although the replies of Pouillon and Cau, who had flown to my rescue, were suppressed – and probably those of many others as well – I had my defenders: among others, Domenach; the Christians were only gently indignant, and on the whole the youth of the nation did not seem excessively outraged by my verbal excesses. Mauriac lamented the fact bitterly. Exactly at the right moment to close his series, an angelic young lady sent him a letter so perfectly calculated to grant his every wish that a lot of us got a great deal of amusement out of what was obviously a godsend for Mauriac! Nevertheless, in restaurants and cafés – which I frequented much more than usual because of Algren – people often snickered as they glanced towards me or even openly pointed. Once, during an entire dinner at Nos Provinces on the Boulevard Montparnasse, a table of people nearby stared at me and giggled; I didn't like dragging Algren into a scene, but as I left I gave them a piece of my mind.

The violence and level of these reactions left me perplexed. Among the Latin peoples, Catholicism has encouraged masculine tyranny and even inclined it towards sadism; Italian men have a tendency to combine it with coarseness, and the Spaniards with arrogance, but this sort of meanness was particularly French. Why? Primarily because in France a man feels himself economically threatened by feminine competition; to maintain, or to assert the maintenance of a superiority no longer guaranteed by the customs of the country, the simplest method is to vilify women. A tradition of licentious talk provides a whole arsenal calculated to reduce women to their function as sexual objects: sayings, images, anecdotes and the vocabulary itself. Also, in the erotic field, the ancestral myth of French supremacy is being threatened; the ideal lover is now generally attributed to the Italian rather than the Frenchman; finally, the critical attitude of liberated women wounds or tires their partners; it makes them resentful. This meanness is simply the old French licentiousness taken over by vulnerable and spiteful men.[1]

In November, the swords were unsheathed once more. The critics went wild; there was no disagreement: women had always been the equal of men, they were forever doomed to be their inferiors, everything I said was common knowledge, there wasn't a word of truth in the whole book. In *Liberté de l'esprit*, Boideffre and Nimier outdid each other in contempt. I was a poor neurotic girl, repressed, frustrated, and cheated by life, a virago, a woman who'd never been made love to properly, envious, embittered and bursting with inferiority complexes with regard to men, while with regard to women I was eaten to the bone by resentment.[2] Jean Guitton, with great Christian compassion, wrote that *The Second Sex* had affected him painfully because one could so clearly see running through it the thread of 'my sad life'. Armand Hoog outdid himself:

1. There exists a hatred of women among American men. But even the most venomous writings, such as Philip Wylie's *A Generation of Vipers*, do not descend to the level of obscenity; their sights are not on degrading women sexually.

2. When Christiane Rochefort's *Warrior's Rest* appeared ten years later, there was less scandal, but there were still plenty of male critics ready to chant the old refrain: 'She's an ugly and frustrated woman!'

'Humiliated by being a woman, agonizingly conscious of being imprisoned in her condition by the eyes of men, she rejects both their eyes and her condition.'

This theme of my humiliation was taken up by a considerable number of critics who were so naïvely imbued with their own masculine superiority that they could not even imagine that my condition had never been a burden to me. The man whom I placed above all others did not consider me inferior to men. I had many male friends whose eyes, far from imprisoning me within set limits, recognized me as a human being in my own right. Such good fortune had protected me against all resentment and all bitterness; my readers will know too that I was never infected by such feelings during my childhood or my adolescence.[1] Subtler readers concluded that I was a misogynist and that, while pretending to take up the cudgels for women. I was damning them; this is untrue. I do not praise them to the skies and I have anatomized all those defects engendered by their condition, but I also showed their good qualities and their merits. I have given too many women too much affection and esteem to betray them now by considering myself as an 'honorary male'; nor have I ever been wounded by their stares. In fact I was never treated as a target for sarcasm until after *The Second Sex*; before that, people were either indifferent or kind to me. Afterwards, I was often attacked as a woman because my attackers thought it must be my Achilles' heel; but I knew perfectly well that this persistent petulance was really aimed at my moral and social convictions. No; far from suffering from my femininity, I have, on the contrary, from the age of twenty on, accumulated the advantages of both sexes; after *L'Invitée*, those around me treated me both as a writer, their peer in the masculine world, and as a woman; this was particularly noticeable in America: at the parties I went to, the wives all got together and talked to each other while I talked to the men, who nevertheless behaved towards me with greater courtesy than they did towards the members of their own sex. I was encouraged to write *The Second Sex* precisely because of this privileged position. It allowed me to express myself in all

1. I by no means despise resentment and bitterness, or any other of those negative emotions; they are often justified by circumstances and one might consider that I have missed something in not having experienced them. If I reject their attribution to me here it is because I would like *The Second Sex* to be understood in the spirit in which I wrote it.

serenity. And, contrary to what they suggest, it was precisely this placidity which exasperated so many of my masculine readers. A wild cry of rage, the revolt of a wounded soul – that they could have accepted with a moved and pitying condescension; since they could not pardon me my objectivity, they feigned a disbelief in it. For example I will take a phrase of Claude Mauriac's which perfectly illustrates the arrogance of the First Sex. 'What has she got against me?' he wanted to know. Nothing; I had nothing against anything except the words I was quoting. It is strange that so many intellectuals should refuse to believe in intellectual passions.[1]

I stirred up some storms even among my friends. One of them, a progressive academic, stopped reading my book and threw it across the room. Camus, in a few morose sentences, accused me of making the French male look ridiculous. A Mediterranean man, cultivating Spanish pride, he would allow woman equality only if she kept to her own, and different, realm; also, he was of course, as George Orwell would have said, the more equal of the two. He had blithely admitted to us once that he disliked the idea of being sized up and judged by a woman: she was the object, *he* was the eye and the consciousness. He laughed about it, but it is true that he did not accept reciprocity. Finally, with sudden warmth, he said: 'There's one argument that you should have emphasized: man himself suffers from not being able to find a real companion in woman; he does aspire to equality.' He too wanted a cry from the heart rather than solid reasoning; and what's more, a cry on behalf of men. Most men took as a personal insult the information I retailed about frigidity in women; they wanted to imagine that they could dispense pleasure whenever and to whomever they pleased; to doubt such powers on their part was to castrate them.

The Right could only detest my book, which Rome naturally put on the blacklist. I had hoped it would be well received by the extreme Left. Our relations with the Communists couldn't have been worse; all the same, my thesis owed so much to Marxism and showed it in such a favourable light that I did at least expect some impartiality from them! Marie-Louise Barron, in *Les Lettres françaises*, confined herself to remarking that *The Second Sex* would at

1. A novelist pamphleteer of the Right, having been sharply attacked by Bost in *Les Temps Modernes*, exclaimed, very hurt: 'But why so much hate? He doesn't even know me!'

least give the factory girls at Billancourt a good giggle; which implies a very low estimate of the factory girls at Billancourt, replied Colette Audry in a 'review of the critics' she did for *Combat*. *Action* devoted an anonymous and unintelligible article to me, delightfully decorated with the photograph of a woman held fast in the passionate embraces of an ape.

The non-Stalinist Marxists were scarcely more comforting. I gave a lecture at the École Émancipée and was told that once the Revolution had been achieved, the problem of woman would no longer exist. Fine, I said; but meanwhile? The present apparently held no interest for them.

My adversaries created and maintained numerous misunderstandings on the subject of my book. Above all I was attacked for the chapter on maternity. Many men declared I had no right to discuss women because I hadn't given birth; and they?[1] They nevertheless produced some very distinct opinions of their own in opposition to mine. It was said that I refused to grant any value to the maternal instinct and to love. This was not so. I simply asked that women should experience them truthfully and freely, whereas they often use them as excuses and take refuge in them, only to find themselves imprisoned in that refuge when those emotions have dried up in their hearts. I was accused of preaching sexual promiscuity; but at no point did I ever advise anyone to sleep with just anyone at just any time; my opinion on this subject is that all choices, agreements and refusals should be made independently of institutions, conventions and motives of self-aggrandizement; if the reasons for it are not of the same order as the act itself, then the only result can be lies, distortions and mutilations.

I devoted a chapter to the problem of abortion; Sartre had already written about it in *The Age of Reason*, and I myself in *The Blood of Others*; people were always rushing into the office of *Les Temps Modernes* asking Mme Sorbets, the secretary, for addresses. She got so irritated that one day she designed a poster: WE DO IT ON THE PREMISES, OURSELVES. One morning, when I was still asleep, a young man knocked on my door. 'My wife is pregnant,' he said distractedly. 'Give me an address ...' 'But I don't know any,' I told him. He swore at me and left. 'No one ever helps anyone!' I didn't know any addresses; and I should scarcely have been inclined to have any confidence in a stranger endowed with so little

1. They went out and questioned mothers; but so did I.

self-control. Women and couples are forced by society into secrecy; if I can help them I have no hesitation in doing so. But I did not find it very pleasant to discover that I was apparently thought of as a professional procuress.

There were people who defended *The Second Sex*: Francis Jeanson, Nadeau, Mounier. It provoked public controversy and lectures, it brought me a considerable amount of correspondence. Misread and misunderstood, it troubled people's minds. When all is said and done, it is possibly the book that has brought me the greatest satisfaction of all those I have written. If I am asked what I think of it today, I have no hesitation in replying: I'm all for it.

Oh! I admit that one can criticize the style and the composition. I could easily go back and cut it down to a much more elegant work. But at the time I was discovering my ideas as I was explaining them, and that was the best I could do. As for the content, I should take a more materialist position today in the first volume. I should base the notion of woman as *other* and the Manichaean argument it entails not on an idealistic and *a priori* struggle of consciences, but on the facts of supply and demand; that is how I treated the same problem in *The Long March* when I was writing about the subjugation of women in ancient China. This modification would not necessitate any changes in the subsequent developments of my argument. On the whole, I still agree with what I said. I never cherished any illusion of changing woman's condition; it depends on the future of labour in the world; it will change significantly only at the price of a revolution in production. That is why I avoided falling into the trap of 'feminism'. Nor did I offer remedies for each particular problem I described. But at least I helped the women of my time and generation to become aware of themselves and their situation.

Many of them, of course, disapproved of my book; I disturbed them or opposed them or exasperated them or frightened them. But there were others to whom I did some service, as I know from numberless testimonies to the fact, especially from the letters that I am still receiving and answering after twelve years. These women have found help in my work in their fight against images of themselves which revolted them, against myths by which they felt themselves crushed; they came to realize that their difficulties reflected not a disgrace peculiar to them, but a general condition. This discovery helped them to avoid the mistake of self-contempt, and many of them found in the book the strength to fight against that condition. Self-knowledge is no guarantee of happiness, but it is on the side of happiness and can supply the courage to fight for it. Psychiatrists have told me that they give *The Second Sex* to their women patients to read, and not merely to intellectual women but to lower-middle-class women, to office workers and women working in factories. 'Your book was a great help to me. Your book saved me,' are the words I have read in letters from women of all ages and all walks of life.

If my book has helped women, it is because it expressed them, and they in their turn gave it its truth. Thanks to them, it is no longer a matter for scandal and concern. During these last ten years the myths that men created have crumbled, and many women writers have gone beyond me and have been far more daring than I. Too many of them for my taste take sexuality as their only theme; but at least when they write about it they now present themselves as the eye-that-looks, as subject, consciousness, freedom.

I should have been surprised and even irritated if, when I was thirty, someone had told me that I would be concerning myself with feminine problems, and that my most serious public would be made up of women. I don't regret that it has been so. Divided, lacerated, in a world made to put them at a disadvantage, for women there are far more victories to be won, more prizes to be gained, more defeats to be suffered than there are for men. I have an interest in them; and I prefer having taken a limited but real hold upon the world through them to drifting in the universal.

It was still beautiful, warm weather when I returned to Cagnes with Sartre in the middle of October. I went back to my same room, to our little lunches on my balcony, to my glossy table under a little window with red curtains. The book Lévi-Strauss let me read had just come out, and I did a review of it for *Les Temps Modernes*. Then I made a start on the novel I had been thinking about for so long already; I wanted it to contain all of me — myself in relation to life, to death, to my times, to writing, to love, to friendship, to travel; I also wanted to depict other people, and above all to tell the feverish and disappointing story of what happened after the war. I dashed down a few words — the beginning of Anne's first monologue — but the blank paper made me feel giddy. I had no lack of things to say; but how to set about it? This was to be no potboiler, oh no! I was high with excitement, but frightened. How long would it take, this new adventure? Three years? Four? A long time anyway. And where would it land me?

To both calm and stimulate myself, I read *The Thief's Journal*, one of Genet's finest books. I took walks with Sartre. Pagniez, who was staying at Juan-les-Pins with Mme Lemaire, came over to see us with his children. His wife's death had brought us closer again. The doctors had not been mistaken. She had dragged on for two years. Confined to her bed, growing weaker and more emaciated all the time, it was heartbreaking to hear her making plans. She was convinced she was on the road to recovery when, during the winter, she died.

We went by taxi to Sospel and Peira-Cava, and took tea on the terrace. We were surprised several days later, on opening *France-Dimanche*, to find an account of our afternoon. The cartoonist Soro, who helped write the gossip column for the paper, was taking his holiday at the Cagnard; he found it ludicrous of us to be entertaining a father and his children. He took a sarcastic tone about my conversations with Sartre, without being able to make up his mind whether it was their hermetic quality he objected to or their simplicity. The contents of such articles were in themselves a matter of indifference to me; but I found it unpleasant to feel that I was being stalked even in my quietest retreats.

The third volume of *The Roads of Freedom*, called *Troubled Sleep*, appeared shortly after our return to Paris. I prefer it to the other two; in the transparency of each particular vision, the world still keeps its opacity; everything is outside, everything is inside; one grasps reality in both its aspects, the heavy weight of things and what we must after all call liberty. Yet the novel was less successful than its predecessors. 'It's a sequel, yet it isn't the conclusion, so people hesitate to buy it,' said Gaston Gallimard, who would have liked to put it out at the same time as the final volume. The readers were also influenced by the critics of course. Sartre shocked the Right by depicting officers deserting their troops. The Communists were indignant because the French people, civilians and soldiers alike, were shown as passive and a-political.

Troubled Sleep left several questions unanswered: Was Mathieu dead or not?[1] Who was this Schneider whom Brunet found so interesting? What happened to the other characters? *The Last Chance* was to answer these questions. The first episode appeared at the end of 1949 in *Les Temps Modernes* under the title: *Drôle d'amitié*. A newly arrived prisoner at the Stalag, Chalais, a Communist, recognized Schneider as the journalist Vicarios who had left the Party at the time of the Russo-German pact; the Communist Party had circulated a warning about him because they supposed him to be an informer. Chalais expressed his conviction that the U.S.S.R. would never enter the war and that *Humanité* was taking collaboration as the order of the day. Uneasy, indignant, distressed, when Brunet discovered from Vicarios that he was going to escape in order to confront his slanderers, he decided to go with him. This shared escape sealed the friendship which Brunet still felt for Vicarios despite the feelings of the others. Vicarios was killed, Brunet recaptured. The rest was still in a rough first draft. Having escaped, Mathieu, tired of being free 'for nothing' all his life, finally and happily decided in favour of action. Thanks to his help, Brunet escaped and reached Paris; there he discovered, with stupefaction, that – with a change of policy analogous to the one that forces Hugo to suicide at the end of *Les Mains sales* – the U.S.S.R. had entered the war, and that the Communist Party had condemned collaboration. Having succeeded in rehabilitating Schneider, he resumed his role as a militant member of the Resistance; but the doubt, the scandal and the solitude he experienced had revealed his subjectivity to him: in the depths of his commitment he had rediscovered his freedom. At the same time Mathieu was moving in the opposite direction. Daniel, who was collaborating, had managed to have him recalled to Paris as the editor of a newspaper controlled by the Germans. Mathieu avoided the post and went into hiding. In the Stalag, his activities had still been those of an individualistic adventurer; now, by submitting himself to a collective discipline, he arrived at genuine commitment: starting in one case from alienation from the Cause and in the other from abstract liberty. Brunet and Mathieu were the embodiments of the authentic man of action as Sartre conceived him. Mathieu and Odette returned each other's love; she left Jacques and they experienced the fullness of a freely shared passion. Then

1. Sartre had an insert printed so that readers would know he was in fact still alive, but you couldn't tell from the story itself.

Mathieu was arrested and died under torture, a hero not in essence, but because he had *made himself* a hero. Philippe too joined the Resistance, to prove to himself that he was not a coward, and also as a revenge against Daniel. He was shot down during a raid on a café in the Latin Quarter. Mad with grief and rage, Daniel hid in his briefcase one of the grenades Philippe used to keep hidden in the apartment; he attended a meeting of German officials and blew up both them and himself. Sarah, having fled to Marseilles, threw herself out of a window with her child when the Germans came to arrest her. Boris was parachuted into the *maquis*. Everyone, or almost everyone, being dead, there was no one left to become involved in the problems that arose after the war.

But they were precisely the problems that at this time interested Sartre; he had nothing to say about the Resistance because he conceived the novel as a form that poses questions, and under the Occupation one knew exactly what to do: there could be no perplexity, no ambiguity about how to behave. For his heroes at the end of *Drôle d'amitié* the die was cast; the critical moments of their stories are those when Daniel wildly rushes along the path to evil, when Mathieu is finally no longer able to bear the vacuum of his liberty, when Brunet abandons his old ideas; all that remained for Sartre to do was to harvest the fruits so delicately ripened; but he prefers to clear the ground, to plough, to plant. Without having abandoned the idea of a fourth volume, he always found work that needed his attention more. To skip ten years and hurl his characters into the anxieties of the present would have been meaningless; the last volume would then have disappointed all the expectations roused by the one before it. The last volume was too imperiously predetermined for Sartre either to change his original intentions or to conquer the distaste which the idea of conforming to them aroused in him.

I was very pleased that Merle's *Weekend at Zuydcoote*, published in *Les Temps Modernes*, won the Prix Goncourt. I saw several films; I shared Cocteau's opinion of *Bicycle Thief*: it was Rome and a masterpiece. With *Festivals of Hell* Paris discovered Ghelderode. At Agnès Capri's theatre, they were doing Queneau's *Les Limites de la forêt*, in which the leading role was played by a dog; there were other acts. I singled out the delicious Barbara Laage who was later to be in the film of *The Respectful Prostitute*.

The audience was largely composed of members of the fourth sex: diamond-covered ladies of about fifty next to the young girls they were manifestly keeping.

Camus came back from South America, he had done too much and looked very tired on the opening night of *Les Justes*; but the warmth of his greeting brought back the best days of our friendship. Perfectly acted, the play seemed to us academic. He accepted all the handshakes and compliments with a smiling and sceptical simplicity. Rosemonde Gérard, humpbacked, ravaged and extravagantly dressed, rushed up to him. 'I like it better than *Les Mains sales*,' she said, not having seen Sartre nearby. Camus turned to him with a smile of complicity and said: 'Two birds with one stone!' for he disliked people treating him as a rival of Sartre's.

We visited Léger's studio; he gave Sartre a painting and me a very pretty watercolour. Since his stay in America his canvases had begun to have much more warmth and colour than before. The Musée d'Art Moderne gave a huge exhibition of them; later, at the same place, I saw the sculptures of Henry Moore.

Since he no longer had a theatre of his own, Dullin had been making exhausting tours of France and Europe. Camille didn't make his life any easier for him, since she was having difficulties of her own and drinking excessively. Crippled and exhausted, he was suddenly seized with such violent pains that they took him to the Saint-Antoine hospital; they opened his abdomen and closed it again hurriedly; he had cancer. As he lay dying, two journalists from *Samedi-Soir* passed themselves off as pupils of his and forced their way into his room. 'Fuck off!' Dullin yelled; but they had already taken a picture. This way of behaving shocked people; *Samedi-Soir* whined and defended itself. After fighting for two or three days, Dullin died. I hadn't seen him for a long time; old and in pain, his end was not tragic in the way Bourla's was, but I am always moved when I recall my memories of him. A whole stretch of my past went with him, and I had the feeling that my own death was beginning.

During our traditional retreat at La Pouèze, Sartre worked at a preface for the works of Genet that Gallimard had asked him to do. I revised my translation of Algren's novel and went on with my own. Having heard on a radio programme that I had described her as a courtesan in *The Second Sex*, Cléo de Mérode brought a suit against me; there was some talk about it in the newspapers; I put the case in the hands of Suzanne Blum and didn't think about it.

In February, Dullin's friends and pupils organized a 'Tribute to Dullin' at the Atelier. We called for Camille to take her there. The door was opened by the ravishing Ariane Borg in dismay. To enable her to face the evening, Camille had been drinking red wine; we carried her, in tears, her hair tumbling down and her clothes in disorder, from the taxi into a box where she hid herself and sobbed through the whole ceremony. Salacrou and Jules Romains made brief speeches; an actor read Sartre's. Olga did a scene from *The Flies* in costume, very well. We heard Dullin's recorded voice in the soliloquy from *The Miser*.

During March, I went to the Théâtre de Poche to attend a few rehearsals and then the opening of two little plays by Chauffard: *Le Dernier des Sioux* and *Un Collier d'une reine*. Claude Martin directed. It was a young troupe who worked together very happily all the time without dissensions. I thought what a pity it was that things were always so different with Sartre's plays! Denner[1] played the king, Loleh Bellon was a charming queen and Olga, who was getting back to acting at last, struck sparks; the critics showered her with compliments. Sartre was hoping to have *The Flies* revived when she was completely recovered.

Just next to my house was a little newspaper vendor and I often used to stop and chat with him. 'I'm Martin Eden,' he told me one day. He used to read a lot and also went to school. He had decided that he would help all the people who were trying to teach themselves in our district: 'Because I found it so very hard myself.' He had managed to organize a sort of club in a room in the Rue Mouffetard and he was asking intellectuals to come and give lectures. Sartre gave one on the theatre, Clouzot one on the film. I spoke about the condition of women; it was the first time I had come into contact with a truly working-class public, and I discovered that, contrary to what Mme Barron had said, they felt very much concerned with the problems I spoke about.

The attempts of the neutralists had come to nothing. On the pretext of joining forces with a conscientious objector called Moreau, Gary Davis tore up his identity papers and started a

1. Whose performance as Landru had just made him famous.

publicity campaign on his own that disgusted his partisans. The R.D.R. had finally collapsed and disappeared. It was now certain beyond doubt that there could be no third course between adherence to one of the two blocs. And the choice between them remained impossible. The State Department continued to support Chiang Kai-shek, who had taken refuge on Formosa, against the Chinese People's Republic that had been proclaimed on 1 November. It had also given financial aid to Franco; it was, as the title of an article published in *Les Temps Modernes* expressed it, 'The End of Man's Hope' for Spain. In Greece, with the connivance of the English, America had assured the triumph of the reactionaries: the Communists and all the others who had opposed that triumph were dying in Makronisos' camp. Yet it was not possible to decide without reservations in favour of the U.S.S.R. when so many half-public, half-concealed dramas still continued to succeed one another in all the Stalinist countries. Our ears were still numb from the admission of Cardinal Mindszenty when Rajk started confessing in his turn – treason and plotting – before being hanged on 15 October in Budapest. Kostov admitted nothing and was hanged in Sofia in December. By the fate of these two 'criminals' who were in fact paying for Tito, Stalin was denouncing 'cosmopolitanism' and 'cosmopolites'.

Sartre had been a member of a committee formed to obtain a retrial in Tananarive, but he had by now practically given up all political activity. He was busy with Merleau-Ponty on the magazine, which was going through a slack period: four years before we had been everyone's friends, now we were looked upon by everyone as enemies. He began two works that had no connexion with our circumstances at that time. *La Reine Albemarle et le dernier touriste* was intended to be the *Nausea* of his maturity, as it were; in it he gave a capricious description of Italy, its present structure, its history and its countryside, and also meditated on what it means to be a tourist.[1] Also his preface to the works of Genet turned into a long book in which he attempted to give an account of one man that would go far deeper than his *Baudelaire*. He had moved closer to both psychoanalysis and Marxism, and it seemed to him at that time that the possibilities of any individual were strictly limited by his situation; the individual's liberty consisted in not

1. He wrote several hundred pages of it, but never had the inclination or the time to revise them and only published tiny fragments of them later.

accepting his situation passively but, through the very movement of his existence, interiorizing and transcending it in order to give it meaning. In certain cases the margin of choice left to him came very close to zero. In others, the choice continued over a period of many years; Sartre was telling the story of Genet's choice; he examined the values which his options brought into play – holiness, demonism, good and evil – in relation to their social context.

Sartre abandoned his work on morals proper that year because he was convinced that

the moral attitude appears when technical and social conditions render positive forms of conduct impossible. Ethics is a collection of idealistic tricks intended to enable us to live the life imposed on us by the poverty of our resources and the insufficiency of our techniques.[1]

He worked mainly in the fields of history and economy. The young Marxist philosopher Tran Duc Thao suggested to him that they have a series of discussions that could afterwards be collected to form a book; Sartre agreed.

In November, Roger Stéphane came to see Sartre; there had come into his hands a copy of the 'Soviet Code of Corrective Labour' which had just been republished in England[2] and though still unknown in France had been the object of a discussion in the U.N. at the beginning of August. It confirmed the revelations made during the Kravchenko case about the existence of labour camps. Did Sartre want to publish it in *Les Temps Modernes*? Yes, he did. Sartre, as I have said, believed in socialism. He expressed his thoughts on the subject a few years later in *Le Fantôme de Staline*: taken as a whole, the Socialist movement

is the absolute judge of all other movements because the exploited experience exploitation and the class struggle as their reality and as the fundamental truth of bourgeois societies . . . it is the movement of man in the process of creating himself; the other parties believe that man is already created. Socialism is the absolute standard of reference by which any political undertaking is to be judged.

Now the U.S.S.R., in spite of everything, had been, and still

1. Unpublished notes.
2. It had been published there as early as 1936; the existence of the camps was already known; but the French Communist Party was too small and the U.S.S.R. too far away for public opinion to pay much attention to them. We had both been so indifferent to politics then, Sartre and myself, that we had never given the matter a thought.

remained, the mother country of socialism: the revolutionary seizure of power had been accomplished. Even if its bureaucracy had become stratified, even if its police had arrogated enormous power to itself, even if crimes had been committed, the U.S.S.R. had never in any way questioned the original appropriation of the means of production; its political system differed radically from those which aimed at establishing or maintaining the domination of one class. Without denying the faults of its rulers, Sartre was of the opinion that if they presented so much ground for criticism it was partly because they refused the excuse provided for bourgeois politicians by the so-called 'economic laws'; they assumed responsibility for everything that happened in and to their country.

It was being said that the Revolution had been betrayed and was now entirely unrecognizable. This was untrue, replied Sartre: it has been embodied; the universal, in other words, has been reduced to the particular. Made real in this way, it immediately encountered contradictions that kept it from attaining the purity of the original conception; yet over the dream of a socialism without defect, Russian socialism had the immense advantage of existing. On the subject of the Stalinian era, Sartre's thoughts were already those expressed recently in an as yet unpublished chapter of *Critique de la raison dialectique*:

> The regime in the U.S.S.R. was really socialism, but socialism characterized by the practical necessity of disappearing from the world or of becoming what it is at the cost of a desperate and bloody effort. ... In certain circumstances, this reconciliation of contradictions may be synonymous with hell.

In *Le Fantôme de Staline*, he also wrote: 'Must we call this bloody monster that tears at its own flesh by the name of Socialism? My answer is, quite frankly, yes.'

Nevertheless, despite this essential right to recognition that he allowed the U.S.S.R., he refused the *either–or* in which both Kanapa on one side and Aron on the other sought to imprison him; he offered the French people the choice of safeguarding their liberty. Such a course implies the necessity of looking truth in the face, no matter what the circumstances. He was determined never to place a mask on truth, not from any abstract principle but because he believed in the practical value of truth. Even if he had been closer to the U.S.S.R. than he was, he would still have chosen to tell this truth, for in his eyes the role of the intellectual is not the same as that of the politician; it is his duty, not by any means to judge an undertaking according to moral rules that are external to him, but to keep it from contradicting its principles and its goal in the process of its development. If the police methods of a socialist country were compromising socialism, then they should be denounced. Sartre came to an agreement with Stéphane that he would publish and comment on the Soviet Code in the December issue of *Les Temps Modernes*.

But on 12 November the *Figaro Littéraire* blazoned across its pages in enormous capitals: APPEAL TO THOSE DEPORTED TO NAZI CAMPS. HELP THOSE BEING TAKEN TO SOVIET CAMPS. The cry came from Rousset. He quoted from the articles of the code which authorized 'Administrative Internment', in other words, all the arbitrary arrests and deportations. With the collaboration of *Figaro*, he was assembling a splendid anti-Soviet machine. The following numbers of the *Littéraire* and the right-wing press in general exploited it to the full. An unbelievable chorus! Hundreds of stories, memoirs, eye-witness accounts suddenly appeared out of drawers and were printed anywhere and everywhere. There were also terrible photographs of armoured trains and 'musulmans' that matched the pictures of the Nazi trains and camps feature for feature. They seemed identical – and they were: old photographs had been unearthed and disguised. This hoax was exposed, but it got no one any nearer to the truth. Perfectly indifferent to the 40,000 people killed at Sétif, the 80,000 murdered Malgaches, the famine and poverty in Algeria, the burned-out villages of Indochina, the Greeks dying in their camps, the Spaniards shot by Franco, the hearts of the bourgeoisie suddenly burst when confronted by the misfortunes of the people imprisoned by the Russians. The truth was that they gave a great sigh of relief, as though all the crimes of colonialism and all the exploitations of capitalism had been annulled by the camps in Siberia. As for Rousset, he had found a job.

Nevertheless, the fact remained that the administration had discretionary powers, there was nothing to protect the individual against the arbitrariness of its decisions. In January, *Les Temps Modernes* published an account of the debates in the United Nations on the work camps and an editorial, written by Merleau-Ponty and signed by Sartre as well as himself, which put the affair in its proper perspective.[1] A serious appraisal and correlation of the information available from various sources placed the figure of those deported at ten million.[2] 'There can be no socialism when one citizen out of twenty is in a concentration camp,' some declared. They accused the Communists of bad faith. Successively and almost simultaneously, we read Wurmser's assertion in *Les Lettres françaises*: There are no camps! and Daix's proclamation that the camps were the U.S.S.R.'s greatest claim to glory. Merleau-Ponty then took Rousset to task: Rousset's demand for the opening of a commission of inquiry was simply another manoeuvre in his anti-Communist crusade. He pointed out those parts of the Russian delegate's reply to the United Nations in which he compared the Russian work camps and the millions of unemployed in the West; when he said: 'The colonies are the labour camps of the democracies,' the Russian was not cheating; the two systems – Russian socialism and Western capitalism – should be considered in their totality; it was not by accident that the Soviet spokesman implicated Western unemployment and colonialist over-exploitation.

This article displeased everyone, or almost everyone. It did nothing to improve our relations with the Communist Party. In any case, the Communist intellectuals were heartily sick of us. Their attitude to *The Second Sex*, however, and the repeated attacks of Kanapa annoyed us less than the hatred with which Aragon was pursuing Nizan. In his novel, *Les Communistes*, he had depicted him as a traitor. Orfilat in the novel was, like Nizan, in charge of the foreign-politics page of *Humanité*; like him he was a philosopher, like him he had demolished Brunschvig and the bourgeois ideologists, like him he had written a study on a Greek philosopher (Heraclitus; Nizan's had been on Epicurus); the non-Communists said of him, as they did of Nizan: 'He's the only intelligent Marxist of the lot, the only one you can talk to.' Having thus made it clear

---

1. *The Mandarins* presents an extremely fictional account of this incident, quite remote from the facts; I even went so far as to use the supposition that French intellectuals had discovered the extent of the concentration camp phenomenon in the U.S.S.R. as early as 1946. It was permissible since the evidence was available, but it was simply an imaginative gesture.

2. The figure is doubtful; so is the number of years that the deported spent in the camps (it was often five years), and equally so the number of deaths and even the meaning and purpose of the phenomenon. Today the Russians consider it as one of Stalin's 'bloody crimes' and do not minimize it; but their appraisals vary.

whom the character represented, without possibility of mistake, Aragon showed Orfilat–Nizan sobbing with fright, after the German-Soviet pact, at the idea of going to the front, and then going off to plead for a post at the Ministry of Foreign Affairs, where an honest liberal made him feel ashamed of his betrayal. The literary vacuity of this portrait did not in the least attenuate its perfidy. Elsa Triolet did her bit by launching 'the battle of the books'; in Marseilles, and then in the suburbs of Paris, the Communist writers gave lectures in which they praised their own merchandise to the skies and treated all 'bourgeois' writing as horse shit: Breton, Camus, Sartre.

The scandal of the slogans which erupted at the beginning of 1950 unmasked the real nature of what Beuve-Méry called 'The war of filth'. This was an affair which brought a great deal of profit to a very few people, but the war continued nonetheless. The victory of Mao Tse-tung had changed the situation. Recognized by China and the U.S.S.R., Ho Chi-minh emerged from the semi-neutrality with regard to the two blocs behind which he had sheltered up till then. The war in Indochina was henceforth presented by the French propaganda services as an episode in 'the anti-Communist crusade'. The West was shaking with fear because on 9 October 1949 General Bradley had announced that the day of the 'Red Atom' had arrived; the U.S.S.R. now possessed atomic bombs. There began to be talk of a new weapon much more powerful even than the atom bomb. In January 1950, on the orders of President Truman the H-bomb went into production. Its effects were described everywhere at great length; *Match* complacently demonstrated on a photograph what would happen if one fell on Paris: eighty square kilometres reduced to nothing. The fear it engendered became cosmic: flying saucers were seen in America and in France, sometimes in the sky, sometimes on the ground; some people had even seen Martians. The newspapers helped to maintain this state of panic. The only one we read with sympathy was *Combat*, but Bourdet resigned from it because Smadja, who was financing it, was trying to interfere with the editorial policy. After that, Rousset and Sérant were able to spread themselves out. Bourdet, supported by Stéphane, started *L'Observateur*; at that time it was only a tiny, boring weekly with very few readers.

I hadn't been away anywhere with Sartre the summer before, so we planned a trip for the spring. Leiris, an ethnographer whose speciality is Black Africa, suggested to Sartre that we go and see what was happening there for ourselves. The Europeans had tried, in vain, to repeal the Houphouet law voted by the Constituent Assembly in 1947 which suppressed forced labour. Having failed to achieve their ends by due process of law, they managed, on each payday, to provoke incidents that were disorganizing the system.[1] The R.D.A. was attempting, through the unions, to protect the small African producers; but the large trading companies were putting pressure on the administration to oppose it. There had been a reign of terror on the Ivory Coast since December of 1949. Many of the R.D.A. leaders had been arrested, tortured or shot down; members of the group, sympathizers and people suspected of sympathizing with it had been massacred or thrown into prison; in February, there were fresh outbreaks whose repression resulted in – officially – twelve people being killed and sixty wounded. To make contact with the R.D.A. and to find out and publish the facts would be a useful piece of work. This project was not favoured – as Leiris discovered while he was trying to get it going – by the Communist Party, to which many of the R.D.A. leaders belonged; but we thought that these latter would be less intractable in the event than their French comrades. Because I wanted to see the Sahara, we devised a plan that would take us from Algiers to Hoggar, then to Gao, Timbuktu, Bobo-Dioulasso, and Bamako, where Sartre would be met by members of the R.D.A. and invited to the Ivory Coast. I rushed around the tourist agencies. The trucks going from Ghardaïa to Tamanrasset carried a few passengers in their cabs; I booked space for two.

This time – it was my third attempt – I managed to get from Algiers to Ghardaïa without a hitch. The town was worthy of my perseverance; it was a magnificently constructed Cubist painting; white and ochre rectangles, brushed with blue by the bright light, were piled on each other to form a pyramid; at the top of the hill was stuck, slightly awry, a piece of yellow earthenware that might that moment have sprung – gigantic, extravagant and superb – from the hands of Picasso: the mosque. The streets were teeming with merchants and merchandise: carrots, leeks and cabbages with skins so shiny that they seemed more like fruit than vegetables.

1. Colonel Lacheroy played a large role in the provocations and the 'repressions' of January 1949.

[215]

Plump, with a look of deep repose, the Mozabites seemed to be very well fed; most of the grocers in Algeria had come from the M'Zab, and returned there once their fortunes had been made. Up above, in the main square, tanned and wiry-looking men from the desert were busy among their kneeling camels.

We liked the hotel and stayed several days; there was a big patio with a gallery running around it giving access to all the rooms; I worked on the terrace in the mornings; towards eleven, the sky would begin to flame and I would retreat into the shade. In the afternoons we went to see some of the other Mozabite towns near Ghardaïa, more provincial but quite as beautiful: Bénis-Isguen, Melika. We wished we could paint; it would have been a good excuse to stay there for hours looking at them. Some officers asked Sartre to give a lecture and he accepted. We were opposed to the colonialist system, but we had no *a priori* prejudices against the men who administered native affairs or supervised the construction of the roads.

I was very excited when I climbed at dawn into the cab of our first truck; even when one is travelling, a real beginning is rare. I had never forgotten the great orange moon behind Aegina, at the moment when our little boat left the Piraeus for the islands. That morning, when the truck had climbed above the cliff that dominates the valley, an enormous redcurrant rose out of the earth: a sun as simple as a childhood memory. Sartre watched it with the same jubilation as myself. In the sky shone, marvellously fresh and still untouched, all the joys we were setting out to reap together. That sun too is inlaid in my memory like a blazon of bygone happiness.

Five miles farther on, we passed two young Germans wearing white caps and sitting on a great pile of luggage under a murderous sun; they were hitchhiking. 'They're mad!' said the driver. The truck was loaded with goods and people, there wasn't room to squeeze in a hummingbird; the road was quite likely to remain deserted the whole day; if by some chance a car did pass, it would certainly be packed to the bursting point. In the Sahara the unforeseen is so strictly limited that there is no margin left for adventure; yet such madmen abound, the driver told us.

We ate lunch in a *bordj* and had two flat tyres; they were both very pleasant stops. The Arabs jumped down from the truck, pulled up some of the thornbrush between the rocks and in the wink of an eye had a fire going and a kettle simmering over it; the water, which they got from a skin bottle hanging on the side of the truck, smelled a bit greasy, but the tea they offered us in painted glasses was excellent. As soon as the wheel had been changed they stamped the fire out and whisked all their apparatus out of sight as if by magic.

The day stretched on over two hundred miles. Three more days, exactly the same, brought us to Tamanrasset, with two stops of twenty-four hours each at El Goléa and In-Salah. To us, the time never seemed long; we were learning a whole new world. First of all there was the road. We discovered with surprise that it was really only an ideal axis around which the navigable track meandered; there were labourers working on it and steamrollers rolling it, but we never drove on it: either it had just been resurfaced for a stretch of several miles and we mustn't spoil it; or else – most of the time – it hadn't been resurfaced, in which case it was so full of crevices, so bumpy, patchy, wavy, lumpy and full of holes that the sturdiest vehicle would have been jolted to bits in five minutes. All of which did not prevent the military engineers from expending an enormous amount of energy and zeal on these six hundred miles, or the 'road' from constituting an object of pride. '*La route, c'est moi*,' we were told successively by the Commandant of El Goléa, who was director of the operation as a whole, by scattered officers who were in charge of particular sections, by engineers who had done the surveying and planning, by contractors and even by one or two foremen. Only the labourers had nothing to say; we came into close contact with one team – one of them having just been bitten by a snake – but they had no boasts to make.

Except when we crossed a *hammada* the colour of anthracite, in which there was literally nothing to be seen – as we were coming out of El Goléa – the Sahara was a spectacle as alive as the sea. The tints of the dunes changed according to the time of day and the angle of the light: golden as apricots from far off, when we drove close to them they turned to freshly made butter; behind us they grew pink; from sand to rock, the materials of which the desert was made varied as much as its tints; sinuous or sharp-edged, their forms produced an infinity of modulations within the deceptive monotony of the *erg*. From time to time we would see a mirage shimmering with metallic lights, it would become still, then vanish into thin air; sand storms would arise, swirling wildly upon themselves, lonely vortices unable to shake the stillness of the world.

We passed two or three caravans. The desert was becoming huger around us, measured by the swinging steps of camels; at least the number of men and beasts and the amount of the loads was in keeping with its size. But where did he come from, where was he going, that man who suddenly appeared from nowhere, walking along with great strides? We followed him with our eyes until he was completely swallowed up again by the great absence that enveloped us.

During the last days of the journey we drove through gorges, beneath giant citadels with battlements and Cyclopean walls black as lava; we crossed plateaux of white sand stuck full of needles and bristling with black lace: the atmosphere had been blown away, and our Earth had changed into a moon. 'Incredible!' we said to each other; and yet a painting or even a photograph of that landscape would have astonished us even more. We were in it, therefore it became natural; the fantastic can exist only in images: once embodied it is destroyed. That's why it is difficult to tell about one's journeys; the reader is taken either too far or not far enough.

Thirsty, dusty, stunned and slightly paralysed, it was pleasant to arrive in the evening, no matter where it was we stopped. At El Goléa, when I went into the hotel with its profusion of patterned carpets, its brass lanterns and all its Sahara bric-à-brac, it seemed like a palace from the Arabian Nights. On the lawn, some Americans had organized a big *méchoui* in honour of Shell. I was jolted back to my own century. In the morning we walked through the town and saw the market and the old slave quarter where the Negroes still live. We had lunch with the head of the engineers. His wife, who was one of our readers, had come to invite us herself; she gave us a French lunch with fresh spring vegetables, and her husband told us about 'his road'.

At In-Salah, Sartre shut himself in his room to work as soon as we got out of the truck; I walked across the dunes, which were fringed with reeds (or, perhaps frayed palms); evening was coming on; the sand I lay down on was as soft as flesh; I almost expected to feel it move beneath my cheek. Along a path I saw tall Negro women passing in single file, draped in blue with their faces uncovered; golden rings swung from their ears. They were coming back from the fields, they did not speak and their bare feet made no sound; in the still of the falling dark, there was something touching in that quiet cortège. I was also moved when I leaned out of my window the following morning; it overlooked a vast square – or rather a stretch of wasteland – across which men and women were moving, quickly, slowly, each absorbed in his or her own progress; I had seen paintings which expressed the maleficent quality of space that separates even as it unites. But in that moment I seemed to surprise it at work in life itself. The houses of In-Salah were made of red earth with battlements; they had been half swallowed up by the sand, despite the barriers and obstacles put up across the streets. In the market I again saw beautiful black women swathed in blue.

Our last stop was only for one night, in the depths of the Arak gorges, at the foot of a black granite fortress; there was a travellers' hut where we found beds, but nothing to eat; two young men were camping out on the terrace and their radio was playing music from another world. They were travelling in a jeep, without an escort, though the rule is that no vehicle has the right to risk travelling alone along the desert tracks. 'It's dangerous,' our driver told us. He was our third, because we had made two stop-overs during our journey, and more loquacious than his predecessors, though sharing their conviction that all tourists are mad. He pointed to the framework of an automobile lying by the side of the track. 'Cross the Sahara in that! It caught fire from spontaneous combustion!' According to him, the heat of the sun had been sufficient to send it up in flames. He told us more stories while we ate lunch in the shade of a thorny bush, the only one we encountered on the whole journey; there wasn't enough shade to cover more than half our heads, but there was water nearby and grass growing as fresh and as green as a Normandy meadow. 'As soon as the rain comes everything is covered with grass and flowers,' the driver told us; he added that the rain came very rarely, but that when it did it was usually torrential. One or two years before, a Dodge had been immobilized by one of these storms; the official period of delay having elapsed, he was sent in his truck to rescue it; at last he saw the car, lost like an Ark amid the waves; but then, before he reached it, he too was caught and held fast by the mud. At first no one was apprehensive when he did not return; in this way he and the tourists spent, they a week and he five days, without food or water other than the muddied water of the flood. As he was talking, a soldier was throwing empty food cans into the air and shooting at them with a distracted air; he in his turn recounted sombre dramas of the desert; our fellow travellers, the people we met by chance when we stopped, were all full of extraordinary and terrible stories, and they all discounted the ones we had already heard: 'I know the man who told you that, he's crazy,' they would say; and then they would assure us that their own stories were guaranteed to be one hundred per cent true. There must have been some that were true out of so many; but which ones?

The evening came when we had finished this first lap of our journey. We arrived at Tamanrasset and the little hotel of the S.A.T.T. It was impossible to choose any other: the S.A.T.T. had a monopoly on the transport and lodging of tourists; moreover, on the pretext of guaranteeing their rescue, should the need arise, they demanded large sums from independent travellers as security. I had often heard protests against these privileges; at Tamanrasset, it was whispered that the lack of any competition encouraged the hotel-keeper to behave like a potentate. Always laughing, with bright snapping eyes, he did indeed seem very confident of his rights; but his hotel, though a terrible barracks of a place, was well run and kept well provisioned by truck and plane. 'At Christmas we had oysters. One of the pilots brought them straight from the sea!' he told us proudly. Everything considered, it was an ideal holiday resort. Because it was more than 5,000 feet above sea level, the mornings were temperate enough for me to work in the garden, facing the black, deforested mass of the Hoggar; there were strips of camel meat hanging from the trees to dry and I was secretly grateful that they didn't serve it to their customers. We had no desire to go climbing up the mountain; it would have been a full-scale expedition, with guides and camels. We contented ourselves with a few automobile rides and the magnificent sunsets that bathed the inky mountains in their light.

The society of Tamanrasset was very closed; the wives of the officers and civil servants lived as though they were at Romorantin; they wore hats, kept tabs on each other and gossiped. We discovered that we were not viewed with favour. A captain bestowed a short visit on us and left it at that. But we were lucky enough to be taken in hand by the teachers, Monsieur and Madame B., and by the explorer Henri Lhote. Mme and M. B. had both French and Tuareg pupils; the latter, they told us, were intelligent but nervous and unstable, and their parents only sent them to class at irregular intervals. In certain villages, at a two or three days' walk in the mountains, the children received no instruction at all; a mobile classroom had been started: at that very moment there was a teacher camping out up in the highlands.

Henri Lhote was searching through the Hoggar for cave paintings and sculptures; he had already amassed a vast collection of photographs and sketches whose authenticity was being somewhat contested at the time. His stories also aroused a certain amount of scepticism. He had narrowly escaped death a hundred times in the course of the most dramatic and extravagant series of events; one day, for example, almost dead with thirst, he reached the edge of a well at the bottom of which he could see the light glinting on a bit of water: the rope tied to the bucket was too short! He twisted an extra length from his clothes and went on, his thirst assuaged, naked across the *erg*; one couldn't help wondering why he hadn't been burned to death by the sun. But it didn't particularly matter; his inventions had a lyric quality that enchanted us.

When we went to visit B. and his wife, we constantly met several tall boys wearing veils who were there playing cards, chatting or dozing: the sons of the Amenokal, their cousins and their friends; they came there as though it were a club; apart from one or two brothels where they found some amusement in the evenings, Tamanrasset had no other distractions to offer them. Now that their wars and raids were forbidden them and they were no longer allowed to exploit slave labour, this warrior people was simply dragging out an empty and almost poverty-stricken existence with all their former occupations gone. Their principal resources were raising sheep and, above all, the salt mines of Amadror, not far from Tamanrasset. From July to September, they came in great numbers from the villages and hewed out the salt with axes. From October to February, they rode in caravans up to the Sudan, where they exchanged their merchandise for millet and manufactured articles. But such trade was beneath the dignity of the great chiefs and their families. I bought some camels made of braided string from Mme B.: 'The eldest son of the Amenokal makes them,' she told me. 'It brings him in a bit of pocket money, but he couldn't bear anyone to know about it.' In the old days the chiefs stuffed their wives with food to such an extent that they needed the help of several servants when they wanted to penetrate one of these lumps of fat. But those days were long past. 'Take a pound of tea,' B. told us when he and his wife drove us out to see the Amenokal; such visits represented for him a by no means negligible source of income. His tent stood among several others about eight miles outside the town; hung with carpets, furnished with coffers, it was luxurious enough, but too small to hold us all; we sat outside around a fire that didn't keep us very warm. Even with blankets thrown around our shoulders, we shivered as we drank our tea; but I enjoyed the strangeness of being there, under those new stars, in this encampment that was really so far away from me in space and time. Freed from the slavery of past opulence, thin, nervous, her face proud and hard, the wife of the Amenokal managed the reception with authority and courtesy; she was in fact, we were told, the real chief. As we left, Mme B. swept the infinitude of the desert with her hand. 'You see what sort of life they have, those boys!' And indeed few people I have seen seemed to me less adapted to the world of today than those young princes, proud and stony broke. They were so impressive in their indigo robes, their sombre eyes glittering above their veils. One afternoon, Mme B. asked one of the Amenokal's sons to uncover his face: 'There's a good boy, take off your veil, just for a moment, Chéri.' (Chéri was his real name, and it was strange to hear this woman quite calmly coaxing him: Chéri, Chéri . . .) He shrugged, laughed, drew away the cloth. His face was disfigured by a great nose like an eagle's beak; every time I caught a glimpse of a Tuareg's face I recognized this same nose, the same disappointing homeliness beneath the dark brilliance of the eyes. The women were luckier. Though it wasn't very easy to get to meet them; the only way Henri Lhote could think of in the end was to invite all the prostitutes of the neighbourhood one evening; most of them were being treated for syphilis at the hospital; he got permission for them to be released for a few hours, and we all sat on a carpet in the school garden and drank tea together.

We spent more than a week at Tamanrassett; we were kept informed of all the gossip circulating between Laghouat and the Hoggar. The Europeans scattered along the more than six hundred miles of the road, surrounded by spaces of dizzying immensity, knew each other, spied on each other, loathed each other, slandered each other, and bickered with each other with all the enthusiasm and attention to detail one would have expected in a small provincial town. All this 'long-distance' chatter was fascinating to us; the night before we left it kept me up very late. After dinner we went up on a roof to see the Southern Cross. Then Sartre went off to bed. I stayed up and stood at the bar drinking and joking with the hotel-keeper and two truck drivers, one of whom was as blond and handsome as Jean Marais at twenty. They talked about the people I had met along the road from Ghardaïa, and in particular about an ex-convict who gave truck drivers very good free bed and board as long as 'the rest' was included; each one gaily accused the other of having profited from this generous offer. Then they began to tell the story of their lives. The stories were interesting and I wasn't bothered by the coarseness of their language; I am perfectly able to use their vocabulary myself when the need arises. We all bought several rounds, the hotel-keeper included, and at about three in the morning I went up to bed still laughing. I was stupefied to hear someone opening my door; it was our host, who came over and propositioned me in a whisper. I was all the more astonished in that his wife did not look at all like a woman with a tolerant disposition. The following morning, he rushed up to me with a wide smile and a basket of oranges. They were a fruit rarely seen in Tamanrasset, so I realized that he was trying to buy my silence. It was a deal; I'd had no intention of making a fuss anyway. He then talked, not about his attempts at seduction, but about my own alcoholic and verbal debauch: opening *Samedi-Soir* several days later, I came across an account of our drinking bout. I read that my trooper's vocabulary had made the truck drivers blush; then there were other kind words that have slipped my mind,[1] but that made me rather uneasy at the time. Since Sartre and I were so closely linked, any filth thrown on me was always intended for him as well; I blamed myself for having provided the opportunity. But did that mean that I must live perpetually on the defensive and calculate every word I spoke and every drink I took? 'The advantage of our position,' Sartre said to me, 'is that we can do whatever we want: it will never be worse than what they say we do.'

A three-hour flight; from above, the diversity of the Sahara was flattened out. It seemed monotonous, but uniformity, so insipid when it indicates the repetition of human effort, fascinates me when I see in it one of the original aspects of our planet; perpetual snows,

1. The article did not appear in the Paris edition. It exceeded in its vileness even the low standards *Samedi-Soir* set for itself.

a sky of flawless blue, a plain of clouds seen from the cockpit, a desert. During the whole journey I riveted my eyes on the redness of the sun. I was not blasé; flying over the Niger seemed to me like a miracle; it was a wide road of grey water, but as the plane wheeled and came down, I caught sight of an island the colour of pale coral opposite a golden beach of sand; at that point the river was made of blue enamel. 'Oh how lucky,' I thought to myself, 'to be alive to-day and not at any other time, and see these things with my own eyes!' But I found the ground itself disappointing; it was no longer pure mineral; it was made messy by clumps of lank grass and sour-looking little bushes. As I stepped from the plane onto the asphalt, the sun hit me on the head like a mallet; we took refuge under a hangar. Yet the sky was as grey as the river. They had warned us: 'Down there, it's never blue; it's like being under glass.' A canopy of vapour filtered the sunlight without lessening the violence of its attack. As we got out of the bus at the hotel, our hostess exclaimed: 'But you must have helmets, you'll be dead by this evening!' Despite our dislike of tourist gear, we walked off to the bazaar she pointed out to us; even crossing those few yards of street we felt as though we were going to collapse. In the shade, the temperature was 104 degrees. 'It's bearable here because it's dry,' people told us; it was certainly dry, but it didn't seem all that bearable. According to our original plans, we should have arrived at Gao three weeks earlier, but Sartre had been detained and we had thought: 'What are three weeks more or less?' Actually, in this place those three weeks mattered: water traffic on the Niger had just stopped for several months.

Duly helmeted, we took a walk through the market on the main square just in front of the hotel. Suddenly, at long last, instead of the veiled phantoms that haunt the Arab towns, there were women. Beautiful Negro women, swathed in brilliant cotton stuffs, their hair piled up in complicated structures of twisted braids, displayed their faces, their shoulders, their breasts, their smiles and their laughter; the young ones, with tawny skins and glistening white teeth, stood resplendent; the textured, dry nudity of the old women had nothing offensive about it; they chattered among themselves and argued with the men. And there was such variety, so many different types, so many different ways of dressing! There were the Peuhls, both sexes so beautiful with their finely cut profiles, the graceful carriage of their heads and the slimness of their waists; the women wore ornaments around their necks, their wrists and in their hair, made of the little cowrie shells that also serve as money. Some of the Negroes wore lurid *boubous*, others were in shorts, with felt hats and sunshades. A few Tuaregs, draped and veiled in blue, wandered through the crowd. Gao was a meeting place of many tribes on market day, and the population was extremely mixed; such variety gave an impression of luxuriance. The impression faded however when we became aware of the poverty of the merchandise being exchanged: poor quality bread, pitiful stuffs, tinplate. In this district, as we were informed later, the natives have almost nothing; even grain has to be distributed to them, otherwise they would have nothing to eat.

The town was built of mud in the Sudanese style; cube-like houses stuck one against the other along narrow alleys. The big attraction was the Niger. We went to look at it at about five in the evening. Flat as a lake, wan, it was bathed in a false dusk that reminded me of the light in Abisko at midnight; we went along it in a pirogue; it might well have been a landscape in Scandinavia, except for the feeling of anguish you only find in hot countries. A whole nation of people was encamped along its banks; they were lighting fires, cooking, getting ready for the night. We went back early in the morning and saw them waking up. Tuaregs, holding mirrors, coquettishly scrutinized their unveiled faces; as we approached they hurriedly replaced their veils. How long were they going to stay here on these banks? How did they live?

The misery and the gaiety of Gao disconcerted us. Roaming through the streets in the afternoon, we heard a tom-tom; we searched to find where the sound was coming from; we came to a courtyard full of laughter and songs: a wedding. There was a group of Negroes watching the festivities through the doorway from the street, and for a long time we watched with them, captivated by the exuberance of the dances and the voices.

To get to know the country a bit we would have had to know people there. We saw almost no one. We were invited over by a young geologist bored by geology; he entertained us on his roof, and we took tea with the Moslems from whom he rented his room; as we talked, I contemplated the town below me, and the undefined country around it, no longer the desert but not yet the savanna. He asked Sartre to look at his pictures: his father was a well-known artist, and he too would have liked to paint. He showed us his canvases, still very immature, but Sartre did not hesitate a moment. 'If you really want to paint, go ahead,' he told him. The young man has since followed that advice.

We had dinner at the home of the administrator; young and a bachelor, he had just lost a lioness he had lovingly raised from a cub. He had little to tell us about the natives, though he did say that their poverty was made even worse by their religion, which forbade those who lived on the banks of the river to eat fish; they were undernourished but did not fish. He placed an automobile at our disposal for the following day. We saw several wretched villages along the banks of the Niger. The countryside seemed to me decidedly unrewarding; its most interesting feature was the ant-hills bristling all over it; if you went to sleep in the shade of one, the driver assured us, you woke up without a stitch left on your body.

One of the places I had wanted to see most of all was Timbuktu, 250 miles from Gao. From Paris the distance had seemed trifling; even if there were no boats, there were sure to be trucks making the journey. I inquired about it and was simply laughed at for my pains: in the present heat, the track – rarely used at any season – was impassable. I resigned myself to this fact with an ease that surprised me. The same thing happened again several times later on; a place that had seemed to me, when we began our journey, the principal attraction of one of its stages, lost its importance when we got nearer to it. From afar, its name had symbolized a whole country; when we got there, the country had many other ways of showing itself to us. In the market at Gao, along the banks of the Niger, I had already seen embodied the images of Timbuktu that I had previously conjured up in my mind's eye.

Perhaps my regrets were also routed by fatigue: twelve hours in a truck under that sun – I hadn't the strength to want anything that much. The heat raged unchecked all day; at siesta time, the electric fan in our room merely stirred up the burning air, and we could not sleep a wink. The shower was a bucket that you tipped; the water fell all over you in one short-lived splash, and it was scarcely any cooler than the air. Towards evening, big birds that they called *gendarmes* began to preen themselves in the trees; they flew about and sang. But the heat scarcely subsided at all. Everyone slept outside; our beds, covered by mosquito netting, were installed in an isolated corner of the roof; I liked going to sleep under the stars, but the nights were so heavy we could scarcely bear the weight of a sheet on top of us. At about four in the morning, a light breeze would begin to catch the netting over us. 'Fair stands the wind for France,' I would think, mistily, and half in a dream I would float for a few minutes over the cool depths of a great lake; a gentle light made the sky opalescent, it was a delicious moment – the only one of the day; the sun soon became savage again. We would go down to our room; couples would be lying with closed eyes in the inner court, more united in sleep than in their daily lives. The last night at dinner, the adjutant and his wife had quarrelled bitterly; now her head was resting gently on her husband's naked shoulder.

Two days after our arrival, Sartre was suddenly prostrated by it all. I called the doctor: 'He's got a temperature of 104.' He prescribed quinine; whereupon Sartre stuffed himself so full of it that he lost his sense of balance and could neither see nor hear. He stayed in bed for two days. Our hostess shrugged. 'A temperature of 104! I get a temperature of 104 every week; it doesn't keep me from polishing the floors!' I managed to keep going, but I was suffering from a complaint as unpleasant as its name suggests: prickly heat. In the hollows of one's knees and elbows, and between the toes, the sweat begins to produce a sort of reddish lichen; it itches a great deal, but the main thing is not to touch it on any account: a scratch, the slightest infection, is enough to produce 'cro-cro', real wounds that can rapidly become running sores. I spent two pretty awful afternoons in a room with Sartre lying there more or less unconscious; at three o'clock, I sat down at my table and worked; what else was there to do? The shutters were closed; outside, a raging sirocco was thrashing among the trees; the darkness and the noise of the wind both suggested the idea of coolness, but the wind was made of flames, and the thermometer on the wall said 110 degrees.

As soon as Sartre could stand on his feet we would leave, we had decided. But at the Tourist Bureau I received an unpleasant shock. Planes only arrived and took off at very irregular intervals; it was impossible to give me a definite date of departure. I loathed the idea of being imprisoned in that furnace.

At last they told me that a plane was to leave the following day for Bobo-Dioulasso. Sartre's fever had abated, and we took it. I looked down nostalgically at the forest beneath us, and at the red roads we would never drive along. There was a short stop at

Ouagadougou. In the airport concourse, a Negro was selling lead figurines – tom-toms, witch doctors, antelopes. I bought an assortment.

'Bobo's unhealthy, it's so humid,' I had been told at Gao. However, when we left the plane I found the moisture in the air a relief. A man with a sallow, puffy face was waiting for us at the airport; in Gao, the people still had tanned, Sahara skins; here, all the faces looked like boiled fish – Bobo was a saucepan with the lid on, perpetually simmering. 'I'll take you to the hotel,' the man said, though we didn't know who he was, and he helped us into the car. He was an official who had come to meet us on behalf of the administration. We drove into the town. 'Bobo-Dioulasso's just like Normandy,' a friend had told me. And the countryside was, in fact, rolling and green, but it was a very suspicious-looking green and the smell of rotting earth was not the same as the smell of meadows in France; long, low, and thatched with dark straw, the houses made it plain that we were in the tropics; a few flowers made bright splashes in the gardens. Our guide deposited us in front of a hotel. Our room was not ready yet, and we sat down in the shade of the veranda on comfortable armchairs, opposite a little open-air dance floor. The assistant administrator, B., found us sitting there and passed on an invitation to dinner with his superior. Then he took us to a fairground around which all the different native districts rose in tiers; he pointed at one of them and said: 'That side's pretty bad; it's under the control of the R.D.A. Whatever you do, don't go walking there!' He didn't show us much. 'Let's go and have a drink before lunch,' he suggested. We went back to the airport, the bar of which was used by the European elite as a meeting place because it stood a few feet above the town and the heat was therefore supposedly less torrid. It seemed to me quite as overpowering as it was down below; the impression of relief I had felt for the first hour had now completely evaporated. Before lunch we took our suitcases up to our room: the same shower as at Gao; it smelled of disinfectant and felt like a steam room. We left the door to the courtyard open and went to lunch. A man we didn't know, a friendly planter from Guinea, came up and offered us an apéritif; we had already had a drink, but he insisted: 'You must drink a lot here!' and told us the story of a young woman, proud of her looks, who drank only very little so as to keep her figure; within a matter of weeks she was dead of dehydration; newborn children had to be watered from morning to night, or else they dried up and died. So we gulped down one or two glasses of black-currant syrup and water. During lunch a storm broke, brief but violent. When we got back to our room for our siesta, the beds were soaked; there were cockroaches coming out of the waste pipe in the shower and crawling all over the floor and ceiling. We fled and wandered around the native town. Steep *marigots*, running almost dry, split the hillsides from top to bottom. The women were doing their washing in the pools of water at the bottom of them, their children playing among the yellow rocks. But apart from these clefts, each district formed a compact and apparently hostile block; the houses presented walls unbroken by any window, and we passed almost no one in the alleys between. It was impossible to penetrate in any way without knowing the inhabitants. Our arrival had been reported in the local press, and Sartre had hoped we would find a message from the R.D.A. at the hotel; we didn't.

We ate dinner with the administrator, B., and his wife, a Creole girl from Martinique who was lamenting that her husband wanted to take her that summer to Paris, which she had never seen. 'It's so cold there!' she said in a frightened voice. 'It's hot in August,' I assured her. 'But August, that's nearly September; in September I'll catch a chill on my chest and it will kill me.' Sitting on the terrace after dinner, I searched the sky for the Southern Cross: 'They showed it to me at Gao.' 'It couldn't have been the real one; it's never the real one they show you.' B. told us about the last elections. 'I got the votes I needed,' he told us, with a wink that made it obvious he had no doubt of our complicity. We left them while it was still early and went for a drink with the planter at the illuminated dance hall; in front of the door, a dressed-up monkey was dancing about on the end of a chain. We were ready to drop with fatigue, but we had difficulty getting to sleep; Sartre barely closed his eyes all night: his bed was still wet, the jazz across the road deafened him, and above all he was frightened of the cockroaches that were trotting about on the ceiling. He spent the night reading a biography of Mme Roland.

In the morning, an automobile provided by the administrator took us into the forest. We visited a village and saw their fetish underneath a tree: a great ball stuck full of very dirty feathers. The women, dressed in loincloths, wore little bits of carved ivory fixed in their jaws by way of ornament (they made me think of the tooth I had pulled out of my own jaw one day); tall and vigorous, their hair smeared with cocoa butter and giving off the most nauseating smell, two of them were pounding grain in a mortar; on a stairway (some of the huts, wretched as they were, had two storeys) among a lot of other naked children, there was a little albino boy; his pale skin didn't look natural; it was as though the top layer had been scoured off with acid and what was left was insufficient to protect him. We were quite close to the town, and yet these people seemed lost in the depths of a forest where time had always stood still. As we left, we passed two young boys coming along the road on bicycles; they were dressed in European clothes, very smart-looking, and they too lived in the hamlet we had just left; in a few years those naked children would become adolescents adapted to this century. We would very much have liked to know how the young cyclists managed the business of belonging to those two worlds.

But to Sartre's great disappointment, we heard nothing from the R.D.A. that day either and were forced to content ourselves with questioning the white people we met at a cocktail party that was given for us. Sartre talked to two future administrators who were making a great display of their good intentions; when pressed a bit, however, it became apparent that they were already preparing to cut their ideas according to their situation. Our trip was becoming farcical and unpleasant. We had set out to make contact with the Negroes who were fighting against the administration; we hadn't met any, and furthermore we were being very honourably entertained by the administrators themselves. Perhaps we would be luckier at Bamako? We took a plane there that evening.

Sartre was coming down with a high fever again; he was shivering when we landed quite late at night. The principal hotel was full; they sent us to the station hotel; a young fellow grabbed Sartre's baggage and dragged him off with an air of authority, while another led me away with equal imperiousness in the opposite direction. I found myself alone, in a sort of cage, furnished with a chair and a pallet, that overlooked the station platforms. Fortunately there were very few trains going by, but on the other side of the wire screen that covered my window the air under the glass roof that covered the railroad tracks was heavy with smoke and soot; I had no idea of the number of Sartre's room and the thought of him lying ill in a prison like the one I was in was nightmarish; I spent an appalling night.

The next day Sartre had somewhat recovered, and the other hotel had saved us a room; there too we suffocated, despite the enormous electric fans, but at least we could sleep out on the balcony: it was an astonishing spectacle in the morning, that balcony piled with half-naked bodies. The food was good; they even gave us strawberries. But what made the stay really pleasant for us was the cordiality of the Air Force Commandant C. He had belonged to the Normandie–Niémen Squadron and spent some time in Moscow, with the result that he was completely without prejudice against left-wing writers; nor did we inspire him with very much curiosity. 'I was in Gao at the same time as you were,' he told Sartre. 'It was told: "Simone de Beauvoir's just arrived with Pierre Dac"; then I found out it was you afterwards. . . .' He hadn't particularly wanted to see us. But he cared very much about a young woman who read a great deal and who had urged him to come and talk to us. He called her Juju. She was a beautiful girl with a lively mind, and he was completely lost in admiration of her intelligence, culture and courage. She was married to an Air Force officer who was away from Bamako at the time. C. had a wife and children who were spending the summer at the seaside in Guinea. But it soon became apparent to us that they were both resolved to divorce and marry each other – which they did in fact shortly afterwards. When love enters into people whose hearts are not withered, it makes them want to love everyone. We reaped the benefit of this kindly predisposition in them and also of their astonishment, for they had expected, they later admitted to us, to encounter monsters and not human beings; they were censured for compromising themselves with us, but the reproaches they received simply created a further complicity between them.

Juju and C. both lived on the outskirts of the town in vast, almost identical houses, surrounded by verandas and equipped with absolutely the latest thing in bathrooms: the tiled floors and light furniture gave an impression of coolness. Juju had a tom-tom displayed on a table just like the one I had bought, only larger; she also had other, well-chosen pieces of native work. We took our apéritifs every evening on her terrace, and she showed us the site of the great ultra-modern hotel that was soon to be built. One of their friends, V. – also a flier – often came and drank with us; his vitality quite revived us. 'You get used to the climate quickly enough; when I get a high temperature, I hop into my jeep and go off and shoot a buffalo, that gets rid of the fever.' He admitted that the prickly heat was unpleasant; 'When you go to bed, you have to dive under the sheet right away,' and he gave a demonstration of an intrepid swimmer hurling himself into icy water. Big-game hunting – for buffalo and even lion – played a large part in their lives; Juju could shoot as well as a man; she often accompanied her men friends in their planes or on their expeditions in jeeps.

The first morning, we went out on our own, in a carriage, through the European part of the town – pretty enough with its old-fashioned colonial houses – and then through the native districts which we didn't get to see much of because the driver refused to stop. But after that we were always with our new friends. They took us to the market; the population of the town was less varied than at Gao, but the goods seemed more abundant and much gayer to the eye; the stuffs the women wore could be bought in profusion: muslins, made in Alsace, but printed in bold patterns that were at that time exclusive to Africa; I bought several rolls. In the evening, Commandant C. drove us in a jeep out to the Niger dam through a dull, thinly wooded landscape; on the road of red laterite I realized the truth of what I had always heard without giving it much credence: that an automobile can only withstand the corrugated surface if it goes more than 50 miles an hour; if it does less, it gets shaken to pieces. There were some Negro prisoners working on the side of the road, under the sur-veillance of armed guards; two of the prisoners, who were pointed out to us, were serving sentences for cannibalism. All their faces seemed to have been moulded into expressions of despair and hate.

Bamako and the surrounding district teems with frightful dis-eases. There are long worms that find their way through the skin on the soles of the feet and dig caves inside for themselves; to get them out, you have to get hold of one end and roll it tight around a matchstick; you give the matchstick a turn every day; it's no good trying to pull it out all at once because it would break and then you'd never get rid of it. We were also given descriptions of the horrors of elephantiasis and sleeping sickness. One of the most widespread scourges was leprosy, and there was a really enormous leper hospital at Bamako.

The doctor in charge of it received us very cordially. He talked to me about *The Second Sex*, which he approved of. We went with him through a big village: huts and markets where men with barrows were offering a variety of products for sale; this was where the lepers lived with their families, for the disease was no longer considered as fatally contagious; furthermore, if caught in its very early stage, it could easily be held in check. The doctor showed us the dispensary where the mild cases were treated; the only indication of the disease on a young Negro woman being given an injection by a male nurse was a slight discoloration on her right arm. 'She may live to be eighty without the disease making any further advance,' the doctor told us. To check the disease they also used chaulmoogra oil, an old Hindu remedy; but at that time *asiaticoside* had just been discovered, and it was hoped that it might prove to be a means of reversing the course of the disease and even of curing it altogether. However, there was a certain number of men and women who had only been hospitalized in the later stages of the malady and were in an advanced state of deterioration; we were taken into the dormitory where they were lying and I thought I would pass out, first because of the smell and then because of the 'lion' faces, the mouths that had become muzzles, the noses eaten away, the mutilated hands. 'Even these won't die as a direct cause of leprosy,' the doctor told us. 'Its progress is extremely slow, it's just that it weakens the organism; all it takes is a bout of flu and a leper will succumb to it.' There were enormous numbers of lepers in the bush, and quite a few walking about in Bamako; we had certainly walked past some in the market. But there was no risk of contamination unless one went out barefoot.

Commandant C. introduced us to one of his Negro friends: a very old doctor who gave Sartre a copy of a voluminous work on the native pharmacopoeia of the region. He didn't discuss politics with us. Every day Sartre waited impatiently for the R.D.A. to contact him; every day brought a fresh disappointment. This silence was obviously deliberate and consequently affected him all the more. After a last evening with Juju and C. in an open-air dance hall, we left for Dakar.

Dakar was part of my private mythology; it was *the* colony: men in white helmets, with yellow faces in the intolerable heat, drank whisky all day long until both their livers and their reason were undermined. People in Bamako thought of it as a haven of cool relief. 'In Dakar you can sleep under a sheet,' they told me nostalgically. Before we landed the pilot of our plane invited us into his cockpit and wheeled over the city so he could show us the port and the sea and the island of Gorée. We touched down, and for the first time since Tamanrasset I felt comfortable inside my skin: seventy-five degrees. We abandoned our helmets in the hotel and went out for a walk in the streets.

We saw no Negroes on the café terraces, no Negroes in the air-conditioned luxury restaurant where we ate lunch; officially, segregation didn't exist; society was split up in such a way economically that there was no need for it; no Negro, or almost none, could afford to frequent the places the whites went to. The European town was uninteresting and the coastline, which we went along for several miles in a taxi, just shabby, despite the splendour of the ocean: frail palms, huts without gaiety, the earth a mess of decayed and decaying vegetable matter. We found the island of Gorée charming, with its tawny, crumbling Portuguese fortress. But our interest was not really caught until the evening, when we went for a walk through the residential area; it was our first contact with natives who had become a proletariat. The muddy streets lined with straw huts had a countrified, village look about them, but they were wide and long and all at right angles to one another; the Negroes living in them were all workers; it evoked – paradoxically, it seemed to us – both the bush and Aubervilliers. We could not begin to imagine what was going on behind those faces, mostly handsome and calm, but closed. Like the boys we saw cycling back to the fetishist hamlet, these men belonged to two civilizations: how did they reconcile them inside themselves? We left Dakar without even beginning to know the answer. Our brief trip through Black Africa had been a failure. Back in Paris we were confirmed in our suspicions that heavy injunctions had been laid upon all the members of the R.D.A. and they had deliberately avoided meeting Sartre.

To recover from our weariness, and to work in peace, we spent two weeks in Morocco. We stopped for a while at Meknès and for a long time at Fez. This time it was spring, the trees were in bloom, the sky was light, and the Djalnai palace had opened its doors. They put me in the sultana's room, decorated with carpets and mosaics and opening onto a beautiful patio; I left my door open while I worked, and often visitors would come in and walk around my table as if I were an exhibit in a museum. The dining room had glass walls and looked out over all the whiteness of the town; we met Rousset there and exchanged unenthusiastic greetings.

Since June, my sister and her husband had been living in Casablanca; I spent a few days with them; we toured by car through the Middle Atlas and as far as Marrakesh where, beyond the red ramparts, I could see the high peaks, glistening with snow.

Boris Vian was fined 100,000 francs for having written *I Spit on Your Grave*. His books, and Sartre's as well, were being held responsible for a good many suicides, criminal offences, murders and the 'crime of the J3' in particular. When Michel Mourre got up into the pulpit of Notre-Dame, this 'sacrilege' too was imputed to the effects of Existentialism.

Sartre's thought, as I have said, was gradually stripping itself of all idealism; but he did not reject the existential postulates and continued to demand, within the realm of *praxis*, a synthesis of the two points of view. In a preface to Stéphane's *Portrait de l'aventurier*, he expressed the wish that the militant might inherit the virtues of those men whom Stéphane termed adventurers.

An action has two aspects: there is the negative aspect that belongs to the adventurer and the constructive aspect that comes from discipline. Negativity, doubt and self-criticism must be re-established within the framework of discipline.

A similar concern inspired the essay he wrote introducing Dalmas' book on Yugoslavia. Stalinist objectivism, he said, annuls the subjectiveness of his opponents by presenting them to the world, often on their own admission, as objective traitors. The case of Tito was unique: he had succeeded and therefore made it impossible for Stalin to recoup his losses in this way. His opposition effectively replaced subjectivism as a force within the Revolution. A truly revolutionary ideology would have to take as its task, in opposition to Stalinism, the reinstatement of subjectivity in its proper place.

Tito was the *bête noire* of the Communists. They had insulted Bourdet, Mounier, Cassou and Domenach, who had spoken out on his behalf, and the last two had even been excluded from the Peace Movement. Sartre's preface provided the Communists with a new grievance. He really didn't have much luck with them. He thought his discussions with Thao so feeble that he opposed their publication; Thao, taking advantage of the bourgeois legal system without the slightest embarrassment, filed a suit against him, and Domarchi, who had sat in on the conversations without opening his mouth except to agree with Thao, joined with the latter in demanding a million francs in damages. The recent trials, the work camps, had so set us against Stalinism that we refused – and we were in the wrong – to have anything to do with the Stockholm Appeal, for which eight million signatures were collected throughout France in the last weeks of June. Yet we were still sickened by 'the West'; we learned with regret that Silone was participating, side by side with Koestler, in the congress 'for the defence of culture' which had been convened in Berlin under the aegis of the *Liberté de l'esprit* movement.

Sartre also had personal troubles. In 1949, he had taken a trip with M. to Mexico and Guatemala, and had also visited Cuba, Panama, Haiti and Curaçao. They were not getting on well any more. Despite Sartre's opposition she had come to live in Paris. They quarrelled and eventually separated.

Algren and I had kept up our correspondence throughout the past year. He had changed his tune since his return to America; the country was changing, very fast. The witch-hunt was affecting a great number of his friends. In Hollywood, which he had visited as a result of winning the National Book Award, all the left-wing film makers were out – many were emigrating to Europe; John Garfield was unable to play the lead in *The Man with the Golden Arm*. On his return from California, Algren had bought a house on Lake Michigan; we were to spend two months there together. For me the idea of having a real life with him was a great happiness.

Just as I was about to catch my plane, the North Koreans penetrated South Korea; immediately the American Air Force and then the American Army intervened. If China attacked Formosa, a world war would break out; the Stockholm Appeal collected three million additional signatures in just a few days. Everyone was talking about France being occupied by the Red Army. *Samedi-Soir* chose as its headline: SHOULD WE BE AFRAID? and concluded that we should. Despite my desire to see Algren and my repugnance at letting him down once again, I hesitated a great deal before leaving France. 'Go,' Sartre told me, 'you can always come back. I don't believe there's going to be a war.' He gave me the arguments that he then repeated in a letter I received during August; in Paris there was panic, gold had soared from 3,500 francs to 4,200, people were queuing outside all the grocers to lay in stocks of canned food and sugar, and everyone was expecting the Red Army to arrive any day, then the bombs. But Sartre still continued to reassure me.

In any case, here is my opinion: A *bloody* war is impossible. The Russians haven't got the atomic bombs and the Americans haven't got the soldiers. Thus it cannot take place, mathematically, until a few years from now. So that leaves us with the fact that both will now, also mathematically, prepare for it. So in the end it comes to the same thing. Either some clumsy move on one side or the other will cause war to be declared without its being a real war: in that case the Soviet troops will come as far as Brest and we get three to five years before we're up against it; or else everyone will wait and arm themselves while they do so: which will result in the mythological spirit of war pervading the whole world, in censorship, espionitis, Manichaeism and, if you like to put it that way, camouflaged occupation by the Americans. If it comes to choice, I believe in the second hypothesis. . . .

I did leave, but with a heart so full of anxiety that it made the sadness of my arrival in America even harder to bear. My first days in Chicago were very much like those Anne spent with Lewis in *The Mandarins* when they meet for the last time. For a whole year Algren had been writing me gay and tender letters; now suddenly he was telling me that he didn't love me any more. 'We'll have a nice summer together, all the same,' he assured me with deliberate thoughtlessness. And the next day he took me to the races with a lot of people I didn't know. I wandered through the crowd of strangers gulping down one drink after another. I had no intention of going back to France, unless there were suddenly some immediate danger. First of all I had to understand with my heart and my body words that I had not yet succeeded in even getting through my head; what a dreary task ahead! It was already enough of an effort to stitch all the little bits of time together. In the little house on Wabansia Avenue, the combination of the stifling heat and Algren's presence suffocated me. I went out: the streets were hostile. At a little hairdresser's in the Polish neighbourhood, the girl who washed my hair asked me in a severe tone: 'Why are you all Communists in France?' A French-woman equalled someone suspect, ungrateful, almost an enemy.

And then, outside, I felt I was melting like the tar on the roads; in American bars one can neither read nor weep. I literally didn't know what to do with myself.

Finally a friend drove us to Miller and gradually time began to resume its flow once more; my days had a routine, and that did me good. I slept in a room of my own, I worked there, beside the window protected by a wire screen; or else, having sprayed myself with 'insect repellent' to keep the mosquitoes away, I lay down in the grass with Sandburg's *Lincoln*; I read a lot of books on American literature and history; and Fitzgerald's heartrending *The Crack-up*; and also science-fiction stories, often disappointing but sometimes casting disquieting lights on the world today. The garden sloped down to a lagoon, and tall hedges on either side protected me from prying eyes; big, grey squirrels ran and jumped around me, and birds sang. Towards noon, we would cross the lagoon in a boat and scramble up and down over the dunes which burned our feet; then we'd get to Lake Michigan, wide and full of movement as the sea. There would be no one else on the sandy, endless beach, only white birds perched high on tall legs and pecking at the sand. I bathed and sunned myself. In the water I took great care not to lose my footing because I could barely swim. But one day, after a few tentative breast strokes, I put my foot down to find the bottom and couldn't; I panicked and sank; I called to Algren, who just smiled at me from a long way off; I called out more explicitly: 'Help!' He still smiled, but all the same my gurglings did worry him in the end; when he did get hold of me, my head was already under the water and my face was wearing, or so he told me, a completely idiotic grin; he added that he had been very frightened, because he was a very poor swimmer too. We returned home on the double, drank a few shots of whisky and, in the euphoria produced by this dramatic rescue, friendship flamed into life between us as vividly as if it had been scoured completely free from the scar tissue of our lost love.

It had its pleasant moments; at night we would walk along the beach; in the distance the tall furnaces of Gary spat out their flames; a great reddish moon hung reflected in the lake, and we talked idly about the beginning of the world or about its end; or else we would watch television: newsreels of famous boxing matches that Algren would explain to me, old films and on Saturday nights an excellent variety show. But quite often, without apparent reason – perhaps because he feared that one of us might be deceived by this apparent harmony – Algren's face would close up; he would move away and fall silent. One day, we had been to the races again with a friend, I had been bored; on the way back the radio in the car announced noisily that war was imminent. To have cut myself off from France in order to live through this private disaster suddenly seemed odious and absurd; so much so that I began to sob. 'It's just propaganda, it doesn't mean anything,' said Algren, who didn't believe in the war. But I had fallen to the bottom of an abyss from which it took me several hours to escape. Another evening Algren went to Chicago: I loved and feared the implacable silence of those days spent on my own; since morning I had mulled over many desolate thoughts before I finally sat down in front of the television screen. They were showing *Brief Encounter*, and I soaked the cushions with my tears.

After a month, Lise came to Miller. I had seen her again in 1947; as in the old days, we had fought a lot but also got on very well together. We fell into each other's arms. She had kept all her beauty and baroque sharpness; in the conventional world in which she lived, her behaviour, which she had refused to correct, got her into all sorts of scrapes that she recounted very amusingly; however, our meeting was darkened by several shadows. Algren had balked at the idea of having a strange woman in his house, and in any case it was too small; he had found Lise a room about five hundred yards away, and that irritated her. She decided to stay for two weeks; I was going back to France in a month, and because of the very difficulty in my relations with Algren I felt the need to be alone with him. Against Lise's frankness I had always had only one weapon – an equal frankness on my part; I used it, and she called me once again 'a clock in a refrigerator'. Despite her coaxing and exuberant manner, Algren found Lise cold; he said she always looked as though she expected him to walk upside down or something; and indeed Lise's natural attitude was one of ironic defiance; to win her over one had to distinguish oneself by some feat or other. Algren even went so far as to tell me one morning that he was leaving for Chicago. We decided finally that it should be Lise and myself who would go there for two or three days.

Her feelings for me were ambivalent; in her opinion I had devoted less time to her during the war years than I ought to have done; she still had a grudge against me for having sacrificed her to my work, and this slight feeling of bitterness was directed against my work; she kept saying, indirectly but with transparent intention: 'It's such a sad thing to be a second-class writer!' This sullenness also reflected her own relation to writing; she wanted to write and she didn't want to write: 'What's the use when we're about to get a bomb on top of us?' The truth was that she was torn between the fact that she had a gift and the fact that she had no vocation; her talent showed itself in the short stories she had had published in magazines, and above all in her letters; she had the gift of concision and also that of choosing the wrong word with the happiest results; but alone in front of a sheaf of blank paper, her heart would sink; I think she wasn't interested enough in other people to have the patience to keep on talking to them page after page.

Her life wasn't going too well. She had come to the States because she was in love with a man and so she could eat; love had grown threadbare, and she was about to be divorced; she had got used to eating. There had been a time when she had hoped that motherhood would compensate for the misfortune of her early years, but that very misfortune had made her ill-suited to the care of a little girl with whom she identified herself both too much and too little. She was grateful to America for having taken her in, but she missed the sort of human and intellectual relationships she had been accustomed to in Paris. She was taking a teachers' training course; she was brilliant at her work, but many of her professors were put off by her aggressiveness. She was both disdainful and easily fascinated, and being cut off from people by the frostiness in her character that Algren had noticed, she would fling herself into the most complicated or impossible adventures. At that time she was obsessed by a pair of male homosexuals and very attached to Willy, the elder one; she was trying to convince him, in the name of Existentialism, that one cannot *be* homosexual: it was rather a question of a choice still reversible at any time. He was very fond of her, but that did not satisfy her. I recall a painful walk we took together through Chicago. I showed her Algren's house, my heart full of heavy memories, while she reiterated with all the scholastic passion of a medieval theologian her proof that Willy could demonstrate his liberty by loving her; one in silence, one aloud, we soliloquized through the heavy city heat, the streets stretching endlessly beneath our feet and neither of us advancing one step.

She left Miller ahead of me to go to Chicago, where Willy and his friend Bernard, who were travelling by car, had arranged to meet her. The morning I was supposed to go to join them the bus that was to take me to the station in Gary didn't arrive. Algren stopped a car on the road and put me in charge of the driver. As soon as he found out I was French, he began attacking me: 'Is it true that you're all Communists? Is it true that in France white women sleep with Negroes?' I pretended I didn't understand English. I rather liked Willy and Bernard but I found it difficult to accept the trio they made with Lise. They wanted to go to sleazy strip joints, and once there they would comment on all the details of the girls' nakedness with snickers that somehow betrayed a resentment against the whole of humanity.

I returned to Miller alone. Algren, who had seen his ex-wife a few months before in Hollywood, told me that he was thinking of remarrying her. So be it, I thought. By that time my despair had drained me of all feelings, and I could no longer react to anything. It was Indian summer by then; I walked around the lagoon, blinded by the beauty of the foliage, red-gold, green-gold, yellow-gold, copper and flame, my heart numbed, believing neither in what was past nor in whatever lay ahead. At brief moments I would come to and throw myself down on the grass. 'It's all over, oh why?' It was a childish distress, because, like a child, I was battering myself against the inexplicable.

We returned, briefly, to Chicago. To keep ourselves in countenance we spent the last afternoon at the races; Algren lost all his cash. So that we could eat dinner he telephoned a friend who came over and stayed with us until the moment we got into the cab taking us to the airport. Algren didn't seem to mind. Chicago glittered behind fine grey gauze, to me it had never seemed so beautiful. I walked like a somnambulist between the two men and thought: 'I'll never see it again. Never. . . .' In the plane, I stuffed myself with sleeping tablets once more and sat there sleepless, my throat torn with the pain of the cry that I was holding back.

Sartre was still reaping a rich harvest of insults. A certain Robichon, in *Liberté de l'esprit* announced that his pernicious influence must be forcibly prevented from making further inroads on our youth, which in any case – he told his readers in the same breath – paid no attention to Sartre whatever. 'Should we burn Sartre?' was the heading of an ironic rejoinder in *Combat*, where we still had a few friends. Sartre had printed several long extracts from his work on Genet in *Les Temps Modernes*; they had aroused interest. But what a fuss at the same time! Although a year earlier apropos of *Deathwatch*, Mauriac had recognized Genet's talent, he now wrote an article in *Figaro* frothing with indignation at what he called 'Excrementialism'. Also some of our friends were expressing astonishment that the magazine had so far not devoted a single article to the Korean War. *L'Observateur* deplored the fact that *Les Temps Modernes* was not coming to grips with the events of our time. Merleau-Ponty, who to all intents and purposes ran the magazine, had been converted to an a-political attitude by the Korean War itself: 'The cannons speak and silence now is all our part' was more or less the substance of his explanation to us.

Sartre's second hypothesis was now proving to be true: the Americans were secretly occupying France. They were helping De Lattre to stabilize the situation in Indochina after his serious setbacks there. In exchange, Pleven publicly endorsed the principle of re-arming Germany and consented to the establishment of American bases in France; when Eisenhower came over to establish his headquarters in Paris during January, the Communists demonstrated in vain. France was accepting the idea of a Europe supported by the Americans and pledged to fight for them. When Beuve-Méry once again defended the idea of neutralism, he merely got called 'emasculated' for his pains by Brisson. 'Is it simply a matter of having balls or not, then?' Beuve-Méry asked. Their argument got a great deal of publicity, but to no good purpose. When it was discovered that Gilson had accepted a chair at the University of Toronto, he was accused of abandoning his country to the Red invasion, and there was indignation at this 'preventive departure'.[1]

In fact there was a good deal of talk about a Russian occupation. After the crossing of the 36th parallel by the American troops, after the 'volunteer' Chinese Army entered North Korea and the American Air Force pounded Pyongyang, the United States announced that mobilization was imminent. MacArthur wanted to bomb China; in that case the Russians would intervene; in

1. Gabriel Marcel wrote a play about it!

America fifty million radiation-resistant identity discs were distributed for the purpose of identifying victims after an atomic attack. Truman declared a state of emergency. If war were to break out, the Red Army would invade Europe as far as Brest in next to no time; what then? 'The day the Russians march into Paris,' said Francine Camus – as we were coming out of a Communist-organized concert, during which we had heard some Bartók dances based on folk tunes – 'I shall kill myself and my two children.' In one lycée class, some teenagers, terrified by their parents' prophecies, made a collective suicide pact that would be effective in the event of a Russian occupation.

It didn't occur to me to wonder what I should do until the conversation we had with Camus at the Balzar: 'Have you thought about what will happen to you when the Russians get here?' he asked Sartre; and then added with a great deal of emotion: 'You mustn't stay!' 'And do you expect to leave?' asked Sartre. 'Oh, I'll do what I did during the German occupation.' It was Loustaunau-Lacau, always one for secret societies, who started the idea of 'armed and clandestine resistance'; but we no longer argued freely with Camus. He was too quickly carried away by anger, or at least by vehemence. Sartre's only objection was that he would never accept having to fight against the proletariat. 'You mustn't let the proletariat become a mystique,' Camus answered sharply; and he complained of the French workers' indifference to the Soviet labour camps. 'They've got trouble enough without worrying about what's going on in Siberia,' was Sartre's reply. 'All right,' said Camus, 'but all the same, they haven't exactly earned the Legion of Honour!' Strange words: Camus, like Sartre, had refused the Legion of Honour which their friends in power had wanted to give them in 1945. We felt a great distance between us. Yet it was with real warmth that he urged Sartre: 'You must leave. If you stay it won't be only your life they'll take, but your honour as well. They'll cart you off to a camp and you'll die. Then they'll say you're still alive, and they'll use your name to preach resignation and submission and treason; and people will believe them.' I was shaken by these words and in the days that followed I remembered Camus' arguments and used them myself. Perhaps they would leave Sartre alone, on condition that he keep quiet; but things would happen – that we could no longer doubt – about which he would not remain silent, and the way Stalin dealt with intractable intellectuals was common knowledge. During lunch one day at Lipp, I asked Merleau-Ponty what he thought he would do; he had no intention of leaving. Suzou turned to Sartre. 'A lot of people will feel disappointed if you leave,' she said with a mixture of innocence and deliberate provocation. 'Everyone's expecting you to commit suicide.' Another day, Stéphane begged Sartre: 'In any case, Sartre, promise me you'll never give in to them!' These heroic tableaux did not appeal to me at all, and I returned to the attack. An alliance with the Fascists against the French workers was out of the question; accepting everything equally impossible; and open opposition would be the equivalent of suicide. Sartre listened to me with a mulish look on his face; he rejected the idea of exile to the very marrow of his bones. Algren, now convinced that some headstrong action on the part of MacArthur might unleash a world war at any moment, invited us both to Miller. But we had never detested America more violently than we did at that moment. In August, Sartre had been disturbed – less so than Merleau-Ponty, but a little all the same – by the fact that the North Koreans had been the first to cross the border and that the Communist press had denied it. We now knew that they had walked into a trap; MacArthur had wanted this conflict, hoping to profit by it in order to hand China back to the Chinese lobby; and we also knew that the feudal leaders of South Korea had their eyes on the industrial power of the North. Manhunts, wholesale bombings, mopping-up operations – the American troops were waging a war as ferociously racist as that being carried on by our own troops in Indochina. If we were to leave, it would have to be for a neutral country. 'Just imagine what it would be like,' Sartre said, 'ending up in Brazil like Stefan Zweig!' He was convinced that by going into exile, no matter how good the reasons for doing so, one lost one's place in the world, and that one could never quite recover it again. And we were considering flight from a regime which was, in spite of everything, the embodiment of socialism! We were finding ourselves in the same boat as the people on the Right; and they weren't just wasting words on the subject, they were using their wealth and their connexions to make sure the necessary boats and planes would be ready for them. We had lunch with Clouzot and his wife Vera; she was dressed with studied casualness: black pants and top, a golden chain around her ankle, her magnificent hair cascading over her shoulders. André Gillois and his wife were there too; during the meal the conversation turned to the practical possibilities of leaving the country. Sartre could not accept being grouped with that camp. 'Between American ignominy and Communist fanaticism, we really don't know whether there's room left for us on earth any more,' I wrote my sister. Sartre was unable either to elude or to accept the now manifest fact that the Communists, by treating him as an enemy, were forcing him to act as though he actually was one. He never put much faith in the likelihood of a Russian occupation;[1] but envisaging it was enough to make him feel very sharply the paradoxical quality of our situation; the shock it inflicted on him played a great role in his subsequent development.

CHAPTER FIVE

My way of life had changed. I stayed at home a lot. The phrase itself had taken on a new meaning for me. For a long time I had had no possessions, neither furniture, nor wardrobe. Now in my closet there hung jackets and skirts from Guatemala, blouses from Mexico, a suit and more than one topcoat from the United States. My room was decorated with objects that were without value but precious to me: ostrich eggs from the Sahara, lead tom-toms, some drums that Sartre had brought back from Haiti, glass swords and Venetian mirrors that he had bought in the Rue Bonaparte, a plaster cast of his hands, Giacometti's lamps. I liked to work facing the window: the blue sky framed in the red curtains looked like one of Bérard's sets. I spent many evenings there with Sartre; I kept a stock of fruit juice for him, since he'd given up alcohol for the time being. And we listened to music. Since 1945, I had listened to Schönberg's *Ode to Napoleon* conducted by Leibowitz, and several other concerts, but really only very few and quite haphazardly. That winter Sartre and I heard *The Messiah*, and at his home we listened with his mother to a broadcast of Berg's *Wozzeck*.

1. 'These preparations did not cause me much alarm because I didn't believe in the invasion: to me they seemed no more than party games in which things were pushed as far as they would go and thus revealed to everyone the necessity of choosing and the consequent results of the choice so made. . . . Surrounded by these gloomy hallucinations, I felt cornered.' – *Merleau-Ponty vivant*.

I wanted a phonograph; I asked Vian's advice about what machine to buy and Sartre helped me assemble a little record library. He was interested in Schönberg, Berg and Webern; he had explained the principles of their music to me, but in France no recordings of their works were to be had. I bought some classics, some early music, Vivaldi's *Four Seasons* which all Paris was suddenly crazy about, a lot of Franck, Debussy, Ravel, Stravinsky and Bartók. The latter we had both discovered separately in America, where he was enjoying a great wave of popularity and at that time – especially his last quartets and the sonata for solo violin – he was the composer who moved us both the most. Also, on Vian's advice, I bought a lot of jazz: Charlie Parker, Ellington, Gillespie. Changing the record every five minutes, and the needle quite often too, what patience it took! And canned music at that time was a long way from being as fresh as the real thing. But it was pleasant to be able to organize my own concerts at home, with my own choice of programme and whenever it suited me.

On Christmas Eve, which brought Olga, Wanda, Bost, Michelle, Scipion and Sartre all together in my room, there was another attraction: a tape recorder that M. had left with Sartre. I recorded several conversations without telling anyone. Words are by nature birds of passage; everyone is dismayed to hear over again, fixed, defined and promoted as it were to the undeserved dignity of a poem, the disparate phrases he or she has unthinkingly thrown out. Scipion had delivered himself of certain impassioned expressions when discussing the charms of Colette Darfeuil (whom he did not know) which it gave him no little stupefaction to hear himself repeat.

I went to the movies now and then. I liked the starkness of Bresson's *Diary of a Country Priest*, and also, despite the abuse of certain surrealist reminiscences, the cruelty of Buñuel's *Los olvidados*. And *Casque d'Or* at last did justice to the beauty of Simone Signoret and revealed her talent to the world.

A new restaurant had recently opened where the old Procope used to be and had taken over the name – marble tables and leather banquettes; I liked it there. Upstairs there was a club where society people dined by candlelight. Below, one came across old inhabitants of the district, among others Louis Vallon, soused. He mumbled insults at me across the room; but then when he was finished he staggered over to talk to me, his eyes streaming with tears, about Colette Audry, whom he had loved before the war in the days when he was a Socialist. It was also at the Procope that I used to meet Antonina Vallentin for lunch every now and again, at least on those occasions when I didn't go over to her place during the afternoon. Badly dressed, in grotesque hats or draped in awful robes, I was amazed to see a photograph of her when she was young and beautiful; but her talent as a biographer was apparent in her conversation: she could talk extremely well about people. A friend of Stresemann's, she had known many politicians well and Einstein, about whom she was writing a book, intimately. She was also the author of works on Goya and Da Vinci which had both been great successes. She was on the staff of *Les Temps Modernes*, primarily as its art critic. We continued to see each other until August 1957, when she died of a heart attack.

Ever since he had taken over *Les Temps Modernes* from Gallimard, Julliard would occasionally invite us to lunch. His wife, the elegant Gisèle d'Assailly, enjoyed bringing together a group of well-known people who didn't always have much to say to each other; in this way we met Poulenc, Brianchon, Lucie and Edgar Faure, Maurice Chevalier and Jean Massin, a bearded priest who was still a believer but had left the Church; he used to say Mass in his bedroom; he explained his reasons for this and his problems. From time to time, Merleau-Ponty would stop him and say: 'You should write this down for *Les Temps Modernes*.' And each time he would reply gently: 'I couldn't care less about *Les Temps Modernes*.' Later he did cease to be a believer, married and collaborated with his wife in writing books of Marxist inspiration, some of which – on Mozart, Beethoven, Robespierre, Marat – are excellent.

Simone Berriau took me up to see Colette, whom she knew very well. When I was a young girl Colette had fascinated me. Like everyone else, I took great pleasure in her style and liked three or four of her books very much. 'It's a pity she doesn't like animals,' Cocteau had said to us one day; it is true that when she wrote about dogs or cats she was only writing about herself, and I preferred it when she did so openly; love, the wings of the music hall, Provence, these subjects suited her better than animals. Her self-satisfaction, her contempt for other women, her respect for a fixed set of values, none of these appealed to me. But she had lived, she had worked, and something in her face attracted me. I had been warned that she was not generally pleasant to women of my age and she received me coldly. 'Do you like animals?' 'No,' I replied. She stared me up and down with an Olympian gaze. I didn't mind; I hadn't expected any contact between us. It was enough for me to look at her. Crippled, her hair in a wild fuzz, startlingly made up, age gave her sharp face and her blue eyes the brilliance of lightning; surrounded by her collection of paperweights, silhouetted against the gardens framed by her windows, she appeared to me, paralysed and regal, like some awful Mother Goddess. When we had dinner with her and Cocteau at Simone Berriau's, Sartre too had the impression of approaching a '*monstre sacré*'. She had made the effort to leave her apartment mainly out of curiosity, because she wanted to see him, and knowing that she was the attraction of the evening for him; she assumed this role with an imperial good humour. She told anecdotes about her life and the people she had known; the vigorous Burgundy tones of her voice did nothing to blunt the pointedness of her wit. Colette's words flowed unimpeded from their source and, compared to this example of one of nature's great talkers, Cocteau's brilliance seemed dim and laboured.

We had dinner with Genet at Léonore Fini's; she had done a portrait of him; together they would go visiting millionaires whom they would urge, with more or less success, to become patrons of the arts. I found her drawings very interesting, her collection of cats less so; and even less still her stuffed mice that enacted a little scene beneath a glass dome.

A person I ran into quite often in Saint-Germain-des-Prés was the painter Wols. He had done illustrations for a text by Sartre, *Visages*; Paulhan would buy a drawing or a watercolour from him from time to time; we liked his work very much. Wols was a German who had been exiled in France for a very long time, he drank a litre of *marc* a day and looked quite old, despite the fact that he was only thirty-six and had blond hair and a rosy complexion; his eyes were always bloodshot and I don't think I saw him cold sober once. A few friends used to help him; Sartre got him a room at the Hôtel des Saints-Pères; the man who ran it complained that they would find him asleep in the corridors during the night and that he would bring friends home at five in the morning. One day I was having a drink with him on the terrace of the Rhumerie Martiniquaise; he was shabby, unshaven and looked like a tramp. A very well-dressed gentleman, very severe-looking and evidently wealthy, came over and spoke one or two words to him. When he had gone Wols turned to me. 'I'm sorry; that fellow is my brother:

a banker!' he said in the apologetic tones of a banker admitting that the bum he has just spoken to is his brother.

Barrault had once told Sartre the story of Cervantes' *Il rufio dichoso* in which a bandit decides to reform on a throw of the dice. At La Pouèze, Sartre began to write a play inspired by this episode though not without altering it: in his version the hero cheated in order to lose. Influenced by his study of Genet and by the reading he had been doing on the French Revolution, he wanted first of all to present an exhaustive picture of society: the nobility was embodied in a certain Dosia who gave him a great deal of trouble and was done away with to make room for Catherine and Hilda. He had finished the first act by the time we got back to Paris. Simone Berriau asked him to read it to Jouvet, whom she wanted to direct it. First of all we had the usual admirable dinner; Brandel told us that often, during Barrault's plays, he went to sleep in his box, hidden behind a pillar. When we had finished eating, Sartre began to read and Brandel to snore; his wife kept pinching him to keep him awake; Mirande too kept dozing off; Jouvet's face was like a death mask. When Sartre had finished there was a leaden silence; Jouvet did not so much as open his lips; Mirande, searching his old memory for some word of praise fashionable in his youth, exclaimed heartily: 'Some of your lines are like vitriol!' But the vitriol didn't seem to have affected anybody that night. They discussed casting. For Goetz, Brasseur could be the only choice. For Heinrich, Sartre had thought of Vitold, but he wasn't free; Vilar, whom we had thought sensational in Pirandello's *Henry IV*, was suggested and accepted. The two women's roles were entrusted to Casarès and Marie Olivier. But first the play had to be finished, and Sartre got down to writing the second act.

Olga was pretty well cured, she had appeared on the stage again several times with success; despite her doctor's advice, she wanted to take on the role of Electra again as soon as possible. Hermantier, who had put on *The Flies* at Nîmes, wanted to do it again at the Vieux-Colombier; it seemed as though things were working out very nicely. As it happened, they were not. Hermantier thought of himself as another Dullin, but he didn't know how to direct the actors, he had no feeling for the text and he chose appalling sets and costumes. Olga still hadn't regained complete control of her powers; her voice, her breath, let her down. Sartre, preoccupied with

Lucifer and the Lord, went to the rehearsals far too infrequently. I was very worried on opening night, and with good reason: the audience found the performance execrable. The supper at Lipp afterwards, with Olga and a few friends, lacked gaiety. After that Hermantier hacked up the text until he was left with no more than a skeleton that was swiftly buried. It would have been a matter of small importance, if that particular failure had not made Olga decide to give up the theatre, when her only mistake had in fact been to return to it too quickly.

To finish the new play, Sartre needed peace and quiet. I wanted to go skiing again, and Bost went with us to Auron. Stretched out in a deck chair, eyes dazzled with whiteness, skin burned by the sun, I rediscovered the taste of a happiness recalled from many years before. The instructors were more tolerant than they had been in 1946 and allowed stems; I had a lot of fun. Sartre was busy disposing of Dosia and also, since it was a long time since he had skied, he would have been an easy target for unpleasant remarks, so he didn't even put his nose out of the door; everyone at the resort assumed he was mad. At Montroc we tumbled headlong together down the trails, nobody knew us, and what a holiday that was! When I went into his room at five o'clock, light-headed from the air and the mountain smell, he would be writing away, rolled up in a cocoon of smoke. It was with the greatest difficulty that he would tear himself away even for dinner in the vast dining room, where a solitary young lady sat reading *Caroline Chérie*.

We had asked Michelle Vian, who had a house in Saint-Tropez, to find us an apartment there; it overlooked a narrow street, it was icy cold, and the chimney wouldn't draw. We moved to the Aïoli; red tiles on the floors, old cretonne on the walls: the rooms, furnished by a homosexual antique dealer who owned the hotel, had great charm and grace. I bought some more skirts from Mme Vachon, still almost unknown then. We visited Ramatuelle again, and Gassin; I worked and read. But Sartre stayed buried in sixteenth-century Germany; I could scarcely drag him out into the streets and along the paths.

Pierre Brasseur, wanting to talk to Sartre about his part, came and stayed nearby for a few days; he no longer resembled the young man who had taken those slaps on the face with so much talent in *Quai des brumes*; bearded now, he had the body and bearing of a hardened campaigner, and Goetz's comic quality. His eyes glittering with uneasy mischief, he would tell stories about the famous people he had met; his imitations of them were a delight. Out on Sennequier's terrace, in the garden of the Auberge des Maures where the bees buzzed around a *gratin dauphinois* spiced with fennel and thyme, while the sun gilded the carafes of *vin rosé*, he gave us several unforgettable recitals. I had often seen his wife, Lina, in the bar of the Pont-Royal in the days when she had been a pianist, sitting alone with her black hair streaming down over her shoulders; she had given up the piano and cut her hair, but she was still as beautiful as ever. They stayed at Mauvannes, and we went over and spent two days with them. Henri Jeanson was there too, with his wife, very friendly but not particularly gay company, I thought; also the director of *Tire au flanc* whom people called Rivers *cadet*, and who wanted to film *Les Mains sales*. He had the reputation of never shooting a scene twice. Since she was expecting *Lucifer and the Lord* to open in May, Simone Berriau was wild with anxiety: 'What's the matter with him? Can't he write any more?' Her stage whisper implied that Sartre was suffering from some shameful disease; she imagined that writing was some sort of natural secretion; if the writer dried up, then his case was more or less the same as that of a cow which stops giving milk: something was wrong organically. But she had every right to be worried. When Sartre got back to Paris the play was put into rehearsal without a line of the last few scenes having been written.

Even without them, the play already lasted longer than any normal theatrical production. Simone Berriau, daily growing more frantic, begged Sartre to finish it with another twenty lines and then demanded enormous cuts; Sartre claimed that her fingers, as she wandered through the theatre, automatically imitated the action of a pair of scissors. She asked everyone who knew Sartre well to try to persuade him; Cau was the only one who yielded; his intervention was very badly received. Brasseur was on her side because his role was already too big for him to memorize. So that every time Sartre wrote a word he did so with the knowledge that the first thought of the producer and the leading actor would be to make him cut it again. The tenth scene gave him a great deal of trouble, even though it had been the first, or almost the first, to come into his mind; however violent Heinrich's indictment of Goetz, the scene still seemed didactic; it suddenly came to life only when Goetz, before a speechless Heinrich, began to arraign himself.

Sartre took the manuscript to the theatre. 'I'll have it typed straight-away,' said Simone Berriau. Cau, who had happened to be passing her room, saw her hand over the text to Henri Jeanson, whom she had been hiding there; she distrusted Sartre and her own judgement. Jeanson reassured her.

Jouvet took no part in these debates. For all practical purposes he was already dead; his heart was bad, he knew he was more or less doomed, and on Ash Wednesday he'd had himself photographed receiving the Ashes. He loathed Sartre's blasphemies. His right thumb riveted to his left pulse, his eye on his watch, he pretended to be timing the scenes but in fact let them run through without making a single observation. Once I had dinner with him and Sartre at Lapérouse. He came to life slightly. It is perfectly possible, he told us, to replace one out of every four of Racine's alexandrines by any rhythmic gibberish you like, or even by obscenities, and the audience will never tell the difference. This contempt for a text made us uneasy.

The actors restored our spirits. Brasseur's version of Goetz in the first act was dazzling; unfortunately he played the second part as though Goetz were a hypocrite, when in fact the character, in the folly of his pride, is detaching himself with utter sincerity from a lying virtue; I thought it a pity, too, that he refused to learn the soliloquy Sartre had written under the inspiration of St John of the Cross. In the last scenes he regained his full powers. Vilar *was* Heinrich; we saw him stop a taxi once and stand aside to let his devil get in first. Casarès, Marie Olivier, Chauffard, almost all the actors were excellent. I found the sets Labisse had designed a bit too naturalistic. And Sartre couldn't persuade them to slash and muddy Schiaparelli's beautiful costumes.

We went on seeing quite a lot of people during the rehearsal period. We got together quite often with Brasseur and Lina. We had dinner with Lazareff, who was helping Simone Berriau finance the production; despite all the things that separated him from Sartre, we had a very pleasant meal together. Camus would often come to pick up Casarès and they would have a drink with Sartre; there was a brief revival of their friendship.

Finally the play was ready; but the cost in intrigues and argu-ments had been so high that by the time opening night arrived we had quarrelled with both Simone Berriau and the Brasseurs; Jouvet had left for the country. I waited for the curtain to go up standing at the back of the house beside Lina dressed in a sumptuous evening coat; both our hearts were gripped in the same iron hand, but we didn't speak a single word to each other. I knew what those three opening cue thuds meant: the sudden apparition, instead of a familiar script, of a public work; it was what I longed for, yet I waited for the moment more anxiously than I had ever done before. I was soon reassured; there was a whistle from somewhere in the house, a few moments of restlessness, but the audience was rapt. I wandered through the corridors feeling more relaxed, I sat down now and then in Simone Berriau's box, though without speaking to her.

Neither the author nor his friends were invited to the supper that she was giving at Maxim's; in any case we wouldn't have gone. We had supper with Camus, Casarès, Wanda, Olga and Bost in a night-club run by a woman from the Antilles called Moune. It was a pretty dismal meal; the old warmth between Camus and ourselves seemed beyond recall. We had spent a much gayer evening – after a preview – with a group of friends, Merleau-Ponty and Scipion among others, at the Plantation, run by Mireille Trépel on the Boulevard Edgar-Quinet; there were Negro musicians playing very good jazz.

For or against, the play's reception was an impassioned one. The Christians were annoyed. Daniel Rops, who wanted to set the tone, had persuaded Simone Berriau to let him see it from the back of one of the boxes four days before the opening; his review in *L'Aurore* tore it to shreds. Mauriac and some of the others claimed that to attack God so violently Sartre must really believe in Him. They took him to task for blasphemies which had in fact been taken from sixteenth-century texts. But the play also had its champions. On the whole, the critics preferred the first act to the others,[1] and the play's meaning escaped them. Kemp was the only one to point out its relation to the study of Genet; the same themes are to be found in both – Good, Evil, holiness, alienation, the demonic – and Goetz, like Genet, is a bastard, bastardy being a symbol of the vital contradiction Sartre had experienced between his bourgeois birth and his intellectual choice. They all made the enormous error of supposing that Goetz, by committing the murder at the end of the last scene, was returning to Evil. In fact, Sartre was once more

1. Ten years later, when Messemer played the second part better than the first, the critics reversed this judgement.

confronting the vanity of morality with the efficacy of *praxis*. This confrontation goes much further than it had in his previous plays; *Lucifer and the Lord* is the mirror of Sartre's entire ideological evolution. The contrast between Orestes' departure at the end of *The Flies* and Goetz's final stance illustrates the distance Sartre had covered between his original anarchistic attitude and his present commitment. He himself has made the following note:

> The sentence 'We have never been freer than we were during the Occupation,' is in opposition to the character of Heinrich, an objective traitor who becomes a subjective traitor, then a madman. Between the two, seven years and the divorce of the Resistance.[1]

In 1944, Sartre thought that any situation could be transcended by subjective effort; in 1951, he knew that circumstances can sometimes steal our transcendence from us; in that case, no individual salvation is possible, only a collective struggle. However, this play differed from its predecessors in that the militant, Nasty, did not triumph over the adventurer; it is the latter who produces the synthesis Sartre had projected in his preface to Stéphane's book: he accepts the discipline of the Peasant War without denying his own subjectivity, within the enterprise he preserves the negative moment; he is the perfect embodiment of the man of action as Sartre conceived him.

'I made Goetz do what I was unable to do.'[2] Goetz transcended a contradiction Sartre had been feeling very sharply since the failure of the R.D.R. and even more so since the war in Korea, without managing to surmount it:

> The contradiction was not one of ideas. It was in my own being. For my liberty implied also the liberty of all men. And all men were not free. I could not submit to the discipline of solidarity with all men without breaking beneath the strain. And I could not be free alone.[3]

This situation was particularly painful for Sartre in the realm closest to his heart: that of communication.

> To talk to the being it is not possible to convince (the Hindu dying of hunger) otherwise all communication is compromised. That is certainly the meaning of my development and of my contradiction.[4]

To have afforded an aesthetic solution to his problem was not enough for him. He was seeking the means of doing what Goetz had done.

1. Unpublished notes. 2. Unpublished notes.
3. Unpublished notes. 4. Unpublished notes.

By June I had finished a first version of my novel; contrary to my usual habit, I had so far shown none of it to Sartre; I found it painful to wrench it out of myself, and I could not have endured any other eyes, even his, to see those pages that were still warm. He was to read it during our vacation. Meanwhile, circumstances and my own pleasure led me to write about Sade. Two or three years earlier, the publisher Pauvert had asked me to do a preface for *Justine*. I didn't know much about Sade. I had found *The Philosopher in the Boudoir* ridiculous, the style of *The Misfortunes of Virtue* boring, and *The 121 Days of Sodom* too abstract and schematic. *Justine*'s epic extravagance was a revelation. Sade posed the problem of the *other* in its extremest terms; in his excesses, man-as-transcendence and man-as-object achieve a dramatic confrontation. But I needed time to study the subject; I sent the proofs back to the publisher. In 1951, Queneau suggested me as a contributor to a series of books in preparation called *Les Ecrivains célèbres*. I chose Sade. Even for a short review I wanted to read everything, and I began an essay intended for *Les Temps Modernes*. In the Enfer[1] of the Bibliothèque Nationale I was duly issued a charming eighteenth-century edition illustrated with engravings in which personages in wigs and court dress abandoned themselves with an air of indifference to the most complicated manoeuvres. Often Sade's narratives were as lifeless as the engravings; then suddenly a cry, a light would spring from the page and redeem everything.

For years I had been having my work typed by Lucienne Baudin, a very pleasant woman my own age; she had a little daughter, about ten years old. Despite several affairs with men, her tastes were more inclined toward liaisons with other women; she lived with a woman in her fifties; they brought the child up together. She used to tell me about her problems, her financial difficulties, her friendships, her love affairs, and the whole lesbian world, so much less well known than the world of the male homosexual. I didn't see her often, but I always got on well with her when I did. After a certain length of time she began to do her work very badly and unpunctually; she became nervous. 'I think I've got something wrong with one of my breasts,' she told me. I urged her to see a doctor. 'I can't stop working.' A year later, she told me: 'I've got a cancer; it's already

1. Collection of proscribed books, so-called from the original rubric *Enfermé*, restricted. – Tr.

the size of a nut.' She was sent to the Cancer Institute at Villejuif; I went to visit her, and when I walked in she burst into tears; she was sharing a room with three other patients; one of them, who had just had a breast removed, kept shrieking with pain between her morphine injections; one of the others had had her right breast removed a few years earlier, and now the left one was infected. Lucienne was reduced to a state of terror. It was too late to operate and they were treating her with radiation. The treatment was not successful. They sent her home and injected her with male hormones. When I went to see her again I could scarcely recognize her; her face was swollen, an incipient moustache darkened her upper lip and she spoke in a man's voice; the only thing that was still the same was the shining whiteness of her teeth. Every now and then she would put her hand to her bandaged breast and groan. I sensed how fragile and painful that bundle of decaying glands was, and felt like running away. She cried. She had written to faith healers, had tried miracle drugs, and dreamed of getting to America to consult specialists. And she cried. They took her to the hospital. In the beds on either side, old women were dying of cancer. They went on with the hormone injections. Puffed up like a balloon, bearded, grotesquely hideous, she went on suffering, unresigned to death. When I came back from Saint-Tropez, her friend told me that she was dying; the next day she was dead, after fighting for twenty-four hours. 'She looks like a woman of eighty,' her friend told me. I hadn't the courage to go and see her corpse.

Lucienne's end made even sadder a year which, despite my work and the pleasure and excitement I got from Sartre's play, was a melancholy one for me. Everyone seemed gloomy. Though MacArthur had been replaced, the fighting went on in Korea all the same, and the French economy suffered in consequence. The Vichyists and ex-collaborators turned Pétain's funeral into what looked like a triumphant demonstration of their return to power, and the June elections, thanks to the system of party alliances, was a victory for bourgeois democracy. Sartre viewed both the year's events and his own situation grimly, and that saddened me too. Olga's failure hurt me as well. And it was hard to write off my relationship with Algren. He hadn't remarried, but that made no difference. It was futile to wonder what his feelings were; even if he found it painful to cut himself off from me, he would still do it if he thought it necessary. The affair was over. I was less devastated by this knowledge than I would have been two years earlier; it was impossible now to change my memories into dead leaves, they had become worth their weight in freshly minted gold. And also, during those two months at Miller, I had shifted from stupefied unbelief to resignation. It didn't hurt any more. But every once in a while a void would open up inside of me, it was as though my life were coming to a stop. I would look at Saint-Germain-des-Prés; there would be nothing behind it. Once my heart had beat in other places at the same time; now, I was where I was, there and nowhere else. What austerity!

We wrote each other only rarely, and even then had little to say. In a letter that reached me in Saint-Tropez, he suggested I spend October with him at Miller. He was offering, in all honesty, the friendship it is always so easy to maintain when a rupture has been made without bitterness and the two people concerned are living in the same city. I consulted Sartre. 'Why not?' he said. I accepted.

At the end of June, Lise came over to Paris with Willy and Bernard. Her friends were overjoyed to see her, and when she arrived she was radiant; the subsequent disappointment was bitter on both sides: she no longer understood us, and seemed far away. She reduced Scipion to a state of stupefaction by scolding him for not working out a budget for himself every month. The United States had become her country; she admired and accepted almost everything about it. On 14 July, I went with her and a whole band of others to all the street balls of the neighbourhood; we stayed for quite a while at the *bal des timides* opposite the Closerie des Lilas. But when I said good-bye to her I knew she had no desire to come back, even just to visit us again. We wrote each other for several years after that; little by little, the animosity in her mixed feelings for me gained ground. I ended the correspondence; as things are, we send each other Christmas cards. She has remarried, has more children, and is doing well, apparently despite serious physical troubles and some disappointments.

In the middle of July, we took a plane to Oslo and I left my melancholy behind me. Sartre's Norwegian publisher put a car and a chauffeur at our disposal so that we could drive across the Telemark; pines, lakes, old wooden churches standing alone in the middle of fields; then Bergen, its abandoned warehouses, its ancient houses of multicoloured wood surrounding the quiet harbour, the animation of the fish market. In the evening we embarked on a boat; at each stop, buses took us on a tour. Sartre had seen all these places long before, with his parents. In the wooden towns to the north, there were gardens where rockeries took the place of lawns and flower beds. During the day, I would sit on deck and read Boswell's *Journal* and his *Life of Dr Johnson*. In the evening I stared for hours at the sun hanging motionless near the horizon, and at the furious activity of the sky above. A ball of fire amid shadows: that was how a little girl in Sartre's first short story had imagined the midnight sun. The reality had disappointed her: it simply stayed light at midnight. I wasn't disappointed; the unaccustomed brightness of the night kept me there on the deck until an hour which elsewhere would have been the dawn. We sailed around snow-covered cliffs plummeting down into the sea. From Kirkenes, a bus took us to the Russian border; through the bushes and barbed wire, we made out sentinels with red stars on their uniforms. I was moved at seeing with my own eyes that forbidden country which meant so much to us. We sailed back, dropping anchor in other ports. The Bergesbne, which is one of Norway's prides, took us back to Oslo; it is the only railroad in the world that goes over glaciers; it never goes above an altitude of 4,000 feet, yet we travelled for hours through perpetual snows.

Sartre, like myself, had once landed in a plane on Iceland, and we had promised ourselves that we would see it. We spent ten days of astonishment there. This young volcano, inhabited only since the tenth century, had no prehistory, not so much as a fossil; the streams smoked, the central heating used water from under the ground; the most difficult thing in the hotel rooms was to get cold water; in the middle of the fields stood cabins that were 'steam baths'. Almost no trees – what we would call brushwood they called a forest; but deserts of lava, mountains the colour of rotten eggs, spitting out sulphurous vapours and riddled with 'devil's cookpots' full of boiling mud; weather-worn rocks that in the distance looked like fantastic towns. These volcanoes were capped with snow fields and glaciers that broke off into the sea. There was no railroad and very few roads; not only was one jostled in the airplanes by peasants carrying cages of chickens, but even the sheep of the island effected their seasonal changes of pasture by air. The peasants looked much more like American cowboys than like the traditional European peasant: well-dressed, well-shod, they lived in houses provided with every modern comfort and travelled on horseback.

But though the landscapes had a strange planetary beauty, the towns, their wooden houses roofed with corrugated iron, were dismal. A tremendous wind roared ceaselessly along the streets that made up the gridiron of Reykjavik. While there we stayed, like all foreigners, at the Hotel Borg. Little flags on the dining-room tables indicated the nationalities of the guests. We were greeted in a friendly manner by the French contingent there, among whom was Paul-Émile Victor. Several times a week he flew out to parachute food, medicaments and tools to the settlements in Greenland. In the evening, he would say: 'I've been to Greenland,' as though he'd been just outside Paris visiting in Meudon for the day. He told us about the Eskimos, about his expeditions, his experiences as a parachutist. There were also two film makers – one of them I had met in Hollywood, and the other was an habitué of the Flore – who were there making a documentary. They took us by car to the lake of Thingvellir, which is very blue and full of little volcanoes and a lot of 'atolls', made of lava clinkers that looked just like gigantic mole-hills. We also met the son of the explorer Scott, who was capturing wild animals, and an Icelandic geologist who was hunting pebbles; he took us for a ride in his jeep through a landscape of rocks more brightly coloured than any flower-bed. We went by plane to sinister Akureyri, and from there I took a hydroplane along the wonderful northern coast as far as the little harbour situated at the extreme north of the island. My only companions were two bearded boys. 'We're hitchhiking around Iceland,' they told me.

The Icelanders were hard drinkers; they were capable of making alcohol out of shoe polish. The principal task of the police was to pick the drunks out of the gutters at night. Every Saturday evening there was a dance at the Hotel Borg, and on that night it would be men in tuxedoes with muddy shirt fronts that the cops were loading into their Black Marias.

There was a reception at the French Embassy; it was one of the only places in the world at the time where Russian and American officials could be seen drinking together. I spoke, in English, to the wife of a Soviet diplomat, who was wearing a whole *jardinière* of flowers on her blonde hair. 'I should love to see Paris,' she told me. 'And I should love to see Moscow.' We left it at that.

After Iceland, we went to Edinburgh. Though less extraordinary than Iceland, Scotland as we went through it by boat, from lake to lake, from island to island, was beautiful. We saw the pale, flat island of Iona with its Celtic remains, and the cliffs of Fingal's cave, which was made inaccessible that day by enormous waves; as we went through the Hebrides I read Boswell's account of the journey he and Johnson made there. We crossed a vast region of heath and hills; on the maps the famous sites were marked with two crossed swords for a battle and just one sword for a massacre. We passed through the landscapes described by Sir Walter Scott, we visited Melrose Abbey. But Scottish austerity was too much for us. It was very difficult to find rooms, and impossible to work in them: no table and no desk lamp. 'If you want to write, go into the writing room,' they told Sartre. He would put his papers on his bed table or just use his knees. Their meal hours were no less strict; once when we were waiting for a boat at ten in the morning in driving rain, not one hotel would serve us so much as a cup of coffee or a piece of bread: it was too late for breakfast and too early for lunch. Our hearts sank at the grimness of the towns.

We stopped in London for two weeks. By chance we happened to run into Mamaine Koestler in a restaurant; she was divorced, as graceful as ever and even more delicate-looking than she had been before. She took us, with her friend Sonia, George Orwell's widow, to one of the private clubs that are the sole refuge of 'night people' in London: the Gargoyle, up on a sixth floor somewhere. We met a few people there – among others, Freud's nephew Lucien, a painter – and drank. In the morning, when we were about to get on the plane back to Paris, I suddenly felt very queasy. 'That one's going to be sick before we start,' I heard a steward murmur, to my great shame.

During our cruise in Norway, I showed Sartre the first version of my novel. It was going to be my best book, he told me, but I still had a lot of work ahead of me. Well-made plots always irritated me by their artificiality; I wanted to imitate the disorder, the indecision, the contingency of life; I had let my characters and the events in the book sprawl in every direction; I left out all the 'necessary scenes'; all the important things happened offstage. I should have adopted an entirely different technique, Sartre told me, or else, having decided that this one suited my subject, I should have pursued it with much greater rigour; as it stood, the book was badly constructed and discouraged the reader. He convinced me that I should link the episodes more tightly, that I should make it clearer what things were at stake for the characters, and that I should introduce some suspense. I had understood the difficulty of the book's dialogue without overcoming it; the intellectuals occasionally talk about their ideas, debate and ratiocinate: even if cut and more skilfully inserted, such conversations are likely to be boring; mine decidedly were. Another thing worried Sartre; to believe completely in my characters, the reader would have had to know their work; I couldn't write their books for them; thus their objective reality escaped; their work, which was the essential element in their lives, was only suggested indirectly, in the margin. This last defect was inherent in the undertaking itself. But for the rest, I decided to rework the whole thing. In such cases, the gossip columnists tell how the writer 'tore it all up and started over'. Nobody does that. One uses the work already done as a foundation.

I spent October with Algren. Plane, train, taxi: I was quite calm when I arrived at the house on Forest Avenue; I had nothing to gain and nothing to lose. Once again there was the splendour of an Indian summer. Once again I bathed in the lake, read in the sun, watched television; I finished my essay on Sade. I scarcely set foot in Chicago. One evening I drank martinis with Algren at the Tip-Top-Tap, some twenty storeys above the lights of the city; then we saw Renoir's *The River*: an indecent lie that put Algren to sleep. Another time, Algren gave a lecture to a Jewish club; since anti-Semitism was very pronounced in Chicago, I imagined that those who suffered from it would be inclined to protest against the established order of things. But when Algren took up the defence of the drug addicts, attacking the society that forced its youth into such sombre avenues of escape, I saw nothing but frowns in the audience. 'He doesn't speak as well as he writes,' they murmured. He also denounced police corruption.[1] A judge answered him with

1. Ten years later, it was acknowledged officially; a great many members of the police force were indicted for burglary, blackmail, complicity, etc. It had taken all that time for the scandal to break out into the open, but things were already going on in 1951 just as they did in 1960, and many people knew it.

a panegyric on the virtues of the 'boys in blue' which received wild applause.

Algren was going to remarry his ex-wife. As I walked along the beach during the last days of October, between the dunes dusted with gold and the changing blue of the water, I thought to myself that I would never see him again, nor the house, nor the lake, nor the sand being pecked at by the little white waders; and I didn't know which I would miss most: a man, a landscape, or myself. We both wanted to keep our good-byes to a minimum; Algren would put me on a train at Gary towards noon; I would go to the airport alone. The last morning, the hours seemed to drag for both of us; we refused to talk to each other and were embarrassed by our silence. At last I said that I had had a very nice time there and that at least we still had a real friendship for each other. 'It's not friendship,' he replied brutally. 'I can never offer you less than love.' These words, suddenly, after those four peaceful weeks, brought all the old uncertainty back: if our love still existed, why these final, these definitive good-byes? All the past flooded back into my heart, all my work was undone, life was unbearable; in the taxi, in the train, in the plane, in a cinema in New York that evening, watching a Walt Disney film in which animals endlessly devoured each other, I wept without stopping. In my room in the Lincoln Hotel, my eyes brimming with tears, I wrote Algren a short letter asking if everything was all over or not. I got back to Paris on All Saints' Day. Everywhere there were chrysanthemums and people wearing black. And I knew the answer to my question.

'One can still have the same feelings for someone,' Algren wrote to me, 'and still not allow them to rule and disturb one's life. To love a woman who does not belong to you, who puts other things and other people before you, without there ever being any question of your taking first place, is something that just isn't acceptable. I don't regret a single one of the moments we have had together. But now I want a different kind of life, with a woman and a house of my own. . . . The disappointment I felt three years ago, when I began to realize that your life belonged to Paris and to Sartre, is an old one now, and it's become blunted by time. What I've tried to do since is to take my life back from you. My life means a lot to me, I don't like its belonging to someone so far off, someone I see only a few weeks every year. . . .'

There remained only to write the words 'the end'. And so I did.

During the Occupation, when Sartre and I were toiling up hills on our bicycles, we used to dream of having a motorcycle. By 1951 it had become easy to realize an even more ambitious project I had been nursing since before the war: buying a car. On Genet's advice, I chose a new Simca model, an Aronde. I took lessons with an instructor in the Place Montparnasse with the predestined name of M. Voiturin. Bost, who had just got his own licence, would take me out on Sunday mornings to practise just outside Paris. What agonies! Going through a village, luckily at less than three miles an hour, I hopped the sidewalk, giving both other people and myself a terrible scare. All the same, having never operated the smallest machine of any kind, it was a miracle that this one obeyed me even approximately. Once I had my licence, our excursions, on which Olga was often included, grew longer; they would last a whole day or even two. I loved the roads through the forests when their reddish pelt was edged with white fur in winter; I loved the spring in Normandy, the tarns of the Sologne, the villages of Touraine; I discovered churches, abbeys, châteaux. I went to Auvers; I saw Van Gogh's café, the church, the plateau and in the cemetery the twin gravestones hidden under the ivy.

To celebrate the hundredth performance of *Lucifer and the Lord*, Simone Berriau summoned *le Tout-Paris* to the Carlton; neither the author nor his friends made an appearance. We went back to the Plantation, where there was a female-impersonation act at the time. Cau dashed over to the Champs-Élysées and came back to tell us how the official celebration was progressing. On Christmas Eve, I gave an all-night party at my place, as I had the year before.

The contributors to *Les Temps Modernes* were still meeting regularly at Sartre's every Sunday afternoon, to the sound of the hornpipe: men in the next building were always doing the dances of their native Brittany while musicians in costume stood in the doorway playing for them. There were a few newcomers – Péju, Claude Lanzmann, Chambure; we'd bought some folding chairs so that everyone would have somewhere to sit. Lanzmann and Péju worked as rewrite men for various newspapers, a job that allowed them to earn a comfortable living and still left them time to do other things. They both had a sound basic training in philosophy, though politics came first for both of them. They helped Sartre 'repolitize' the magazine, and it was they more than anyone else who oriented it toward that 'critical fellow-travelling'[1] which Merleau-Ponty had abandoned. Lanzmann I liked very much. Many women found him attractive; so did I. He would say the most extreme things in a completely offhand tone, and the way his mind worked reminded me of Sartre. His mock-simple humour greatly enlivened these sessions. We drank *framboise* and debated hotly; we made suggestions, digressed, and swapped the pearls we had culled from *Aspects de la France* or *Rivarol*. In November Sartre asked for a volunteer to review Camus' *The Rebel*. He wouldn't let anyone say anything bad about it because of their friendship; unfortunately none of us could think of anything good. We wondered how we were going to get out of the dilemma.

These meetings account for most of the red-letter moments in a period which was one of the darkest of my life. Both in France and abroad, things were going from bad to worse. In France 'the most backward collection of employers in the world' stubbornly buried its head in the sand of Malthusianism; production just managed to reach the same level as it had in 1929, the price inflation continued while wages had scarcely budged. The bourgeoisie remained indifferent to this state of decline and pursued its savage war against Communism. The big financiers and the government paid Jean-Paul David to intensify his propaganda against 'the Fifth Column'; he had a radio programme and inundated Paris with posters and tracts. The Left was divided and unable either to stop the war in Indochina or make any dents in the current colonialist policy,[2] despite the trouble brewing throughout Black Africa; except for a few *graffiti* – U.S. GO HOME – they had no way of fighting the ichneumon-like invasion Sartre had predicted a year before. In the States, MacArthur had gone so far as to attack General Marshall during June, and then Dean Acheson as well; investigations were instituted into the lives of American officials working for the United Nations. These persecutions were presented undisguised as the preliminaries of a preventive war Eisenhower himself announced in an interview he gave to *Paris-Match* in October: the armies of the West were to prepare for imminent battle in the suburbs of Leningrad. An issue of *Collier's Weekly* printed a report on the state of the world five years after the end of the atomic war in

1. *Merleau-Ponty vivant.*
2. In December occurred the trial of the 460 Ivory Coast Negroes arrested in the circumstances I have already described.

1960. My imagination balked at envisaging such catastrophes; but I didn't believe we were going to have peace either. As in 1940, the future lost all perceptible shape, and I vegetated without living; the subjection of France was almost as painful to me as it had been then. One evening, at the end of a long day's outing in my car, I had dinner with Olga and Bost in a hotel in Chinon; the dining room was pleasant, we were drinking a good wine and we were gay; two American soldiers came in and I felt a sudden tightening around my heart that I recognized. Bost said out loud, 'They give me exactly the same feeling as the Chleuhs.' Seven years before we had loved them, these tall soldiers in khaki who had looked so peaceful; they were our liberty. Now they were defending a country which was supporting dictatorship and corruption from one end of the world to the other: Synghman Rhee, Chiang Kai-shek, Franco, Salazar, Batista. . . . What their uniforms meant to us now was our dependence and a mortal threat.

Time grows shorter as we grow old: seven years means yesterday. That beautiful summer when everything had begun again still remained the true reality of my life, so much so that I wanted to call the novel I was working on *The Survivors*. But truth and reality had been made into a mockery and though my disillusionment had begun in 1948, I had not yet reached its depths. My feelings of revolt only aggravated the discouragement I was now sharing with most of my fellow countrymen.

The young men of 1945 had certainly changed their tune. The French cinema was drooping; except for the Communist newspapers the left-wing press no longer existed; budding film-makers and journalists, where were the fruits by which we were to know them? As for literature, their doubts about the age they were living in, and consequently their doubts about themselves as well, were too deep for them to devote themselves to it with any fervour. Vian, once the most ambitious, had virtually given it up; he composed songs and sang them, he wrote a column on jazz in a newspaper. They were interested enough in politics to argue in the bars of Saint-Germain-des-Prés, but not interested enough to find a way of life or a reason for living. It wasn't their fault. What could they do? What could anyone do just then in France? Once, hope had united us; now we scarcely saw them any more. We were still bound to our older friends by the past but – except for Genet, Giacometti, Leiris – we were not entirely in agreement with any of them about the present and the future. Those who had filled our lives before the war had all – except Olga and Bost – more or less vanished. Mme Lemaire lived in the country, Herbaud abroad. Pagniez had turned against Sartre once again, and they had more or less quarrelled. Since Dullin's death, Camille had become a recluse.

I had buried my memories of Chicago a second time, and they no longer caused me pain – but what sadness to feel the pain subside! 'Well, that's that,' I said to myself; and I no longer even thought about my happiness with Algren. Less inclined than ever to what are called adventures, my age and the circumstances of my life left little room, it seemed to me, for a new love. My body, perhaps as the result of a deeply ingrained pride, adapts easily; it made no demands. But there was something in me that would not submit to such indifference. 'I'll never sleep again warmed by another's body.' Never: what a knell! When the realization of these facts penetrated me, I felt myself sinking into death. The void had always frightened me, but till now I had been dying day by day without paying attention to it; suddenly, at one blow, a whole piece of myself was being engulfed before my eyes; it was like some brutal but inexplicable amputation, for nothing had happened to me. In the glass my face still looked the same; behind me a burning past was still not far away, but, in the long years stretching ahead of me, it would not flame up again; it would never flame again. I suddenly found myself on the other side of a line, though there was no one moment when I had crossed it. I stood there, bewildered by astonishment and regret.

The future was barred to me by History – both personal and public – and even my work was of no help to me in finding my way into it. I was by no means certain I could remedy the weaknesses that Sartre had pointed out; and in any case it would be another year or two before I finished the attempt. The horizon was so black that it took almost as much courage to keep going as it had to continue with *L'Invitée* in 1941. This book meant a great deal to me. In 1943 and 1945, my successes had satisfied me; they did so much less now. *L'Invitée* was a long way away; *The Blood of Others* had faded; *All Men are Mortal* had never been a success. *The Second Sex* was still going strong, but in France it had earned me only a very equivocal reputation. I wanted something more. Unfortunately, this book was not going to make much of a stir, of that I was convinced. I wrote, I crossed out, I began again, I tormented myself, I wore myself out, without hope. History was no longer on my side, far from it. There was no place left for those who refused to become part of either of the two blocs. Sartre agreed with me that the novel would offend both Right and Left; if I managed to get three thousand readers I should be doing well! This failure, which seemed to both of us a foregone conclusion, saddened us not only in itself but also because it was a sign of our exile. All political action had become impossible for us and even our writing was going to trickle away into the sand.

As always, Sartre was a great help to me. Yet he seemed further away from me than ever before. His successes had not changed him, but he had created a situation which in cutting him off from the world also broke some of our ties; he no longer even set foot in the cafés we had so loved before; he had not followed me down the ski trails at Auron; the unknown partner of our life together had become, by the pressure of circumstances, a public figure. I had the feeling that he had been stolen from me. 'Oh, why aren't you an obscure poet!' I used to say to him. Overhauling his political position, he was pursuing at the same time an exhausting inner development and studies which devoured his days. I missed his old insouciance and the golden age when we always had so much time: our walks, our strolls through Paris, our evenings at the cinema we never seemed to go to any more. He invited me to follow him along his path. 'You should read this!' he would tell me, pointing to the books piled up on his desk; he would insist: 'It's fascinating.' I couldn't; I had to finish my novel. And then, although I too wanted to know more about the world I was living in, it wasn't a necessity for me as it was for him. The year before, he had been forced into the position of making a hypothetical choice, in the event of a Russian occupation, between two solutions, one impracticable – to stay, without submitting – the other odious – to leave; this had led him to the conclusion that it was impossible to be what he was, and it was impossible for him to go on living without finding a way of surmounting that situation; thus, the urgency he felt now was forcing him back into the project which he had never abandoned: the construction of an ideology which, while enlightening man as to his situation, would also offer him a practical approach to life. Such an ambition was foreign to me; my objective importance was too slight for a putative Russian occupation to pose any personal problem for me; I could not expect, and at the same time I did not desire, to play even the smallest political role. So that for me to read the same books as Sartre, and to meditate upon the same themes, would have been a gratuitous activity; what he had undertaken concerned him too intimately for anyone, even myself, to help him with it. I knew all this; yet it seemed to me that his solitude was isolating me from him. 'It's not like it used to be,' I said to myself; loyal to my past, these words were enough to upset me. I put into my heroine's mouth in *The Mandarins* the words I was saying then to myself: 'It makes me unhappy not to feel happy.' I also told myself: 'There are people more unhappy than I am,' but it was a truth from which I drew little consolation – on the contrary; the delicate sadness inside me was like a resonator that captured the vibrations of a whole concert of laments from the outside world; a universal despair crept into my heart until I began to long for the world to end.

All these circumstances explain the panic to which I fell a victim towards the beginning of spring. Until then, I had never been under any threat from my body: in 1935 I had been unaware of the seriousness of my state. Now, for the first time, I believed myself to be in danger.

'It's nothing,' I told myself at first; then I wondered: 'But is it something?' I kept getting a stab of pain in my right breast, and in one particular spot there was a swelling. 'It's nothing,' I told myself more and more often; and more and more often I fingered the unaccustomed little swelling. I remembered the hairy face of Lucienne Baudin, and her agony; for an instant, fear gripped me: 'What if it's cancer?' I thrust the thought aside; I was feeling well enough. Then the stabs of pain returned and with them my anxiety. My body no longer seemed invulnerable; from year to year it was deteriorating insidiously; why should it not have begun to decay quite suddenly? With a show of offhandedness I mentioned it to Sartre. 'Then you must go and see a doctor, so he can put your mind at rest,' he told me. I was given the name of a specialist. I went to see him on one of those April days when summer suddenly falls prematurely out of the sky; I had put on the fur coat I had been wearing the day before, and I was almost dying of the heat as I walked up one of the gloomy avenues that branch off the Place de l'Alma. The surgeon was reassuring at first: in view of my age, it would be wise to perform an exploratory operation and have a biopsy immediately; but I didn't look like a cancer patient and the suspicious swelling moved about when he rolled it between his fingers, which meant that it was benign. However, to lend the consultation a gravity worthy of the price he was charging, he left a certain amount of doubt hovering in my mind; he asked me if I would agree to the removal of the breast if it should turn out to be a malignant tumour. 'Yes, of course,' I replied. And I left, shaken. This time I would get off with an amputation at most; but I recalled the old women in the room with Lucienne: ten years later the other breast becomes infected,[1] one dies in appalling agony. Sweltering in my fur coat, sweating, my mouth thick with anxiety, I looked up at the blue sky and thought: If I really did have cancer, it would happen just like this, there would be no portents ... I repeated to Sartre, in a strangled voice, what the doctor had said. His way of consoling me shows what clouds were lowering on our horizon: if the worst came to the worst, I could count on twelve or so more years of life; twelve years from then the atomic bomb would have disposed of us all.

I was to be operated on the following Monday; on Sunday I went out in the car with Bost to see the beautiful abbey of Larchant; I drove badly and kept stalling the motor the whole time. Bost grew impatient. Instead of learning, I was regressing; he couldn't see the connexion between my nervousness and what he took to be a very minor operation. 'You know,' I said to him as we came back into Paris, 'I may have cancer!' He looked at me with stupefaction. 'Don't be silly! How could that happen to *you*!' I marvelled at the way he kept intact my old optimism. I went into the clinic that evening. I had dinner, I read, I went to bed early. A sister shaved my armpit. 'In case they have to take everything off,' she said with a smile. They gave me an injection and I went to sleep. I was resigned to what was to come – not out of curiosity, as I had been when the threat of the sanatorium had been hanging over me, but out of a kind of bitter indifference. Next morning, after another injection, they wheeled me out on a trolley, covered with just a sheet. At the door of the operating theatre they put little white boots on my feet, which intrigued me a great deal; then a needle went into a vein in my left arm. I said: 'I can taste garlic' and then all sensations stopped. When I came to, I heard a voice: 'There's absolutely nothing wrong with you,' and I closed my eyes again; angels came and rocked me to sleep. I came out after two days, my

1. This isn't always true, far from it; but it is what I believed.

breast covered with bandages, but full of wonder at finding myself still whole and delivered from my fear.

Now the gaiety of springtime won me. We drove to the south of France, Sartre, Bost, Michelle and I. Michelle had separated from Boris, and Sartre, who had always found her very attractive, had become intimately involved with her. I liked her very much, everyone always liked her because she never put herself first. Gay and rather mysterious, very discreet and yet very much there, she was a charming companion. We had a pleasant journey down, visiting the Abbey of Saint-Philibert at Tournus and the house of the postman, Cheval, at Hauterive. Bost and I fought fiercely about who was to drive; we both loved driving for long distances. Bost didn't stay long at Saint-Tropez; I took him one evening to the station at Saint-Raphaël and on the way back I was suddenly moved at the thought that I was driving alone for the first time. I became bolder. I left the Hôtel de l'Aïoli at dawn, and as I drove through the town with all its shutters closed I felt once more the way I used to feel on those holidays long ago. I would hitchhike in those days. What a marvellous feeling, when a car stopped and carried me off down the road! To me it was miraculous to be taken in ten minutes a distance it would have taken me two hours to walk. Now, driver and passenger at the same time, I kept wanting to say thank you to myself. Walking had brought me a different kind of pleasure; but the new pleasure I got from my car made me almost forget the old one. I saw Provence once more as I had loved it twenty years ago, and yet I saw it in a different light as well: past and present made an alliance in my heart. I became so bold that I even drove out along the little byways of Les Maures with Merleau-Ponty and his wife, both new arrivals in Saint-Tropez. They displayed great courage; it's true that they had driven down from Paris with a couple without a licence between them; on the dangerous bits of road, the husband and wife had come to blows over who was to drive. A great many of the people I knew were learning to drive; after the postwar shortage, it was beginning to be possible to obtain cars again.

I worked a little; Sartre was writing on Mallarmé; on Sennequier's terrace, in the bar of La Ponche, he told me about what he was doing and explained some of the poems. He had meetings to attend and went back to Paris by train. I drove on alone to Avignon, proud of my powers, but with the fear that I might break down and not know what to do always in the back of my mind. At Avignon, I met Bost at the early morning train, and he helped me drive back to Paris as we had arranged.

I left again soon afterwards; Sartre was spending three weeks in Italy with Michelle, so Olga, Bost and I took a motor tour there, exploring side roads and finding places it was difficult to get to without a car: Volterra for example. It was very pleasant to be able to go where we wanted when we wanted, just as the fancy took us. I got back to Paris in time to see the magnificent Mexican Exhibition.

Two things marked the beginning to that summer: Sartre quarrelled with Camus and effected a reconciliation with the Communists.

I saw Camus, for the last time, with Sartre in a little café on the Place Saint-Sulpice in April. He made fun of a lot of the criticisms of his book; he just took it for granted that we liked it, and Sartre had great difficulty in knowing what to say to him. A little later, Sartre met him in the Pont-Royal and warned him that the review in *Les Temps Modernes* would be fairly cool, if not harsh. Camus seemed disagreeably surprised. In the end, Francis Jeanson had accepted the task of doing the piece on *The Rebel*; he had promised to do it circumspectly; as it turned out, he got carried away. Sartre persuaded him to soften some of his strictures, but there was no censorship on the magazine. Camus, affecting to ignore Jeanson's existence, sent Sartre an open letter in which he addressed him as '*Monsieur le directeur*'. Sartre replied in the next issue. And everything was over between them.

As a matter of fact, if this friendship exploded so violently, it was because for a long time not much of it had remained. The political and ideological differences which already existed between Sartre and Camus in 1945 had intensified from year to year. Camus was an idealist, a moralist and an anti-Communist; at one moment forced to yield to History, he attempted as soon as possible to secede from it; sensitive to men's suffering, he imputed it to Nature; Sartre had laboured since 1940 to repudiate idealism, to wrench himself away from his original individualism, to live in History; his position was close to Marxism, and he desired an alliance with the Communists. Camus was fighting for great principles, and that was how he came to be taken in by the hot air of Gary Davis; usually, he refused to participate in the particular and detailed political actions to which Sartre committed himself. While Sartre believed in the truth of socialism, Camus became a more and more resolute champion of bourgeois values; *The Rebel* was a statement of his solidarity with them. A neutralist position between the two blocs had become finally impossible; Sartre therefore drew nearer to the U.S.S.R.; Camus hated the Russians, and although he did not like the United States, he went over, practically speaking, to the American side. I told him about our experience at Chinon. 'I really felt I was back in the Occupation,' I told him. He looked at me with an astonishment that was both sincere and feigned. 'Really?' He smiled, 'Wait a little while. You'll see a real Occupation soon – a different sort altogether.'

These differences of opinion were too radical for the friendship between the two men not to be shaken. Also, compromise was not easy for a man of Camus' character. I suppose he felt how vulnerable his position was in some way; he would not brook challenge and as soon as he saw one coming he would fly into one of his abstract rages, which seemed to be his way of taking refuge. There had been a sort of reconciliation between him and Sartre at the time of *Lucifer and the Lord*, and we had published his article on Nietzsche in *Les Temps Modernes*, although we weren't at all satisfied with it. But this tentative attempt had not lasted. Camus was ready, at the slightest opportunity, to criticize Sartre for his permissiveness with regard to 'authoritarian socialism'. Sartre had long believed that Camus was wrong all along the line and that furthermore he had become, as he told him in his letter, 'utterly insufferable'. Personally, this break in their relations did not affect me. The Camus who had been dear to me had ceased to exist a long while before.

During that year, some Communists had asked Sartre to be a member of the Committee for the Liberation of Henri Martin, and to collaborate on a book making the facts of the matter public; he was happy that the first step towards a reconciliation had been made. Circumstances had convinced him that the only path still open to the Left was to find a way back to unity of action with the Communist Party. And the contradiction that was tearing him apart had by then become intolerable.

I was a victim of and an accomplice in the class struggle: a victim because I was hated by an entire class; an accomplice because I felt both responsible and powerless . . . I discovered the class struggle in that slow dismemberment that tore us away from them (the workers) more and more each day . . . I believed in it, but I did not imagine that it was total . . . I discovered it *against* myself.[1]

Sartre told me one day: 'I've always thought against myself.' But he had never done so as savagely as he did in the years from 1950 to 1952. The work he had begun in 1945 with his article on the writer's commitment was finished; he had utterly demolished all his illusions about the possibility of personal salvation. He had reached the same point as Goetz: he was ready to accept a collective discipline without denying his own liberty. 'After ten years of rumination, I had reached breaking point: one light tap was all that was required.'[2] It was a book that struck him first: Guillemin's *Le Coup du 2 décembre.* In his youth, in opposition to Politzer, for whom the bourgeois were defined exclusively by their situation as exploiters, he had supported the view that they could, in their relations with each other, display certain virtues; he had a respect for his stepfather, an engineer, severe both with others and with himself and a hard worker who lived a life of austerity. The Collaboration[3] had first aroused Sartre's suspicion that all bourgeois virtues are inevitably perverted by alienation. *Le Coup du 2 décembre* showed him what men just as upright as his mother's husband were capable of thinking and writing. All capitalists must speak with the voice of Capital; yet the bourgeois are nonetheless individuals of flesh and blood who, to defend their interests, employ means whose violence is scarcely masked. It was Guillemin who tore away the veils hiding this process. From that moment, Sartre saw the class struggle in all its clarity – men against men; from that moment too, friendships and rejections became a matter of passion. He was overwhelmed with anger when he learned in Italy of the arrest of Duclos, on the evening of the demonstration against Ridgeway,[4] then during the strike that failed on 4 June, at the triumphant reaction of the Right, the arrests, the appropriations, the lies, including the most grotesque of them all, the story of the carrier pigeons.

In the name of the principles it had inculcated in me, in the name of its humanism and its 'humanities,' in the name of Liberty, Equality and

1. Unpublished notes.   2. Unpublished notes.
3. Most of his stepfather's friends collaborated, though his stepfather himself was a Gaullist.
4. Ridgeway was coming to take over from Eisenhower as the head of S.H.A.P.E. Three days earlier, André Stil had been arrested for having referred to him in *Humanité* as the 'General of the bacteriological war'.

Fraternity, I swore a hatred for the bourgeoisie that would die only with my own death. When I returned abruptly to Paris, I had to write or choke.[1]

He wrote the first part of *Les Communistes et la paix* with a fury that frightened me. 'In two weeks, he's spent five nights without sleep, and the other nights he only sleeps four or five hours,' I wrote my sister.

The article appeared in *Les Temps Modernes* a month before his 'Réponse à Camus'. These two pieces of writing had the same meaning: the postwar period was over. No more postponements, no more conciliations were possible. We had been forced into making clear-cut choices. Despite the difficulty of his position, Sartre still knew he had been right to adopt it. His mistake up to that point had been, he thought, to try to resolve the conflict without *transcending* his situation.

I had to take some step that would make me 'other'. I had to accept the point of view of the U.S.S.R. in its totality and count on myself alone to maintain my own. Finally, I was alone because I did not wish to be alone enough.[2]

This epoch we had just lived through was what I had tried to evoke in *The Mandarins*. The book was to take me several more months of work to finish. But everything about it had already been decided. This is the moment for me to explain my intentions in writing it.

From 1943 onward, my happiness had been carried along by the stream of events; I felt myself so joyfully at one with the times I lived in that I had nothing to say about them. *All Men are Mortal* reflects my new awareness of History, but diffused in a moral fable that took me away from my own century; when I asked myself in 1946: 'What shall I write now?' I thought of writing about myself and not about the world and time I lived in; I took that for granted. And then, while I was working on *The Second Sex*, things around me changed. The triumph of Good over Evil ceased to be a matter of tacit assumption; it even seemed gravely threatened. From our collective halcyon, I had fallen, like so many others, to the dusty earth below: the ground was littered with smashed illusions. As in the past, failure, disturbing my private life, had brought forth

1. *Merleau-Ponty vivant.*   2. Unpublished notes.

L'Invitée, so once again it made me step back from my recent experiences to see them better, and filled me with a desire to redeem that failure with words. It became possible and necessary for me to embody it in a book.

An experience is not a series of facts, and I had no intention of composing a chronicle.[1] I have already explained what is for me one of the essential purposes of literature: to make manifest the equivocal, separate, contradictory truths that no one moment represents in their totality, either inside or outside myself; in certain cases one can only succeed in grouping them all together by inscribing them within the unity of an imaginary object. Only a novel, it seemed to me, could reveal the multiple and intricately spun meanings of that changed world to which I awoke in August 1944; a changing world that had not come to rest since then.

It swept me into its flux, and with me all those things in which I had believed: happiness, literature. What good is happiness if it not only does not bring me truth, but even hides it from me? Why does one write if one no longer feels oneself charged with a mission? Not only was I not weaving my life, but its shape, the shape of the time I lived in, the shape of all I loved, depended on the future. If I thought that humanity was on the road to peace, justice and plenty, my life would be coloured very differently than if I thought it was rushing towards war or wading through seas of pain. The practical side of politics – committees, meetings, manifestoes, discussions – bored me as they had always done; but I was interested in all the things that made our world. I had felt what was then called 'the failure of the Resistance' as a personal defeat: the triumphant return of bourgeois domination. My private existence had been deeply affected by it. In stormy quarrels, or else in silence, the friendships that had glowed around me after the Occupation had all more or less died down; their death had become inseparable from the death of the hopes we shared, and that death was the centre around which I organized my book. To talk about myself I had to talk about *us*, in the sense in which we used that word in 1944.

The danger of the enterprise was only too plain: we were

1. Today I am telling the story of my past in an historical mode, but I am doing so as a result of a project – on which I shall interrogate myself later on – entirely different from the one I formed in 1949, in the light of a disappointment which I had neither overcome nor even understood at the time, and which was still painful.

intellectuals, a race apart with whom novelists are advised to have nothing to do; merely to describe a collection of peculiar animals whose adventures would have been interesting as a series of anecdotes but nothing more – that was a project that could never have held my interest; but, after all, we were human beings, just a little more concerned than most people with giving our lives an integument of words. If the desire to write a novel became imperative for me, it was because I felt situated at a point in space and time at which each of the sounds that I could draw from myself had a chance to awaken echoes in a great many other hearts.

To represent us, I wrought a great number of characters and singled out two of them as 'subjects'. Although the central plot was the breaking and subsequent mending of a friendship between two men, I assigned one of these privileged roles to a woman, since a great many of the things I wanted to say were directly linked to my condition as a woman. There were many reasons that persuaded me to put a masculine hero beside Anne. First of all, to convey the density of the world it is convenient to employ more than one point of view; then, I wanted the relationship between Henri and Dubreuilh to be lived internally by one of the pair; above all, if I entrusted to Anne the burden of expressing the totality of my experience my book would have been, contrary to my intention, the study of one particular individual. Depicting, as I was, a writer, I wanted the reader to envisage him as a fellow being and not as an exotic animal; but a woman with a literary vocation is even more of an exceptional being than a man with that vocation. (By exceptional being, I mean not a monster or a natural marvel, but a rare statistical entity.) I entrusted my pen, therefore, not to Anne but to Henri; to Anne I gave a profession that she pursues with discretion; the axis of her life is the lives of others – her husband, her daughter; this dependency, which relates her to the majority of women, interested me in itself and also afforded one great advantage: Anne, being profoundly involved in the conflicts I was recounting while remaining outside them, envisaged them from an entirely different point of view than either Dubreuilh or Henri. I wanted to present images of my postwar period that would be at once decipherable and confused, clear but never fixed; Anne provided me with the negative of the objects that were shown through Henri's eyes in their positive aspect. My attitude with regard to literature was ambiguous. There was no longer any question of didacticism or salvation-seeking; in the face of the H-bomb and the hunger of millions words seemed futile; and yet I worked at *The Mandarins* with a furious doggedness. Anne did not write, but it was necessary to her that Dubreuilh should continue to do so; Henri sometimes wanted to stop writing, sometimes not; by combining all their contradictions, I could throw light on these things from different angles. The same thing was true when I tackled the characters' actions and the scandals aroused by them; similarly with the misfortunes of the others, their death, my death, the passage of time. Again I used the basic opposition on which I had built *All Men are Mortal*, giving Anne the sense of death and its concomitant taste for the absolute – which suited her passivity – while Henri contented himself with existing. Thus the two accounts of life that alternate throughout the book are not symmetrical; rather, I attempted to establish between them a sort of counterpoint, each reinforcing, diversifying, destroying the other.

Describing Henri as he experienced himself, in his familiarity with himself, I also wanted to show a writer in his excess, his mania; famous, already ageing, much more fanatically devoted than Henri to politics and literature, Dubreuilh occupies a key position in the book, since it is in their relation to him that his wife, Anne, and Henri define themselves. While approaching him fairly closely, thanks to Anne's intimate knowledge of him, I retained his opacity; the acuity of his experience and the strength of his mind place him above the other two; and yet, because his soliloquy always remains secret, I conveyed much less of it through him than through them.

I took particular pains with two portraits: Nadine and Paule. When I began, I intended to avenge myself on Nadine for certain traits that had offended me in Lise and some of my other younger women friends – a sexual coarseness that revealed rather nastily their underlying frigidity, an aggressiveness that was a poor compensation for their feeling of inferiority; demanding their independence without having the courage to pay the price of it, they converted the anxiety to which they were condemning themselves into bitterness. I had also observed, in other contexts, that the children of famous parents often have difficulty achieving maturity; the character I was drawing seemed to me suitable, by her very ingratitude, for the role of Dubreuilh's daughter. Little by little, the circumstances which explained her unpleasant qualities began to appear to me as full of valid excuses; Nadine began to seem to me more to be pitied as a victim than to be blamed; her egoism flaked off; she became, beneath her touchy uncouthness, generous and capable of attachment. Without deciding whether she would take the opportunity, at the end of the book I offered her a chance of happiness.

Of all my characters, the one that had most trouble taking shape was Paule, because I approached her by so many paths that did not intersect. In Anne's case, dependence was palliated by a direct and warmhearted interest in people and events; I conceived Paule as a woman radically alienated from herself by an exclusive attachment to one man, and tyrannizing him in the name of her slavery: a woman in love. Even more than at the time of *The Blood of Others*, in which I had given a sketch of one of these unfortunate creatures under the name of Denise, I now knew how dangerous it is for a woman to commit all of herself in a liaison with a writer or an artist dedicated to his work; giving up her own predilections, her own occupations, she exhausts herself in an attempt to imitate him without ever being able to reach him, and if he should turn from her, she finds herself stripped of everything. I had seen many examples of such a bankruptcy, and it was a subject about which I felt I had something to say. I was thinking, too, of certain women, beautiful and extravagantly brilliant in their youth, and then exhausting themselves later in their attempts to make time stand still; many such faces haunted my memory. And I still remembered the ravings of Louise Perron. It took me some time to compose from these specific intentions, these tattered images, these burning memories, a character and a story that I could fit into the book as a whole.

I have sometimes been criticized for not having chosen, to represent my sex, a woman who assumed an equal role with men in the realm of professional and political responsibilities; in this novel I was avoiding exceptions; I depicted women as, for the most part, I saw them, and as I still see them today: divided. Paule clings to traditional feminine values, they are not enough, she is torn to the point of madness; Nadine manages neither to accept her femininity nor to transcend it; Anne comes nearer than the others to true freedom, but all the same she does not succeed in finding fulfilment in her own undertakings. None of them can be considered, from a feminist point of view, as a 'positive heroine'. I agree, but unrepentantly.

I have said that at first I only wanted to establish the loosest of links between all these characters; 'well-made' novels always bored me. This was one of the criticisms Sartre made on reading the first version; given the form I had chosen, the vagueness of the plot was a weakness and not a clever device; I tightened it up. But it did not worry me that one long and important episode should remain marginal: the love affair between Anne and Lewis. I wrote it because it gave me pleasure to transpose into a fictional world a real occurrence that meant so much to me; and also, imprisoned in her role as a witness, Anne would have lacked reality. I wanted to give her a life of her own; also, in the years just after 1945, it was one of the things I found most wonderful, the way space had suddenly been opened up to us; I expressed this feeling of liberation by involving my heroine in a transatlantic affair. The extent to which I have made my account of it convincing is a direct function of its adventitious character; for when she meets Lewis, Anne has already existed a long time for the reader, he knows the world she moves in, he has had time to become attached to her. I was able to make her a familiar figure even before anything exciting happened to her, because the novel had other centres of interest. That is what people didn't understand when they said they liked the love story itself, but that they would have preferred it if, for the sake of unity, I had given it a separate treatment; by detaching it from the whole I should have emptied it of its content since, whether imaginary or real, what is called a character's richness is the interiorization of his or her environment. Lewis, it is true, does not benefit from any context; but he is seen through Anne's eyes; it suited my purpose that he should not exist until the moment he exists for her, and that one should be able to get inside his skin only insofar as Anne herself is able to do so; if one believes in her, one is inclined to believe in him. Of all my characters, Lewis is the one who approaches closest to a living model; external to the plot, he was exempt from its necessities, I was completely free to depict him as I wished; it so happened – a rare coincidence – that Algren, in his reality, was very representative of what I wanted to represent; but I did not content myself with a mere anecdotal fidelity: I used Algren to invent a character who would exist without reference to the world of real people.

For, contrary to what has been said, it is untrue that *The Mandarins* is a *roman à clé*; I loathe *romans à clé* as much as I loathe fictionalized biographies: it is impossible to sleep and dream if my senses remain awake; it is equally impossible to move into the world of fiction while still remaining anchored to the real world. If he tries to encompass both real and imaginary worlds at the same time, the reader becomes confused; and one would have to be a very cruel author indeed to inflict such a palimpsest on him. The extent and the manner of the fiction's dependence upon real life is of small importance; the fiction is built only by pulverizing all these sources and then allowing a new existence to be reborn from them.[1] The gossips who poke about among the ashes let the work that is offered them escape, and the shards they rout out are worth nothing; no fact has any truth unless it is placed in its true context.

Then Anne is not me? She was made from me, true, but I have explained for what reasons I made her into a woman in whom I do not recognize myself. I lent her tastes, feelings, reactions and memories that were mine; often I speak through her mouth. Yet she has neither my appetites, nor my insistences, nor, above all, has she the autonomy that has been bestowed on me by a profession which means so much to me. Her relations with a man almost twenty years older than herself are almost like those of a daughter and, despite the couple's deep understanding, leave her solitary; she had only tentatively committed herself to her profession. Because she does not have aims and projects of her own, she lives the 'relative' life of a 'secondary' being. It was mainly the negative aspects of my experience that I expressed through her: the fear of dying and the panic of nothingness, the vanity of earthly diversions, the shame of forgetting, the scandal of living. The joy of existence, the gaiety of activity, the pleasure of writing, all those I bestowed on Henri. He resembles me at least as much as Anne does, perhaps more.

For Henri, whatever people have said, is not Camus; not at all. He is young, he has dark hair, he runs a newspaper; the resemblance stops there. Certainly Camus, like Henri, was a writer, enjoyed being alive and concerned himself with politics; but they both shared these traits with a great many other people, with Sartre, with myself. Henri's language, his attitudes, his character, his relations with others, his vision of the world, the details of his private life, his

1. A successful historical novel satisfies this demand. Alexandre Dumas projects history into an imaginary dimension; his Richelieu is unequivocally an imaginary character.

ideas – all these things differ completely from those of his pseudo-model; Camus' profound hostility to Communism would alone be sufficient – both in itself and in its implications – to set a deep gulf between them; my hero, in his relations with the Communist Party and in his attitude to Socialism, resembles Sartre and Merleau-Ponty, and not Camus in the slightest; and in fact, most of the time they are my own emotions, my own thoughts that inhabit him.

The identification of Sartre with Dubreuilh is no less aberrant; the only similarities between them are their common curiosity, concern with the world and fanaticism in work; but Dubreuilh is twenty years older than Sartre, he is marked by his past and fearful of the future, between politics and literature it is politics to which he gives his preference; authoritarian, tenacious, closed, unemotional and unsociable, sombre even in his moments of gaiety, he could scarcely be more different from Sartre. Nor do their stories intersect; while Dubreuilh's creation of the S.R.L. is almost an act of fanaticism, Sartre simply linked himself, without any show of frenzy, to certain groups that asked for his support; at no time did he ever give up writing; he published the 'Soviet Work Code' without hesitation as soon as he became aware of its existence. The plot that I elaborated also differs deliberately from the facts. First by a transposition in time; I described as happening between 1945 and 1947 events, problems and crises that actually took place later. The R.D.R. came into being at the time of the struggle for neutralism; the scandal of the Russian camps did not break out until 1949, etc. The intimacy which exists between Henri and Dubreuilh is much more like that which in fact existed between Bost and ourselves than like the distant friendship that linked us to Camus. I have described the way in which the final quarrel between Camus and Sartre was simply the final moment of a long disagreement; the rupture between Henri and Dubreuilh is so entirely unlike theirs that I had written a first version of it in 1950, and it is followed by a reconciliation, which did not happen between Sartre and Camus. As soon as we had been liberated, their political attitudes were already beginning to diverge. Camus belonged neither to the *Temps Modernes* group nor to the R.D.R.; there was never any collusion between the R.D.R. and *Combat*, which *L'Espoir*, incidentally, resembles far less than it does *Franc-Tireur*; Camus left his newspaper for reasons that had nothing to do with Sartre. He no longer had anything to do with it at the time of the 'Soviet camps' affair, and he was never faced with the question of whether or not to make their existence public. The same things hold true of the secondary characters and events: all the material I drew from memory was refracted, diluted, hammered thin, blown up, mixed, transposed, twisted, sometimes completely reversed, and in every case re-created. I would have liked people to take this book for what it is; neither autobiography, nor reportage: an evocation.

Nor is *The Mandarins*, in my opinion, a novel with a message. Such thesis-novels always impose a certain truth that eclipses all others and calls a halt to the perpetual dance of conflicting points of view; whereas I described certain ways of living after the war, without offering any solution to the problems that were troubling my main characters. One of the principal themes that emerges from my story is that of *repetition* in the sense in which Kierkegaard uses that word: truly to possess something, one must have lost it and found it again. At the end of the novel, Henri and Dubreuilh once more take up the threads of their friendship, their literary work and their political activities; they return to the point they started from; but in between there was a time when all their hopes had died. From that moment on, instead of being content with a facile optimism, they take upon themselves all the difficulties, the failures, the scandal implied in any undertaking. Their old enthusiastic adherences are replaced by austere preferences. I described their apprenticeship; but I offered no proofs. The final decision of these two men does not have the value of a lesson; given what they are and the circumstances in which they find themselves, the reader can understand that they should make that choice; but he can also predict that in the future their hesitations may return. More radically, their point of view – that of action, of the finite, of life – is implicitly questioned by Anne, in whom I embodied the point of view of being, of the absolute, of death. Her past inclined her to this contestation and in the novel's present it is imposed on her by the horror into which the world is plunged. That is another important theme of the book, which it has in common with *The Blood of Others*; but when I wrote *The Blood of Others* I had just discovered that horror. I tried to protect myself against it, and I asserted, through my hero, the necessity of taking it upon oneself; that is how the book became didactic. By 1950, the horror had become a familiar dimension of the world. I no longer sought to elude it. Dubreuilh does attempt to transcend it, but Anne allows herself to remain immersed in it, and contemplates the idea of affirming its intolerable truth by her own suicide; between these two attitudes I made no choice. In the end, Anne does not kill herself; this is because I did not want to repeat the error I made in *L'Invitée* of attributing to my heroine an act motivated by purely metaphysical reasons. Anne is not made of the stuff of suicides; but her return to an acceptance of the everyday world seems more like a defeat than a triumph. In a short story I wrote at the age of eighteen, the heroine, on the last page, came down the stairs leading from her room to the living room: she was going to mingle with the others, she was going to submit to their conventions and their lies, betraying the 'real life' she had glimpsed in her solitude. It is no mere coincidence that Anne, leaving her room to go and join Dubreuilh, walks down a staircase: she too is betraying something. And then, tomorrow for her as well as for Henri, is uncertain. The basic confrontation of being and nothingness that I sketched at the age of twenty in my private diary, pursued through all my books and never resolved, is even here given no certain reply. I showed some people, at grips with doubts and hopes, groping in the dark to find their way; I cannot think I proved anything.

In *The Mandarins*, I remained faithful to the technique of *L'Invitée*, though using it more flexibly; underlying Anne's narrative is a monologue occurring in the present, which allowed me to break up the narrative, elide it and comment on it freely. I know the drawbacks of this form, even though I kept to it; but if I had eluded the conventions it imposed on me, I should only have been obliged to adopt others that satisfied me even less. Just after the publication of *The Mandarins*, Nathalie Sarraute wrote an article condemning this traditional approach. But in my eyes her critique is null and void because it is based on a metaphysic that does not hold water. According to her, reality 'today' has been forced to take refuge in 'scarcely perceptible impulses'; a novelist who is not fascinated by the 'dark places of psychology' can be nothing more than a *trompe l'oeil* artificer. This is because she confuses exteriority with appearances. But the exterior world does exist. It is not impossible to write good books based on an outmoded psychologism, but one certainly cannot deduce from it a valid aesthetic system. Nathalie Sarraute allows that there exist, outside herself, 'great sufferings, great and simple joys, powerful needs' and that one might think of 'evoking the sufferings and struggles of men in a plausible enough manner';

but these are tasks below the dignity of a maker of literature; with amazing unconcern, she abandons them to the journalists. At that rate, one could divert one's readers with clinical studies, psycho-analytic memoranda, the verbatim ravings of schizophrenics and paranoiacs. So scrupulous when it is a question of anatomizing an ambition or a grudge, does she think that the life of a factory or an H.L.M. can be accounted for by reports and statistics? Collective enterprises, public events, crowds, the relations of men to each other and to things, all these very real phenomena, that cannot be reduced to the terms of our subterranean palpitations, deserve and demand to be explored in terms of art. That dialogue is a problem for a novel-ist I quite agree; but I certainly don't think speech is 'the extension of subterranean movements'; it has a great many uses; most often, it is an act, demanded by a situation, which explodes into daylight, breaking with the silence, and we denature it by encysting it within the continuity of an interior monologue. Means must be invented which will aid the novelist to unmask more efficiently the truth of the world, but not to turn him aside from it to imprison himself in a maniacal and untruthful subjectivism.

As for the style of *The Mandarins*, it either pleases or fails to please, but it has often been criticized in an academic manner, as though there existed a standard 'good style' from which I diverged. I deliberately kept close to the spoken word. These memoirs are written differently. A certain rigour is suitable for a narrative deal-ing with a past already fixed. But in my novel I was attempting to evoke existence at the moment it springs into being, and I wanted my sentences to correspond to that movement.

INTERLUDE

WHY this pause, suddenly? I know perfectly well that an existence cannot be analysed into clearcut periods, and 1952 did not represent a milestone in mine. But the country and the map are different things. My narrative demands a kind of summing-up before I can continue it.

One defect of diaries and autobiographies is that usually what 'goes without saying' goes without being said, and thus one misses the essential. I too am falling into this trap. In *The Mandarins*, I failed to make clear how important their work was to the characters in the book; I was hoping to do better for myself this time. I was deceiving myself. There is scarcely any way of describing work; you do it, and that's all. And so it is that in this book it takes up very little space, whereas in my life it takes up so much; my whole life is organized around it. I am insisting on this point because the public is more or less aware of the time and trouble it takes to write an essay; but, on the whole, they imagine that a novel or a book of memoirs can just be dashed off in no time at all. 'There's not so much to that. I could've done as much myself,' a lot of young women said after reading *The Memoirs of a Dutiful Daughter*; it is no coincidence that they did not in fact do as much. With one or two exceptions, all the writers I know work enormously hard; I am like them. And contrary to popular belief, novels and auto-biographies absorb me much more than an essay; they also give me more pleasure. I think about them for a long time in advance. I thought about the characters in *The Mandarins* until I believed they really existed. For my memoirs, I familiarized myself with my past by rereading letters, old books, diaries, newspapers. When I feel ready, I write three of four hundred pages straight off. This is arduous work: it requires intense concentration, and the rubbish that I accumulate appalls me. At the end of a month or two, I am so sickened I can't go on. I begin again from scratch. Despite all the material I have at my disposal the paper is blank once more, and I hesitate before taking the plunge. Usually I begin badly, out of impatience; I want to say everything at once; my narrative is lumpy, chaotic and lifeless. Gradually I become resigned to taking my time. Then comes the moment when I find the distance, the tone and the rhythm I feel are right; then I really get under way. With the help of my rough draft, I sketch the broad outlines of a chapter. I begin again at page one, read it through and rewrite it sentence by sentence; then I correct each sentence so that it will fit into the page as a whole, then each page so that it has its place in the whole chapter; later on, each chapter, each page, each sentence, is revised in relation to the work as a whole. Painters, Baudelaire says, progress from first sketch to finished work by painting the complete picture at each stage; that is what I try to do. So that each of my books requires two to three years' work – four for *The Mandarins* – during which I spend six or seven hours a day at my writing table.

People often have a much more romantic idea of literature. But it imposes this discipline precisely because it is more than just a profession: it is a passion or, let us say, a madness. When I wake up, an appetite or an anxiety obliges me to pick up my pen straight away; it is only in the dark periods when I doubt everything that I observe an abstract schedule; and in the dark times even the schedule may be of no avail. But, except when I am travelling or when extraordinary events are occurring, a day when I do not write tastes of ashes.

And of course inspiration comes into it: without it, mere diligence would be no use at all. The desire to express certain things in a certain way is born, reborn, enriched and transformed in capricious ways. I do not decide the resonances an incident, a sudden understanding, or a flash of memory awaken in me, nor what image or what word may spring into my mind. I keep to my plan, but I leave room for my moods; if I suddenly want to write a certain scene, treat a particular theme, I do so, without holding myself rigidly to a pre-established sequence. Once the main body of the book exists, I willingly trust myself to chance. I let my thoughts wander, I digress, not only sitting at my work, but all day long, all night even. It often happens that a sentence suddenly runs through my head before I go to bed, or when I am unable to sleep, and I get up again and note it down. Many passages in *The Mandarins* and my memoirs were written in one fell swoop under the influence of a sudden emotion; sometimes I retouch them the next day, sometimes not.

When finally, after six months, a year, or even two, I submit the results to Sartre, I am not yet satisfied, but I feel I'm at the end of my tether; I need his severity and his encouragement to revive my energies. First of all he reassures me: 'You've done it . . . It will be a good book.' And then little things begin to annoy him: it's too long, too short, that's not right, that's badly expressed, it's a mess, it's hopeless. If I weren't accustomed to his harsh way of putting things – mine is no softer when I'm criticizing him – I would be utterly crushed. As a matter of fact, the only time he really made me feel uneasy was when I was finishing *The Mandarins*; ordinarily his criticisms stimulate me because they show me how I can improve the defects I am already more or less aware of, and which often jump out and hit me in the face as soon as he begins reading a book. He suggests cuts and changes; but most of all he urges me to go further, to go deeper, to face up to obstacles instead of trying to get around them. His advice is always directed the way I myself want to go, and then I need only a few weeks, or a few months at most, to give the book its final shape. I stop when I have the impression, not of course that the book is perfect, but that I can't do any more with it.

In the years I am describing, I took a great many vacations; that means, generally speaking, that I went and worked somewhere else. However, I did go on long journeys during which I did not write. That is because my desire to know the world is closely linked with my desire to express it. My curiosity is less barbaric than it was when I was young, but it is still almost as demanding: one never stops learning because there is never any end to ignorance. I do not mean to imply that no moment is ever gratuitous for me; no instant has ever seemed wasted if it brought me a pleasure. But through the dispersion of my occupations, my diversions and my wanderings, there is a constant desire to add to my store of knowledge.

The further I go, the more the world fills my life to the bursting point. To tell it, I need a dozen registers and a pedal to sustain the feelings – melancholy, joy, disgust – that have coloured whole periods of it, through the heart's intermittences. Every moment reflects my past, my body, my relations with others, the tasks I have undertaken, the society I live in, the whole of this earth; linked together, and independent, these realities sometimes reinforce each other and descant together, sometimes they interfere with, contradict, or neutralize each other. If their totality does not remain always present, I shall say nothing exact. Even if I surmount this difficulty, I stumble over others. A life is such a strange object, at one moment translucent, at another utterly opaque, an object I make with my own hands, an object imposed on me, an object for which the world provides the raw material and then steals it from me again, pulverized by events, scattered, broken, scored yet retaining its unity; how heavy it is and how inconsistent: this contradiction breeds many misunderstandings. I was not as shaken by the war as I claim, some have said, since in 1941 I was enjoying going for walks; some will say, no doubt, that I was little affected by the war in Algeria because Rome, because music, because certain books still held their attraction for me. But, and everyone must have experienced this, it is possible to be amused even as the heart mourns. The most violent, the most sincere emotion does not last;

sometimes it instigates action, engenders obsessions, but it disappears. On the other hand an anxiety, temporarily laid aside, does not cease to exist: it is present in the very care I take to avoid it. Words are often no more than silence, and silence has its voices. During the time Sartre was a prisoner, was I unhappy, or still happy? I was as I have described myself, with my moments of gaiety, my anxieties, my discouragements, my hopes. I have tried to capture reality in its diversity and its fluidity; to summarize my story in final words is as aberrant as to translate a good poem into prose.

The background, tragic or serene, against which my experiences are drawn gives them their true meaning and constitutes their unity; I have avoided linking them by transitions that would be unequivocal, hence artificial. Yet if this ever-present totality seems so necessary to me, why have I subjected myself to chronological order instead of choosing some other construction? I have pondered this matter, and I have hesitated. But what counts above all in my life is that time goes by; I grow older, the world changes, my relation with it varies; to show the transformations, the ripenings, the irreversible deterioration of others and of myself – nothing is more important to me than that. And that obliges me to follow obediently the thread the years have unwound.

So that after this interlude I take up my story at the point where I had left it.

PART TWO

CHAPTER SIX

YOUNG women have an acute sense of what should and should not be done when one is no longer young. 'I don't understand,' they say, 'how a woman over forty can bleach her hair; how she can make an exhibition of herself in a bikini; how she can flirt with men. The day I'm her age . . .' That day comes: they bleach their hair; they wear bikinis; they smile at men. When I was thirty I made the same sort of resolution: 'Certain aspects of love, well, after forty, one has to give them up.' I loathed what I called 'harridans' and promised myself that when I reached that stage, I would dutifully retire to the shelf. All of which had not kept me from embarking upon a love affair at thirty-nine. Now, at forty-four, I was relegated to the land of shades; yet, as I have said, although my body made no objection to this, my imagination was much less resigned. When the opportunity arose of coming back to life, I seized it gladly.

July was almost over. I was about to drive down to Milan; Sartre would join me by train, and we were going to tour Italy for two months. Meanwhile, Bost and Cau were happily preparing to fly off to Brazil, where the publisher Nagel was sending them to gather material for a Guide. They bought white dinner jackets and Bost invited us to celebrate their departure around an *aïoli*. I suggested he invite Claude Lanzmann as well. The party lasted late, we drank a lot. Next morning my telephone rang. 'I'd like to take you to the movies,' Lanzmann said. 'To the movies? To see which film?' 'Oh any one.' I hesitated; my last days were crowded, but I knew I mustn't refuse. We agreed on a place and time to meet. To my great surprise, as soon as I had hung up I burst into tears.

Five days later I left Paris; standing on the side walk, Lanzmann waved as I put the car into gear. Something had happened; something, I had no doubt of it, was beginning. I had rediscovered my body. Distracted by the emotion of our good-byes, I got completely lost in the suburbs before I finally emerged onto Route Nationale 7, delighted to have ahead of me that long ribbon of kilometres on which to remember and to dream.

I was still driving in a dream two mornings later as I left Domodossola, where I had spent the night; I had two passengers, English girls hitchhiking from Calais to Venice with return plane tickets from Munich to London in their pockets. It was raining over Lake Maggiore; I skidded and tore a milestone out of its socket; neither girl so much as flinched. Some Italian men straightened my mudguard and soothed my pride by telling me that the road was notorious for the camber that caused innumerable accidents; but the shock, far from bringing me to my senses, simply confused me more than ever. I dropped the English girls at a crossroads, went on into Milan, meandered along looking for a garage and suddenly noticed that my right door was flapping open; as I was trying to close it I went over the kerb. 'I'm losing my head,' I told myself, and stopped the car; then I noticed that my bag with all my papers and a great deal of money in it was no longer on the seat beside me. I left the car there and ran back the way I had come as fast as my legs would take me. Then I saw a cyclist coming towards me, holding the bag at arm's length with a disgusted look on his face.

The car finally entrusted to a mechanic, I went to the Café della Scala and collected Sartre and my wits; but I was still upset that afternoon when I got back behind the wheel. Would this new mode of travelling appeal to him? I was afraid I would discourage him for good by some awful display of clumsiness; but no, my awkward manoeuvring in the towns didn't make him at all impatient; on the open road, nothing disturbed his phlegmatic attitude except the boorishness of certain Italians, who would pass and then dawdle in front of me: 'Pass him, go on, pass him.' The Italian would accelerate or even start zigzagging to keep in front; Sartre wouldn't leave me in peace until I had finally got in front again; if I had yielded to all his exhortations, we'd have been killed a hundred times over; but I preferred this enthusiasm to prudent warnings.

From Cremona to Tarento, from Bari to Erice, we rediscovered Italy: Mantua and the frescoes of Mantegna, the paintings in Ferrara, Ravenna, Urbino with its Uccellos, the Piazza d'Ascoli, the churches of Apulia, the troglodytes of Matera, the *trulli* of Alberobello, the baroque beauties of Lecce, and in Sicily those of Noto. We went last to Agrigento; we revisited Segeste, Syracuse. We went through the Abruzzi. I took a ski-lift to the top of the Gran Sasso and saw the gloomy-looking hotel where they had shut Mussolini away. Thanks to the car, we were no longer restricted by timetables, and nothing was inaccessible. All the same, something had been lost, Sartre said, and I agreed: the surprise of finding yourself suddenly plunged into the centre of a town. If you arrive by train, or by plane, a city seems like a new world; when you travel by car, a city is the end of a stage on the journey, a knot linking it to the next, and not a universe; its streets merely extend the roads outside and lead to other roads; its originality fades, for the colour of its walls, the design of its squares and façades, are already adumbrated in the little towns near by. The advantage is that although the city becomes less striking, it is also more easily understood. The real meaning of Naples came to us only after we had seen the extent of the poverty in southern Italy. A new familiarity sprang up between the countryside and ourselves; we stopped off in villages and mingled with the *braccianti*, who sit in the cafés for hours without drinking, without hoping; often men along the road would make timid signs to us and we would stop to give them a lift; most of them were unemployed; they asked us if we could find them work in France.

Besides, the car also had surprises in store for us. I remember the 15th of August; we left Rome for Foggia in the morning, drove all day under a blazing sky, continually delayed by roadwork and barriers; night had fallen; for two hours the white glare of the Italian headlights had blinded me, and I was exhausted. At Lucera we stopped and got out for a drink; I parked the car against the city wall and we walked through the gates. Suddenly we were in a great hall streaming with light, full of people dancing, and the ceiling was the sky; other halls led out of it, one after the other, every piazza in the town was lit up like day, and each had its own orchestra and ball.

That summer, the thermometer stayed over eighty almost without exception all over Italy. Sartre was writing the sequel to *Les Communistes et la paix*; he wanted to work, I wanted to go sightseeing: we succeeded in combining our obsessions, but not without considerable discomfort. We would sight-see, wander, walk, eat up the miles until the middle of the afternoon, braving the hottest hours of the day on foot and by car; then, broken with fatigue, we would retire to our rooms – usually suffocatingly hot – and instead of resting, hurl ourselves at our desks. More than once I had to leave mine to soak my burning blotchy face in cold water.

On the way back I stayed with my sister in Milan for several days; while there I read Pavese's journal and took it back with me to Paris so we could publish extracts from it in *Les Temps Modernes*.

During our vacation, Lanzmann had been on a trip to Israel; we had written to each other. He returned to Paris two weeks after I did, and our bodies met each other again with joy. We began to build our future by telling each other the past. To define himself, he said first of all: I'm a Jew. I knew the weight of those words; but none of my Jewish friends had ever made me fully understand their meaning. They let their situation as Jews pass without comment — at least in their relations with me. Lanzmann insisted that his be recognized. It was the ruling force of his life.

As a child, he had lived at first in a state of pride: 'We are everywhere,' his father would tell him proudly as he showed him a map of the world. When, at the age of thirteen, he discovered anti-Semitism, the whole world was shaken, nothing survived intact. He would admit: 'Yes, I'm a Jew,' and language was immediately abolished, the questioner became a blind, deaf, savage animal; he felt personally to blame for this metamorphosis. At the same time, reduced to the abstract notion, a Jew, he felt expelled from his own being. To such an extent that he no longer knew, in the end, if it was more of a lie to say yes or no. Rejected because of this difference at the age when all children want most to conform, his exile left its mark on him for good. He regained his pride thanks to his father, one of the very first members of the Resistance. He himself started a Resistance organization while still at a *lycée* in Clermont-Ferrand, and, from 14 October 1943 on, fought in the *maquis*. So his experience had presented an image of the Jews not as people resigned, humiliated, persecuted, but as fighters. The six million men, women and children exterminated by the Nazis belonged to a great people not predestined to martyrdom, but the victim of gratuitous barbarism. Weeping with rage at night as he evoked these massacres, by the hate he vowed against the murderers and their accomplices he withdrew again into the exile once forced upon him but now desired of his own free will: he wanted to be a Jew. The names Marx, Freud, and Einstein filled him with pride. He beamed whenever he discovered that some famous man was a Jew. Even today when people praise the great Soviet physicist Landau without mentioning that he's a Jew, Lanzmann flies into a rage.

Although he had many friends among them, his bitterness towards the *Goyim* never disappeared. 'I want to kill, all the time,' he told me. I could feel, buried inside him, flexing its muscles, a violence always ready to explode. Sometimes in the morning after some disturbing dream, he would wake up shouting at me: 'You're all kapos!' He assailed our world with buffoonery, outrageous behaviour, extravagances of speech and manner. At twenty, when he was a senior at the Lycée Louis-le-Grand, he rented a cassock and went around knocking on rich people's doors and collecting money. Yet scandal was only an expedient. He still looked back nostalgically to the days of his childhood, when he was a Jew but all men were brothers. He had been torn apart, the world had been given over to chaos: he tried to make himself whole again and rediscover order in the world. At twenty, he believed in the universality of culture and he had worked zealously to make it his: he had the feeling it didn't quite belong to him. He had put his hopes in the mediating power of truth; but men answered him with their passions and their interests, they remained divided. Neither knowledge nor reasoning could provide an escape from his solitude. Isolated, unjustified, he experienced his own contingency to the point of disgust. He knew that no inner cunning would ever free him from it; his only salvation lay in sustaining himself by some objective necessity. Marxism affected him as a truth no less self-evident than his own existence; it revealed the intelligibility of human conflicts and released him from his subjectivity. Ideologically in agreement with the Communists, recognizing his own dreams in their objectives, he put his trust in them with an optimism that sometimes irritated me, but which was the obverse of a profound pessimism: he needed a vision of a redeemed future to compensate for the laceration he suffered. His Manichaeism astonished me, for he had a subtle, even a cunning, intelligence; he often blamed himself for it, but without being able to keep from relapsing into it. Because he had been dispossessed of everything, he could not bear to be deprived of anything. He had to be able to see his adversaries as the representatives of absolute Evil; the army of Good had to be without defect if it was to restore the lost Paradise. 'Why don't you become a member of the Communist Party?' I asked him. He shied away from the idea. Between sympathy, even unconditional sympathy, and commitment there lies a distance he could never bridge, because nothing seemed real enough to him, especially not himself. In his childhood, by forcing him to renounce either his

'Jewishness' or his individuality, the world had stolen his Self: when he said *I* he always felt like an impostor.

Lacking any frame of reference, he adopted very easily the viewpoints of people he respected; but he was also stubborn and wilful. He could find no means inside himself to oppose the voice of his emotions and desires, or the violence of his imagination; he refused to try to control them. Indifferent to the usual constraints and conventions, he allowed his sadness to express itself in tears, his feelings of revulsion in fits of vomiting. Sartre, most of my friends, myself – all of us were puritans; we kept our reactions under control and externalized our emotions very little. Lanzmann's spontaneity was foreign to me. And yet it was by his excesses that he seemed near to me. Like him, I would make plans with frenzy and follow them through with maniacal stubbornness. I would weep violently, and there still lurked within me a sort of nostalgia for my old rages.

A Jew and an eldest son, the responsibilities with which Lanzmann had been burdened from childhood on had produced a precocious maturity in him; sometimes he seemed to be carrying the weight of a whole ancestral experience on his shoulders: while I was talking to him, it never occurred to me that he was younger than I. Yet we were aware that there was seventeen years difference between us; but the gap did not alarm us. For myself, I needed some sort of distance if I were to give my heart sincerely, for there could be no question of trying to duplicate the understanding I had with Sartre. Algren belonged to another continent, Lanzmann to another generation; this too was a foreignness that kept a balance in our relationship. His youth doomed me to being only a moment in his life; it also excused me, in my own eyes, for not being able to give him today the whole of mine. Not that he asked me for it in any case: he accepted me as I was, with my past and my present. All the same, the harmony between us was not achieved all at once. In December, we spent several days in Holland; along the frozen canals, in the taverns with their close-drawn curtains where we drank our *advokat*, we talked. The vacations I took every year with Sartre presented a problem: I didn't want to give them up; but a separation of two months would have been painful for both of us. We agreed that Lanzmann would come every summer and spend ten days or so with myself and Sartre. As we talked, other sources of uneasiness, our last doubts, were dissipated. When we got back to Paris, we decided to live together. I had loved my solitude, but I did not regret it.

Our life together developed its own pattern. In the morning we worked side by side. He had brought back some notes from Israel that he wanted to work up into an account of his visit. He had been much struck by what he had seen there: in Israel, Jews were not outsiders, they were the people with all the rights; with pride and, with a certain sense of scandal, he had discovered that there were Jewish ships and a Jewish navy, towns, fields, trees that were Jewish too, there were rich Jews and poor Jews. His astonishment had led him to ask himself certain questions about himself. Sartre, to whom he described this experience, advised him to write a book combining an account of Israel with his own story. Lanzmann found the idea attractive; as it turned out, it was not a happy one. At the age of twenty-five he lacked the necessary perspective to write about himself; he began very well, but then came up against obstacles within himself and was forced to stop.

Lanzmann's presence beside me freed me from my age. First, it did away with my anxiety attacks. Two or three times he caught me going through one, and he was so alarmed to see me thus shaken that a command was established in every bone and nerve of my body never to yield to them; I found the idea of dragging him already into the horrors of declining age revolting. And then, his participation revived my interest in everything. For my curiosity had become more temperate. I was living on an earth limited in resources and a prey to terrible and simple ills, and my own finite state – that of my situation, my destiny, my work – restricted my desires; for behind me were the days when I had expected everything in every sphere of life! I still took an interest in what was happening: books, films, painting, theatre; but I was more concerned with controlling, deepening, completing my earlier experiences; for Lanzmann, these things were new, and he threw an unexpected light on all of them for me. Thanks to him, a thousand things were restored to me: joys, astonishments, anxieties, laughter and the freshness of the world. After two years in which the universal marasma had coincided for me with the break-up of a love affair and the first warnings of physical decline, I leapt back enthralled into happiness. The war was receding. I immured myself in the gaiety of my private life.

I continued to see Sartre as much as before, but our habits

changed. A few months before I had been awakened by an unaccustomed noise: someone was tapping lightly on a drum. I switched on the light. Drops of water were falling from the ceiling onto a leather armchair. I complained to the concierge, who informed the agent, who spoke to the owner. And the rain in my room continued, slowly rotting everything. When Lanzmann lived with me the furniture and the floor were submerged in books. It was still possible to work and sleep in the room, but it was no longer a very pleasant place to live. From then on, to eat and talk and drink, I moved my headquarters with Sartre to La Palette, on the Boulevard Montparnasse, or sometimes to Le Falstaff, which reminded us of our youth. I also went quite often with Lanzmann or Olga to La Bucherie, on the other side of the square; when I arranged to meet people it was usually there; the place was a meeting place for left-wing intellectuals; through the bay window you could look out at Notre-Dame and greenery; there was a phonograph quietly playing the Brandenburg Concertos. Like myself, Sartre was happiest in the tiny circle I assembled in the Rue de la Bûcherie for New Year's Eve: Olga, Bost, Wanda, Michelle, Lanzmann. There was so much understood between us that a smile conveyed as much as a whole oration. In a group like this, conversation can be the most amusing pastime in the world; when the complicity we shared is lacking, it becomes hard work, and often futile as well. I had lost the taste for ephemeral encounters. Monique Lange offered to take me out to dinner with Faulkner; I refused. The evening Sartre had dinner at Michelle's with Picasso and Chaplin, whom I had met in the States, I preferred to go with Lanzmann to see *Limelight*.

With spring came a great satisfaction: *The Second Sex* appeared in America with a success unsoiled by any salacious comment. The book has always remained dear to me and every time it has been published in another country, I have been pleased to receive fresh proof that the scandal it aroused in France was the fault of my readers and not myself.

Towards the end of March, I went down to Saint-Tropez with Lanzmann; he took me to see his part of the *maquis*; there were still great piles of rubble blocking the roads of La Margeride. We joined Sartre at the Aïoli; Michelle was living with her children on a little square near by. Chatting with Sartre on Sennequier's terrace, we again met Merleau-Ponty and also Brasseur, who had a house at Gassin. He asked Sartre to do an adaptation of Dumas' *Kean* for him, and Sartre, who adores melodramas, didn't say no. In the evening, we would sit by the wood fire in the dining room of the Aïoli: before long this spruce little hotel was to disappear beneath a layer of dust, and Mme Clo, so respectable with her white hair, her high-necked pullover, her discreet make-up, was accused of complicity in a holdup; I had great difficulty in recognizing her as the old, haggard-looking woman whose picture appeared in all the newspapers in 1954. I showed Lanzmann Les Maures, Estérel, the coast, the corniches. As we drove we talked about my novel, which I had given him to read in manuscript; he had an acute and painstaking critical sense; he gave me some good advice and I learned a lot from his objections; at first they irritated me, but then I gradually became aware of the defect that was provoking them. I was taking enormous trouble over this book. I had reworked it from start to finish since our Norwegian trip: when Sartre re-read it at the end of autumn 1952, he was still not satisfied. Irked by the conventions of the novel, I had accepted them but had not done so wholeheartedly; it was too short, too long, scattered; the conversations didn't ring true; I wanted to show particular individuals, with their certainties and their doubts, ceaselessly challenged both by others and by themselves, wavering between clear-sightedness and excessive simplicity, between prejudice and sincerity; and now, suddenly, instead of creating people, I seemed to be expounding ideas. Perhaps it really was impossible to take writers as heroes, or at any rate impossible for me; perhaps my resources were not equal to the task. . . . 'I'm just going to shelve the whole thing,' I decided. 'Keep working at it,' Sartre told me; but his uneasiness counted more heavily for me than his encouragement. It was actually Bost and Lanzmann who convinced me to keep going; they were reading it for the first time, and they were more affected by its positive value than by its weaknesses. So I went back to work. But there were many times during that last year of labour when I had to champ hard on the bit when people asked with polite astonishment: 'Aren't you writing any more? Why doesn't she write any more? It's been a long time since she wrote anything . . .' And I would feel a stab of jealousy when I caught sight of the crisp cover of a new novel fresh from the press, and written by some talented writer with a nimbler pen than mine.

In November, Sartre had published in *Les Temps Modernes* the second part of his study, *Les Communistes et la paix*, in which he gave an account of exactly how far and why he was in agreement with the Party. He went to Vienna, and on his return gave us a detailed account of the Congress of the Partisans for Peace. He had spent a whole evening drinking vodka with the Russians. There were – relatively – only a few Communists there: twenty per cent. Many of the delegates had come to the convention without the permission of their governments; some of them, to get out of Japan and Indochina, had been forced to make long and devious journeys on foot; others – the Egyptians particularly – were running the risk of being thrown into prison when they went back. France, apart from Communists, was poorly represented; the intellectual Left, which Sartre had hoped to induce to accompany him, was missing. I went with Lanzmann to the meeting at the Vel' d'Hiv' where the delegates gave an account of their experiences; there was a certain piquancy in seeing Sartre and Duclos sitting next to each other and exchanging smiles. The Communists were surprised as well, I think; the committee member who was supposed to introduce Sartre hesitated slightly: 'We are happy to have among us Jean-Paul . . .'; there was a slight gasp; people thought he was going to say 'David'. He recovered himself and Sartre took the microphone. I was always moved to hear him speak in public, I suppose because of the distance that the listening crowd created between us; one after the other, his sentences landed easily, but to me each one seemed a precarious miracle. He produced a great deal of amusement with his mockery of the left-wingers who had been too frightened to go to Vienna; he took Martinet and Stéphane to task; the latter was sitting in front of me, I could see him acknowledging the hits, and from time to time he turned around with a wan smile.

The *Temps Modernes* staff approved of Sartre's political attitude for the most part; he himself has told[1] how his relations with Merleau-Ponty were altered by it. Many people dissociated themselves from him, with greater or lesser publicity, either by a profound and genuine disagreement, or because they found it compromising to be linked with him. He was rather coldly received at Freiburg, where he went to give a lecture. He spoke for three hours. 'I got quite caught up in it; you won't catch me at

1. *Merleau-Ponty vivant.*

another!' said the wife of the director of the French Institute as she came out. Out of the twelve hundred students who had heard him, barely fifty understood French well enough to follow. 'We understood the ideas, but not the examples,' one of them said. Sartre struck them as too close to Marxism. He paid a visit to Heidegger, perched on his eyrie, and told him how sorry he was about the play Gabriel Marcel had just written about him.[1] That was all they talked about, and Sartre left after half an hour. Heidegger was going in for mysticism, Sartre told me; then he added, his eyes wide: 'Four thousand students and professors toiling over Heidegger day after day, just think of it!'

He had finally decided to write most of the book devoted to the defence of Henri Martin himself. Some of his friends were a bit worried: hadn't he anything better to do? I had felt that way too, in prehistoric times: before the war. Now, literature was no longer sacred to me; and I knew that when Sartre decided to go in a certain direction it was because he felt it was necessary. 'He should finish his novel. It's high time he finished his Ethics. Why does he remain silent? Why did he speak out?' Nothing could be more futile than the criticism and advice with which people inundated me on his behalf. It is impossible to understand from the outside the conditions in which a man's work develops; the person in question knows better than anyone what he needs to do. At that time, Sartre needed to smash a great many things in order to discover others:

I had read everything; I had to read everything again; I held but one thread in my hand, but Theseus had no more, and it was enough for me too: the inexhaustible and difficult experience of the class struggle. I read everything again. There were still closed doors inside my head; I broke them down, not without an exhausting effort.[2]

He re-read Marx, Lenin, Rosa Luxembourg and many others. That was how he prepared for his sequel to Les Communistes et la paix. But before that he wrote a long reply to the criticisms Lefort had levelled at him in the pages of Les Temps Modernes.

Sartre's new attitudes filled Lanzmann with joy, for politics seemed to him more essential than literature, and I have already mentioned that if he was not a member of the Communist Party,

1. *La Dimension Florestan*, a painful satire on Heideggerian Existentialism, was not broadcast until the following year. But there had been a public reading of it.   2. *Merleau-Ponty vivant*.

it was only for subjective reasons. When he had read the draft of *The Mandarins*, he had persuaded me to explain more fully the reasons for the distance both Henri and Dubreuilh try to keep between themselves and the Communists; till then, it had seemed to me to need no explanation. I was far from disapproving of what Sartre was doing, but he had not persuaded me to follow him because I evaluated his development by referring to his point of departure: I was afraid that his *rapprochement* with the Communist Party would take him too far from his own truth. Lanzmann was at the other end of the road: every step that Sartre took towards the Communists he called a step in the right direction. Established from the outset and almost by nature at a point where their perspective became his own, he forced me to give explanations when I had been used to asking for them; every day, I was put in the position of having to challenge my most spontaneous reactions, in other words, my oldest prejudices. Little by little, he wore away my resistance, I liquidated my ethical idealism and ended up adopting Sartre's point of view for my own.

All the same, to work with the Communists without renouncing one's own judgement was scarcely any easier – despite the relative relaxation of the French Communist Party – than in 1946. Sartre did not feel concerned with the internal difficulties of the Party, with the expulsion of Marty and of Tillon. But there were things he could not accept: the Prague trials, the anti-Semitism rampant in the U.S.S.R., the articles Hervé was writing in *Ce Soir* against Zionism in Israel, the arrest of the 'murderers in white coats'. He received visits from Jewish Communists who wanted him to make his position clear. Mauriac, in *Le Figaro*, demanded that he condemn Stalin's attitude towards the Jews, and he replied in *L'Observateur* that he would do so in his own good time. He would soon have been forced into having to quarrel with his new friends, if the course of events had not broken this mounting deadlock. One day, Sartre was to lunch with Aragon; Aragon finally arrived, an hour and a half late, unshaved, completely shattered: Stalin was dead. Malenkov immediately released the doctors who had been accused and took measures to relax the tension in Berlin. For weeks, our little group, like everyone else in the world, was immersed in hypotheses, commentaries and prophecies. Sartre felt strangely relieved! The reconciliation he was hoping for would finally have a chance of success. The article by Péju on the Slansky affair,[1] published in *Les Temps Modernes*, was not attacked by the Communist Party.

The war was still going on in Indochina. Things were beginning to stir in North Africa. After two years of peaceful efforts and disappointed hopes, Bourguiba no longer saw any way of making Tunisia independent other than violence; his arrest[2] provoked riots and a general strike throughout the country; order was restored by scouring Cap Bon, arresting 20,000 people, terrorizing the population and by torture. In December 1952, there was a protest strike in Casablanca after the murder of Ferhat Hached;[3] a deliberately provoked riot and the killing of four or five Europeans enabled M. Boniface to bludgeon the budding Moroccan trade unionism to death; he had five hundred workers massacred. Neo-Destour and Istiqlal were bourgeois parties, but all the same they embodied the desire of Tunisia and Morocco for independence, and Sartre supported them with all the inadequate means at his disposal: going to see people, meetings, *Les Temps Modernes*.

There was one diversion that still kept all of its old allure for me – travel; I had not seen all I wanted to see, and there were many places I wanted to go back to. Lanzmann, for his part, had seen almost nothing of France or the world. Most of our leisure time we spent on excursions, some long, some short.

I think that trees, stones, skies, the colours and sounds of the countryside will never lose their capacity to touch me. I was still as moved as in my youth by a sunset over the sands of the Loire, a red cliff, an apple tree in bloom, a meadow. I loved the grey and pink roads under the endless hedge of plane trees, or the golden rain of the acacia leaves in the fall; I loved the provincial towns, not of course to live in but to pass through and remember, the excitement of the markets in the square at Nemours or Avallon, the quiet streets with their low houses, a rose-bush climbing across a stone façade, the murmuring lilacs rising behind a wall; gusts of my childhood would come back to me with the odour of mown

1. A large portion of the documentation had been supplied by the Czecho-slovakian ambassador.
2. One hundred and fifty members of the Neo-Destour were arrested with him.
3. The leader of the Tunisian trade-union movement, shot down by the Red Hand.

hay, ploughed fields, brambles, the gurgling of springs. When time was short, we would content ourselves with going out to dine in the countryside near Paris, happy to smell the greenery, to see the lights flowering along the highways, to feel the city's breath as we drove back. We drank new wine on a hillside, red and green stars passed winking over our heads before gliding down on to a glittering plain bristling with red-eyed pylons, and their hum troubled me the way a train whistle across the fields used to. Yes, for a few more years I could take pleasure in the gilded tiles of the roofs in Burgundy, in the granite of the Breton churches, in the stones of the farms of Touraine, in those hidden roads running beside streams greener than their own grassy banks, in the garden taverns where we stopped to eat a trout or a *fricassée*, in the glitter of cars at night, along the asphalt of the Champs-Élysées. Something was secretly undermining this sweetness, these pleasures, this country; but for the moment I was not being obliged to go nosing after it, and I let myself by lulled by the glamour of appearances.

In June we left on our first long trip. Lanzmann was ill, the doctor had prescribed the mountains, and we went to Geneva; but it rained; it was raining all over Switzerland; we wandered around the Italian lakes, then we reached Venice, where Michelle and Sartre were staying. The final outcome of the Rosenberg affair was expected at any moment. It was by then two years since they had been condemned to death, and all that time their lawyers had been fighting to save them. The Supreme Court had just rejected any further stay of execution. But the whole of Europe and the Pope himself were clamouring so loudly for their reprieve that Eisenhower would surely be forced to grant it.

One morning, after spending a few hours on the Lido, Lanzmann and I took a *vaporetto* back to the Piazza Roma, where we were to join Sartre and Michelle and have lunch with them in Vicenza. We caught sight of a newspaper with the enormous headline: I ROSENBERG SONO STATI ASSASSINATI. Sartre and Michelle disembarked a few moments later. Sartre was grim. 'We really don't want to go to see the theatre at Vicenza again,' he said, and then added in an angry voice: 'We don't feel particularly gay, you know.' Lanzmann telephoned to *Libération* and they agreed to publish an article about it by Sartre. He shut himself up in his room and wrote all day; that evening, in the Piazza San Marco, he read us what he had written; no one was particularly taken

with it; nor was he. He began over again that night: 'The Rosenbergs are dead, and life goes on. That's what you wanted, isn't
it?' That was the sentence he telephoned to *Libération* next morning,
followed by the rest of the article.

Life was going on. What could one do about it? What could
one do? Lanzmann and I talked about the Rosenbergs as we drove
on toward Trieste. But we also looked at the sky and the sea, at
the world in which they no longer existed.

'If you're going to Yugoslavia, I can get you some dinars,' the
porter at our hotel in Trieste told us. Go to Yugoslavia? Was it
possible? Nothing simpler. In twenty-four hours the Putnik agency
had provided us with visas, maps and advice. Armed with two
spare wheels, a jerry-can, candles, oil, planks and various tools,
we filled up with gas. 'Yugoslavia by car! You're going to have
fun!' said the station attendant. We were very excited as we
crossed the frontier: almost an Iron Curtain. And it was, in fact,
a different world we drove into. Not a vehicle on the road along
the sea; the pavement was so full of holes we soon had to edge
into the fields; even then it was impossible to do more than
twenty-five miles an hour. Night fell, we were dying of hunger
by the time we found a hotel in Otocac. 'We'll serve you dinner,'
we were told, 'but you'll have to wait for the porter to see about
a room.' The porter: he couldn't have been a more important
character if we'd been in a novel by Kafka. A room? The porter
has the key. Gas? Only the porter can start the pump or open the
stockroom. Where is he? Never there. Finally he is found. He
hasn't got the key; he's gone to get it. He will come back; but
when? That evening, we waited patiently in a smoky dining
room, chewing meatballs and drinking *slivovitz*. 'There's a French
lady here who'd like to speak to you,' the man serving us said.
A toothless old schoolteacher came and sat down at our table;
she knew a prince, whom she was dying to have us meet and who
would have plenty to tell us about Tito's extortions; as for herself,
her husband was in prison and she had great difficulty earning a
living. He had fought as a colonel beside the Germans, and she
had lived in Paris, hiding like a little grey mouse, she added. We
took a turn around the town, drowned in night and silence, and
it looked like a town in a fairy tale, so amazed were we to find
ourselves there at all.

The Italian station attendant would have laughed himself silly if he could have followed our progress. Tourists were only just beginning to come back; few hotels, few restaurants, the most frugal of meals; it was hard to find gas. The smallest repair job presented a problem; garages had neither tools nor spare parts; the mechanics just banged about haphazardly with a hammer. We didn't find it funny at all. The country itself had been the poorest in Europe before 1939, and since then it had been ravaged by war. The causes of the general austerity were first its resistance against Fascism, and second its refusal to revive the old system of privileges; for the first time in my life, I did not see opulence side by side with poverty; no one we met showed either arrogance or servility; everyone had the same sense of dignity; and towards us, foreigners as we were, everywhere the same cordiality without reticence; we were asked for help and were offered it with equal naturalness.

We liked what we saw. Around the Plitvice lakes, amid the sound of rustling foliage and waterfalls, children were selling birch-bark baskets full of wild strawberries; beautiful blonde peasant girls watched us from the roadside as we drove by; I re-experienced a remembered joy: seeing the Mediterranean suddenly appear, from the side of a mountain, and the olive trees terracing down, down toward the infinite blue of the water; steep, full of ravines, bristling with promontories and studded with sparkling islets, the coast was as beautiful as my memories of Greece. We saw Sibenik, Split and its palace; in the churches there were old women mumbling away in front of ikons. Suddenly, we were in the East – Mostar, with its domes and slender minarets; but the temperature there was over 95 degrees, the air was humid, Lanzmann ran a fever and I remembered with remorse the orders his doctor had given us. We decided to hurry back up to Belgrade and return to Switzerland. We stayed a day in Sarajevo; though so close to the Mediterranean, its wide avenues and the heavily furnished hotel belonged to Central Europe; the graceful and dilapidated mosques to the East; and what a strange hodgepodge of women in black kerchiefs, booted peasants, embroidered clothes in the wretched market that evoked a word from before the other war: the Balkans.

To get to Belgrade, we chose the shortest route on our map, which crossed the Sava. Passing through villages and hesitating at crossroads, we asked several times: 'Beograd?' The reply was invariably a series of voluble sentences in which the word *autoput* recurred, accompanied by gestures that seemed to be urging us to turn back. While trying to avoid the rabbits that kept leaping into our headlights, Lanzmann asked me: 'Do you think this is the right road?' I showed him the map. In the middle of the night we arrived at the edge of a vast stretch of dark water: no bridge. We had to go back the way we had come for 120 miles before getting onto the highway. I took over the wheel from Lanzmann, who was exhausted, and ran over a hare. 'Stop and pick it up,' he said, 'we can give it to someone.' It was an enormous hare, and was scarcely bleeding at all.

Dawn was breaking as we drove into Belgrade. We slept, and then went out to have a look at the city, with its massive heart surrounded by big peasant villages; stores, restaurants, streets, people, everything looked poverty-stricken. In the old part of the city, we got out of the car, determined to get rid of the hare, which I was carrying by its ears. We didn't dare offer it to anyone; but all the same we couldn't just throw it away! Finally we stopped in front of a young couple pushing a baby carriage, and I held the hare out to them saying: 'Autoput'. They thanked us, laughing.

The following evening we set out again along the deserted *autoput*, which we had all to ourselves except for a few haycarts; a storm of terrifying violence forced us to stop at Brod, a big metallurgical centre; there was a dance in progress at the hotel, and the workers of both sexes seemed to be having a good time. The man in charge of the hotel commented on how gay they all were, and then went on to catalogue his country's grievances against the U.S.S.R. Lanzmann knew German, a language many Yugoslavs could also speak. Everyone we talked to hated the U.S.S.R. at that time almost as much as they did the Germans. Among others, I remember a stop in a village where we had two inner tubes repaired. Some road workers invited us to have a drink with them in a shed decorated with paper wreaths and flags; they began to tell stories of the *maquis*, and Lanzmann did the same. For them, too, one of Tito's greatest claims to glory was his break with Stalin.

After stopping for a few hours in Zagreb, then in Ljubljana, we left Yugoslavia; not without regret. Its poverty was extreme; there was a terrible lack of roads, bridges; we had driven over a viaduct that was used not only by cars but by pedestrians and trains as well. But beyond this penury, there was something that touched me, something I had never seen anywhere else: a simple and direct relation between man and man, a community of interest and hopes, fraternity. How rich Italy seemed to us, as soon as we got across the border! Enormous tank-trucks, automobiles, gas stations, an intricate network of roads and railroads, bridges, shops bursting with goods – all these things suddenly seemed like privileges. And with prosperity, we returned once more to hierarchies, distances, barriers.

At last we were back in Switzerland, its snow, its glaciers. We explored every col, every peak accessible by car. After the hazards of our Yugoslavian itineraries, we found it disappointing to drive along heavily frequented roads; crawling up steep and ice-covered roads at night, more than once we squeezed a delicious sense of adventure from our fear. Once we slept nearly 10,000 feet up, at the foot of the Jungfrau, and saw the sun rise on the Eiger. And then we walked: I still could walk. Wearing espadrilles, we would walk for seven hours at a stretch across the glacier snows. Lanzmann was discovering the world of mountains; at Zermatt, he learned by heart all the dramas of the Matterhorn. After a few days in Milan with my sister, we took a look at the Val d'Aosta; on a sign at the edge of a meadow, we read: RESPECT NATURE AND THE RIGHTS OF PROPERTY. Back in Paris, we unpacked our memories and were amazed to find the olive trees of Dalmatia all mixed up with the blue of the glaciers.

I left Paris again almost immediately with Sartre. We spent a month in a hotel in Amsterdam that overlooked the canals; we worked, we visited the museums, explored the town and all of Holland. An exceptionally severe strike had just broken out in France and was paralysing all the public services, including the post office and the telephones;[1] to keep in touch, Lanzmann and I each took our letters to the air terminals and entrusted them to passengers. Once he tried to soften up a telephone operator by pleading the ardour of his sentiments. 'Love is not an emergency,' she answered him curtly.

From Amsterdam, Sartre and I drove out to see the Van Goghs in the Kröller-Müller Museum set among woods and fields; we drove along the banks of the Rhine, then of the Moselle. On the

1. Provoked by Laniel's decrees aimed at the Post Office workers, it then spread to the railroads and many other industries; some three million employees stopped working.

terraces of the *Weinstübe* we drank scented wine in beautiful thick glasses the colour of pale grapes. Sartre showed me the remains of the Stalag where he had been a prisoner, on a hill above Trier. I was struck by the site; but the rusty barbed wire and the few huts that were still standing told me much less than his stories. We crossed Alsace, drove down as far as Basel where I saw the Holbeins and the Klees again.

Lanzmann was supposed to join us there for a few days, as we had arranged, and I awaited his arrival with impatience. I received a telegram: he was in the hospital; he had had an automobile accident just outside Cahors. I was alarmed. I rushed with Sartre to Cahors where Lanzmann was lying, scraped and bruised. It was not as serious as had been feared. He was soon out of bed, and the three of us went touring together around Lot and Limousin; we visited the caves of Lascaux. We drove as far south as Toulouse, revisiting Albi, Cordes, the forest of Grésigne. My vacation with Sartre ended up with a tour of Brittany: it seemed very beautiful to us in those stormy autumn days. But I was anxious. At first I had been afraid that Lanzmann would not be able to accept my relationship with Sartre; now he was taking up so much room in my life that I was beginning to wonder if my understanding with Sartre was not going to suffer in consequence. The life Sartre and I led together was no longer quite the same. He had never been so absorbed by his political activity, his writing, all his work; in fact he was overworked. I was profiting from my rediscovered youth; I gave myself to each moment as it came. Of course we would always remain intimate friends, but would our destinies, hitherto intertwined, eventually separate? Later I was reassured. The equilibrium I had achieved, thanks to Lanzmann, to Sartre, to my own vigilance, was durable and endured.

1953 ended well. The deposition of the Sultan was a victory for colonialism, but a precarious one in our opinion. The armistice had finally been signed in Korea; Ho Chi-minh, in an interview given to a Swedish newspaper, the *Expressen*, let it be known that he was ready to negotiate. The riot on 17 June in East Berlin, in the course of which the police had fired on the workers, the fall of Rakosi, and Nagy's abolition of the concentration camps had obliged the Communists to acknowledge certain facts they had been denying up till then; some of them were asking themselves questions; others 'gritted their teeth'. To sympathizers, the development of the U.S.S.R. brought an unqualified feeling of satisfaction: the work camps and Beria were disappearing; the standard of living of the average Russian would rise, favouring a greater political and intellectual democracy, for light industry was no longer sacrificed to heavy industry; and already there were signs of the 'thaw', as Ehrenburg called it in the title of his latest novel. When Malenkov announced that the U.S.S.R. possessed the H-bomb, the likelihood of a world conflict seemed to be removed for some time to come. A 'balance of terror' is at least better than terror without any balance. In this context, Adenauer's victory, which portended the creation of a European army, seemed less grave an event than it might have been otherwise.

In a few weeks, and with a great deal of enjoyment, Sartre had made the adaptation of *Kean* Brasseur had asked him for; for once the rehearsals went off without any fuss. I saw *Waiting for Godot*. I am always mistrustful of plays that use symbols to present the human condition in its universal aspect; but I was full of admiration at the way in which Beckett succeeded in captivating us, simply by depicting the indefatigable patience that despite everything, against all odds, keeps our species and each one of us clinging to this earth; I was one of the actors in the drama, with the author as my partner; as we waited – for what? – he talked, and I listened; with my presence, with his voice, we kept alive a useless and necessary hope.

Hemingway's *The Old Man and the Sea* had just come out in a French translation, and all the critics were lauding it to the skies. Neither my friends nor I liked it. Hemingway knew how to tell a story, but he had overloaded this one with symbols; he had identified himself with the fisherman who carries the Cross on his shoulders, in the falsely simple guise of a fish. I found this senile narcissism irritating. I was not entirely in agreement with Lanzmann about von Salomon's *Fragebogen*. Germany had become the most prosperous country in Europe; Antonina Vallentin, who had just come back from a trip there, told me about her encounters with German Neo-Nazism; despite the 'questionnaires', the ex-Nazis and the businessmen who had supported Hitler were regaining the upper hand. I could understand how Salomon's self-justification was being greeted with anger. I recognized how much bad faith there was in his work, and indeed it was apparent in the style itself. But the liveliness of his narratives reawakened my old desire to recount my own memories.

Soon in fact I would have to be asking once more: What shall I write? For at last – and it was a factor that made no small contribution to the gaiety of that fall – I had finished my book. I was worried about the title. I had given up the idea of calling it *The Survivors*; after all, life hadn't actually stopped in 1944. I would have gladly used *The Suspects*, if the word hadn't already been used a few years earlier by Darbon, for the theme of my novel was essentially the ambiguous condition of the writer. Sartre suggested *The Griots*; we rather liked comparing ourselves to those blacksmiths-cum-witchdoctors-cum-poets whom certain African societies honour, fear and despise all at the same time; but it was too esoteric. 'Why not *The Mandarins*?' Lanzmann suggested.

The beginning of that winter was a severe one; the Abbé Pierre launched his big charity drive, middle-class ladies eagerly divested their households of a few cast-off garments, everyone felt kind and generous, and the New Year's celebrations were very lively. Our little group gathered at Michelle's. Now that the manuscript of *The Mandarins* had been turned in to Gallimard, and Lanzmann was having a two-week holiday in January, I dreamed of sun. For the time being, Morocco was quiet; Lanzmann wanted to see it and I wanted to see it again; we booked seats on a plane. The day before we were due to leave, the newspapers carried the headline: Alert in Morocco. It was the beginning of a wave of terrorism and counter-terrorism unleashed by the deposition of the Sultan. We changed our plans, and two mornings later we embarked, with the car, for an Algiers that proved to be rainy, full of beggars, men out of work, and despair. Behind this dismal façade, a people in ferment was being organized by militants with stubborn patience, but we were not aware of it then. We made a beeline for the desert. In front of the hotel in Ghardaïa were parked trucks with slogans painted on their sides advertising the purposes of the expedition. 'To sell electric cookers and study parasitology across 20,000 miles of Black Africa.' An American woman, who was preparing to drive across the Sahara, was polishing up her Willys Overland. Why shouldn't we go on down to El Goléa as well? Lanzmann asked me. The people in the hotel assured him that the Aronde would be in pieces by the time we got there. I suggested we go to Guerrera first. The city rose up red and resplendent, above the sands; in the square, surrounded by an attentive circle of people, a man carrying a sheep on his back was walking up and down very fast, yelling out words. It was an auction sale; we looked at the people and the streets, walked through the oasis. But to get there and back, what an ordeal! We had to drive along a bumpy, gullied road, switching abruptly from fifty miles an hour to three; on the way back, night was falling; under a storm sky of terrifying beauty we got stuck in a sand dune; we had a shovel and planks, so Lanzmann managed to get us out; but he gave up the idea of El Goléa.

At Ouargla, the apricot-coloured sands and the burnt-almond cliffs that had so moved me eight years before were still exactly the same. Touggourt we disliked; we slept there and couldn't get away quickly enough, despite a sandstorm and the advice heaped on us from all sides. Visibility was less than thirty feet, and at the end of five minutes we found ourselves driving across a wasteland. Each encouraging the other's pigheadedness, we found our way back on to the track and switched on our headlights; a car stopped: a Moslem notable and his chauffeur. 'Follow us.' Their Citroën plunged on at sixty miles an hour through the thick, white darkness. Lanzmann kept his foot on the accelerator and his eyes riveted to the back of their car. They stopped in a village and we went on, at the same pace – as soon as Lanzmann slowed down, the car would shake and every piece of it begin to bang against the piece next to it – with the certain knowledge that we should be smashed to bits if any obstacle suddenly appeared in front of us. At last we emerged from the storm, but the wind had drifted sand across the road; at the end of two miles we were stuck. A team of workers servicing a narrow-gauge railroad came to our aid; then we got stuck again. Two vans passed, at less than six miles an hour, carrying workers; they got us out of that one. Finally, fifty miles from El Oued, we got stuck for good and all; it was dusk, and very cold; we were going to have a bad night of it. We thanked our stars when we saw a Dodge coming towards us: the stationmaster, his wife, two Moslem drivers. They pulled us out; we got stuck again. Finally we transferred our baggage and ourselves to the Dodge; we locked the car, but refused to let one of the Arab drivers stay and guard it all night.

Next morning the drivers went out to fetch the car. The stationmaster, fearing that if his train weren't used it would be withdrawn from service, wanted us to make use of it the following day in order to get the car back to Biskra. 'It will break down,' predicted Salem, a young man with a very positive manner who said that for the sum of four thousand francs he was perfectly willing and able to drive it across the desert to Nefta. I had travelled the route myself once in a truck, but could the Aronde get through? No, people told us. As we were wandering, perplexed, through the beautiful, funnel-shaped gardens, we saw Salem approaching; he was in a jeep full of children, and it was leaping from dune to dune like a mountain goat. We turned to each other. 'Well, if you don't object, let's try it!' That evening we said good-bye to a very upset stationmaster. His wife, who had not been in Algeria long, was still dazzled; a big house, a vast garden, as many servants as she needed, it was beyond her wildest dreams: 'When I write my parents that I drove a hundred miles a day just for fun, they won't believe me!' They were good people, but they objected to Lanzmann's remunerating the two drivers, who were employed at the station. Lanzmann did it all the same, behind their backs; they found out and were offended.

Next morning, all of El Oued turned out to watch us leave; Salem had let some of the air out of the tyres; he started the motor and we moved off, raked by a battery of sceptical looks: 'You'll never get through in that thing.' We were worried; if anything went wrong, we would have to wait eight days for the next train. Alas! in less than three miles the car was stuck; some peasants helped us get free, but the next time there wouldn't be anyone around, I told myself with consternation. And, then, the Aronde began to fly over the sand; from time to time, as he got to the top of a dune, Salem would put it in reverse so as to attack the summit from another angle, and over we would go. At three that afternoon we were drinking his health in a Moslem café in Nefta, while the other customers came clustering around to gaze at him in admiration. He was lively and intelligent as well as physically adroit; he must have joined the A.L.N. at the first opportunity; what happened to him?

Thanks to him, we had been well received; but a little later, coming back from a stroll through the oasis, the few merchants still standing frozen behind their stalls in the almost deserted square stared at us with hostile eyes; the hotel was closed; a nearby bistro, apparently open, refused to serve us so much as a glass of water. We visited Tataouine, Médenine, Djerba, but felt a veil of hostility cutting us off from the country. Outside Gabès I heard for the first time a phrase that was soon to become familiar: I asked an officer if we could get through to Matmata, I was afraid the road would be too sandy; he gave me a superior smile. 'Are you frightened of the fellagha? You don't need to worry; we're always around, they don't try anything with us!' One evening, at dusk, we drove around Cap Bon. We were coming back from Tunis by plane, so we put the car on a boat; a young Tunisian docker read Sartre's name on the car; he called the others: 'Hey! Jean-Paul Sartre's car! We'll put it on first one! Say "thank you" to him for us!' I envied Sartre: on those faces France had doomed to hatred, his mere name could bring forth smiles of friendship.

I began to write again, but halfheartedly. The only project I really cared about now was to resuscitate my childhood and my youth, but I lacked the courage to approach it directly. I took up the threads of some tentative efforts begun and abandoned a long while before, and set to work on a novella about Zaza's death. When I showed it to Sartre after two or three months, he held his nose; I couldn't have agreed more: the story seemed to have no inner necessity and failed to hold the reader's interest. Then there was a period during which I contented myself with reading and correcting, very badly, the proofs of *The Mandarins*.

1954 disappointed many of our hopes; the Berlin Conference having failed, France was preparing to ratify the C.E.D. Supported by America, which, beaten in Korea, at least wanted to keep Indochina from going Communist, France rejected Ho Chi-minh's advances. On 13 March, the day General Navarre began the battle of Dien Bien Phu, I suffered a distressing experience that was new to me: I felt myself radically cut off from the great mass of my compatriots. Press and radio were predicting that the Vietminh army would be wiped out; not only did I know, from reading the left-wing and foreign newspapers, that this was untrue, but, together with my friends, I was glad it wasn't true. The war had caused hundreds of thousands of deaths on the Vietminh side, both among the civilian population and in the army, and those deaths affected me more than the casualities of the garrison: 15,000 légionnaires, of whom at least a third were ex-S.S. men.

The heroism of the suicide units was more extraordinary than that of Geneviève de Galard and Colonel de Castries, who were indecently exploited by our propaganda services. Bidault used their courage as an argument for refusing to negotiate even a cease-fire long enough to evacuate the wounded. When Dien Bien Phu fell I knew that the Vietminh had for all practical purposes won its independence, and I was glad of it. For years I had been opposed to the official governments of France; but I had never before been in a position where I found myself rejoicing over a defeat; it was even more shocking than spitting on a victory. The people I passed in the street imagined that a great misfortune had just befallen their country and mine. If they had had any inkling of how pleased I was, they would have thought I deserved to be stood up against a wall and shot.

The ultras and the Army attempted to blame the suffering, the agony, the deaths that occurred at Dien Bien Phu on the civilian population in general and the Left in particular; if Laniel and Pleven got their bottoms kicked, so much the better – at least there were some kicks not going to waste; but after all, it was not the Ministers who had chosen to trap the Expeditionary Force in a 'chamber pot'. The Army, which was afterwards to nurse its rancour with so much self-satisfaction on the memory of this 'humiliation', was entirely to blame for the affair. As for the Left, not only had it at all times desired peace, but its newspapers and its politicians had even denounced the dangerous extravagance of the Navarre plan. There was a murderer in the government: Bidault; but his crime was not that of betraying the Army; he he had even gone to the point of risking a world war in order to support them. There was no telling what extremities we might be reduced to by the paraphrenia of an army which, refusing to admit its own mistakes, was now returning to France thirsty for vengeance. Yet, while the Parliament was overthrowing Laniel and Bidault, opposing the departure of a fresh contingent of troops and charging Mendès-France with the task of negotiating peace, while a majority of the country approved these steps, at the same time a bitter chauvinism, encouraged by those defeated in Indochina, began to infect public opinion. Ulanova was scheduled to dance in Paris; the parachute regiment assumed they would be avenging the defeat of Dien Bien Phu by using threats that so intimidated the authorities that her performance was cancelled.

In March, the Americans had exploded a bomb on Bikini which had surpassed even their expectations by its results.[1] Oppenheimer, who had been active in the preparations for this explosion, was nonetheless accused of un-American activities. The witch-hunt showed no signs of slackening; yet American imperialism seemed to be in the best of health; those oppressed by it, and those who attempted to resist it, were immediately crushed. To gain world attention, some Puerto Ricans fired on Congressmen while they were actually sitting in the House: in vain. Arbenz, in Guatemala, had attempted to shake off the yoke of United Fruit; a band of mercenaries, christened an 'Army of Liberation', landed and drove him out.

In February, Elsa Triolet asked Sartre to participate in a conference of writers from East and West that was about to prepare the ground for a sort of Round Table at Knokke-le-Zoute; he accepted. Michelle, Lanzmann and I went with him in the car; by day, we went for drives and looked at paintings; in the evening he would tell us how his sessions had gone. The bourgeois intellectuals, Mauriac among others, had refused Elsa Triolet's invitation; the little group of Communists and Communist sympathizers that she had mustered were drawing up an appeal with a view to a much larger meeting. They didn't want to frighten anyone away and therefore had to weigh each word very carefully; Carlo Levi was there, feeling the cold despite his fur hat, Fedin, Anna Seghers and Brecht, charming but throwing the whole conference into an uproar, when the text had been finally settled, by asking in an innocent tone if it wasn't possible to add a protest against the American atomic tests; Fedin and Sartre wisely bypassed his suggestion. The Queen of the Belgians, an old progressive, received the members of this little congress in Brussels. The Russian writers invited Sartre to go to Moscow in May.

He had overworked the whole year; he was suffering from high blood pressure. His doctor had prescribed a long rest in the country; he did no more than take a few drugs. He scarcely slept for several nights before he left because he had to finish his preface to Cartier-Bresson's book of photographs, *D'une Chine à l'autre*; he was to stop over in Berlin and take part in a meeting of the Peace Movement, and he was intending to prepare his speech for that on the

1. It claimed a great many victims among Japanese fishermen and also among the customers who bought their fish.

plane: he was decidedly overdoing things and I was getting worried. He seemed terribly tired. His first letters reassured me a little. In Berlin he had talked about History's universalization and its paradox: one of its aspects was the appearance of weapons capable of demolishing the earth; the other was the intervention in world affairs of countries that had been wholly or partly colonialized, and which, in order to win their independence, were launching national wars against which atomic bombs were powerless.

Now, he assured me, he was recovering from his fatigue. From his Moscow hotel, the National, he could see Red Square covered with flags; they were celebrating the anniversary of the union of the Ukraine with Russia. He watched the procession. 'With my own eyes I counted a million men,' he wrote. He had been unpleasantly struck by the boorishness of certain foreign diplomats, who sniggered on their grandstand: 'Their bad manners would not have been tolerated on the Champs-Élysées on the fourteenth of July.' He visited the University, talked to students and teachers, listened to workers and technicians in a factory discussing the works of Simonov; he went sightseeing a lot; his interpreter had given him 500 roubles in case he wanted to go out alone, which he did often. He was invited by Simonov to the latter's *dacha* and subjected to a severe ordeal: a four-hour banquet, twenty toasts in vodka, and at the same time his glass continually refilled with Armenian *vin rosé* and red wine from Georgia. 'I am watching him eat,' said one of the guests. 'He must be a good man, because he eats and drinks sincerely.' Sartre felt that he owed it to them to remain worthy of this praise all the way to the end. 'I managed to keep the use of my senses, but I did partially lose that of my legs,' he admitted to me. They put him on the train to Leningrad, which he reached the following morning. He was captivated by the banks of the Neva and all the palaces; but they didn't let him rest. A four-hour drive around the city, a tour of the monuments, an hour off, a four-hour visit to the Palace of Culture. Similar programme the next day, followed by an evening at the ballet. He returned to Moscow, then left by plane for Uzbekistan. After that he was due to accompany Ehrenburg to Stockholm for a Peace Movement meeting and return to Paris on 21 June.

In June, my sister exhibited her recent paintings in a gallery on the Right Bank. Preoccupied with technical problems, she was still keeping her spontaneous gifts too much in check, but some of her things were striking. At the private viewing I met Françoise Sagan, who had come with Jacqueline Audry. I didn't care for her first novel much; later on, I was to like *A Certain Smile* and *Those Without Shadows* better; but she had a delightful way of avoiding the child-prodigy label they had stuck on her.

It was a beautiful summer. I went with Lanzmann to a small hotel on the Lac des Settons; we took a library with us, but as it turned out spent most of our days driving up hill and down dale, looking at châteaux, at abbeys, at churches; the hills were yellow with flowering broom. The day we came back to Paris I found a note from Bost in my pigeonhole at the bottom of the staircase: 'Come over and see me at once.' I thought: something's happened to Sartre. And in fact Ehrenburg had telephoned to d'Astier that morning from Stockholm, asking him to let Sartre's friends know that he had been admitted to a hospital in Moscow; d'Astier had got in touch with Cau, who had passed the message on to Bost. I was alarmed, as I had been on that day in 1940 when I had received the letter from an unknown woman telling me Sartre's new address: *Kranken-revier*. Bost seemed badly shaken too. What exactly was the matter with Sartre? He didn't know. I wanted to talk to Cau; he was at the Sorbonne attending some meeting or other; we went there; d'Astier had said something about blood pressure, Cau told me, it's nothing serious. I wasn't satisfied. I knew already that Sartre was suffering from high blood pressure; had he had an attack? Together with Bost, Olga and Lanzmann, I decided to go to the Soviet Embassy and ask the Cultural Attaché to telephone to Moscow. In the entrance hall we ran into some officials and I explained my request to them; they looked at us with astonishment: 'Telephone yourself . . . All you have to do is pick up the receiver and ask for Moscow.' The image of the Iron Curtain was still so firmly fixed in our minds at the time that we had some difficulty believing them. We went back to the Rue de la Bûcherie, I asked for Moscow, for the hospital, for Sartre. At the end of three minutes, I was stupe-fied to hear his voice. 'How are you?' I asked anxiously. 'I'm very well, thank you,' he answered in polite tones. 'How can you be well if you're in the hospital?' 'How do you know I'm in the hospital?' He seemed mystified. I explained. He admitted that he'd had a sudden attack of high blood pressure, but it was over and he was returning to Paris. I hung up, but my mind was not at ease; this warning had a completely different meaning from the one in

1940; then, it had been external dangers that were threatening Sartre; suddenly I realized that, like everyone else, he was carrying his own death within him. It was something I had never faced up to; to counter it, I invoked my own disappearance from the world, which, though it filled me with terror, also reassured me; but at that moment I wasn't involved: what did it matter whether or not I was on earth the day he disappeared from it? What did it matter whether I survived him or not? – that day would still come. In twenty years, tomorrow, the threat was still the same: he was going to die. A black enlightenment! Sartre recovered. But something irrevocable had happened; death had closed its hand around me; it was no longer a metaphysical scandal, it was a quality of our arteries; it was no longer a sheath of night around us, it was an intimate presence penetrating my life, changing the taste of things, the quality of the light, my memories, the things I wanted to do: everything.

Sartre returned; apart from the huge ugliness of the new architecture, he liked what he had seen. Above all, he had been interested by the new relations that had been formed between men in the U.S.S.R., and also between people and things; between a writer and his readers, between the workers and their factory. Work, leisure, reading, travel, friendships: all these things had a different meaning there. It seemed to him that Soviet society had to a large extent overcome the solitude that gnaws at ours; the disadvantages attendant on the collective life of the U.S.S.R. seemed to him less regrettable than our individualistic loneliness.

The trip had exhausted him; every day, from early morning till the following dawn, there had been meetings, conversations, visits, journeys, banquets. In Moscow, his programme had been spread out over several days and allowed him slightly more respite; elsewhere, the various regional organizations allowed him none. He was supposed to spend forty-eight hours in Samarkand. 'One day with the officials, one day on my own,' he had stipulated. They were surprised by this caprice: beauty doesn't cease to be beauty just because there are forty people looking at it at once; it was put down to his bourgeois individualism, but they did finally agree to his request. At the last moment, the Union of Tashkent Writers shortened the excursion to a single day; there were factories to visit, children's books to look at. 'But we'll leave you alone,' the interpreter promised. An archaeologist and several of the local

[319]

notables escorted Sartre through the city; the car stopped in front of palaces and mosques, superb vestiges of the reign of Tamburlaine; everyone got out, the archaeologist delivered an account of each particular building. Then the interpreter spread his arms and shooed everyone away: 'And now, Jean-Paul Sartre wishes to be alone.' They all moved off, and Sartre was left standing there, waiting until he could decently rejoin them.

The worst ordeals were the moments of relaxation, which were very festive occasions, moreover: banquets and drinking bouts. He was obliged to repeat several times feats similar to those he had accomplished in Simonov's *dacha*. The evening he was to leave Tashkent, an engineer as strong as three cart-horses had challenged him to a vodka duel; his challenger then accompanied him out to the airport, where he sank into a heap on the asphalt, a great moment of triumph for Sartre, who then managed to get to his seat and immediately sank into a leaden sleep. When he woke up, he was in such a bad way that he asked his interpreter to arrange a day's rest when they got to Moscow; as soon as he got out of the plane, he heard his name being called over one of the concourse loudspeakers: Jean-Paul Sartre. . . . It was Simonov, who had telephoned the airport to ask him to lunch. If he had known Russian he would have asked for the lunch to be postponed till the following day, which Simonov would have been quite agreeable to; but neither of his 'aides'[1] – apart from his interpreter, he was accompanied on all his trips by a member of the Writers' Union – was willing to take the responsibility of suggesting this change to Simonov. Accordingly, the meal took place that same day; wine again flowed freely and at the end Simonov presented Sartre with a drinking horn of imposing dimensions and brimming with wine: 'Empty or full, you shall take it with you'; and Sartre found himself standing there holding it; it was impossible to put it down unless it was empty. Sartre did what was expected of him. After the meal he took a solitary walk along the bank of the Moskova, and he could feel his heart battering against his ribs. It went on pounding so violently during the night and the following morning that he felt unable to attend the meeting with a group of philosophers that had been arranged for him. 'But what's the matter with you?' his interpreter asked. She took his pulse and rushed out of his room to call a doctor, who immediately had Sartre admitted to the hospital. They treated him, he

1. In the sense Kafka gives this word in *The Castle*.

slept, rested, thought he was better. In fact, he wasn't. I invited a few of our closest friends in, and it was visibly a great effort for him to tell us about his adventures. He gave an interview to *Libération*; he rushed through it, and when they offered to let him read what they had taken down, he begged off. He went with Michelle to Italy for a rest and began an autobiography; but he couldn't put two ideas together, he wrote to me. At least he was sleeping an enormous amount and seeing only people he found interesting: he had been received with great friendliness by the Italian Communists. He had an alfresco dinner on the Piazza Trastevere with Togliatti; the restaurant musician proudly showed his Party card to Togliatti and sang some old Roman songs in his honour; a whole crowd gathered, applauding warmly, but some Americans began hissing; the Italians growled back; to prevent a riot they had to leave quickly.

Meanwhile I was travelling in Spain with Lanzmann. A lot of anti-Franquists had been going there without scruples for several years now; so I stifled my own. Except at Tossa, which had been turned into an ugly tourist centre, I found little change. Poverty had increased; in certain spots in Barcelona, and almost everywhere in Tarragona, the streets were like sewers, full of famished children, beggars, cripples and sickly-looking prostitutes. The capital was different, we could see that Franco had been taking pains over it; the filthy slum districts I had seen in 1945 had been razed; but where had their inhabitants been relocated? The apartment blocks that had sprouted up on the sites were full of well-off civil servants.

Actually, we had known what was going on in Spain before we went there. If we had come all the same, it was because the country still had ways of reaching us: its past, its soil, its people. I revisited the Prado; I found I now preferred Goya and also Velázquez to El Greco. At Ávila, in the Escorial, in the *cigarrales* of Toledo, in Sevilla, in Granada, I found the same delight I had experienced there in the old days.

Both Lanzmann and I liked to understand, to learn, but we also enjoyed the fugitive emotion to be found in an apparition: a red castle rising on a hill beside a lake; a valley, seen from a high pass, melting away into infinity beneath its veils of mist; a shaft of light suddenly breaking through a cloud and bathing the fields of Old Castile with an oblique radiance; the sea, far off. And Lanzmann got caught up in my old obsession of combing every detail of the regions through which we passed: coral-coloured mountains, swollen, livid plateaux, plains of stubble fired by the setting sun, and that steep and ragged coastline whose terror and splendour Dali has caught so well. The heat held no terrors for us; a burning wind was sweeping the high plains of Andalusia when we visited its hamlets of cave dwellers in a temperature of ninety degrees. We rested on beaches or in deserted creeks, bathing at leisure in the sea and the sun. In the evening we went into the villages and watched the young girls in their pale dresses walking up and down, laughing.

At Lerica it was fiesta; little girls dressed up as grown women in the Andalusian costume – long frilled skirts, fans, mantillas – their lips, cheeks and eyelashes made up, strutted between the shooting galleries, the lottery tents, the roundabouts, the open-air cafés; fireworks were going off on every street corner. Lanzmann saw his first bullfight, a bad one, but it moved him nonetheless. Then we headed for the north, which I had never visited; I saw the windows of Léon, the museum in Valladolid, the little ports of the Basque country, Guernica. Finally San Sebastian, and from there we drove straight home.

I found it hard to sort out exactly how I felt now about the Spanish people. Defeat is a disgrace; it is impossible to survive it without compromising with what one hates. I was troubled by what seemed to be a patience no longer illuminated by the slightest hope. As we drove by them in our car, the road workers ought not to have smiled at us. Yet they knew the rich were no friends of theirs, these peasants who never lifted so much as a finger to ask us to stop for them; they looked at us with blank astonishment when we suggested they might like a lift; one old woman even thought we were trying to kidnap her. One evening we picked up a very old man carrying a large sack. 'Where are you going?' 'Oh . . . the capital!' he answered with a grand gesture; he meant Badajoz, forty miles away. 'That's a long way!' 'Oh yes! I would have walked all night.' In Sevilla, in the bars of the Alameda, the little prostitutes ought to have regarded us with hostility; but no. One very young girl sat down at our table and begged me; 'Take me to Paris; I'm good at washing and ironing, I'm a hard worker, I'll take good care of you. . . .'

A conversation finally made me see it all clearly. In Granada, while we were having dinner at the Alhambra Hotel, Lanzmann, annoyed with the maître d'hôtel who wouldn't let him take off his jacket, sounded off against the soldiers and priests who ran the country; the maître d'hôtel began to laugh: he didn't like them either. During the Civil War he had worked in the hotel in Valencia where Malraux and Ehrenburg stayed. He reminisced for a minute, then his voice hardened. 'It was you who encouraged us to fight; then you dropped us; and who paid for it? We did. There were a million people killed; dead bodies everywhere, on the roads, in the squares. We're not going to start all over again, never, not at any price.' Yes; these peaceful-looking men had risked their lives for a different future; they were the sons, the brothers of the men who had given theirs; England and France were as responsible for their resignation as Germany and Italy. Another generation would have grown up, less crushed by its memories, before hope could return, before the struggle could begin again.

By the time I got back to Paris, Mendès-France had signed an agreement with Vietnam and gone to Tunis for negotiations with the Tunisian leaders. He had successfully urged the Chamber of Deputies to vote against the C.E.D. Although he had refused the support of the Communist vote, his policies were those desired by the Left.

Sartre was still in a pretty bad way when we left by car at the end of August; the first evening, in his hotel room in Strasbourg, he stayed for a long while just sitting in his chair, hands on his knees, back bent, eyes blank. We had dinner in a restaurant in La Petite France. 'Literature is a lot of horseshit,' he told me; he sat through the whole meal emanating a feeling of disgust. Fatigue was making him see everything in the worst possible light; writing was such an effort for him that he could no longer see any meaning in it. We drove through Alsace, the Black Forest, Bavaria. So many ruins! Ulm had been pounded to pieces, Nuremberg to dust. *Swastikas waved at every window.* Rothenburg, skilfully restored, took us back twenty years: in 1934, we had walked along those ramparts, refusing to face the catastrophe that was almost upon us, unable, even Sartre with his gift for envisaging disaster, to sense the enormity of what lay ahead. In the painted streets of Oberammergau, it was difficult to believe that anything had ever happened. In Munich we found the giant beer halls still filled with Bavarian gaiety. In 1948, in Berlin, the distress of the Berliners had softened my bitterness; but I detested Munich, loudmouthed and cosy, full of strutting profiteers bursting with delight at the good thing they had made out of their defeat. I have only one pleasant memory of it. One morning, in the middle of the almost dried-up river, two men in evening dress and top hats were staggering about in the water; with their black dress clothes, their bewildered looks, their uncoordinated attempts to get back on to the bank, they were the very embodiment of that grotesque sense of fantasy so peculiar to Germany.

At Salzburg, in a hotel in the old town that mirrored all its age-old graces, Sartre began working again; he was finding himself. We revisited the surrounding countryside, the lakes and mountains, then after a week we headed for Vienna. As a consequence of contracts signed by Nagel without Sartre's assent, a production of *Les Mains sales* was in rehearsal there; the Peace Movement warned Sartre of this; he protested, and explained his position to a press conference. At last I saw the Breughels in the museum, the Danube, the Ring, the Prater and the old cafés I had heard so much about; in the evening we would sit down to dinner in medieval-looking cellars in the heart of the city, or in cabarets farther out, at the foot of hills covered with yellow vines.

I had wanted to take another look at Prague; Sartre got us visas without difficulty; the idea of crossing the real Iron Curtain excited my curiosity. It was no mere metaphor; the little grassy road we had followed to an isolated frontier post suddenly ran slap up against a metal grille, flanked by dense and threatening barbed-wire fences; a sentinel was walking nonchalantly back and forth on top of a lookout tower. I sounded the horn. He paid no attention whatever; I sounded the horn again; a soldier came out of the guardroom and examined our passports through the bars; he made a sign to the sentinel who felt in his pockets and threw down a key; the soldier opened the iron grille as though he were a lodge keeper on some large private estate.

It was Sunday; no cars; but lots of people picnicking along the road, in the meadows and under the pines. I drove through countryside and villages, astonished at feeling so immediately at home in a People's Democracy. When we reached Prague, Sartre asked a passer-by in German how to get to the hotel we knew was reserved for foreigners; he telephoned to the poet Nezval, who seemed relieved when Sartre told him not to bother to come and see us immediately, for his wife was giving birth just then. We borrowed some money from the porter and walked around the town; it was very moving to recognize everything again – the avenues, the bridge, the monuments, and also the cafés and restaurants – when in fact nothing was the same. (It was in front of that tavern, in that exact spot, that we had looked over someone's shoulder and read the name Dollfuss and a word beginning with M.) There were neon signs, elegant displays in the shops, an animated crowd, and lots of people in the cafés, which were pretty much like the ones in Vienna. We wandered a long while through the streets and our memories.

The next day, the fat poet Nezval – who loved Paris so much, and used to sit for hours, a beret on his head, on the terrace of the Bonaparte – showed us 'the small beer' – the churches, the Jewish cemetery, the museum, the old taverns; some of his friends came with us. We passed a gigantic statue of Stalin; forestalling any comment we might have made, a young woman said sharply: 'We don't like it at all.' We saw an opera that was mediocre, and several puppet films at a private showing. The most amusing was one exhorting drivers to sobriety; the main character was a charming little stoned motor-cyclist who went whizzing past cars and trains and finally smashed himself up trying to go faster than an airplane. We left Prague loaded with gifts: art books, records, lace and crystal. Only one shadow darkened our visit, but it was a big one; we were sightseeing in a library one day, when for an instant we found ourselves alone with one of the curators; abruptly he whispered: 'There are terrible things going on here, you know, these days.'

On the way back, we went through a perfunctory customs inspection without difficulty, but on the Austrian side a young Russian soldier refused to let us go on into Austria: we had neglected to ask for permission to drive through the Russian zone. While he was telephoning to his captain, an Austrian soldier engaged Sartre in conversation. 'Paris – oh I know Paris well,' he said amiably. 'I was there in 1943.'

Lanzmann came to join us in Vienna. I had never before had the experience of waiting for someone dear to me at an airport. It's a poignant business: the vast, empty sky, the silence, suddenly the tiny whisper up there, the little bird growing larger, approaching, wheeling away again, suddenly hurtling down towards you. We drove into Italy. I suggested we take the Grossglockner Pass and Sartre was indignant: the historic route was the Brenner Pass. As we drove over it, he evoked the pomp of Maximilian's panoplied cavalcade riding down from the dark German forests towards the Roman sun and the imperial diadem. We rested up from our Central European expedition in Florence and Verona.

Sartre caught a train back from Milan, where I stayed for a short while with my sister. I returned to France with Lanzmann, driving through Genoa and along the coast. Some of my Czech presents had been stolen in Florence one night, when I had left them in the car; I still had some books and records that the customs officers at Menton sniffed at suspiciously; whatever came from Prague was dubious. I explained they were works of art and folk songs. 'Prove it!' they replied. I showed them the photographs illustrating one of the books: 'You see: they're just landscapes.' 'Landscapes, there are plenty of those here,' said one of the officials, indicating the coastline and the sea with a sweeping gesture. Both books and records were confiscated.

From the first of October on, I was expecting *The Mandarins* to appear in the bookshops any day; *The Second Sex* had taught me a lesson; I could almost hear all the unpleasant gossip in advance. I had put so much of myself into this book that there were moments when my cheeks burned at the idea of indifferent or hostile eyes moving across its pages.

On the way back from Nice to Paris with Lanzmann, I went into a hotel in Grenoble at about midnight; a *Paris-Presse* was lying on the reception desk; I opened it and my eye was immediately caught by an article by Kléber Haedens devoted to *The Mandarins*. To my great surprise – for we didn't see eye to eye on most things – he spoke well of it. When I telephoned Sartre the next day, he told me that a very friendly notice had appeared in *Les Lettres françaises*: was I going to be greeted with approval from all sides? On the whole, yes. Reversing my expectations, it was the bourgeois critics who found that my novel had a pleasing odour of anti-Communism, while the Communists took it, quite rightly, as an expression of sympathy for them. As for the non-Communist left wing, it was in its name that I had been attempting to speak. Only a few Socialists and the extreme Right attacked me with any venom. Forty thousand copies were sold in the first month.

'They're putting you up for the Goncourt,' Jean Cau told me. I was shocked: I was too old. 'You'd be foolish to refuse,' my friends told me. If I won the prize, the book would reach a really wide public. And I'd earn a lot of money. I had no pressing need of it, since I had access to Sartre's; but I'd have liked to make my contribution to our common funds. And apart from that, the rain in my room was growing steadily heavier; the Goncourt would enable me to buy an apartment. All right: if they offered it to me, I would accept it.

From what was said at the preliminary discussions, I was told that I had a pretty good chance of winning. Since I had no desire to be swooped down on by a flock of journalists, on the evening before the final deliberations I moved, with Lanzmann, to a lodging procured for me by Suzanne Blum. I waited for the result beside a radio, not without nervousness, for I had been encouraged to make plans I should not be able to abandon without disappointment; at noon I learned that I had won the prize. We had a 'family' celebration, consisting of a lunch at Michelle's, during which Sartre presented me with a very appropriate gift – a book on the Goncourts by André Billy which had just been published; the celebration continued with a dinner that evening with Olga, Bost, Scipion and Rolland. I had warned the jury and also Gaston Gallimard that if I were chosen I should not make an appearance either in the Place Gaillon or the Rue Sébastien-Bottin. At thirty-five, in my innocence, I should have enjoyed exhibiting myself; now I found it repugnant. I have neither braggadocio nor indifference enough to offer myself as willing fodder for the curious. Some journalists, sitting on the stairs, vainly besieged a door behind which a cat was meowing, and which was in fact the Bosts'. Two or three days later, some photographers posted themselves in the street to catch me coming out of the Café des Amis; I left through the veterinary clinic, the door of which opened onto another street. The only interview I gave was to *Humanité-Dimanche*. I wanted to make it clear that my novel was not hostile to the Communists and that it had not aroused their enmity.

'If you accepted the prize, you should have played the game,' people said to me. I fail to see in what respect the decision of the Goncourt jury can be said to have created an obligation on my part towards the television, the radio and the press, nor why it should have induced me to smile at the camera, answer foolish questions or publish what was better left in a drawer. 'The journalists are only doing their job.' Agreed; I have nothing against them; some of my best friends are journalists – I just don't like the newspapers they work for. Furthermore, with the best will in the world, or the worst, publicity disfigures those who fall into its hands. In my view, the relations a writer entertains with the truth make it impossible for him to acquiesce to such treatment; it is quite enough that it should be inflicted on him by force.

The prize brought me a great many letters. A good many readers automatically buy the book that wins the Goncourt, and to them I was anything but a satisfying choice; the letters they sent me were angry, hurt, indignant, moralizing, insulting. I have chosen the following pearl, of Argentine origin (which does slightly tarnish its orient): 'Why must the love scenes in a work of this sort be described in the manner of the *Diary of a Chambermaid* or *The Princess of Cleves*?' People I had known more or less intimately in the past congratulated me as though on some sort of promotion; this surprised me, but I had the pleasure of seeing certain ghosts rise up out of the past: pupils, fellow students, an English teacher at the Cours Désir. Rouen, Marseilles, the Sorbonne, my childhood itself: the past suddenly began to fall into place. A great many people I didn't know also wrote to me, from France, from Poland, from Germany, from Italy. The Portuguese Embassy let its displeasure be known, but students in Lisbon and Coimbra wrote thanking me. Some young Malgaches sent me a wooden statuette to show how touched they were at my writing about the repression of 1947. I believe too fundamentally in death to worry about what will happen to me after it; in those moments when the dream I dreamed at the age of twenty – to make myself loved through my books[1] – comes true, nothing can spoil my pleasure.

My only problems came from the legend, planted and nurtured by the critics, that I had written an exact and faithful chronicle; this legend turned my inventions into indiscretions or even into denunciations. Like dreams, novels are often prophetic simply because they deal with possibilities; thus Camus and Sartre quarrelled with each other two years after I began to recount the avatars and the breakup of a friendship. Several women wanted to recognize Paule's story as their own. These coincidences finished off the process by which my fables became accepted as accredited truths. Did Camus or Sartre bear false witness as I described

1. This is of course a desire common to a great many writers. 'I write to be loved,' Genet has written; and Leiris quoted this phrase in an interview as an expression of his own feelings.

Henri doing? people have asked me. When did I practise psycho-analysis? In one sense, it pleased me that my story carried such conviction; but it upset me that people thought me so unscrupulous. One of the secondary characters, Sézenac, gave rise to a mis-understanding that I found very unpleasant. He had certain traits reminiscent of Francis Vintenon, whom I mentioned earlier, and whose strange and violent death was attributed to an ex-collaborator; in *The Mandarins*, Sézenac was done away with in a somewhat similar fashion, but by one of his comrades, since I had made the character a double agent guilty of having betrayed some Jews. A woman friend of Vintenon's asked me for an appointment. She thought I had some secret information about him; she had identified the imaginary murderer as one of her friends. She left without my having been able to disabuse her. I'm afraid my book engendered a great many other misunderstandings besides this one, so deter-mined are people to take it as a faithful account of reality.

Bombs, attempted assassinations: the Moroccan nationalists were not going to give up the struggle until the Sultan was reinstated. When the rebellion broke out in the Aurès, I believed that the days of colonialism, at least in North Africa, were numbered. Mendès-France sent reinforcements into Algeria; after him, Edgar Faure refused to negotiate; the Algerian police began imprisoning and torturing people;[1] Soustelle became Governor-General and was converted to 'integration'; the Army took a solemn oath never to relinquish Algeria; the Poujadist movement, which had come into being eighteen months before, was spreading like wildfire. But the insurrection that had just exploded was an irreversible event, the example of Indochina and the general trend of the world as a whole convinced me of that; it was a conviction confirmed by the Bandoeng Conference, which heralded the imminent de-colonization of the entire planet.

The appearance of my street began to change. Leather-jacketed North Africans, looking very well groomed, began to frequent the Café des Amis; all alcohol was forbidden; through the windows I could see the customers sitting down in front of glasses of milk. No more brawls at night. This discipline had been imposed by

1. From January 1955 on, in the *Bloc-Notes* he had been writing since April 1954 for *L'Express*, Mauriac, under the heading *La Question*, denounced the use of torture in Algeria.

the F.L.N. militants, who had gained a dominating influence over the Algerian proletariat living in France. The influence of the M.N.A. had greatly declined. In Algeria itself, it represented a harmful dissident faction, according to Francis and Colette Jeanson in *L'Algérie hors la loi*; the French left wing as a whole was hesitating between the F.L.N. and the M.N.A.; and in any case its position was not clear on any one point; it wanted a 'liberal' solution of the conflict: it was a word capable of many interpretations. Sartre and *Les Temps Modernes* joined with Jeanson in demanding independence for the Algerian people, and regarded the latter as embodied by the F.L.N.

The events in North Africa and the fall of Mendès-France brought to a head the opposition between those French people who wanted things changed and those who had an interest in maintaining the status quo. A certain amount of regrouping was going on in the first camp. *L'Express* rallied *La Gauche nouvelle* to the cause of Mendès-France, who was also supported by Malraux and Mauriac. On 31 December Mendès-France had persuaded the Assembly to approve the Paris Agreements reviving the Wehrmacht; he defended himself against the accusation of wanting to 'abandon' Algeria; his faction was proposing to remodel capitalism and colonialism in order to bring them into line with a new technocracy: really no more than a right-wing policy with a facelift. The *Nouvelle Gauche*, the idea of which had been launched a year earlier by Bourdet, was more deserving of its name.

It became evident to us that we would have to make distinctions between our real allies and our adversaries in this new 'Left'. The *Temps Modernes* team took upon itself the task of elucidating the meaning of this now devalued label. Lanzmann made a frontal attack on the question by writing an article on 'the left-winger'. Others studied and instituted inquiries into more detailed aspects. I approached the problem from the other side, attempting to define the principles professed by the Right today. I had enjoyed unravelling the myths spun around woman through the ages; in this case, too, it was a matter of laying bare the practical truths – the defence of privileges by the privileged – whose crudity is concealed behind systems and nebulous concepts; I had already read a lot, I had swallowed a great deal of nonsense; I now had to gulp down much more. It was boring and irritating work, but I did it joyfully, since all this nonsense was a sign of the ideological collapse of the privileged classes. The economists were sharpening up new theories for the defence of capitalism much less unwieldy than those used by their predecessors; but they no longer knew what ethic, what ideal to invoke as a justification for the combat itself. The conclusion I drew was that their thought is really no more than a counter-thought. The future has proved me right. Through the mouth of Kennedy, of Franco, of Salan, of Malraux, the 'Free World' invokes no other reason for its being, no other rule of life than this: to oppose Communism; it is incapable of proposing any positive ideal of life to put in its place. It is a pitiful thing to see the United States Government desperately hunting for themes of propaganda; it cannot hide from the world the fact that the only values being defended by the United States are the interests of America. Even the word Culture has become unusable; against Spender and Denis de Rougemont, the Russian intellectuals would risk insisting on it. Of course there will always be a Thierry Maulnier or two, brandishing a sheaf of threadbare phrases in the face of the future. Such delaying tactics never really delay anything.

In June, Merleau-Ponty, who was becoming very irritated by Sartre's political attitude, published *Les Aventures de la dialectique*, in which he remodelled his philosophy in the most fantastic manner. He was linked at the time with *La Gauche nouvelle* and served it by discrediting Sartre's 'ultra-bolshevism'; this produced great rejoicings on the extreme Right: ingeniously selecting one of Merleau-Ponty's most unfortunate phrases – in which he confuses need and liberty – Jacques Laurent announced that with these few words he had given Sartrism its death blow. Sartre's ideas were already so ill-understood that it seemed to me deplorable that they should be distorted even further. It was so often forgotten that in *Being and Nothingness* man is not just an abstract point of view, but an embodied presence, so often man's relation with the other was reduced to a matter of the *regard* alone! Gurvitch, in one of his lectures, had recently claimed that the Other, in Sartre's thought, is an 'intruder'. I wanted to re-establish the truth; Sartre applied the dialectical method in a great many domains; he left the door open for a general theory of dialectical reason; his philosophy was not a philosophy of the subject, etc. The sentences I quoted from his work contradicted, point by point, the allegations Merleau-Ponty had made.

It has been said that it was Sartre's job to reply. There was no compulsion whatever for him to do so; on the other hand, any Sartrian had the right to defend a philosophy that he had made his own. I have also been blamed for the virulence of my reply; but Merleau-Ponty's attack was in its essentials extremely harsh. And he himself did not hold a grudge against me for it, or at least not for long; he was able to accept the existence of purely intellectual anger. And in any case, though we both felt great friendship for each other, our differences of opinion were often violent; I would often get carried away, and he would smile.

Generally speaking, I take too peremptory a tone in my essays, some people have told me; a more temperate approach would be more convincing. I don't think so. The best way to explode a bag of hot air is not to pat it but to dig one's nails into it. I am not interested in making appeals to people's better natures when I think I've got truth on my side. In my novels, on the other hand, I set great store by nuances and ambiguities. That is because my intentions are not the same. Existence – others have said it and I have already repeated it more than once myself – cannot be reduced to ideas, it cannot be stated in words: it can only be evoked through the medium of an imaginary object; to achieve this, one must recapture the surge of backwash, and the contradictions of life itself. My essays reflect my practical choices and my intellectual certitudes; my novels, the astonishment into which I am thrown both by the whole and by the details of our human condition. They correspond to two different orders of experience which cannot be communicated in the same manner. Both sorts of experience are to me equal in importance and authenticity; I see myself reflected no less in *The Second Sex* than in *The Mandarins*, and vice versa. If I have used two different modes of self-expression, it was because such diversity was for me a necessity.

That winter, we drove down to Marseilles with Lanzmann; despite the devastation and the ugliness of the new buildings, I still liked the place, and he liked it too; it was a pleasure to open my eyes every morning on the sight of the flotilla in the Vieux Port and to see the smooth water turning golden in the evening light. We worked at our articles, we took walks, we talked, and we read the newspapers assiduously. One morning a big front-page headline informed us that Bulganin was replacing Malenkov as Premier of the Soviet Union; Malenkov had retired from the government and Bulganin was to have Khrushchev as his right-hand man. Heavy industry was to have priority over light industry once more. Rakosi had returned to power in Hungary, ousting Nagy. But there was no return to Stalinism. There began to be talk of co-existence. In June, Bulganin and Khrushchev paid a visit to Tito.

None of which prevented the professional anti-Communists from pursuing their extremely fruitful careers in France. They inspired Sartre to write a farce, *Nékrassov*. It was still not finished when Jean Meyer began rehearsals, with Vitold in the role of Valéra, the false Nékrassov; Sartre had difficulty finishing it, because he didn't want to make his hero into an out-and-out bastard, but he also didn't want to make him into a convert. After rehearsals had been going on for a day or two, he brought in the script of a new scene in which he depicted the terrors of the bourgeoisie in farcical-lyrical style. While the club of those-to-be-shot was having a lugubrious party at Mme Bounoumi's, strikers began parading up and down outside the windows, and the hitherto nebulous sense of impending disaster among the guests slowly turned into wild terror. Simone Berriau went white: 'They'll smash my chairs.' Meyer, alarmed, also protested: 'It's much too long!' Valéra, fleeing from the police, was to jump out of the window among the strikers who then opened his eyes to the truth. On second thought, this Jadnovian optimism didn't appeal to Sartre. He cut the riot; the scene immediately lost all its vigour. It was also shorter; however, the play when finally finished was still longer than it should have been; the prologue was dropped. Meyer directed *Nékrassov* without either invention or gaiety, and Sartre has since regretted not having centred the plot on the newspaper rather than on Valéra. Which does not keep the play, when performed by good actors, from being an extremely funny comedy; the terrors, the ravings, the petty obsessions, the near-sightedness, the slogans and the fantastic inventions of the anti-Communists – among others the myth of the 'suitcase bomb' lately propagated by Malraux – all of these had provided Sartre with a series of irresistible effects. The opening-night audience, made up of critics and society people, was hostile; they could not help laughing and made up for it afterwards by saying how much they had yawned. But the press could not forgive Sartre for having dared to ridicule it; it wanted his head. Françoise Giroud got herself invited to a dress rehearsal and quickly took over the theatre column of *L'Express* from Renée Saurel, who resigned from the paper; she then tore *Nékrassov* to pieces. All the other newspapers, or almost all of them, followed suit. A play can weather the attacks of the critics when it can command the favours of the orchestra; this is the case with Anouilh: he appeals to the rich. But *Nékrassov* was an attack on precisely those people who assure the box office of its receipts; the ones who came found the play amusing but made sure to tell their friends they had been bored stiff. In the name of culture, the bourgeoisie will swallow a great many affronts; this particular bone stuck in its throat. *Nékrassov* lasted for only sixty performances.

My articles took up a great deal of my time during that year because of all the reading I had to do for them. I did have some time off all the same. I went for drives with Lanzmann, I went out, I visited friends. I made the acquaintance of Lanzmann's brother Jacques when he came back from America. Stammeringly, he poured into our ears a series of comic adventures in which reality and his own fantasies were freely intermingled. His first book, *La Glace est rompue*, gave a picture of Iceland both extravagant and exact; we were sorry that the ambassador was offended by the fragments of it we published in *Les Temps Modernes*. Lanzmann also had a sister, called Evelyne Rey, who belonged to the Centre de l'Ouest theatre company; she acted in the provinces for the most part, but the Centre brought their production of *The Three Sisters* to Paris and I saw her work for the first time. Shortly after that she took over the part of Estelle in *Huis clos* at the Théâtre de l'Athenée. At twenty-two, penniless and inexperienced, she was red-haired, fat, made up like a *femme fatale*, and wore black velvet dresses. Paris improved her taste with amazing rapidity. Within the year, I watched her become blonde, slim, fresh-looking and elegant. Evelyne was very funny, which is rare in women, and so pretty that people were amazed by her intelligence. We often went out with her. I liked her very much.

With Lanzmann, I went to the cinema. *The Salt of the Earth* was a touching story, simply told. I enjoyed Buñuel's variation on *Robinson Crusoe*, and also Fellini's masterpiece *I vitelloni*. I had picked up a taste for Westerns from Sartre in the old days. Above all the rest, I preferred Huston's *Treasure of the Sierra Madre*, made from the novel by Traven, the mysterious author of best-sellers who lived in Mexico and whose identity no one had ever discovered. But Gary Cooper in *High Noon*, Marilyn Monroe in *River of No Return*, and the violence of *Shane* had also held me breathless. And that was the year I saw Joan Crawford again in *Johnny Guitar*, more beautiful than ever in the lustre of her fiftieth year. But most of the time the Americans were now spoiling this sort of film by working the same old political 'message' into them all. A hero or heroine, sometimes a child, would have an almost neurotic repugnance towards violence; for an hour and a half, sometimes two, the wickedness of the 'bad people' would fail to have any effect on this attitude; suddenly, at the last moment, to save a friend, a fiancée, a father, the main character would kill. The audience then returned home convinced, it was hoped, of the necessity of the preventive war.

I went to see *Porgy and Bess* delightfully performed by a visiting American company, and *The Crucible*, very well staged by Rouleau. *Ping-Pong*, with some of our friends in the cast – Evelyne, Chauffard – seemed to me Adamov's best play. I don't know how I came to miss the 1954 production of *Mother Courage* that introduced Brecht to French audiences; he was revealed to me[1] by *The Caucasian Chalk Circle*, which the Berliner Ensemble brought to the Sarah-Bernhardt in June of 1955.

Except for those that informed me about the world I was living in, few books made a great impression on me. But there was Pavese's *La bella estate*, which offered me all one can ask of a work of fiction: the re-creation of a world that envelops my own, that belongs to my own, that takes me into another country and enlightens me, which leaves its mark on me forever with all the reality of an experience I have lived through myself. In Leiris' *Fourbis* I found again those qualities that had riveted me in his *Bifures*: those spirals of words coiling in on themselves and unrolling again into infinity, drilling into the abysses of the past and the heart, yet glittering there in broad daylight, reflecting from image to image towards a secret that vanishes at the very instant it seems it must appear, the search having no other outcome than itself in the slow revolution of its thousand mirrors.

Towards the end of spring, Violette Leduc's *Ravages* appeared, a tense and violent novel in which the author hurled her experience

1. *The Threepenny Opera*, which I had seen performed by a French Company in 1930, had given me no real idea of his work.

down before the public without the slightest complicity; with the result that the book was found not only shocking but unpleasant as well, by the Gallimard readers in the first place. The first part related without compromise – though also without obscenity – the love affair of two college girls; the Gallimard readers asked that it be cut. Certain scenes were considered unpublishable, although they were no more daring than many others that had been printed; it was just that the erotic object was in this case woman and not man, which to the Gallimard readers was an outrage. Amputated in this way, the story lost a great deal of its point without gaining any of the graces Violette Leduc had deliberately avoided. Nevertheless she had the impression that it was getting off to a good start. We strolled down the walks of the Bagatelle, among the beds of tulips and hyacinths, in the sun, and on the strength of Gallimard's sales figures we dreamed of a success for her. The figures were wrong. There were critics who liked *Ravages* and said so; people still didn't buy it. 'I'm a desert that talks to itself,' Violette Leduc wrote to me one day. Usually writing that attempts to evoke aridity betrays it, the reader makes his way through a pleasant, dappled landscape; but in Violette Leduc's case, beneath the hard brilliance of the words the desert remained bare, spiky with rocks and thorns. That was her great success; it was also her failure. It threw her into a terrible state of depression.

I wanted very much to visit the U.S.S.R.; but I wanted even more to get a look at China; I had read the report by Belden and all the books that had come out in French on the Chinese Revolution, though there were still only a small number at that time; we had gazed for hours at Cartier-Bresson's book of photographs. All the travellers we met who had been to Peking spoke of it in dazzled tones. When Sartre told me we'd been invited there, I didn't dare believe my ears. In June, as we sat watching an extraordinary performance given by the Peking Opera, I still wasn't sure it was true.

Meanwhile, I took a trip more modest in scope but nevertheless very important for me; the Congress of the Peace Movement was held in Helsinki; my political evolution had led me to a point where I wanted to take some part in that event. I accompanied Sartre. We stopped for a few hours at Stockholm; then our plane rose over a sea so coldly green that I felt it must be solid, like liquid ice. I could make out a scattering of abandoned islets, seeming even more solitary when one house stood on a headland; the islets multiplied, then came a point when I no longer knew if I was flying over waters sprinkled with earth or land punctuated with water; victory went to the land: pines, lakes as elusive as reefs. These inaccessible, invisible, sequestered places were violated by my eyes, and yet my eyes united them too, bestowing on this section of the planet, for a while, an aspect that existed only for me, yet very real all the same. I found it as disturbing as when my eyes in childhood were re-creating the world, as disturbing as that age-old sadness: in a moment, all this will no longer exist for anyone.

I experienced in Helsinki what Sartre had felt in Vienna. In the vast auditorium hung with decorations and flags almost every country in the world was represented; the members of the Committee sat in tiers; the other members of the Congress sat behind desks provided with headphones, or else walked up and down the aisles whispering. A variety of costumes: Hindus, Arabs, Roman Catholic priests, Greek Orthodox prelates. It was moving to see these people all drawn together by the same hope, often at great risk and personal danger, from every corner of the earth. I talked to some American students who had come in secret to Helsinki at the risk of losing their passports. Sartre introduced me to Maria Rosa Oliver, a beautiful, paralysed Argentinian woman who went all over the world in a wheel-chair; she had been forced to go through Chile in order to get to Finland. I met Nicolas Guillen, the Cuban poet, and Jorge Amado, the Brazilian writer, whose novels I admired. Once again I saw Anna Seghers, with her extraordinary blue eyes. During a lunch, Lukács started a discussion with Sartre on liberty, less ferocious than the letters they had exchanged the year before, but more fruitful; Sartre listened politely as Lukács explained that man was conditioned by the age he lives in; he still hadn't finished when it was time for the afternoon session to begin. I had dinner with Surkov and Fedin; as we drank Georgian wine on the brink of a night undecided whether to fall or not, listening under the pale sky to the murmur of the trees, I remembered the rather doleful curiosity with which, four years earlier, we had gazed, up beyond the North Cape, at the Russians' barbed wire and their red-starred sentinels; for us the Iron Curtain had dissolved; no further embargo, no more exile; the realms of socialism were now part of our world.

I met Ehrenburg several times. I remembered him as I had seen him before the war, hirsute and thickset, on the terrace of the Dôme. Now he was dressed with a casual daring that recalled Montparnasse in the old days – a pale-green tweed suit, an orange shirt, a woollen tie; but his body had caved in; under the white, carefully groomed locks, the face had lengthened. He had a full-bodied voice and his French was flawless. The only thing about him that made me uncomfortable was his self-confidence. He was aware of being the cultural ambassador of a country that held the future of the world in its hands; a good Communist can never be in doubt that he is in possession of the truth; there was nothing surprising in the fact that Ehrenburg should speak *ex cathedra*. His dogmatism was balanced by his charm, at once various and acute. He rebuked Sartre, in a friendly and almost grandfatherly tone, for certain details in an interview that Sartre had given to *Libération* on the subject of the U.S.S.R. He asked him earnestly not to attack the U.S.A. too fiercely when his turn came to speak; conciliation was the order of the day; he had intended to suggest to a certain magazine that it publish certain extracts from *America Day by Day*, but at the moment he didn't think that it would be opportune. He talked to me about *The Mandarins*; in Moscow, all the intellectuals who knew French had read it and discussed it favourably, although the love story had seemed superfluous to them. 'However,' he added, 'we can't see that it's possible to translate your work at the moment.' He gave me two reasons for this: first the traditional Russian prudery with regard to literature; secondly, a few years earlier the discussions about the camps would not have worried anyone; people would just have smiled and said: 'Even our sympathizers are getting mixed up in anti-Communism!' But now, these things were known to be true. The return of those who had been deported was even creating difficult problems; which meant that the reading public would not easily tolerate having a knife turned in the wound. He told us some strange stories about Stalin, the following among others: Stalin was chatting, very informally, with some writers. 'There are two ways of being a great writer: painting powerful, tragic frescoes, like Shakespeare, or else describing the tiny details of life in depth, with great precision, like Chekhov.' He paused, then said: 'If I had been a writer, I should have been a Chekhov.' Ehrenburg was making a considerable effort to 'thaw' Soviet writing; in his magazine he was trying to create as many contacts with the West as possible; he was a protector of non-official painting. With his subtle intelligence, his taste formed by what used to be termed the 'avant-garde', he had applied himself to bringing about an effective reconciliation of this acquired liberalism with Soviet orthodoxy; it was a task that had not always been without danger.

I went out, with Sartre or by myself, to look at the town. It was ugly, but lashed by a glorious sea barred with reefs and breakwaters. At its gates, there was an enormous park planted with birches and pines; we had dinner there one evening, all sitting at little tables in a big glass pavilion, and I found it very pleasant chatting first to one little group then to another. Vercors and his wife told me about Peking, the covered market, the imperial palace, and I said to myself: 'Only three more months!' We went for a stroll along the paths with Dominique Desanti and Catherine Varlin Guillen, who had arrived at the end of the meal dying of hunger; at eleven in the evening it was still light, some festival was being celebrated, and among the pines we passed bands of Finnish men singing in chorus as they walked through the park to celebrate one of their heroes and watch the firework displays. Back in Helsinki, Guillen was dreaming of hot dogs; but there was not a single café open, not a shop, not even a street stand. Silence everywhere; the hotel bar was closing; we tried to buy a bottle to drink up in my room. 'It's two minutes past midnight,' one of the hotel employees told us severely. We made do with water. Guillen fulminated against Nordic puritanism. Another evening, when Sartre had been delayed, I went to the hotel bar up on the fifteenth floor. I sat there for a long time in front of a glass of whisky, watching the sun hanging just at the edge of the horizon, the coast and its reefs being battered by a tumult of waves, whose foam slowly faded back into the advancing night. It was beautiful to see, and I was happy. What Ehrenburg had said about *The Mandarins* had been a pleasure for me; the American students prophesied a great success for me in the U.S.A.; I was lucky; while I was writing it, the cold war had seemed to doom it to failure, now the world thaw was helping it. After years of fighting against the current, I once more felt myself borne along on the stream of History; and I wanted to plunge deeper into it. The example of the men and women I was moving among here stimulated me. For three years, I had devoted a great deal of myself to my private life. I regretted nothing.

But old directives began to awaken in me: to be useful in some way.

The sessions of the Congress were not very interesting; there were orators in abundance; they had not come from the corners of the earth just to sit and say nothing. But the real work was done in the sub-committees. The Algerian delegation wanted to have a talk with the French delegation; Boumendjel presided over the meeting. He described to us the situation of their country. They called to our attention the fact that a few days before, the rebellion had entered a new phase; it was spreading throughout the entire country; the 120,000 French soldiers stationed at that moment on Algerian territory would be powerless to contain it. We ourselves, they said, can scarcely control it; tomorrow we won't be able to control it at all. They urged the French to act immediately in order to break the vicious circle of repression and rebellion: 'Negotiate with us!' Vallon and Capitant smiled. 'The problem is an economic one; if we made the necessary reforms, your political demands would no longer have any *raison d'être*.' The Algerians shook their heads. 'We'll put the reforms into operation ourselves. Our people wants its freedom.' Some of the French delegation supported them. Sartre did not enter the discussion because he was not well enough informed about the problem, but he knew very well that no valid economic reform could be effected within the framework of colonialism.

When we got back to Paris, the vicious circle had not been broken. In the Assembly, an M.R.P. deputy, the Abbé Gau, denounced the methods used by the police in Algeria, which he said were worthy of the Gestapo. He was listened to with half an ear,[1]

1. In February, Vuillaume, Inspector General of the Administration, had been given the task of instituting an inquiry; it was not till much later, when it was published by *Témoignages et documents*, that I was to see his report of 22 March 1955. He described the different tortures in use by the police and added that they seem to him to be necessary: 'One must have the courage to speak out directly about this delicate problem. In effect, either people take shelter behind the hypocritical attitude that has prevailed up till now and which consists of wanting to remain ignorant of what the police is doing . . . or else they adopt the mock-indignant attitude of someone who is pretending he has been tricked. . . . Now neither of these attitudes is admissible, the first because the veil has been lifted and public opinion alerted, the second because Algeria, particularly in the present circumstances, has need of an especially effective police force. To restore its confidence to the police force and set it back on its feet there is only one remedy: to recognize and condone certain procedures.'

then a little later a state of emergency was declared. Marshal Juin formed a committee pledged to keep Algeria French at any cost. The fabric of colonialism was cracking everywhere: Bourguiba's triumphal re-entry into Tunis, Lemaigre-Dubreuilh's assassination in Morocco, riots in the Cameroons. But even these proofs did not convince those whose interests lay in ignoring them.

I went back to Spain with Lanzmann. We had decided to see some bullfights. In these days when words cost so little, I can appreciate the value of these trials in which a man engages his body in this hand-to-hand grapple with death. On condition, of course, that he does so of his own free will. In our society, the will of the exploited is never free; and the defects of capitalism have a thousand different repercussions both in the ring and the arena. Given this one reservation – and it is an important one – I find the attacks directed against boxing and bullfighting on moral grounds to be without foundation. The bourgeois moralists are pure spirits, or almost; they pay no attention to the needs, defections, resources, limits, strength and fragility of their bodies; they admit them as relevant only in the case of sex and death. These two words spring immediately to their pens when they interpret an event in which the body commits itself in its brute state to an ultimate conflict, without the intermediary of some mechanism. If they fling about words like barbaric and sadistic, it is because they are shocked by the identification of a man with his body. To the crowd, which accepts this struggle naturally, because it corresponds to their inner experience, they attribute 'low' and 'suspect' instincts. They forget that traditional celebrations are not susceptible of explanation by individual perversions; as for death, it is less present in a bullring than on an airstrip. The enthusiasts of the *corrida* usually irritate me as much as its opponents because they talk in terms of the same myths as the latter, except that their tone is ecstatic instead of indignant. These myths did not exist in the peasant communities where bullfighting was born; they were cultivated when the landed aristocracy and their parasites took it over and used it for their own advantage. If one sweeps such myths away, despite all the frills and

---

Soustelle did not officially ratify these conclusions but did subscribe to the following, which includes all the others: 'The attempt to establish the limits of personal responsibility is one of extremest difficulty. Furthermore, it is to my mind inopportune.'

furbelows, the ceremonies, and a whole literature, the bullfight still retains its original significance: an intelligent animal fights and overcomes an animal that is more powerful but less mentally skilled. It is precisely because I have a materialist view of man that such a combat interests me. It has been spoiled by gimmicks simply because it has become (like boxing) a financial enterprise whose mainspring is desire for profit. But sometimes the daring, the sincerity of a bullfighter restores its original purity.

We started off in Barcelona, where we saw Chamaco, idolized by the Barcelonese although he was still a *novillero*. Then we went to Pamplona; the *feria* was in progress and bore scarcely any resemblance to Hemingway's descriptions. In the squares, in the cafés, in crowds, in gangs, in brotherhoods, nothing but men, men singing and dancing heavily and enjoying being with other men. We spent three afternoons at bullfights; I liked Gijon very much, and that year he won the golden ear.

We went on to the west coast and stopped at Toja, lured by the pine groves and the solitude of the immense beaches. But in those districts Spain had no smile for us. When we walked along the jetties of the little nearby port, the faces of the fishermen, bent over their nets, grew hard. In the towns and villages of Asturia, throughout the mining district, every look we surprised was a reproach; children threw stones at the car. We preferred this rage to resignation, but we did not find it pleasant to be its target. And we hated all the mystifications even more than we had the year before. Too many fireworks everywhere, imitating gaiety; too many priests patrolling the little towns, thirsty for visions of the life beyond. They swarmed everywhere like insects, those clergymen with velvet hats who have reduced the hatred around them to silence only by force of arms. At Oviedo, as we drove in, a procession was filling the avenues of the town with whining, sing-song chants, with orphans, with women in black, with gloomy adolescents in long robes; not a glimmer of light in these faces stupefied by the shabbiest and narrowest sort of devotions. Santiago de Compotela, despite its cathedral and the glory of its name, put us to flight: the streets smelled so strongly of holy water and venality. We went through forests whose acorns are used by those who live in them as food; and we wanted to visit the valley of Las Hurdes, disclosed to the world before the war by Buñuel's film. There was one road leading down into it, the only entrance to the valley, and so steep that from below, the wall of rock it clings to like a snake appears impassable. Over a sort of gateway we read: 'You are entering the valley of Las Hurdes'; and it seemed to us as though the gates of a world cut off from the world outside were closing behind us. Up in the mountains, I knew that a luxurious monastery had recently been built only a few miles away; that represented the furthest extent of public solicitude. The houses were stables, in which goats, chickens and human cattle all lived pell-mell together; children, adults, all suffering from goitre, all with the same look of animal despair stamped on their faces; and we only saw the bottom of the valley, where at least there is a tiny stream of water and a layer of soil that produces a few plants; but up on the rocky plateaux, water and even earth has to be brought up on the men's backs. It was dark as we drove back; not a light, not a single voice; a few doors stood open to reveal a dark silence in which animals and people lay huddled together; and in our mouths, too, words froze and refused to form.[1]

Salamanca was beautiful: plaza, arcades, stone buildings, statues, all with a classical quality unexpected in Spain. Without stopping, we drove straight on to Valencia through the tumultuous winds of La Mancha dotted with the tall windmills of Don Quixote. The *feria* was beginning; we liked it much better than the one at Pamplona; nothing folksy – the genuine effervescence of a twentieth-century city. We watched the *apartado* on the first morning and then all the *corridas* on the following days. In between we strolled in the Albufera and watched the white sails gliding along among the orange trees of the *huerta*. There was a water shortage in Valencia for those three days; we drank beer or wine, and took sunbaths till our skins grew sticky. Lanzmann bought a magnificent red and yellow poster of Litri facing a bull, which I pinned up on one of my walls.

Having resisted Andalusia, we reached Huelva; Litri was making a comeback there – once again – to which the press was giving enormous publicity. He was a local boy, and the day of the *corrida* there was a large crowd of men and women gathered at his door waiting with a kind of devotion for him to appear. I have a very vivid memory of that country bullring, crudely whitewashed and dominated by a hill whose colours were those of Africa; among

1. The scandal was too flagrant. In the last year or two, some superficial remedies have been applied. The road now runs through the valley; electricity has been installed; some schools have been started.

the tawny rocks and eucalyptus trees, people were standing, dressed in brilliantly coloured stuffs, and watching. Nothing very interesting happened. Ortega, blond and getting paunchy, was more like a matador in an opera; Bienvenuda was careful not to take too many risks or too much trouble, and Litri, his cheeks as red as those of a Zurbarán madonna, did not quite deserve all the applause he drew from the crowd. Suddenly, as a new bull hurtled into the ring, a young boy leapt over the balustrade, carrying a red handkerchief; faced with the bull, still untaught but intact, he made several daring passes and I could already feel the two horns gouging into my belly; none of the toreros, or any of their teams, made a move. Finally, a policeman reached over the barricade and knocked the kid out; he fell onto the sand and was carried off.

A great eucalyptus wood, a grey plateau planted with umbrella pines, bare sierras; Madrid. We liked it that year, perhaps because we explored it with people who lived there. One night, as we were drinking *manzanilla* at a counter, beneath the head of a famous bull, one of them, struggling through the barriers of his bad French and our bad Spanish, took a liking to us; he went and woke up his brother who spoke French fluently; in a very old tavern with painted walls, we ate shrimps together, served boiling hot with oil and garlic in earthenware bowls; we talked and drank to the sound of guitars in the little bars near the Puerta del Sol until dawn; from time to time, a woman or a man, suddenly inspired, would begin to sing or dance. Our friends were lower-middle-class people quite comfortably off; they didn't like the present regime. 'Nobody likes it,' they assured us; but they did not meddle much with politics. One of them believed fervently in God. 'If I didn't,' he told us, 'I'd kill myself here and now.' They didn't let us pay for a single thing we had: 'This is our home.' The following Sunday, we took them and their wives to see a bullfight out at the Escorial, unfortunately a bad one.

I have already written the story of my journey to China.[1] It was not like my other trips. It was not just a wandering, not an adventure, not a journey made just for the experience, but a field study in which caprice played no part. It was a country fundamentally foreign to me; even with the Yucatán and Guatemala I had been able

1. *The Long March.*

to establish some common ground because I had already been to Spain. In China there was none. I was able to get to know a little about the work of the writers I met there through English translations that I read at the time; but until then they had not existed for me; and – except for two or three French-literature specialists – neither my own name nor Sartre's meant anything to them; the newspapers explained that Sartre had just written a 'Life of Nékrassov',[1] and the people we talked to frequently expressed a polite interest in this work; then we would move on to gastronomy. This mutual ignorance restricted our conversations even more than the various political constraints. Added to which, Chinese culture – as I have explained at length elsewhere – is essentially a culture of civil servants and courtiers; it had little to say to me. I liked the Opera, the ritual grace of the gestures, the tragic imminence of the music, the slender, birdlike voice. I liked the grey *huntungs* of Peking and its flawless nights set in the splendour of autumn. In the theatre sometimes, or occasionally walking along a street, the things I perceived became part of me, I forgot myself. But for the most part I was consciously there, faced with a world which I was struggling to understand and to which I could not find the key.

It was not easy to decipher. I was encountering the Far East for the first time; for the first time I understood fully the meaning of the words underdeveloped country; I saw what poverty meant when it involved 600 million men; for the first time, I was there watching a people at that hardest of labours: the construction of socialism. These new experiences overlapped and blurred each other; the poverty of the Chinese only appeared to me through the vision of their attempts to overcome it; and it was to that poverty that the constructive efforts of the regime owed their severity; the crowds I was jostled by, their pleasures and their pains were all hidden from me by an exotic veil. All the same, looking, asking, comparing, reading, listening, I did finally experience one fact that emerged clearly from the half-shadows of my perception: the immensity of the victories won in only a few years over the scourges that had once held sway in China – dirt, vermin, infant mortality, epidemics, chronic malnutrition, hunger; the people had clothes and clean housing, and something to eat. Then I saw how very real was the impatient energy with which this nation was building a future for

1. The great nineteenth-century Russian poet.

itself. Other points became clear. However incomplete my experience was, I began to think that it might perhaps be interesting to write an account of it.

On the way to China, I had spent only a single day in Moscow, though without anyone or anything spoiling the pleasure of it for me. With Sartre as my guide, I walked through the streets from morning until the moment when the ruby stars are lit on the towers of the Kremlin. We stayed there a week on our way back from Peking. After two months of Chinese poverty, Moscow dazzled me, as New York had once done, coming from the chronic shortages of Europe. It was dark when Simonov came to fetch us from the airport; the University, so ugly by daylight, was glowing with a thousand lights; we had dinner with Simonov and his wife – a well-known actress whom everyone kept staring at – at the Soviet-skaia, which turned its dining room into a cabaret at night. What joy to come back to the sort of food and drink one can get high on! There was an orchestra, a floor show, and couples dancing, their cheeks aflame; we were a long way from the phlegmatic teachings of Confucius. Across the city they were building wherever you looked but not with trowels and little baskets of earth: trucks, steamrollers, cranes, bulldozers, there was nothing they didn't have; there were one or two of the old *isbas* still standing in almost every neighbourhood, but bristling with television aerials.

Olga P., our interpreter, took us around without a set programme, wherever we felt like going or she had the sudden impulse to take us. She showed us the monastery of Zagorsk, just outside Moscow; the churches were very beautiful and full of old women mumbling; in the classrooms, dirty bearded seminarists were leafing through books; the priests we passed on the walks outside seemed just as unkempt; as soon as one of the devout old ladies caught sight of one she would hurl herself at his hand and kiss it gluttonously. But the archimandrite who gave us lunch was superb; purple gown, long beautifully combed hair and long well-groomed beard. 'I hope you will excuse us, today is a day of abstinence,' he said, as a novice covered our plates with caviar; there were enormous photographs of Marx and Lenin nailed up on the walls. The archimandrite explained to us the ways in which the Revolution had helped religion: nowadays people knew that one became a priest by vocation and not for motives of personal gain. Olga P., who was Jewish, was almost choking with rage. 'I translate,' she would say in a stiff voice, and then she would repeat what the priest had said in a completely flat voice. 'I know we must instruct the people and not rush them,' she said as we came out, taking herself to task, 'I know we must respect their beliefs; but all the same they go too far.'

We ran into Carlo Levi. He was delighted by the 'dated' quality of so many things in Moscow: the ruffled curtains, the beaded lampshades, the plush, the acorns, the fringes, the lustres. 'It's my childhood, it's Turin in 1910,' he said. We watched for quite a while as passers-by charitably tried to keep a drunkard leaning against a wall on his feet: if you fell down and stayed down you were picked up and locked up until midday, and then you were late for work.

We saw several shows: *The Lower Depths*, staged in the classic Stanislavsky style; a comedy by Simonov with his wife acting in it, and Mayakovsky's *The Bedbug* at the Satirical Theatre. Olga P. had told us the story of the play in great detail and then translated long bits of it on the spot; the play was helped by a very swift production done with a very light touch and teeming with invention, also by a remarkable actor who played the lead in the 'alienated' Brechtian style.[1] During intermission I glanced around the audience and recognized Elsa Triolet's pretty nose, but the eyes were different and the hair was red; it was in fact her sister, once Mayakovsky's mistress. She exchanged a few words with Sartre. 'People have called it a play against Communism,' she said very loudly and clearly, 'but it's simply against a certain sort of hygiene.' At the end, Prissipkin came to the front of the stage and apostrophized the audience: 'Why aren't you all in cages too?' Jumping so swiftly from the imaginary to real life, he put us all in the same boat. Olga P. criticized *The Bedbug* for its didactic character. For us its meaning was quite clear: it is impossible to accept bourgeois society with its defects and excesses; but when one has been formed by it, it is impossible to submit to the 'hygiene' demanded by the U.S.S.R. during the early years of socialist construction. The author's suicide seemed to us to confirm this interpretation which, it turned out, was also that of the company and the director. Later, I am told, the play was put on by another company in Moscow

1. I have since been informed that Brecht himself saw the show several days after we did and warmly approved of the art with which the leading actor presented Prissipkin without identifying with the character.

which removed all its ambiguities and presented it as a straight-forward moral lesson.[1]

I understood why Sartre had ended up in hospital the year before: the Russian writers all enjoyed terrifyingly good health, and it was difficult to avoid their imperious offers of hospitality. A congress of critics from all regions of the U.S.S.R. was being held in Moscow. Simonov asked Sartre to participate in one of the afternoon sessions; beforehand we would lunch with him and some of his friends from Georgia. 'Excellent! But I won't drink,' Sartre said. They agreed to that. All the same, there were four bottles of different kinds of vodka on the restaurant table, and ten bottles of wine as well. 'Just sample the vodkas,' Simonov said, and went on, inexorably, to fill our glasses four times; then we had to drink some wine to go with a barbaric and sumptuous banquet: an enormous quarter of mutton, cooked on a spit and streaming with blood. Simonov and the three other guests told us laughingly that they had been celebrating all night, Muscovites and Georgians challenging each other with glass after glass of vodka and wine; Simonov hadn't slept the night before; he'd started working at five in the morning. They went on till they'd finished every single bottle, without any apparent effect. Olga P., who had done her best to refuse any drink, nevertheless discovered by the time we got to the Congress that she was too tired to translate; my own head was on fire, and I was full of admiration when Sartre managed to get up and talk quite sanely about the role of the critic. There was a debate on the relative amount of space that should be allowed to tractors and men in the peasant novel; I found the discussion tedious, but not more so than usual in that sort of argument. I don't imagine that any writer, in the West any more than in the East, has ever learned very much about his job from conferences attended by other writers.

I had to write two articles, give interviews, speak on the radio; I spent my last day in bed, partly, I admit, because I had caught cold, but mainly because I was so exhausted. I spent it reading *The Road to Calvary* by Alexis Tolstoy, enjoying my solitude, and the silence.

1. Neither the translation that appeared in *Les Temps Modernes*, nor the adaptation staged by Barsacq at the Théâtre de l'Atelier had the slightest success. I conclude that, out of context, *The Bedbug* has remained hermetic to the French public.

CHAPTER SEVEN

WHEN I came back from China, my confidence in history had been restored: the exploited would ultimately conquer in the Maghreb too, and the day of their victory might even be near at hand. On 20 August, at Oued Zem, the Moroccans avenged their brothers massacred by the ultras, by the police, by the Glaoui. On the same day, in the Constantine district, the A.L.N. had shot seventy Europeans.[1] The government had sent troops to North Africa – 60,000 men to Algeria alone – but this move had not been allowed to pass without protest. On 11 September everyone who was available turned out at the Gare de Lyon, and with cries of 'Morocco for the Moroccans' prevented the departure of the train. *L'Express* exhorted the youth of the country to obey its government and was immediately inundated with letters of protest. When *Les Temps Modernes* urged the young not to give in, it was with the approval of a large part of the nation. At Rouen, at Courbevoie, and in several other barracks, the soldiers, backed up by the Communist workers, refused to leave, and submitted to orders only by main force.

The left-wing press attempted to strengthen this resistance and mobilize public opinion against the war by trying to print the truth about it; it offered convincing proofs that the A.L.N. was not merely a gang of pirates but a well-disciplined people's army and a political entity. It denounced machine-gunning, bombings, the burning of villages and the use of torture. In November, two articles in *Les Temps Modernes* analysed and destroyed the myth of integration. A group of intellectuals started an Information Centre[2]; a Committee of Intellectuals opposing the prosecution of the war in North Africa was also formed.

In November, the Sultan was to return to Morocco; Tunisia was to be granted 'independence with interdependence' in the words of Edgar Faure; the problem of Algeria, a heavily settled colony, was more complicated than that of the two protectorates, but it

---

1. Thirty-five of them at El Halia. The reprisal caused the death of 12,000 men, women and children.
2. Which published *Témoignages et documents*.

seemed to us that France could not avoid granting it a new status analogous to those of its neighbours. After the elections of 2 January – despite the unexpected success of the Poujadists – we believed that the moment for this concession was at hand; the Front Républicain gained a majority of votes and had committed itself to a rapid termination of this war, described by Mollet as 'cruel and lunatic'. In his inaugural address, given on 31 January, he spoke of the 'particular personality of Algeria'. From the Socialist benches, Rosenfeld delivered the decisive opinion: 'that the fact of Algeria's existence as an independent nation must be recognized'.

We were not surprised by the reaction of the Army and the *pieds noirs* – Soustelle's passionate farewells to Algiers, the tomatoes thrown on 6 February, the Committees of Public Safety; Mollet's capitulation, when he replaced Catroux by Lacoste, we did find unexpected. Elected to conclude a peace, he intensified the war. We looked on with stupefaction as the Front Républicain gave him their support and the Communists, on 12 March, voted him special powers. This sudden change of policy was justified by a spate of propaganda that included statements preposterous beyond belief. The population of Algeria, it was said, had a great affection for France. The rebellion there was the result of an 'Islamic conspiracy', with Nasser and the Arab League in the role of puppeteers. French deputies in the course of their public duties were forced by Soustelle to applaud a philosophy of history which one normally expects to find only in the novels of Mickey Spillane, in American comic strips and in pulp spy thrillers. The press disseminated it and the public was both delighted with such exciting fare and flattered to be made privy to such very unsecret secrets. The newspapers kept from their readers the true nature of the reprisals by means of lies and omissions. It was known that since 'pacification' was not the same thing as war, the A.L.N. was not entitled to the protection of international law; people avoided asking themselves what happened to the prisoners that were taken. In April, only *Humanité* carried any mention of the 400 Moslems of Constantine who were beaten and hacked to death or hurled down ravines, all in the course of a single afternoon, by the forces of law and order. Only *L'Observateur* and *Humanité* disclosed the truth behind the tragedy of Rivet.[1] When Lieutenant Maillot went over to the A.L.N. on 6

1. A policeman was killed at Rivet on 8 May, then two Moslems as a reprisal; then, on 10 May, a European baker. This unleashed a bloody spate of

April the press showered him with insults without so much as asking what his reasons were. No one even mentioned the living conditions of the North Africans in metropolitan France, the shantytowns of Nanterre, except for two or three left-wing journalists.

And even those the government set about muzzling. Bourdet was arrested, Mandouze suspended, and a search warrant issued against Marrou, who had protested on 5 April in *Le Monde* against collective reprisals, against the concentration camps, and against the use of torture: he had made comparisons with Gurs, Buchenwald and the Gestapo. *Humanité* was seized several times, and André Stil indicted. An attempt was made to disgrace the Left by involving it in a shady 'secret information leak'; the Right blamed Bourdet, Stéphane, d'Astier, and Van Chi's negotiations for the loss of Indochina: such traitors should not be left free to stab their mother country in the back a second time. Even so, before settling down to war, the country, which had after all voted for peace, did shy once or twice. In several places there were protests against the departure of recalled conscripts. There were meetings, processions, strikes and walkouts everywhere; petitions circulated, and delegations of constituents asked to see their deputies. The Communists either organized or supported these demonstrations. After the friendly reception given to Mollet and Pineau during their visit to Moscow in June, the Communists became less vociferous, however. Sartre wanted the Peace Movement to condemn the war in Algeria. A Soviet delegate of some importance who happened to be passing through Paris told him that such a motion would be inopportune; he himself wanted a motion passed declaring that the Movement was opposed only to wars of aggression: the French in this case were not aggressors. We thought that the U.S.S.R. was holding back because it was afraid the Maghreb would become part

---

machine-gunning and troops were called in. They surrounded the Moslem district, loaded all the men – about forty – into trucks and shot them. They also picked up and shot some young men from neighbouring *mechtas*; after that they set fire to the place; almost all the inhabitants were burned alive except for a handful who managed to escape and begged the soldiers to spare their lives. The rightist papers published a picture of them: 'The population of several Arab encampments express their allegiance to France'; Rivet became a small fort, the murdered peasants were referred to as 'fellaghas', and this Oradour [French town burned and its population massacred by the Germans, 10 June 1944] was turned into a victory for the French army.

of the American zone of influence. Also, the Communist Party feared it would be cutting itself off from the masses if it appeared to be less nationalistic than the other parties. Officially it expressed its opposition to the government; but it no longer urged all those who could to defy it. It made no effort to combat the racism of the French workers, who considered the 400,000 North Africans settled in France as both intruders doing them out of jobs and as a sub-proletariat worthy only of contempt.

The electoral campaign had been based on a tissue of ambiguities and rivalries for power; the Front Républicain promised peace while at the same time rejecting the idea of abandoning Algeria, and without mentioning the word independence, which was so unpopular that even we at *Les Temps Modernes*, who both desired it and considered it inevitable, avoided calling it by its real name. If he had not capitulated, would Mollet have succeeded in his negotiations? What is certain is that by the end of June all resistance to the war had ceased. Giving not a thought to what it was going to cost, convinced that 'the loss of Algeria' would make them poorer, their mouths full of slogans and clichés – French Empire, French *départements*, abandonment, selling out, grandeur, honour, dignity – the entire population of the country – workers and employers, farmers and professional people, civilians and soldiers – were caught up in a great tide of chauvinism and racism. If Poujade suddenly lost his importance, it was because everyone in France had become a Poujadist. Our young men were sent without a qualm to the *djebels*, where they consoled themselves by playing soldier at the expense of the *bicots*.[1] We were able to observe, then and for several years to come, in all its dismal splendour, the phenomenon that Sartre calls 'recurrence',[2] each side finding in the conduct – or misconduct – of the other sufficient reason for its own attitude, which serves in its turn as sufficient reason for the actions of the other side. When Mollet had two prisoners guillotined on 20 June and another on 5 July, actions which provoked the Moslems of Algeria to a general strike, no one in France raised so much as an eyebrow.

We had begun by loathing a few men and a few factions; little by little we were made forcibly aware that all our fellow countrymen were accomplices in this crime and that we were exiles in our own

1. In March, there were 190,000 men in Algeria; on 1 June, 373,000. The half-million mark was soon reached.
2. *Critique de la raison dialectique.*

country. There were only a very few of us who did not join in the general chorus. We were accused of demoralizing the nation. We were treated as defeatists – *Those people over there are defeatists, said my father as we passed in front of the Rotonde* – as 'the fellaghas of Paris', as anti-French. But for what reason could Sartre and myself – without mentioning the others – be possessed by a mad rage against France? Our childhood, our youth, our language, our culture, our interests – everything bound us to our country. We were not misunderstood there, or hungry, or persecuted in any way. When it has turned out that we were in agreement with its politics and its feelings, we were delighted by such an understanding. There was nothing enviable in our present state of desolation and powerlessness. It was forced on us by evidence we could not ignore.

The A.L.N. now numbered 30,000, and its forces were no longer armed with shotguns but with rifles and automatic weapons; they controlled, as Lacoste himself admitted, one third of Algeria, which meant that the population was on their side. Ferhat Abbas had rejoined the F.L.N. From the mass of the people right up to its leaders, the combat was deepening, intensifying, and in the struggle Algeria's unity as a nation was being forged. Algeria would win. The prolongation of hostilities was in our opinion – as in Mollet's once – 'cruel and lunatic', because it meant condemning hundreds of thousands of Algerians to death and torture; on the French side it meant the sacrifice of thousands of young men, the necessity of systematically misleading public opinion, the restriction of liberties, the perversion of ideologics, the decay of a country fed with lies to the point where it had lost all sense of the truth and become alienated, disorganized, passive, ripe for every concession and for the first dictatorship to come along.

We refused to feel indignant about the methods of fighting used by the F.L.N. 'We're not fighting against choirboys,' was the habitual refrain of the French 'paras'. Yet when militant Algerians in France liquidated traitors, that was murder. Whereas the Frenchman was proving his virility by slitting throats, torturing prisoners and raping, the Algerian terrorist who did such things was demonstrating his ancestral 'Islamic barbarity'. In fact, the A.L.N. had no choice; it fought with any means that came to hand. And yet, even among those who recognized the validity of its aims, there were only a handful of us who insisted that terrorism and reprisals were inevitably the two sides of an equation. Partly out of caution,

but also with virtuous sincerity, most people began their denunciations of the use of torture and machine-gunnings by saying: 'Of
course we realize that the other side is guilty of terrible excesses.'
What excesses? The word had no meaning when applied to either
side. Camus' language had never sounded hollower than when he
demanded pity for the civilians. The conflict was one between two
civilian communities; the enemies of the colonized people were first
and foremost the European colonists, the army defending these was
only an accessory, and that army could win the war only by destroying the people from which the A.L.N. drew its strength; and
it was precisely that necessity which far from justifying the army's
actions condemned it. The massacre of a poverty-stricken nation
by a rich one (even if it was carried out without hatred, as was
asserted by a young parachutist[1]) is an action that can only turn
one's stomach. Our convictions derived from simple common
sense; and yet they cut us off from the rest of the nation and isolated
us even among the rest of the Left.

Hervé's *La Révolution et les fétiches* represented the first attempt
made by a French Communist intellectual since the death of Stalin
to criticize the official ideology of the Party. Unfortunately the
work itself was slight and muddled. Hervé was strongly attacked
by orthodox Communists, in particular by Guy Besse, and finally
found himself excommunicated from the Party altogether. In *Les
Temps Modernes*, Sartre dismissed both Hervé and Besse at the
same time. He was very emphatic about how important Marx's
thought had always been for him:

Men of my age are well aware of this fact: even more than the two
world wars, the all-important thing in their lives has been a perpetual
confrontation with the working class and with the ideology of the
working class which afforded them an irrefutable vision of the world
and of themselves. For us, Marxism is not merely a philosophy, it is
the climate of our ideas, the environment that nourishes them, it is the
movement of what Hegel calls the Objective Spirit.

But he also deplored the fact that Marxism had become stagnant;
Naville, who thought he had been drawn from cover, attacked
Sartre in *L'Observateur* and Sartre replied. The Communists let
Sartre's article go by without much reaction. One of the editorials

1. Perrault: *Les Parachutistes*. In what way is an atrocity less atrocious
because it has been committed without hatred? It seems to me to make the
atrocity worse.

in *Les Temps Modernes* blamed them for voting special powers to Mollet; but we remained their allies.

That February it seemed to us that the whole face of the Communist world was about to undergo a great change: Khrushchev announced at the 20th Party Congress that war was not inevitable, that a peaceful withering away of imperialism was possible, followed by a triumph of the working class without an armed struggle; he spoke of each nation's right to determine its own road to socialism. But hope gave way to surprise when his report of 25 February was made public; the brutality of this indictment, its suddenness, its 'anecdotage' – all disconcerted us. It was not enough to demolish Stalin; there should have been some analysis of the system that had made his tyranny and his 'bloody crimes' possible. Disturbing questions remained unanswered. Was there no risk of a police dictatorship springing up afresh in the service of some new team of rulers? The people who were denouncing the 'cult of personality' today had all worked with Stalin. Why had they said nothing? How far did their complicity extend? And how far could they be believed?

No one, either in the U.S.S.R. or elsewhere, has yet given a satisfactory explanation of the Stalin era. On the other hand, the purpose and the meaning of Khrushchev's report were soon apparent. It was a premeditated move. He had wanted to establish the fact that the changes made in the past three years were not merely a chance conglomeration of unconnected events but were to be taken as constituting a sort of revolution, deliberate, coherent and irreversible; he had chosen to demonstrate this by an act rather than by abstract explanation; his condemnation of Stalin had created a definite break between the past and the present; henceforth, the bureaucrats trained under Stalin were to abandon their old ways and adapt themselves to the new order, and if they did not, they would appear unequivocally as an opposing faction.

The rehabilitation of Rajk on 29 March marked the beginnings of de-Stalinization in the People's Democracies. It was to be hoped that it would extend to the Communist Parties of other countries; but the French Communist Party held back. At the end of March, *Humanité* reprinted a *Pravda* article against Stalin; but in their commentaries on the 20th Party Congress Thorez, Stil, Courtade, Billoux and Wurmser all made it their business to ignore the issue. One or two allusions were made to the 'report attributed to

Khrushchev' and during the 14th Congress of the French Communist Party, held at Le Havre, it was not mentioned at all. The Party was not going to become democratic.

However – as in East Germany after 1953 – the process of de-Stalinization in Hungary and Poland turned into a revolt against their Stalinist rulers. In Budapest, the Petoefi circle, whose meetings had been encouraged by the regime, suddenly turned against it: Mme Rajk spoke there on 19 June. On 27 June, several thousand intellectuals gathered to rehabilitate some hundreds of journalists who had been condemned as 'bourgeois'. Tibor Dery and Tibor Meray attacked the present rulers. They demanded freedom for the press and free access to information. There were cries of: 'Down with the government! Long live Imre Nagy!'

In Poznan the following day, thousands of metalworkers went on strike with cries of: 'We want bread! Down with Old Guard!'; their immediate target was the food shortages, but they were also protesting against a government that was stifling their freedom without providing them with a decent standard of living. The police fired on the crowds, and forty-eight workers – according to official statements – were killed. The French Communist Party explained away this riot as the result of 'provocation' by foreign agents. Courtade denounced what he called 'irresponsible Polish rebelliousness'. However, only a very few days afterwards the Polish government and the official press of the country acknowledged that the demands of the workers were well founded.

After winning the Goncourt, I had bought myself a studio. I had greatly enjoyed furnishing it with Lanzmann's help, and when I came back from China we moved into it. I am very fond of this ground-floor apartment with its high ceiling, so full of light and colours and all the souvenirs of my travels. Through the bay window I look out on an ivy-covered wall and the wide sky; if I go up the inside staircase to the floor above I can look out over the Montparnasse cemetery, low houses and deserted streets; here and there a red bunch of flowers punctuates the grey stones. Perhaps because of this view, but above all because I have always liked things to be settled and decided, when I went to bed for the first time in my new room, I thought: This is the bed I shall die in. I still say it to myself sometimes. It is doubtless here in this workroom that I shall end my days. Even if I actually die elsewhere, it is here that my friends will have to settle things after my death: go through my papers, throw things away, give away or sell the few objects that belong to me. This room, as it looks now, will survive a little while after I have disappeared. When I look around it, I feel my heart contract sometimes, as if I were seeing here the absence of a dear friend who is never coming back.

But when I lean out of the window on the upper floor, I know nothing of the future; I am completely possessed by the present. I often watch the sunset; then night comes; beneath the leaves along the Rue Froidevaux there is the glow of the sign outside a big *café-tabac* and the traffic lights at the intersection, while the Tour Eiffel ceaselessly sweeps Paris with its long arms of light. In winter, in the early morning when it is still dark, the tall display windows light up, yellow, orange, dark red. But it is in summer, above all, at about five in the morning, that I linger oftenest at the window, breathing in the dawn before I go back to sleep; already there is a premonition of the heavy heat to come hanging in the blue-grey sky; trees cluster above the graves, the ivy climbing up the wall gives off a thick green odour that mingles with the scent of the lime trees flowering in a square nearby, and with the songs of the birds; I am ten years old, I am in the park at Meyrignac; I am thirty, I am setting out for a long walk across the countryside. No; but at least these smells are given to me, this birdsong, this vague hope.

When I returned, my decision to write about China became even stronger. I knew, and I still know, that well-fed Westerners are incapable of putting themselves for a single instant in somebody else's shoes. All the same, I was stupefied by the ignorance that seemed to affect them – or which they seemed to affect. The anti-Communists, having been slightly shaken by the changes inside the U.S.S.R., were now turning to China as the main object of their attacks. They expressed pity for the Chinese because they all have to wear blue,[1] and omitted to mention the fact that until recently three quarters of them had not worn anything at all. Such excessive examples of deliberate misrepresentation spurred me on. And then I remembered the promise I had made myself in Helsinki; by giving the lie to the propaganda issuing from Hong Kong, I should be making myself useful. The austerity of the task did not displease me. It was one that demanded considerable effort on my part. To

1. This is only true, moreover, in Northern China, where such monotony of dress is traditional.

fill in the gaps in my documentation, I went to libraries and information centres to consult reports, articles, studies, books and statistics devoted to the China of both yesterday and today, without omitting from my reading the accusations of Communist China's enemies. I visited several sinologists who helped me and answered my questions. All this collection of material took some time, and I needed a lot more in which to assimilate all I had found out and to arrive at a synthesis. I have rarely worked so hard so continuously as I did for the whole of that year. I worked at home in the morning and at Sartre's during the afternoon; sometimes I would sit at my worktable in either place for four hours at a stretch without once lifting my head. Sometimes too Sartre would get quite worried because my face turned red: I felt I was on the verge of an attack of congestion and threw myself on his divan for a few moments.

It goes without saying that when *The Long March* was published I was severely taken to task by the anti-Communists; in the United States especially, when the translation came out there, there was a tremendous outcry. What naïveté! they screamed in chorus, those same Americans who were so voraciously swallowing the nonsense served up to them by Allen Dulles. Nevertheless, in the six years since it has been published, several specialists, none of whom can be suspected of Communism – René Dumont, Josué de Castro, Tibor Mende – have confirmed what I said then. China is the only large underdeveloped country that has won the battle against hunger; if it is compared to India, Brazil, etc., this victory seems almost miraculous.

I personally profited from this study a great deal. As I confronted my own civilization with another very different one, I discovered that many traits I had once believed to be common to both were in fact not so at all; simple words like field, peasant, village, town, family did not mean at all the same thing in China as in Europe; and this made me see my own environment in a fresh light. During that period I read *Tristes tropiques* by Lévi-Strauss, and one of its merits – among many others – in my eyes was to make me see the whole face of the earth again as if for the first time, not because of the extent of his explorations, but simply because of the point of view he adopted; it was the same one I was trying to use to describe Peking and the other places I had been to see. Generally speaking, this journey had swept away all my old touchstones. Until then, despite my wide reading and my few perfunctory glimpses of Mexico and

Africa, I had always taken the prosperity of Europe and the United States as my norm, and the rest of the world had existed only vaguely, somewhere on the horizon. Seeing the masses of China upset my whole idea of our planet; from then on it was the Far East, India, Africa, with their chronic shortage of food, that became the truth of the world, and our Western comfort merely a limited privilege.

The Long March could not be as lively a book as *America Day by Day*, and there are some passages in it that are already deadwood. But I do not regret the trouble I took over it; simply by writing it, I acquired a framework of knowledge, certain keys that have helped me to understand other underdeveloped countries.

Sartre was working very hard too. Two years earlier he had published the third part of his essay *Les Communistes et la paix*, which he had practically given up the idea of finishing. The circumstances which had inspired it were now far in the past; and his relations with the Communists had changed since 1952. The books he had read and his own reflections had brought him to see things from a different point of view. He had been converted to the dialectical method and was attempting to reconcile it with his basic Existentialism. Also, Garaudy had suggested to him that they take a particular topic and use it to compare the usefulness of the Marxist and Existentialist methods; they had decided that they would both make a study of Flaubert and his works, each in his own way. Sartre wrote a long essay crammed with material, but too carelessly put together for him to think of publishing it. He was also still working on his autobiography, searching through the years of his childhood for the reasons which had made him become a writer. Lastly, he was adapting a film scenario, called *Les Sorcières de Salem*, from Arthur Miller's play *The Crucible*, which Raymond Rouleau was to direct.

I did not have much time for holidays that year. All the same, I occasionally allowed myself little vacations. In January, I spent some time with Lanzmann at the *col* of the Kleine Scheidegg. The first morning he could scarcely keep upright on his skis; I had not put mine on for six years; as I heard the gentle crackle of the snow once more, I felt that I had won a little victory over time. We took lessons and made progress, quickly in his case, slowly in mine; but I quivered with pleasure every morning, when I turned my face to the rising sun and felt the sting of the cold on my skin. We went down to Grindelwald; a chair lift hauled us back up over gorges bristling with black and white pine trees, right up to the peak of the First Run; going up, it was four degrees below zero, and our teeth chattered despite the heavy oilskin capes the attendant had wrapped around us; once we were there, we stood in the sun gazing out at a dazzling panorama: the Eiger, the Jungfrau. Soon we were making long expeditions together, broken by halts on the terraces of the chalet-restaurants which smelled of damp wood and orange peel. In the evening, when the little funicular railway had stopped working for the day, the hotel was wrapped in silence and solitude; we would lie down on our beds and read. *The Kingdom of This World* by Alejo Carpentier, about the revolt in Haiti, was a brilliant novel, but not as rich as James' historical account called *Les Jacobins noirs*. In *The Lost Steppe*, although he subscribed rather unthinkingly to the current myths about primitive life and femininity, Carpentier took me through the virgin forest on the most beautiful journey a book has ever afforded me.

In the spring we took the car to London, which we both liked, despite the austerity of its night life; we also flew to Milan where my sister was having an exhibition of her latest pictures. For a quarter of an hour, in the luminous early light, the pilot circled over the Cervin and Mont Rose; it seemed unfair that we should be able to see without effort this extraordinary landscape for which the Alpine climbers risk their necks. We went for a tour of Brittany: the promontory of Le Raz, Morbihan, Quiberon. A man asked us for a ride; in the car he told us something about himself in a desperate, gravelly voice. He had just come out of prison where he had been confined for vagrancy; he was looking for work, no one would hire him because he had just come out of prison, where he would very soon be put again because he was still a vagrant. We passed two policemen. 'If I had been walking, they'd've picked me up,' he said. He told us a little about his life: the child of poverty-stricken parents, he had never learned to read nor prepared for any trade. He pointed to the pylons alongside of the road. 'One of these days I'll climb up there and touch the wire; then they'll have to do something about me.' One often reads in the papers about bums climbing up pylons and electrocuting themselves; that day I understood what lay behind such suicides: creatures so destitute, so utterly alone, that their only way to gain recognition as men is to change themselves into corpses. And the hobo has no hesitation about the way to do it; the pylons are his horizon and his obsession.

I lunched at Ellen and Richard Wright's with my American publisher. He was pleased with the translation of *Les Mandarins*, but apologized for having had to make a few cuts here and there, just a few lines. 'In the States, it's all right to talk about sex in a book,' he explained, 'but not about perversion.' The book was a great success in the United States.

I went to see the retrospective exhibition of works by Nicolas de Staël, who had killed himself a year before for reasons to do with his private life, but also, apparently, because in the end painting had not provided him with the certainty he had been seeking; he had followed his talent to most of the dead ends of modern art. At the Palais des Sports I saw the Moscow Circus and Popov; socialist humanism had forced him to express respect for his own species and – although Charlie Chaplin managed it – it is very difficult for a clown to make people laugh without making fun of his fellow men. I went to the opening of *Soledad*: it seemed to me that my friends Colette Audry and Evelyne Rey were both very talented, the first as an author, the second as an actress. The Bochum company did *Lucifer and the Lord* at the Sarah-Bernhardt; Messemer acted the second half much better than Brasseur, but was not so good in the first; unfortunately the other actors were mediocre, the production was expressionist and there were enormous cuts, all of which combined to ruin the performance. However, the press was much more complimentary than for the original production at the Théâtre Antoine; I think the critics must have merely been reflecting the snobbery of the audience, which didn't understand German and because they weren't called upon to understand the play felt free to be enthusiastic about it.

I went to a private screening of Resnais' *Night and Fog*. As we were coming out, Jaeger, a film director I had once known slightly at the Flore, suggested that I do a commentary for a documentary which Mènegos had shot in China; the film was badly put together and spoiled in places by bits of sentimentality and camera tricks, but there was one astonishing sequence: the building of a railroad through sheer mountains, and across the Yangtse-Kiang; they had used a bulldozer, brought over piece by piece in boats, in combination with unbelievably archaic construction techniques of which I had seen examples myself. I agreed to write an accompanying text.

I went to the studio several times, and as I ran the reels to and fro on the moviola I realized that I was going to find it a difficult job; my sentences had to follow the rhythm of the shots, they could not say anything that the images on the screen could say for themselves and yet they must not distract attention from them; Mènegos and Jaeger were eager to reach a wide audience, so I was forbidden to make any political references; they had even gone so far as to cut all the shots that showed portraits of Mao Tse-tung; so I was condemned to fill in the silences with that false poetry which is the trap into which most film commentators fall; I couldn't bring myself to do it. Also the film depicted the hardships and dangers of the work that had been accomplished; it was my task to exalt its heroism. I don't like having to be enthusiastic to order. My literary and moral scruples forced me into a dryness of tone which was doubtless excessive. The director and the producer altered what I had written, made it more flowery. I could never bring myself to go and hear it.

In June or thereabouts, *The Fall* by Camus was published. I was angry with him because of his articles in *L'Express*; he had been one of the first to protest against the living conditions of the Algerians in 1945; now the humanist in him had given way to the *pied noir*. All the same, I was upset when I discovered to what extent he had been hurt by the attacks on *The Rebel*; and I was also aware that he had been having a bad time in his private life; his self-confidence had been shaken, he had been through a period of painful self-questioning. I opened this new book of his with a great deal of curiosity. In the first few pages I recognized the same Camus I had known in 1943: his gestures, his voice, his charm, an exact portrait, without any overemphasis, of a person whose severity was in some secret way softened by his very excessiveness. Camus was at last attaining his old dream: he was filling in the gap between the truth and his public image. He was usually so starchy that I was deeply touched by the simplicity with which he talked about himself now. Then suddenly, this vein of sincerity ran out; he began to gloss over his failures with a series of conventional anecdotes; he switched from the role of penitent to that of judge; he took all the bite out of his confession by putting it too explicitly at the service of his grudges.

One morning, at about nine, we were all gathered in front of the Coupole, Michelle, Sartre, Lanzmann and myself. We were going to Greece. I gazed, with incredulous gaiety bubbling up inside me, at our shiny cars parked at the kerb, and pictured them as they would look in ten days, sweeping into Athens covered with dust.

Two days of wandering through Venice, and then we set off for Belgrade, where we met some Yugoslav intellectuals. One of them, a very old man, asked us fearfully for news of Aragon; he had just served a prison sentence for his loyalty to Stalinism and hardly dared utter the names of his French comrades. Socialism and literature, art and commitment – we discussed all the classic problems; but the writers in Belgrade had one that was peculiar to themselves; most of them had been influenced, in some cases very deeply, by Surrealism, and they wanted to find a way of integrating it with the popular culture of their country. 'Now that socialism has been made a reality here,' said one novelist very decisively, 'everyone is free to write just as he chooses.' The others protested. For they made no secret of the fact that the country was beset with great difficulties. Collectivization had not worked, the peasants had gone as far as killing people to prevent its being imposed on them.

As we left Belgrade, we were struck by the poverty of its outer suburbs, and also by the desolation of the villages along the dusty, dilapidated road. We stopped at Skopje, a dismal, dirty Balkan town inhabited by sad-looking peasants and women in black kerchiefs that they pulled right down over their faces. Here too the writers were in a state of perplexity; they were worried by the Surrealist vogue in Belgrade; being Macedonians, they wanted to write for the people of their own province; their language was still crude and unformed; they must make it richer, suppler, mould it until they could use it to say what they wanted to express: the problems of their own time, of their own country. What help could Éluard be to them, or Breton? But could they choose any other point of departure? This simple question seemed to them to verge on the blasphemous. We continued on our way. At the frontier post, we were surprised to see that the customs officers were making the tourists leaving Greece wash their tyres and their feet in troughs.

In Greece we noticed immediately that we were regarded without friendliness. Wherever we stopped we had to let it be known pretty quickly that we were French. A year earlier, in July 1955, there had been bombs exploding in Nicosia; the Greeks in Cyprus had been demanding that the island be restored to Greek rule. For a whole year now, Cyprus had been torn by bloody attacks and reprisals. In June, some terrorists had been hanged. The British were well aware of the enmity the Greeks felt for them: we didn't see one Englishman during the whole journey.

Then Salonika, with its glowing green gardens, its glazed tiles, its basilicas. We left Sartre and Michelle and went on to Athens along difficult roads that wound around the outer bastions of Mount Olympus. The Acropolis, Delphi, Olympia, Mycenae, Epidaurus, Mistra, Delos: I saw everything again except for Santorino. And I went to new places – Cape Sounion, the coast of Euboea, the cyclopean splendour of Tiryns, the feverish wilderness of the Morea, where, it is said, fathers still cut off the heads of fallen daughters with their axes; I walked through the beautifully named Malvasia, simmering almost deserted between the dilapidated ramparts that still seemed to defy the pirates. Not a cloud in the sky, and my heart had not rusted. Once or twice we went outside Athens in the evening to drink a glass of whisky at Chez Lapin, with its terrace overhanging the little inlet where the yachts are moored and fronting the sea like a ship's prow; the city's countless glittering lights and the shimmering stars carried me far, far away from everything, away from myself, as it had in the old days. I loved Delphi, the open-air café above the olive groves, where the country people danced in the evening; there was a little three-year-old girl there, spinning and swaying in time to the music, her face made unrecognizable by ecstasy, seemingly quite crazed; we could sense the sea in the distance. The countryside seemed tragically poor; there were women breaking stones along the roads, and peasant women would come out of their houses to beg for alms. Yet in the evening, in the villages, there were bright dresses and laughter.

In Paris I don't have much time to read. When I go away on vacation, I always take a suitcase full of books. In the penumbra of our rooms, or lying on the sandy beaches, I steeped myself that summer in Bénichou's *Morale du Grand Siècle*, Lucien Goldmann's *Hidden God*, and Desanti's study of Spinoza. They were all works that furthered the progress of Marxism by establishing the precise links of a given work with the society from which it emanated. I would have liked to revise all the culture I had ever acquired from this point of view.

We went over to Brindisi by boat and rejoined Sartre in Rome. After we had all spent a few days together in Naples, Amalfi, Paestum, Lanzmann took the train back to Paris.

We were both, Sartre as well as myself, a bit worn out with all the travelling we had done; above all other countries we loved Italy, and above all other cities, Rome; so there we stayed. Since that year – except in 1960, when we were visiting Brazil – Rome is where we have spent all our summers, with short excursions to Venice, Naples, Capri. Even when its bricks are being scorched by the heat of the *ferragosto*, when the asphalt is melting along the deserted avenues, occasionally punctuated by a solitary, useless policeman in a white helmet, we still feel comfortable there. This great bustling, crowded city still calls to mind the little town founded by Romulus. 'They should build cities in the country, the air is much cleaner,' goes the old joke; for me, Rome is the country. No factories, no smoke; there is nothing provincial about Rome, but often in the streets, on the piazzas, one feels the harshness, the silence of country villages. The old designation 'people', in which all factions were dissolved, really applies to the inhabitants of Rome, who sit in the evening along the Trastevere, on the Campo di Fiori, on the fringes of the old ghetto, at the tables on the wine merchant's terraces in front of a carafe of Frascati; children play around them; calmed by the coolness of the streets, babies sleep on their mothers' knees; through the fragile gaiety hanging in the air, impetuous cries rise up from below. You can hear the popping of the Vespas, but a cricket sings as well. Of course I like those massive cities that press you on all sides, cities where even the trees seemed to have been made by man; but how pleasant it is not to have to leave the bustle of the world and still be able to breathe clean air under an untainted sky, between walls which still retain the colour of the earth from which they grew! Rome offers another even rarer opportunity: in Rome you can experience simultaneously today's effervescence and the peace of past ages. There are many ways of dying: falling to dust like Byzantium; being mummified like Venice; or else doing half the one, half the other; museum pieces amid the ashes. Rome endures, her past still lives. People live in the theatre of Marcellus, the Piazza Navona is a stadium, the Forum a garden; between the tombs and pine trees, the Appian Way still runs towards Pompeii; and one has never finished discovering it; from the depths of the past something is always appearing as though newly minted in the freshness of each instant: a delight that never palls for me. Classical and baroque, calmly extravagant, Rome combines gentleness with severity; no affectation, no languor, but never harshness or aridity either. And what lightheartedness! The piazzas are irregular, the houses built on a slant. A Roman campanile will have a little bell tower like a wedding cake just next door, and these caprices generate a harmony; gently swelling, delicately receding, even its most monumental esplanades avoid solemnity; the lines of the buildings – here a cornice, there the coping of a wall – curve in and slowly wheel, avoiding immobility without ever losing their balance. Sometimes they have a severe symmetry of design; but this austerity is tempered by the mellowness of the lines, by the ochres, the time-softened, burned-out terra-cottas that coat them. The travertine is wan, but the Roman light makes it shimmer. Between marble toes, the grass blades sprout. Rome. Artifice and truth melt one into the other. The eye is caught by an eighteenth-century print, flat and white, then it springs to life: it is a church, a staircase, an obelisk. On every side I glimpse theatre sets that marvellously deceive the eyes; and then, no, they're not lying, the balustrades, grottoes, terraces and columns are all real. One evening, we looked down a complicated perspective of buildings and saw, as though through the tiny hole of a souvenir penholder, a reproduction of a street in which were walking tiny reproductions of men; what we saw was in fact a street and men quite close to us. Rome. At every bend in the road, at every street corner, at every step, some detail catches my attention; which shall I choose? At the far end of a courtyard, a dark clock face surrounded by greenery, with a double horizontal pendulum, pointed and menacing, like a story by Poe; the stone barrel near the Corso where lovers come to drink; the touching dolphins in front of the Pantheon, pressing themselves against the tritons with their cheeks full of water; and all those little houses, with their own courtyards and gardens, built on the roofs of the big houses. Rome, its shells, its volutes, its conches and its basins: in the evening the light transforms the jets of the fountains into diamond aigrettes, while the stone turns to rippling liquid beneath the streaming reflections of the dappled water; in the velvet of the night sky, the roofs glow with the colours of dying suns, bordering flower beds of stars; on the Capitol the scent of pines and cypress trees makes me long for immortality. Rome: a place where what we must call beauty is the most ordinary thing in the world.

We used to drink our coffee every morning in the piazza in front of the Pantheon, among the street vendors in their felt hats, carrying on their trade and making deals as though they were at a country fair; smalltime smugglers keeping an eye on the stocks of American cigarettes stuck under the mudguards of the cars in front of the Hotel Senato. We would read and discuss the day's newspapers, then go back home to work. At about two, we'd set off on an expedition around one of the seven hills or out into the countryside. I spent some pretty appalling afternoons that year; my room, in a hotel on the Piazza Montecitorio, overlooked a little courtyard being refaced by a team of masons wearing their traditional headgear of old newspapers; my window was barred by their scaffolding; I was slaving away, trying to finish my book on China, and every now and then I was choked by the *afa*. In the evening, the heat would abate; we would eat dinner in various places, quite often on the Piazza Navona or the Piazza San Ignazio, and then we'd decide where to go and have a drink. We rather liked the Piazza del Popolo, but at Rosatti's, the Flore of Rome, we met journalists, who demanded interviews, and all sorts of people who bothered us. Sometimes we sat in a little bar at the foot of the Capitol; I always felt that at any moment the bronze warrior sitting in the middle of the piazza, lit up as though for a ball, would put his spurs to his horse and come galloping down the staircase. Our favourite spot was – and still is – the Piazza Sant'Eustacchio, facing the church with its dreamy stag's head; late into the night the cars move past, luxurious or modest, families, couples, gangs stopping at the counter to gulp down cups of what is supposed to be the best coffee in Rome; often the women stay in the cars and let the men get out to argue and laugh among themselves; a horribly depressing old man came around trying to sell little dolls that pissed, and every ten minutes he would refill them with dismal concentration, though no one ever bought any. Here, and in many other spots where we could watch the night people of Rome leading their strange lives, we would sit for hours, drinking and talking. Sartre was less confident about the future than he had once been, more severe about the past, and sometimes everything looked dark to him; he would lament the fact – as Camus once had, though in a different sense – that it was impossible for a writer to re-create the truth; one tells truths, and that's better than nothing, but they are fragmentary, insubstantial, mutilated by a thousand and one restrictions. When we talked together we made it our particular endeavour to go as far as it was humanly possible in the search for truth, to consider it from every aspect, to abandon ourselves unstintingly to the pleasures of argument, of extravagance, of blasphemy; it was our way of deciding where we stood, and also a way of blowing off steam, a game, a purification.

A committee of left-wing writers invited us to a dinner in the Via Margutta. The president, Repacci, white-haired, pink-cheeked, clear-eyed, confessed to me that he amazed himself by the rapidity of his pen; he could knock off two novels in a single week. Sartre was seated next to an eighty-year-old lady novelist, Mme Sybille, still very beautiful and once rather famous, about fifty years ago; she had every right to believe she was still young considering the grace deployed by the Italians – who can be coarse, but in an altogether different way from Frenchmen – in paying court to her; even a formal banquet doesn't stifle their imagination, and I wasn't bored at all. In fact the dinner we were invited to by Alba de Cespedès I found very entertaining indeed; like her friend Paula Massini, she combined the usual salty Italian malice with a caustic and very feminine turn of phrase; together they lacerated for us the underside of Roman literary life. Visconti was there, intelligent and lively, demonstrating his conversational brilliance; and a young man who, going over to Visconti and Sartre, asked nonchalantly: 'You both know all about the film world. Why is it that directors are always so stupid?'

From time to time we saw Carlo Levi, Moravia, Guttuso the Communist painter and Alicata. Part of Rome's charm was that the unity of the Left had never been broken since our first trip there after the war in 1946. What Sartre had tried to bring about in France he could see here in reality. Almost all the intellectuals were in sympathy with the Communists and the Communists had remained faithful to their humanist traditions. This alliance with the Communist Party, so austere in France, found expression here in warm and openhearted discussions. Sartre responded very strongly to this friendly atmosphere. And also, in Italy there was no flourishing anti-Communist movement; besides which, they were lucky enough not to have any colonies; the people you passed in the street were not, like people in the streets of Paris, like us, accomplices in mass murders and torture.

Thanks to the liberal attitude of the Italian Communist Party and its fortunate situation, there are some very good left-wing newspapers in Italy that reach a very wide public; reading them is one of our pleasures. We pay close attention to the smaller news items – the whole of Italy is reflected in them. For several days the press was kept in copy by the tragi-comedy of Terrazzano. Two brothers, inmates of the gloomy asylum of Aversat, near Naples, were granted a leave of absence for good conduct. They managed, without much difficulty, to buy submachine guns and explosives, then took over the school at Terrazzano and demanded two hundred million lire in exchange for the lives of the ninety schoolchildren and three women teachers whom they had captured and tied up; they also demanded a radio, a television set and food. Their requests were granted; the money was brought in a truck; but they were afraid of a trap and wouldn't come out; for six hours they continued to threaten the crowd outside and the children inside, while the police, the town officials and a priest tried to reason with them. They killed a young workman who tried to get in through a window. Finally, with the help of one of the teachers, who had managed to untie herself, the police rounded them up.

In *Unità* and *Paese sera* we followed the Poznan trial that had begun in September. Contrary to normal usage, the police did not 'prepare' the trial. The accused had counsels who defended them and witnesses who gave evidence in their defence. The galleries applauded when the rulers of the country were vilified. They were supported by riots and demonstrations. The people demanded the reinstatement of Gomulka, who had been imprisoned in 1948 by the Stalinists and since rehabilitated. The government made considerable concessions; the prisoners on trial were given very indulgent sentences. In October, the masses demanded that Poland become autonomous, and that as a first step the Soviet troops under Rokossovsky be withdrawn; they asked for worker-management to be introduced in industry, that the hasty and badly executed collectivization that had been introduced be slowed down, and that the country be 'democratized'. On 19 October the 8th Plenum was inaugurated; Gomulka, who had been named a member of the Central Committee, immediately demanded the exclusion of all pro-Soviet leaders and Rokossovsky's recall.

Theatrically, Khrushchev, Molotov, Zukov, Mikoyan and Kaganovitch suddenly flew to Warsaw; they opposed the departure of Rokossovsky; Russian tanks began to advance on Warsaw; Gomulka called up Polish troops and armed the workers. There were clashes, the beginnings of riots. Suddenly, Khrushchev and his men flew back. What had happened? Whatever it was, Gomulka was now First Secretary of the Polish Communist Party, and Poland was already on the road to de-Stalinization.

In Hungary, Rakosi had left the government. On 6 October an enormous crowd followed Rajk's funeral cortege. On the 14th, Nagy was reinstated as a member of the Party. On the 23rd, the students of the country decided to celebrate the victory in Poland with a demonstration.

What a shock when we bought *France-Soir* at a kiosk in the Piazza Colonna on 24 October and read the headline: REVOLUTION IN HUNGARY. SOVIET ARMY AND AIR FORCE ATTACK REBELS. In fact, the Air Force had not been involved. But this did not make the events as described in *Paese sera* any less distressing: 300,000 people had paraded through Budapest demanding the return of Nagy, political independence from the U.S.S.R., and even in some cases secession from the Warsaw Pact. The A.V.O. had fired on the crowd. Soviet tanks, rushed into Budapest, had fired too; there were at least 350 dead and thousands of wounded. When Nagy seized power the following morning, the Russians and the rebels were already at grips, and the crowd was lynching members of the A.V.O.

That evening we had dinner at the Fontanella with Guttuso and his wife; he took us on to Chez Georges near the Via Veneto, where a guitarist was playing old Roman songs. Nervously, we repeated what had happened again and again, without understanding what it all meant. Confronting an unpopular, or even a hated regime, rebelling against excessively harsh living conditions, de-Stalinization had unleashed an explosion of nationalist and vengeful feelings just as it had in Poznan; as in Poznan, the police had fired on the crowd; but why had Russian tanks been so quick to intervene, thereby giving the lie to the promises of the 20th Party Congress, violating the principle of non-intervention, covering the U.S.S.R. with the taint of a crime that would convict it in the eyes of the world of being an imperialist power and an oppressor? Shattered though he was, Guttuso could still not envisage breaking the innumerable bonds attaching him to his party; he fought back his despair with words, gulping glasses of whisky that brought tears to his eyes. Sartre, who was almost as committed as Guttuso by the efforts he had made to reach an agreement with the Communists, defended himself in much the same way. We thought too about the

Left in France, which at that moment needed more than ever to keep its ranks tightly closed – we had just heard about the idiotic capture of Ben Bella – and which would be completely and finally split apart by this unjustifiable tragedy. The appearance of Anna Magnani made a diversion; she sat down at our table and sang a few songs very quietly, accompanied by the guitarist. Then we returned to our perplexities. There were moments when I felt like parodying Dos Passos: 'Sartre emptied his glass of whisky and said agitatedly that the U.S.S.R. was Socialism's last chance and had betrayed it. "We could neither approve of this intervention nor condemn the U.S.S.R.," said Guttuso. He ordered another drink and the tears came to his eyes.' But this humour was shattered in an instant at the thought of the real anguish which at that moment, as we well knew, was holding millions of men in its grip.

Paese sera and *Unità* printed extremely impartial comments on the facts. In Turin, one day when one of the issues of *Unità* defended the Russian intervention – the local editions varied from place to place – a group of workers forced their way into the office and protested. We were able to derive some comfort from the honesty of the Italian Communists. And the situation looked as though it might evolve in the direction of agreements similar to those that had been reached in Poland. Nagy proclaimed an amnesty; workers' councils and revolutionary committees were formed throughout the country; he promised, and obtained, the withdrawal of the Russian troops stationed in Budapest. When I left Sartre at Milan, where I was to stay with my sister for a short while, we were feeling better about things. But with Cardinal Mindszenty out of prison and talking on the radio, the demands of the rebels and the concessions made by Nagy, our anxiety revived. Nagy announced that the old parties were to be reconstituted and that there were to be free elections; despite a visit from Mikoyan and Suslov, he repudiated the Warsaw Pact and insisted on Hungary's remaining neutral; the hunt for members of the A.V.O. was still going on, and 'refugees from the interior' were beginning to appear; the situation had reached the point where socialism was in danger. Russian tanks surrounded Budapest. On 3 November, A. Koethly, a Socialist, and members of the various other parties became members of the government, which now included only three remaining Communists: Nagy, Kádár and Malester.

The following afternoon, Lanzmann having come down by

plane to meet me, we left Milan in the car, spending the night at Susa; it was drizzling; we bought the newspapers and sat shivering in a dismal café to read them. Moscow was accusing Nagy of having chosen 'the Fascist path'; the Russians had attacked Budapest and bombarded the Cespel factories. We chewed anxiously on this news all evening. We were worried about what was going on in Egypt, too. The whole summer, ever since the nationalization of the Suez Canal, there had been a violent propaganda campaign against Nasser in England and France. On 30 October, Mollet and Eden had delivered an ultimatum. Mollet had been urging on the Israeli Army against him and, strongly supported by the French Air Force, it had just won the battle of the Sinai desert. Despite the opposition of the rest of the world, an Anglo-French landing was expected at any moment.

The following morning we drove out of Italy over the Mont-Genèvre Pass; between a bright blue sky and the glowing russet of the land below, the snow sparkled in sheets of joy; Budapest and Cairo were a long way off; we talked about them; but all that seemed real to me was the splendour of the mountains under the sun. Then we went into an inn and ordered lunch. The owner was laughing as he talked to some of the other customers, and slapping himself on the thigh: 'Oh they caught them all right – in mid-air, like a lot of butterflies!' Immediately I understood what it meant to be back in France: I had fallen into a cesspool. By giving the order to shoot down that Moroccan plane, Max Lejeune and Lacoste had deliberately sabotaged the possibility of a negotiation. On the international level, France had chosen the solitary and shameful path from which it was never to deviate again. And without gaining anything by it, for in Algeria new leaders were already taking over. There had been anti-French riots in Tunis; in Meknès, some Europeans had been massacred. But the innkeeper and his customers, and so many millions of others besides, all thought it was very, very funny; the phrase was so French, so witty. 'Like butterflies!' they said again and again. And the calm splendour of the autumn was forced to give way to their hilarity. I felt the war inside me again, all wars, all the things that divide us, that tear the world apart.

When I got to Paris, the country was expressing public indignation at the new 'national humiliation' that had just been inflicted on it. On 5 November, English and French paratroopers had landed in Egypt; on the 6th, under pressure from the U.N., from the United States, from Khrushchev, from the British Labour Party, they had left again. In fact, in the privacy of their homes, what really concerned my fellow countrymen was the gas rationing that the blockade of the Canal entailed.

On his return from Italy, Sartre was disgusted by the French Communist newspapers. Referring to the events in Hungary, *Libération* used the phrase 'Fascist putsch', André Stil called the workers of Budapest 'the dregs of the fallen classes', and Yves Moreau labelled them 'Versaillais'. In an interview in *L'Express*, Sartre expressed his unqualified condemnation of the Soviet aggression; he said that he was 'regretfully but completely' breaking off all relations with his friends in the Soviet Union, and even more definitively with these responsible for the policies of the French Communist Party. He had made such efforts, for such a long time, to reach some sort of agreement with them and keep it intact! Nevertheless he did not hesitate for an instant: the Russian intervention had to be denounced in the name of that very socialism it was claiming to defend. I joined with him and some other writers in signing a protest against the Russian intervention that was published by *L'Observateur*. After a few days of fighting, the rebellion was stamped out; but the Hungarian workers went on a long strike in protest against this 'return to order'. We were infuriated by the lies printed in *Humanité*, according to which the members of the A.V.O. who had been lynched were workers murdered by Fascists. But from another point of view we could not help but wonder at the generous internationalism of our French chauvinists: because Russian tanks had fired on the Hungarian workers, they demanded that the French Communist Party should be suppressed. These purehearted lovers of justice – their hands dripping with Algerian blood – delivered themselves of the highest-sounding phrases on the subject of a people's right to self-determination; to strengthen this argument, they set fire to the headquarters of the Communist Party and led an attack on the offices of *Humanité*. Budapest: what a godsend for the reactionaries! Their old weapons had been blunted by the changes inside the Soviet Union and by the events in Poland that October; now they had a brand-new one handed to them on a platter; they are still using it. When Malraux is asked if he has no regrets about betraying *La Condition humaine*, he answers: Budapest. Written, spoken, all through that year the interminable dialogue went on: 'What about Suez? – Well, what about Budapest?' You were forbidden to speak out against the Suez landing unless you had shouted equally loudly about the Russian tanks. The Thierry Maulniers were very disappointed that Sartre had in fact shouted, and they congratulated him on his adroitness with very sick-looking smiles on their faces.

The events in Hungary, disguised and interpreted in so many different ways, seemed to us to be less and less easy to disentangle the more we heard about them. The Hungarian workers were certainly not 'Versaillais'; but when Radio Free Europe broadcast encouragement to the rebels there was no doubt that the Right had been counting on nothing less than a counter-revolution. Was this the case? And if so, since we believed that socialism, even a distorted, impure form of socialism, was the only hope of mankind today, how should we judge the Soviet reply?

I remember one long evening we spent, among others, discussing this problem at Fejtö's; his wife was there, Sartre, Martinet, Lanzmann, the Polish Ambassador, and a Polish journalist on *Tribuna-Ludu* who had actually been present during the insurrection. Fejtö had already written a book and an incredible number of articles on the subject; he was so exhausted, his wife told us, that she had been forced to give him injections to keep him going. The Polish journalist was of the opinion that initially the insurrection was a unanimous expression of the people's discontent; he didn't believe for an instant that there had been any émigrés, National Socialists, or Fascists playing roles of any importance. But he did think that without the second Russian intervention, the slide towards the Right which began between the 23rd and the 31st of the month would have led to civil war; if Hungary had rallied to the Western bloc, there would have been such violent repercussions in the satellite countries that a world war would have broken out. Fejtö, who was savagely anti-Soviet, admitted that the reactionary forces had tried to keep the rebellion going for their own profit, especially in the western part of the country; yes, there was a threat of civil war and the victory of socialism was not certain. Then should the Russians have risked its being defeated? the Pole insisted. Sartre's reply – which he developed later in *Le Fantôme de Staline* – was that the refusal to face this test automatically implied the choice of a certain political standpoint: that of the blocs and the cold war, in short a Stalinist standpoint. Hungary, all the Communist Parties and the Soviet Union itself would pay dearly for this decision on the part of the Russians; better to have allowed free elections than to do this violence to a whole people.

The Communist press dug itself in behind its barrage of lies; André Stil's 'smile of Budapest' stuck in a good many throats. Several of the Party's intellectuals expressed their disapproval more or less discreetly. Rolland was excluded; Claude Roy, Morgan, Vailland, received warnings. There was a violent altercation within the headquarters of the C.N.E., of which Sartre was a member, between Aragon and Louis de Villefosse who then left the Committee, taking several sympathizers with him; Vercors and Sartre decided it was preferable to stay; but they were very dissatisfied with the text of the declaration that Aragon finally produced for signature. Fearing a general hostility, the C.N.E. cancelled its annual sale. The Committee of Intellectuals was shaken by violent disputes; certain members, some ex-Communists in particular, wanted to railroad through a motion containing a radical condemnation of the U.S.S.R.; it would have been tantamount to throwing all the Communist members off the Committee. Others thought that for us, as Frenchmen, peace in Algeria still remained the primary objective and that we shouldn't allow ourselves to be disunited. This was the position held by most of my friends, and Lanzmann defended it.

Nagy, who had taken refuge in the Yugoslav Embassy, was kidnapped by the police. We heard news of fresh arrests. The writers of the Soviet Union sent a letter to the writers of France deploring the attitude taken by the latter and defending the attitude of the U.S.S.R.; the signers of our original protest replied with a new declaration quite as unequivocal as the first but giving the reasons for our attitude in more detail and also leaving a door open: 'We are prepared to meet you in a country of your choice in order to continue this discussion.' Sartre, Claude Roy and Vercors intervened at the C.N.E. on behalf of the Hungarian journalists who had been condemned to death. This time Aragon was in agreement with them.

In January *Les Temps Modernes* published a special issue on Hungary that had been almost entirely produced between the time of the 20th Congress and the events of October. In *Le Fantôme de Staline*, Sartre explained his position in the matter: 'True political action must necessarily contain an implicit moral evaluation of itself.' This was the basis of his criticism of the Soviet Union's relations with the satellite countries and of his disapproval of the Russian interventions. Nevertheless, he reaffirmed his adherence to socialism as embodied in the U.S.S.R., despite the errors of its leaders. Budapest had been a heavy blow to him. But, in the final analysis, he had at least been able to test on this occasion the line of conduct he had laid down for himself: to side with the U.S.S.R., and to count on no one but himself to maintain his own point of view.

He did not fall back into solitude, he was not reconverted into an enemy of the people. Coming after the 20th Congress and the events of October in Poland, Budapest forced the Communist intellectuals to ask themselves certain questions. Many 'sealed their lips' and refused to yield an inch. But many others felt that their very deepest beliefs had been jeopardized. 'When I think of my articles on Hungary!' said one woman I knew who was a Communist sympathizer. 'How could I have painted such a rosy picture? Though of course, that was under Nagy' Certain militant Communists noisily reproached themselves for having insisted on the guilt of Rajk and Slansky. Others, like Hélène Parmelin, while refusing to indulge in what she called a 'mental strip-tease', a form of entertainment the anti-Communists could watch with a jubilant sense of their own virtue, nevertheless did reawaken their critical faculties; several groups were formed with the intention of remaining within the Communist Party, but without accepting all its orders. *La Tribune de discussions*, founded in the spring of 1956 by some militant Parisian workers dissatisfied with the attribution of special powers to the government, won the support of a certain number of intellectuals. In December, others started *L'Étincelle*, which in April was to be amalgamated with *La Tribune*. What they wanted was not to *revise* Marxism from the outside, but to *change* it, for far from having surmounted them, they were finding themselves caught inside the various Socialist contradictions. Sartre had never ceased to demand a living Marxism; discussions between him and the Communist opposition grew more and more frequent; he had many with the Polish intellectuals as well. Polish–Soviet agreements were signed in Moscow on the Leninist basis of equality of rights; the Stalinists were removed from power, a large number of militants were rehabilitated, and the unions were encouraged in their defence of the workers' interests. The Congress of Writers expressed its condemnation of Socialist Realism. Gomulka was attempting to allow liberty its rightful place, without weakening socialism. Sartre's independent attitude towards the Communist Party meant that to the writers of Poland his words seemed specially intended for them. In November we were invited to the Polish Embassy; there we met Jan Kott and Lissowski, who asked Sartre to write an article for a magazine he was running. Sartre's plays were put on in Warsaw, and *Les Temps Modernes* on its side devoted an issue to Poland.

Even with the orthodox Communists, even with the Soviet Union, our bridges were not burned. Sartre had broken with the French Communist Party but not with the C.N.E. and not with the Peace Movement. He found that *The Respectful Prostitute* was still being performed in Moscow; it was put on in Czechoslovakia and even, a little later, in Hungary. Towards the spring of 1957, he twice met Ehrenburg, and, although neither man changed his position, they were able to carry on a very cordial conversation. Shrewd and faithful to the spirit of the 20th Congress, the Russians had decided not to alienate the sympathizers who had refused to accept Budapest; Vercors, one of those who had protested, received an invitation from them in 1957. It was a new and important development, the discovery that one could attack the U.S.S.R. on a specific point without being considered a traitor. This moderate attitude allowed us to work side by side with the French Communist Party on the issue that was most burning for us all: Algeria.

CHAPTER EIGHT

IT was not of my own free will, nor with any lightness of heart, that I allowed the war in Algeria to invade my thoughts, my sleep, my every mood. Camus' advice – hang on to your own happiness, no matter what – was exactly suited to my temperament. There had been Indochina, Madagascar, Cap Bon, Casablanca: I had always managed to regain my serenity. After the capture of Ben Bella and the Suez crisis, it was destroyed. The government was going to persist with this war. Algeria would win its independence; but not for a long time. At that moment, when I could not even glimpse the end of it all, the truth behind the restoration of peace in Algeria was finally brought into the light of day. Recalled conscripts had talked; information flowed in: conversations, letters written to myself or to friends, the reports of foreign journalists, more or less secret accounts distributed by small groups. We didn't know everything, but we knew a lot, too much. My own situation with regard to my country, to the world, to myself, was completely altered by it all.

I am an intellectual, I take words and the truth to be of value; every day I had to undergo an endlessly repeated onslaught of lies spewed from every mouth. Generals and colonels explained that they were waging a magnanimous, even a revolutionary war. We were treated to a spectacle fit only for a circus freak show: an army that thinks! The *pieds noirs* were clamouring for integration when the mere idea of a single University was enough to make them recoil in horror. They declared that aside from a few ringleaders, the population liked them. Yet during the 'rat hunt' that followed Frogier's funeral, they made no attempt to distinguish between the *good* Moslems, *their* Moslems, and the others; they lynched anyone they could lay their hands on. The press had become a lie factory. It would not breathe a word of the mass graves that had to be dug for the victims of Fechoz and Castille,[1] but shrieked blue murder at the assassinations that began the battle of Algiers. The paras surrounded the Casbah, the wave of terrorism was brought to a halt; we were not told by what means. The newspapers were afraid not only of seizure and legal proceedings but also of a drop in circulation; they simply printed what their readers wanted to hear.

For, provided it was properly costumed for them, the people of France were prepared to accept this war with a light heart. I was not at all upset when the ultras demonstrated on the Champs-Élysées; they demanded that we fight 'to the very end', and that the Left be outlawed; as they went by, they smashed the windows of the tourist agency underneath the offices of *L'Express*. They were just ultras. What did appal me was to see the vast majority of the French people turn chauvinist and to realize the depth of their racist attitude. Bost and Jacques Lanzmann – who had taken my old room in the Rue de la Bûcherie – told me how the police treated the neighbourhood Algerians; there were searches, raids, and man-hunts every day; they beat them up, and overturned the vendors' carts in the open-air market. No one made any protest, far from it;

1. The plastic bomb placed in the Casbah by Fechoz in July killed fifty-three persons and wounded innumerable others. On 6 August, Castille left another one, only slightly less murderous, there.

the people there – who had never had so much as a finger laid on them by a North African – congratulated themselves on being 'protected'. I was even more stupefied and saddened when I learned with what docility the young soldiers sent to Algeria became accomplices in the methods of pacification.

My natural inclination to torture myself was so slight that when Lanzmann gave me the *Dossier Müller* to read, my first reaction was just to put it out of sight. Today, in this grim December of 1961, like most of my fellow creatures I suppose, I am suffering from a sort of tetanus of the imagination. I read Boudot's statement in the Lindon trial:

One evening, I saw some men coming up to my table with leaden faces; they were members of the engineering corps who had just buried alive four fellaghas between the ages of twenty and seventy-five. The old one had been the last to die. He was so afraid, they told me, . . . that the sweat from his body rose like steam in the night air. They died gradually as the bulldozer threw the earth on top of them.

Then I read Leuliette's statement:

These prisoners had been hung by their feet. I saw them in the morning, and in the evening they were still there. Their faces were quite black, and they were still alive. I should also like to instance the use of electric current. It was when the genital area was affected that the victims cried out most. It was also used on the inside of the mouth.

I read this and moved on to another article. That, perhaps, is the final stage of demoralization for a nation: one gets used to it.

But in 1957, the broken bones, the burns on the face, on the genitals, the torn-out nails, the impalements, the cries of pain, the convulsions, they reached me, all right. Müller had publicly related his experiences while serving as a soldier in Algeria, and his courage had earned him his death from a French bullet; it was our duty to read it and make it as widely known as possible. But I had to force myself. There were many other accounts of the same kind to inflict on myself. For every one we published in *Les Temps Modernes*, we received ten. Some appeared in *Esprit* as well. Whole battalions were looting, burning, raping, massacring. Torture was being used as the normal and indispensable method of obtaining information; it was not a matter of 'incidents', of isolated excesses, this was a system. In this war a whole people had risen against us, and every individual member of that people was a suspect. The only way to stop the atrocities was to stop the war.

My compatriots did not want to know anything about all this. In the spring of 1957, the truth was already available, and if they had greeted it with as much zeal as they had the revelations about the Soviet work camps, then nothing could have prevented its being brought to the eyes of the world. The plot to hide it succeeded only because the whole country was an accomplice to it. The ones who did speak were not listened to, the others shouted louder to drown them out, and if people did hear a few rumours in spite of themselves, then they went about forgetting them as fast as possible. Pierre-Henri Simon's book *Sur la torture*, which introduced the public to the *Dossier Müller*, was repeatedly discussed in the columns of *Le Monde* and *L'Express*, which are not, after all, secret publications. The entire left-wing press reviewed the collection called *Les Rappelés témoignent*, and Sartre wrote an article about it called *'Vous êtes formidables'* in *Les Temps Modernes*; the authors of these accounts were mostly seminarists and priests, certainly not people in the pay of Nasser or Moscow; in any case, no one accused them of lying; people simply stopped their ears; nor was Servan-Schreiber, who had been recalled a few months earlier to serve as a lieutenant in Algeria, in the pay of the Arab League or the U.S.S.R. His eye-witness account, which appeared first in *L'Express* and later in book form, received an even greater degree of publicity when an official inquiry was instituted against him. Despite his respect for the Establishment and military tradition, even though he readily swallowed the mystique of the 'black commandos', the crimes he described should have had some effect on public opinion: Arabs shot down 'for the fun of it', prisoners brutally murdered, villages burned, mass executions, etc. No one turned a hair.

Murderers with bazookas were allowed to go where they liked. Yveton, who had placed a bomb in an empty factory after taking every precaution to avoid killing anyone, was guillotined. Why had this Frenchman taken up the cause of the Algerian people? Why were doctors, lawyers, teachers and priests in Algeria helping the F.L.N.? People said, 'Oh, they're traitors,' and felt that was answer enough. The public was told about the 'suicide' of Larbi Ben Mihidi, who was found hanged from one of the bars of his window, bound hand and foot. After the 'suicide' of Boumendjel, who had been kept in solitary confinement and tortured by the paras for several weeks and then thrown off a roof, Capitant, a

[380]

professor of law at the University of Paris, stopped his lectures as a protest; his gesture caused violent repercussions. On 29 March General de La Bollardière caused a sensation: he asked to be relieved of his command because he disapproved of the methods the French army was using. The case of Djamila Bouhired was reported both throughout France and abroad. The Left's campaign against the use of torture must have been a matter of public knowledge, since the government was sufficiently worried by it to set up a 'Safeguard Committee' to protect itself.

I had been labelled, along with several others, anti-French. I became so. I could no longer bear my fellow citizens. When I dined out with Lanzmann or Sartre, we hid away in a corner; even so, we could not get away from their voices; amid the malicious gossip about Margaret, Coccinelle, Brigitte Bardot, Sagan, Princess Grace, we would suddenly hear a sentence that made us want to run for the door. I went with Lanzmann to Les Trois Baudets, where Vian was singing. In one of the sketches the actors unfolded newspapers: rebel units destroyed, a *mechta* captured. I read: Rivet, Oradour; and the laughter of the audience filled me with loathing. Another evening we went to hear Greco sing at the Olympia. A *pied noir* stood on the stage and told stories about the '*bicots*'; my palms were wet with shame. At the cinema we had to swallow newsreels showing the fine work the French were doing in Algeria. We stopped going out. Just having a coffee at a counter or going into a bakery became an ordeal. We heard things like: 'It's all because the Americans want our oil', or: 'Why don't they just put all they've got into it and get it over with?' Outside the cafés, the customers would spread *L'Aurore* or *Paris-Presse* on their tables, and I knew what was going on in their heads: the same thing that was there in the paper; I couldn't sit down near them any more. I had liked crowds once; now even the streets were hostile to me, I felt as dispossessed as I had when the Occupation began.

It was even worse, because, whether I wanted to be or not, I was an accomplice of these people I couldn't bear to be in the same street with. That was what I could least forgive. Or else they should have trained me from childhood to be an S.S., a para, instead of giving me a Christian, democratic humanist conscience: a conscience. I needed my self-esteem to go on living, and I was seeing myself through the eyes of women who had been raped twenty times, of men with broken bones, of crazed children: a Frenchwoman.

My sister and her husband had come back to live in Paris. He was a Socialist and defended Mollet's policies. 'All the same, we've put a stop to the terrorism in Algiers,' he told me. I knew – only partially, but already enough for my peace of mind – what this mock peace had cost. 'After all, these cases of torture are only exceptions,' was another thing he told me. When he said such things I would fly into fits of rage I tried to repress. But whenever I said good-bye to him, I could tell from the pounding of my heart, the weight on the back of my neck, the buzzing in my ears, that the tension inside me had mounted.

I wanted to stop being an accomplice in this war, but how? I could talk in meetings or write articles; but I would only have been saying the same things as Sartre less well than he was saying them. I would have felt ridiculous following him like a shadow at the silent demonstration he took part in with Mauriac. Today,[1] however little it might affect the outcome, I could only throw all my weight into the struggle. In those days, I still wanted to feel that an effort would not be in vain before I was willing to make it.

We knew Francis Jeanson very well. He had visited Sartre in 1946 with the manuscript of *La Morale de Sartre*. During the war he had crossed the Spanish frontier to join the Free French; he had been captured and put in a concentration camp. He was released after several months, but the life there had ruined his health, and in Algeria he had been obliged to accept an office job. He became friendly with many Moslems. After the Liberation he had gone back to Algeria quite often and followed events there very closely; this was how he had been able to write *L'Algérie hors la loi*. He was a contributor to *Les Temps Modernes* and its manager for four years. In 1955 Éditions du Seuil had published his *Sartre par lui-même*. There were very few people who understood Sartre's thought as well as Jeanson. After Budapest he had blamed Sartre for what he considered too intransigent an attitude, and relations between us had been cold since then. Mutual friends informed us about his work with the F.L.N. Neither Lanzmann, Sartre, nor myself were yet ready to follow him. In Algeria there was only one choice, Fascism or the F.L.N. In France, we thought, it was different. It seemed to us that the Left had nothing to teach

1. Winter 1961.

the Algerians, and that *El Moudjahid* was quite right to put them in their place. But we still believed that it was possible to work for their independence by legal means. Knowing Jeanson as we did, we were sure he had not committed himself in such a way without mature consideration; there was no doubt that he must have had very good reasons. I shied away from the idea all the same. I had met two people who were working with him,[1] and they had shocked me by the flippancy of their chatter; I wondered whether clandestine action might not be a way of getting rid of guilt. Perhaps those who had taken this path already nursed a desire to cut themselves off from the French nation, bound up with feelings of resentment and unresolved hostilities?[2] I defended myself against the doubts their choice aroused in me by the absurd manoeuvre I so much detest of attributing it to a psychological rationalization on their part, without asking myself if my own distrust was not dictated by subjective motives. I had not understood that Jeanson was not rejecting his status as a Frenchman by helping the F.L.N. Even if I had been more lucid in my appraisal of what he was doing, the fact remained that participation would have meant going over to the traitors' camp in the eyes of the country as a whole; something inside me – timidity, vestiges of mistaken beliefs – still prevented me from contemplating such a thing.

In October 1956, my essay on China completed, I set out to tell the story of my childhood. It was an old project. I had tried to write about Zaza several times, in novels and short stories. I had attributed my own desire to write about myself to the character of Henri in *The Mandarins*. On the two or three occasions I had allowed myself to be interviewed I had always been disappointed: I would have liked to ask the questions as well as give the answers:

I have always had the secret fantasy that my life was being recorded, down to the tiniest detail, on some giant tape recorder, and that the

1. They soon stopped doing so, moreover.
2. Jeanson's reply to these doubts was unexceptionable: 'When we undertook the action we are being blamed for, none of us lacked work, we all loved our respective professions, and none of us was considered mediocre in our exercise of them. Nor could we possibly have been ignorant of the fact that France was the only country in which we had a chance of feeling completely at home and of finding work that would suit our various aptitudes.

day would come when I should play back the whole of my past. I am almost fifty, it is too late to cheat: soon everything will sink into the abyss. My life can only be recorded in a general way, on paper and by my own hand; so I shall make a book of it. When I was fifteen I wanted people to read my biography and find it touching and strange; all my ambitions to become 'a well-known author' were directed to this end. Since then I have often thought of writing it myself. I have long been a stranger to the exaltation this dream once aroused in me; but the desire to make it a reality has always remained in my heart . . .

. . . I spent the first twenty years of my life in a big village that stretched from the Lion de Belfort to the Rue Jacob, from the Boulevard Saint-Germain to the Boulevard Raspail: I still live there. From my worktable I look out and watch a group of schoolgirls walking across the Place Saint-Germain-des-Prés: one of them used to be me. She walks home just as the first street-lamps come on; she will sit down in front of a blank sheet of paper, she will make marks on it just as I am doing on this sheet now. There have been wars and journeys, and deaths and faces; nothing has changed. In the mirror, I should see a different picture, but there is no mirror; there wasn't then. There are moments when I don't quite know whether I am a child playing at being a grown-up or an ageing woman remembering her childhood.

No. I do know; I am myself, today. The little girl whose future has become my past no longer exists. There are times when I want to believe that I still carry her inside me, that it is possible to tear her free from the wrappings of my memory, smooth her worn eyelashes, and sit her down beside me just as she used to be. It isn't possible. She has disappeared without leaving even a tiny skeleton to remind me that she did once exist. How am I to call her back from this oblivion?

For eighteen months, sometimes up, sometimes down, through difficulties, through joys, I kept at this work of resurrection: of creation, for it made as many demands on my powers of imagination and reflection as it did on my memory.

Sartre meanwhile, at Lissowski's instigation, was examining the relation between Existentialism and Marxism; he wrote an essay which later became *The Question of Method*. Once under way, he began the work he entitled *Critique de la raison dialectique*. He had been pondering the subject for years, but had felt that his ideas were not yet ripe; he had needed some external stimulus before being able to take the plunge. At the same time, a publisher asked him for a study of a painter to be published as one of a series of art books; Sartre had always loved Tintoretto; even before the war, and increasingly since 1946, he had been interested by the Venetian master's conception of space and time. He decided to devote a long essay to the subject.

My *Memoirs* absorbed me less totally than my study of China; I read more. My friends lent me various books by Americans concerned with analysing the society of their own country, all of which tended towards the same conclusions: Riesman's *The Lonely Crowd*, the essays of Wright Mills, Whyte's *The Organization Man*, Spectorsky's *The Exurbanites*. They described both the causes and the consequences of the conformism that had so disappointed me in 1947, and which had become even more pronounced. America, having become essentially a consumer society, had passed from the inner-directed society of the Puritan era to the other-directed stage in which the individual is governed not by his own judgement but by the behaviour of other members of society; these books gave an account of the startling ways in which the morals, education, life style, science and feelings of the nation had been transformed. This country, once so passionate about individualism and still scornfully calling the Chinese 'a nation of ants', had itself become a nation of sheep; repressing originality, both in itself and in others, rejecting criticism, measuring value by success, it left open no road to freedom except that of anarchic revolt; this explains the corruption of its youth, their refuge in drug-taking and their imbecile outbreaks of violence. Of course, there were still men in America who were using their eyes to see with: these books themselves, other similar ones and certain films were proof of that. There were a few literary magazines, a few almost secret political newsletters that still dared oppose public opinion. But most of the left-wing newspapers had disappeared. *The Nation* and *New Republic* preserved only the narrowest margin of intellectual independence. The *New Yorker* had become as much a part of the Establishment as *Partisan Review*.

My aversion to America had not diminished since the Korean war. The government was fighting segregation more or less vigorously; a large part of the country was rejecting it outright, and the industrialization of the South doomed it to eventual extinction. Yet it had provoked several appalling scandals during the past few years: the execution of MacGee; the lynching of Emmet Till, accused at the age of fourteen, without proof, of having raped a white woman, and the acquittal of his murderers; the violence inflicted in Alabama on coloured students who attempted to mix with whites;

even without these outbreaks I knew what the implications were, and that they had not changed. As for the anti-Communist fanaticism of the Americans, it had never been more virulent. Purges, trials, inquisition, witch-hunts – the very principles of democracy had been rejected. Algren had seen his passport taken away simply because he had belonged to the Rosenberg Committee. In foreign affairs, America was using its dollars to support, against the demands of its own people, men it had bought who, furthermore, were often more concerned with their own interests and served the Americans very badly. If voices were raised against this policy, they must have been effectively silenced: I never heard one.

What then had happened to the writers I had liked and who were still living? And what did I think of them today? Reading them with a fresh eye, discussing them with Lanzmann, I revised many of my earlier judgements. The early novels of Wright, Steinbeck, Dos Passos and Faulkner still kept the merits, however unequal, I had previously seen in them. But we were no longer politically in agreement with Wright, who had become openly anti-Communist; he no longer seemed interested in writing. Steinbeck had foundered in patriotism and foolishness; Dos Passos' talent had dried up ever since he had rallied to Western values: instead of a world of verminous depths, determined to mask its own putrefaction by words and gestures, he was now describing only the diseased, hardened skin. In *A Fable*, Faulkner too, though on the surface it was just the story of the Unknown Soldier, was in fact retelling the Passion of Christ; as if we needed that again! *Intruder in the Dust* showed that racism in the South often conceals nuances and values incomprehensible to Northerners blinded by a simplistic rationalism. In 1956, Faulkner had said in an interview that the South should be left to settle the Negro problem in its own way; he openly declared himself on the side of the whites, even if it meant going out into the street and shooting Negroes. As for Hemingway, I still admired some of his short stories, but *A Farewell to Arms* and *The Sun Also Rises* disappointed me on a second reading. He had done a great deal to further the technique of the novel, but now that the freshness of his innovations had faded, the tricks and the shallowness of his characters had become only too apparent. Even more important, I discovered that his conception of life was antipathetic to me. His individualism implied a deliberate complicity with capitalist injustice; it was the individualism of a dilettante rich enough to finance costly hunting and fishing expeditions and treating his guides, his servants, the natives he encountered, with ingenuous paternalism. Lanzmann pointed out the taint of racism in *The Sun Also Rises*; a novel is a microcosm: if the only coward in it is a Jew, the only Jew a coward, an inclusive if not a universal relation is established between these two terms. Apart from which, the implication of the complicity Hemingway invited us to feel with him at every turn of his plots is that we too are aware of being, like himself, Aryan, male, endowed with wealth and leisure, and experiencing our body only in confrontations with sex and death. He speaks as one seigneur to another. The geniality of the style may mislead, but it is no coincidence that the Right has woven him so many laurel wreaths; it is the world of the privileged that he has described and exalted.

I was not very familiar with the young writers. I had liked the work of Carson McCullers very much, and met her once in Paris, ravaged by drink, puffy, almost paralysed; it appeared she was no longer writing. I had also glimpsed Truman Capote once at the Wrights', lying on a divan in pale-blue velvet pants; he had talent, but didn't seem to do much with it. People had praised Salinger's *Catcher in the Rye* rather too much; I found it little more than promising. And unfortunately poetry was beyond me; I didn't know the language well enough to judge for myself, and I mistrusted translations. In short, in writing as in other things, I could find nothing in America that could touch me, except perhaps for its past. It aroused the same bitter feeling of disappointment as France itself. I still retained vivid and grateful memories of its landscapes, its cities, its great spaces, its crowds and its smells; I liked its swift, swarming language, informal, vigorous, and so well suited to catch the very movement of life; I thought with affection of my American friends who had given me so much pleasure by their cordiality, by the openness of their laughter and their sudden humour. But I knew that if I were to go back to New York or Chicago, the air I breathed there would be, like that of Paris, polluted.

The best moments of that year were the two weeks I spent at Davos with Lanzmann. There I had rediscovered the pleasures of sun and snow, and experienced the relief of not having to listen to French people talking. In the early summer I once more felt the joy of leaving this country, where a Socialist government was suppressing celebrations on the 14th of July. I went with Lanzmann to the south of Italy. The roads were better than in 1952, the hotels more comfortable; the cities had all grown larger, and many had managed to do so with elegance. But the country seemed to be as poor as ever; around the Gulf of Tarento a few empty gestures had been made towards agrarian reform; there were cottages, each named after one saint or another, sticking up in the middle of the marshes which had been parcelled out among the peasants; they had no water or fertilizers, so nothing grew. We passed *braccianti* on the village squares, and the life of the provinces hadn't changed since Fellini had portrayed it in *I vitelloni*; drinking *grappa* at about eleven one evening on a deserted street in Cantazaro, we watched a scene that was a faithful evocation of the spirit of his film: some young men were running along after a *topolino*, they caught it, shook it, stuffed up the exhaust with paper, it started up again, the plug shot out to the sound of laughs that sounded more like yawns; the *topolino* turned around, the whole thing began over again. Over and over again. We got tired first.

We went on down towards Sicily; one evening, as we came around a bend in the road, it appeared in front of us in the fading dusk, speckled with lights and fringed with mist; we stopped; another car drew up behind us. 'Looking at the view?' asked the driver. 'Me too. Every time I pass this way I stop and look at it.' He was a policeman. He made a sweeping gesture with his hand and said emphatically: 'It's the second most beautiful view in the world.' 'Oh?' I said. 'And which is the most beautiful?' He hesitated. 'That I don't know.' I visited Sicily again; I saw Ragusa, sullen and prosperous, its baroque beauties girdled by a zone of very pretty new apartment houses. We fled from Lipari, where the water was black with oil and infested with French tourists. After a stop at Cape Palinuro, which Darina Silone had pointed out to me years before, we drove back up to Rome. We took with us a Yugoslav refugee who hitched a ride as we were leaving Eboli; he had been given several days' leave from the Italian camp where he had been interned with other stateless Yugoslavs so that he could look for work, but he was penniless, and if he was late getting back to camp he risked penalties: another instance of the almost inextricable situations I have so often encountered along the road.

I stayed in Rome with Sartre for over a month. Our Communist friends kept their distance and we saw very few people, but I was very happy at the Hôtel d'Angleterre, just off the Piazza di Spagna, and I worked well. Sartre wanted a rest after the *Critique*. He had been to Venice to take another look at the Tintorettos, and began writing about them. He also did a preface for *The Traitor* by Gorz.[1]

I felt I should like to spend two or three weeks breathing a less citified air than that of Rome. Sartre suggested we go to Capri. The Roman newspapers were saying that Naples was being ravaged by an epidemic of Asian flu; but Capri is not Naples, and the epidemic would undoubtedly move north. We set out. In Capri, we read in the Neapolitan newspapers that the Asian flu was ravaging Rome. Each city delighted in exaggerating the disaster that had befallen the other.

I had been afraid that Capri would be flooded by tourists and snobs; as it turned out, they all descended on the same places at exactly the same times – as they do in Venice, or Florence, as they do everywhere. We had no difficulty avoiding them. We stayed in an uninviting hotel right in the centre of the town; but since it was in a district where no car could penetrate we enjoyed both solitude and silence. We walked along the sea, we gazed at the Faraglioni, which gave Sartre as much pleasure as Giacometti's sculptures; we passed above the lurid red villa Malaparte had left in his will to the writers of the Chinese People's Republic, who were finding it rather an embarrassment; sometimes we climbed up as far as the palace of Tiberius; generally we stopped lower down in some deserted open-air café, or else we lunched off a cake or a sandwich with a glass of white wine, while we sat and watched the sun on the rocks and the sea. When he was writing *Le Dernier Touriste*, Sartre had done research on all these places; he also knew a great many anecdotes and bits of gossip about life on Capri. I persuaded him to let himself be hauled up with me by chair lift from Anacapri to the top of Monte Soláro; his delight in the charms and glories of this ascent was rather less than mine, but he took great satisfaction in being able to take in the subtle lines of the whole island at a glance.

To drink our coffee in the morning, and every evening after

1. Ten years after our meeting in Geneva, Gorz, who was then living in Paris, had brought Sartre a philosophical work, intelligent but too obviously derivative of *Being and Nothingness*. After that he had written an essay about himself which was excellent.

dinner, we went and sat on a terrace of the *Salotto*, either before the *Führungen* invaded it or after they had evacuated it. After midnight, there would only be a scattering of people left at the bottom of the staircase that looked as noble and remote as a set for a play; alone, in couples, in groups, people would walk up or down it, stop at the top of the steps, sit down on them, or melt away into the darkness beyond.[1] They seemed to be acting in some mysterious and very beautiful play; their gestures, their poses, the colours of their clothes, among which we recognized the same pink Tintoretto used in his paintings, all seemed preordained and inevitable; and in a flash the illusion, so long forgotten, lived again: our life was as rich, as rigorous, as the stories people tell. Sartre talked to me about his book. He was working slowly, carefully, shaping each sentence; there were some I said to myself over and over again with delight, in the velvety silence of the night. In Capri that summer, the stones were as beautiful as statues, and words sometimes shimmered with light.

My sister was no longer living in Milan; we stayed there only one day, waiting for Lanzmann to join us. We went over the Tenda Pass to Nice, and from there to Aix where we spent the night. As we were driving under the starry sky, we glimpsed the coppery flash of a meteor: the Sputnik! The newspapers next day confirmed that it had in fact passed over that exact spot at that time. We thought with friendship of this ephemeral little companion in space, and we gazed with new eyes at the old moon on which men might land within our lifetime. Against all expectations, the first satellite had been launched by the U.S.S.R.; that pleased us no end. The enemies of socialism were always trying to prove that it had failed by pointing out Russia's industrial and technical backwardness; this would give them the lie with a vengeance! The Americans talked about a 'scientific Pearl Harbour'. This achievement gave the Russians a military superiority on which we congratulated ourselves: if the country which has the least interest in starting a war has the greatest likelihood of winning it, then so much the better for peace. The 'anti-Party' faction had been superseded; the spirit of the 20th Congress was taking root. Our hopes for peaceful coexistence were to become even stronger in April, when Moscow announced the Russian suspension of nuclear tests.

Revolts against American imperialism were brewing all over South America. There was a great deal of talk about the Cuban

1. A brightly lit store has now ruined this décor.

rebels when they walked into the entrance hall of a hotel two days before the Havana Grand Prix, kidnapped the famous racing driver Fangio, and released him after the race. Their leader, Castro, a lawyer exiled to Mexico by Batista, had returned with a few comrades in a boat. He was described as being a sort of bearded Robin Hood. The little guerrilla army under his command included some women members, a fact which caused a good many sniggers among the French bourgeoisie; apparently he could count on support from the Cuban population, from students and intellectuals among others; but it was difficult to believe him when he announced that he would shortly overthrow Batista by strikes, riots and open fighting.

The French Left was finding it difficult to recover from Budapest. The severity of the penalties inflicted on the rebels – Tibor Dery, among others, was sentenced to nine years in prison – outraged the non-Communists, while the Party continued to assert its solidarity with Kádár. *L'Étincelle* was discontinued. Vercors, who had been a zealous supporter of the Party, explained in a rather funny little book called *P.P.C.* that he had had enough of being used to dress up the set and was now making his final exit. Even more serious than these dissensions among the intellectuals was the political apathy of the proletariat. At the end of October, after the success of the gas and electricity workers' strike, the C.G.T. and the C.F.T.C. launched others. At Saint-Nazaire, strikes broke out with such violence that a worker was killed and the journalist Gatti was wounded. The Renault workers struck, as did the Civil Service and the teaching profession. But the very fact that these movements were launched at the height of a governmental crisis proved that they were a-political. Neither the parties nor the unions linked them in a struggle against the Algerian war. Nevertheless, the Right became extremely uneasy; there was talk of conspiracies. *L'Express* created regional Forums as weapons against the threat of Fascism.

Lacoste's 'last quarter of an hour' had been going on for over a year, and the methods of pacification being used were exactly the same as at the beginning. Telling some friends about the contents of an issue of *Les Temps Modernes*, Daniel, a contributor to *L'Express*, ended by saying: 'And then of course there's the usual torture ration.' It was monotonous, certainly: electric goads, immersions, hangings, burnings, rapes, funnels, stakes, nails torn out, bones broken; always the same boring programme. But we saw no reason to change our tune until the army and the police changed theirs.

A university graduate called Audin had been arrested in Algeria on 1 June; he had not been heard of since. The staff of the Lycée Jules-Ferry had demanded an inquiry; in vain. Early in December, one of his friends defended his thesis in mathematics at the Sorbonne; the event was actually a funeral attended by a great number of professors and writers.

Even the readers of *Figaro* were kept informed of cases of arbitrary arrest, disappearance and torture, by Martin-Chauffier.[1] After weeks of continual postponements, the report of the Safeguard Committee appeared in *Le Monde*. The Committee spokesman began: 'Acts which in other times and in normal circumstances might appear exorbitant are perfectly legal in Algeria.' So there was, of course, no need to denounce them. The report limited itself to stating the facts, which, even when covered by this 'exorbitant' legality, nonetheless seemed excessive. They were shocking enough and numerous enough to create a scandal. *Le Monde* was severely criticized for having printed the report; the events themselves seemed to be of little interest for the reading public.

On 10 December the trial of Ben Saddok began. Several months earlier, at an exit of the Colombes stadium, he had shot Ali Chehkal, the former vice-president of the Algerian Assembly and one of the most notable Moslem collaborators. Pierre Stibbe, his lawyer, called several left-wing intellectuals as witnesses for the defence, among them Sartre. Sartre was very much moved as we made our way to the Palais de Justice; in conferences and meetings, words may sometimes be taken lightly enough, but that day a man's life was at stake. If Sartre helped save his life, in a few years' time there would be an amnesty to make him a free man again; the difference between life and death sentences was therefore much greater than in ordinary trials. Hence the anxiety of the witnesses, since each of them could assume that his testimony might well be the deciding factor in the jury's decision.

Sartre was sequestered with the others, out of earshot of the preliminary arguments. I took a seat on the crowded benches beside some young lawyers. Mme Ali Chehkal, draped in mourning veils

1. He had made an investigation in the name of the International Commission Against Concentration Camps.

and sitting just beneath the judge's bench, represented the case for the prosecution. I looked at the young, open-faced man in the dock. Acts analogous to the one he had committed had been acclaimed during the Resistance as heroic deeds; yet the people of France were now going to make him pay for his, perhaps with his life.

Some of Saddok's comrades spoke about his qualities as a man, a worker, as a friend; his ageing parents wept. After that, teachers, writers, a priest, a general and some journalists got up to explain how Saddok's action was caused by the conditions of life imposed on his fellow Algerians; and they described those conditions. 'So that's it!' said two of the young lawyers sitting near me, in bitter tones, 'We're the ones they're putting on trial. They're saying that whatever happens to us in Algeria is just a fair exchange!' The prosecution had called Soustelle. He appeared, in black tortoiseshell spectacles and an overcoat that made him look like a big manufacturer; without looking at anyone, he launched precipitately into a eulogy of the dead politician. After that, a young girl with artificial legs came forward, supported by some of her relations; she had been a victim of the bomb-throwing at the Casino de la Corniche.[1] She began to shout in a jerky, strident voice: 'There's been enough horror! You don't know what we go through! There's been enough bloodshed! No more blood! No more blood!' This melodrama had been rehearsed by the prosecution as part of its case against Saddok, but the embarrassment it caused had rather the opposite effect. Émile Kahn, old, frail, his hair completely white, staggered to his feet, demanding on behalf of the League of the Rights of Man, of which he was the president, that the great number of extenuating circumstances involved in Saddok's case be taken into account. A pastor read a letter from his son, who had been recalled and sent to Algeria; the youth told how he had seen a territorial unit – in other words, *pieds noirs* – torturing an old Arab man; supported by a few friends, he had been forced to threaten them with arms before he could succeed in wresting their victim from them. This narrative – hanging, beatings, torture – was read out in stony silence; not one gasp of surprise or disgust: everyone knew already. My heart froze inside me as I once again faced this truth: everyone knew and didn't give a damn, or else approved.

Sartre was one of the last to be heard. He did not betray how nervous he was, except perhaps at one point when he was speaking

1. Subsequently transformed into a torture centre.

with formal deference of the dead man and referred to him as Ali Jackal. Comparing his own attitude to Ben Saddok's, he explained that young men could not be expected to display the same patience as their elders because all they knew of France was a bloodstained face. He went on to emphasize the fact that Saddok's action was a political murder and must not be treated as a terrorist attack. He made a great effort to speak in terms that would not shock the court, and the court in its turn seemed relieved by this moderation.

Massignon gave his evidence after Sartre, then Germaine Tillon; France, she pointed out, had forced the youth of Algeria into hatred. A teacher there had assigned the following subject to his class of ten-year-old Moslems for an essay: 'What would you do if you were invisible?' She herself had read some of their compositions; every single student had given the same answer, expressed in different specific fantasies: 'I would kill all the French People.'

I left the court. In the corridor, General Tubert was thundering against the French in Algeria. All the witnesses were praising the impartiality of the president of the court and the freedom he had allowed them. There were harsh comments on Camus' absence. His voice would have carried added weight because he had just been awarded the Nobel Prize. Stibbe had asked him to do no more than read aloud a passage from one of his recent essays in which he condemned the death penalty; he had refused to appear in the witness box or even to send a written message to the court. Several witnesses had quoted him in their pleas to the judge for clemency, though with a slight touch of sarcasm in some cases.

I ate dinner at La Palette with Sartre and Lanzmann. Would Saddok lose his head or not? We were full of anxiety. To release the accumulated tensions of the day, Sartre drank some whisky. He hadn't been able to drink for some time, and he grew still more agitated; before long, he had fallen into a fit of angry depression. 'To think that I stood there and eulogized Chehkal! and spoke against terrorism: as if I was against terrorism! All to please the Poujadists on the jury! Just think of it!' His rage and frustration brought tears to his eyes. 'To go through all that for a few Poujadists!' he repeated. I was frightened by the violence of his emotion: it was caused by more than his disgust at the concessions he had made in court; his nerves had already been stretched to breaking point for weeks, for months.

The newspapers next morning made depressing reading. They carried reports of what the witnesses had said, and without realizing it had drawn up an excellent indictment of the war; the reading public was going to get the truth at last in this unexpected manner. But every paper was violently against Saddok. 'What a nice-looking boy he is, Chehkal's murderer!' read one of the headlines. The press generally accused the witnesses of having cast a stigma on the fair name of France that only the blade of the guillotine could remove. We were afraid that the jury would be influenced by these articles.

It was with great relief that we learned the verdict that evening. Life imprisonment; but the prison gates would be opened when the war was over. We were happy for Saddok first of all, but it was also a comfort to find that there were still men in France capable of judging an Algerian according to their conscience.

In Algeria, such notions no longer existed. Scapegoats were chosen simply by chance: six Moslems confessed under torture to the murder of Frogier; one was picked out for execution, and although there was no proof against him, Coty refused to pardon him.

Towards the end of January 1958, Maître Bruguier asked me to testify to the good character of Jacqueline Guerroudj, who had been one of my best pupils at Rouen. She had gone as a teacher to Algeria, where she had married a Moslem teacher and with him become a member of the urban groups of the A.L.N.; she had passed on to Yveton the bomb that he had placed in the headquarters of the E.G.A. Both of them, along with Taleb, one of those accused with them, were condemned to death in December 1957. The Left started a campaign to save them, and I helped as best I could. We managed to win a remission of their sentence. But Taleb, convicted only of having prepared the explosives and denying all participation in this particular attack, was beheaded.

The bombing of Sakiet upset a large section of the French Right. Oradours were committed every day, as one corporal put it;[1] but smashing up a Tunisian village was a mistake. In an attempt to justify it, the newsreel *Actualités* inserted a piece of film showing A.L.N. soldiers stationed in Tunisia: another mistake; in uniform

1. Quoted in 1957 by a recalled conscript; in August 1956, a corporal of the 2nd B.E.P. had told him: 'If there's ever another Nuremberg trial we'll all be condemned: we have an Oradour every day.'

[395]

and well disciplined, they constituted an army, not just a gang of malefactors.

It was being said that Massu, a pious and scrupulous man, had insisted on sampling the electrodes himself. His verdict: 'Very rough; but a brave man could take it.' A book appeared to remind us all of the intolerable truth about torture: *The Question* by Henri Alleg. Sartre reviewed it in an article called 'A Victory', which was published by *L'Express* and bitterly criticized. The book nevertheless sold tens of thousands of copies and was translated all over the world.

The use of torture was by now such a well-established fact that even the Church had been forced to make a pronouncement on its legality. Many priests rejected it, both in word and deed, but there were also chaplains on hand to encourage the *corps d'élite*; as for the bishops, most of them carried tolerance pretty far, and not one of them risked raising his voice in reprobation. Among the laity, what a deafening silence of consent! I was revolted by Camus' refusal to speak. He could no longer argue, as he had done during the war in Indochina, that he didn't want to play the Communists' game; so he just mumbled something about the problem not being understood in France. When he went to Stockholm to receive his Nobel Prize, he betrayed himself even further. He boasted of the freedom of the press in France: that week, *L'Express*, *L'Observateur* and *France-Nouvelle* were all seized. In front of an enormous audience, he declared: 'I love Justice; but I will fight for my mother before Justice,' which amounted to saying that he was on the side of the *pieds noirs*. The fraud lay in the fact that he posed at the same time as a man above the battle, thus providing a warning for those who wanted to reconcile this war and its methods with bourgeois humanism. For, as Senator Rogier was to say a year later, in all seriousness: 'Our country ... needs to colour all its actions with a universal and humanitarian ideal.' And there my fellow countrymen were, indeed, all trying as hard as they could to preserve that ideal while they were trampling it underfoot. Every evening, a sentimental audience wept over the past misfortunes of little Anne Frank; but all the children in agony, dying, going mad at that moment in a supposedly French country was something they preferred to ignore. If you had attempted to stir up pity for them, you would have been accused of lowering the nation's morale.

This hypocrisy, this indifference, this country, my own self, were no longer bearable to me. All those people in the streets, in open agreement or battered into a stupid submission – they were all murderers, all guilty. Myself as well. 'I'm French.' The words scalded my throat like an admission of hideous deformity. For millions of men and women, old men and children, I was just one of the people who were torturing them, burning them, machine-gunning them, slashing their throats, starving them; I deserved their hatred because I could still sleep, write, enjoy a walk or a book. The only moments of which I was not ashamed were those in which I couldn't do any of those things, the moments when I would rather have been blind than go on reading the book in front of me, deaf than hearing what people were saying, dead than knowing what we all knew. I felt that I was suffering from one of those diseases whose most serious symptom is the lack of pain.

Sometimes, some parachutists would appear in the afternoon and set up a sort of stall in front of Saint-Germain-des-Prés. I could never bring myself to go up to it. I never knew exactly what they were up to; in any case, it was some sort of propaganda. As I sat at my desk I could hear the sound of military music; they gave talks and made collections, and I think they showed photographs, carefully selected ones, of their campaigns. I could feel the familiar lump forming in my throat, the old impotent, raging disgust: exactly the same symptoms the sight of an S.S. man had always produced. French uniforms were having the same effect on me that swastikas once did. I looked at those boys in their camouflaged battle uniforms, smiling and parading with bronzed faces and clean hands: those hands . . . People stopped to watch, interested, curious, friendly. Yes, I was living in an occupied city, and I loathed the occupiers even more fiercely than I had those others in the forties, because of all the ties that bound me to them.

Sartre protected himself by working furiously at his *Critique de la raison dialectique*. It was not a case of writing as he ordinarily did, pausing to think and make corrections, tearing up a page, starting again; for hours at a stretch he raced across sheet after sheet without re-reading them, as though absorbed by ideas that his pen, even at that speed, couldn't keep up with; to maintain this pace I could hear him crunching corydrane capsules, of which he managed to get through a tube a day. At the end of the afternoon he would be exhausted; all his powers of concentration would suddenly relax, his gestures would become vague, and quite often he would get his words all mixed up. We spent our evenings in my apartment; as soon as he drank a glass of whisky the alcohol would go straight to his head. 'That's enough,' I'd say to him; but for him it was not enough; against my will I would hand him a second glass; then he'd ask for a third; two years before he'd have needed a great deal more; but now he lost control of his movements and his speech very quickly, and I would say again: 'That's enough.' Two or three times I flew into violent tempers, I smashed a glass on the tiled floor of the kitchen. But I found it too exhausting to quarrel with him. And I knew he needed something to help him relax, in other words something to destroy himself a little. Usually I didn't protest strongly until the fourth glass. If he was swaying when he left, I blamed myself. I was almost as worried about him as I had been during those agonizing weeks in the summer of 1954.

I was hoping that the snow would do something to raise my spirits, but the two weeks I spent at Courchevel disappointed me. Two years before, I had felt rejuvenated when I put on my skis again; now I could tell I was getting old because I could make no progress. Lanzmann rarely accompanied me to the slopes; he was writing an article for *Les Temps Modernes* about the curé of Uruffe. It was an astonishing story: a priest murdering the woman he had got with child, slitting her open so he could baptize the foetus, sounding the alarm, denouncing the crime and helping his parishioners look for the murderer. The trial had been even more astonishing; Lanzmann's piece exposed its true meaning with great point and clarity: 'The reason of the Church' demanded at one and the same time that the priest should be neither understood nor punished. So the curé saved his head while the two murderers of Saint-Cloud, no less deserving of clemency – two half-retarded boys who had spent their childhoods in orphanages – were condemned to death.[1] The other people at our hotel found it quite natural that they should go to the guillotine; I couldn't help overhearing what they said at mealtimes. This was the main reason why our stay there was not very pleasant: we were still in France. In Paris, I managed to avoid the horrors of the French bourgeoisie I suddenly found myself swamped by here. The couple who complained about no longer being allowed to beat the Negroes in the Congo were Belgians; but the French people felt for them in their affliction. When Lanzmann and I wanted to go away for a few days

1. One of them was reprieved.

in April, we picked England: the south coast, Cornwall. The only Frenchmen I felt sympathy for as a group were the young people; some left-wing students asked me to give a talk on the novel at the Sorbonne and I accepted. I had been living such a retired life that when I walked into the lecture hall it was a shock to realize, from the welcome they gave me, that they knew who I was. This expression of friendship warmed my heart, something it badly needed.

CHAPTER NINE

THE bombing of Sakiet had provoked the intervention of the English and American good offices; there was talk of a diplomatic Dien Bien Phu; the Army began to protest very loudly that it would not allow such a thing. People began to talk about De Gaulle's returning to office. It was useless to count on the police being able to maintain order within the Republic. A certain number of cops having been shot in Paris by Algerians – not by chance in the majority of cases, but as isolated reprisals – the police staged a mass demonstration in front of the Chamber of Deputies on 13 March. The Dides network had set up nuclei within the force, which as a result was sympathetic to Fascism. When the Left began to hold increasing numbers of forums and meetings after the fall of Gaillard, brought down by Soustelle and Bidault on 15 April, the 'patriots' who came to smash the faces of the speakers were therefore assured of police protection. It seemed impossible to arrive at any combination of Ministers that would stand together as a government, and De Gaulle's name was heard more and more often on everyone's lips. On 6 May Pflimlin was mentioned, but he was unable to form a government without the votes of the Independents and they could not reach a decision.

The F.L.N. had to a large extent absorbed the M.N.A. and won a spectacular number of adherents to its cause.[1] It was insisting that the conventions of international law be applied to the A.L.N. When the French Government sent two Algerian fighters to the guillotine,

1. On 18 April, nine Algerian soccer players from the national French team, ten Algerian N.C.O.s from Saint-Maixent, and the Grand Mufti Lakdam left for Tunis.

[399]

three French prisoners were shot. The city of Algiers decided to demonstrate against these reprisals on 13 May.

That evening, I was in my apartment with Lanzmann when Pouillon, the recording secretary of the Assembly, telephoned. The demonstration in the Forum had developed into an insurrection; the crowd, led by Lagaillarde, had seized the Gouvernement Général; Massu was now president of a Committee of Public Safety; in short, with the support of the army, Algeria was cutting itself off from France in order to remain French. Other telephone calls followed – journalist friends giving us the latest news. Pouillon called again to tell us that the Chamber of Deputies had been quite firm in its reaction; it had voted Pflimlin in by 280 votes against 120, the Communists having abstained on principle. I went to bed feeling reassured. The following morning there was a rumour that when the colonels had heard about last night's vote in the Chamber they had panicked; one of them was supposed to have said, 'It's all fucked up!' Pflimlin severed all communications between Algeria and France; against such a blockade the seditious faction would not be able to hold out a week. On 14 May none of the people I knew was particularly uneasy. Lanzmann had been invited to visit North Korea with a delegation of other extreme-left journalists: he had wondered during the night if the trip would be cancelled; now he didn't think it would.

The following day we learnt that during the morning Salan had stood in the Forum and cried: 'Vive De Gaulle!' Pflimlin restored communications with Algeria and took no further action. The day after that, the newspapers described the masquerade that had been organized in Algiers and throughout the country in the name of fraternization.

The evening I went to the Sarah-Bernhardt theatre to hear Brecht's *Trial of Lucullus*, a grim attack on war and generals, the audience nearly brought the roof down with its applause; but it was entirely composed of left-wing intellectuals who had already been isolated in their own country for a long time. The Communists professed to be optimistic. Lanzmann represented Sartre at the Committee of Resistance against Fascism; every time they met, Raymond Guyot would say: 'To start with, we should congratulate ourselves. Committees are being formed everywhere . . . the situation is excellent . . .' But on the 19th the general strike launched by the unions collapsed. That same day De Gaulle gave a press conference;

Lanzmann told us about it as we ate dinner in the Rue de la Bûcherie with Bost and his wife; he had recognized all the old R.P.F
faces in the crush. While insisting on an exceptional method of investiture, De Gaulle had made it understood that he wanted to be
called to office legally by the country. There were society women listening in ecstasy; Mauriac was swooning with joy. Bourdet asked
De Gaulle if he didn't think he was playing into the hands of the
various factions. 'Your world is not my world,' was the gist of De
Gaulle's reply. He was going to pull it off, Lanzmann had no doubt
on that score; our bourgeois democrats would much rather put
themselves in the hands of a dictator than revive the Popular Front.
Bost didn't want to believe it; they bet a bottle of whisky on it.

Some Americans who landed at Orly refused to leave the plane
because they imagined Paris to be in the throes of a bloody revolution; we laughed, but it didn't really seem all that funny. Everything
was happening so quietly it felt like a funeral. The country allowed
itself to be persuaded that there were only two alternatives: De
Gaulle or the paras. The army was Gaullist, the police Fascist;
Moch had suggested the mobilization of civilian militias. But the one
thing the Right and the Socialists were worried about, as the paras
got ready to advance on Paris, was to avoid 'le coup de Prague'.
The 'appeal' De Gaulle sent Mollet on the 19th was couched in such
blunt terms that it shocked the recipient himself; then he prevailed
on himself to answer it. As for the apathy of the proletariat, it had to
be interpreted as consent; without De Gaulle, the working class
would no doubt have shaken itself awake, but his government between 1945 and 1947 had been no worse than those that had succeeded it; he still retained his prestige as a liberator, and since he was
not venal he passed for honest. Thanks to him, Algiers would
triumph.

What on 13 May had seemed impossible appeared inevitable by
the 23rd. The *pieds noirs* and the Army had won. Everything was
going to be settled without any struggle. It was so easy to see it all
coming that the delegation with which Lanzmann was going to
Korea decided not to delay their departure. He himself would have
liked to stay, but couldn't stand out against the others. I went with
him to Honfleur, which we both loved, and we spent two days
there. Pointing at the little meadows full of flowering apple trees,
he said in a desolate voice: 'Even the grass won't be the same
colour any more.' What upset us most was the sudden vision of

what France had gradually become: politically apathetic, inert, ready to hand itself over to the men who wanted to fight the war to the bitter end.

I drove Lanzmann to Orly on the morning of 25 May. During the afternoon, news came through of the uprising in Corsica. These were upsetting, uncertain days, for me as for so many others. I had stopped working. *Memoirs of a Dutiful Daughter* had been given to Gallimard in March. I hesitated to go on with them. My state of idleness and the general anxiety led me, as in September 1940, to start writing my diary again. I also began it again to a large extent so that I could show it later to Lanzmann, with whom it was almost impossible to correspond. I shall transcribe it here, as I have done before.

26 May

Strange days, in which we listen hour after hour to the radio and INF 1, and buy every edition of the newspapers. Yesterday, Pentecost Sunday, 800,000 Parisians left the city, the streets were quite empty; it was heavy, but not hot, with a grey sky. From Sartre's window you could see the fire engines, bright red, their long ladders on top, rushing along the Boulevard Saint-Germain. A great many police cars on patrol. The new Algiers Committee (Massu, Sid-Cara, Soustelle) announced on Saturday: 'De Gaulle or Death.' They have sent Arrighi to Corsica, but they also declare they have severed all relations with Corsica.

Lanzmann left the day before yesterday for Korea. Telegram from Moscow, where he is to spend three days.

Talks with Sartre in the evening about my book while we ate at La Palette. He reminded me how happy we used to be at Rouen, in the anonymity of youth (I can still see the Brasserie Paul where I used to correct my pupils' work). Mustn't falsify this period when I write about it.

Icy weather today. The wind is shaking the ivy on the cemetery wall and getting into the studio around all the window frames. The work I'm starting will take me three or four years, which is a rather frightening thought. Better start by getting all the material together.

Yes, for another whole day, all of Pentecost Monday – Paris was as deserted as yesterday, newspapers censored, foreign papers forbidden – the same muted atmosphere of disaster. It's rained, and there was a big thunderstorm. Lunch at La Palette with Nazim Hikmet. Seventeen years of prison, and now he has to lie down twelve hours every day because of his heart. Very charming. He told me how a year after he came out of prison there were two attempts to murder him (with cars, in the narrow streets of Istanbul). And then they tried to make him do military service on the Russian frontier: he was fifty. The doctor, a major, said to him: 'Half an hour standing in the sun and you're a dead man. But I shall have to give you a certificate of health.' So then he escaped, across the Bosporus in a tiny motor-boat on a stormy night – when it was calm the straits were too well guarded. He wanted to reach Bulgaria, but it was impossible with a high sea running. He passed a Rumanian cargo ship, he began to circle it, shouting his name. They saluted him, they waved handkerchiefs, but they didn't stop. He followed and went on circling them in the height of the storm; after two hours they stopped, but without picking him up. His motor stalled, he thought he was done for. At last they hauled him aboard; they had been telephoning to Bucharest for instructions. Exhausted, half dead, he staggered into the officers' cabin; there was an enormous photograph of him with the caption: SAVE NAZIM HIKMET. The most ironical part, he added, was that he had already been at liberty for over a year.

Lanzmann telephoned from Moscow. It was seven here, nine there, and night was just coming down over the Moskova. So near, so far. Some young fellows had come up to him at the entrance to his hotel and murmured in English: 'Business?' They wanted to get clothes from him in exchange for girls. He was feeling completely at sea, very worried about events, which he could only learn about through the Moscow correspondent of *Humanité*.

Found it difficult to work. We're waiting, though we don't know for what. Spent the evening with Sartre and Bost. Speculated about events.

Tuesday 27 May

Lunch with Sartre at the Coupole. The C.G.T. had given orders to go on strike. The F.O. and C.F.T.C. weren't following their lead, but all the same we were expecting something from them. Nothing; buses and métro still working. In the taxi, on the radio, end of De Gaulle's statement. Yes, it's 'the last quarter of an hour' as Duverger puts it. The driver: 'Well that's it! Now they've got him in it, along with taking all our money, and sending those kids to get killed in Algeria.' He was furious with the '*cocos*' because they voted the government special powers and then a tribute to the army; they're just making jackasses of everyone: 'Look how their so-called strike is going!' Doubtless some sort of Leftist, ready to accept De Gaulle out of anger. What self-deception! Everything will be managed very gently, then they'll get tough afterwards. Just a country that's given up; and it's been going on so long one feels only disgust. How stale defeat tastes! An impression of living 'historic' moments, but not in the same acute, agonizing way as in June 1940; days of deceit, slimy, like the ones Guillemin describes. We're sloshing through the messy materials of some book by a future Guillemin.

Last night there were terrible black things, twisted like vine shoots, falling out of the sky; one landed beside me, it was an enormous python, and my fear stopped me from running away. A sort of police car was going by, I leapt inside; they were hunting the snakes, which had already been falling on the country for hours – a strange country made up of jungles and worn-down roads. But the only memorable sight was the vision of those great, apocalyptic shapes above my head, still falling.

Telephone calls all day, as on the night of 13 May. And my young friend in Marseilles writes me almost every morning. We all feel the need to talk, even if we have nothing to say.

Péju has just called (at six o'clock) to tell me that Pflimlin left Coty looking very disturbed, that De Gaulle has left Colombey, he's on his way back. No strike anywhere, except among the miners in the north. De Gaulle said tonight that if he hasn't been given power within the next forty-eight hours, he will seize it. The army is for him. In Toulouse, they asked the military commandant to guarantee order in the town (because of the demonstration expected this evening) and he refused.

Sartre is working on his play; and I'm trying to interest myself in my past. On our way to Honfleur, Lanzmann told me: 'Even the grass won't be the same colour any more.' I look out at the Place Saint-Germain and I think: It won't be the same city any more.

Radio at half past seven: still hope perhaps.

Wednesday 28

Spent yesterday evening with Leiris and his wife. Listened to the radio with them; impossible to get Radio Luxembourg, could hear only French national stations. Night session of Parliament. Pflimlin made them vote on the law to change the Constitution. Remembered the time I listened to the radio with them when the Germans were retreating into Belgium.

This morning, glorious weather. Found out what was happening. Pflimlin got a majority of 400 votes against a little more than 100, the Independents have left the government, he has resigned, but without creating '*la vacance du pouvoir*'. Coty has announced that a new government will be formed by this evening.

There is supposed to be a huge demonstration this afternoon; we are going to it.

Friday 30 May

I can't write anything except this diary, and I don't really want to write that, but I've got to kill time somehow. Wednesday, lunch at La Palette with Claude Roy, who has asked to be reinstated as a member of the Communist Party and no doubt will be. He quoted something De Gaulle said about Malraux which is all over Paris: 'He blamed me for going all the way to the Rubicon just to do some fresh-water fishing, and now that I've crossed it he's off fishing in the lagoon.' Malraux has in fact been away in Venice all this time, lecturing on art; but he came back the evening before last and is expecting, according to Florence, to be made Minister of Information and Culture.

We went by taxi – on Wednesday – at quarter to six in the evening, to the Reuilly-Diderot métro station. Long procession on the left-hand sidewalk; Communists, obviously so, carrying placards: LONG LIVE THE REPUBLIC. We were expecting the Committee of the 6ième at the station, but the C.N.E. had chosen it for *their* meeting place as well. The métro began disgorging a whole heap of people we knew: Pontalis, Chapsal, Chauffard, the Adamovs, the Pozners, Anne Philipe, Tzara, Gégé with his family and the people from his studio, my sister. Everyone was amazed to see such a huge crowd there; each of us had been afraid that the demonstration would be a flop. The Place de la Nation was black with people. We walked behind the banner of the 'Beaux-Arts', only to find ourselves suddenly behind the 'Rights of Man', then somewhere vaguely in between. We saw old Republicans in a state of jubilation, feeling fifty years younger because of it all; they jumped up in the air to see over the heads of the crowd, and when they saw how long the procession was their faces beamed. People were perched on the traffic signs down the middle of the streets, climbing on the shoulders of friends and waving approval; the procession was endless in either direction. Along the sidewalks, a great many people were applauding and shouting with us; they were in fact demonstrating. A gay crowd, and a well-behaved crowd, obeying orders. There were a few cries of: 'Long live the Republic', but the favourite was: 'No Fascists in France'; there was a lot of 'Hang Massu hang Soustelle'; some: 'Down with De Gaulle', though not shouted very loudly. The slogans: 'De Gaulle in the museum – the paras in the factories' were a big success. (Was this discretion the result of a sense of law and order, or the respect for De Gaulle that S.L. was talking about yesterday? In any case, when someone began to shout 'Hang De Gaulle', they always shut him up.) We sang the *Marseillaise* and the *Chant du Départ*. Sartre sang with all his might. There were two tall, good-looking boys, each with a pretty girl on his arm, who never stopped yelling the whole time. People were staring out of windows, and many of them expressed sympathy; children applauded. Over the Berceau Doré, three very old ladies in white wigs, leaning on faded gold cushions, saluted us with regal gestures as we passed. The lights went on changing from red to green, even though all traffic had been stopped. However, from time to time the procession would get jammed; we stopped, then set off again. In front of the police station, the cops stood motionless, impassive, and the crowd turned towards them aggressively with cries of: 'Hang Massu!' It was a heart-warming, moving, unanimous procession. There were men who had been deported walking along in striped uniforms, and invalids and cripples in cars. The arrival at the Place de la République was disappointing; nothing had been arranged beforehand. There were people who had climbed up on the plinth and were waving flags, but no orders had been given; we began to disperse. There were some shouts of 'To the Place de la Concorde!' but no one made a move; it would have been impossible to get through in any case. There wasn't a single cop on the route, but both ends were guarded by C.R.S. cars. The crowd was not in a fighting mood. What was surprising was the spirit that had swept everyone along: even the least politically minded sort of people from Le Village had come. But some of us couldn't help remarking that people in general seemed too good-humoured, they seemed quite happy to shout and sing, but not at all determined to act. And the evening before, the strike had failed; the F.O. and the C.F.T.C. congratulated themselves the next day on having demonstrated 'independently of the C.G.T.' There will certainly be no general strike. Bost, Olga and the Apteckmans went up to the second floor of the Hôtel Moderne, where some American journalists were working, with the help of a great deal of whisky; the view from up there was very striking, they say. However, down in the dining room on the ground floor, there were some English-women drinking soup with complete indifference. Apparently Mendès was acclaimed in the Place de la Nation, but after he arrived, when all the groups were dispersing, some Fascists tried to attack him. They didn't have much luck.

We went back to Sartre's apartment, feeling moved, and with a glimmer of hope in our hearts. We immediately heard bad news: the parachutists had landed (a rumour that's been going around for four days); neither the army nor the C.R.S. will support the Government; De Gaulle had left Colombey and Coty was to call him to the Élysée during the night. Sartre had an engagement for the evening, and I couldn't bear being on my own; I went to join the Bosts and Apteckman in a restaurant on the Rue Stanislas. We went back to the cars we'd left in the Rue du Faubourg-Saint-Honoré and prowled around the Élysée Palace, which was all lit up; it was nearly midnight; the people who had come in great numbers to watch during the evening were beginning to disperse; we could hear chants of: 'Massu in Paris! The paras in Paris!' It was a handful of distinguished-looking forty-year-olds (I forgot to say that there has been a joyful recovery on the Stock Exchange, and that the napoleon has gone down seventy francs). The cops headed them off very politely. Regiments of C.R.S. men in their dark cars, or standing in the street, pistols in hand, had cordoned it all off; if they had been Gardes Républicains one would have felt protected, but in the circumstances they inspired fear more than anything else. They were letting the crowd move by – pedestrians and cars. Barbara Apteckman tried her charm on them and they answered back good-humouredly. She asked them: 'What are you waiting for?' 'De Gaulle; but we've been here two hours and he still hasn't arrived.' Others said: 'We've been sent from Bordeaux, they treat us like shit here.' And others: 'We're waiting to fight.' There was a vast procession of elegant cars crawling along because of the bottleneck. 'Where are you going?' 'To see De Gaulle.' A taxi from Chez Maxim's, very old-fashioned, with a very chic old driver and Maxim's crest on the door; inside, a man in evening dress and a superb woman in a red dress, covered with jewels. They were like film extras: that little typical and unexpected touch in a film shot ten years later. A car drove out of the Élysée; it looked as though it was over and De Gaulle hadn't turned up. We drove past the Chamber and went for a drink in the Bûcherie. It was full of people who had demonstrated that afternoon, all of whom were expressing astonishment at the size of the turnout. But no one knew what was happening at the moment, and the Bosts' radio was broken. I called Péju. The parachutists had definitely not landed, and the Socialists were standing firm against De Gaulle. In fact, he went back to Colombey during the night. Apteckman was as convinced as I that the Socialists would betray us. The next day (yesterday, Thursday) was a strangely sad morning. It was marvellous weather, I went out to read the newspapers, birds singing in the squares, chestnut blossoms falling. Sat on the terrace of a café, on the corner of the Avenue d'Orléans. *Le Figaro* criticized the demonstration. *Humanité* announced that there had been 500,000 demonstrators, which disappointed me because I thought there had *really* been 500,000. *L'Express*, ready to scuttle itself, with Mauriac shamefully at the helm. Went home, unable to read through the papers properly, or write, or do anything. I was tied in knots with anxiety. The trash cans were overflowing with garbage along the sidewalks because the collectors were on strike.

And that day the betrayal began. The letter from Auriol to De Gaulle was published: if De Gaulle would promise to cut himself off from Algiers, then sixty-nine Socialists had declared that they would vote for him, 'in order to avoid civil war'. Lunched at the Pouillons'. It was there we heard Coty's message to the two Chambers; he threatened to resign if De Gaulle was not put in office. That evening De Gaulle came back. He called the leaders of all the 'national' groups together at the Élysée. During the night, he went back to Colombey yet again. There's going to be one more day of machinations, and then the trick will have been played: slick scenario, perfect execution.

At lunch, Pouillon talked very amusingly about parliamentary customs and rites. Lévi-Strauss was there, taciturn as ever. He asked in an amazed tone of voice: 'But why does De Gaulle find mankind so despicable?' which was charming, because he always affects to be much more interested in the fauna and flora of the countries he goes to than in their inhabitants; but in fact he is a humanist, and there is nothing he finds more repugnant than the idea of 'greatness'.

At Sartre's at five in the afternoon: papers, radio, anger. He goes on working all the same.

Evening with Olga. She asked Bost to join us at the Coupole. A young left-wing journalist who came with him refused to believe that De Gaulle could have been involved in any sort of plot. He began to speculate about his 'character', which just set my nerves on edge. Got home in a state of violent exasperation.

Saturday 31 May

I'm calm again, I don't know why; perhaps because Sartre has decided to stop taking corydrame, is making himself sleep and be calm, and it's contagious. And above all, because it's all settled, the game is lost and, as Tristan Bernard said after he was arrested, we've got nothing to fear now, we can start to hope. De Gaulle's investiture will take place this evening without any doubt. At least the S.F.I.O. will make a show of protest. The teachers' strike, supported by the pupils' parents, was a success yesterday in the primary and technical schools, and half successful in the secondary schools. There will still be considerable opposition forces, and they're bound to make themselves felt in one way or another.

There were incidents in Saint-Germain-des-Prés on Thursday evening. Evelyne was there. Some elegant cars were going up towards the Champs-Élysées; there was a traffic jam. They began to sound their horns: 'Algeria for the French!' The cafés all emptied out into the street, the 'villagers' all came out, and since there happened to be some cobblestones in front of the church, they picked some up and threw them at the cars. Evelyne got into Robert's car with him and they followed. Around the Élysée, the ladies in their evening dresses, their long kid gloves and their jewels were fraternizing with the helmeted C.R.S. men.

Even people we know are giving in. Z. the other day: 'After all, at least De Gaulle is one better than Massu,' and X. explained to me today that if the Socialists refused to vote for De Gaulle it would mean civil war. He's waiting for De Gaulle to get together with

Mendès-France and revolutionize the economy. His wife, when we were left alone, said to me: 'You understand how it is; we need to think that Jean [her husband] won't be forced to resign.'

Sartre had lunch with Cocteau, who was in disagreement with the appeal the Academy had sent to De Gaulle.

Press conference at the Lutétia on use of torture. Only moderate applause when Mauriac announced that he was a Gaullist. Big attendance. Not many journalists, actually, but five hundred intellectuals.

At the moment I'm doing much more reading than writing. In *Critique*, an interesting article on operational research. If a computer had to work out the 'optimum answer' in a case such as the following: the shortest route to visit twenty American cities, it would take it two hundred and fifty thousand years. Whereas man takes 'short cuts'; each man has to deal with others who also decide things by 'short cuts'. So we do everything at a level where the 'optimum answer' doesn't exist.

Lanzmann arrives in Korea today. Curious situation.

As I was coming back along the Rue Blomet yesterday, at about three in the afternoon, I saw some groups of young men wandering about on the Boulevard Pasteur. 'The cops chased them away, but they're coming back,' the taxi driver told me. They were right-wingers trying to get the classes at the Lycée Buffon going again. The taxi driver: 'I've finished with strikes myself. Got the message. You don't work, so the others get it all. It's not worth it. . . . What's going to happen? Well it's not going to be any worse than what we've had already.' (That's what one hears people saying everywhere: at least things will change, they can't get worse.) However he had one footnote to add, on the subject of De Gaulle: 'It's all his fault, all this. All he needed to do in 1945 was chuck out all the Jews.' I laughed out loud at that, so he ended up: 'I don't know what it all means. No idea at all. No one else has either. And I've got a son in Algeria!'

INF 1 has announced that there were other demonstrations along the Champs-Élysées last night, with car horns and 'Vive De Gaulle'. Then counter-demonstrators shouted: 'No Fascism in France'. Riot; several people seriously wounded; the Communists got the best of it.

This morning I read all the weeklies through again quietly and all the passages on De Gaulle in Werth. The business of the postcards sent to Colombey is farcical. Certainly nothing of the 'great figure' about him.

Lunch and quiet day with Sartre. Still incapable of working, but tried to read Lacouture's *Le Maroc à l'épreuve*. The radio announced that De Gaulle's investiture would be tomorrow: the Socialists haven't reached an agreement among themselves (77 for, 74 against; in the Chamber, about 40 for and 50 against, Guy Mollet possibly resigning); they will vote individually. De Gaulle has climbed down a step; he's going to make a personal appearance in the Chamber, and he'll allow himself to be photographed. The government is expected to be very right-wing, but without anyone from Algiers. They must be worried in Algiers, despite the demonstration yesterday evening.

As I was leaving Sartre's, I met Evelyne, Jacques, Lestienne and Bénichou. They were going up to the Champs-Élysées, where a lot more action was expected. The little Fascists were already in Saint-Germain with their newspapers and their placards; police everywhere. There were obviously going to be some heads broken.

Evelyne is on permanent duty on the Committee of the 6ième and goes out rioting every night. An intense longing to be young again cut through me, a desire to go to the Champs-Élysées, driven by a genuine youthful impulse, with her gang. Perhaps I might even have done it if I hadn't had a date with Violette Leduc. I went home. It's eight in the evening, and all my anxiety has come back. I'll take her out to Saint-Germain in any case, I can't stay shut up here this evening – the last one of the Republic. The committees expect to stage demonstrations tomorrow, but it's all still vague, and that just adds to the tension.

Question number one: What will De Gaulle do in Algeria?

A strange evening; V.L. arrived and threw herself into my arms: 'Chantal is dead!' And then I was swamped with all the goings-on in the house where she lives: the hermit on the third floor she took rice pudding to, who received her in his underpants, then got dressed, put on his tie, went out on to the landing to deliver 'political' speeches and finally got sent to the asylum at Villejuif by the concierge; Chantal, a girl of fifteen with enormous quantities of hair and three holes in her heart, who lay on the operating table for twenty-six hours and died that morning without a drop of blood left in her. V.L. poured out all these sinister tales which didn't concern me and stopped my thinking about the things that did. We ate dinner at the Bûcherie, where I saw Claude Roy, and then went for a drink in Saint-Germain. People everywhere, not a single empty chair on the terrace of the Deux Magots; we found a place outside the Royal and stayed there almost two hours just looking, without saying a word. We looked at the women's extravagant dresses, the infinity of faces, and above all the cars, the cars coming and going, packed with arrogant women and delighted men. Every now and then a police car or a little patrol van. Nothing to put your finger on except, half an hour past midnight, this enormous crush of automobiles, like traffic coming back into the city after a weekend or afternoon traffic on a busy weekday. Riveted to my chair, beside V.L., I felt quite empty, possessed entirely by this beautiful evening without a sky (the lights devoured it) in which, after all, nothing was really happening any more, because everything was over, but which formed a setting nevertheless, with its shining automobiles, its ladies and gentlemen riding the streets in triumph, where something hideous was taking off its mask.

Sunday 1 June

Didn't sleep much; am astonished by the civic classicism of my dreams: they were drowning a naked woman, half flesh, half statue, who was the Republic. Investiture this afternoon. A young woman rang the bell and handed me my committee invitation (the 14th), for 3.45 p.m.

Telegram from Lanzmann. He's arrived at Pyongyang.

Monday 2 June

Not a spare minute yesterday to write about what was happening. The committee telephoned. It was V. who called, and when I said: 'Speaking,' he still sounded incredulous: 'Mlle de Beauvoir herself?' 'Yes, yes.' 'In person?' 'Of course.' Sartre tells me it's just Communist distrust. V. told me what the committee had decided: we had to go and lay flowers at the foot of the statue of the Republic. I asked if I was to join the committee of the 14th Arrondissement; and what about Sartre? V. hesitated, he didn't know, he told me to go to headquarters but to walk with the 14th group as well, and he asked me to pass on the order because they had been forbidden all communiqués and hadn't been able to distribute pamphlets. It all seemed very badly organized to me.

I had to meet Rolland at the Deux Magots because he wants to publish a small extract from my *Memoirs* in *L'Observateur*, together with a short interview. He had got his orders from the Communists: get to Sèvres-Babylone with a car to help block the road (?). Went up to see Sartre; from the window I could see Bost talking to Evelyne, in a flowered skirt and pink jumper with a pink scarf on her head, looking ravishing. She sweeps up the head-quarters of the 6th every evening; she had spent the morning running around the police stations with Reggiani trying to get out a girl who'd been arrested for distributing pamphlets; they hadn't found her. She suggested we join the committee of the 6ième which was to meet at half past three at Sèvres Croix-Rouge.

We left at 3.25; passed Adamov and some others who were 'part of the act'. Got into the car, in which Olga and Evelyne were already waiting for us. I bought some blue and white irises and some red gladioli in the Rue Jacob; who would have thought, seeing us twenty years before, that one day we'd be going to lay red, white and blue bouquets at the feet of the statue of the Republic! There were a great many demonstrators with placards and flags at the Sèvres Croix-Rouge crossroads, some of them scattered, some in a tight group. A car passed and sounded its horn: '*Al-gé-rie fran-çaise!*' We rushed the car; the driver zigzagged his way through, sneering at our shouts. There were cries of: 'Down with De Gaulle!' and the customers on the terrace of the Lutétia replied with 'Long live De Gaulle!' Argument. The Desantis and some others said we should go to the Place de la République; however, the Communist instructions were different; the procession moved up the Boulevard Raspail chanting slogans. Since we were part of the 'Anti-Fascist Committee', we got back in the car and moved on towards the Place de la République; I was rather glad about this, because I had the impression that the procession was going to run into trouble (which is what happened – it was rather a bloody fight in fact). We left the car and the flowers in the Boulevard Voltaire. At a quarter to four, not many people, but cops everywhere, an army of them – helmeted squads on foot, cars packed; the statue was cordoned off, impossible to get near it. It was very hot and very sultry; we went around the square; a lot of people, but scattered, perplexed; some of the women carrying bouquets (we saw lots in the streets that morning, but for another reason: it was Mother's Day). Near a métro entrance, a woman had given way to hysteria and was shrieking. We sat down on a terrace; Apteckman and his wife were passing and they came and sat with us, just waiting; the old lady sitting next to us had a bouquet. Apteckman went to see how things were going and came back at a run: we could get through. Bost ran to get our flowers, but he took too long and we joined the procession without him, moving across the square in little groups under police control; a little girl carrying a bunch of daisies came and handed one to each of us. We laid them in front of the statue and went and stood on the sidewalk; there was beginning to be quite a crowd; behind us stood rows of flower stalls, put up, or anyway increased in number, for the occasion. The crowd sang the *Marseillaise* and shouted: 'The police are with us.' Some boys in leather jackets were hurriedly buying peonies or hydrangeas and carrying them solemnly across the square; there was a marvellous old man – long yellow beard, pince-nez, ecstatic smile on his face – who looked like a believer walking back from Communion. They were still shouting: 'Republican Police. De Gaulle to the Museum!' Suddenly, everyone began to run. In the rush, an invalid fell down, some men stopped to pick him up. Evelyne tried to get behind the grille gates of a cinema, but they chased her out; the concierges were closing the main gates of the apartment houses (as they did when Paris was liberated). We took a cross street back to the Boulevard and looked for the car which Bost must have moved somewhere else (that's why he took so long) to leave everything clear for the C.R.S. cars. It was about four-thirty. We drove back through the square, and it was quiet again. (It was ten minutes later, I think, that Georges Arnaud got his arm broken by a blow from a truncheon and the blood started flowing.) There was a rumour that there were demonstrations in Belleville, so we started up towards the Buttes-Chaumont. How green and gay it is there, with such pretty streets and sudden wide vistas out over Paris, blue in the distance! It was a quiet Sunday, people taking the air on benches, children playing, little girls walking in procession to Communion. And then, in the Avenue Ménilmontant, we ran into a procession; we got out of the car and joined it; they were Communists, men from the neighbourhood cells; they wound up and down the streets where I used to go once to do 'social fieldwork'; they shouted up to the people in the windows: 'All Republicans down with us!' Sartre gave the same full-throated rendering of the

Marseillaise that I'd heard on Wednesday; he was there, not as a member of a delegation, nor even as the writer Jean-Paul Sartre, but just as an unknown citizen; he no longer cared what people thought, he felt at home in this crowd, he who had always had such difficulty accepting elites, and felt so ill at ease being part of them. We got back on to the Avenue; as we passed the terrace of a café packed with North Africans, the demonstrators shouted: 'Peace in Algeria!' The Algerians scarcely smiled. A woman said quietly: 'There aren't many of them demonstrating.' 'And quite right too, it'd be too big a risk; they're always the ones who get it, with things like this,' the woman next to her answered, sympathetically. People began to pick up stones along a stretch of the street that was being repaired; but another procession, with placards and flags, came marching to meet them and put a stop to that; there were parleys; the leaders urged the crowds to disperse. Had they come from the Place de la République? When we went through it once more in the car, it was quiet; but this time, as well as the cops, there were Red Cross orderlies in helmets, stationed at the street corners.

We listened to the latest news in Mme Mancy's room. There had been riots in a lot of places; at the city gates and at the exits from the big railroad stations, the C.R.S. were stopping people coming into Paris (mostly members of Communist cells); this hadn't prevented meetings in the Place de la Trinité and near the Bastille though; or in other places. Good speeches by Mendès and Mitterand, both declaring: 'We will not yield to blackmail'; more than half the Socialists, 50 out of 90, are going to vote No. The counting begins at seven-thirty.

Evelyne called; Jacques had been picked up on Saturday evening on the Champs-Élysées, and sent to Beaujon; he had spent the night wandering through the corridors and yards, and the day without anything to eat because he went on a hunger strike; his fellow prisoners were Fascists, and they'd been fighting each other with stones. They were beginning to release the prisoners, but only in little groups. Jacques had been let out at nine in the evening. (Evelyne quoted a charming thing that Lestienne had said; he was complaining about Palle. 'Palle is a Gaullist and keeps on spouting Gaullist propaganda at me; it's quite sickening, because he knows I'm a right-winger underneath it all and that it's only too easy to influence me!')

[415]

Spent the evening with Sartre, first at La Palette, then here at my place. Hope (vague) that the Left may pull itself together, and intense curiosity about Algeria. Malraux talked to De Gaulle for three hours on Saturday; no doubt that he's to be Minister of Information.

As for personal matters; Sartre saw Huston and Suzanne Flon on Saturday; it's agreed that he will do the film on Freud.

At about eleven, the storm that had been threatening all day finally broke. Flashes of lightning all around a helicopter glowing with red lights, the police helicopter that was flying over Paris during the procession on Wednesday, and still keeping watch on us; the Eiffel Tower floodlit; they call it its 'robe of light'; I liked it better dark, with those beautiful rubies glowing around its head. Rain bucketing down, tremendous wind, not very propitious weather for any demonstrations of enthusiasm, and the fact is, nobody's tried to start any. The investiture tonight was as dreary as that of any old Président du Conseil. Nevertheless, my head is ready to burst; the apprehension has all gone, but I'm so tense I've been taking sarpagnan.

This morning I read Herbart's *La Ligne de force*, in which there are some very malicious but very funny passages on Gide, and a nice little anecdote about Aragon.

I gave Rolland some pages of my *Memoirs*; lunch with J., the American student, who staggered me with her widely misconceived opinions about Gaullism. She told me about her childhood: a horrific membrane over one eye, a childish, dominating, hysterical Jewish mother, complexes everywhere. An operation at the age of nineteen made her bad eye look normal again, and she contends that Sartre and I taught her through our books that one is marked by one's past but not determined by it. From that time on she was saved. She wants to make me a present of her private diary in eighteen manuscript volumes. She is haunted by the atomic bomb, and can't understand why people in France worry about it so little. She has written to Oppenheimer. She showed me a brochure about the four Americans who went by boat across the Pacific and wouldn't move from the area where the next test was to take place; they soon found themselves in prison. Her dream is to get a boat crammed with people of all nationalities to do the same thing; then the U.S.A. couldn't just put them all in prison. Or else she wants to offer herself as a martyr on whom they can do experiments to find out the results of the explosion. It's typically American, this naïve idealism projected on a world scale (Gary Davis). She's not a fool, however; far from it. Perhaps she'll move out of this phase when she has a profession and some solid ground beneath her feet.

Spent the day with Sartre, reading newspapers and taking notes. He lunched with S.-S. and Giroud. They had a referendum at *L'Express* ten days ago; everyone was decidedly opposed to De Gaulle except F., from sheer despair, and, of course, Jean Daniel.

None of the Algerian faction in the government; nor any demonstrations of enthusiasm in Algiers. They're terrified they've been betrayed. Beuve-Méry has capitulated entirely. The last issue of *L'Express* is much more accurate than the one before. The most stubborn of them all, the one who's really standing firm, is Bourdet. His reply to Sirius (Beuve-Méry) in *Le Monde* was really excellent. In any case, there's a split inside *Le Monde*; some of the contributors are holding out. *France-Soir* is beginning to turn its coat; today they started a series of extracts from De Gaulle's *Memoirs*.

We were saying yesterday evening with Sartre:

The intellectual can be in agreement with a regime; but – except in underdeveloped countries which are short of trained people – he should never agree to fill a technical function as Malraux is doing. Even if he supports the government, he should remain a latent source of opposition and criticism, in other words, he should judge policies, not execute them. Even so, he will find a thousand problems confronting him; but his role must not become confused with that of the rulers; this division of labour is infinitely desirable.

Tuesday 3 June

After the tension, depression. I was so little inclined to put my nose out of the door this morning that I slept until half past twelve. The weather still muggy and cold. Yesterday evening with Sartre and Bost. Lunch today with Sartre, Pontalis and Chapsal. Waited for them at the Falstaff; at the next table, a young gentleman looking like a rather superior civil servant[1] was chatting to a beastly woman: 'All the same, Mendès did applaud De Gaulle . . .

1. Possibly he was a small-time con man. In 1963, he bumped into Sartre again in the Falstaff. 'It's going to start getting tough now,' he warned him.

No, X. doesn't want a Popular Front; that means he can be brought around ... Try to convince your group ... That's unfortunate; apparently Lazareff is basically anti-Gaullist ...' When Sartre came in they whispered: 'There's Sartre,' and then left after a little while. We were just beginning to eat when there was a telephone call for Sartre: 'Monsieur Sartre, I felt I must tell you that the General is getting ready to make peace in Algeria, that he's not going to have you arrested, and that we regret the attitudes you have adopted in the pages of *L'Express*.' Very polite; he wanted to *bring Sartre around*!

I don't find it amusing any more, jotting down these little things. But I'm too down to write. Or am I down because I'm not writing? We leave next week for Italy; that makes these last days feel even more provisional and contingent. I find it difficult to get interested in my past; I don't really know what to do.

A very good article in *Saturday Review*, with my photograph on the cover. But *Time* and *The New York Times* don't like it at all. What annoys them is that I should speak well of China when I'm not a Communist.

To describe the demonstrations on Wednesday and Sunday as a 'detotalized totality' would be a real literary challenge; Sartre managed it up to a point in *The Reprieve*. It seems to me a much more interesting way to attempt things than what they are calling 'aliterature'.

Sartre was telling Pontalis just now that whenever he tries to think of a subject for a play an immense void forms inside his head; then, at a certain moment, he hears the words 'The Four Horsemen of the Apocalypse' echoing inside it. It's the title of a novel by Blasco Ibañez that he read when he was young. He is also having trouble getting back to work. He's taking corydrame again. 'I'm not sad,' he told me, 'but I'm asleep. It's like a morgue.'

Thursday 5 June

I don't know what it was that drove me to such a pitch of exasperation yesterday evening; probably irritation at seeing all those newspapers and hearing all those people wondering what 'he' is going to say, going round in circles trying to interpret his silences. Also hearing him, against a background of all that shouting in Algiers, with his ageing voice and his enigmatic grandiloquence. And thinking that they'll all start trying to decipher the oracle yet

[418]

again, insisting at all costs on squeezing some drop of hope from his words, when in fact everything is settled now, immutably: years of war and massacres and torture.

Yesterday morning I went to the dentist. L., a Communist and a Jew, was as lugubrious as myself. He said that he found the vigour, the optimism of the Communists insupportable; just because half the Socialists had voted with them they thought they'd won. As for his patients, some of them were saying things like: 'Oh come on, De Gaulle isn't going to send you to a concentration camp.' 'I know.' 'Well then, what does it all matter to *you*?' Lunch with Bianca, still very taken up by her committees. She said she had met some groups of parachutists on the street in civilian clothes. (It ties up with a piece of news censored from *L'Express* but revealed today: Lagaillarde had landed with six men at a nearby airfield to try to contact the parachutists stationed near Paris. They were nevertheless politely shipped back to Algeria.) She also told me that in Passy and in Neuilly, 'urban militias' of a sort are being formed, with block leaders, etc., much the same as under the Occupation.

Spent the afternoon at Sartre's, vainly attempting to think about my book. I too found myself wondering: What is De Gaulle going to say? Now, I know. He has given his blessing to the 'renovation' and 'fraternization' of which Algeria has given us such an example, and he hopes these things will spread all through France itself. Soustelle never leaves his side. Then, in the Forum, he paid tribute to Algiers, to the Army, and without actually using the word integration, said that Moslems must become 'Frenchmen in the full sense of the word'; he mentioned a 'single university'. Algiers is disappointed because this is still not Fascist enough for them, and because *real* integration would put them up the creek. In spite of all our suspicions, we were still amazed that he should have taken over Algiers and their policies so completely. At least it makes everything quite clear. All evening at La Palette we talked about nothing else. I blamed myself for not having tried to do more. Sartre pointed out exactly what I had always told myself: that I can't very well go around mimicking him all the time; our names are so closely linked we're almost thought of as only one person. All the same, when I come back from Italy I'll try to commit myself more actively. I should find the present situation less intolerable if I had been more energetic and militant. When I got home, feeling very nervous and humiliated in a way, as well as angry, I found an absolutely insane letter from Y. about Gorz's book *The Traitor* and Sartre's article in *L'Express*; it was a flood of anti-Semitism. I was seized by a fit of anger against the world in general that kept me in a state of near suffocation for an hour before I finally managed to drug myself to sleep.

I slept badly and woke up with my nerves in knots. There was a letter from the 'Ministry of National Defence', signed by a Mme de —, asking me to write some articles for *Bellone*, a magazine intended for the 'Women's Armed Forces', of which she enclosed a copy. Were they going to make advances to us, on top of everything else? Went to buy the newspapers and read them in the café on the corner (the corner of the Avenue d'Orléans). *L'Observateur* still very good, *L'Express* had some good bits and some wishy-washy articles. Both were guarded. They were waiting to see what De Gaulle was really up to in Algeria; they said we must regroup against him 'even if . . .'; today everything is clear, and I suppose that Bourdet is, in Mauriac's famous phrase, 'agreeably disappointed'. Abbas, Tunis, Rabat, are all categorical: De Gaulle's offers are unacceptable. Only that nut Amrouche gives a military salute in *Le Monde*: 'I take you at your word, *mon Général.*' We are also informed that there are now more than three hundred and fifty Committees of Public Safety in France. With all this encouragement from De Gaulle, the hatches will soon be well battened down. Sartre says that there is nothing we can do – he and I – for the moment. So, off we go to rest a bit, we can work when we come back.

Lunch with Reggiani and his wife. Sartre told them about his play, which he wants to have put on in October; after October it might not get put on at all.

I bought myself a dress as a distraction, but it only took five minutes and didn't distract me in the slightest. The brackish taste of defeat.

I really don't understand why I'm as upset as I am. The country will end up Fascist, and then, whether it's jail or exile, things will go badly for Sartre, but it's not fear that's got hold of me; I haven't reached that stage yet, unless I'm beyond it. What I find physically intolerable is being forced to be an accomplice of drumbeaters, incendiaries, torturers and mass murderers; it's my country all this is happening to, and I used to love it; and without chauvinism or jingoism, it's pretty difficult to be against one's own country. Even the countryside, the sky over Paris, the Eiffel Tower, are poisoned for me.

This morning, as I was reading on the corner of the avenue, two cart vendors – they were selling cherries – both North Africans, suddenly went for one another. How they fought! All the same there were two passers-by in leather jackets – not middle-class people, of course – who hurried over to try to separate them. It wasn't too easy, because one of them had got his teeth firmly fixed in the other's shoulder through his check shirt. Then a cop strolled up, swinging his truncheon and smiling; but it was all over, he missed his chance of clouting anyone.

Friday 6 June

This morning, for no particular reason, something inside me had loosened; I felt relaxed. Card from L. in Irkutsk; he found Siberia enchanting. How well I remember those little airfields with their ruffled curtains! I took the car out to Fontainebleau and back to see how things went; it's all right – I'm in good working order and so is the car. I can't wait to start.

Joan left all eighteen volumes of her diary with the concierge. It's interesting, despite all the rubbish, because she has revealed herself completely. Generally speaking, I find personal diaries fascinating, and this one is quite extraordinary, one really does take a dive straight into someone else's life, another frame of reference, and in a sense that's the severest test of all: while I'm reading it, she's the absolute subject, not me any more.

De Gaulle is still on his tour of Algeria, obviously displeased. In Oran, they yelled: 'Soustelle! Soustelle!' and he said: 'Stop, I beg you.' He evidently doesn't like this Fascism, which will try to go further than he wants. He may be playing into their hands. But enough of this commenting and prophesying and interpreting. I will just make a note of the fact that the press is lukewarm about the whole thing. The fact is, this 'comeback' hasn't produced much enthusiasm on either side.

Saturday 7 June

Almost two weeks without working, and yet I feel so impatient to begin on the morning of the 25th. But you can't expect to work well in a state of anxiety, especially when it's a question of invention, getting yourself started. Letter from Joan this morning; listening to De Gaulle speak has put her off him; a purely sentimental reaction, but shared by a great many other people. He has a Fascist style when he speaks, military, grandiloquent; it makes a lot of things clear when you hear it. Interesting letter from A.B.[1] He talks about how frightened the Moslems are in the little villages; they're avoiding him because to be seen with him would be compromising; terrible pressures are being used to create the mock fraternization; the arrests still go on underneath it all, and the murders.

I must answer letters; grey, dull morning.

Sunday 8 June

Finished with the radio three times a day, INF 1, every edition of the newspapers. Things will move slowly for the next few days. At Mostaganem, on Friday evening, De Gaulle finally came out with the words 'French Algeria'; but the 'left-wing Gaullists' insist on the fact that he avoids saying 'integration'. For a man of 'character', he has proved to be singularly accommodating; for after all – without mentioning the other things – in Algiers they put the two Ministers accompanying him under house arrest; and instead of insisting that they should appear at all the various functions during the next few days, he accepted the snub. Obviously he's prepared to bow and scrape if he has to.

I'm still wading through Joan's extraordinary diary, wallowing in it. I find it touching, because she's read me as though I were part of her own life, because many of her criticisms are very much to the point, because she defends me with so much warmth all the time, and often with intelligence. But even here I'm blasé; ten years ago it would have had quite an effect; now, I find it quite pleasant, but troubling too. I ought to be writing new books, better ones, I ought be proving my worth afresh, proving that I really deserve to exist like that for other people. And I'm hovering between two projects without being able to decide.

Tuesday 10 June

Malraux said to S.-S., who repeated it directly to Sartre: 'We have received completely reliable information about fraternization: it is a reality.' When mythomania is blown up into a political system,

1. A soldier in Algeria.

[422]

things are becoming serious. He made a short speech about French 'generosity' so far-fetched that even Clavel protested in *Combat*. Bost is on the Cinema Vigilance Committee and is furious because they're so cautious: ten out of the fifteen members are Communists. Sartre says it's simply a question of getting into position and that the committees can't really do anything until the referendum comes up.

Dinner on Sunday with Suzanne Flon, nice, and Huston; he has that American attractiveness, despite a big stye on his eye. We talked a lot about Freud, a virgin until he was married at the age of twenty-seven, and a completely faithful husband. Huston had the idea for this film after shooting a documentary on battle neuroses; the film turned out so anti-militaristic that it was suppressed.

Wednesday 11 June

Since I had the evening free yesterday I called Joan and asked her to come over. It gives my heart a slight pang to think that she spent five years wanting to see me, was tenacious and clever enough to succeed in doing so, and now all that success amounts to is these three rather everyday conversations. At this point, having read her diary, I wanted to talk to her about herself. How unhappy she had been! What a beautiful little 'private hell' she had built for herself with that curious and very American mixture of freedom and taboos. And what a solid foundation it had: her appallingly cruel deformity and her tortured relationship with a mother at once pretty, famous and completely off the rails ever since her husband – a calm, attractive man – had left her and gone off to the other end of the earth. Joan, with her membrane-covered eye, her crooked teeth, afflicted by tics and shyness, spent a lonely and haunted childhood entirely in her shadow. At sixteen, there was an idyll with Bodenheim, a poet famous in the twenties, by then a half-mad, impotent alcoholic; he used to grope her in parks. The mother, informed of what was happening by a police-woman, wrote him a letter, purporting to come from a professional boxer, in which she threatened to beat him up. He explained to Joan that he had to break with her because he had piles and a hernia; and also because he had been mixed up in so many affairs with minors that he might be jailed if it happened again; or at the very least there would be a scandal, and then his publisher wouldn't reprint any of his books. He died five years later, caught in bed with a fairly attractive woman by her jealous husband, who stabbed Bodenheim in the heart, strangled his wife and ended his days in a lunatic asylum. The whole of Greenwich Village went to Bodenheim's funeral, but not one person followed the wife's coffin. After that, Joan's story was one long series of more or less sordid affairs and unfortunate passions. She spent two years at Yale: more unfortunate passions. Although she was a brilliant student, people shied away from her because she was so vehement and excitable, as well as being mixed up with Communists and Trotskyites. Finally she came to Paris. That was how she had managed to be at my lecture, interrupt me and then write to me. We had dinner at the Falstaff. A half-crazed woman selling flowers came in singing and writhed about on the floor, to the great amusement of the customers. I advised Joan to go back to America, to stop keeping a diary, to think about something besides herself, and to read instead of talk. I also advised her to write, it seems to me that she could: something does 'come across', and strongly, in that extravagant diary of hers. She doesn't dare; she wants to work in a factory so she can be 'close to the working classes'. But I think writing is the only way she's going to find of defeating her solitude. She had on a black velvet dress with a rather pretty blue brooch, she'd had her bangs curled. 'I'm not *ugly*, I'm just *plain*,' she told me. She's going back to America in August. I'll be surprised if she does decide to become a writer.

Stopped in at Gallimard's this morning. Chatted for an hour and a half with Jacques Lanzmann at the Deux Magots. He told me about his trip to Mexico, Cuba, Haiti and San Domingo. He assured me that in Santiago de Cuba he had seen men hanged by the balls, and a tiger that was given the corpses to eat. But he's a poet. Every day the Batista-controlled newspapers publish pictures of the people he's had tortured and killed: more than a hundred each day. It made Claude Julien sick, and he'd been tortured himself during the Resistance. They found a way of getting out into the *maquis*, hoping to do a story on Castro and the rebel army. They were arrested an hour before they were due to leave. They had the bright idea of saying to the general (who is not averse to castrating prisoners with his own hands): 'We have had problems similar to yours in Algeria, so we thought we'd come and see how you coped with them.' Thanks to his papers, Julien was able to get back to Havana, whereas Jacques was put on a plane to Haiti.

Yesterday evening, the Committee of Public Safety in Algiers delivered itself of an incendiary declaration. Did Salan approve it or not? After some hesitation, De Gaulle finally decided to say that he was displeased.

Corrected my proofs and took notes at Sartre's. He's as happy as I am about starting for Venice. It's impossible for me to start work till I'm settled there. I had the impulse three weeks ago, but it suddenly stopped short.

Jules Moch (*En retard d'une guerre*) divides the history of destruction into epochs: individual, artisan, small-scale, large-scale, quasi-universal. Why am I (Sartre is the same) so little affected by the atomic threat? Perhaps because we can do absolutely nothing about it; all one can do is think about it, an idle occupation, especially when the problems in Algeria are so real and urgent, and concern us so directly.

Friday 13 June

Very friendly letter from a twenty-year-old girl student. At the moment, everything seems to be encouraging me to be narcissistic: Joan's diary, heaps of friendly letters, Gennari's book about me, my own memories as I go through my *Memoirs*, correcting proof. It has all made me decide to go on with my autobiography; Sartre said again that in any case I've already gone far enough for the attempt to be legitimate. I'll get down to it in Italy then. Usual contingent days before a departure; errands, mail, enormous bundles of proofs to correct. I've borrowed Monique Nathan's *Virginia Woolf* from V. Leduc; now that I've read her *Diary of a Writer* I wanted to have another look at the extraordinary faces of this woman – what a lonely face!

Malraux and his 'psychological shock'; complete insanity.

Monday 16 June – Milan

Suddenly, a completely new viewpoint: holiday. I woke up on Saturday at 6.30 in the morning, and what was stopping me from leaving right then? I left. To dive back into solitude, into freedom, as in the days of my walking tours – what rejuvenation! A beautiful morning. I know that road through the Morvan by heart, it's sign-posted with my memories. . . . Annecy too is a memory, from further back; after twenty years, I still recognized its canal, the streets with their arcades, the little restaurants at the edge of the water. I ate dinner in the old town and drank a Scotch on the lake as I read Hlasko's *Eighth Day of the Week*. I love starting off early in the morning, before the curtain rises. Pretty road, still deserted, along the side of the lake, and gradually the villages filled up with people in their Sunday clothes. On the Little Saint Bernard there was snow, and even some skiers slalom-racing. Seeing the snow and the mountain scenery made me a little nostalgic, because all that is lost forever now: the long walks, ten or twelve hours, between six and nine thousand feet or even higher, sleeping in tents or barns – I loved it all so much. Lunch at Saint-Vincent. 'How are things in France?' my hostess asked me. 'It depends which side you're on. It depends whether you like generals or not,' I answered. To take advantage of the sun, I stopped in a meadow where I had a superb landscape on every side of me, a dilapidated castle far away on my right, another off on the left, and buried in the high grass I finished Hlasko's book: a lot of vodka, very little love, because there was nowhere to go indoors and make love, a general atmosphere of sarcasm produced by the author's dissatisfaction with the world and with himself as well; cleverly written, but nothing more. I drove through a few more little towns bubbling with Sunday spirits and paved with yellow pebbles, then came the Autostrada and the Piazza della Scala.

Six in the evening. I had absolutely nothing to do, which was rather disconcerting but pleasant too. I drank two gin fizzes in the hotel bar; they're still as good as ever. I remember the same bar in 1946, how luxurious it seemed to me! That was a real second youth, even more head-turning than the first. I was thinking of those past days as I wandered out into the streets of Milan, tepid, idle, almost empty: Sunday evening. All the Italian women were wearing shirt dresses, some made for them, some off the rack, all, in my opinion, regrettable. New skyscrapers, new blocks of apartments – things change quickly in Italy. The Autostrada had changed since the year before, with that enormous bridge that joins it to the city.

Sartre arrived this morning at half past eight; we read the newspapers in the Café della Scala. Marvellous Italy! One slips into the atmosphere immediately. All Milan is talking about a great artistic drama: a madman, who calls himself 'an anachronic painter', yesterday morning at the Brera attacked Raphael's *Marriage of the*

Virgin with a hammer. One of the guards managed to keep the destruction from becoming total, but traces of the 'sacrilege' will always remain, a fact which has apparently thrown the entire world into a state of consternation. There isn't much about France in today's papers, but at the hairdresser's I found an issue of *Oggi* with a very amusing article called 'The Gaullist's Ten Commandments'; it drew a parallel between the present events in France and those in Italy during 1922; it's our turn to have a taste of Fascism, and they find it rather entertaining. The Left is laughing too, but they're worried; a right-wing dictatorship in France is a serious danger to Italy too.

This morning we wandered around Milan, then lunched with the Mondadoris at the Ristorante della Scala. He has scarcely changed in twelve years, still looks like a swashbuckling pirate; she's blonde now, but still has the same smile, the same unaffected manner, the same charm. He's begun writing poems, *engagé* poems, because he's left-wing. We talked about Hemingway. M. said that at Cortina, he was still drinking as usual, but that he was in a state of terror about his liver, his heart, and the idea that drink might kill him. One day, after a meal, he got hiccups. He called his doctor in a state of panic. 'You must use the elevator,' the doctor told him. So H. went up and down, up and down, six times, supported on one side by the doctor and on the other by Mondadori. The hiccups stopped. He pulled down his green eyeshield, and went off to bed.

We went to see the exhibition of ancient Lombard art; nothing particularly good in it, except for a big altarpiece. Sartre got annoyed: 'It's all military art! This is the sort of painting you get when a country is ruled by soldiers!' (Mondadori said, with slightly ironical sympathy: 'For twenty years now, we've had neither art nor literature. . . .')

We ate dinner at dusk in the Piazza del Duomo, relaxed, relieved at having escaped from France. Sartre said that he hadn't felt so calm for a long time.

Tuesday 17 – Venice

All the same, I still have bad dreams; I'm eager to wake up in the morning.

We left a little before ten in the morning; blue-grey sky, sunny, damp weather: north Italy. Lunch in Padua. We took our coffee in a café reputed to be the largest in the world. I bought a newspaper. On the front page: Nagy shot, also Malester and two others. 'We mustn't buy any more newspapers!' said Sartre, his calm suddenly shattered.

Venice; for the tenth time, or is it the twelfth? Pleasantly familiar. 'Canal closed – work in progress.' We turned off down canals we'd never seen before, so narrow it was almost impossible to pass. Charming rooms at the Cavaletto. Sartre ordered 'three teas', and settled down to work. Festy has sent me some proofs; I went to the Piazza San Marco, but there was too much music; I made myself comfortable on the bank of the canal and corrected forty pages; now I've come back here. The sky is pale with a slight wash of pink, there is a faint murmur coming up from the gondola moorings and the quays. I must get back to work tomorrow or I'll begin to droop and pine.

Wednesday 18 June

The big headlines of the Italian newspapers read: LE MANI SPORCHE. No one talks about anything except the execution of Nagy and Malester. Why? We discuss it endlessly without reaching any conclusions. It's sinister as far as France is concerned because the Communists are going to be even more isolated, the Left more demoralized, and Gaullism strengthened. The counterdemonstrators won't be feeling so enthusiastic today. And just when Sartre was trying to forget politics for a few days!

Long letter from Lanzmann; he was dazzled by Siberia, and the Koreans got him drunk on ginseng. He heard about De Gaulle's investiture on the Okinawa radio.

Friday 20 June

I'm very pleased with my room, with the ripples of light and shade moving across the ceiling and the *battie-becco* of the gondoliers. But until this morning I've been working badly, done nothing but read, and been tired. This morning I decided to take the plunge. I ought to make myself write ten pages of rough draft every day. Then at the end of the vacation I'd have something to work on, a nice bundle of 'rubbish' I might then make something of. There are so many memories to be assembled that I can't see any other way of going about it. I've read *L'Invitée* from cover to cover and made notes of what I thought about it now. I discovered things in it that I've said again almost word for word in my *Memoirs*, and others which recur in *The Mandarins*. Yes – and there's nothing discouraging in the fact – no writer ever writes anything except *his* books.

We went to see San Rocco again, and the church there and the Accadèmia. I compared what I saw with what Sartre had to say last year about Tintoretto.

Apparently almost nothing happened on 18 June, except for a few brawls with the Fascists in Ajaccio, Pau, Marseilles.

Saturday 21 June

Received some letters. One of them from a Roman woman, married, mother of two grown children, once an opponent of Fascism and now a member of the Communist Party, in despair over Nagy's execution and wondering what point there is in living: nothing to do, powerless to affect the world by her actions. There are so many people who write to me and say: 'It's terrible to be a woman!' I wasn't wrong when I wrote *The Second Sex*, in fact I was even more right than I thought at the time. A series of extracts from the letters I have received since that book came out would make a very moving document.

Yesterday, at the Correr Museum, we saw an Antonello da Messina, not particularly good, but certainly concrete proof of what Sartre had told me: that he was the link between Vivarini and Giorgione's *Tempest*, and even more definitely between Bellini's first and second styles. Our tastes haven't really changed much in twenty-five years; I still experience the same astonished admiration in front of the Cosimo Turas and remember my surprise when I first came upon them years ago.

We're settling down into a rhythm here. Up at 9.30, long breakfast with the newspapers in the Piazza San Marco. Work till 2.30. A snack. Sightseeing or a museum. Work from five till nine. Dinner. A Scotch at Harry's Bar. A last Scotch at midnight on the Piazza, when it's finally free of all the musicians, the tourists, the pigeons, and despite the chairs on the café terraces regains the tragic beauty Tintoretto captured in his *Abduction of Saint Mark*.

Yesterday afternoon I corrected an enormous bundle of proofs sent by Festy; for once one of my books is giving me pleasure to re-read. Unless I'm mistaken, it should be a success with young girls who are having problems with their family and religion, and aren't yet liberated enough to liberate themselves. Also, I think I've really got my new book started at last.

Newspapers from Paris. In his *Bloc-Notes*, Mauriac has reached the stage of eulogizing Guy Mollet! Letters from Paris. The meeting of the Committee of the 6th Arrondissement, at which Reggiani read out Sartre's piece, was a success on 17 June; more particularly, there was an ovation for Sartre after the first few sentences, and an even bigger one at the end. (There were almost seven hundred people there, at the Sociétés Savantes hall.) Henri Lefebvre has been excluded from the Party for a year because he joined the 'Club de Gauche'.

How pretty it was, as we sat in the Piazza San Marco last night, that single *oeil-de-boeuf* lit up under the eaves, amid the vast expanse of all those flat façades, and that man's silhouette inside it. He was just looking; it was as though he were unable to tear himself away from the sight of the Piazza at night. Suddenly the light went out, so unexpectedly that Sartre and I both said together: 'Oh! It was like a shooting star.'

Sunday 22 June

Yes, I think I'm off to a good start, and for at least two years. In one sense it makes me feel secure. That good little schoolgirl is still there inside me, worrying if I 'sit doing nothing' for a week or two. A trip is a kind of activity, so I can give myself up to it without guilt. But in Paris I was just drifting, and I blamed myself for that. All the same, I haven't been completely wasting my time. Apart from writing this diary and correcting my proofs, I've amassed material for my book, re-read my old novels and letters, jotted down some memories. I think I really will get through my ten pages a day now. There's something disheartening about doing it all so messily, but I can't afford to hold myself back by *writing* a single page before I've got the whole canvas blocked out. This is the way I worked on *America Day by Day*; though not on the *Memoirs* – those I wrote in little sections.

Tuesday 24 June

On Sunday afternoon we went out towards the Arsenal; there was a crowd on the Fundamenta Nuova, but no tourists; they were Italians who had come to watch the regatta. Boats, canoes, gondolas, packed with people, clustering around great posts with green decorations painted around the top. Everywhere in the green lagoon – exactly the same green as the trees – there were processions of gondolas, and gondoliers, dressed in dazzling white, bent over their poles, their buttocks modelled just as one sees them in the pictures of Carpaccio. A few russet or purplish sails; two or three yachts in the distance. We left before the regatta began. The streets were so peaceful: the provinces. Then little by little – rather like cars on the road as one approaches a big town – there were more and more people walking, suddenly we were in a crowd, the *Führungen*, peasants in Tyrolean hats, real rustics straight off their mountains (one of them with an enormous red beard), fat German women in transparent dresses and straw hats, and then we were back in the Piazza San Marco; the pigeons, the photographers, the city.

After dinner at La Fenice, where the owner insisted on taking us on a tour of the kitchen, we went to Harry's Bar. As we came out, two Italian men accosted Sartre very graciously. They invited us to go and have a drink at Ciro's. 'Turn to the left; with Sartre, one must always go left,' they said as they showed us the way. One of them was a tiny sculptor; the other, a man of about forty, with a curiously mobile, rather shifty face, said he was a 'scientist'; he works with microbes and runs a laboratory. 'Me, I'm just someone whose job it is to make people piss'; he's called 'Charming' he informed us. He once read *The Wall* and found it so good he doesn't want to read anything else Sartre has written. Like many Italians, he enjoys playing on words; he uses a nice expression that I didn't know: *faire du casino* (make a disturbance, a row). They bought us Venetian white wine while they talked on charmingly about Venice, how it manages to be so provincial and still support a large working-class population. 'No one works so hard as the Venetians,' he assured us. 'Besides, there are 300,000 of them in Milan.' We finished the evening on the dance floor of the Martini Tavern, almost deserted because by then it was two in the morning.

They arranged to meet us at eleven the following evening in Harry's. By then, we said to each other: 'It's going to be a hell of a bore; for one thing we had a few drinks in us last night; and also they're bound to bring other people along.' We weren't wrong there, but it turned out quite differently from what we expected.

'Charming' was eating with a dark-haired man at a round table;

he came over to us. 'He's an American, a ghastly bore, who's just arrived from New York.' He was in fact an Italian who had a business in America, but he was from Genoa, and the Genoese, C. explained, are not Italians. The 'American' spoke not a word of French; the conversation began badly; enter an Italian woman, blonde, heavy but with beautiful pale eyes, very much made up, more or less dotty about the 'American'; she didn't speak French either. They were all making fun of her because a burglar had recently tied his boat up alongside her house, slipped in through a window and stolen all her brassieres and panties. 'The tools of her trade,' said C., who has a touch of the pederast's misogyny about him (he is obsessed with pederasty). He suggested animatedly that we should go and have a drink at a very beautiful new hotel on the Giudecca, where his friend wanted to check in; we agreed, and got into the hotel's private launch; it was charming crossing the canal on a beautiful night, starry for once, with an orange crescent of moon that looked as though it had been stuck up there just for the tourists; in the distance, we could see the lights of the Lido, bright yellow, and the Doges' Palace floating away. The hotel had a garden going right down to the lagoon, really lovely. But we wandered about uncertainly in the enormous vestibules; the barman had 'shut up shop' we were told by the porter. The 'American' went up to pick a room and we sat down to wait for him. The sculptor telephoned; we set off again, and as we stepped out of the launch once more, Sartre and I agreed that we felt like people in one of Pavese's stories: all these enthusiastic schemes perpetually falling flat. The sculptor was waiting for us with some of his friends; we went out onto the Campo della Fenice, where there is a pleasant café set in the middle of greenery. C. ordered us some strange drinks: a concoction of mint and grappa, a Venetian speciality consumed by the Venetian worker, or so he claimed, at five in the morning, and mixtures of pernod and whisky. I stuck to straight grappa. Poor Sartre had by now become prey to a short young man with starry eyes who worked in films; he had collaborated on the scenario of *Le amice*; he said to me: 'You're famous here, people in Venice adore *The Mandarins*,' and C. asked me: 'Was that you, *The Mandarins*?' Though he hadn't in fact read it. 'Yes, now I think of it, one might expect you to be a writer,' he said, looking perplexed. Things seemed to have turned formal, the charm was broken. We said good night and went off in the direction of our usual hangout, a tavern on the little Piazza dei Leoni off Saint Mark's. The big Piazza was deserted; a red-haired woman was sobbing and screaming; she had one hand wrapped in gauze and was making a scene with two well-dressed characters who were obviously plain-clothes policemen; she was lying prostrate under one of the arcades; suddenly she left off weeping, leapt up after the two men and began protesting with wild gestures; all the neighbourhood whores came out of the shadows to see what was going on. Finally the redhead moved off, grumbling to herself. We sat down in front of two Scotches. A man came running out of a nearby café – quite well-dressed, middle-aged, Italian – followed by a waiter who was hitting him; the customer suddenly turned, seized a chair and brandished it; the waiter knocked him down. A tremendous outcry from the onlookers: 'No!' and they all rushed over to pull them apart. We were agreeably affected by this reaction; in France, people wouldn't have felt this impulse to interfere, they would have let them go on till they drew blood. The waiter was led back to his café; the customer walked off; two minutes later he was back, accompanied by two guards carrying sabres. We went and joined the group of idlers in front of the café (all Italians, because it was late). The waiter got irritated, he asked them to move on, saying in French: 'If you had any education, you wouldn't stand around.' 'Are you telling me I'm uneducated?' Sartre asked. The discussion looked as though it might become ugly, but the café owner, annoyed now, made the waiter go inside. A tall, dark-haired prostitute shouted after him in Italian: 'He's French and you've insulted him; that's not good manners!' We went back to our table. The Italian who'd been knocked down came over to the counter of our tavern and drank a coffee with an arrogant but chastened expression; he went away again. Two cleanly dressed bums with beautiful white hair and sharp faces helped the waiter of the nearby café take in his chairs while they listened to his account of the affair; he gave them a few coins; they divided them up and disappeared nonchalantly into the night. We left too, and suddenly found ourselves surrounded by three or four café waiters, among them the protagonist of the recent drama. He wanted to explain matters to Sartre; but the tone he took was so aggressive that the quarrel seemed more likely to be resumed than settled. 'That customer comes and makes trouble for us every single night,' said one of the waiters in defence of his colleague. The latter insisted: 'I wasn't attacking you, I was talking generally, to everybody.' 'But they were all Italians, and you spoke in French,' Sartre answered with a smile. They all laughed, and the waiter held out his hand with a smile. 'True. All right. I apologize.' The whole of this affair was conducted in a style quite peculiar to Italy.

Rain today, Venice melting in mist, the churches and palazzos deliquescing. A few gondoliers have swathed themselves in black capes.

De Gaulle is still negotiating Mollet's visit to Algeria; he wants a reassurance that he won't be forced to leave him behind in the cloakroom. Under pressure from Algiers, one of the radio reporters has been sacked and the staff in general has been overhauled; Delannoy is leaving. Nocher is back. More and more, Algiers is giving the orders.

Wednesday 25 June

The *Corriere della sera* found Malraux's press conference very amusing. Photographers, television cameras, big production number; Malraux spoke in the tones of some mystical preacher, and the four hundred journalists expressed surprise. Not many facts, said the Italian correspondent, but everyone learned a good deal about 'the psychological and choreographic style of the regime'. Malraux wants to make another Tennessee Valley out of Algeria, and send the three French Nobel Prize winners to investigate the prisons. As Sartre says: 'We've fallen out of cowardice into the symbol.'

Thursday 26 June

Letter from Lanzmann, admiration mixed with irritation. He says the Koreans are extraordinarily likeable, but that the official optimism there is worse than in China.

Legal proceedings have been instituted against *L'Observateur* and *L'Express.* At least we know where we are now as far as freedom of the press is concerned. And anyway, a comparison with the Italian newspapers makes it clear how much the French press censors itself, it's been castrated. The articles they're being prosecuted for are about Algeria, of course; among other things, there was an interview with an F.L.N. leader. However, Algiers is fuming; Malraux's press conference has infuriated them.

Monday 30 June

We revisited Torcello and saw the Carpaccios at San Giorgio again; we went up the campanile and the bells rang out in our ears. We visited the Biennale: a very bad Braque exhibition, a very lovely one of Wols; interesting sculptures by Pevsner. And we've had some charming evenings; to avoid meeting people, we've migrated from Harry's Bar to Ciro's, where a German pianist plays lovely old tunes. I was amused by two young Americans who sat side by side for hours on end without opening their mouths, but with their eyes perpetually starry and smiles on their lips, as though they just couldn't get over the fact that they're alive, that they're Americans, and that the rest of the world exists. A big, pasty Belgian decided, without knowing who he was, to make a portrait of Sartre; it was pitiful. He had just arrived from Brussels in the company of a homosexual count obviously a victim of one of those terrible love agonies homosexuals suffer from so often: dark, empty eyes, haunted by some distant image; great difficulty in regaining his presence of mind when the other man spoke to him.

This evening, our last, we went to Harry's to say good-bye to 'Charming' and the sculptor. They were drinking white wine with a rich Swedish arms manufacturer and his wife. He touched my heart because he had bought *The Mandarins* and spent a whole night reading 137 pages of it; he told me enthusiastically that he thought it was 'even better than *Gone With the Wind*'. He said: 'Naturally, I'm a snob; what else have I got?' He gestured towards the Swedish woman. 'She loathes *The Mandarins*.' Then she, not at all embarrassed: 'Yes, there's too much politics in it; I loathe politics.' Then she added graciously: 'Besides, I'm a conservative. I have a husband, an official lover and a great deal of money; so of course I'm conservative.' Then, with a slightly worried air, to the arms manufacturer: 'I do have a great deal of money, don't I?' He shook his head and she laughed. 'No! Then I'm ruined.' She attacked C.: 'You're such a pig.' To which he replied with animation: 'Yes, but such a human one!'

Tuesday 1 July

Left Venice. But first we breakfasted on the Rialto, on the Grand Canal, and read the papers. De Gaulle has set out with Mollet for the Algerian 'front'. The business of the Perpignan teacher who killed one of his pupils seems quite clear. Perpignan is full of 'Africans' from Morocco and Tunisia; they are completely Fascist and have formed a sort of 'Committee of Public Safety' against the teachers who went on strike in May and against all left-wing teachers in general. The Amiels were left-wing, and life was systematically made impossible for them; in class by constant riots, at home by fireworks in their letter-box; they had seriously threatened to kill him. A few days beforehand, when some pupils came to make trouble in front of his house, he had fired over their heads. This time, the rumpus outside his windows had been even worse than usual; he had fired on them. And now the teachers are brawling among themselves in the school courtyard, Fascists against anti-Fascists. Bianca had been telling me about the tension, even in Paris, between pupils and teachers in the 'high-class' *lycées* like Pasteur, Janson, etc.

Stopped at Ferrara. Arrived at Ravenna at six. It's pleasant in the falling dusk, but there's nothing noisier than these little Italian towns with their motorbikes and their scooters. It's already six years since I was last here, driving for the first time on a long journey, just having met Lanzmann.

Wednesday 2 July

How beautiful Spoleto is, with its streets all ramps and stairways, and paved with little pebbles. There are big lanterns hung from black façades and so much shadow that the spiders think they're in a barn and spin immense webs between the telegraph wires. Our hotel overlooks a little square paved with irregularly shaped stones, surrounded with greenery, with a little fountain sobbing in the middle, just like a private garden. The scent of lime trees in bloom mingles with a vague odour of leatherwork and incense. All around are the dry hills, the blue distances of Italy.

I haven't been to look at the Ravenna mosaics again, I didn't particularly want to and I no longer feel I have a duty to perform; on trips, I only do what I feel like doing now. I enjoyed revisiting Urbino where we lunched and drank coffee under the arcades. The waiter asked Sartre: 'Are you French? Are you a writer? Are you Jean-Paul Sartre?' He claimed he recognized him 'from the newspapers'. But a few moments later three young Italian teachers came over and asked Sartre for his autograph; it was they who had discovered his presence.

In Spoleto, Alleg's *La tortura* is on sale. There are posters on the walls: De Gaulle, *il dittatore*, Mollet, *il traditore*, Pflimlin, *il codardo*. And the caption: THIS IS WHAT ANTICOMMUNISM LEADS TO: FASCISM ... BEWARE OF THE POPE! Marvellous blue sky and the pleasure of coming back to Italy again: Venice isn't Italy.

In the evening, I walked with Sartre through the streets smelling of lime-flower tea. The big lanterns were all lit up.

Friday 4 July

Yesterday we saw the streets, the Duomo and the superb bridge with its tall arches stretching across a narrow and rather shallow valley. Why this bridge? In front of the hotel, the waiters were putting out tables and lamps, they were painting the barricades violet for some celebration or other. We left for Rome. We could see Saint Peter's and the Monte Mario from twelve miles away.

It was raining and the afternoon was not very enjoyable, despite the pleasure of staying in the Piazza Rotonda at the Hotel Senato. When I nap for an hour in the afternoon, I am always seized by panic just before I wake up: we're going to be seventy years old, and then we'll die, it's a fact, it's certain, it's not just a nightmare! It's as though waking life were a too-rosy dream with death hidden in the misty distance, and in sleep I reach the truth, the heart of the matter.

Today is very beautiful, very blue, I feel the happiness of being in Rome for a long time take hold of me again, and the desire to write. And I write. A long letter from Lanzmann, torn between his love for the Koreans and the irritation of having to travel as part of a delegation.

De Gaulle is coming back from Algeria. He did not receive the Committee of Public Safety; they are furious in Algiers. But the ambiguity persists, the symbols, the disputes of terminology. There's an article in *Le Littéraire* by Mauriac, in which he exalts De Gaulle and talks with rancorous affection about Malraux, who has fallen in love with power and been given a 'ministry to nibble at'.

Sartre is happy in Rome and is enjoying the play he's settled down to. I still haven't read any of it. Evidently Simone Berriau is going crazy in Paris waiting for it.

When I feel the desire to write these days, I get on with my book; when the desire leaves me, even this diary bores me. I don't know if I'm really giving it a chance.

Tuesday 8 July

Huge headlines in the newspapers: SOUSTELLE REPLACES MALRAUX.

The Socialists are rallying more and more. Mollet still hasn't given an inch.

No, I really haven't anything to say at the moment in this diary. Rome is empty of tourists, not too hot, blue, ideal. Same daily rhythm as last year. At about ten, long breakfast out in the Piazza, still full of rustics in floppy hats; work till two or three; we eat a sandwich on a terrace and go for a little walk. Work again till five. We dine at Pancracio's, with spaghetti *à la carbonara* and some Barolo. And then we drink a little bit too much whisky in the Piazza Santi Apostoli or the Piazza del Popolo. And it's all so familiar, so happy, that there's no need for words.

Friday 11 July

And perhaps there are other reasons, too, for my not having anything to say. Yes, Rome is a happy place, and my work, though it's a bit sickening, interests me, and Sartre's is difficult but it absorbs him. Only there's France. As we drank our last Scotch in the Via Francesco Crispi, watching the hostesses at the neighbouring dance-hall (and the very funny girl, all in pink and very feminine one evening, and the next day in jeans and fascinated by Sartre's shoes), we admitted to each other that our hearts were not light. We put on a show of living a humdrum, peaceful life, but nothing really tastes quite right.

Beautiful storm yesterday over Rome, and in the evening the Via Veneto was still wet and almost deserted. I don't like Fellini all that much; but it's impossible not to see the Via Veneto through the shots of *Cabiria*.

Florence wrote in a friendly way in *Le Monde* about the extracts in *Les Temps Modernes* from *Memoirs of a Dutiful Daughter*. I do so hope that people will like the book, and it would help me in writing the next one.

The Socialists have asked De Gaulle to do away with the Algeria Committees; as the *Corriere della sera* put it, it's very significant and of no importance whatever. Silence, resignation throughout the French press. *L'Express* and *L'Observateur* both call attention despairingly to this sickening apathy, and the scarcely veiled, quiet, inevitable rising tide of all the things we hate.

'Before the invention of window glass, it was impossible to be a genius outside those regions where the olive tree grows.' That is the sort of observation I find enchanting. I read Sauvy's things with passion; now I am reading Fourastié's, which amuse me a great deal. Though he irritates me too, with his Mme Express-Technocrat side. Frightening vision of technocratic man; the other side of his optimism is 'the Organization Man'. These tertiary towns in which Le Corbusier, Francastel, Fourastié, etc., want to make people live are actually 'suburbs'; American residential districts. They give me the shudders. Space, light, air, order – fair enough; but what do they mean by 'harmony'? Doesn't 'man' (which man?) need aggressiveness in his environment as much as calm, doesn't he need resistance, the unexpected, and to feel when he looks about him that the world is not just a big kitchen garden? Must we really choose between hovels and high-status subdivisions?

What a beautiful day! We lunched at the Tor del Carbone off the Appian Way. Cypresses, umbrella pines and bricks under a pale sky, and that endless road, for even in a car the eye still takes its measure as it was when you travelled it on horseback or on foot to far-off Pompeii: straight between the straight cypresses, it suggests a flat and limitless country to the mind. I loved it today with almost the same intensity of feeling as at twenty-five.

This evening, people in Paris are going to dance, with the most magnificent fireworks, the biggest orchestras that have been seen for years. And last year was a mockery: a Socialist government forbidding the Fourteenth of July balls. But this 'national renascence' that's being celebrated tomorrow is sickening. I used to love our Fourteenth of Julys so much. I'm glad I'm not in Paris. I'd have been grinding my teeth every night.

Amusingly enough, across the narrow street, my bathroom window frames my neighbour's window opposite exactly, while his forms a frame for his television screen; he is sitting alone on a chair, and I can see perfectly what he is watching. This evening, a woman in a spotted dress is meditating, alone, against the white background; then she says a word and there's applause. It's one of the *lascia-raddopia* programmes we're always reading such impassioned accounts of in the newspapers; in Italy it's really a national sport.

The storm has cleared the air; it's had a similar effect on me, too. I feel relaxed now for no good reason. So much the worse for the Fourteenth of July balls; just now I was in the Piazza Navona, there was the dark blue sky of the Roman night over the dark red houses, with the *oeil-de-boeuf* windows lit up, and all the people strolling about – a moment of perfection. Tonight, once more, life sinks its teeth into my heart.

Tuesday 15 July

From now on the Fourteenth of July will also be a day of national celebration for Iraq: revolution in Baghdad! Which smashes the Baghdad Pact to pieces, Iraq supporting the 'Arab Republic', Nasser in the seventh heaven, and the rebels in Beirut likewise. I imagine the F.L.N. is jubilant about it, too.

Meanwhile, there's been a parade on the Champs-Élysées. De Gaulle didn't watch it because he would have had to take third place in the stand: still that acute sense of *grandeur*! Malraux delivered an address in the Place de l'Hôtel-de-Ville, but the 'people of Paris' he was purportedly speaking to were in fact Moslem and French soldiers under orders to be there. One interesting incident. Several young Algerian soldiers, brought to Paris by force as a symbol of fraternization, as they passed the stand, instead of saluting Coty, pulled green and white banners out from under their shirts and waved them defiantly. That night the Algerians killed eleven people, six of them Moslem collaborators.

Another long letter from Lanzmann. There isn't a single man in Korea who isn't either a widower or an orphan, he writes; many of them weep as they tell their story. The Americans completely destroyed towns and villages just for the fun of it, and the Koreans hate them for it. They figure in all the plays and all the films there as villains with cardboard noses, and the booing that greets their appearances is by no means a mere convention. He watched a parade that was much more rigid and military than the one in China on 1 October, according to Gatti who saw both. They are still tense with the feeling of the war; it is the peculiar feature of the country, this perpetual background of war.

Sartre was seeing people yesterday evening. I went to the movies, a bad American film about the crimes committed in the name of journalism. There was a trailer for *Paths of Glory*. It seems to be rather good and I scarcely have the courage to go see it. The present is bad enough without going and making myself ill watching the horrors of the 1914–18 war and all that military beastliness. As Georges Bataille used to say: 'I have my schedule for suffering.'

While lunching with Sartre, met the Merleau-Pontys, very lively and gay on their way to Naples. A little Italian girl, very shy, planted herself firmly in front of our table and began showering me with compliments; which is always enjoyable. (How enjoyable? etc. That's one of the points I must go into in my next book.)

If I were like the famous writer in Fourastié's book, who couldn't work because of the noise two children made with their roller skates, I should be in a very bad way indeed. This piazza is the noisiest in Rome: scooters, motorbikes, cars braking savagely with loud squeals, horns blaring despite its being forbidden, clanging scaffolding, shouts, the lot. But it doesn't bother me. The women in Rome all look terrible in their shirt dresses, which are even more of an eye-sore along the Via Veneto in the evening than they are on the housewives around here in the morning. The big dress designers have given their homosexual sadism full rein, from the look of it.

I'm reading Jones' book on Freud; what's astonishing is the curious mixture of conscience and frivolity, naïveté and sagacity in this 'adventurer'. He and his cocaine were fundamentally responsible for the death of at least one man, and the story of Fliess is horrible. Freud had 'guilt feelings', but he was guilty. Admirable story about Breuer. He was treating Anna O. (or rather, as Camille would say, 'she was treating herself with him', for it was she who discovered the *catharsis*). He fell in love with her without admitting it to himself, but his wife became aware of what was happening. He decided to call a halt to the treatment and informed Anna, who was in any case almost cured, that he intended to do so; the evening of the break, a telephone call revealed that she had suffered a complete relapse; she was hysterically miming a childbirth. Breuer understood what this meant, got his hat, fled to Venice with his wife and got her with child – a daughter who killed herself sixty years later in New York. Meanwhile Anna became the first social worker in Europe; she saved numbers of Jewish children during the pogroms just after 1900.

[441]

On 25 May I set to work on this book with a light heart; now I'm having difficulty with it and beginning to have doubts; perhaps it's because of the heat – 95°; and I dashed off four hundred pages of appallingly sloppy stuff without stopping; that takes the pleasure out of it. I'll go on for another month, dragging material out of my head and stockpiling it, then when I get back to Paris, I'll just have to use it somehow to revive a little interest in myself, a little enthusiasm. I still don't begin to know what the tone of the book is going to be like, or how it'll be planned.

According to *Paese sera*, the Americans have invaded Lebanon; 'landed' in the Lebanon is the word the *Messagero* uses. Nuances.

The young Moslems with the F.L.N. banners have been apprehended; there were four of them apparently. According to *Le Monde*, they shouted: 'Down with French Algeria.' The French have killed Bellounis,[1] who was accused of having shot four hundred of his men; the Italian newspapers say the French have killed Bellounis *and* the four hundred men.

Jones doesn't explain very well what Freud's own particular neurosis was, nor how he got rid of it. Perhaps the fact that Freud's daughter is still alive embarrasses him, but there are certain questions he doesn't ask: Freud's relationship with his wife, for example. It's easy enough to say that they were 'excellent'; but Freud's depressions and migraines are either directly linked to his domestic life or they are not. Which? After all, he was an extremely vital man; witness his passionate love of travel. Monogamous, all right; but why, exactly? Jones avoids the question. On the other hand, what he does describe in great detail, and very well, is Freud's work, so different from that of both the philosopher and the scientist. The most moving moment is the one where he discovers his mistake about hysteria. He had believed that all his women patients had been 'seduced' by their fathers and expounded this theory to his colleagues, despite general reprobation on their part; then he reflected that there could hardly be so many incestuous fathers, that his own had not been, even though his two sisters displayed symptoms of hysterical disorders; he realized that his patients had invented it all. What a slap in the face! What a shock!

1. Bellounis had made overtures to France on behalf of the M.N.A. and organized a 'Popular Army of Liberation' in opposition to the A.L.N.

It was only after a terrible struggle that he mustered the courage to continue practising, and he scarcely earned any money at all for a long while afterwards. And yet he wrote to Fliess that he had a feeling it was a victory rather than a defeat; this unanimous lie appeared to him pregnant with meaning, and opened a new path. And it was in fact the starting point of his discovery of infantile sexuality. 'I am an adventurer, a conquistador, and not a scientist,' he used to say, regretfully sometimes. It is moving to watch these concepts that have become so scholastic, mechanical – transference for example – reveal themselves in such vital experiences. The first time one of his women patients flung her arms around Freud's neck, he remembered the story of Breuer and suddenly sensed the existence of the transference principle. In one of his letters he gives a ravishing description of the Piazza Colonna and of the Italians; he was staying at the Hotel Milano. His face, in his photographs, grew more and more intense as he advanced in years, and also more and more closed, and above all sad.

Joan fights against her tendency to idolize people by searching out the weaknesses in her 'heroes'; but if, on the contrary, one starts by taking a 'hero' as a man, then one begins to admire him for what he has gone on to do despite his weaknesses.

I have read through this diary and found it entertaining. I ought to go on with it, but taking more trouble over it. Everything that 'goes without saying' has been passed over in silence; for example, our reactions after Nagy's execution.

Why are there some things I want so much to say and others I want to bury? Because they are too precious (sacred perhaps) to be written about. As though death alone, only oblivion, could suffice for certain realities.

If only I could write when I'm drunk; or be more excited when I write! There ought to be a way of combining the two!

Rain, Roman rain; it's beautiful outside the shutters, at midnight, with the grumbling thunder and all that noise of water. Storms are becoming to Rome. I have opened my shutters; the sky is full of waterfalls, from the dome of the Pantheon, from the roofs, from the gutters. There are three black silhouettes, tiny, motionless, with their shirts making white splashes, under the sudden immensity of the Pantheon colonnades; now they are moving, walking calmly across the black and white porch while the water and the lightning rage around them. It's a beautiful sight. The street is becoming a torrent, a piece of paper is caught up in an eddy of wind, hovers, and is flattened against a wall. When the lightning flashes, it scatters strings of brilliants along the pavement. A powerful smell of the earth, suddenly, in this city of stone. The cars leave wakes behind them like boats. But suddenly there are no more cars, and the electric lights in the street have just gone off. There are people trying to leave the Sacristy; the waiter has opened an umbrella and there is the roar of the taxi starting up. And all the time, the men still there, alone, calm and unaccountable, tiny figures hardly moving, black and white against the black and white of the paving stones.

The storm dies down. A street sign lights up again: PIZZERIA. Last rumblings. A pink and blue man goes running by. It is one in the morning.

Friday 17 July

I always have this feeling when I begin a new book, that it's a gigantic, impossible undertaking. I forget the way work is done, how one gets from the first shapeless jottings to the final draft; I always feel that this time it's not coming off, that I'm not going to make it. And then, in one way or another, the book gets written; it's just a matter of time.

Sunday 17 August – Paris

Well, there's no doubt that I have a happy disposition. I enjoyed my vacation, but it's a pleasure all the same to find myself back in Paris, sitting in front of my desk, in this room invaded at the moment by all the souvenirs of the Far East that Lanzmann has scattered over the coverless divans. It's the first time in six years that I haven't spent the summer holidays with him, because of Korea. But I'm getting old. My desire to rush about all over the world has become decidedly blunted, the desire to work has increased. I begin to feel the sense of urgency Sartre has inside him all the time. How hot it was in Italy! My arms stuck to the table, and the words got gummed up inside the cells of my brain. I couldn't get them down into my pen. Here it's cool, almost too cool, and I've got at least eleven straight months of work ahead of me; it's going to seem long, but at the moment the thought encourages me. And Lanzmann tells me that people like the extracts from my *Memoirs* already published – that encourages me too.

It was because of the heat that I stopped keeping this diary for a month. It has to be written quickly, with a gaiety that keeps the hand skipping across the page. I was able to make myself work – I got through some sixty pages, which for me is a lot – but that drained me of the impulse to do anything else. This is my first morning back in Paris, and I'm starting it again.

Perhaps it was also the fact that there wasn't very much to say on Capri. This year we had delightful rooms in the Hotel de la Pineta I discovered the year before when I was living in the smoke from the kitchens of the Palma. There was a vast tiled room that looked cool, although it wasn't, a big terrace with deck chairs and tables; you could see the sea, pine trees, Monte Soláro, and for a whole week there was the most beautiful moonlight. I liked the crowing of the cocks in the morning. The island was full of the good smell of Mediterranean scrub, but there was an over-sweet scent of crushed strawberries lurking in some spots. Breakfast with Sartre at the *Salotto*, the newspapers, work from eleven-thirty to three or thereabouts, walk in the heat of the day, with a stop for something to eat; at the Metromania they had a delicious cake that brought back my childhood, and what a beautiful view! Work again till nine, and long evenings watching the people in the piazza, as we drank our Scotch. The five-and-dime-store aspect of the place had unfortunately been accentuated by the lamps hung up over the *Salotto*.

Was it because we were less lighthearted this year that we were more sensitive to the weaknesses of Capri? We were perpetually disheartened by the situation in France, which has fallen into such a state of apathy that I don't feel I even want to talk about it any more. And then, the previous year Sartre had been happily writing about Tintoretto, whereas at the moment his play is getting off to a slow start; he's not in the mood to write 'fiction' these days. He's only doing it because he's contracted to.

We saw the Clouzots briefly, and had dinner twice with Moravia, very amusing, relaxed, friendly; instead of discussing general ideas, he talked about himself, about Italy, and talked very well. Speaking about his accident, he admitted with disarming candour: 'Ah! I have accidents all the time, I drive very badly, I'm too nervous and I like to go fast; once, coming from Spoleto to Rome, the road was empty and I never went less than eighty-five the whole way, it was all right that time; but if it hadn't been . . .' In Rome he had once mistaken reverse for first and squashed two peasant women up against a wall; two days before he had almost crashed into a truck while driving a Cadillac belonging to a princess, and he braked so sharply that the car caught fire 'inside the wheels'. He agrees that Carlo Levi is more careful: 'But he has to get help from the attendant to get out of a parking lot; he can't manage reverse. And he never goes over twenty-five miles an hour.'[1] He's very funny when you get him on to the subject of his colleagues. He says that all the writers from the provinces have *one* thing to say, about their own region, something local, and after that they've got nothing left; whereas he has the whole of Rome (which is to say Italy, and mankind). The speed at which he works! He writes for two or three hours in the morning, never more, and he produces two short stories a month and a novel every two or three years! We talked to him about his early works. He told us a little about his life, in snatches, with much grace. He had a bone disease from the age of nine until he was sixteen, had hardly any schooling, wrote *The Time of Indifference* at twenty; it had a success in Italy greater than any book had had for a long time, and greater than any was to have since. For six years he felt empty; he wrote nothing. Then he wrote *Wheel of Fortune*; this second novel was not given *one line* of criticism in Italy because of Fascism: it was decadent literature, and one thing led to another until he was first forbidden to sign his newspaper articles and then to write them at all. He had inherited money, so he travelled abroad to escape Fascism: China, France, America. He spent several years on Capri with his wife, Elsa Morante. He talks about her with affection and respect, and considers her books to be the best contemporary Italian novels being written, but he seemed extremely alarmed when I said I'd like to meet her. It irritates him that she surrounds herself entirely with homosexuals. He claims that eighty per cent of the men in Rome have slept with other men. He talks about them almost enviously because their sexual adventures are so easily come by, and because they have such a gleeful gluttony for them; he quoted a remark made by P., one of Elsa Morante's friends: 'How many

1. A little later, in Rome, Carlo Levi told Sartre: 'Moravia? But you know he has many more accidents than he says. He has them every day. Only little ones, of course. They don't put them in the newspapers. It's his psycho-motor mechanism that doesn't work properly, the connexion between his head and his arm. He doesn't know what he's doing, he tries to shift into first and finds himself shooting off in reverse.'

people are there on the earth?' 'More than two billion.' 'That means there are more than a billion men I'll never sleep with!' He also tells charming stories about the Church, like all Italians. There was a Pope who had a real ambition to be a saint, a canonized saint; the Cardinals prayed for him: 'May the Lord open the eyes of Our Holy Father – or else close them.'

The pleasure of writing for the pleasure of writing; I am just writing whatever comes into my head. When we came back to our hotel, no matter what time it was, there was always one little pale waiter, fifteen years old, with a woman customer putting his apron straight for him one day; he was always there, morning and night. One day I asked him: 'Don't you ever sleep?' 'Sometimes,' he answered, without bitterness, without irony, in an absolutely matter-of-fact tone, as the English say. The next day I asked him: 'How long did you sleep last night?' 'Four hours.' 'And during the day?' 'An hour.' 'That's not much.' 'That's life, Madame.' I suppose he was content just eating well and being properly dressed: he was one of the privileged. Possibly even more heart-breaking was the waiter in a striped sweat shirt at the Capranica; the third evening we went there, he said to Sartre stammeringly: 'Factory? Me work . . .' He wanted to get work in a factory in France. He didn't like the job he was doing. 'Business not lovely tonight,' he said to us once very sadly; business was never lovely for him, except once, when he lit up suddenly: 'Oh! Tonight the bill is lovely!'

There was Lanzmann's lightning trip to see us: six hundred million Chinese, without counting the Koreans, suddenly invading the little island of Capri. I went with him to Naples where the civil airport was guarded by an army of American soldiers because it was covered with United States fighter planes in transit to Lebanon. Then the return with Sartre along the new Naples–Rome *corniche*; the pines and the Etruscan green of the Domitiana gave us both the feeling, at exactly the same moment, that we had suddenly been transported straight back to classical times. An evening in Rome with Merleau-Ponty, whom we bumped into near the Pantheon. Then Pisa. The Pisanos in the museum – the dancing woman without a head, and the woman hiding behind her dress; it was as though the marble had been immersed in a volcano, matter is tragic, and movement astounding.

Return with Sartre as far as Pisa, where he is meeting Michelle.

Inferno of the Pisa–Genoa road. And on the morning of 15 August, on the 'truck route' to Turin, hell again. Then the pleasure of driving, especially yesterday, Bourg to Paris in five and a half hours.

Sign of old age: distress at all leave-takings, all separations. And the sadness of memories, because I'm aware they're condemned to death.

Wednesday 24 August

Work. For two afternoons at the Bibliothèque Nationale I have been steeping myself in old copies of the *N.R.F.* and *Marianne*. It's amazing finding oneself back *before* events that now make up the past. I want more and more to write about old age. Envy of the youth of today, so much ahead of us at their age, and partly thanks to us. How undernourished we must have been! How rudimentary everything we were told about philosophy, economics, etc. An impression (unjust) that mankind wasted a great deal of time at my expense. And it's hard to keep the future as a dimension in one's life when one already feels one's been buried by those who are coming *after*.

The night before last, the F.L.N. committed a spectacular series of acts of violence in metropolitan France: gas storage tanks set alight in Marseilles, cops killed in Paris. De Gaulle was booed in Dakar and Guinea. I am reading Duverger and Sternberg's *Le Conflit du siècle*, which is as entertaining as a thriller. First fine day after all the rain and cold; it's warm, golden, rather autumnal and sumptuous.

The Committee of Resistance against Fascism is getting up a big counter-demonstration for 4 September; how will it go off? Lanzmann is doing a lot for it and tells me that the preparatory campaign is being very well organized. He has spoken at many meetings, in Paris and in the provinces.

Monday 1 September

Telephone call from Sartre. He's seen Servan-Schreiber in Rome. He's doing three articles for *L'Express* which will appear on the 11th, 18th and 25th.

Thursday 4 September

There's a vaguely sinister feeling about this morning. Sartre still in Italy, Lanzmann not back yet from Montargis where he spoke yesterday evening, Paris seems empty. The workmen bang so loud on the wall that it's impossible to sleep after eight and difficult to work; anyway I'm too nervous. Pale blue sky with yellow clouds above the yellowing trees; it's fall now among the graves in the cemetery of Montparnasse. I feel panicky about this afternoon. No, not fear (though there may be some of that too), apprehensive because it may be a failure; I dread having to swallow a whole hour of that sickening ceremony without there being anything to show for it. Yes, they're bringing Pétain back to life; a hundred picked workers will be awarded the Légion d'Honneur, and Malraux will explain that De Gaulle has taken up the left-wing challenge and that he will dare to speak in the Place de la République. I went through it the day before yesterday evening with Lanzmann. It's been arranged in such a way – with stands which will be packed with guests, cops, veterans, etc. – that the public will be miles away and won't even be able to hear us. Yesterday it was announced that the local authorities have forbidden the carrying of placards. At the Committee they have given us yellow papers with a NO at the top; we're to bring them out when De Gaulle appears. Instructions vary from committee to committee, though. Evelyne's isn't coming till five instead of four, and they're going to unroll their banners right away, which is idiotic. Everyone's just hoping we'll be able to improvise something when the moment comes. But whatever happens, there are going to be so many cops among the crowd (even *Paris-Presse* has admitted this, with a smile), that I don't think there's a chance of doing much against these farcical displays, these masquerades that turn my stomach.

A tiny young lady rang my bell two days ago in order to 'contact' me. So I went to my neighbourhood committee yesterday evening. It was pitiful and touching. I made the mistake of getting there at nine: no one. The concierge handed me a key after a lot of grumbling, but I preferred to wait on one of the benches. After half an hour a young woman arrived and led me into a big, empty studio at the other end of the courtyard. Other women began to arrive, little by little; there were eight of us finally, and not a single man. Muddled discussion; still, I admire their dedication, they didn't go home till midnight, and three of them offered to stick up posters and distribute pamphlets between six and seven in the morning; and they have children, and a career. Very mild evenings, lots of people and neon signs in the streets.

The North Africans are no longer allowed to go out at night. At Athis-Mons the cops fired at some Italians because they thought they were North Africans.

9 September

I was wrong, on the morning of 4 September, when I envisaged a complete fiasco. At one, in the Place Saint-Germain-des-Prés, I ran into Genet, we fell on each other's necks and went to have lunch on a café terrace. He talked with great enthusiasm about Greece and Homer, and very well about Rembrandt; there had been some extracts from his *'Rembrandt'* in *L'Express*, but cut – what he said was really much better. He too remakes the man in his own image when he says that he changed from pride to goodness because he wanted there to be nothing separating him from the world; anyway it's a beautiful idea. He said some nice things about the bits of my *Memoirs* he'd read: 'They give you more density.' Then he launched into a passionate apologia for F.L.N. terrorism, but my attempts to get him to go to the Place de la République were in vain.

Bost decided to wear his Croix de Guerre and Lanzmann sported his Resistance medal. We went together, and arrived shortly before four at the barriers in the Rue Turbigo separating the guests from the general public; the cops were there, checking invitation cards. Seeing the way they'd set up the barriers, we both immediately thought: 'It's a police trap.' We went back up towards the Lycée Turgot, where I was supposed to meet the others. Nobody there; all along the sidewalk buses full of C.R.S. men, ugly women got up to the nines walking in front of them brandishing their passes roguishly; they were feeling very important.

I realized that the others wouldn't be able to get to the Lycée because the street had been made into a blind alley by the blockade, so I got out of it myself. Three hundred yards farther down there was already a first cordon of police. L. had gone to join the leaders of the Resistance Committee[1] at Saint-Maur; I waited for the Sixth Committee at the Réaumur métro station, where Evelyne had told me they were supposed to meet. And I did in fact see Evelyne, the Adamovs, etc., arriving. By then, people were flowing in, in groups, in crowds, in masses. We took hope again; we formed a group near the Arts-et-Métiers métro station, right next to the first police

1. Which was coordinating all the neighbourhood committees.

barrier. A man who wanted to get by insulted them; they hit him and the crowd yelled, showering them with little pieces of paper: NO. The courage of some of the demonstrators took my breath away. Someone said nonchalantly: 'They're going to charge, they're putting on their gloves,' and we backed away a little, so that we'd be able to get into the cross streets. People were still arriving, *en masse*, but they all got a shock when they saw the tremendous barricades. Adamov grew irritable and said: 'Let's try somewhere else!' I myself thought we should stay there, not scatter about but keep opposite the stands, as many of us as possible. I think I was right too, except that we'd have got truncheons on our heads; Adamov's impatience saved us from that. We began to wend our way around the Place de la République, vainly searching for a way to get closer in. There was a rumour that some groups had gone off to the Place de la Nation, but I persuaded mine to go back and demonstrate opposite the stands, near the Arts-et-Métiers station. We passed other processions, going where? They didn't know. We told each other: 'You can't get through there.' 'Not back there either.' Finally we ended up in the Rue de Bretagne and people got out their little banners and posters and placards and balloons with the word No on them, and there was a lot of applause. There were cries of 'Down with De Gaulle', shouted out syllable by syllable as though we were at a sporting event, and Adamov said angrily: 'It's all too gay, this isn't how we should be behaving.' Clusters of balloons rose up into the sky just above the stands, and there were Noes floating in mid-air. We had run into Scipion and Lanzmann's father; they had just been in the Rue Turbigo; the people there had been allowed to get into the street in fairly large numbers and then discovered they were caught like rats in a trap. They began to demonstrate when Berthoin started his speech, to such good effect that no one could hear him; whereupon the police went into action, from behind, from the front, there was no way out, the crowd was savagely punished by their truncheons. While Scipion was telling us all this, Adamov got thirsty and we all went into a bistro; suddenly, outside, there was a stampede; the police were charging. (One charge had already been started earlier, and we had taken refuge under the main gate of an apartment building; the concierge let everyone come in who wanted to, saying: 'If *they* turn up, close the door.') Two blood-spattered women came into the bistro, one calm, the other screaming, really knocked out of her senses, and they made her lie down on one of the banquettes in the back room. One blonde woman had blood streaming through her hair; there were men with blood on them going past in the street. Evelyne shed one or two tears of emotion, and someone said sternly: 'You're not going to faint!' We went out and began demonstrating again. There was a market all along the Rue de Bretagne, and the tradespeople appeared to be on our side. The crowd was very likeable – hard, excited, and gay; it was the liveliest demonstration I've ever taken part in. Not legal like the big funeral procession of the Republic, nor hesitant like the Sunday of the investiture; it was serious and for some, dangerous. V.'s wife was very pale when they arrived at five, green at 5.15, vomiting at 5.30; her husband was holding her against a wall and coaxing her. 'She's ill,' a friend said; and another corrected him: 'She's scared.' And then added, by way of a complete explanation: 'She's always like that.' I asked why she didn't stay at home. 'Ah! Then she gets such a bad conscience about it, it makes her even sicker than being scared does.' They left her in a café in the Rue des Archives.

At about 7.30 we decided to get out of it. Lanzmann's father took us in his car; we went back through the Arts-et-Métiers intersection. The ground was littered with Noes; along the Rue Beaubourg some of the cobbles had been torn up; there were groups of people arguing along the Boulevards. We went to Bost's. He had been demonstrating with Serge. We all had dinner at Marie-Claire's, telling each other about the events of the day and tearing apart Germaine Tillon's article, which Bost, Lanzmann and I thought was disgusting.

Ignominy of the press the next day. All the same, *Le Figaro*'s 'hundreds of demonstrators' was going a bit too far. The Préfecture announced that there had been 150,000 people present; there were 6,000 invited guests, 4,000 sightseers, foreigners or even mystified Gaullists; therefore there had been 140,000 of us. (When I called Sartre to give him the figures he was disappointed; in Rome, the newspapers had been talking about the 250,000 demonstrators.) Shots had been fired in the Rue Beaubourg; four people wounded. *Humanité* and *Libération* gave accounts that coincide exactly with the one Lanzmann had written for the Committee of Resistance newspaper; the sad thing is that no one reads them, except those already on their side. All the same, despite all its efforts to slant things, a few truths emerged in *France-Soir*; there were the letters published in *Le Monde* the following day, and the tone of *Paris-Presse* was scarcely triumphant. They admitted that there was a certain 'contact' which did not materialize between De Gaulle and the public. We heard his speech at Marie-Claire's – not live, but retransmitted half an hour after the event, so that they had time to filter out the background of Noes; the voice and the speech of a far from hale-and-hearty old man. The real gem of the day, recounted by a great number of newspapers: 'Six Swedish journalists were brutally beaten with truncheons, taken to the police station, and given another going over. Their protests finally got through to their Embassy; as they released them the police said: 'We apologize, we thought you were Dutch.' Another journalist said: 'I'm an American'; one of the police blacked his eye and said in English: 'Go home!'

M. was one of the invited guests; even up there, everyone didn't applaud, and the Noes sounded terrifically loud; the foreign diplomats couldn't take their eyes off the truncheon work going on at the end of the street. During De Gaulle's speech people kept turning their heads to look at the crowd, and from time to time the whisper went around: 'They've broken through the barriers.' Whereupon all the gentlemen up there had the same reflex; they loosened their belts in order to use them as weapons. Basic misrepresentation by the newsreels, the radio and the television. Nevertheless, De Gaulle has given up the idea of his big propaganda tour; when he leaves here on the 28th it will be to visit only a few towns, and even then he will limit himself to making contact with the 'official bodies'.

On the subject of propaganda, here is one detail among others. I found another inland revenue summons waiting for me at home. I wrote to the tax inspector: 'Very well, fix a day.' He answered. 'If you pay in November, there will be no summons.' And then I learned that the inland revenue offices had been given a 'confidential' warning not to insist too brutally on taxes being paid, and not to seize any goods. A matter of soft-soaping the taxpayer.

Sunday 14 September

A sumptuous autumn. Yesterday, at about 8.30 in the morning, I had the impression I was back in Peking. There was the same golden softness in the sky and in the air, and there I was waiting for a car to

take me to a boring meeting; it was a conference of Protestant teachers at Bièvre; I had accepted their invitation because of the referendum, hoping to drag a few Noes out of them. It was lovely, the old
bulbous manor house sitting in the middle of its undulating grounds.
The audience seemed very pleasant; a lot of pastors, among them
Mathiot, who had just spent six months in jail for helping an F.L.N.
member to get to Switzerland. I spoke about commitment among the
intelligentsia; we discussed it a bit, and they seemed to agree with
me. But the ride home in the car was a let-down; one white-haired
woman thought as I did but the two others, a psychiatrist and a
woman doctor, were afraid of parachutists and Communists. They
said that De Gaulle was, after all, De Gaulle; that on the Left there
was no one but Mendès, and he has such an unpleasant personality!
All these people suffocating themselves like this by sticking their
own heads in the sand are not Fascists; but they are so terrified of
Communism!

In the evening, Lanzmann took me to dinner at the Vanne
Rouge. When I got back to Paris I was so sleepy and so nervous at
the same time that I couldn't even face a drink at the Dôme, so I
went home to bed. I still feel tense this morning. Is it going to be
like May all over again? The idea frightens me. I'm frightened of
staying tense like this till the 28th. And after that? I can't imagine
October this year.

I'm eager to keep this diary again now, partly because any other
work is so difficult while I'm in this state of tension. The meeting of
the 'Liaison Committee' of the 14th Arrondissement on Friday
evening was pleasant and friendly. I decided to walk to the Rue du
Château; it gave me a gentle poetic feeling, walking along the Rue
Froidevaux, passing the Hôtel Mistral and the Trois Mousquetaires.
I've been diving back into my past so much recently that at the
moment it's a dimension of my life. The little room, which must be
a C.G.T. headquarters, was packed. Jusquin asked me to sit up
with the committee. I was next to Francotte, a Senator, ex-
Municipal Councillor and a Communist, looking very much the
cunning old left-wing politician. He said to me: 'Ah! *The Mandarins*! That was good. . . .' And then laughing: 'It's exactly the
same situation, the same problem: with us or against us. . . .' I
answered: 'Yes, and the same solution; we're *obliged* to work with
you.' To which he replied, in an inimitable tone: 'What can you
expect, the fact is we trip up sometimes, we make mistakes. Who

doesn't? But by and large, we're in the right.' Jusquin outlined the situation, not bad, but my God! why all this optimism? Why say 'The victory of the Noes is assured' when the problem is to know whether there will be just slightly more Noes than Communist votes? They asked me to do some articles for the little local paper, and I also agreed to go and see some students at the Cité Universitaire. Then someone passed me a note: 'How pleasant to see you again, etc.' It was from Françoise d'Eaubonne, whom I hadn't seen for a long time. I took her off with me to the Trois Mousquetaires, where I had a bite to eat. She had been working for *Travail et Culture*, but there had been political dissensions and she left. She still writes for *Europe* and is a reader for Julliard.

Sartre will be back tomorrow; he told me on the phone that he's pretty tired. The article he sent – I helped S.-S. cut it – gives the same impression; he wasn't inspired. But he had to write it.

Excellent speech by Mendès-France. Lanzmann was at the conference; also, curiously enough, Genet. Evidently Mauriac looked touched, but that didn't prevent him from repeating in his *Bloc-Notes*, like some old dotard: 'All the same, there is De Gaulle; there is De Gaulle.' He accuses himself – only too truthfully I'm afraid, for his sake – of having sought all his life for the deplorable sort of isolation you get in a sleeping car.

16 September

I met Sartre yesterday in the rain at the Gare de Lyon, and then we spent the day chatting. He's very tired. I'm still being 'militant'; writing posters, lectures, articles. Lanzmann is completely taken up by the electoral campaign. During his lecture at Montargis, before two hundred and fifty teachers, he spoke of 'the rape of conscience'. Z., a Communist, said to him: 'You shouldn't have used that word; there were women present.'

Wednesday 23 September

Up till this morning, it's been like a madhouse all around me. Sartre got a liver infection on Sunday, just as he was due to begin working on his next article for *L'Express*. He was so worn out, so feverish and weak-headed on Sunday afternoon that it looked as though it would be impossible for him to write it; and since he'd been irritated at the slight dullness of his first article, the idea that this one might be the same infuriated him. He worked for twenty-eight hours at a stretch, without sleep and almost without a break; he slept a little on Sunday night, but when I left him harassed, at eleven on Monday evening, he started working on it again and went on till eleven the next morning; by that afternoon he gave the impression of being deaf and blind; I wondered how he could possibly hold up through the meeting. And it appears he spoke very well. He didn't go to bed until half an hour past midnight. Meanwhile, on Monday evening, I went to see Lanzmann and found him completely absorbed in his article about China, which he spent all that night and the following day completing – and which is very good. I was spending that same Monday evening making cuts in Sartre's article, an ungrateful task, and pretty tiring when it's got to be done fast. L'Express has just been delivered at Sartre's, finally. The article is really very good indeed, and the joints aren't too obvious.

I don't know if it's exhaustion or irritation, but my constant state of tension, which I feel especially in the back of the neck, the eyes, the ears, the temples, makes work difficult. I've written the articles I promised; it's insane how the tiniest paragraph takes me ages to write. Still, for better or worse, I've started revising my book, beginning with Chapter One.

Yesterday a Trappist rang at my door: Pierre Mabille. He was bringing me some of Zaza's notebooks to help me complete my Memoirs. Nothing very interesting; her letters say everything.

Lunch this morning with Baudiou, the boy from the École Normale. He talked to me about the Socialist Party, about the paras 'occupying' Toulouse on the 14th of July; they pushed everyone off the sidewalks, ordered drinks in the cafés, refused to pay, and forced the girls to dance with them. The officers were shouting at them through loudspeakers: 'That's it, boys, make them dance, you're all worth more than these civilian pimps.' But it didn't have the effect of anti-Gaullist propaganda; on the contrary, people thought: De Gaulle will protect us from this sort of thing. Baudiou told me that his father was in serious danger on 27 May, when the Tunisia-Morocco veterans, of whom there are a great many in Toulouse, tried to stage a nationalist putsch. We talked about Algeria, of course. And about the referendum. He is extremely pessimistic.

Everybody is waiting for Sunday: 60 per cent? 70 per cent? We're putting our money on 65 to 68 per cent; probably 68. After that comes the election campaign, which seems to be getting off to a bad start.

The various tortures are all thriving more than ever, even in metropolitan France. The police and the North Africans have machine-gun fights every day.

Saturday 27 September

Yes, it does me good to get out of my shell a bit. I had often regretted living so pent up all last year. I enjoyed yesterday evening very much. Not that I got the same little personal satisfaction out of it that I felt when I gave my lecture at the Sorbonne, before six hundred people who'd come just to hear me and gave me such a warm reception; but I too am 'a true democrat', and that's the sort of contact that moves me most, when one gets the benefit of a collective sympathy.

I prepared a few words of introduction in a bistro in the Rue d'Alésia, then I went on into the school. About two thousand four hundred people, half of them suffocating in the heat of the hall, the other half shivering out in the courtyard. 'The finest meeting of the whole campaign,' said Stibbe. Jusquin piously claimed that only a third of them were Communists; but even reversing the proportions, one-third non-Communists rubbing elbows with the Communists wasn't so bad. Beneath the dais, some old gentlemen – one bearded, some bald – very agitated. There was a U.F.D. meeting in the Mairie of the 14th Arrondissement a few hundred yards away, and they hadn't been warned that ours was taking place; individually, no one could have cared less, but one must have consideration for the feelings of others, etc. In short, it was decided to exchange delegations. Then my co-president stood up to speak, I said a few words, and the speakers came up one by one: Madaule, Gisèle Halimi, very persuasive; she spoke unrhetorically, in a conversational tone, but passionately, with smiling intensity and tiny gestures. She had been at a meeting in Toulouse the evening before, had spent the day on a train, was going the next day to ask the President of the Republic for a favour; she has children and a career that must take a toll of her nerves and her heart; yet another of the super-active young women to whom I take off my hat. We got on well together and exchanged addresses. After that, Yves Robert did a charming act, supported by Danièle Delorme, fresh as a flower in a smart yellow suit; we ought to use

[457]

'theatre folk' more; he made everyone laugh a lot. An amazing speech from a lawyer who until recently had been a left-wing Gaullist, well-groomed, impeccable, 'the man-most-likely' type, fundamentally different from everyone else there, and juggling with incomprehensible words; he told how at the meeting on Thursday in the Salle Pleyel the applause had been so wild that it had drowned Soustelle's speech; they had shouted: 'Death to the Communists!' and Soustelle had egged them on. 'They'll kill him!' someone had shouted. (People were interrupting as though it were a Victorian melodrama with cries of 'Yes! No! Bravo!' It was all very appealing.) The lawyer finished up with a great rhetorical gesture. 'I saw that meeting, and now I look at this one; and I have chosen!' He was acclaimed, everyone present feeling that they had been chosen personally. Next came d'Astier, a classic performance; a Communist, reading (as they always do) a long treatise without skipping a single word and without a single inflection; then Stibbe, who gave a detailed commentary on the Constitution. All the other speakers were sweating; when he gave me his hand, it was like ice. There was one farcical incident: a U.F.D. delegate from the other meeting made a speech heavily underlining the divergencies between the U.F.D. and the group he was addressing; but he 'was made happy by the thought of these parallel existences that were going to converge in a unanimous No'. While the co-president was asking for money, it was announced that Bourdet was in the hall: ovation. 'Let him speak!' But he refused to do so. He had just come from the U.F.D. meeting, which apparently only ninety-three people had attended. I very much enjoyed watching the faces of the people there, and their reactions. There was one very poor-looking woman, almost a female bum, who had brought two kids with her: a little dark girl with a Modigliani face under her black pudding-basin of hair; and a little boy of ten who laughed and clapped and seemed passionately interested in everything that went on.

As we came out, students, very nice people, and a blind man with his wife. He had read *The Mandarins* in Braille, he runs a Braille library, had put out a Braille anthology which was honoured by the Académie, and wanted me to be a patron of his magazine for blind poets; he already has Fernand Gregh and Duhamel! I got out of it. In the big *brasserie*, I joined up with C. Chonez, Françoise d'Eaubonne, Renée Saurel. At a nearby table were Hélène Parmelin, O. Wormser, Pignon; at another table were the U.F.D. group:

Stibbe, Bourdet, Halimi. We sent each other delegations from table to table; it was all very gay, and I stayed till 1.30 in the morning. Everyone spoke very highly of Sartre's article.

Today, work; the first chapter is taking shape. It's not impossible that the whole book will be finished in two years.

Tuesday, the books have been sent out from Gallimard's. I remember the feeling of dread when *The Mandarins* came out; I had put so much of myself into those pages, and I couldn't help thinking of all those eyes moving across them. This time it's different, I can keep myself more aloof; the critics and readers don't bother me. But I do feel uneasy – almost remorseful – when I think of all the people I've brought into it and who'll be furious.

A beautiful fall, warm, golden, shady and sunny; but people are beginning to come to blows all over France.

Latest conversation with a taxi driver; he observed that Paris is full this Saturday because of the voting. 'And how will they vote?' I asked. 'Come now, little lady, that goes without saying; for honesty ... He's honest, that man, you know; if he wasn't, you can imagine what the parties would have said about him. . . . No, I can't see him being a dictator; and what if he was? After this, we'll be electing our deputies, we'll have our say too. . . . Anyway, it's got to change, hasn't it, and it can't be any worse than it was before. . . . You've got to have a bit of faith.'

Sunday 28 September
Referendum.

Monday 29 September
Well! Now we know what defeat tastes like, and it's bitter, on the whole. It was a beautiful day, golden, clear, people went to vote with a smile, the polling stations seemed to be almost empty, despite the enormous number of people who voted, doubtless because it was all so well organized. I voted in the morning, lunched with my sister, went with Sartre to the Rue Mabillon; the polling officer smiled and said to him: 'There were some photographers round this morning asking what time you were going to vote.' We went for a walk, without much enthusiasm, then sat out on a terrace near Saint-Michel. We felt useless, empty; but there was no great anxiety, the government, the Communists and our own common sense told us that a figure of between 62 and 68 per cent was a more or less

foregone conclusion. We ran into Boubal; he said with conviction: 'Ah! The Occupation, those were the good old days!' and he lamented the fact that all one ever sees in the Flore these days is queers. After that we worked, then had dinner at La Palette. Sartre was still rather tired. I extorted a promise from him to go see his doctor. Lanzmann turned up at about midnight, already overwhelmed by the impending disaster, but trying not to show it too much, because Sartre is always accusing him of being pessimistic. The results already announced filled us with dismay: more than 80 per cent. Sartre went off to get some sleep. We visited *France-Soir*, humming with activity. All the provinces were in, except Marseilles, and they made it more than 80 per cent. We went home, in complete gloom, and began the same merry-go-round of phone calls as on 13 May. First Péju, who had piles of detailed and very upsetting figures. At *Humanité*, Lanzmann got through to T. and asked: 'The Communists must have betrayed us; how is it possible?' and T. answered sombrely: 'Read your friend Sartre's article.' I began to cry, I'd never have believed it could affect me so much; I still feel like crying this morning. It's rather dreadful to be against a whole country, your own country; you feel as though you're already an exile. We called L.'s father; he told us that all the rightists were out gloating on the Champs-Élysées. It's almost as hard to bear as the disappointment of the people on our side. There was a moment of false hope; according to Europe No. 1. the last count made it only 72 per cent. But it was an error – 77 per cent of Paris voted Yes. A large section of them, an enormous section, don't know what they're doing, people like my taxi driver the other day: Well, things have got to change, we'll just have to hope. Only what they've done is irrevocable; how many years before they realize that there's no hope in that direction? And when they do? On the telephone, Lanzmann asked an information operator how he had voted: Yes. 'You were wrong,' Lanzmann said. While I was waiting to be connected to someone who was out, I too asked: 'Are you happy with the results?' 'Why do you ask that?' came the uneasy reply. 'I just wanted to know.' 'I've already had someone jumping down my throat just a moment ago.' 'Because you voted Yes?' 'Yes.' 'Ah! Well, it *is* a pity you did, isn't it?' I replied as I hung up. He wasn't sure he was in the right; but all the same, it was another Yes.

Nightmares the whole night. I feel as though I've been put through a grinder.

When I bought *France-Soir* and *Libération*, then opened them in the Place Denfert-Rochereau, it made me think of the war, when I opened the papers and burst into tears: 'The Germans have marched into Belgium.' This time I was prepared; but I felt almost the same distress. How gloomy *Libération* was! *Humanité* too, apparently, but there weren't any tears left. I telephoned: Sartre wasn't expecting this. I can feel death in my heart.

It was my *département*, the Corrèze, that voted the best! That impoverished country of wasteland and chestnut trees was already radical when I was a child.

The horror people have of Parlement; Sartre points out in his article that people think of the deputies as 'loafers' who just ham-string the executive all the time with a series of mutinies. Then there are other things as well. To begin with, the stink of old scandals still clings: Panama, Oustric, Stavisky; there hasn't been one during the Fourth Republic (the piastres affair was something else again), but people still have the idea that the Chamber is choc-a-bloc with Freemasonry, backstage intrigue, bribery, and they feel they're always being stabbed in the back. The heart of the matter is that *they don't want to be governed by their equals*; they have too low an opinion of them, because they have too low an opinion of themselves and of their next-door neighbours. It's 'human' to like money and watch out for one's own interests. But if one is human like everybody else, then one is not capable of governing everyone else. So people demand the non-human, the super-human, the Great Man who will be 'honest' because he's 'above that sort of thing'.

It's a sinister defeat because it's not merely the defeat of a party or of an idea, but a repudiation by eighty per cent of the French people of all that we had believed in and wanted for France. A repudiation of themselves, an enormous collective suicide.

Wednesday 1 October

A day overcast by the referendum and Sartre's illness; he has a bad head, but won't go and see the doctor before Saturday, which worries me. I have nightmares and then feel uneasy all day long.

Last night I had dinner with Han Suyin, who is enchanting. I met her at the Pont-Royal: light-coloured suit, tall, slender, her face hardly Asiatic at all, beautiful for her forty years. Her daughter, by a Chinese father, is distinctly Asiatic-looking; she doesn't know a word of French and must have been very bored. We had dinner at Chez Beulemans. Han Suyin is interesting. She decided at a very early age to accept her condition as a half-caste; she chose not to choose. She feels as much a Westerner as an Oriental, she says, but her heart belongs entirely to Asia. She lives in Singapore, and devotes every day, from nine in the morning till five in the afternoon, to her Chinese patients (she's a practising gynaecologist); then she drives back to her house and writes. Since 1952, she's visited China every year; she has enormous admiration for the Chinese leaders: they're saints, she says. She told me that in Singapore and even in Canton, despite the new regime, there are still communities of women (about thirty thousand in Canton) who are officially recognized as lesbians; they marry within the community and adopt children. They may leave the community and marry a man. In that case they cut their hair. They have their tutelary goddess, ceremonies, etc. She says that Chinese puritanism is really stifling, that in the beginning the Russians caused a scandal because they tried to flirt with the Chinese girls. She thinks that for at least five years it will go on being difficult for Chinese intellectuals.

Thursday 2 October

Dark days. *L'Express* makes depressing reading; an issue full of resigned defeat and distractions. *L'Observateur* puts up a better show. Sartre had lunch with Simone Berriau. I'm grateful to her for frightening him; he's going to the doctor in a moment, and I'll accompany him. Qualified satisfaction: she threatened him with hemiplegia and infarctus; he seems terribly tired; he stuffs himself with Optalidon, belladénal and corydrame, one after the other; he has attacks of vertigo and incessant headaches.

Lunch at the Coupole with Gisèle Halimi. In the course of the conversation she told me about her life. Oh, how much there is still to be done about the condition of women! She told me about the Philippeville trial. There wasn't a single hotel-keeper there who would give her or her colleagues a room; the lawyers in the town had to give them lodgings in their own homes. The chief of police had asked for nine death sentences; the bench pronounced fourteen, which is to say one for each of the accused (who had been picked at random after the riot and were doubtless all innocent), except one decoy. The trial has in any case been disallowed, there's going to be a retrial in Algiers any day now.

Monday 6 October

Sartre saw the doctor. He's a little better now, although he still gets headaches.

It's been raining so much that all the trees along the Paris avenues still have green leaves. It scarcely seems like autumn at all.

The future has no face. We feel unemployed, useless, abashed.

Tuesday 14 October

These really are days of horror. It was like this in the plane that had lost an engine six hours out of Shannon: constant fear, with brief respites followed by a fresh onslaught of fear. It's the same with Sartre. Now and then he seems better; then, like yesterday, he stumbles over words, has difficulty walking, his handwriting and his spelling are appalling, and I am appalled. The left ventricle is tired, the doctor says. He needs a real rest, which is just what he won't take. Our death is inside us, but not like the stone in the fruit, like the meaning of our life; inside us, but a stranger to us, an enemy, a thing of fear. Nothing else counts. My book, the criticisms, the letters I get, the people who talk to me about it, everything that would otherwise have given me pleasure, rendered utterly void. I haven't even the strength to go on with this diary.

Tuesday 21 October

Days of horror. Especially Saturday, when I went to the doctor's. Sunday, yesterday, one long suffocating nightmare!

Tuesday 28 October

Coming out of the nightmare, the illness. I must be already benumbed by old age to be able to bear it.

I think I'm going to stop keeping this diary.

And, in fact, I did stop keeping it. I put the pages in a folder, and wrote on it, impulsively: *Diary of a defeat*. And I never touched it again.

What happened during those days of horror was that Sartre had just missed having a heart attack. He had been putting his health to a terrible test for a long time, not so much because of the exhaustion his desire to make 'full use' of himself was inflicting on him as because of the tension he had set up inside himself. To think against oneself is all very well – it has fertile results – but in the long run it tears one to pieces; by forcibly smashing a way through to new ideas he had also done damage to his nerves. Once before, writing *The Psychology of Imagination* had got him into a very bad state; to complete the *Critique de la raison dialectique* had required a considerably more violent effort. But it was the defeat of the Left, above all, and De Gaulle's accession to power that had really stunned him. In Rome, stuffing himself with corydrame the whole time, he had worked on a play; I knew the general outline of it, and at Pisa, before I said good-bye to him there, he had shown me the first act. Outside, it was a hundred degrees, but he had regulated the air conditioner in his room until it was like being inside a glacier. I shivered as I sat reading a text that was full of promises but didn't keep one of them. 'It's like Sudermann,' I told him. He agreed. He would begin again, but he needed time, and as usual he had made a lot of rash commitments. The fear of spoiling a work that was enormously important to him also aggravated his state of excitement and irritability. Finally, when he got back to Paris, a serious liver infection flared up. The twenty-eight hours of uninterrupted work, followed by the evening meeting, all of which I had noted in my diary, finally finished him off. Shattered by continual headaches, stumbling over his words in a thick voice, handwriting and spelling completely out of control, he began to suffer from vertigo and lose his sense of balance. While lunching with Simone Berriau he very carefully put his glass down an inch from the table; she immediately picked up the telephone and made an appointment for him with Professor Moreau. Waiting for him in a nearby bistro, I fully expected to see him come out of the doctor's office on a stretcher. He walked out, and showed me the prescription: certain drugs, no drinking, no smoking, rest. He more or less obeyed, but went on working. The headaches persisted. He had once been so lively, so decisive, and now he walked along with his neck stiff, his limbs leaden, his face puffy and fixed, speech and gestures completely unsure. His mood too was unusual: a dopey calm, punctuated by acute fits of anger. The doctor must have been struck by his apathetic expression, because he promised him straight away: 'I can restore your aggressiveness.' Yet when I saw him tense at his desk, his pen scratching wildly across the paper, his eyes heavy with sleep, and told him: 'Take a rest,' he answered me more violently than I ever remembered. Sometimes he gave in. 'All right, five minutes,' he would say. He would lie down, exhausted, and sleep two or three hours. 'He's tired today,' his mother said to me one afternoon when I got back to his apartment ahead of him. 'Are you tired?' I asked him when he came in. 'Of course not,' he said, sitting down at his desk. I persisted. 'I assure you I feel perfectly all right'; he smiled: 'Everyone has his own distillations. . . .' 'What d'you mean?' 'You know perfectly well: the thickets of the heart.' And he began drawing unnamable things on a piece of paper. I pretended to work, expecting to see him collapse at any moment. He had an appointment the next morning with a woman friend; I succeeded in making him write a *pneu* to call it off; he made four tries before he managed to write it, and when she received it she burst into tears: the words were all on top of each other, distorted, incoherent. I went to see the doctor. 'I won't try to conceal from you,' he said, 'that when I saw him coming into my surgery I thought: That man is going to have a heart attack.' He added: 'He is a very emotional man. He has overworked himself intellectually, but even more so emotionally. He must have moral calm. Let him work a bit if he insists, but he mustn't try racing against the clock. If he does, I don't give him six months.' Moral calm in France today! I went straight to Simone Berriau; she agreed to put off *Altona* until the following fall. I hadn't informed Sartre of these visits; when I did tell him a few hours afterwards, he listened with an indifferent smile; I'd rather he'd flown into a rage. For a while he only worked a very little at a time; then, slowly, he began to get better. The most painful part for me during this crisis was the solitude his illness condemned me to; I couldn't share my worries with him because he was the object of them. The scars left by the memory of those days have never left me, especially of the one when 'the thickets of the heart' first threw their mysterious shadow between us. Death had become an intimate presence to me in 1954, but henceforth it possessed me.

This subjection had a name: old age. Towards the middle of November we had dinner at La Palette with Leiris and his wife; since the last time we'd met him he had swallowed a fatal dose of barbiturates and been saved only by a very difficult operation and then a long course of treatment. We talked about sleeping pills, drugs, sedatives, and the anti-depressants Leiris was taking; I asked him what effect they had exactly. 'Well, they de-depress you.' Then, when I asked him to be more precise: 'It means you know everything's just as awful as it was before; only you're not depressed.' As he was sitting there with Sartre thrashing out the differences between tranquillizers and anti-depressants, I thought: Well that's it, we're on the other side now, we're old. A little while later, chatting with Herbaud, a very old friend, I said that, basically, there was nothing else for us to look forward to except our own death or the deaths of those close to us. Who'll go first? Who'll see the others out? Those were the questions I was asking now when I thought about the future. 'Now, now,' he said to me, 'we haven't reached that stage yet; you've always been too old for your years.' And yet, I wasn't wrong. . . .

The last thread that kept me from my true state snapped: Lanzmann and I drifted apart. It was natural, it was inevitable and even, on reflection, desirable for both of us; but the moment for reflection had not yet come. The action of time has always disconcerted me, I regard everything as definitive, so that the business of separation was difficult for me; for him, too, though the initiative had been his. I wasn't sure that we would manage to salvage the past, and it meant too much to me for the idea of giving it up not to be odious. It was with a heavy heart that I reached the end of that intolerable year.

CHAPTER TEN

Ever since May, great gusts of words had been sweeping across France; the simple syllable 'lies' was inadequate to describe them; they were *lecta*, without any positive or negative relation to reality, rumours engendered in the air by human breath. There were teams of specialists to interpret them. They produced the translation 'generous offer' for the phrase 'peace for the brave', which to the Algerians meant capitulation.

The press went into hiding. The elections were a farce in Algeria, and in France a victory for the U.N.R. who, with the obligatory Moslem candidates also elected, formed a bloc of two hundred and sixty Gaullist deputies. The Communists lost ground. Many people who had up till then been left-wing opted for what they called 'realism'. One particularly striking case was that of the Unionist

Serge Mallet who, early in 1958, had talked very intelligently to Sartre about the new tactics the employers were using and the difficulties they were creating for the unions; at that time he was searching for a means, within the framework of the class struggle, of overcoming them. The long essay in which he repeated these explanations in print had amazed Sartre by its clumsiness; Mallet lost no time in correcting this error. He wrote some excellent articles for *Les Temps Modernes* and several other left-wing newspapers in which he analysed neo-capitalism and described the present working conditions of agricultural and factory workers. I made his acquaintance at the Coupole at the time of the referendum, and he surprised me. He knew from a completely reliable source that an emissary from De Gaulle was in Tunis at that moment conducting negotiations; the peace would be signed within two days. I saw him again a few weeks later; he described the manoeuvres being used by the young employers to split up the working class, he criticized the trade unionists for clinging to outdated attitudes, and I realized that beneath a pretence of adapting the working class avant-garde to the new methods of neo-capitalism he was really subscribing to collaboration between the classes. He was rallying to the economic theory that had become the new regime's perpetual refrain. *Les Temps Modernes* accepted no more of his articles on economic theory.

The result of the referendum had severed the last threads linking me to my country. There were to be no more trips through France. Tavant, Saint-Savin, and other places I had never seen no longer held any attraction for me; the present was even spoiling the past for me. From that time on I lived through the pride of our autumns in humiliation, and the sweetness of summer in bitterness. Sometimes I still feel a catch in my throat at a landscape's sudden grace, but it is the memory of a love betrayed, it is like a smile that lies. Every night when I went to bed, I was afraid of sleep, afraid of the nightmares twisting through it, and when I woke up I was cold.

'The time of battles is over,' De Gaulle announced at Touggourt. But they had never been more serious. Challe achieved several military successes, he smashed the *katiba*. But his psychological warfare failed, he did not win over the population. In the early spring of 1959, a new and as yet little-known aspect of this war of extermination was revealed to us: the prison camps. It was learned that from November 1957 on, the so-called 'redistribution' programme had begun to assume increasingly large proportions. Since the A.L.N. – despite official propaganda – existed among the population 'like a fish in water', the only thing to do was remove the water: empty the *mechta* and the *douars*, scorch the earth and herd the peasants together, under the control of the army, behind barbed wire. This principle was applied on a grand scale. On 12 March 1958 *Le Monde* made a fleeting allusion to the existence of these camps. In April, the Secretary-General of Catholic Aid, Mgr Rodhain, led an inquiry into the matter and then, on 11 August, published certain of its findings in *La Croix*: 'I discovered that there were more than a million human beings involved, generally women and children. . . . A notable proportion, particularly among the children, suffer from hunger. I have seen these things and bear witness to them.' He estimated the numbers of the 're-distributed' at more than 1,500,000.[1] Some of them, as he had seen with his own eyes, had been reduced to eating grass. Tuberculosis was rampant. The people there were in such bad physical condition that even drugs did not affect them any more. On 15 April an even more appalling report was made public, this one addressed officially to M. Delouvrier on his request. From this it emerged that more than a million redistributed peasants were living in 'extremely precarious' conditions.[2] On an average, 550 out of every thousand inmates were children, and one of those 550 was dying

1. This is also the figure arrived at by Paillat – *Dossier secret de l'Algérie* – who is generally little moved by the misfortunes of Moslem populations: 'From May 1958 to July 1960, the number of displaced persons rose from 460,000 to 1,513,000. Their number is still increasing.' The paragraph heading 'The Piteous Horror of the Redistribution Centres' and the material following it make it quite clear that he is referring to the camps. And he too emphasizes, on the strength of a report by General Parlange, their 'deplorable material conditions'.

2. The report stated: 'Any displacement of populations entails an appreciable, *and in some cases a total*, curtailment of the material resources of those involved.' These people were obliged to leave behind their goats, their chickens and their meagre land, they were losing at least a third of their resources; the more fortunate among them sometimes managed to get a new piece of land to cultivate, but since there were very few adult males among them – all in the *maquis*, in prison, or dead – those that did could not possibly provide for the needs of the women, children and old people composing almost the entire population of the redistribution centres. In fact, these 1,500,000 displaced persons were living on relief of staggering inadequacy. 'The sanitary situation is almost everywhere *deplorable*. . . . When a group of displaced persons reaches the thousand mark, approximately one child dies every two days.'

every two days; since many of the women and old men were also unable to withstand the conditions, it may be estimated that these camps killed more than a million people in three years.[1]

Delouvrier forbade the creation of further centres. He was ignored, and the numbers of the 'redistributed' only increased. In July, Pierre Macaigne published in *Le Figaro* an account of his visit to the Bessombourg camp:

Crammed together in unbroken wretchedness, fifteen to a tent since 1957, this human flotsam lies tangled in an indescribable state. There are 1,800 children living at Bessombourg. . . . At the moment, the whole population is fed entirely on semolina. Each person receives about 4 ounces of semolina a day. . . . Milk is given out twice a week: one pint per child. . . . No rations of fat have been distributed for eight months. No rations of chick-peas for a year. . . . No ration of soap for a year. . . .

From young soldiers and from journalists who had been in Tunisia and met Algerians torn from camps near the frontier, I discovered further details: systematic, organized rapes – the men were taken out of the camp or herded into a corner while the soldiers went in and performed; dogs set on old men for diversion; torture. But these reports as they stood should have been enough to disturb people. Mgr Feltin, Pastor Boegner, both spoke about them with indignation; scarcely anyone listened. The press kept quiet. The French Red Cross, which the International Red Cross had been asking to do something about these displaced

---

The sanitary situation, the writers of the report continued, is an outcome of the standard of living: 'In one of the most tragic cases we encountered, a medical report specifies that the physiological condition of the population is such that drugs no longer affect them.' And under the heading 'standard of living' it states: 'It is in this realm that the situation of these displaced persons is at its most tragic, the sanitary situation being only a consequence of it. . . . The almost total absence of domestic animals is a characteristic common to all the redistribution centres; this means that milk, eggs and meat are of necessity excluded from the diet of those living in them. . . . The rations distributed by way of relief are extremely meagre; in one of the cases we observed, they were limited to 24 lbs. of barley per adult, per month, which is not much when there are young children as well. The most serious lack in this matter is the total absence of regularity in these distributions. . . . Means of existence must at all costs be provided for these people if the experiment is not to end in disaster.' The redistribution centres very rarely numbered less than 1,000 and sometimes as many as 6,000.

1. This was also the figure given by the Algerians.

persons for two years, still took no action. Whereas when the floods in Madagascar left 100,000 homeless, the government, anxious to demonstrate the advantages the island gained from its adherence to the French Commonwealth, launched a relief campaign, and the French people rushed to prove how '*formidable*' they were.[1] It is always nicer to get emotional about a natural cataclysm than about crimes to which we are accomplices.

There were other sorts of camps: internment camps, transit camps and selection camps, in which men were imprisoned by arbitrary decisions of the police or the army; they were then tortured, physically and psychologically, till they went mad or, in many cases, died. Abdallah S. described in *L'Express* how between beatings and tortures he was forced to deny the F.L.N. and tell them how much he loved France, in words straight from the heart. There were camps of this sort in France; Larzac – once this had been the name of a plateau I used to rush gaily over in my youth, on foot, or on my bicycle; now it was a name for hell. The people living in the vicinity were aware of this, despite the precautions that had been taken. The entire French people was aware that camps had been set up on their own soil similar to the ones in Siberia they had once denounced with such a hue and cry; no one protested now. Camus did not raise the slightest objection – Camus, who had been so disgusted only shortly before by the indifference of the French working class to the Russian camps.

As for the use of torture, in about March 1958, De Gaulle, after continual requests for a public condemnation, coolly announced from on high that torture was a product of the 'system' and would disappear with it. 'The use of torture has ceased,' Malraux had assured the nation after 13 May. In fact, it had spread to France itself. In October, in his defence of the priests being tried at Lyons for having helped the F.L.N., Cardinal Gerher invoked the tortures to which Moslems were being subjected in the police stations of the city. An Algerian being 'interrogated' in a Versailles police station hanged himself from the bars of his cell. *Témoignage Chrétien* and *Les Temps Modernes* published the complaints of the

1. At the beginning of his report, Mgr Rodhain remarked: 'A natural disaster in Madagascar and a man-made disaster in Algeria. . . . In the first case, 100,000 left homeless, in the second, a million refugees. . . . The public is passionately concerned about Madagascar. . . . For the refugees in Algeria, no one will lift a finger.'

Algerian students so savagely 'questioned' by the D.S.T. in December. In February, during the trial of the Algerians who had shot at Soustelle, one of the accused pointed to one of the police officers packing the court, Commissioner Beloeil: 'That man tortured me.' The Commissioner disappeared from sight and was not questioned. In Algeria, the use of torture was an accepted fact. 'There was a time,' Gisèle Halimi told me, 'when if I said: "My client's admissions were extracted from him by torture," the President of the Court would hammer on the table and say: "That is an insult to the French Army." Now, he simply says: "I accept them, nevertheless, as true."' Thirty young priests, shattered by their experiences in Algeria, wrote to their bishops, and a military chaplain publicly condemned the use of torture. But the legal reforms which in March made secret hearings legal, made the isolation and ill-treatment of prisoners even easier. In June, the students who had been tortured in December – Boumaza, Khebaïli, Souami, Fancis, Belhadj – spoke out. They brought action against M. Wybot who had been present in person at several of the interrogations. The book was seized and the affair hushed up.

In March a meeting protesting at the use of torture was to be held at the Mutualité; I was in the middle of preparing my protest when the Commissioner of Police for our district came around to warn me that the meeting had been forbidden. He was most polite about it; then he pointed to a strip of black crepe on his lapel. 'I lost a son in Algeria, Madame.' 'It is in all our interests to make an end of this war,' I replied. His voice became threatening. 'There's only one thing I want, and that's to go down there and finish off a few of them myself.' I shouldn't have liked to have him 'question' me. There was a press conference that evening. Later, we managed to organize two or three meetings. A great many people turned out at the Montparnasse cemetery to attend the burial of Ouled Aoudia, killed by a policeman shortly before the trial of the Algerian students arrested for having re-established the U.G.E.M.A., in whose defence he was to appear. At the end of the academic year, a 'fortnight of action for peace in Algeria' was organized. These demonstrations were not entirely useless, but so inadequate that a growing number of young people and adults were opting for illegal action.

After the whip-cracking of June 1956, there was no further open and collective opposition to the war among young people. There were more or less secret committees of young people still protesting, but in words only. In September 1958, I received the first mimeo-graphed, anonymous issue of a publication called *Vérité pour …* which limited itself at first to economic and political analyses, but very quickly began to preach desertion and support of the F.L.N. It was run by Francis Jeanson, who was thus attempting to over-come a difficulty: 'that of making public a means of action that should theoretically remain underground'.[1] It was at this time, too, that the Young Resistance Movement was started.

My friends and I had very different opinions now on the subject of supporting the F.L.N. We had seen Jeanson again and been con-vinced by the reasons he gave that his movement was politically justified. The French Left could not now resume its former revolu-tionary attitude except in collaboration with the F.L.N. 'You are stabbing French soldiers in the back,' he had been told. This accusation reminded me of the sophistry of the Germans when they accused the *maquisards* of preventing the return of prisoners. It was the professional military men and the government that were killing the youth of France by prolonging the war. The lives of Moslems were of no less importance in my eyes than those of my fellow countrymen; the enormous disproportion between the French losses and the number of their adversaries they had mas-sacred revealed this emphasis on the shedding of French blood to be no more than a sickening piece of blackmail.[2] Since the Left had completely failed in its attempt to carry on the struggle within the limits of legality, if one wanted to remain faithful to one's anti-colonialist convictions and free oneself of all complicity with this war, then underground action remained the only possible course. I admired those who took part in such action. But to do so de-manded total commitment, and it would have been cheating to pretend that I was capable of such a thing. I am not a woman of action; my reason for living is writing; to sacrifice that I would have had to believe myself indispensable in some other field. Such was not by any means the case. I contented myself with giving what help I could when I was asked for it; certain of my friends did more.

Malraux was dropping Labiche and Feydeau from the Comédie-

1. *Notre Guerre* by Francis Jeanson.
2. Jeanson later revealed that his connexion with the Fédération de France had in fact enabled him, on several occasions, to influence it and to save French lives.

Française repertory; he cast a veil of high-sounding speeches over the machinations of the Philips Corporation which had had the idea, to the great despair of the Greeks, of exploiting the commercial resources of the Acropolis by presenting a *Son et Lumière* performance there. 'Not since the Nazis set foot on the Acropolis have we experienced such a humiliation,' we read next day in a Greek newspaper, and a conservative one at that. France's degradation continued. The University was crying out for financial help, and the government was preparing to subsidize private schools. The anti-Sovietism of the middle classes persisted. The Soviet scientists announced when they launched the first Lunik that it would pass close to the moon; the newspapers insinuated that they had intended to hit it and failed. The Pasternak affair was a godsend. It is true that the Union of Soviet Writers showed itself in a clumsy and sectarian light by insulting and expelling Pasternak; but he was after all allowed to live in peace in his *dacha*, and the Swedish Academicians were being intentionally provocative when they conferred their prize on a Russian novel that expressed a rather cool attitude towards Communism and which they considered as counter-revolutionary; they were forcing the Soviet Writers' Union, which until then had turned a blind eye, to act in some way. Pasternak is a very great poet, but I could not get through *Doctor Zhivago*. Reading it taught me nothing about a world to which the author seemed to have made himself deliberately blind and deaf, and then he enveloped it in a mist in which even he himself melted away. To swallow these lumps of solidified fog, the middle classes must have been sustained by a fanaticism of no mean power. The same fanaticism later inspired them with a no less far-fetched passion for Tibet, about which they knew nothing whatever except that it had rebelled against Chinese domination; the Dalai Lama immediately became the embodiment of liberty and Western values. If there was one thing they hated more than the U.S.S.R., it was China. On his return from Peking, Lanzmann had told me a great deal about the Chinese experiments with communes; apparently the success of these had varied greatly according to different regions and conditions, but it was an interesting attempt to decentralize industry and link it more closely with agriculture. In France, it was accused of destroying the family as well as of crushing individuality, and only its difficulties were publicized.

I greeted the Pope's death with a certain amount of pleasure, as well as that of John Foster Dulles. The Cyprus incident was settled to the advantage of the Cypriots. But the most astonishing revolutionary victory was the one brought off in Cuba by the rebels of the Sierra Maestra. As winter began, they marched westwards from their mountains, Batista fled, Castro's brother led his troops into a Havana mad with joy, and Fidel was received there in triumph on 9 January. In the cellars of the city, in the surrounding countryside, tremendous mass graves were unearthed: more than twenty thousand people had been tortured and shot, whole villages had been pounded to pieces by the air force. The people demanded reprisals; to satisfy them and keep them within bounds, Castro instituted a public trial that resulted in roughly two hundred and twenty death sentences. The French newspapers presented this inevitable purge as a crime. *Match* published photographs of the condemned men kissing their wives and children, but without, needless to say, showing any pictures of the bodies of their victims, without saying how many there had been, without even mentioning them. Castro was well received by Washington; but when he began to put his agrarian reforms into effect and they discovered that their Robin Hood was in fact an out-and-out revolutionary, the Americans – who had fried the Rosenbergs when they were accused of espionage in peacetime – waxed indignant because he had sent some war criminals to the firing squad. Castro had the whole Cuban population behind him; when he handed in his resignation in July, as a means of settling his conflict with Urrutia, the President of the Republic, a million peasants flowed into Havana. Striking their *machetes* together, producing a deafening din, they demanded that he remain at the head of the country and that Urrutia go instead – which he did. He was replaced by Dorticós.

During my vacation I had decided, as I said, to go on with my autobiography; I continued to waver in this determination for a long time; it seemed to me presumptuous to talk so much about myself. Sartre encouraged me. I asked everyone I met whether they agreed; they did. My question became increasingly pointless as the book progressed. I compared my recollections with Sartre's, with Olga's, with Bost's; I went to the Bibliothèque Nationale to get my life back into its historical frame. For hours on end, reading old newspapers, I became involved in a present heavy with the uncertainty of its future and already become a past left far behind; it was disconcerting. Sometimes I became so absorbed in my task that time fell away from under me. As I came out of the library court-yard, unchanged since I was twenty, I no longer knew what year I was walking into. I looked through the evening paper with the feeling that the next day's issue was already on the shelves, within arm's reach.

I was spurred on by the success of my *Memoirs* which, once Sartre was out of danger, affected me more intimately than the reception of any of my other books. In the morning when I got up, and when I came home to go to bed, there were always letters on the floor inside my door to drag me out of my depressions. Ghosts rose up out of the past, some annoyed, some kindly; school friends I'd treated rather sharply smiled at the awkwardness of their youth; friends I'd written about sympathetically got angry. Some ex-pupils of the Cours Désir approved of the picture I had painted of our education; others protested. One lady threatened me with court proceedings. The Mabille family were grateful to me for having made Zaza live again. They sent me details about her death that I did not know, and also about her parents' relations with Pradelle, whose reticence I understood much better as a consequence. It was romantic, this discovery of my past brought about by my writing an account of it. As I re-read Zaza's letters and notebooks, I was plunged back into it once more. And it was as though she had died a second time. Never again did she come back to see me in my dreams. Generally speaking, since it has been published and read, the story of my childhood and youth has detached itself from me entirely.

In October, the *Temps Modernes* staff got together for a lunch at Lipp's to celebrate the return of Pouillon, who had spent the summer near Lake Chad among the Corbos on an ethnographical expedition. He had been quite insensitive to the heat and was bothered only by the flies that covered him from head to foot every time he washed in front of his tent. He had been quite happy eating the lump of millet that they kneaded for him every morning. His sole occupation was talking to the natives all day with the help of an interpreter. It seemed to me that if I had been in his place I should have died of boredom. 'Every morning,' I told him, 'I'd have been panic-stricken wondering: What am I going to do until this evening?' 'In that case, never go there!' he answered vehemently.

Unfortunately he hadn't been able to collect much information; the life of the Corbos is extremely rude. 'They've lost the bow,' Pouillon explained, 'they had it, and now they've lost it. It's worse than never having discovered it; you can never discover it a second time!' The neighbouring tribes used them; but what's the good? they said. Given these conditions, there was no modern invention capable of dazzling them; automobiles, airplanes: what's the good? Occasionally they would kill birds with stones and eat them. They owned cattle, but the pastures where they were turned out to graze were so far off that they were scarcely more than an imaginary form of wealth. The women did the work of cultivating the land, so naturally all the men were polygamous except one idiot, a bachelor who lived on charity, and an old man better off than the others who explained to Pouillon: 'I don't need to have more than one wife; I'm rich.' Their traditions appeared to be as rudimentary as their way of life; to perpetuate them would have required an intelligent old man and a curious child. This conjuncture did not occur very often; many had fallen into oblivion. They lived without religion and without rites, or almost. Pouillon's voice was vibrant with enthusiasm as he talked. These people escaped want by rejecting all wants; they had nothing, yet they lacked nothing. We were afraid he was going to become a naturalized Corbo.

Outside the circle of my intimates, I only enjoyed talking with people when we could be alone, since we could often get through the small-talk stage very quickly then; I was sorry I had never managed to do so in the course of my rare meetings with Françoise Sagan. I very much liked the light touch of her humour, her determination not to be fooled by anyone and not to strike attitudes; every time I left her, I said to myself that next time we must have a real talk together; and then the next time we didn't – I'm not quite sure why. Since her conversation makes its points by way of ellipses, allusions, implications and unfinished sentences, I always felt it would be pedantic of me to finish mine, but I just couldn't get used to breaking them off halfway through, and always wound up unable to think of anything to say. I found her intimidating, as I do children and adolescents and everyone who uses language differently from me. I suppose she felt ill at ease with me too. One summer evening we happened to meet on the terrace of a café on the Boulevard Montparnasse; we exchanged a few words; as usual she was very charming and funny and I would have enjoyed nothing more than just staying there with her. But she told me immediately that there were some friends waiting for us at the Epi Club. Jacques Chazot was there, Paola de Saint-Just, Nicole Berger and a few others. Sagan drank in silence. Chazot told a lot of Marie-Chantal stories, and I was astonished to think that there had been a time when nothing could have been more normal than to find myself sitting in a nightclub, with a glass of Scotch in front of me – I felt so out of place! Though it's true that I was surrounded by a group of strangers, and that they had no more idea what I was doing there with them than I had.

I read a little. Aragon's *Holy Week* bored me almost as much as *Doctor Zhivago*; once I got the point he was making, and realized the virtuosity with which he was doing it, I could see no reason to go on with this scholarly allegory; I like Aragon's voice direct and uncluttered, as it comes through sometimes in *Le Roman inachevé*, and in *Elsa*; I found him moving when he was talking about his youth and his visions, his ambitions, the ashes left by fame, life passing and killing as it goes. Though *Zazie* won such an enormous public, I had liked other books by Queneau better, from *Chiendent* to *Saint-Glinglin*. But I plunged with great enjoyment into the intricacies of *Lolita*. With disquieting humour, Nabokov was disputing the transparent rationalizations about sex, about the emotions, about the individual, so necessary to the Organization World. Despite the pretentious clumsiness of the prologue and his failure to sustain the end, I was gripped by the story. De Rougemont, who writes idiotically about Europe but not at all badly about sex, has praised Nabokov for having discovered a new embodiment of the idea of love-as-fatality, love-as-curse; and it is true that in our age of Coccinelle and sentimental ballads love doesn't seem to entail damnation for anyone any more; whereas, from the very first moment that he sets eyes on Lolita, Humbert Humbert is in hell. With *La Révocation de l'Édit de Nantes*, Klossovski had written, in incomparable style, a novel of deep and baroque eroticism. Usually in erotic books the characters are reduced to a single dimension; their debauches are inadequate to restore life to bodies the author has cut off from the real world, and thereby drained of their life's blood. But Klossovski's heroine, a much-honoured Radical-Socialist member of Parliament, really lived; when he led her into dungeons worthy of Eugène Sue and delivered her up to flagellations one believed in her masochistic jubilation. The treatment he doled out to those who put their trust in heaven was no better than that reserved for those who laughed in its face; in each case, the distortions of their sexuality demonstrated the inability of today's bourgeoisie to assume their bodies, and thus to be men.

It was generally during the afternoon, before working, that I read. In bed at night I occasionally glanced through one of the advance copies of novels that had been sent to me; at the end of ten minutes my light would be off. One evening it didn't go off. The book was by an unknown woman, and it began without any great fuss; a nice young girl met a mixed-up boy, she saved him from suicide, they were going to love each other: banal enough, only this wasn't. Disturbing, equivocal, their love forced the reader of *Warrior's Rest* to question the nature of love itself. This unschooled young girl spoke like a woman rich with experience, and in a tone of voice that held me right up to the last page, despite a certain number of slack passages. It's a rare pleasure, being struck unexpectedly by a book that no one has even mentioned to you. Christiane Rochefort: who was she? I only found out a short while later, when the verdict of the public had sustained my own.

The complete version of *Ivan the Terrible* was shown in Paris. The first part was a little stilted; the second, unfettered, lyric, epic, inspired, perhaps outstripped anything I had ever seen on a screen. The Central Committee having condemned it, in September 1946, Eisenstein wrote to Stalin, who received him, and then sat through the film in the Kremlin projection room; Stalin remained impassive throughout, or so Ehrenburg had told us, and then left without a word. Eisenstein had been given official permission to shoot a third section which was to be amalgamated with the second; but he was already very ill and died two years later.

For a long time Bost had been singing the praises of a new film which he had seen at a private screening and which broke with the usual pattern of French films: *Le Beau Serge*. As soon as it was released, I went to see it. The actors were all unknowns, and it depicted a village in the central part of France with such fidelity that the images on the screen seemed to me like memories; Chabrol told the story of its inhabitants' narrow lives, their shortcomings, without ever seeming to look down on them. In *The Cousins*, this gift for compassion and for presenting the truth in all its freshness was no longer in evidence, but here again the tone was original. In *The Four Hundred Blows*, Truffaut portrayed the world of grown-ups rather badly, but that of childhood extremely well. The 'New Wave' directors were always operating on too meagre a budget to be able to use the costly production methods of their elders; this helped them shake off a lot of the dust that had settled.

In about May, Lanzmann took me one evening to watch Josephine Baker rehearsing at the Olympia; actors in street clothes were walking through sets that were only half up and bumping into other half-naked actors in imitation classical garb; I greatly enjoyed the disorder, the frenzy of the technicians, the bad temper of those in charge, the unexpected effects produced by this conjuncture of sumptuous artifice with the routine of everyday life. But as I recalled the Josephine of my youth, I kept repeating to myself that line of Aragon's: 'What's happened? Life . . .' Baker managed with a heroism that compelled one's admiration; but that only made it seem all the more indecent to watch her. I could detect in her face the disease that was gnawing at mine.

Shortly after that – exactly ten years after the doctors had told him: 'You've got another ten years' – Boris Vian died of anger and a heart attack during a private screening of his film *I'll Spit on Your Graves*. I learned the news one afternoon when I arrived at Sartre's and picked up *Le Monde*. I had seen him for the last time at Les Trois Baudets. We'd taken a drink together; he had scarcely changed since the first time we talked. I had been very fond of him. Yet it was only several days later, coming across a picture in *Match* of a bier covered with a piece of cloth, that I realized: it's Vian under there. And I understood that if nothing in me revolted at that, it was because I was already used to the idea of my own death.

I spent a month in Rome with Sartre. He was much better, he was well. He was finishing his play. He had rewritten the first act and gone on to write the next few scenes, which were all I could possibly have wished. One evening he gave me the manuscript of the last act, which I read in the little Piazza Sant' Eustacchio: a family council had been called to judge Franz; each of them explained his or her point of view, then we got back to Sudermann. When one of Sartre's works disappoints me, I always try at first to put myself in the wrong, and then I get angry as I go on and find myself more and more in the right. I was in a very bad temper indeed when he rejoined me and I had to tell him how let down I felt. He wasn't particularly disturbed. His first idea had been for a dialogue between the father and the son, and he wasn't even sure why he'd changed it. So he went back to that idea, and this time the scene seemed to me to be the best one in a play I rated above any of the others he had written.

He in his turn gave me some stern criticisms of the first draft of my book. I have already said that when Sartre is not satisfied with what I've done, he doesn't mince words either. I would have to do it all over again. But finally he added that it was going to be more interesting, for his taste, than the *Memoirs*, and I went back to work with renewed pleasure. In the hottest part of the day, lying on my bed, I read Métraux's *Le Vaudou, Hopi Sun*, the amazing autobiography of an Indian that describes his double commitment to American civilization and to the traditional life of an Indian village; in *The Planetarium* I revisited the world of Nathalie Sarraute's lower-middle-class paranoiacs. And I rediscovered Rousseau's *Confessions*.

Sartre left me in Milan; I was to meet Lanzmann there a week later. I went to stay at Bellagio, a little intimidated at the prospect of being alone with myself for so long, since I'd got out of the habit. The days seemed too short. I had my breakfast at the edge of the lake, leafing through the Italian newspapers; I worked in front of my open window, enchanted by the calm landscape of hills and water before me; in the afternoon I read Massin's *Mozart*, which I had wrested from Sartre before he even finished it. He had found it excellent; it was a book so rich and so passionately written that I had difficulty tearing myself away from it and getting back to work. I was delighted to plunge back into it after dinner, as I sat drinking grappa on the terrace. Then I would walk in the moonlight. I spent ten days at Menton with Lanzmann. He read my manuscript and gave me some good advice. Our lives were moving apart, but the past had been preserved intact in our friendship. When I had first known him, I was not yet ripe for old age; he hid its approach from me. Now I had found it already established inside me. I still had the strength to hate it, but no longer to despair.

During the summer, Malraux made a public-relations tour of Brazil. They confronted him with the political attitude taken by

Sartre; Malraux accused him, in public addresses, of never having resisted the Germans, and even of having collaborated, to the extent of allowing his plays to be put on during the Occupation. A Minister of Culture insulting one of his country's writers while in a foreign country – that was something quite new. He also claimed that during his three months as Minister of Information the use of torture had been suspended; as people pointed out, that wasn't being very nice to M. Frey.

In about July, the Red Cross announced that an increasing number of Moslems were disappearing as Audin had 'disappeared'. Vergés and Zavrian had established themselves in Aletti on 10 August in order to give a hearing to the Algerian women whose husbands, sons and brothers had vanished in this way; they came in droves. Though expelled, the two lawyers still had time to collect a hundred and seventy-five statements, which appeared in *Les Temps Modernes* in October, as well as in *L'Express*. No bodies, therefore no proofs, was the answer of those people to whose advantage it was to deny these murders. *La France catholique* explained in one and the same breath that no one could affirm that Audin had been tortured and strangled because no one had been there to witness it, and that the tortures suffered by Alleg could hardly have been much of an ordeal since he had lived to tell the tale. When the trade unionist Aïssat Idir died in the hospital in August as a result of burns, an inquiry was started. Interned in the camp of Bitraria he had awakened one January night to discover his pallet in flames. Despite the insistant protests published for once by the press, and in particular by *Le Monde*, it was decided that he had set himself on fire, through negligence.

On 16 September, De Gaulle came out with the word 'self-determination', in November he agreed to include the G.P.R.A. among 'those with a right to be heard'; Fascist plots and regroupings multiplied; meanwhile the restorers of peace in Algeria continued to devastate the land and decimate the population. An official army communiqué showed that 334,542 Moslems had been confined in redistribution camps between June and September.[1] In Novem-

1. In *Réforme*, on 14 November 1959, Pastor Beaumont published some travel notes made between 14 and 29 October: 'In many of the redistribution centres the average ration, counted in calories, is only a quarter or a third of the *minimum* necessary to sustain life.' The number of those interned in the centres had increased by 30 per cent since March, and the camps would certainly not be suppressed before the end of the war. The people in them were

ber, there appeared in *L'Express* an eye-witness account by Farrugia, an ex-deportee, of the internment camp at Berrouaghia[1] which was indisputably nothing but an extermination camp. There were others like it. Between 15 October and 27 November the International Red Cross made surveys of the redistribution, selection, internment and transit camps, which it then collated to form a general survey of about three hundred pages, incorporating eighty-two reports; they were so shocking from the French point of view that after negotiations with the government the Red Cross released only a few extracts, from which *Le Monde* then published certain conclusions. But the complete text was circulated under cover. *L'Observateur* reminded its readers of the circumspection with which the International Red Cross had spoken of the Nazi camps. Their investigators had not seen the gas chambers with their own eyes; the camp officers had assured them that the parcels sent to the internees were faithfully distributed, etc. It was obvious that everything had been done to fool them in this case as well, and they had more or less acquiesced. Nevertheless, even though I was inured to these things, it was only with difficulty that I forced myself to read their report through to the end.

In December, *Témoignage chrétien* and then *Le Monde* made public the report of a priest, a reserve officer, on the instructions given in August 1958 at the 'Training Centre for Subversive Warfare' at the Jeanne-d'Arc camp:

Captain L. gave us five points of which I have a precise record, together with the objections and the replies to them. 1) Torture must be kept clean; 2) it must not be carried out in front of young soldiers; 3) it must not be carried out in the presence of those with sadistic tendencies; 4) it must be carried out by an officer or some responsible person; 5) above all, it must be humane, which means that it must cease

---

getting an average of about 5 ounces of hard wheat, or 700 calories, per day per capita, but in one of the cases he encountered the daily ration was as low as 3 ounces or 400 calories. In another extreme case, at the Michel farm, 500 out of 1,000 had died. In a 'normal' camp, Pastor Beaumont had seen with his own eyes children dead and dying of hunger: 'Children with tibias and fibulas covered by no more than skin, children in the last stages of rickets, children with malaria for whom there was no quinine, and who lay shivering on the bare ground without even a covering over them.'

1. He confirmed the account given of it in July by *El Moudjahid*; there were 2,500 prisoners there: men considered particularly dangerous and 'intellectuals'. They were being treated with brutality, tortured, beaten up, murdered; many went mad; many killed themselves.

as soon as the prisoner has talked; and even more important, it must leave no trace. Given these conditions – was the conclusion – you have the right to use water and electricity.

This report passed more or less unnoticed. The French people were by then drifting in a state of indifference in which the words knowledge and ignorance were more or less equivalent, a state in which even the most startling revelation made no impression on them. The Audin Committee proved that Audin had been strangled to death. But wind of it scarcely reached the general public, and they had no desire to find out more.

After the days of the barricades, De Gaulle had the bill for plenary powers voted through. The atmosphere became more unbreathable every day. On street corners, in front of police stations, you saw the cops standing, submachine guns in hand, eyes constantly alert; if you went up to them at night to ask the way, they levelled their weapons at you. On New Year's Eve, one of them killed a boy of seventeen in Gennevilliers as he was going home from a dance. Once Bost was driving home very fast at about two in the morning when he was chased and stopped by a police car. He had to show his papers; profession: journalist. 'An intellectual!' said one of the policemen with hate in his voice. While he kept his submachine gun trained on Bost, the others went through the boot. You couldn't go a hundred yards along a street without seeing North Africans being loaded into a police truck. As I passed the Préfecture, I saw one lying on a stretcher covered in blood. One Sunday, I drove with Lanzmann along the Rue de la Chapelle. There were cops, snug in their bullet-proof vests, Sten guns in their hands, searching some men they'd lined up against a wall with their hands in the air: Algerians, shaved, well-groomed, wearing their best clothes. It was Sunday for them too; the hands delved into their pockets and came out brandishing their pitiful personal belongings: a pack of cigarettes, a handkerchief. I gave up going out in Paris.

Yet it was certain that Algeria would obtain its independence; all Africa agreed about that. When Guinea had the courage to reply No to the referendum on 28 September 1958 France broke off relations; she did not break off relations with the other nations which, a year later, made as if to follow the same path.[1] In an attempt to prevent

1. The truth is, that with the exception of Mali, they didn't really attack colonialist exploitation, and the genuine revolutionaries had to continue the struggle. In the Cameroons it was, and still is, a bloody one.

a revolution in the Congo and safeguard its own economic interests, Belgium was decolonizing as fast as it could. The last of the English colonies had received assurances of their imminent emancipation. In Monrovia, during the summer, the young African nations had made a demonstration of their solidarity with Algeria.

Things in the rest of the world seemed less gloomy than in France. The tension between the blocs still subsisted on certain points, especially in West Germany, where a fanatical anti-Communism was now being supplemented by a renaissance of anti-Semitism; swastikas appeared on the synagogues on Christmas Eve. But Khrushchev's trip to Washington and the one Eisenhower was to make to Moscow were events without precedent. Lunik 2 and Lunik 3 confirmed Russia's superiority in space; that was a guarantee of peace.

In much the same way as airline passengers involved in an accident are advised to get straight into another plane, old Mirande had urged Sartre, after the failure of *Nékrassov*: 'Write another play right away; if you don't, you've had it, you'll never dare to again.' Although he'd let several years elapse, Sartre had dared to. I liked *Altona* so much that it revived my old illusions: a work, perfectly brought off, transfigures and justifies the life of its author; yet Sartre, possibly because of the circumstances in the midst of which he began work on it, never felt any great liking for this play. Vera Korène put it on at the Théâtre de la Renaissance and, once back in Paris, I watched almost all the rehearsals, often delighted, often disappointed. My pleasure was unalloyed on the afternoon when Reggiani, after going through it again and again, correcting himself with subtle severity at each attempt, taped the monologue at the end, which I found so beautiful; it was reassuring to realize that not one of those intonations could ever, now, be changed again. For the actors varied. I wasn't entirely satisfied with the scenery and the costumes, and, for a change, the play went on too long. I helped Sartre make a few cuts and encouraged him in refusing to make others demanded by the management. Vera Korène and Simone Berriau, who was associated with the production, prophesied disaster; cabals, scenes, tantrums – I was used to all that. But this time there was something serious at stake. I had never seen Sartre so anxious about the reception his work was going to get. Once, between two work sessions, we were striding out along the boulevard under a stony sky, and I felt his uneasiness infecting me. 'Even if it's a bomb, you'll still have written your best play,' I told him; perhaps, but what a disaster for the actors who would have blown their whole season on it! And it would disgust Sartre with the theatre for good. I thought of all the enemies who had been announcing for years that Sartre was finished and would rush around with glee to bury him. Spiteful rumours had already begun to circulate when the first performance had to be postponed because the technicians and actors weren't ready. But it opened at last. Standing at the back of the orchestra, I studied the invited audience; it was stifling in the badly ventilated auditorium; that wasn't going to help anyone follow a play of such rich and difficult content. Yes, I was sure Reggiani had been wrong not to muss up that far too handsome uniform. Suddenly other imperfections began to hit me in the eye. More moved than ever by the public unveiling of a work that affected me personally to the very marrow of my bones, dripping with sweat, clutched by panic, I hung on to a pillar, expecting to faint at any moment. At the final curtain the applause was so loud that I knew we had won. All the same, I was nervous when the curtain rose a few evenings later before the sullen audience of the first public performance. I went for a walk with Sartre along the boulevard. There was an apartment house on fire, we stopped to watch the firemen fight the blaze. Back at the theatre, I stood in one of the boxes, then another, watching the play in snatches and noticing that, as always happens, the company was acting less well than on the previous evenings. During intermission, Vera Korène and her friends went off into a chorus of lamentation about the length of the play; that did nothing to boost the morale of the actors, who were already half dead with nerves. After the final curtain, the dressing rooms, the staircases, the corridors backstage, were inundated with everyone's friends. They liked the play, but complained about not being able to hear very well and being too hot. My nerves were in shreds by the time I got up to the second floor of the Falstaff, where Sartre was giving a supper for the company and his close friends. We were all worried. Sartre had resigned himself to making more cuts, but reluctantly, and I could sense his inner torment. He downed a drink, two drinks; once it had never occurred to me to count; the more he used to drink the funnier he became, but that was in the old days; he poured himself a third, I tried to stop him, he laughed and took no notice; my head

[485]

was suddenly filled with memories of the winter before – the distillations, the thickets in his heart – and what with the Scotch inside me as well, I was suddenly seized by such a feeling of panic that I burst into tears; immediately, Sartre put down his glass. Amid the general excitement the incident passed almost unnoticed.

Sartre cut or deleted some of the scenes, reducing the playing time by about half an hour. And without having read almost any of the reviews he flew off to Ireland, where Huston was waiting for him to bring the Freud scenario. As soon as I woke up on Thursday, I went out to buy the dailies and weeklies and glanced through them, sitting in the sun on a café terrace: it was a beautiful October morning. Almost all the critics agreed with me in placing *Altona* above all Sartre's other plays. I sent him a cable immediately, and the reviews.

By the time Sartre came back ten days later, the play's success was assured. He gave me a lighthearted account of his stay in Ireland. Huston had greeted him on the threshold of his house dressed in a red tuxedo; it was an enormous building, still unfinished, crammed with a costly and bizarre assortment of *objets d'art*, surrounded by grounds so vast that it took hours to cross them on foot. In the morning, Huston would go prancing about them on horseback, sometimes falling off. He would invite all sorts of people out there and then suddenly go off and leave them, in the middle of a conversation, which Sartre would struggle vainly to keep going. Sartre had been forced in this way to entertain an Anglican bishop, a maharajah and an eminent authority on fox hunting, none of whom spoke French. During the day he was always occupied by discussions with Reinhart and Huston, so he didn't see much of Ireland, but he had been taken with its funereal charm. He was finding the profession of scenario writer an ungrateful one.

I too made my first attempt in that field. Cayatte suggested that I work with him on a film about divorce; I hadn't the slightest desire to write about 'the problems of the couple', but I knew a lot about them. I had received so many letters, heard so many case histories; the idea of making use of all this material in a scenario was a tempting one. Two things bothered me. First, the cinema does not leave room for the same frankness as the printed page; impossible to refer to the Algerian war, and consequently to locate my main characters in their true social situation; but their story, detached in this way from its background, no longer seemed real in my eyes; could I succeed in interesting myself in it? Second, Cayatte wanted the woman's and the man's differing versions of the conflict that divided them to be presented in two separately narrated episodes. I objected that the life of any couple is a story with two faces, but not two distinct stories. He insisted, but when he read my script admitted that this binary form was ruining it. I amalgamated the two sections. It would have been better to start again from scratch, but I had already got caught up with my characters and with the situations I had involved them in; my imagination was no longer free. Before long, I realized that, despite our mutual goodwill, there was a misunderstanding between Cayatte and myself; I think he had approached me because I am generally thought of as having a taste for 'problem novels', whereas, as I have already said, I don't like them at all. In my scenario I was at pains not to prove anything whatever, all the sequences were ambiguous, the links between them varied and fluid. Was Cayatte right or wrong in finding it confused? It also lacked, according to him, the necessary 'gimmick' that surprises an audience and guarantees success; I would have preferred to capture the audience by less obvious methods, by the underlying tone, by a style as Bresson did, for example, in *Les Dames du Bois de Boulogne*, with its intense austerity of effect. But after all, I had no complaints; Cayatte knew what he wanted, and it wasn't what I was giving him. I understood perfectly why he decided not to go on with it.

During the few weeks I was busy with the scenario, I did not stop reworking my book. Spurred on by the favourable comments, and even more by the criticisms I received from Sartre and Bost and Lanzmann, I cut, amplified, corrected, tore up, began again, pondered, made decisions. For me, it's a privileged interval, the period when I finally escape the vertigo of the blank page and haven't yet bogged down in the minutiae of the final draft. I was also spending hours reading and re-reading the manuscript of the *Critique de la raison dialectique*; I groped my way along many dark tunnels, but when I emerged I was often transported by a feeling of pleasure that made me feel twenty years younger. *Altona* and the *Critique* redeemed all the marasmas, all the fears of the previous autumn. Through Sartre, and on my own account too, the adventure of writing regained its exalting taste.

To spend hours, months, years, talking to people one doesn't know – a strange activity. Luckily, chance makes me a little present from time to time. In the summer of 1955, I walked into a bookshop in Bayonne. 'There's one book I really like,' a young woman was just saying, 'it's hard, it's peculiar, but I like it: *The Mandarins.*' It gives me pleasure to see flesh-and-blood readers who really like me. I also rather like getting to see the ones who loathe me. There was another summer when I was lunching with Lanzmann in a hotel in the Pyrenees; some Spanish people and a Frenchwoman married to a certain Carlo were dining at a nearby table; she talked about her domestic life: 'I've got a chauffeur, and it's so convenient for getting the children out.' She was depressive and narcissistic; going on to analyse the subtle reactions of her heart, she said: 'I only like what's completely the opposite of myself.' Then her voice rose. 'A madwoman, she's abnormal, a disgusting book . . .' She was talking about *The Second Sex*, and me. We left the restaurant first, and as we got back into the car I gave the waiter a signed postcard with the words: 'To Madame Carlo, who has the good taste to like only what is completely the opposite of herself.'

Ever since *The Second Sex*, I have received a great many letters. Some are merely tiresome: autograph hunters, snobs, gossips, busybodies. Some are insulting; that doesn't worry me. The invectives of an anti-Semite who wittily signs himself Merdocu, Rumanian Jew, or of a *pied noir* who accuses me of coprophagia and describes my banquets, can only divert me. The ones from a 'French Algerian' lieutenant who wanted to see me stood up against a wall and riddled with bullets simply confirm my opinions about the military profession. And there are other letters, envious, sharp-tongued, angry, that help me understand the resistance aroused by my books. The majority of my correspondents tell me of their fellow feelings, confide their difficulties, ask for advice or explanations; they encourage me and sometimes enrich my experience. During the Algerian war, young soldiers who felt the need to talk to someone shared their lives with me. I am often asked to read manuscripts. I always accept.

Among the people who wish to make my acquaintance, many are simply inconsiderate. 'I'd like to talk to you to find out what you think about women,' was how one young woman phrased her request. 'Read *The Second Sex*.' 'I haven't time to read.' 'I haven't time to talk.' But I'm always happy to meet students of either sex.

Many of them know both Sartre's books and my own very well and want to discuss and elucidate particular points; to see them is therefore not merely doing them a service but also an opportunity for me to find out what young people are thinking, what they know, what they want, how they live. The acquaintance of young girls whose lives have not yet become settled is a great comfort to me. Once, when I was expecting to greet someone who sounded, from her letters, like an oppressed wife and mother, I was agreeably surprised to see a beautiful twenty-year-old blonde girl walk into my studio. A French Canadian who found no stimulus in her family, her environment, her country, she had pursued her education as far as possible and then won a scholarship to study theatre direction in Paris. Her letters of reference, her beauty and her intelligence soon enabled her to make her way in the Paris theatre world; she attended several courses; she watched rehearsals, going every day to those for *Tête d'Or*. She used to tell me about them; nothing escaped her lively and critical eye. Her own difficult personal problems never kept her from being ardently interested in those that affected the world at large. I missed her when she went back to Canada. Though very different, Jacqueline O. had also succeeded in wrenching herself free from a stifling background and overcoming serious personal distress; twenty years old, a schoolteacher in Switzerland, she was studying for a diploma, writing short stories feverishly, reporting for newspapers, working actively for Socialism, and for votes and independence for women; dark-haired and plump, her long green or purple nails and exaggeratedly large earrings made a curious contrast with the calmness and maturity of her manner. Later, she was to quit Europe and as a teacher move to Mali, where she is quite happy.

I also felt great friendship for a young man from Marseilles who had been writing me comradely letters for some years. After a difficult adolescence, he had been a sailor, then a washer-up in a London restaurant, and I don't know what else. 'I'm a classic misfit,' he told me modestly, the first time he came to see me. He had a closed face, but when he managed one of his awkward smiles he looked like a little boy. He was against society, against adults, against everything. He arranged matters so that he could earn a living and at the same time continue his education and pass his exams. From his original tentative anarchism he progressed to an extreme and even dangerous state of commitment. He often took me severely to task.

When *The Long March* came out – a much less vigorous book than *America Day by Day* – he asked me uneasily, making a downward, slithering gesture with his hand: 'Are you going to keep on like this?'

It is mostly young women who come to see me. Many have reached the age of thirty and feel trapped in a situation – husband, child, work – which they have helped to create, though in a way despite themselves; some of them manage better than others in such situations. Often they try to write. They discuss their problems with me. Some of them make extravagant confessions. I saw Mme C. two or three times about a manuscript of mediocre quality she had sent me; she was about thirty, married, comfortably off, with two children, and she described her marital difficulties to me. She was frigid; her husband was consoling himself with her best friend, Denise, and the two went off on car-hopping orgies together. 'Why? What do you get out of it?' she had asked Denise. 'An extraordinary feeling of complicity; and afterwards, tenderness,' Denise had answered. One morning Mme C. telephoned me; she had to see me, right away. She rang my bell that afternoon, came in and began her story. Unable to contain her curiosity about the complicity and the tenderness, she had gone with her husband and Denise in a car to the Avenue des Acacias in the Bois de Boulogne, where the participants do their car hopping. C. decided on two little cars filled with nothing but men. 'Well, you won't have the time to be bored, my dears,' he said to the women, leading two men into the apartment, followed by four others: mechanics, garage hands, delighted by this piece of good luck. Everyone drank a lot. The husband contented himself with looking on. As soon as the guests had departed, he went over to Denise and began murmuring endearments to her; the tenderness was for her! Despair, scene; Denise left. 'You've spoiled everything,' C. shouted at his wife, rushing out and slamming the door. She ran after him, he got into his car, she got into hers, they both drove off, one behind the other, at top speed. In the middle of Les Halles, he stopped short and she drove into the back of his car. She'd left her licence and insurance at home; the police kept her at the station until her husband brought them. They went back home and were immediately disturbed by two of their nocturnal visitors in an ugly mood: one of the four others had taken their wallets. Exhausted, she lay down on her bed, thinking over all her trials and tribulations. 'And suddenly,' she told me, 'I felt something I'd never experienced before. . . .'

Why had she insisted on letting me in on all this? At all events, it provided me with a curious glimpse of Parisian morals. One evening, Olga, Bost, Lanzmann and myself drove to the Avenue des Acacias. Cars were cruising slowly up and down, passing, waiting, smiles were exchanged. The social hierarchy was respected. Posh cars followed posh cars; little cars formed groups of their own. We got in on the act too, and soon we had a 403 and an Aronde tagging along behind us. Bost accelerated fiercely and we shook them off, aware that we had violated all the rules of polite behaviour. As for Mme C., she has slipped out of my life.

Every writer who is at all well-known receives crank letters from nuts. I should be doing no service either to them or to myself by replying; I refrain from doing so. But sometimes they are insistent. One morning, in Rome, I received a cable – in English – from Philadelphia: 'Trying vainly to reach you for two weeks. Will telephone Tuesday noon. Love. Lucy.' Apparently this person knew me, knew me well even; who was it? The voice on the telephone spoke to me quite intimately; but in English, and over such a distance, I could scarcely make out what was said. 'Excuse me,' I said, 'but when did we meet? I can't place you. . . .' There was a long silence. 'You can't place me!' She hung up. I was a bit upset, imagining that Lucy, whoever she was, had met someone in Paris pretending to be me. She telephoned again during the afternoon. 'Madame de Beauvoir,' she said in a distant voice, 'I shall be in Paris on 17 December and I'd like to talk to you about Existentialism.' 'Gladly,' I answered and hung up; I had realized what it was all about. I found out later that to get my address Lucy had telephoned first to my American publisher, and then, at their suggestion, to Ellen Wright in Paris. Letters began arriving – three or four a week. Lucy owned an antique shop, she was going to sell out so that she could come and live with me, she was buying a new topcoat, she described my joy when I would open my door to welcome her! 'There is a misunderstanding,' I wrote her on several occasions. Then I would receive a cable or a formal letter: 'Would you be kind enough to grant me an interview so that we can discuss *The Ethics of Ambiguity*.' Meanwhile, I was advised that the customs office was holding certain packages on which I was supposed to pay duty: a bust of Nefertiti, an 'engagement ring' worth

50,000 francs. I had them returned to the sender. Once more I wrote: 'Do not come.' Whereupon Lucy telephoned Ellen Wright: 'Should I come or not?' 'No,' Ellen said. I received a final letter: 'I have sold my shop, I am penniless, and now you reject me! You have taught me a lesson, but I am a bad student; I haven't understood it. I cannot even blame you for anything, you have been so careful to protect yourself.' A month later, a parcel from Philadelphia was delivered; it had been very carefully wrapped, and contained a single chair rung.

In 1958, in our opposition to the Algerian war and to Fascist threats, we had drawn much closer to the French Communists. Sartre had intervened in the Peace Movement with his request that it should fight for Algerian independence as it had fought for that of Vietnam. In April, he had gone with Servan-Schreiber to meet some Communists at the Hôtel Moderne with a view to creating anti-Fascist committees. From May on, we had fought side by side. Through Guttuso, whom he had met again in the spring of 1958, Sartre had renewed his contact with the Italian Communists. In 1959, Aragon had passed on an invitation to him from Orlova, who was playing Lizzie in *The Respectful Prostitute*, and her husband Alexandrov. He didn't think he could accept, but when the Soviet Embassy asked us to dinner, we went. Maurois and Aragon, who were preparing to write parallel histories of the U.S.A. and the U.S.S.R., were there; also Elsa Triolet, Claude Gallimard and his wife, the Julliards, and Dutourd, who avoided shaking our hands, thus sparing us his. I found myself beside Vinogradov, who was beaming with joy because Khrushchev was due to visit Paris very shortly; on my other side was Leonid Leonov; I had read *The Badgers* twenty years before, but Leonov spoke scarcely any French. He did manage to tell me: 'Philosophy's finished. ... Einstein's equation makes all philosophy useless.' Elsa Triolet sat opposite me, between the ambassador and Sartre; her hair had gone grey, her eyes had stayed very blue, and her pretty smile contrasted sharply with the bitter expression of her face. As we were talking about discoveries for rejuvenating the old and prolonging life, she said abruptly: 'Oh no! It lasts long enough already; I'm nearly through it now, don't make me go back again.' Camus had told me in 1946 that she and I had one characteristic in common: the horror of growing old. One day, talking about the beginning of *Le Cheval roux* – in which the narrator has been so appallingly disfigured by an atomic explosion that she wears a stocking over her head to hide her face – Sartre had asked Elsa Triolet how she had had the courage to imagine herself with this scarecrow face. 'I only had to look in a mirror,' she replied. At the time, I said to myself: 'But she's wrong. An old woman isn't the same as an ugly woman. She's just an old woman.' In the eyes of others, yes; but for oneself, once past a certain stage, the looking glass reflects a disfigured face. Now I understood her. After dinner, I found myself in a corner of the drawing room with Maurois. I was hoping he would talk to me about Virginia Woolf, whom he had known; but the conversation didn't 'take'.

In October, Lanzmann told me about a book he'd only glanced through, but which seemed to him very good: *The Last of the Just*. After so many real-life stories, after Poliakoff's *Le III⁰ Reich et les juifs*, what could a work of fiction possibly say? I opened the book one evening, and could not stop reading it all night. When the book subsequently became so famous and so widely discussed, I rebutted many of the criticisms that were levelled at it. Nevertheless, I did have some reservations to make on a second reading: some crudities in the writing; a religiosity still apparent beneath all the skilful camouflage. Perhaps, too, the book's authenticity is tainted by a little too much ingenuity; but after all, that is what literature is, as Cocteau says: *un cri écrit*, a written cry.

Lanzmann made Schwartz-Bart's acquaintance, and he invited us over together one Sunday afternoon. Schwartz-Bart was dressed like a worker, but it was the head and face of an intellectual that emerged from his turtleneck sweater; he had restless eyes, a sensitive, mobile mouth, and spoke very volubly in such a whispering voice it was difficult to catch what he said. Although completely indifferent to worldly values, money, honours, privileges, fame, he made no attempt to seem annoyed by the interest he had aroused. 'At the moment I'm not working, so the interviews and all that don't bother me; it's just part of the trade.' He had spent four years writing his book as well as he could; it seemed to him logical that he should now do his best to make sure people read it. Nevertheless, he had reacted vigorously to the importunity of certain journalists. He was no lamb ready for the slaughter; if he professed non-violence, it was, it seemed to me, because it seemed to him to be the most appropriate and effective weapon at the time – which doesn't mean that he wasn't quite sincere about it. He believed in human nature, and he believed that it was good; he wanted society to be content with what he called 'the human minimum' instead of running after progress; in short, his inclinations were far more towards the saintly ideal than towards that of the revolutionary. Lanzmann and I disagreed with him on these points, but he was a difficult person to argue with. Being spontaneous and warm-hearted, he gave at first an impression of openness and relaxation; then one realized that by adjusting his ideas so exactly to his emotions, he had constructed an almost unassailable system of defences for himself; for him, to shift from any position by so much as an inch would have entailed a total demolition and a total reconstruction of his whole attitude to the world. We noticed afterwards that he had in fact told us nothing he did not subsequently repeat to the press and television; that was natural enough, but it belied the illusion of sharing his secret confidences which his ease of manner created. Even reduced to a rather official version, the story of his early life was fascinating; he had a very quick mind, and a charm that combined gentleness and pride, sharpness and patience, sincerity and reticence; instead of the two hours I had expected to be with him, I stayed six. The next time I saw Schwartz-Bart was once again with Lanzmann, at the Coupole; the success of his book, which the juries of the Goncourt and the Fémina were fighting over, had annoyed several little-known writers who regarded Judaism as their province; they had persuaded Parinaud, who wanted the honour of the Goncourt for a writer in his own circle, to write an article which, thanks to the comments Bernard Franck made on it in *L'Observateur*, was soon the laughing-stock of Paris. Schwartz-Bart was accused of some harmless enough errors and also, a more serious matter, of plagiarism; there was in fact, in the first part of his novel, a passage of about ten lines that very closely resembled a similar passage in an old chronicle. There was nothing to make such a fuss about. This first section was in any case a pastiche; to imitate the style of a text one has to steep oneself in it; certain sentences fix themselves in one's mind, to such an extent that one ends up by thinking they are one's own. I had experienced the same thing myself when I was writing *All Men are Mortal*. But as I had already divined, if Schwartz-Bart took such pains to protect himself, it was because he was vulnerable; this intrigue had upset him badly. He sat across from me, quivering with calm. 'It's

all over, I've decided not to worry about it any more,' he told me.
'I spent the night thinking it all over quietly. The prize I don't care
about; as for money, I've already earned quite enough. It's losing
my reputation that's so terrible, but I'll get it back. I'll disappear for
four years; I'll come back with a new book; and they'll see that I
really am a writer.' We assured him that the Goncourt jury
wouldn't be taken in by the plot, and that none of his readers had
any doubts about his being the real author of his book. He scarcely
listened. 'I prefer to expect the worst; that's how I do things; I
imagine exactly what it will be like, I accept it and then I stop
worrying about what's going to happen.'

After the Goncourt, announced prematurely to the fury of the
ladies of the Fémina, I invited Lanzmann and Schwartz-Bart over. I
was flabbergasted when I saw him come in and almost began to
laugh. He had disguised himself in a long green raincoat, a green
hat with a turned-down brim, and dark glasses. 'I'm being hounded,'
he said wildly. 'People come up to me in cafés and ask for autographs, they call me Monsieur Schwartz-Bart. Monsieur! Can you
imagine!' He was sincerely frightened by the realization that
celebrity limits you and cuts you off from others. And he was disturbed by the obligations it was imposing on him; he received so
many letters! Confidences, confessions, thanks, complaints, requests, pleas; apparently he felt he ought to pay a personal visit to
everyone who wrote him; he thought of himself as accountable in
the eyes of the entire Jewish community. I thought there was a hint
of self-satisfaction in his panic, and I felt the impulse to assure him
that in a few months' time he would be able to walk along the
street in perfect peace. But no one, after all, can pass so quickly
from obscurity to fame, from poverty to riches, without being
disturbed by the process. What was he to do with the millions of
francs that were suddenly showering down on him? There were
people around him who needed a helping hand, but no more than
that, and there weren't many of them. As for himself, there was
nothing he wanted. Did he need to buy an apartment? Obviously
not. A car? He wouldn't know how to drive it. 'I have no dreams,'
he told us; he paused. 'Yes, one little one: a motorbike to ride out
into the country on Sundays.' Then he added with a half-smile:
'And you can get around so easily on a motorbike; they're very
convenient.' We suggested a phonograph and some records. He
only wanted three records: 'I could listen to the Seventh Symphony

for ever; I don't see how I'd get any more out of buying fifty records.' He had a sincere antipathy to luxury and enormous scruples with regard to money, for he always thought of the price of anything in terms of a worker's salary; he had taken a taxi to get to my studio – that represented two hours' work for a labourer. I understood this attitude, because as soon as I made any money it had presented me with problems I have never solved. He also talked about his future plans – a novel on the situation of the Negro; sensitive to the oppression women suffer, he was going to take a Negro woman as his main character. I wondered if he would be able to bring her to life as convincingly as he had done with Ernie. In any case, he was leaving for Martinique.

I didn't see him until a year later, when he came back to sign the Manifesto of the '121'. He hadn't yielded at all to the blandishments of fame and money, though using the latter seemed to come to him more naturally, and asceticism was no longer his ideal, either for himself or for humanity in general. His friends in Martinique had converted him to a belief in revolution by violence; he had utterly approved of the first chapter of *Les Damnés de la terre*, published by *Les Temps Modernes*, in which Fanon demonstrated that the oppressed have no other way of attaining their rightful status as human beings. Schwartz-Bart was inwardly freer than before, more open and, it seemed to me, had his feet more firmly planted on the ground. These changes were proof that he was putting the truths of reality before his own opinions, risk before the comfort of certainty.

I was alone in Sartre's apartment one January afternoon when the telephone rang. 'Camus has just been killed in a car crash,' Lanzmann told me. He was coming back from the south of France with a friend, the car had smashed into a plane tree, and he was killed instantly. I put down the receiver, my throat tight, my lips trembling. 'I'm not going to start crying,' I said to myself, 'he didn't mean anything to me any more.' I stood there, leaning against the window, watching night come down over Saint-Germain-des-Prés, incapable of calming myself or of giving way to real grief. Sartre was upset as well, and we spent the whole evening with Bost talking about Camus. Before getting to bed I swallowed some belladénal pills; I hadn't taken any since Sartre's recovery, I ought to have gone to sleep; I remained completely wide awake. I got up, threw on the first clothes I found, and set out walking through the night. It wasn't the fifty-year-old man who'd just died I was mourning; not that just man without justice, so arrogant and touchy behind his stern mask, who had been struck out of my heart when he gave his approval to the crimes of France; it was the companion of our hopeful years, whose open face laughed and smiled so easily, the young, ambitious writer, wild to enjoy life, its pleasures, its triumphs, and comradeship, friendship, love and happiness. Death had brought him back to life; for him, time no longer existed, yesterday had no more truth now than the day before; Camus as I had loved him emerged from the night about me, in the same instant recovered and painfully lost. Every time a man dies, a child dies too, and an adolescent and a young man as well; everyone weeps for the one who was dear to him. A fine, cold rain was falling; along the Avenue d'Orléans, there were bums sleeping in the doorways, hunched up in another world. Everything tore at my heart: this poverty, this unhappiness, this city, the world and life, and death.

When I woke up, I thought: He can't see this morning. It wasn't the first time I'd said that to myself; but every time is the first time. Cayatte came over, I remember, and we talked about the scenario; the conversation was just a pretence; far from having left the world, Camus, by the violence of the event that had struck him down, had become the centre of it and I could no longer see anything except through his dead eyes. I had gone over to the other side where there is nothing, and realized, with a dumb pain, how everything still continued to exist though I was no longer there; all day I teetered on the edge of that impossible experience: touching the other side of my own non-being.

That evening I had planned to go see *Citizen Kane* again; I got to the theatre too early and sat down in the café opposite, in the Avenue de l'Opéra. There were people reading newspapers, quite indifferent to the big headline on the front page and the photograph that was blinding me. I thought of the woman who loved Camus, of her agony at encountering that face on every street corner, a public face that must seem to belong to everyone else now as much as to her, a face that could no longer speak and tell her it wasn't so. What a refinement of torture, I thought, one's secret despair proclaimed and trumpeted to the wind at every street corner. Michel Gallimard had been badly injured; he used to come to our celebrations in 1944 and 1945; he too died. Vian, Camus, Michel: the series of deaths had begun, it would go on till it reached mine, inevitably too soon, or too late.

That winter I explored again a realm that I had left unvisited for a long time: music. I had given away my phonograph, I didn't go to concerts any more. My young Canadian friend, who used to go to those given by the Domaine Musical, urged me to go hear one; it was very near Sartre's apartment, at the Odéon, and she promised to get the tickets. I was afraid of not understanding anything. But Sartre was curious enough to have a try. As it turned out, we felt completely lost. Why were they sniggering? Why were they clapping? Wahl, Merleau-Ponty and Lefèvre-Pontalis, all of whom we saw in the intermission, couldn't make head nor tail of it either, but that didn't seem to bother them at all. Sartre felt piqued at finding himself out of things. I bought a hi-fi and some records, adding to my collection every month. Sartre helped me pick out the tone rows, identify the structures. We spent a whole winter on Webern; I found his music as dense as a sculpture by Giacometti: not an ounce of superfluous flesh, not one unnecessary note. I worked my way backwards into the past; every kind of music interested me. I spent all my free time near my turn-table. Two or three evenings a week, I would settle down on my divan with a glass of Scotch and listen for three or four hours. I still do it quite often. Music has assumed much greater importance for me than at any other period in my life.

I wondered why. No doubt the main reason is a material one: the existence of the long-playing record, the quality of the recordings. The old seventy-eights were difficult to keep in order and handle; you couldn't concentrate on the music and give yourself up to it at the same time because it was cut up into such little pieces. Today, the ends of the sides almost always coincide with the natural divisions of the music and are therefore geared to the natural rhythm of one's attention. There are a great many works available, which means that one can put together extremely rich and varied concerts for oneself. Circumstances too played a part. I very rarely go to the movies or to the theatre any more, I stay in. Of course, I could read; but when the evening comes, I feel I've had enough words, my mind is swimming with them; I feel worn out by this world of ours and books are no escape from it. Novels do invent other worlds, but they're very similar to this one, and usually more insipid. Music takes me into another universe, ruled by necessity and composed of a substance, sound, which I find physically agreeable. It is a universe of innocence – at least it was until the nineteenth century – because man is absent from it; when I listen to Lassus or Pergolesi, even the idea of evil no longer seems to exist. And then I was so ignorant about music. It brought me something that the other arts no longer afford me; the shock of great works that are completely unknown to me. I discovered Monteverdi, Schütz, Perotinus, Machaut, Josquin, Victoria. I learned to appreciate better the composers I was already familiar with. My books are piled helter-skelter on their shelves, they don't mean anything to me; but I love looking at my multi-coloured record sleeves, austere or gay, concealing such tumults and harmonies beneath their glossy surfaces. During these past few years, it has been through music that art has mingled familiarly with my everyday life, inspired me with violent emotions, permitted me to experience its power and its truth, as well as its limits and its hoaxes.

Often, on Sunday walks with Sartre along the banks of the Seine, behind the Pantheon, in Ménilmontant, we would lament the way in which age had blunted our curiosity; for we were being offered splendid opportunities to travel. When he was passing through Paris, Franqui, the editor of the largest newspaper in Cuba, *Revolucion*, came round to see me with a few friends, one of whom spoke French. Hair and moustache black, very Spanish, he told me authoritatively that it was our duty to take a look with our own eyes at a revolution actually in progress. We felt great sympathy with Castro; yet Franqui's offer to us – for Sartre had met him too – left us almost indifferent. Some Brazilians invited us to visit their country the following summer, and our reaction was just as half-hearted. 'I wonder,' Sartre said to me, 'whether it's not just physical exhaustion that stops us, rather than moral fatigue.' This explanation appeared to him to be truer and more optimistic than the other, and certainly the fear that he would overtax himself kept a firm rein on my desires. There was another reason for our apathy: the war in Algeria was blocking our horizon. Yet the rest of the world did still exist, and we had no right to be completely uninterested in it. What Franqui said was true: Cuba's experiment did concern us. A visit to Brazil would enlighten us about the problems of underdeveloped countries; Amado and other Leftists there wanted us to come because they hoped that by giving lectures and writing articles, Sartre might be useful to them. To remain deaf to these invitations, to anaesthetize our curiosity, to brood in impotence over the misfortunes of our own country, was a sort of resignation from life. Sartre was the first to decide that we should shake ourselves out of our inertia.

When we took off, halfway through February, relations between Cuba and the United States were strained, and the American ambassador had returned to Washington. The Spanish ambassador had also left Havana, having forced his way, dead drunk, into the television studios there, because, according to him, they were insulting Franco. The bonds between Cuba and the U.S.S.R. were strengthening; Mikoyan had just paid Castro an official visit. It was a fine February morning; I watched the precise outlines, the clear-cut colours of a geographical map unroll beneath me; as in my atlas, the Gironde fanned out its muddy waters from Bordeaux to the green-tinted ocean; the snow-covered Pyrenees sloped gently down to a sea already hinting at spring; soon, quite suddenly, we were in Madrid, hitherto so far away. Sartre, who hadn't set foot there for thirty years, got no joy out of seeing it again. At about three in the afternoon all the shops were shut, it was raining, the few people we saw in the streets seemed badly dressed and dismal-looking. 'There's a pleasure in imagining what's going on inside those people's heads,' he said as we sat drinking *manzanilla* in a café on the Gran Vía. The next day he went to look at the Goyas and Velásquezes in the Prado. And then we left for Havana. In the plane we deciphered as much as we could of some Cuban newspapers and then dropped off into fitful sleep. When I awoke, I looked out and saw another, different sea, islands, then the coast and a green plain with palm trees sticking up out of it.

The bewilderment of our arrival: temples still throbbing, ears humming, the sun beating down, bouquets, compliments, questions all jumbled together ('What do you think of the Cuban Revolution?' one journalist asked Sartre. 'That's what I've come to find out,' he answered), and all those strange new faces. An automobile drove us along a wide road between palm trees and huge flowers; as we went, someone gave me a running commentary on the places we passed, the monuments, but I scarcely heard any of it, I could only see the wildness of the sea on my left; I was sleepy, I was hot, I wanted a shower, then there I was sitting at a second-floor window looking out over a grey stone square facing a very beautiful church, holding a *daiquiri* as voluptuous as in Sartre's descriptions, and the

[500]

voices still explaining and asking questions. They even began to grow in number when, after a short respite, we went to have lunch in a restaurant which was a de-luxe imitation of a rustic *bohio*. A few days later I knew I would be able to put names to these smiles, to decide which I liked and which I didn't, but at that moment I could make no distinctions between all these mouths interrogating me about abstract painting, Algeria, the commitment of French writers, of American writers, and Existentialism. I should have delighted in all this noise and fuss, if only I could have shaken off the burden of fatigue that had been made so much heavier by all the hours we had lost in flight.

Next day my weariness had gone. After Madrid, after Paris, the gaiety of the place exploded like a miracle under the blue sky, in the gentle darkness of the night. Sartre has explained at length in his account of our visit what advantages their revolution afforded the Cuban people. To watch the struggle of six million men against oppression, hunger, slums, unemployment, and illiteracy, to understand the mechanisms of the struggle and discover its significance was a passionately interesting experience. The discussions, the visits, the briefing sessions very rarely took a formal turn; our guides and our interpreter, Arcocha, very quickly became our friends; after a few initial moments of stiffness, our three-day trip with Castro was spent in an atmosphere of familiarity. Striking out with him into the warmth of the crowds, we experienced a joy we had not known for a long time. I liked the simple expansive Cuban landscapes. The pale-green of the sugar-cane harmonized perfectly with the deep green of the palm fronds at the top of their smooth silver stems; one of my biggest shocks was seeing cows grazing at the foot of these trees whose image had always been linked for me with that of the desert. I liked Santiago with its black crowds and Trinidad, austerely embalmed in its colonial past, yet fresh too with all the exuberance of its flowers. I loved Havana. Vedado, where our hotel was, displayed all the seductions of a rich capitalist city: wide avenues, long American automobiles, elegant skyscrapers and, in the evening, brilliant displays of neon signs. The windows of my room overlooked a park that extended down to the sea; in the distance I could see old Havana, the headland battered furiously by tall waves. I would drink my very black, almost bitter coffee with Sartre in the morning, eat some tender, succulent pineapple and then, while he was writing a preface for Nizan's *Aden-Arabie* which Maspéro wanted to reprint, I would sally forth out of the air-conditioned coolness of the hotel; I went out to read on the lawn, breathing in the scents of the grass and the ocean; in the evening, leaving the air-conditioned foyer, I would feel the dampness of the night against my face, its smell of hothouses and swooning flowers. Sartre knew old Havana a bit; he showed me its packed, old-fashioned streets, its arcades, its squares full of people daydreaming. We used to eat dinner there, alone or with friends. When I went into a restaurant, it was as though someone had dropped a cool scarf around my shoulders. Often we'd go and sit in Ciro's, which Hemingway used to frequent. One night we had supper, a Chinese stew, at a stall in the market with the poet Baragagno, the photographer Korda and his wife, a model and member of the Women's Armed Services, amid a strong smell of vegetables and fish. Every day the newspapers carried pictures of Sartre with Guevara, with Jiménez, with Castro; after he'd given a talk on television, everyone recognized him. 'Sartre, it's Sartre!' the taxi drivers would shout as we went by. Men and women stopped him in the street; before the talk they'd never even heard his name; their friendly effusions were addressed to the man Castro had told them was their friend, thereby giving us some idea of the extent of his popularity.

It was carnival time. On Sunday evenings, troupes of amateurs appeared in the streets, joyfully putting on shows they'd spent the whole year preparing; costumes, music, mimes, dances, acrobatics – we were dazzled by the taste, the invention, the virtuosity of these *comparsas*. Two ballets illustrating peasant ceremonies were performed by Negro dancers with magical abandon; the second of them appeared, at first sight, to be danced by only women: bewigged and made up, the men too were wearing the coloured skirts, the petticoats, the laces, the shawls of their remote ancestresses. With a crowd of friends, we stayed out until dawn, joining in the delirious joy of this crowd still drunk with victory. In the theatre we also saw some Negro ceremonies still very close to those of Africa, despite certain Catholic influences; the manager had invited several groups to stage their rites in his theatre just for one evening; they were not giving a theatrical performance, they were actually living a moment of their religious life. Many of the spectators were amazed at having been made to pay to see these familiar ceremonies; some of them were annoyed at not having been asked to perform and criticized those who were doing so. 'I can do that much better,' they murmured. After the final curtain, we saw the women dancers in the wings still not entirely released from their state of trance. This transformation of ritual into spectacle was an indication both of the Cubans' respect for their African traditions and their desire to tear away the veil of secrecy which had hitherto concealed them.

On 5 March we were lunching out of doors on a sort of ranch outside Havana, with Oltuski, the very young Communications Minister, and two of his colleagues, when we heard a loud noise; the Minister of the Interior was called to the telephone. La Coubre had just blown up; some dockers, all Negroes, had been killed. Then came the foggy day when we stood shivering in the stand with Castro, watching their funeral. The hearses went by in procession, each one followed by its weeping family of mourners; it was as though the carnival floats and the *comparsas* had undergone some funeral metamorphosis. Then Castro spoke for two hours. Five hundred thousand people listened to him, strained and serious, convinced and rightly so, it seemed to us, that the sabotage was due, if not to America, at least to Americans.

The Sunday evening processions and celebrations were cancelled. A fund-raising campaign was started to make possible the purchase of a fresh consignment of arms. Along the Prado – that long, wide terrace stretching along the fringes of the old town – young women stood selling fruit juice and snacks to raise money for the State; well-known performers danced or sang in the squares to swell the fund; pretty girls in their carnival fancy dress, led by a band, went through the streets making collections.

'It's the honeymoon of the Revolution,' Sartre said to me. No machinery, no bureaucracy, but a direct contact between leaders and people, and a mass of seething and slightly confused hopes. It wouldn't last forever, but it was a comforting sight. For the first time in our lives, we were witnessing happiness that had been attained by violence; all our previous experience, especially the war in Algeria, had presented us with its negative aspect: the rejection of the oppressor. Here, the 'rebels', the people who had supported them, the soldiers of the militia who might soon perhaps be fighting again, were all radiant and bursting with gaiety. It restored a pleasure in just being alive that I had thought I had lost forever. It was counteracted by the news which reached us from France.

Lanzmann sent us letters stuffed with newspaper cuttings: the police had arrested several members of Francis Jeanson's underground movement, though he himself had escaped. The comments of the press were enough to make one vomit. The men in the movement had been bought; as for the 'Parisiennes' involved, whose photographs were printed on the front page of *Paris-Presse*, they had supposedly been seduced into it by handsome men sent over for this purpose by the F.L.N. Money and sex: it was impossible for my fellow countrymen to conceive of any other motives for human behaviour.

It was without much joy, therefore, that we prepared to return to France. As far as New York, we travelled with Chanderli, who was representing the G.P.R.A. at the U.N. as an observer, and whom we had met once in Havana. Plump and jovial, he was taking back some of those farmers' straw hats with the brims teased into a fringe for his children, and kept putting them on and laughing.

I had never been in New York with Sartre before. We landed at two in the afternoon and were due to take off for London at ten – only a brief visit. And suddenly there was a Cuban attaché telling us that he'd organized a cocktail party for the press at four o'clock in the Waldorf! I realized then that I was still far from the resigned wisdom of old age. Sartre told him firmly that we were not free until six. In a cab, on foot, in another cab, we ploughed through the town. It was a Sunday and a cold one. After the multicoloured tumult of Havana, its blue skies, its passionate jostling people, New York seemed bleak and almost poverty-stricken; people in the streets looked shabby and seemed rather bored; there were some new skyscrapers, designed with daring elegance, but many neighbourhoods had been rebuilt in the style of our own H.L.M.s. The contrast we had noticed in 1947 between American luxury and European poverty no longer existed, and I was looking at the United States with new eyes; it was still the most prosperous country in the world, but no longer the one that was creating the future; the people I was seeing were no longer in the vanguard of humanity, but members of a society afflicted with Organization sclerosis, poisoned by lies, cut off from the rest of the world by a Dollar Curtain; like Paris in 1945, New York gave me the impression of a Babylon after the fall. Though no doubt the way in which I passed through it helped dim its effect. There was no time to relive the past, to begin a future. When we emerged from the Sherry-Netherland, where we rediscovered the taste of real martinis, I suddenly recognized the Central Park I had known, Manhatten's beauty reviving as night fell – but it was time for us to go to the Waldorf.

There were a lot of people there: malicious Sauvage from the *Figaro*, French and American journalists, and also nice old Waldo Frank and my friend Harold Rosenberg who still contributed to *Les Temps Modernes* occasionally, and other people who were sympathetic to the Cuban Revolution. To be genuinely left-wing in the United States takes a great deal of character and independence as well as openness of mind. I felt a great surge of friendship for these lonely and courageous men and women.

After the summer of 1951, I had continued to correspond with Algren. I told him all about Paris, about my life; he wrote that his marriage with A. was not faring any better than the first, that America was changing, that he no longer felt at home there. Finally, silence fell between us. From time to time I would hear rumours about him, always extravagant ones. He had torn up fabulous contracts, signed disastrous agreements, lost fortunes at poker; once, on a winter morning, he had fallen into a hole full of water and, unable to get out, had all but frozen to death, standing there with only his head visible; he had arranged to meet a woman literary agent in a Philadelphia brothel which then caught on fire, whereupon he made his escape through a window; shortly afterwards, the literary agent had put a bullet through her head. In 1956, the translation of *The Mandarins* was published in America at the same time as his latest novel; the journalists subjected him to a battery of questions which he rebuffed with a bluntness apparently directed at me. I wasn't offended; I knew all about his moods. However, when Lanzmann said to me one evening: 'Algren will be telephoning you in a moment from Chicago, they've just said the call was coming through,' I realized that he wanted to explain his reaction. I got into a terrible state of nerves at the thought of hearing that familiar voice coming from so far away: five years, more than 4,000 miles. He didn't call; he'd been afraid, too. One day I dropped him a line; he replied. We began writing to each other again, very occasionally. He'd been divorced again; he was living in Chicago once more, in an apartment; there were enormous new buildings now where the old Wabansia house used to be. He was vaguely hoping he would be able to get a passport and come over to Paris. 'Yes,' I wrote to him once, 'I'd so much like to see you again before I die.' As he read these words, he realized suddenly that neither of us had so much longer to live. In November 1959, a letter arrived announcing that he had finally been granted permission to travel abroad again, that he was landing in London at the beginning of March, and that ten days later he would land at Orly. I wasn't going to be in Paris until the 20th, I answered, but he could make himself at home in my apartment.

I was feeling worked up and a little uneasy when I rang my front doorbell; there was no reply, yet I'd sent a telegram. I rang again, harder; Algren opened the door. 'You?' he asked me, with stupefaction; Bost, who had gone with Olga to meet him at the airport and whom he was seeing a lot of, had assured him there would be no plane from New York before the following day. Algren's eyes were naked; he had replaced his old spectacles with a pair of contact lenses which he hadn't been able to get used to and decided to do without. Apart from this detail he didn't seem to me to have changed at all; it was when I hunted up some old photographs that I realized how much he had aged; that first moment – forty, fifty, thirty, anything – all I saw was that it was Algren. He told me later that it had taken him, too, several days to discover that time had left its mark on me. We weren't surprised to find that right away, despite the years of separation and the stormy summers of 1950 and '51, we felt as close as during the best days of 1949.

Algren had just come from Dublin; he told me about his stay among the Irish mists, surrounded by inspired beer drinkers; Brendan Behan, whose work he admired enormously, had been too deep in an alcoholic stupor to be able to respond with more than a few grunts. He told me about Chicago, old friends, new friends, also drug addicts, pimps and thieves; the arrogance of the respectable he found more intolerable than ever; society was always in the right, its victims were treated as criminals: that was one of the changes in America that Algren was least able to forgive. He was awakened every morning by his own anger: 'I've been eaten alive, made a sucker of, betrayed.' He had been promised one world and then found himself in a quite different one, a world directly opposed to all his convictions and all his hopes. His anger always lasted till the evening. 'Once I used to live in America,' he said to me, 'now I live on American-occupied territory.'

And yet it was still there under his skin – this country in which he felt himself as exiled as I did in mine. Chicago came alive again in my studio; he was wearing the same corduroy pants as he had there, the same worn jackets, the same cap in the street; he had put out his electric typewriter and reams of yellow paper on one of the desks; the furniture and the floor were piled with cans of American food, American gadgets, products, books, newspapers. I read the New York *Herald Tribune* every morning; we listened to the records he'd brought over: Bessie Smith, Charlie Parker, Mahalia Jackson, Big Bill Broonzy; no cool jazz, it left him cold. Often, Americans passing through Paris would ring at the door; he would take them around and show them the Musée Grévin. The only one I saw was his friend Studs who was doing free-lance work for a Chicago radio station; I let him do an interview with me about Cuba which earned me several friendly letters when it was broadcast. Algren became friendly with some fellow Americans living in the building; through them he got to know others – among them James Jones – who had formed an exclusive colony in Paris, cut off from the French, whose language they could not even speak, and from the United States which they had all left, indifferent to politics but marked by their origins. Algren preferred his daily bouts of anger to their rootlessness.

I was living a much more retired life than in 1949, so I had fewer people to show him. After the Bosts, he met Sartre and Michelle again; I introduced him to Lanzmann, Monique Lange, who was accustomed to shepherding Gallimard's foreign writers around Paris, and her friend Juan Goytisolo. Algren surprised our visitors with an apparatus consisting of a battery hidden in one of his pockets and a little red light bulb that lit up in the middle of his bow tie.

Especially when he first arrived, I went for long walks with him around Paris. We made a pilgrimage to the Rue de la Bûcherie: all my links with the old house had been broken, and there was some talk of its being pulled down. Jacques Lanzmann had left it, Olga and Bost had moved elsewhere, and so had the dressmaker and her husband; Betty Stern was dead, the little concierge had been killed in an automobile accident. All that remained of my past was Nora Stern and her dogs. We revisited the Flea Market and the Musée de l'Homme. Bost took us for a drive. Algren, alas! had borrowed a movie camera, and used it as shamelessly as ever. He was enchanted by the Rue Saint-Denis and its prostitutes. He leaned out of the window and took a long shot of one group around the entrance of a hotel as we passed; the traffic lights changed to red and the car stopped; the women began shouting abuse at him, and I thought they were going to spit in his face. I began to go out to restaurants again. Algren was very fond of the Akvavit in the Rue Saint-Benoît because the bottles were all encased in sheaths of ice and the spirits as they were poured out looked so clear and cool; he also enjoyed the Baobab, where they served 'witch-doctor chicken' and pineapple flambé to a background of African music. We went to Les Halles for onion soup, and to masses of bistros for steak washed down with Beaujolais. One evening we ate dinner on a Seine pleasure boat, watching the quays with their bums and their lovers slide past before our eyes.

Algren was fed up with American films and didn't know any French, so we didn't go to the movies much. I took him to see Becker's *Le Trou*, since I was sure that silent story of an escape would interest him; he liked Reichenbach's *L'Amérique insolite* more than I did, possibly because he couldn't understand the commentary which kept spoiling the photography for me. Despite its occasional clumsiness, we were both struck by *Come Back Africa*; it was a topical film; a state of emergency had just been declared in South Africa following an outbreak of rioting that had, officially, killed 54 Negroes and injured 195 others.

I went to a great deal of trouble thinking up places to go that Algren would enjoy. I enjoyed myself too, trailing around Paris at night like a foreigner. We went to the Olympia to hear Amalia Rodriguez, so beautiful in her black dress, seducing that audience into rapt attention for her recital of *flamencos* and *fados*. At Les Catalans, we drank *sangría*, heard more *flamencos* and saw some excellent dancing. Since he liked cherries in brandy and old French songs, we went to the Lapin Agile, though the clientele and the acts there had deteriorated pitifully; and to the Abbaye as well, where old French airs were interspersed with American folk songs. I saw Harold again after a gap of many years, at the Ecluse, where he was presenting several very successful new acts. Olga and Bost went with us to the Crazy Horse Saloon; according to Algren, striptease had been developed into a much more refined art in Paris than in Chicago.

The most memorable evening was one thought up by Monique Lange and Goytisolo. After dinner at the Baobab, Monique suggested a drink at the Fiacre. I had certainly got out of touch with things, because I was a bit taken aback by the crush of boys and much older men who were there chattering away and coaxing each other, their hands sliding quite openly under the angora pullovers: it was stifling, and as soon as our glasses were empty we made for the exit; a teenager whom Monique knew gestured in my direction. 'What's she doing here?' 'She's just interested.' 'Ah! Then she's on our side?' he said, quite delighted. Algren was even more astounded than I was.

At the Carrousel, charmed by the first set of strippers, he was so mystified when he discovered that they were of the masculine gender that he almost flew into a rage. At Elle et Lui he lost his head completely: there were women, and men dressed as women; then there were women dressed as men, and men too; he didn't know which sex to turn to.

Monique had invited him to Formentor, where a lot of publishers and writers from various countries were meeting to establish an annual international prize. I let him set off on his own, and then ten days later took a plane to Madrid, where he was waiting for me with Goytisolo. It was early May, the weather was beautiful. Algren had enjoyed himself enormously, meeting all sorts of different people. He'd quite fallen in love with Barcelona; he'd spent three days climbing up onto the roofs and wandering round the Barrio Chino and the docks. Meanwhile, Goytisolo had been in Madrid wearing himself out trying to get his brother Luis out of gaol; he'd been incarcerated several weeks earlier, after a trip to Czechoslovakia, and was very ill. We spent an interesting evening in an old tavern with painted walls talking to some young intellectuals who explained to us the efforts and the difficulties of the opposition; they pointed out to me that Sartre's books were forbidden but that Camus' were on display in all the bookshop windows.

Algren found Madrid dull, so I flew with him to Seville; trees covered with dazzling violet flowers relieved the aridity of its streets. At Triana, in sleazy dance halls, beneath ceilings hung with paper wreaths, we listened to the harsh sobbing of the *flamenco* singers. At Málaga we rejoined Goytisolo and his friend V., a photographer, who took us by car to Torremolinos. Goytisolo knew a great many stories about the homosexuals and society ladies packing the resort. We found somewhere to sleep in a little port whose whitewashed houses roofed with shiny tiles were terraced up the side of a hill. 'The more dilapidated it is inside, the more whitewash they put on outside,' Goytisolo told us as we walked through the streets the next morning. It was true; we saw naked children in the streets and caught glimpses of sordid interiors. At the top of the village, Algren took some pictures. 'Yes, you think it's picturesque,' a woman grumbled at him, 'but when you've got to go up and down all day!' All the fountains were at the foot of the cliff. I had no hesitation, therefore, when we reached Almería the next day and Algren decided to go and take pictures of the troglodyte settlements, in deciding not to accompany him; Goytisolo went off with him to revisit some places and people he knew while I went up to the Alcabaza with V., amazed to think that I had been through this town twice and had both times neglected to visit these gardens and terraces, their violent-looking blooms, their bristling, scaly, contorted cactuses. V., too, was taking pictures of the cave-riddled cliffs and their poverty-stricken inhabitants moving up and down along the almost perpendicular paths, but he was doing it with a telescopic lens. I read Cela's *The Hive*, feeling very lighthearted in the morning sun surrounded by friends, and thought it a very good book. Then there was the wonderful road to Granada over red, ochre, ashen and bloated terrain. I spent three days at the Alhambra with Algren. Spain had conquered a much larger place in his heart than Italy.

Algren was counting on staying five or six months, and I didn't want to spend as long a time as that away from my normal routine. I continued to work at home in the morning, then at Sartre's during the afternoon, also spending several evenings a week in his company. Algren had articles to write, he had no lack of friends, and he liked being alone; this arrangement suited him as well.

A few days after our return from Cuba, Sartre and I attended the reception given by Khrushchev at the Soviet Embassy. What an aviary! There were the Gaullist ladies wearing amazing hats made of ribbons, of feathers, of lace, of flowers, and low-cut gowns covered in furbelows, costly and very complicated; prejudices apart, the ladies of the Left really did produce the better impression, without hats and wearing quiet suits. As for Nina Khrushchev, her placid smile and her black dress disqualified the very idea of elegance from the start. Debré made a speech. There was a crush as people moved forward to catch a glimpse of Khrushchev; he walked through the crowd and shook hands with people. Sartre had missed a meeting of writers and journalists at which he would have been able to see more of him. Khrushchev was to meet Eisenhower shortly in Paris: doves were hovering over the champagne glasses.[1]

The *Critique de la raison dialectique* was published; attacked by the Right, by the Communists and by the ethnographers, it gained the approval of the philosophers. Nizan's book *Aden-Arabie* and Sartre's preface to it were also very well received. In Havana, Sartre had often been irritated at having to write this piece when there were so many other things to do; but the confrontation of his own youth with the youth of Cuba today had been of use to him; his preface was particularly affecting to girls and boys of twenty or so. Young people loved him; I had a further chance of observing this the evening he talked at the Sorbonne about theatre. He was applauded as much as if he had been a great conductor, and when he left, the students escorted him in a body to his taxi; these feelings were aroused not only by the writer but also by the man and by the political choices he had made. As exhaustive as ever, he had begun an enormous work on Cuba that was going to be far larger in scope than the reporting he had offered to do for *France-Soir*. Lanzmann helped him abstract a series of articles from it. He went on with this work until our departure for Brazil.

When I returned from Spain I gave Gallimard my new book, still untitled, and *Les Temps Modernes* printed the beginning of it under the noncommittal heading *Suite*. I wanted to continue it, so went off to the Bibliothèque Nationale to refresh my memories of the years 1944 to 1948. I had given an account of these years in *The Mandarins*, feeling that the best way to reveal the meaning of an experience was to project it into an imaginary dimension. But it was a matter of regret for me that a novel always failed to render the contingency of life: the imitations of it a novelist may attempt are soon belied by exigencies of form. In an autobiography, on the other hand, events retain all the gratuitousness, the unpredictability and the often preposterous complications that marked their original occurrence; this fidelity to real life conveys better than even the most skilful transposition how things really happen to

1. Shortly after this, the U-2 incident brought the plans for a summit conference to a halt – though Khrushchev may have had other reasons for declining it as well.

people. The danger is that the reader may not be able to discern any clear image amid this welter of caprice, just a hodgepodge. In the same way that it is impossible for a doctor to define both the position of a corpuscle and the length of the wave attached to it, so the writer is unable to depict the facts of a life and its meaning at one and the same time. Neither of these two aspects of reality is any more true than the other. So *The Mandarins* was no excuse for not continuing these memoirs, which in any case were to extend much further in time than the novel.

I had for some time been interested in the efforts of a woman, Doctor Weil-Hallé, to gain wider acceptance for the use of contraceptives in France. Having received so many confidences, I knew the tragedies caused by unintended pregnancies and by abortions. 'For a woman, freedom begins in the womb,' one woman had written me. I agreed with her, and the Communists' attitude had annoyed me, four years earlier, when Mme Weil-Hallé, Derogy, Colette Audry and several others had mapped out a campaign for the encouragement of birth control. Thorez accused them of Malthusianism: they wanted to weaken the proletariat by depriving it of children. A delegation of women attempted a debate with Jeannette Vermersch; Colette Audry was still wide-eyed when she told me about the interview. The language Jeannette Vermersch had used to vaunt the beauties of conception had been worthy of Pétain: 'You are trying to take all the poetry out of love!' A little later she suddenly became very practical and added: 'These young working people do it in the corridors, you know, on their way from one room to the next. . . .' In fact, the majority of those whom the lack of contraceptives forces into abortions are married women. With an optimism worthy of that which inspires M. Louis Armand today, the Communists used as their argument against planned parenthood the prosperity France *might* achieve, which would enable her to provide for a population of seventy million: the private misfortunes of working-class women today just didn't exist for them. I wrote a short preface for Mme Weil-Hallé's book *Le Planning familial* and another for *La Grande Peur d'aimer*. When this latter work came out, I attended the author's press conference in the new Julliard offices. There were about a hundred people present; psychoanalysts, doctors, various more or less qualified specialists in the human heart. Mme Weil-Hallé in a white dress, blonde, fresh, virginal-looking, expounded in her musical voice the advantages of the pessary; some fifty-year-olds asked uneasily if the use of such things was not harmful to the romantic side of love. The vocabulary employed was edifying in the extreme. They talked, not about birth-control but about the joys of maternity, not about contraception but about orthogenesis. At the word abortion, faces were turned away; as for sex, that wasn't allowed in the room at all.

Towards the end of April, Francis Jeanson called a meeting in the heart of Paris of all the correspondents of the principal foreign newspapers. Georges Arnaud was present and published an eye-witness account in *Paris-Presse*; the newspaper itself was left in peace, but Arnaud was arrested on 27 April for 'failing to denounce a malefactor'. Meanwhile, although completely discredited by the Audin Committee during the court proceedings they had instituted in Lille against *La Voix du Nord*, Captain Charbonnier was awarded the Legion of Honour. In Algiers they were beginning the Alleg trial, as well as preparing a case against Audin for 'desertion'. It was at this time, too, that the 13th Arrondissement introduced auxiliary Moslem police – the *harkis*; as I walked round Paris with Algren we often passed these blue-uniformed men paid to betray their fellows.

One morning towards the end of May Gisèle Halimi telephoned to ask me to see her at once; we met on the sunlit terrace of the Oriental in the Avenue d'Orléans. She had just arrived from Algiers, where she had gone to appear for the defence in the trial of an Algerian woman on 18 May. Since her entry permit didn't allow her to take up residence there until the 16th, she had succeeded in having the trial postponed until 17 June. The girl had told her how she had been tortured; pale and emaciated, visibly in a state of shock, she still had burns on her skin and could cite witnesses. Gisèle Halimi had urged her to make an official deposition and request an inquiry, which would necessitate a further delay: would I agree to write an article insisting on it? Yes, of course I would. I limited myself, more or less, to transcribing Djamila's own account of the affair and sent the article to *Le Monde*. M. Gauthier telephoned me. 'You know, what we've found out about Djamila Boupacha doesn't look too good!' he said, as though I'd recommended her as a house-maid. 'A high official who knows all about the case says she's under the gravest suspicion,' he added. 'I don't see that that's any justification for sticking a coke bottle into her,' I said. 'No, obviously not. . . .' And while we were on the subject, he asked me to change the word 'vagina', which was the one Djamila had used, to 'womb'. 'In case teenagers read the article,' he explained. 'They might start asking their parents for explanations. . . .' Is that the only question they're likely to ask? I wondered to myself. Beauve-Méry also found it shocking, M. Gauther added, that I had written: 'Djamila was a virgin'; would I not paraphrase this somehow? I wouldn't. They printed those four words in parenthesis.

Le Monde received fourteen letters of sympathy addressed to me, and three furious ones. 'Everyone knows that these torture stories are a stock weapon in the arsenal of the F.L.N. lawyers; and even if some of them should happen to be genuine, all one can say is that it is one of the forms of immanent justice,' wrote one woman, a *pied noir* who had taken refuge in Paris. More friendly letters reached me. 'No, we're not becoming inured to these horrors; but we don't hear about them!' one man wrote. Then there was a woman who wrote in great distress: 'My husband and I thought people weren't tortured any more after De Gaulle came back.' We organized a committee for the defence of Djamila Boupacha. Telegrams were sent to the President of the Republic asking for a postponement of the trial. Françoise Sagan wrote an article in *L'Express* supporting this campaign. *Le Monde* was suppressed in Algiers because of my article and a page on the Audin affair. 'We lose four hundred thousand francs each time!' M. Gauthier told me over the telephone, his voice heavy with reproach.

A congress 'for Peace in Algeria', scheduled for 12 June in the Mutualité building, was forbidden. Georges Arnaud's trial took place on 17 June; Sartre was a witness; I got there early and waited a long time outside the gate of Reuilly barracks with Péju, Lanzmann, Evelyne and Arnaud's wife; he was very pleased about this spell in prison, she told us, because it had given him a chance to talk with the Algerian prisoners there. I sat near the front; it was a packed house, and a very Parisian one, all the left-wing intelligentsia having arranged to meet there. Doctor Lacour, one of the outstanding figures in the Lacaze affair, was in evidence with his fiancée, a very pretty Negro girl who was Vergès' secretary. Arnaud spoke very well, without trying for effects or overdoing it. Several witnesses confined themselves to defending him on a professional level; many, helped by the questions of the lawyers, strengthened the prosecution's case. Through Arnaud, the trial aimed at intellectuals in general, and Maspero got a big laugh when he introduced himself with the challenging words: 'I am an intellectual, I am proud of being an intellectual from an old intellectual family, three generations of intellectuals.' The heat in the overcrowded room was appalling, and shortly after Sartre had finished giving his evidence I left with him. Arnaud was convicted – that was in the nature of things – but with a suspended sentence. He was released that same evening.

A journalist had informed me during the trial that Djamila's had been postponed. Gisèle Halimi had been turned back by the authorities in Algiers, and the court, knowing the scandal the affair had aroused, hadn't dared try the girl in the absence of her defending counsel. There remained the matter of prosecuting her torturers; if the case were tried in Algeria, the evidence would automatically be thrown out of court. The Algiers courts had to be forced to relinquish the case, and only Michelet, the Minister of Justice, was qualified to request this in the Court of Appeals.

A delegation consisting of Germaine Tillon, Anise Postel-Vinay, both ex-deportees, Gisèle Halimi and myself went to see him on 25 June. The Melun talks were just beginning, and despite the gulf between De Gaulle's point of view and that of the G.P.R.A., these governmental gentlemen considered the war and its horrors as already a thing of the past. This was how I explained the Chancellor's attitude to myself; nervous, evasive, he didn't even bother to contest the facts we presented to him. 'The Boupacha family has been through a terrible ordeal,' Germaine Tillon said. 'Everyone has!' he replied in a clipped, hurt tone, as though he were talking about some unavoidable misfortune in which the government had played no part; he made no attempt to dispute the truth of Djamila's claims: torture was nothing new to him! He simply hesitated about the decision he should make. As he escorted us to the door, he said to me in anguished tones: 'It's terrible, this gangrene the Nazis have bequeathed us. It infects everything, it rots everything, we simply aren't able to root it out. Roughing up is one thing – you can't have a police force without it; but torture! . . . I try to make them understand; the line must be drawn somewhere. . . .' He shrugged his shoulders to indicate his powerlessness. 'It's a gangrene,' he repeated. Then he recovered himself. 'Fortunately it will all be over soon!' he concluded with a sprightly air; I didn't feel particularly proud of having to shake hands with him.

In the afternoon, escorted by M. Postel-Vinay, we presented ourselves in M. Patin's office. Gisèle Halimi has already given an account of this interview,[1] but it made too strong an impression on me for me to leave it out. Bald, bug-eyed, glancing evasively from behind his glasses, M. Patin's lips wore the infinitely superior and rather weary smile of a man it is impossible to take in. He sat opposite his assistant, M. Damour, who didn't speak more than three sentences the whole time we were there; he just nodded when Patin was speaking. Germaine Tillon led the attack: she had been intimately connected with a great many cases of torture, and not one complaint had ever resulted in a punishment; hence she had decided that this time we must appeal to public opinion. Patin turned to me: I had committed a misdemeanor in publishing Djamila's complaint. 'And you didn't give an accurate account of the facts,' he said reproachfully. 'It was a group of soldiers under the command of a captain that searched the house, not a rabble.' 'In my version it was *harkis*, police inspectors and *gardes mobiles*,' I said, 'it's you who are calling them a rabble.' There were gestures warning me to tone down my answers, and I realized that it would be to our advantage if I kept my mouth shut as much as possible. 'Your Djamila made a bad impression on me,' he continued. 'She doesn't like France. . . .' And when Gisèle Halimi quoted the words of old Boupacha, who still retained a naïve faith in France despite the tortures, he shrugged his shoulders. 'He's a coward and a clown. . . .' He went on: 'These officers you're attacking are such fine men. . . . I had lunch the other day with a young lieutenant; you know, in civilian life he's an agricultural engineer,' he said compassionately, as though studying agriculture somehow put one above suspicion. 'They find articles like yours very damaging,' he added with reproach in his eyes. Germaine Tillon again made the point that no member of the Army had up till now been publicly reprimanded; yet the number of Moslem civilians massacred was infinitely greater than that of the European victims. He stretched out one hand towards a heap of folders. 'I know,' he said, 'I know.' How I wished that all the sceptics could have seen that almost conciliatory gesture on the part of the President of the Safeguard Committee! Rapes, deaths, tortures, it was all recorded there,

1. *Djamila Boupacha.*

he admitted it; and he seemed to be asking us: What can I do? 'Try to understand; Algiers is a big city; the police is insufficient to maintain order there; the Army has to take over their job, but they're novices. . . . The suspects are brought into the guardroom; at night, the officers go back to their homes; and there the prisoners are, left to the mercies of a rabble that sometimes goes a bit too far. . . .' This time it was the National Servicemen he was calling a rabble. Anise Postel-Vinay became indignant. 'Even the Germans never left prisoners alone with ranking soldiers. There was always an officer on duty.' (In fact, the tortures in Algeria, too, were always supervised by one or more officers; which doesn't improve the situation.) Nettled, he burst out: 'Try to understand: if the Army weren't allowed some leeway it would be impossible to go out into the streets of Algiers at all.' 'In other words, you are saying that the use of torture is justified!' Gisèle Halimi protested. He looked worried. 'Don't force me to say that!' She thought it scandalous, she told him, that a lawyer hadn't the right to assist his client during the preliminary examination. 'Oh come, come,' he said with a weary smile, 'if there had to be a lawyer there, there wouldn't be any examination at all. The suspects would just get a bullet through their heads on the q.t. We're protecting them.' I could scarcely believe my ears. Patin was freely admitting that his dear, irreproachable officers would not hesitate – hadn't hesitated – to murder any of their adversaries whom a due process of law threatened to release from their clutches.

We got back to Djamila. 'Exactly what did she tell you about the bottle?' he asked Gisèle Halimi with a slightly suggestive look. She told him, he nodded his head. 'That's right, that's right!' He smiled knowingly. 'I was rather afraid they'd *sat* her on a bottle, the way they used to do in Indochina with the Viets.' (Who did *they* refer to, if not his beloved, guiltless officers?) 'That means the intestines are perforated and the victim dies. But that's not what happened. . . .' Various murmurs of reaction. He went on quickly. 'You claim she was a virgin. But after all, we have photographs of her taken in her room; she is between two A.L.N. soldiers with guns in their hands, and she herself is holding a Sten gun.' What did that prove? She never made any secret of her work for the A.L.N.; that had nothing to do with whether she was a virgin or not, we said. 'All the same, she was running a bit of a risk in that respect, wasn't she?' he replied; then he complained: 'When I questioned her in the prison in Algiers, she refused to talk to me.' 'Naturally. She has pretty good reason to mistrust the French and their police.' 'Police! She took me for a policeman? Do I look like a policeman?' We answered with polite circumspection: 'Neither more nor less than anyone else, to the eyes of a young Moslem girl in jail.' 'But that's enough to make one give up in despair: what good are we doing?' M. Patin's eyes sought those of his assistant. 'What good are we doing, M. Damour?' 'When you went to see her again, Djamila suggested that you visit the selection camps at El-Biar and Hussein-Day; but you didn't do so,' Gisèle Halimi said. 'What! Did you expect me to? I should have got myself thrown out!' Patin's voice swelled with terror and indignation. 'I might even have been arrested!' He mused for a moment. 'You don't seem to realize! They're very tiring, these investigations. And they cost me a great deal. Isn't that so, M. Damour? We don't get all our expenses back; a lot of it comes out of our own pockets.' He'd touched a sensitive spot; M. Damour came to life. 'Your Djamila cost us twenty-five thousand francs,' he told us reproachfully. 'Any way, at least we're coming to the end of all these dramas!' M. Patin concluded. He still had a few observations to make on Djamila's psychology: 'She thinks she's another Joan of Arc!' 'In 1940, when we were twenty, there were quite a lot of us who thought we were Joan of Arc,' said Anise Postel-Vinay. 'Yes, Madame,' Patin replied, 'but you were French!' When I told Sartre and Bost about this interview that evening, they were as stunned as I had been by so much frankness. We must have allowed our disgust to show, because Patin later told Vidal-Naquet: 'I like the Audin Committee much better, I really got on very badly with the Boupacha Committee.' Shortly after that, the judges in Algiers intimated in so many words that they were ready to make a deal: Djamila was to agree to be examined by an expert who would declare her insane and not responsible for her acts; she would be released, and at the same time her complaint would lose its validity, thereby making the case null and void. She refused. At the end of July, she was transferred to Fresnes, and a judge from Caen was put in charge of the investigation.

The Melun talks ended in failure; but the youth of the country would not consent to a recurrence of the inertia into which their elders' cowardice had let the country sink in 1956. The U.N.E.F. recognized the U.G.E.M.A.; the Minister of Education cut off its supply lines. Non-violent demonstrators walked in procession through Vincennes, where some Algerians had been arbitrarily interned; we could not accept their principles, but the method had its effectiveness. The number of those who would not submit to the regime was increasing. One afternoon, in the Rue Jacob, we met Rose Masson, torn between pride and anguish; her eldest son, Diégo, had been arrested at Annemasse while helping conscripts to cross the frontier. Before the examining magistrate, he claimed full responsibility; born of a Jewish mother, exiled in the United States since early childhood, he had sworn to himself never to compromise in his fight against racism. His cousin, Laurence Bataille, was also arrested and charged with the possession of arms and having transported an important member of the F.L.N. in his car. In *Esprit*, Jean le Meur, who had been imprisoned, expounded a Christian's reasons for civil disobedience. A novel, *Le Déserteur*, written by someone who called himself Maurienne, explained why some conscripts preferred exile to this war. It was because of the pressure brought to bear on them by these young rebels that Blanchot, Nadeau and several others decided to draw up a manifesto expressing the intellectuals' recognition of the right to disobey; Sartre signed it, as well as everyone working at *Les Temps Modernes*. In opposition, the Communists presented us with a truncated version of a passage from Lenin: one opposes war by participating in it; but apart from the fact that this does not apply to colonial wars, there wasn't a single place, either in the barracks or in Algeria, where the Communists had produced anti-militaristic agitation. Servan-Schreiber and Thorez joined in condemning us in the name of 'action of the masses' – but at that time the masses were on vacation. Undoubtedly only a small minority would take the path of illegal opposition; by giving support to that minority and thereby implicating ourselves as well, we hoped to restore some radical feeling to a Left that had become deplorably 'respectful', as Péju put it; and we thought that this piece of avant-garde action might create serious repercussions.

My sister exhibited her latest pictures at the Synthèses gallery, and I found them very beautiful. At the private viewing, I met Marie Le Hardouin, very upset over the execution of Chessman, about whom she was writing a book. The war in Algeria was mobilizing all my emotions, I had none left over for anything else, but I understood how she felt. In Marseilles, where I spent several days with Algren, we wondered about the future of his country. In Seoul, the students had driven out Syngman Rhee; in Japan, they had demonstrated violently against Hagerty. Che Guevara had predicted to the United States: 'You are going to lose the whole planet,' and his prophecy was coming true. Algren was not counting on either Nixon or Kennedy to make any great change in American politics. 'Whoever wins,' he said to me, 'my only consolation will be that the other one has lost.'

A little later, I took a plane with him for a two-week trip to Istanbul and Greece. We were on a jet, and I felt something almost approaching anguish as it compressed vast stretches of my past into the space of a few hours; I felt that I was dead, and flying over my own life, looking down on it from high in the sky. Lake Geneva: I had seen it for the first time in 1946, with Sartre. It was stupefying to be able to see Milan and Turin at the same time, separated by the hundred miles of *autostrada* I had impatiently driven along so many times. And already I could make out Genoa, the coast road Sartre and I had taken so many times from Rome to Milan; we used to lunch at Grosseto, in the Bucca San Lorenzo. . . . Suddenly I awakened Algren, who was dozing beside me; we were flying over Capri, invisible beneath us, and the light was so bright and clear that from our 38,000 feet we could make out quite clearly the contours of Ischia; I recognized Forio and the rocky headland we had visited by a horse-drawn cab; Algren pointed out a crevasse with wisps of smoke coming out of it that were actually from his cigarette, and he laughed at my credulity. Then came Amalfi, the Galli, the whole coast with its layer upon layer of memories, and the south, with a sea on either side. Dusk was falling over Corfu. I made a great leap into the past, back as far as the deck of the *Cairo City*, when the coast of Greece appeared, the islands and the Canal of Corinth. As we surged on towards Istanbul through the purple and sulphur sky, my heart ached with the memory of how alive I had once been, and how new the world. Yet at that moment I felt happy: but on the other side of a line that I could never turn and recross ever again.

Istanbul at night looked deserted. Next morning it was teeming with life. Buses, automobiles, handcarts, horse-drawn carriages, bicycles, porters, people walking, the traffic was so thick on the Eminonu bridge that one could scarcely cross the road without risking certain death; all along the wharves, there were clusters of ships: steamships, tugboats, tenders, barges. Their sirens were wailing, their engines hiccuping; on the road, overloaded taxis rushed up, skidded, screaming, to a stop, then drove away again in a series of minor explosions; there was the clanging of metal, yells, whistles, a vast discordant uproar reverberating inside our heads already battered by the violent bombardment of the sun. It was like a sledgehammer, yet no reflections spattered the blackish waters of the Golden Horn, cluttered with old tubs and pieces of rotting wood jammed between the warehouses. In the heart of old Stamboul, we clambered up dead streets lined with wooden houses more or less in a state of collapse, and along others with shops and workshops opening off them. Shoeshine boys, cobblers, crouching inside with their gear in front of them, gazed at us with hostility; we got the same looks in the wretched bistro where we drank our coffee at wooden tables; was it Americans they hated, or just tourists? Not a woman in the place; almost none in the streets; nothing but masculine faces, and not one wearing a smile. The covered bazaar, bathed in a flat grey light, made me think of a vast hardware store; everything about the markets in the dusty streets was ugly – the utensils, the stuffs and the cheap pictures. One thing roused our curiosity: the quantity of automatic scales and the number of people, often quite poverty-stricken, who were prepared to sacrifice a coin to weigh themselves. Where were we? These jostling crowds, entirely male, were a sign of the East, of Islam; but the colour of Africa and the picturesqueness of China were missing. It felt as though we were on the fringe of a disinherited country, and of some dismal Middle Ages. The interiors of Sancta Sofia and the Blue Mosque lived up to all my expectations; I had seen and liked smaller mosques, more intimate and more alive, with their courtyards, their fountains and pigeons circling overhead; but there was almost nothing left in them of the long-extinguished past. Byzantium, Constantinople, Istanbul: the town did not live up to the promises of these names, except at that hour when its domes and their slender, pointed minarets were silhouetted along the hilltop against the glowing sky at dusk; then all its sumptuous, bloodstained past appeared through its beauty.

We wanted to get to know some Turks. A few weeks earlier, a military *coup d'état* had ousted Menderes; there had been riots in the city with the students joining in: what were they thinking now, what were they doing? Organized tourism has its disadvantages, but our isolation had even more. Annoyed at not being able to get beneath the décor of the place, we left after three days.

Athens, by comparison, seemed feminine, almost voluptuous; we spent a week on Crete: wonderful landscapes, several affecting ruins, especially those at Phaestos. Then we went back to Paris and the moment came to part. Not a single shadow of disagreement had troubled our five months together. I wasn't tearing myself to pieces, as I used to, at the thought that our intimacy had no future: we ourselves didn't have much left either; I no longer felt that our relationship was being thwarted, but instead completed, saved from destruction, as though we were already dead. Our old times together didn't even inspire in me the nostalgia that betrays a lingering hope. Algren told me how, at the end of a walk one day, his steps turned automatically towards the Rue de la Bûcherie. 'As if my body hadn't given up the past,' he said with regret in his voice. 'Was it so much better, the past?' I asked him. 'When I was forty, I didn't realize I was forty; everything was beginning!' he blurted out impulsively. Yes, I could remember that. But it was already quite a while since I had heard the news; I was ageing, I was old. By the way we had rediscovered each other, we had erased ten years from the score, but the serenity of our farewells was a reminder of my true condition: I was an old woman.

Our visit to Havana had given us new reasons for going to Brazil. Cuba's future would be settled for the most part in Latin America, where Castroist currents were already becoming apparent; Sartre had made it his intention to talk to the Brazilians about Cuba. We had witnessed a revolution in triumph. To understand the world outside the Cold War, we had to get to know an under-developed, semi-colonized country where the revolutionary forces had not yet been unleashed, and perhaps would not be for some time. The Brazilians we met persuaded Sartre that by combating Malraux's propaganda in their country he would be rendering a useful service to Algeria and the French Left; their insistence finally convinced us that we should make the trip.

We were away only two months; if I give a detailed account of all that we saw there, I shall probably be criticized for breaking the line of my narrative. But Brazil is such a fascinating country, and one so little known in France, that I should always regret not having shared the whole of my experience there with my readers. Those who are bored by this piece of reporting can always skip it.

Before taking the plane for Recife, where a congress of critics was being held, we were invited to dinner at the home of M. Diaz, a painter who had been kind enough to get our tickets and visas for us. In his apartment, pleasantly decorated with some of his own paintings, a hot buffet had been laid out according to the custom of his country, which I decided was much more civilized in this respect than ours: we could move about and talk to different people. There were some pretty women, very well turned out, and some intellectuals, many of whom had served jail sentences under Vargas; among others, the painter Di Cavalcanti, gay and corpulent beneath his thick head of white hair. We chatted with Freyre who had described the way of life in north-east Brazil during the colonial period in his *Maîtres et esclaves*; he gave me an illustrated book about Ouro-Prêto. There was a lot of talk about Brasília; while admiring the conceptions of Lucio Costa and the buildings of Niemeyer, most of the people there thought it a pity that Kubitschek should have sunk such a fortune in this abstract city where none of them would ever want to live. 'All the same,' Di Cavalcanti said, 'in the chapel of the Presidential palace I see there is now a little bunch of flowers made out of shells: At last a touch of bad taste! At last a sign of life! It's a beginning.'

And once more, in the middle of August, I was arrowing through the solitudes of the sky. Beneath my feet, forming then melting away, lie roads, beaches, oceans, islands, mountains and gulfs that I see with my own eyes and which don't exist. Nothing changes, neither the climate, nor the smells, nor the multiform monotony of the clouds, and suddenly, without having budged, I find myself *elsewhere*. I set off once more, my heart assailed by a strange weariness at the thought of circling like this around the earth as it circled in its turn, trailing its lights behind it, putting them out too soon as my watch lost count of the hours. There was the sombre ribbon of the Tagus, then Lisbon airport; a voice called through the loud-speakers: all passengers for Elisabethville; I looked curiously at the men and women making their way towards their plane – and towards what destiny? A little later, I stepped off my plane into a muggy, black country. Dark men in white jackets bustling noiselessly among the tables; Dakar, Africa, that enormous continent with the Congo bleeding at its heart; I glimpsed some soldiers wearing shorts and blue helmets: the United Nations had just decided to intervene in Katanga.

Another morning was born, and with it a green sea, breakers, a coast fringed with white foam. Recife: rivers, canals, bridges, a grid of roads, hills, on one peak a Portuguese church, palm trees. The docks again, and the bridges, and the church; again; again; we circled, and another tiny plane circled beside us. 'They can't get the landing gear down,' Sartre told me. But they will, I thought. Nothing bad could happen to me at that moment, under that sky, at the edge of that new continent. Half an hour later, the wheels appeared, the plane landed. Ambulances and fire engines were massed out near the runway; the little military aircraft escorting us was to have transmitted orders to our pilot in case he had to make a crash landing.

Sartre was not in very good shape; he was suffering from an attack of shingles brought on by overwork and persistent depression. I too swayed slightly when I stepped out into the fresh air and the sun. There were so many hands stretched out to us, flowers, journalists, photographers, women with bare arms, men in white jackets, the face of Jorge Amado. Police, customs; as in Havana, I was dopey with fatigue by the time a car came to take us into the centre of town: first to our hotel, then along a riverbank, then to a cool, gay restaurant. I drank my first *batida*: a mixture of sugar-cane brandy – *cachaça* – and lemon juice. It was a first link between these strangers and myself, this new taste so familiar to them; I also learned to enjoy *maracuja* – passion fruit – whose rich, tango-coloured juice filled the carafes on all the tables. I noticed that there were also bottles of flour on all the tables; this was powdered manioc which they sprinkle over all their dishes. It was difficult to predict which of these people we were going to like or dislike, which we should see again, or when: the Congress had drawn people from all the states of Brazil. We learned with satisfaction that Amado, who was there specifically to welcome us, would act as our guide for at least a month.

We spent a few minutes at the Congress, and then Amado took us off with a group of people to rest in a friend's *fazenda*. It fitted exactly the descriptions I had read in Freyre's book: below, the workers' quarters, the sugar-cane mill, a chapel farther off; on the hill, the house. The master of it painted, and his pictures filled it with light; the gently sloping garden, its trees, its flowers, the undulating landscape of sugar-cane, palm trees and banana palms seemed to me such a paradise for the senses that I let myself slide away for an instant into the most heretical of dreams: to slip under the skin of a great landowner. Amado's friend and his family were away; I had a first glimpse of Brazilian hospitality: everyone found it quite normal to sit on the terrace and ask for drinks to be served. Amado filled my glass with the pale yellow juice of the *cajou*; he felt, as I do, that one learns to know a country to a large extent through the mouth. At his request, some of his friends invited us the following day to visit them and eat the most characteristic dish of the north-east, the *fetjuada*: for the *caboclo* a hash of black haricot beans, for the middle-class gastronome a sort of rich cassoulet.

I had read in Freyre that girls in the north-east used to marry at thirteen, in the full bloom of their beauty which, at fifteen, had already begun to fade. A professor introduced me to his daughter, very pretty, very heavily made up, with smouldering eyes and a red rose stuck in a bosom already full: she was fourteen. I met no teen-age girls at all – either children or grown women. The latter, how-ever, now fade less quickly than their grandmothers; Lucia and Christina T., at twenty-six and twenty-four, both sparkled with youth. Despite the patriarchal customs of the north-east, they had a certain amount of freedom. Lucia was a teacher, and Christina, since their father's death, was managing a luxury hotel near Recife that belonged to the family; both did a certain amount of journal-ism; both travelled. It was they who took us around Recife in their car.

We saw Olinda, the first town to be built in the country – three hundred years before Brasília – according to the plans of an archi-tect. Maurice of Nassau, who governed the district between 1630 and 1654 on behalf of the Dutch, had it built by Pieter Post, then decorated by a team of painters and sculptors. It is built in tiers on a hillside three miles outside Recife and a good many of its old houses are still intact. When the Dutch had been driven out, the Portuguese artists built churches there in a sober baroque style. I recognized the same staircases, the same porches and façades, bathed in the steamy odour of the tropics, that had moved me when I saw them rising from the dry earth of Portugal. We went down to an endless beach. How I loved the indolence of the tall coconut palms fringing the imperious tumult of the ocean! How white against the water shone the triangular sails of the *jangadas* – masted rafts, made of five or six tree trunks held together with wooden pegs; they are quite seaworthy on calm days but don't stand up well in storms. Every year there are many fishermen who don't come back. We went into a kiosk and tasted coconut milk: they bore through the fibre and the shell, then you suck it out through a straw; it was lukewarm and insipid.

Recife also contains some beautiful baroque churches; their windows, decorated with wrought-iron balconies, give them a charming frivolous expression. In the market-place, people clustered around the storytellers; some were improvising songs; others were reading from clumsily illustrated paperbound books. They would stop before they reached the end; to know how it came out, you had to buy the book. In the centre of town there were old squares planted with dark trees, streams, small shops, pedlars; but as soon as one ventured away from them into the grid of dry streets with scaling walls and roads of beaten earth one saw nothing but decrepitude and desolation. 'In Recife, there is a beggar under every palm tree,' Bost had told me. No, this year it had rained and the peasants around the city had a few roots to gnaw at; but when the drought comes they swarm into the city. There are twenty million of them suffering from chronic starvation in an arid polygon as large as France. Christina showed us an area on the outskirts where a completely destitute section of the population was stacked in little wooden shacks. She told us about the peasant leagues which, encouraged by Julião, a Socialist member of Parliament and a lawyer in Recife, were trying to unite the peasants and promote agrarian reform; several of her friends belonged to it. 'When I first took on the hotel,' Christina told us, 'I was still very young, and I wanted to be thought of as a hard taskmaster. I made my employees work as much as possible for the least possible money. Then I saw how they lived . . .' She was a sincere Catholic, and revolted by social inequalities. On Sunday morning she went sailing with the most exclusive club in town and raced her boat passionately; but she would quarrel with the other members and, generally speaking, with all the people of her own class. She drove like a fury through the residential district of Recife, with the express purpose of frightening the pedestrians. 'They have to be reminded that they're mortal,' she said with a laugh.

As a result of one of those complicated arrangements in which the Brazilians excel, we found that we had ended up with four airplane tickets for just the two of us; Amadó then arranged for Lucia and Christina to use them. He had spent his youth in Bahia where we had an extra guide in the person of a young professor of ethnography, Vivaldo, a half-caste with the stocky figure of a football player. Zelia Amado joined us too; she arrived a night late; another aircraft having overturned on the runway, hers was unable to land. So we made up a group of seven people, all French-speaking and all happy in each other's company. To get around, we had a sort of minibus with a driver at our disposal. Sartre was feeling better; our only official obligations were a lecture and two official lunches. We spent a very happy week together.

Bahia consists of two towns connected by elevators and funiculars, one of them running along the coast, the other perched on top of a cliff. That was where our hotel was, very modern, enormous, elegantly proportioned. From my room, and from the immense glass-walled bar full of green plants and birds, where we drank *batidas*, there was a view, under a perpetually agitated sky, across the 'Bay of All Saints', its reefs, its beaches, its tranquil coconut palms, its boats and their trapezoid sails; brief squalls would lash the ocean as we watched. Amado showed us the commercial streets in the upper town. On the door of the University there was a notice: PHILOSOPHY ON STRIKE. The rector and the students were having a disagreement. Churches everywhere. One of the best known was built by Spanish artists; not a square inch of plain stone: shells, volutes, lace. The Portuguese façades are sober; inside, however, good taste yields to richness of ornament: facings of gold chased in the most extravagant patterns, bosses and pendentives, birds, palms, demons hiding like the policeman in the child's puzzle amid the protuberances of walls and ceiling; the sacristies have displays of rosewood or black jacaranda chests, Delft pottery, Portuguese tiles, porcelain, gold plate, life-size wax saints worthy of the Musée Grévin – emaciated, scarred, contorted with pain or ecstasy beneath their wigs of real hair – and Christs, scourged, bruised, bristling with thorns, long red ribbons bleeding from their wounds. They made me think of Bobo-Dioulasso's fetish.

The narrow old streets where Amado spent his childhood all run parallel down a steep slope to the sea; on one side is the neighbourhood of the 'professional women'. We went into bazaars packed with all sorts of merchandise jumbled together; walls and ceilings were passed over with dazzling butterflies cut out of magazine covers. The car plunged along precipitous ramps and brought us out onto the docks, near the covered market. Except for the lack of hygiene, it reminded me of the one in Peking; in its narrow alleys are sold the plainest of foodstuffs, salted things, leather, textiles, millinery, cast-iron ware; but there is also an extraordinary profusion of popular art, articles indicating the survival of an ancient and varied culture. Both for us and for himself, Amado bought necklaces and bracelets of coloured seeds, pottery, earthenware figurines, black-faced dolls dressed in traditional Bahian clothes and ornaments, brass Exus – spirits that are more mischievous than evil, though the forks they carry suggest our devils – musical instruments, heaps of knicknacks; he explained to us the meanings of all the amulets, pictures, plants, drums, and jewels connected with their religious ceremonies. The stalls spilled out into the open air, right up to the edges of the docks where a flotilla of *saveiros* rose and dipped on the swell, their hulls touching, their masts rising like a dense thicket from the water; there were pedlars selling lengths of peeled sugar-cane, which one chews and then spits out once all the juice is gone, coconut cakes, bean fritters, large pots, amphoras, more pottery, some pretty, some hideous, bananas and other fruit; the smell of palm oil mingled with that of brine; coming and going all the time, on the boats as well as on land, was a crowd of men and women with skins shading through all variations of brown, from chocolate to white. We went through a barber's shop where the occupants were placing bets on the *bicho*, or animal game, a sort of lottery which together with soccer is the most popular form of amusement in Brazil. On the second floor, a Negro woman was running a bistro which looked pretty nondescript but was in fact famous; on the wall, a picture of Yemanja, goddess of the sea; in a pot, some 'swords of Ogun', cactus leaves shaped like large knife blades, very common in France and extremely necessary in Brazil for the protection of houses and property. Sartre didn't touch the oily stews they served – vermilion, coral, pistachio-coloured – though I tasted them with caution; the crab soufflé won me completely.

Several days later, as we were leaving the city we saw another market. 'The Brazilians won't take you there,' a Frenchwoman had told me. But Amado took us everywhere. It had been raining and we had to splash our way through all sorts of filth; except for some rather beautiful pottery, the wares displayed reflected the poverty of the customers: hunger was an ever-present threat in Bahia too, especially in the places Amado referred to as the 'invasion areas' because so many squatters had settled there. One of them was built over a lagoon; it was obvious no one would try to claim that piece of land back; the hovels were built on stilts over the water and joined to the mainland by shaky catwalks. It reminded me of the 'water district' in Canton, except that here the people had let themselves go completely and were living without the slightest effort at hygiene. There were other poor districts scattered about over the green hills, among the banana palms with their slashed leaves; they were crisscrossed with telegraph wires forming a cemetery for the kites the children played with; the rich, brown earth gave off a country smell; these suburbs were almost villages, still preserving the traditions and organic ties of rural communities.

The fact is that the population of Bahia, seventy per cent of which is Negro – this was the sugar-cane and consequently the slave-owning region – shares an intense communal life. The Nago African rites were perpetuated here, cautiously concealed behind a façade of Catholic liturgy with which they eventually fused, forming a religious amalgam similar to the voodoo of Haiti and called here *candomblé*.[1] It is a complex tissue of beliefs and practices, without any formal church hierarchy and therefore comprising many individual variations. Roger Bastide's book *Les Religions africaines au Brésil* had just come out and I read it. There is a supreme God, Father of Heaven and Earth, with an entourage of spirits, the Orixa, which correspond to certain of our saints; Oxala approximates Jesus, Yemanja the Virgin Mary, Ogun St George, Xango St Jerome, Omuh St Lazarus. Exu, who is more like the Greek Hermes than our Devil, serves as a mischievous intermediary between mankind and the 'enchanted ones'. These latter live in Africa, but their power extends over great distances. Every individual belongs to a particular Orixa (the priests reveal to him which one) who protects him if he offers the required gifts and sacrifices. Certain privileged people, who have submitted to the long and complicated rites of initiation, are called upon to serve as 'horses' for their god: he is brought into their bodies by means of ceremonies which – as with the descent of God into the wafer in the Catholic religion – constitute the culminating moment of the *candomblé*.

1. The word signifies the religion as a whole, the communities which carry on its traditions and the religious ceremonies themselves.

At Recife, an evening's entertainment had been organized for us in which Negroes disguised as Indians danced a number of very sophisticated ballets; but we had not been able to see a Xango.[1] In Bahia there are religious celebrations almost every day, and the entire intelligentsia takes an interest in them. Amado, who had been enthroned in office while still a youth, is one of the highest dignitaries of the *candomblé*; Vivaldo occupies a less exalted position in it, but he knows all the 'mothers of the saints', and the *babalaô* (soothsayers, half priests half witch-doctors) of the town. Twice our car took us at night, through the Russian-looking mountains that form the suburbs of Bahia, out to distant houses throbbing with drums. On both occasions the mother of the saints first took us into a kitchen where a woman was preparing food, both sacred and profane, then into the room where the altar stood. Amid a mysterious jumble of fetishes – ribbons with the colours of the gods, offerings, stones, pots – the Orixa are represented by statues in the sentimental Catholic style: St George and his dragon, St Jerome, St Cosmos and St Damian (the twins with multiple and important powers), St Lazarus, etc. In a fenced-in courtyard there was a crowd of Negroes – mostly women – the members of that fraternity and their guests; a few white people, too: a painter who had often drawn inspiration from the dances, a journalist from Rio – Rubem Braga – and the Frenchman Pierre Verger, a great initiate, we were told, and the man who knew most about the inner secrets of the *candomblé*. There were men beating the sacred drums and others playing instruments we didn't recognize. The 'mother of the saints' joined the dance of the 'daughters of the saints': women who had already been initiated and 'ridden' by their god in the course of previous ceremonies of a similar kind. Some were very young, some very old; they had on their very best finery, long cotton skirts, embroidered bodices, bandannas – and also jewellery and amulets; they moved in a circle, walking to a swaying rhythm that sometimes became more jerky but was always quite calm; most of them were joking and laughing together. Suddenly a face would be transformed; the eyes would go blank; after a period of anxious concentration varying in length, or sometimes instantaneously, the woman's body would be shaken by a violent agitation, she would begin to stagger; as if to support her, the initiates – Amado and Vivaldo among others – stretched out the palms of their hands towards her. One of the saints' handmaidens –

1. In the Pernambuco region this is the equivalent of the Bahian *candomblé*.

an initiate deprived on this occasion of a divine visitation – having calmed the possessed woman by pressing her in a close embrace, unknotted her bandanna, took off her shoes (to make her into an African once more) and led her off into the house. At both ceremonies all the women dancing fell into trances, as did two or three women guests, who were led off with the others. They returned, dressed in sumptuous liturgical costumes corresponding to their particular saint and holding various emblems in their hands, among others a sort of horsehair whisk which they twirled in the air; the solemnity of the gestures and the grave expressions on their faces were signs that they bore a god within them. They resumed their dancing, each one intensely absorbed in her own ecstasy yet always in harmony with the movements of the group. Sartre had told me about the frenzy of the voodoo; here, the individual manifestations were kept under control by a collective discipline; some of the women were affected very violently by these manifestations, but without once becoming isolated from their companions. At one of the two ceremonies we attended a young Negro woman was just finishing her cycle of initiation. She remained lying on the ground during the whole of the first part of the evening, her head shaved, dressed in white; she was trembling slightly, her eyes fixed on something invisible, both with us and elsewhere, like my father on his deathbed. Towards the end, she went into a trance, was led off, and came back transfigured by a mysterious joy.

I asked the classic question: 'How can these trances be explained?' Only the 'mother of the saints' has the right to simulate them, in order to help bring about the descent of the Orixa; and it seemed to me that one of the two I saw did in fact avail herself of this prerogative. Everyone who has watched these rites agrees that the others employ no trickery, and I'd swear that they don't: their metamorphosis, when it comes, is as much a surprise to them as it is to the spectator; nor did they look at all like neurotics or drug addicts. The old women in particular, lively and ironic as ever, turned up for the *candomblé* with all their everyday good sense. What then? Vivaldo talked quite openly about supernatural intervention; Pierre Verger too, though rather more guardedly. Amado and all the others admitted their ignorance. What is quite certain is that these things are entirely of a cultural nature and have nothing pathological about them; analogous results may be found wherever people are torn between two civilizations. Forced to bow before the strength of the

Western world, the Negroes of Bahia, once slaves, now an exploited class, live in a state of such oppression that they can scarcely call their lives their own; to preserve their customs, their traditions, their beliefs, is not a sufficient defence; they also cultivate those techniques which will help them attain a state of ecstasy and so tear themselves free of the false earthly manifestation in which they have been imprisoned. At the moment when they seem to lose themselves in the dance, they in fact find their true selves; they are possessed, yes, but by their own truth. Even if the *candomblé* does not change men into gods, at least it uses the mediating action of imaginary spirits to restore their humanity to a group of men who have been forced to the status of cattle. The Catholic religion hurls the poor down on their knees before God and His priests. By means of the *candomblé*, on the other hand, they are enabled to experience that sense of personal sovereignty all men should be able to claim. All present do not achieve the state of ecstasy, even among the group previously disposed to it by initiation; but if only a few experience it, that is enough to save them all from their state of abjection. The supreme moment of her individual life – when she is transformed from pancake vendor or dishwasher into Ogun or Yemanja – is also the one in which the 'daughter of the saints' becomes most closely integrated with the rest of the community. Few societies offer their members such an opportunity: to realize one's ties with all those around one, not just in the banality of everyday life, but through all that one holds most secret and most precious. The *candomblé* is not particularly entertaining or picturesque, being slow-moving and rather monotonous; if the leftist intellectuals pay such attention to it, it is because – in the absence of the changes they hope one day to see – it enables these disinherited people to maintain a sense of their own dignity.

After plunging up and down steep streets – luckily Zelia had an amulet in her possession that was sovereign against all accidents – we drew up one morning at the door, guarded by an Exu, of the oldest, the largest and the most famous *candomblé* in all Bahia. This sanctuary is to Bahia what Montserrat is to Spain, and the most venerated of the 'mothers of the saints' reigns over it: except that this religion is for the poor and not the rich; instead of marble, gold plate and great organs, here there is beaten earth, cheap pottery and a few drums. Situated on a hilltop, the enclosure contains the little houses where the neophytes live during their initiation period, and to which in certain circumstances the daughters and hand-maidens of the saints return; there is a large hall for the dances, constructed, like our own churches, according to the rules of a complicated symbolism; the 'mother of the saints' lives in the main building. The divinities of the various towns – in the form of sentimental plaster figures – stand all together on an altar; those of the country districts have their chapels outside: they are arranged so as to recall the location of the temples on the gods' original continent, for every *candomblé* is a microcosm of Africa. After glancing around these outbuildings – some of which are hidden in the surrounding countryside – we went back to the quarters of the 'mother of the saints'; in front of her door, pecking rather listlessly at the ground, were two chickens singled out for an approaching sacrifice. Amado and his sister belonged to her *candomblé*; they took her aside to settle the question of their obligations, which they never fail to fulfil. Warned in advance of our visit, she had put on her most magnificent costume: skirts and petticoats, shawls, necklaces, jewels. She was lively, talkative and mischievous; she complained about Clouzot, who had tried to violate her secrets, then delivered an ardent eulogy of Pierre Verger, who had brought her certain objects from Africa that had strengthened her relations with the Orixa. She had been to Africa herself, and I understood her to say that when presented with a choice between the two sets of gods she had inherited, she had opted for the Nago cult. She spoke Nago a little: a knowledge of the African tongue is obligatory for one who wishes to have dealings with the saints. While we went off to the kitchen, where a young woman served us various kinds of food, the 'mother of the saints' consulted some shells in order to find out which of the spirits we were dependent on: Sartre was Oxala and I was Oxun. Along the road, we had noticed chickens lying at the foot of trees with their throats cut; we told her about them: they certainly had something to do with black magic, of which she expressed disapproval. 'I work only for good, never for evil,' she declared. It is the sorcerers who with the aid of the 'dog' – the devil – make people fall sick, ruin them or kill them. The mothers of the saints, the fathers of the saints, and the *babalaô* intercede for the good of mankind. We talked with her for quite a while. The marriage of *candomblé* and Catholicism does sometimes produce individual absurdities; but on the whole, the native peasant fetishism absorbed by the Christian tradition blends very well with the surviving strain of African fetishism, and the people of Bahia feel as much at ease in the church of San Francisco as on their own *terreiros*.

The half-pagan, half-Christian ceremonies, in which the blood of chickens is spilled amid the fumes of incense, take place above all in the church of Senhor do Bonfim. We went on a long and beautiful trip to take a look at it, following the intricate indentations of the coast, gazing as we passed at the old fort of Monteserate and the chapel with its porch extending out into the sea. The church rises above a large square. In front of the porch you can buy ritual necklaces and beads, crucifixes and amulets, pictures of the Sacred Heart and of Yemanja, advancing across the waves with her long hair streaming behind her. In the vestry there is an astonishing collection of ex-votos: plaster casts and canes, photographs, paintings, casts of the organs the Senhor has cured.

At night, in the streets of Bahia, the young toughs still practise the ancient French sport of foot-boxing or *savate*; when they attach razor blades to their ankles, it becomes a fight to the death. This sport has inspired a dance which I saw once in a sort of open-air café in the middle of an 'invasion area', another time in the centre of Bahia in a big room decorated with wreaths and flags and multi-coloured streamers. The dancers are all men, each one lifting his partner in the air, hurling him to the ground, then gesturing menacingly at the fallen man's face with his foot, though without actually touching it. Both the attacks and the evasion tactics are susceptible of numerous variations. There are musicians who play an accompaniment to this mock combat. The champion and teacher of the dance, an old, thin, very tiny Negro with a knowing air, gave an astounding exhibition of his art.

Amado's father had been a cacao planter; at nineteen Jorge had written his first story, *Cacao*, describing the condition of the agricultural workers. Later, in *Violent Earth*, he depicted the courage and the misdeeds of the first conquerors of the forest, the 'colonels', who exercized the right of life and death over hordes of slaves and settled their quarrels with bullets. *La Terre aux fruits d'or* evokes the generation that followed them: speculators and exploiters who respected the outward appearances of legality. In his book *Gabriela*, which was having an enormous success that year, Amado had gone on to describe Ilhéus, the cacao port. He wanted to show it to us.

We flew off over a moving landscape of hills and forests swollen with water. It was raining the evening when we reached Itabuna, though it didn't look any less dismal the next morning in sunlight. To get acquainted with a country, Amado was of the opinion that one should first of all know what they eat there. He took us to the market: red beans, manioc, bad rice, pumpkins, sweet potatoes, bars of raw sugar that looked like black soap, beef dried in the sun – nothing fresh; on the backs of the little donkeys, amphoras swathed in hay; set out on the ground, ropes and goatskin gourds; we were in the open air, but it smelled like an old barn. The people – Indian and Portuguese half-castes with very little or no Negro blood – all had gloomy faces. The land here is rich, but all in the hands of a privileged few; the tobacco and cacao plantations leave no room for growing food. Amado and a few notables escorted us to a *fazenda*, a model one we were told. We followed the course of a torrential river through lovely country. The master's house was built on a rise in the middle of a garden. Like the great majority of big land-owners, he preferred to live in Rio rather than on his own domain. It was his bailiff who received us. With a smile on his lips he led us to the place – more like stables than a village – where the workers lived. No water, no light, no heating, no furniture: four walls surrounding a square of beaten earth; a few packing cases. These rooms formed the sides of a courtyard where we saw some naked, swollen-bellied children and some tattered-looking women dragging themselves about; the dark-skinned, dark-haired men watched us go by, their *machetes* in their hands, hate in their eyes. *In Cuba, they had the same skin, the same hair, the same* machetes, *and their eyes fixed on Castro burned with love.* In a corridor was thumbtacked a ludicrous poster of an elegantly dressed woman traveller stepping down from a sleeping car; I saw no other decoration. The cacao beans darkening on the roofs in the sun gave off a sweetish fermenting odour that mingled with other, unnamable smells. We walked along a muddy path into the forest where the golden fruits grow: the cacao shrubs need the shade of the tall palms around them and the damp, soft earth our feet sank into. Amado picked one of the husks and split it open; white, rather slimy, the bean did very faintly suggest the taste of chocolate. On the way back I asked why we had been told it was a model *fazenda*. 'I suppose because a doctor drops by once in a while; because the place where they get their water is less than half a mile away; because the roofs keep out the rain. In any case,' he added, 'compared to the peasants of the Sertan, these people are privileged: they eat.'

Along a road that ran by the river, with forests on either side, through a countryside which looked as though one could be happy in it, we drove to Ilhéus. Bales of cacao piled in the warehouses; men, mostly Negroes, loading them on to little boats moored in the peaceful bay whose waters, joined to the ocean by the narrowest of channels, were the same shade of soft green as the palm trees, softened by the evening light. The dockers work hard, but they are unionized and earn good money. We could see from their muscles, from their healthy appearance, from the songs and laughter that seemed natural to their lips, that they could eat as much as they liked. The ocean outside the harbour of Ilhéus is so rough that big ships cannot get near the port; we could see two of them standing a long way out, waiting for their cargoes to be brought to them. In *Gabriela*, Amado demanded that the port of Ilhéus be modernized; such is his credit in Brazil that work has already begun. Battered by wind and spray, we went out to the end of the jetty they had begun to build.

Another of the region's resources is cattle. We set out one morning for the Feira de Santa Ana, about sixty miles from Bahia. It was market day. There was a thick, jostling crowd that stretched for more than two miles; musicians dressed up as *cangaceiros* were using their guitars and their vocal chords to make as much noise as they could; there were pancakes being sold, fruit tarts, coconut cakes, candies; but this illusion of gaiety was swiftly dissipated: the market was almost as meagre as the one in Itabuna; no popular art, with the exception of some nondescript earthenware figurines. A far cry from Bahia, this place was lapped by the desolation of the surrounding country, where living means simply exhausting oneself in the effort to survive; there is no room for superfluities. At the edge of the town, there were corrals in which we could see enormous herds of steers, and *vaqueiros* galloping around them, raising the dust. To protect the men from the cactuses and thorns out in the brush, they are armoured with leather from hats to boots. Their herds do not belong to them; they receive a very small share in the profits from raising them, but it is not at all a profitable business because of the droughts and epidemics. Lying spread out on the ground were hats, shoes, pants, jackets, belts, overalls, all made of a pretty fawn-pink leather, but with a strong animal smell.

There now remained – since Amado is systematic – only the

tobacco industry to inspect. 'Cachoeira is only an hour's drive from here,' the professor with whom we were lunching told us. It took us three hours, and the jolts from the craters pitting the road painfully reawakened Sartre's shingles. We glimpsed two or three isolated shacks with tobacco plants growing around them. The town lay stretched out peacefully on both sides of a river; old houses, old churches; we wandered around a bit. Then we went into a dim shed where some tired-looking women were trampling tobacco leaves with their bare feet; the acrid odour of the dead plants was reinforced by the smell of the latrines where piles of filth were decomposing in the sun; it all seemed like the vision of a hell in which women were condemned to splash continually through their own excrement. On the way out they all rushed to soak their feet in a trickle of muddy water by the door: no washbasins, no running water, yet there was a river flowing only a few feet away. Many of the women workers were wearing sacred necklaces. 'Ah!' Vivaldo said to one of them. 'You are a daughter of Oxun then?' He questioned her about the *candomblés* in Cachoeira. Hesitant at first, her face lit up later, he told us afterwards, when she realized that he was himself an initiate. Having seen the abject conditions in which these women were forced to live, I understood fully what a miracle the *candomblé* effects.

Our last excursion took us out one morning to the oil town at the end of the bay. One of the Brazilian's sources of pride is that the oil industry is now nationalized. In 1953, impelled by a violent wave of anti-American feeling, Vargas established a state monopoly called Petrobraz: from that moment onward, no foreign capital could be invested in Brazilian oil, a move that came as a blow to the American companies. A year later the 'American' faction forced Vargas to suicide, but the state monopoly remained. Petrobraz sometimes hires foreign technicians, but there are no longer any oil fields which it does not own. A giant refinery stretches along the sea; we looked down on it from the nearby hillside where the very comfortable workers' quarters have been built. Compared to the peasants, the industrial working class in Brazil forms an aristocracy, and the workers of Petrobraz occupy the highest rung. We also went into the forest and saw the derrick of a drill that was working at a depth of 13,000 feet.

These trips made us familiar with the physical aspects of Brazil, the indentations of its coast, the colour of its forests. And at the same time our friends were straightening out our initial difficulty in understanding the political situation.

We had arrived in the middle of an election. Added to which, Rio, recently deprived of its status as a capital in favour of Brasília, henceforth constituted the new State of Guanabara, whose first governor and representatives were about to be named. There were three men running for President. Since Adhemar – to whom the slogan 'I steal but I act' was being attributed – stood no chance at all, it was virtually a straight fight between Jânio Quadros and Marshal Lott; Jânio was the right-wing candidate; once in power, he would favour the interests of the great capitalists, though he had sent declarations of friendship to the Algerians and Cuba. Christina had decided to vote for him; she wore shoes decorated with the little broom that was his emblem: he was promising that he would put a stop to corruption. 'He'll just put a new lot of profiteers in power,' Lucia said. 'He supports Cuba and Algeria, he'll do something for the peasants,' Christina replied. 'He's a hysteric; he's full of promises, but he won't keep them,' her sister retorted. She was going to vote for Lott, as was Amado and all the Left. A Nationalist and an anti-American, he was promising to fight for Brazil's economic independence. He was supported by Kubitschek – who was forbidden by the constitution to stand for office, but whose prestige was very high – and by the Communists; the drawback was that Lott was a soldier, one of the old guard, and very reactionary in his foreign policy: he was opposed to the new Cuba. On the subject of his stupidity, stories as distressing as they were laughable were being circulated even by his own supporters. Prevented by illness from taking part in some manoeuvres, he once decided to reproduce them in his own home. He set off with his orderly to march twenty-five miles around and around his own garden. Halfway they came to a halt. The soldier felt thirsty and, realizing he had left his water bottle behind, walked over to get it. Lott stopped him. 'It's twelve miles away,' he said. For six weeks there were banners, posters, records and loudspeaker cars noisily informing us of the merits of the rival candidates; there were fireworks displays in their honour.

We followed the campaign in the newspapers, which our knowledge of Spanish enabled us to make out more or less. I read most of the works on Brazil written or translated into French; I got to know a little about its literature from French translations.

We said good-bye to Christina and Lucia, and to Vivaldo, who was waiting with feverish impatience for the arrival of an African teacher from whom he was going to learn Nago. When we left Bahia, its showers and its laughter, its yellow mud, its black crowds, its churches where the Christs are fetishes, its altars where the plaster saints have the faces of African gods, its markets, its folklore, its peasant magic, we knew that we were going into another world. Three hours in the plane. The ground began to bristle with saw-toothed mountains, with 'God's fingers', with stark needles, with sugar loaves; I made out a bay sown with innumerable little islands and so vast that my eyes could not encompass it all: Rio. A populous, ugly road, several overcrowded avenues flapping with election banners, a tunnel, and we had reached our hotel in Copacabana.

The beauty of Copacabana is so simple that it doesn't show on the postcards, and it took some time before it got through to me. I opened my window on the sixth floor; a warm vapour wafted into my room carrying the fresh scent of iodine and salt and the noise of the ocean breakers. For three miles the tall buildings faithfully follow the gentle curve of the vast beach that receives the ocean's dying waves; between the two, an avenue rigorously bare. There is nothing to break up the curved encounter of vertical façades and flat sand; the austerity of the architecture is in harmony with the nakedness of land and water. Only one splash of colour breaks the whiteness of the beach: kites for hire, red and yellow, speckled with black. It was winter, I could make out only a very few silhouettes, some stationary, some moving, between the roadway and the sea. Early in the morning, the neighbourhood domestics appear, then at about eight, the white-collar workers, people who work during the day, then the people who don't have to work, and the children. People don't bathe much, the sea is too high; there are creeks and beaches which offer more shelter elsewhere; here they paddle, lie in the sun and play soccer. It was difficult to believe that this carefree solitude, the brute splendour of the ocean and its rocks, was part of a compact and feverish great city. In the evening, a steamy-smelling mist filtered the lights of the apartment houses and the glare of the neon signs, and there was nothing else in the world left to desire but that soft glitter, that cool, moist air.

Copacabana has 300,000 inhabitants, mostly upper or lower middle-class; it was pleasant walking among its handsome apartment buildings, often built on piles in the style of Le Corbusier. The district comes to an end at the foot of a cliff one usually goes through by tunnel, though there are several roads climbing up over the top. The whole of Rio is convulsed into sudden hills and sugar loaves suddenly blocking its streets in mid-career and pierced by subterranean avenues. These stone humps are covered with greenery, and the town, already besieged by the ocean, is also invaded by the forest; no other great city belongs so entirely to nature. A car ride in Rio is a succession of steep climbs and bends, of unexpected engulfments, of abrupt downward plunges, with sudden magnificent views of the rocky coast and its necklace of beaches. Looking down from the Corcavado, where they have erected a sixty foot figure of Christ 2,200 feet above sea level, one is dazzled by this wild yet urban landscape.

None of the buildings are very high except in the richer districts; the city stretches so far that the taxi drivers have divided it into two zones: the taxis of the northern zone never go over into the southern zone, and vice versa. We drove several times through the ugly industrial agglomerations of the north, but we only became really familiar with the south. The Avenida Presidente Vargas intimidated us with its vast width, but we often wandered along the Avenue Rio-Branco: a sea of pedestrians on the sidewalks, the roadway packed with vehicles; stores, kiosks, posters, bars opening out onto the street with coffee machines glittering beside big jars of juices – pineapple, orange, *cajou*, passion fruit; then banners and slogans. It was all so animated that it seemed gay at first, but the people in fact looked sad. Off to the right and left, the no-traffic streets were black with people; then even pedestrians became rare, the stores turned into meagre little shops; right in the heart of the city we found ourselves wandering through a little old-fashioned village. Several times we climbed into a street car, which we liked because it went so slowly and kept stopping. We visited the buildings designed by the various young Brazilian architects: the Museum of Modern Art, Affonso Reidy's new housing project, Nino Levi's apartment buildings, and others by Niemeyer and Lucio Costa, two of Le Corbusier's pupils who helped him on the Ministry of National Education building; their work was more elegant to look at than his. There was very little of Portugal left. I've forgotten the name of the tiled *largo* we saw, which forms a big courtyard with only one exit, far from the city's noise, surrounded by colonial houses and gardens full of fine old trees. One of the places we liked best was the square of the wharf: there were steamboats getting under way for their trips around the islands in the bay; ferryboats transporting passengers, cars, and merchandise over to Niterói, which with its 200,000 inhabitants and its skyscrapers seems to stand on the other bank like Rio's mistreated stepsister. The boats are always overloaded, and one quite frequently reads in the newspapers that thirty or fifty passengers have been drowned. Taxis and street cars keep flowing into the square; there are itinerant pedlars and vendors selling food and drink out of stalls. Along one side stretch the great covered markets, giving off a smell of fresh vegetables and pineapple, as well as fish and dried meat. From a restaurant on the second floor we could watch the boats in the bay and all the activity on land. One Sunday, as we were walking along a dingy avenue split in two by a canal, we noticed in the distance a lot of men in bright-coloured shirts: pink, yellow, green especially (green is the Brazilians' favourite colour). They were laughing and chatting with groups of women leaning out of the windows of some big, low houses. Through the half-open doors we caught glimpses of beautiful mulatto girls sitting on the staircases in bathing suits. Nothing clandestine; openly, in the middle of the afternoon, it was just like a village celebration.

In the evening, Rio was resplendent: necklaces, belts, bracelets of brilliant stones encircled her sombre flesh. Still more, I loved the little streets with their shops all closed in the blue-grey falling light of dusk. There is something tired and faded about Rio – the black and white mosaic sidewalks are full of cracks, the asphalt is warped, the walls scaling, the pavements filthy – that is hidden by the sun and the crowds. The poorer districts, when they are allowed to slip back into silence and darkness, are full of floating phantoms and regrets.

Out of Rio's three million inhabitants, 700,000 live in *favelas*; the starving peasants who come, often from a long way away, to seek their fortune in the town crowd together on bits of land that the owners have allowed to become derelict – marshy stretches, rocky hillocks; when they have managed to get together enough planks, cardboard and old scraps of iron sheeting to make themselves some sort of hut, the authorities no longer consider themselves entitled to expel them. The steep slopes of the rocky hills, in the very heart of Rio, teem with these *favelas*. An official in the town's tourist office suggested that they might look less poverty-stricken if they had patterns painted on them, like circus wagons. The project never reached fruition, but a few of the huts are now brightly coloured; from a distance, perched on the highest hills dominating the city and the ocean, some of these neighbourhoods look just like contented villages. The Brazilians don't like showing you their *favelas*. However, Teresa Carneiro, whom we had known in Paris, did take us to see one. It was in Copacabana, an agglomeration of about four thousand souls, mostly Negroes, rising in tiers up the sides of a hill more than 300 feet high. Poverty, filth, disease – it was an exact copy of all the others, except for one detail: there was a nun living there called Sister Renée, or quite simply Renée. Daughter of a French consul, she had been so overcome in her youth by the poverty of the Spanish people that she had taken the veil and followed in the footsteps of the worker-priests. She had been advised to come to Rio. She had 'squatted', with the approval of the owner, on a piece of land where the men of the *favela* had helped her set up a dispensary and a school. Blonde, pink-faced with high cheekbones, almost beautiful, she wore a blue nurse's smock. She surprised us by her intelligence, her culture, and her good sense about material things. 'The people here need a bit of water before we begin telling them about God. . . . Morality yes, but sewers first. Sewers first, morality afterwards.' She spoke in their defence: 'People accuse them of all sorts of crimes; I think they commit very few, considering the conditions they live in.' She pointed to the club at the seashore where the rich young girls and boys of the town came to play tennis and bask in the sun. 'I was born to that, but I'd willingly go down and strangle the lot of them all the same. The poor people don't get enough to eat, that's why they haven't got the energy to fight back.' There was a vast tome on hemp lying on her table: both men and women here were in the habit of intoxicating themselves with drugs that threw them into a state of acute delirium. On Saturday nights, there were several huts where they celebrated their *macumbas*, a very different thing from the beneficient *candomblés* of Bahia; among this sub-proletariat, cut off from all rural tradition, possession was an individual as opposed to a collective adventure; in their trances, the initiates would burn and wound themselves, sometimes seriously; on Sunday mornings they came to Renée for treatment. But they themselves possessed magic remedies, she said; she had seen deep cuts which an hour later had formed scar tissue. 'There's something in their religion,' she declared, though the idea didn't worry her, presumably because she believed that there are many ways to reach God. Her methods of administration were very similar to those I had seen applied in China: she had persuaded the population to work for its own good. Some of the men had laid out cement paths and were digging sewers as best they could; she helped them steal electricity from the town; at the same time she was pressuring the municipal authorities to provide it legally, together with a water supply and a real sewage system. Several women in the neighbourhood were assisting her, and she was trying to train them as her auxiliaries. There was a fairly large white minority living among the Negroes, and she was fighting their racist attitude. She had her problems. The place was over-populated; both the municipal authorities and common sense forbade the acceptance of newcomers; she was flying in the face of both. 'But it isn't charity,' she said. 'It just isn't right to refuse people a roof over their heads.' During the month off her superiors allowed her, she was hoping to work among the Indians on the Amazon. 'One has to have something to do with oneself on a holiday,' she said with a smile. Direct, spontaneous, without a shadow of self-consciousness, she disarmed in advance all the criticisms one can usually make of lady do-gooders and sisters of charity; she didn't look at the people in her care through the eyes of society or the eyes of God, but rather at God and society through their eyes.

Zelia could drive, and Christina, who had come to Rio with her mother, had a car; they showed us the surrounding countryside: the wild cliff road that extends up from the beaches; and 3,000 feet above sea level, along the sides of the Pico da Tijuca, the magnificent luxuriance of the forest that today replaces the now-exhausted coffee plantations. Amado and his sister took us up the mountain to Petrópolis; in the summer, when Rio lies suffocating in the heat, they rent rooms there in an enormous hotel that was to have been a casino. Gambling is now forbidden; and there are long vistas of deserted saloons, one leading into another. We saw the villa where Stefan Zweig killed himself. Another day we went with Zelia by boat to the island of Paquetá and drove round it in a horse-drawn carriage; the carriage was old and harmonized perfectly with the beautiful faded mansions we passed, whose abandoned gardens exhaled the ancient scent of eucalyptus.

In the evening we would eat dinner on one of the terraces of the Atlantica, absorbed by the glittering lights, the murmur of the waves, the warm, damp caresses of the air. We often lunched in one of the *churrascarias*. Here quarters of pork, mutton and beef are spitted on iron pikes which are then stuck upright into the ground in front of wood fires; this is the gaucho method of cooking meat in the south. The *churrasco* is served in a piece of equipment that holds the pike in a horizontal position; nowhere in the world have I eaten more succulent meat. Europeans don't usually care very much for the manioc served with it; fried and well prepared, I found it delectable. The air was scented with the smell of burning wood.

In Brazil, the more modest sort of hotel-restaurant is called a *boîte* (the French word); there are also a good many small nightclubs in Copacabana, which is what the French usually mean by the same word, but Amado and his wife weren't familiar with them. We visited only the dim bars they term 'little hells' on account of the more or less venal love affairs that come to fruition there in an atmosphere of dance music and drink. It was in these places that Graham Greene, having come to Rio for the PEN-Club congress and fleeing literary discussions, spent most of his time in the city.

We had felt an immediate sympathy for Jorge and Zelia when we first met them; in Rio, we became intimate friends. At our age, having seen so many links snap or disintegrate, we had not expected to experience again the heady sensation of budding friendship. The daughter of a Communist killed by the police and a Communist herself, Zelia had first met Jorge in the course of an election campaign; he had won her in an open fight from a husband whom she no longer loved; for fifteen years they had maintained a happy and vital relationship together. Zelia possessed a childlike naturalness and spontaneity which she owed to her Italian origins; she had character and warmth, a sharp eye and a lively tongue; her presence had a tonic effect on me, and she is one of the rare women with whom I have been able to laugh. In Jorge, too, passion and reserve were in equilibrium; one sensed, behind his deliberate manner, the violence of the forces held in check. He appreciated what he called 'the good little things of life': food, landscapes, a woman's charm, conversation, laughter. Sensitive to others, always ready to understand and help them, he also had very decided aversions and a good deal of irony in his make-up. Solidly rooted in the soil of Brazil he enjoyed a privileged position there: at a time when a country is struggling to overcome its internal divisions, it honours as heroes the writers and artists who reflect an image of the national unity to which it aspires. Everyone in Brazil who could read was familiar with *Gabriela*; and in no other country in the world have I seen an author who enjoyed such universal popularity. As much at ease in an 'invasion area' as in the home of a millionaire, he was able to take us to see President Kubitschek exactly as he took us to visit the 'mother of the saints'.

As a young man, he had served a prison sentence under the Vargas regime. Later, when the Communist Party was declared illegal, he had gone with Zelia into exile. They had spent two or three years in Czechoslovakia during a difficult period. They had been to Paris, Italy, Vienna, Helsinki, Moscow, Pakistan, India, China, and I can't remember where else besides. He often teamed up with the Cuban poet Nicolás Guillen and the Chilean Pablo Neruda at congresses and on trips; to relieve the tedium of official visits, he used to play practical jokes on them. Watching an opera in Peking, between Guillen and their interpreter, he relayed a version of the plot to Guillen that shocked him by its obscenity. A few days after that, they had a discussion with some Chinese writers about the theatre. 'I fail to understand,' Guillen told them indignantly, 'how you can respect tradition to the extent of preserving whole scenes of pornography in the plays you present for the people.' The Chinese looked quite stunned; Amado was choking with laughter, and Guillen suddenly understood. 'Oh, you!' he said, without finding it funny at all. In Vienna, Amado sent Neruda a series of telegrams addressed 'To the greatest poet of Latin America' just to annoy Guillen. However he did include the latter in his confidence when he wrote a letter, purportedly by a woman admirer who offered herself to Neruda. Over breakfast Neruda read it to them, then suddenly grew morose: 'What a fool she must be! She's forgotten to give me her phone number!' Both Zelia and Jorge knew scores of stories about scores of people.

Zelia attended classes at the Alliance Française and spoke French very well. Jorge spoke less correctly, but very fluently, as did the majority of Brazilians we encountered. Both had a few 'Brazilian-isms' in common; instead of individual, man, fellow, or character, Amado would always say *monsieur*. 'I don't much care for the face of that monsieur over there. . . . I think he's a rather unpleasant monsieur.' When telling us about our appointments for the day, he would say: 'You have three compromises this afternoon'; there was a subtlety in his use of these expressions that we found too enjoyable ever to correct.

The Amados lived two minutes from our hotel in a big apartment with tiled floors, huge windows and a great many books; their shelves were filled with pieces of folk art; from every corner of the earth they had brought back vases, pots, toys, boxes, dolls, statuettes, earthenware, pottery, musical instruments, masks, mirrors, embroidery, jewels. A delicately coloured bird flew at liberty around the studio. They had a son and a daughter of about twelve and eight respectively. The son, Juan, though urged by his high-school newspaper to get an interview from Sartre, refused to do so for a long while. 'He says he hasn't anything to say to young people any more,' he objected.[1] They had a friend staying with them, a Frenchwoman, and Jorge's brother, a journalist, was a frequent visitor. It was like a home to us. We went there almost every evening to drink passion fruit, *cajou*, lemon, or mint *batidas*; sometimes we ate dinner there or, if we dined out, the Amados accompanied us. Jorge decided whom we should and shouldn't meet, he protected us from troublesome people with a stubborn patience that infuriated more than one; one journalist to whom he had shown the door wrote a poisonous article accusing Jorge of keeping us under lock and key. The official lunches with university professors, writers, journalists, all took place at the edge of the bay; the place was so beautiful and the food so good that I scarcely got bored at all.

Ultima hora was publishing *Ouragan sur le sucre*. Rubem Braga and one of his friends, a left-wing Catholic, decided to put it out in book form. We discussed it with them. We saw Di Cavalcanti again. We drove along a series of sharply winding roads over the Tijuca to see Niemeyer. He lived up on the heights in a villa of his own design that looked more like an abstract sculpture than a house; there was a roof over the terrace, and the studio was open to the sky. He made us gin-and-tonics, and we sat down to chat as though we had known each other for ages. To build a whole city from scratch is an extraordinary opportunity for an architect; he was very grateful to Kubitschek for having offered him that chance and then upholding his choice against all comers. But he was a Communist – as was Costa, who had conceived the plan of the new capital – and he was asking himself a number of questions that he hoped to discuss with us at greater length in Brasília itself.

Apart from Villa-Lôbos, we scarcely knew any Brazilian music.

1. Alluding to the preface Sartre wrote for *Aden-Arabie*.

The 'samba schools' where the carnival is rehearsed were not yet open. Amado played us some records. He invited over a composer who sang and accompanied himself on the guitar. The author of the play *Orfeù negro* got up a musical evening for us. (He didn't like the film at all because it had betrayed the original, he said. All the Brazilians I meet blamed Marcel Camus for having given such a facile and untruthful picture of their country.) We went to his house and met a group of boys and girls from the *Bossa Nova* who played piano, guitar and sang in a style of such discretion that 'cool' jazz would have burned one's ears by comparison. As we left, Sartre told me that he felt the same embarrassment in the presence of the young girls there that Algren had experienced when confronted with the transvestites at the Carrousel. He would let his eye rest with pleasure on the pleasing face, the generous proportions of a young woman, and then suddenly wake up to the fact that he was ogling a little girl of thirteen!

We spent an evening at the home of Josué de Castro, whose enemies were saying of him, with great injustice: 'Hunger feeds him well.' He was as interesting as his books, and funny as well. There were some young technocrats who told us about the Brazilian economy; that started a furious discussion. One of the subjects we touched on was the frequency of various kinds of accidents in Brazil. The Rio streetcars are always overloaded with clusters of people hanging on outside, and a single jolt is enough to send them flying. 'And that's nothing compared to the suburban trains,' Amado told us; passengers often fall off onto the tracks and get injured or killed. Castro and Amado, despite the fact that they'd both flown around the world almost three times, admitted that they almost died of fear every time they flew in a Brazilian plane,[1] and Niemeyer, they said, whenever he had to make one of his frequent trips between Brasília and Rio, always did the eighteen-hour journey by car rather than spend an hour flying it. Because there are so few roads and railroads, Brazil has the most extensive airline network of any country in the world except the United States, but its plant and equipment are very inadequate. As a country – and this is the reason for one of the most striking traits in the Brazilian character: bluff – it is living far beyond its means. It already has

1. Two years later, in the summer of 1962, Castro was with his daughter and infant grandson in the plane that crashed into the sea after taking off from Rio. The baby was drowned.

one foot in the future: prosperous industries, modern cities, abundant oil; yet it walks forward with only the poor tools it has inherited from the past: old tubs and flivvers, rattletraps and roads full of holes, inadequate laboratories, techniques, and administration; so it keeps falling flat on its face. Added to which, as in all countries under the domination of foreign imperialism – Cuba before Castro, China before Mao – corruption is rife; faced with a defenceless people in bottomless misery, the rich form a sort of Mafia which thinks of nothing but filling its own pockets as fast as possible; in building, transport, vaccines, food, the most elementary standards of safety are ignored. At a time when their undertakings have suddenly multiplied out of all proportion in every sphere – manpower, raw materials, space – the Brazilians have scarcely succeeded at all in reducing the risks inherent in all such enterprises during the nineteenth century.[1] Fires in the *favelas*, scaffolds collapsing, ferries sinking, overloaded trucks careening into ditches – something about these disasters reminded me of Italy on a gigantic scale; in Italy they wait for the workers to be killed before they start to get worried about the conditions they have to work in, but they do at least get worried; in Brazil they don't: there is a superabundance of unskilled labour, human lives aren't worth a pin.

Towards the end of the evening, Prestes arrived. I had read the book Amado wrote about him. In 1924, while still a captain in the army, he had taken his battalion with him and joined a Paulist revolution that had failed; for a period of six years, with a column of fifteen hundred men, he cut his way through Brazil, pursued by the police, preaching revolt. In the course of this first 'long march', he was converted to Communism. In 1935, he attempted to stir up the army against Vargas and was sentenced to forty-six years and eight months in jail. His wife, of German origin, had her breasts cut off by the 'green shirts' and was handed over to the Germans; she died in a concentration camp. In 1945, when Vargas left office, Prestes was released and took over the leadership of the Brazilian Communist Party, at that time the largest on the continent. The Party was dissolved in Dutra in 1947, and Prestes went underground. But from 1955 on, having succeeded in winning all the Communist

1. The dramatic affair of the Fortaleza vaccines and the monster fire in the Niterói circus have since provided tragic illustrations of what I have written here.

votes over to Kubitschek, the Nationalist candidate, he had been able to live out in the open again. The position of the Communists in Brazil is curious. The Party still remains illegal; but every person has the right, on the grounds of individual liberty, to be a Communist and to meet with other people of the same opinions. Prestes no longer bore any resemblance to the handsome young 'knight-errant of hope' he had been in more heroic days. He delivered a long, dogmatic harangue attacking the peasant leagues and preaching moderation: Brazil would only become a Socialist country by doing nothing to try to become one. He was making the rounds of the public squares, speaking in favour of Lott, the governmental candidate, whom my friends were finding increasingly distasteful every day. 'I'll vote for him, but he'll arrest me,' was how Amado put it. Why didn't the Communists run a candidate who, without saying so openly, would be their representative? There were too few of them, they didn't like the idea of being counted. Only half the population was involved in the election battle: illiterates don't vote, and the peasants can neither read nor write. Yet the Brazilians claim they are democratic, and up to a certain point it's true. Arrogance is entirely foreign to them; superficially, masters and servants live together on an equal footing; in Itabuna, when the bailiff of the *fazenda* offered us a drink, our driver stayed in the salon and drank with us. The split occurs lower down in the scale; the bailiffs don't treat the plantation workers as equals, or even indeed as men. Up to a certain point, too, the Brazilians refuse to adopt racist attitudes. Almost all of them have Jewish blood, for the majority of the Portuguese who emigrated to South America were Jews; almost all of them have Negro blood. Yet I observed a marked anti-Semitic attitude in middle-class circles. And not once, either in their drawing rooms, in their universities,[1] or in the audiences at our lectures, did we see a single dark or light-brown face. Sartre commented aloud on this fact once, during a lecture at São Paulo, then he corrected himself; there was one Negro in the hall, but he turned out to be a television technician. It may be that the segregation is economic; the fact of the matter is that all the descendants of the slaves have remained in the working class, and in

1. Vivaldo was the only exception; this was in Bahia, and although he was a half-caste, his skin was very pale in colour.

the *favelas* the poor whites consider themselves superior to the Negroes.

This doesn't prevent the Brazilians from being attached to their African traditions. All the ones I met were under the influence of the Nago cults. Even if they were not, like Vivaldo, convinced of the existence of the saints, they all believed in their powers at least. When the 'mother of the saints' revealed to us the names of our divine patrons, Amado assured us that a consultation with another priestess would give the same results. He was a high dignitary of the *candomblé* and observed its precepts. Pushing away a dish of kidney beans, he said to Sartre: 'My saint forbids me to eat them; you're Oxala; you're allowed everything white.' He smiled as he said it; but he certainly preferred to yield to such superstitions than to risk flouting them. Sartre questioned Zelia, a practical, rationalist daughter of the cities: without believing in the supernatural, she couldn't bring herself not to believe in it. Amado's father was suffering from a cancer and believed that an evil spirit was torturing him. Zelia conjured up a good spirit; the whole household took part in the rite, and the housemaid went off into a trance; the old man's pains disappeared; every time they came back, the good spirit drove them away again. 'What is one to think?' Zelia asked. She usually wore a consecrated necklace in the colours of her saint. One little incident seemed to us significant. Someone had given Sartre an amulet which would assure him of Oxala's protection. After dinner one evening at a journalist's house, the guests all congratulated the cook. Zelia pointed to Sartre and said to her: 'He has the same saint you do.' Sartre showed her his amulet; the cook thought he was giving it to her and took it with thanks. The following day the journalist telephoned to Amado: Was Sartre sure he hadn't changed his mind about this gift now that he'd thought it over? Didn't he want the amulet back?

One morning, Zelia told us, one of their friends, O., who was running for Parliament, asked her to drive himself and his wife to the top of Tijuca before dawn. Obeying the prescriptions of a *babalaô*, they got out of the car, took a basket of eggs, and rubbed a dozen of them over their bodies, throwing each one into a ravine when they'd finished with it. They were supposed to distribute alms during the night; they scoured the town looking for a beggar and finally awakened a hobo sleeping on a bench. O. was not elected. He ran again while we were there and organized an *umbanda* ceremony which Amado suggested we attend. We crossed Rio in Zelia's car behind O.'s electoral van covered with stickers: *Vote for O.* Little Juan Amado was in the van and started shouting through the loudspeaker: 'Vote for O. Vote for Sartre, for Amado. Don't vote for O.' The man kept making detours to pick up O.'s campaign workers. It took us two hours to reach the northern sector; we wandered through the outlying suburbs for some time before we found the garden full of banners announcing the meeting O. was holding in the later afternoon. There was a hedge of shrubs around a big country-style house where a 'mother of the saints' was raising a dozen adopted children; they slept anywhere and played under the trees. Very black, very fat, magnificently attired, she proudly showed us an altar, similar to those in Bahia but much more sumptuous. The vast table where we were to eat lunch was still bare. In the open-air kitchen women were bustling around the stoves. We were almost faint with hunger by the time three o'clock came around and they served us shrimps and rice, fried pork, all succulent but slightly spoiled by a pompous speech from O. Since we had some 'compromises' in Rio that day, we slipped away in the middle of the banquet. O. was defeated in the elections again.

The Brazilian Left was hoping to establish close economic relations with the young nations of Black Africa. It was therefore critical of Kubitschek's visit to Salazar. The Brazilians have experienced dictatorship and loathe it, and colonialism is repugnant to them; the Portuguese exiles we met, democrats in Portugal, had a Fascist attitude with regard to Africa: they wanted the Angolan revolt suppressed. The Brazilians, who won their own independence only 140 years ago, are always on the side of any people fighting for it now. That is why Sartre was able to awaken such a response by talking to them about Algeria and Cuba; about Cuba especially. The Castroist revolution involved them directly; they too were living under the thumb of the United States and deeply pre-occupied with agrarian reform.

In Recife, to the great relief of the French consul, a big, kindly man, Sartre spoke about Algeria without openly attacking the French Government. He maintained this moderate attitude in Bahia too. When the University of Rio – thereby demonstrating its liberal attitude – offered one of its amphitheatres for his press conference Sartre decided to take the bull by the horns. When he was asked questions about De Gaulle, about Malraux, he replied without equivocation. All the newspapers printed accounts of these conversations, and from that time on, all the newspapers in Rio and São Paulo, dailies and weeklies alike, carried pictures and detailed accounts of Sartre's activities in every issue. An enormous number of people attended the lecture he gave at the University, and also the one on the colonial system sponsored by some young technocrats; it was given at their Educational Centre, and the hall was too small to accommodate the audience, which crowded onto the balconies and into the gardens. Lecturer and listeners were all sweating like pigs, to such an extent that when Sartre finally tore himself away from the applause at the end, the dye in his jacket had run and turned his shirt blue. Rubem Braga managed the *tour de force* of bringing out *Ouragan sur le sucre* before we left, and Sartre agreed, as a demonstration of solidarity with Cuba, to sign copies of it publicly; for the same reason, and despite my scruples, I sat beside him in a brightly decked hall, behind a table loaded with copies of his book fresh from the press, and signed some too. One person who bought a book, thinking to give Sartre pleasure, had brought him a portrait of De Gaulle that he had painted and framed with his own hands. At the University I spoke – not because I wanted to, but because I had been asked – on the position of women.

The French colony showed us unequivocal hostility. Not only was Sartre expounding his point of view – in lectures, articles, radio and television interviews, etc. – on Algeria and De Gaulle, he also paid a visit to the G.P.R.A. representative living in Copacabana with his wife, a Frenchwoman who had been a teacher in Algeria. It was at their house that we saw some bogus issues of *El Moujahid* that had been doctored by the psychological service of the French army. They considered the work Sartre was doing on behalf of their cause in Brazil very important.[1]

Our stay in Rio was interrupted by the week or so that we spent in São Paulo, about an hour's plane journey away. 'Wouldn't you rather have a nice quiet night in a sleeping car?' Amado suggested.

1. When Ben Kheddah visited Brazil in the fall of 1961, he was struck by the services Sartre had rendered to the Algerian cause. He told Lanzmann and Fanon how, when he landed, the authorities had wanted to keep him out of the country; but the students who had come *en masse* to greet him marched him out of the airport in triumph. And immediately began talking about Sartre.

He yielded with good grace. There was a crowd at the airport when we arrived, mostly young people carrying placards – CUBA SI, YANKEE NO – and acclaiming Sartre and Castro. We were taken under the wing of the 'Sartre Society', consisting of students and very young professors.

The town isn't beautiful, but it's full of life. It's one of the cradles of Brazil; the Jesuits set up a headquarters here in the middle of the sixteenth century, and it was from here that the *bandeirantes* set out to conquer the interior. It is also the most modern city in Brazil: wide arterial roads, viaducts, tall buildings, bustling crowds, dense traffic, a profusion of little shops and luxury stores. Between 1900 and 1960, its population jumped from 80,000 to 3,500,000 and the city is still under construction; half-finished apartment blocks are everywhere. We noticed, however, that the construction workers only functioned in slow motion and, on certain sites, not at all. The enormous inflation into which the country had been forced was bringing on a recession; many projects had been abandoned. We were shown the Italian quarter, which has no character, and the Japanese quarter, which has a great deal; its inhabitants are almost all Japanese; the stores sell Japanese products, the restaurants serve Japanese specialties in the Japanese style. There is a very rich residential district: gardens full of flowers, colonial-style houses, ultra-modern villas. There are also some *favelas*; there was a great deal of talk about the diary kept by a Negro woman called Caroline which gave a day-by-day description of the life of her *favela* in the harshest terms. A young reporter had discovered it by chance and the book was on the way to becoming a best-seller.[1] We noticed a great many posters in the busier streets vaunting the merits of the spiritist religion or announcing spiritist séances. I went down into Santos; it was a Sunday and the port was asleep. The promenade along the sea, with its palm trees, its squares, its kiosks, its baby carriages, reminded me of the beauty of Copacabana.

Intellectually, São Paulo, more industrialized, was even more alive than Rio. Press conferences, television appearances, meetings, discussions with young sociologists and economists, book signings, lunches with writers, a visit to the Museum with a group of painters who – what an ordeal! – looked at us while we looked at their paintings: we were kept busy. The more we got to know them, the more warmly we felt towards the Brazilian intellectuals. Conscious

1. It has since been translated into French under the title: *Le Dépotoir*.

of belonging to a country on the way up, with the whole future of Latin America dependent on it, their work was for all of them a battle to which they had committed the whole of their lives; their curiosity was vast and insatiable; since they were on the whole very cultured and had quick minds, it was profitable and pleasant to talk to them. They were acutely conscious of social problems. With so many *favelas* dotted about their towns, the Brazilians can never forget the existence of poverty; it is a perpetual wound to their national pride; it is a challenge to their democratic sentiments; even the right-wingers worry about it and try to fight it.[1] The middle-class leftists and the intellectuals are forced to take up revolutionary attitudes. We were struck by one phenomenon that is to be observed all over Latin America: there are great land-owners and very rich businessmen who are Communists. This is because they feel that only socialism can enable their countries to free themselves from the imperialist yoke of the United States and so save the great mass of their compatriots from a degradation that reflects on them. Obviously these are exceptions, and the intellectuals play only a very small role. It must not be thought that revolution is just around the corner.

One morning *Ultima hora* arranged a meeting for Sartre with the trade-union leaders. They didn't all give the same answers to his questions, but several definite facts emerged from this conversation which further talks later confirmed. The workers of Brazil have only just emerged from the peasant class; either they have been peasants themselves or their fathers were; since their standard of living is considerably higher than that of the country districts, they think of themselves as a privileged class. They have no solidarity of interest with the starving people of the north-east or the day labourers in the south. Some of them are strongly aware of belonging to an exploited class; but all believe that at the moment a certain degree of collaboration with the great capitalists is necessary. The attitude of the latter is ambiguous. They would like to appropriate for themselves the entire resources of Brazil, which at

1. It goes without saying that the immense majority of the privileged classes are fighting tooth and nail, above all else, to defend their privileges, and it is they who are largely responsible for the poverty. At least they do not evince the same indifference to it that one finds in other countries. The *Estado de São Paulo*, which is a right-wing publication, printed a noteworthy study of the city's *favelas* while we were there.

the moment are for the most part in the hands of American corporations; but in order to develop their resources, they need the financial support of the United States; consequently they end up fighting imperialism and playing into its hands at the same time. Insofar as the capitalists aim at making the country economically independent, the working class sees their success as a promise of future prosperity; this is the explanation of the support accorded first to Kubitschek and then to Lott by the Communists. Leaving aside its state of subordination to the United States, the situation of Brazil as a nation recalls that of Italy, conditions in the north and the south being reversed, but it is more tragic because of the underdevelopment and the extent of the territory concerned. National unity works against the north, because the great landowners in that region invest their profits in the industries of the south, thus denying the north any opportunity for development. Doomed to hunger, the peasants are in a revolutionary situation; but their dispersion, their apathy, their ignorance, all work against the possibility of their acquiring class-consciousness, and they are almost entirely unable to come to grips with the situation; the working class is awakened and possesses the practical means necessary for the struggle, but it is not in a revolutionary situation. As for the lower middle class, in Cuba their lack of opportunities roused them against Batista; here, their hopes are fed by the growing industrialization, and they accept the status quo. It would be a long while, in the opinion of the people we talked to, before socialism would stand much chance in Brazil.

Once more I found myself talking about women in a large flower-decked and scented hall, addressing a lot of bedizened ladies who were thinking exactly the opposite of what I was saying; but a young woman lawyer thanked me on behalf of all working women. The condition of women in Brazil is difficult to define. It varies from region to region. In the north-east, a young girl – even if she lives in a *favela* – has no chance whatever of marrying if she isn't a virgin; she is kept under strict surveillance by those around her. The big industrial towns of the south are much more liberal. In Brazil, divorce does not exist. But if a man and a woman, one of whom is already married, decide to start living together, they put an announcement in the newspaper. They are then accepted as a legitimate couple even in the starchiest and most old-fashioned circles, and their children have the right to bear the father's name and inherit his property. All well and good, but the price a mother has to pay is that when she leaves her home, she forfeits all rights to her children. And when a man dies, only his first wife can inherit his property; the companion who has shared his life without an official contract doesn't get a cruzeiro.

Sartre gave a lecture on literature and another on colonialism in a theatre holding six hundred; it was full when we arrived, and the police were holding off a crowd of about four hundred milling around outside the doors; their shouts of frustration could still be heard as Sartre began to speak. Suddenly, having broken through the cordon, they surged into the auditorium, sat down in the aisles and clung to the walls to the accompaniment of loud applause. There were two Frenchmen who demanded to be allowed to speak in defence of 'French Algeria'; one might almost have thought they were accomplices deliberately planted by Sartre to make fools of his adversaries; one of them, in any case, was a notorious eccentric. A French professor and a French priest also in the audience both assured Sartre of their solidarity.

There is an attempt on foot in Brazil to decentralize higher education. A university had just been founded at Araraquara, a town of some 80,000 inhabitants a few hours' drive from São Paulo. Professor L., hoping to gain some publicity for himself, manoeuvred so persistently and so cleverly that Sartre finally agreed to go there and talk on dialectics to the philosophers and on colonialism to the students. We left as darkness fell and then stopped for the night at the *fazenda* owned by M., the editor of the *Estado de São Paulo*, as Amado had arranged. M.'s newspaper is a right-wing publication, but very different from the ones at home. I have already mentioned that it was conducting a campaign against poverty in the *favelas*; left-wingers also wrote for it; it was giving Sartre and his lectures a great deal of favourable publicity. As a 'liberal' opposed to Vargas's semi-dictatorship, M. had been in prison with Amado, and they still maintained a polite relationship. Some reporters photographed us on behalf of the paper. During dinner, M. talked to us about the Negro problem. 'We're not at all racist here,' he explained, 'only – and it's our fault – we haven't managed to educate the Negroes to our own intellectual and moral level. So of course they inevitably stay at the bottom of the social scale.' At the other end of the table, his three grown-up sons sat grinding their teeth; they would doubtless have expressed the same ideas, but with more subtlety. The father, astonishingly hale and hearty, despite his great age, launched into a diatribe against women who smoke: the neuroses particular to our sex, according to him, are all exacerbated by tobacco. His wife, who seemed to have her nerves under perfect control, then showed us to the vast, old-fashioned rooms that had been prepared for us.

When I awoke, I was dazzled by the brilliance of the trees, the grass, the passion flowers, the hibiscus, the yellow, orange, pink, purple bougainvillea. We inspected the plantation. The coffee torn up by the roots, burned, thrown into the sea – that abstract scandal of 1928 or so – was these dark-green plants stretching across the plateaux; the whitish seed inside the tiny fruits had almost no taste. Vast and monotonous, but with pleasant valleys, and great trees on the horizon, the countryside looked contented under its pale sky. But Amado had already described to us the drudgery of the harvest; it only lasts a few weeks, during which the agricultural workers are given lodgings by the owner; sometimes he keeps them on till the following year, but if he decides to reduce his labour force, or re-new it, he is within his rights: they simply have to leave and look for an opening somewhere else. Below the M. family's estate, along one side of the courtyard where the coffee beans were drying, was a schoolhouse containing twenty or so children. Next year they would probably be a hundred miles away; it wouldn't be easy for them to learn to read. The quarters for the day labourers were better than the pig-sties we'd seen at Itabuna, but still very poor.

At Araraquara, Sartre bolted down a few sandwiches and then, at about two, went into the banner-hung amphitheatre: 'Viva Cuba! Viva Sartre! You've talked about the *bohios*; now talk about the *favelas*.' The students had a discussion with Sartre about the possibilities of a revolution in Brazil similar to the one in Cuba. Sartre asked them questions about the peasant leagues, and spoke to them about the necessity of agrarian reform. 'They all seem to be revolutionaries to a man!' I said to Amado, with whom I took a walk later on through the deserted Sunday streets, while Sartre was looking over his notes. 'It will pass when they've become doctors or lawyers,' he answered. 'Then they'll ask for nothing better than a national capitalism independent of the United States. The peasants won't be any better off.' As we neared Professor L.'s house on our way back, we saw a great stream of automobiles, trucks, vans and coaches appear. It was the enormous crowd coming back from a soccer match; the Brazilians are fanatical about them.

Sartre spoke on dialectics. We left late, ate dinner in a *churras-caria*, and the night was already far advanced when we drove off the main road in order to get to M.'s *fazenda* where we were to spend the night again; the driver got lost on the dirt roads that connect the plantations. At last we glimpsed a tiny light in the distance, we began navigating by it, losing it, finding it again, circling around it without being able to reach it. It was two in the morning before our car finally drew up at the foot of the steps; the lamps were lit, the doors wide open; we went in and found our rooms. Yet another example of the Brazilian hospitality which added so much charm to our trip. When I came down next morning, there was Amado in the corridor, hilarious at the reactions of Professor L., whom he didn't like. 'That poor monsieur almost had a heart attack!' he told me. Unfolding his paper that morning, L.'s eye had fallen upon the headline: SARTRE PREACHES REVOLUTION. He had given a great groan: 'I'm ruined!'

Sartre had become very popular with the young people. Two or three times in São Paulo we arranged to spend the evening on our own. The harshness of the city was softened in the dusk, the pedestrians walked less quickly, a Negro went by singing; after the tumult of the day, we enjoyed this dreaming calm. Often, cars would draw up: 'Can we take you anywhere?'

In Rio, students would accost us on every street corner. 'What do you think about yourself, Monsieur Sartre?' one girl asked at the end of a lecture. 'I don't know,' he answered with a laugh. 'I've never met myself.' 'Oh! How sad for you!' she cried impulsively. There happened to be a representative of the French Government in Rio at the same time as ourselves; there was a cocktail party in his honour; a Brazilian friend of ours, more than a little tight – according to his own account – took the guest of honour aside: 'It isn't you who represents France; it's Jean-Paul Sartre.' The official smiled; since Brazil was according Sartre a triumph, it would have been a blunder to try to clip this feather out of France's cap. 'We represent two different aspects of France,' he said. The Brazilian intellectuals were grateful to Sartre for embodying the *other* aspect. Rio awarded us the title of 'honorary citizens'. There was a brief reception during which our diplomas were presented to us.

It was difficult for us to get hold of French newspapers, but our friends kept us up to date on what was happening in France by letter and telephone. The Jeanson trial began on 7 September; Jeanson's lawyers wanted Sartre to be there, but he had accepted commitments in Brazil and did not want to abandon the action he had engaged there on Algeria's behalf. He was of the opinion that a letter would carry just as much weight as his oral testimony. The mail service from Rio to Paris is not quick, and letters even risk getting lost en route. Sartre telephoned Lanzmann and Péju and explained to them at length what he wanted to include in his declaration to the court. He then charged them with the actual writing of the text which was read out on 22 September:

Finding myself unable to attend the hearing of the military court, a state of affairs I profoundly regret, I should like to explain myself in greater detail on the matter discussed in the telegram that I dispatched earlier. Merely to have affirmed my 'total solidarity' with the accused is, in fact, not enough: I must still say why. I do not think that I have ever met Hélène Cuènat, but I am fairly familiar, through Francis Jeanson, with the conditions surrounding the work of the 'organization of support' now on trial. Jeanson, I repeat, was a colleague of mine for a long time, and if we were not always in complete agreement, as is natural enough, the Algerian problem in any case brought us together again. I followed his efforts day by day and they were those of the French left wing attempting to find a solution to this problem by legal means. It was only when confronted by the failure of those efforts, by the manifest impotence of the Left, that he resolved to engage in a clandestine action that would provide concrete support to the Algerian people in their struggle for independence.

But it is as well to clear up an ambiguity at this point: this practical solidarity with the Algerian fighters was not dictated to him solely by the nobility of his principles or by his general wish to combat oppression wherever manifested; it sprang too from a political analysis of the situation in France itself. The independence of Algeria has in fact been won. Whether it will occur in a year's time or in five years' time, with the agreement of France or without it, after a referendum or through internationalization of the conflict there, I do not know, but it is already a fact, and General De Gaulle himself, brought into office by the champions of French Algeria, now finds himself constrained to admit: 'Algerians, Algeria is yours.'

This independence therefore, I repeat, is a certain fact. What is not certain is the future of democracy in France. For the war in Algeria has made this country rotten. The increasing restriction of liberties, the disappearance of political life, the general acceptance of the use of torture, the permanent opposition of the military to the civil powers, are all marks of a development that one can without exaggeration qualify as Fascist. In the face of this development, the Left is powerless, and it will remain so as long as it refuses to unite its efforts with those of the only force which today is truly fighting the common enemy of Algerian and French liberties. And that force is the F.L.N.

This was the conclusion reached by Francis Jeanson, it is the conclusion I have reached myself. And I think I may say that there are now more and more French people every day, especially among the young, who have decided to translate it into action. One is able to see things more clearly when one comes into contact, as I am doing in Latin America at this moment, with public opinion abroad. Those whom the right-wing press is accusing of 'treason', and whom a certain section of the Left is hesitating to defend as they should be defended, are widely considered abroad as the hope of the France that is to be and its noblest manifestation today. Not a day passes without my being asked about them, about what they are doing, about what they feel; the newspapers are ready to open their columns to them. The representatives of the 'young resistance' protest movements are invited to their congresses. And the declaration of the right to disobedience in the Algerian war, which I signed together with a hundred and twenty other university teachers, writers, artists and journalists, has been acclaimed as a reawakening of the French intelligence.

In short, it is important in my opinion to understand clearly two points that you will excuse me for setting out rather superficially, but it is difficult in a statement of this kind to get to the bottom of things.

Firstly, those French people who are helping the F.L.N. are not animated simply by noble sentiments with regard to an oppressed people, nor are they putting themselves at the service of a foreign cause; they are working for themselves, for their own freedom and for their future. They are working for the establishment of true democracy in France. Secondly, they are not isolated, but benefit constantly from an ever more numerous body of helpers and from an active or passive sympathy that never ceases to grow. They were in the van of a movement that will perhaps have awakened the Left, recently bogged down in a despicable caution. They will have made it better prepared to face the inevitable trial of strength with the Army that has been hanging fire since May of 1958.

It is obviously difficult for me to imagine, far away as I am, what questions the military court would have wished to put to me. I suppose, however, that one of them would have concerned the interviews that I gave to Francis Jeanson for his broadsheet *Vérité pour . . .*, and I shall reply to it without evasion. I do not recall either the exact date or the precise terms of this conversation. But you will be able to find it easily enough if the text in question is included in the prosecution's file.

What I am certain of, on the other hand, is that Jeanson came to see me in his capacity as the prime mover in the 'organization of support' and of this broadsheet which was its mouthpiece, and that I received him knowing exactly what was at stake. I met him two or three times more after that. He concealed none of his activities from me, and I approved of them entirely.

I do not believe that there exist noble tasks and common tasks in this field, activities reserved for intellectuals only and others that are unworthy of them. During the Resistance, the Professors of the Sorbonne did not hesitate to carry messages and work as contacts. If Jeanson had asked me to carry dispatch cases or give shelter to militant Algerians, and I had been able to do so without risk to them, I should have agreed to do so without hesitation.

These things must be said, I think; for the moment is now approaching when each one of us must assume his responsibilities. It so happens that those most deeply engaged in political action, hampered by some lingering respect or other for the outward forms of legality, still hesitate to go beyond certain bounds. So that it is in fact the young people, supported by the intellectuals, who, as in Korea and Japan and Turkey, are beginning to tear aside the mystification of which we have been made victims. Hence the extraordinary importance of this trial. For the first time, despite all the obstacles, all the prejudices, all the promptings of caution, Algerians and Frenchmen, fraternally united by a common combat, are standing side by side in the prisoner's box.

All efforts to separate them are vain. Vain, too, will be the attempt to present these Frenchmen as lunatics, as criminals, or as romantics. We are beginning to be tired of false indulgence, of 'psychological explanations'. It must be said quite openly, quite clearly, that these men and these women are not alone, that there are hundreds of others who have already taken over where they left off, and thousands who are ready to do so. A contrary fate has temporarily separated them from us, but I dare to say that they stand in that box as our representatives. What they represent is the future of France, and the ephemeral power that is now preparing to pass judgement on them has already ceased to represent anything at all.

The entire French press considered this statement as a challenge that the government must, for its self-respect, take up. M. Battesi, the deputy for Seine-et-Marne, in a written question, asked that legal action be taken against Sartre.

Sartre [wrote P.-H. Simon] has presented the government with the choice of either sparing him, in other words, showing themselves to be weak, or of taking action against him, in other words weakening themselves by entering into conflict with a great mind.

Meanwhile, in the matter of the Manifesto of the 121, disapproved of by *L'Express* and *Humanité*, an investigation of persons unknown had been opened. On 8 September, *Paris-Presse* carried the front-page headline: JEAN-PAUL SARTRE, SIMONE SIGNORET AND 100 OTHERS RISK FIVE YEARS IN JAIL. The French Embassy in Rio was letting the whole world know that Sartre would be arrested when he got back to Paris. The French Government announced that in future the penalty for incitement to disobedience would be from one to three years' imprisonment; it would be more severely punished on the part of a civil servant. By the time we left Rio, several signatories had been charged; among others, Daniel Guérin, Lanzmann, Marguerite Duras, Antelme, and Claude Roy. In the course of a banquet, M. Terrenoire, then Minister of Information had declared:

Sartre has replaced Maurras and represents an anarchic and suicidal dictatorship aiming to impose itself on a bewildered and decadent intelligentsia.

Whole pages in the newspapers were devoted to the Jeanson organization, to the '121' in general and to Sartre in particular. A cloudburst of insults and threats.

With Amado, his brother and Zelia, we landed one morning at Belo Horizonte, the capital of Minas Gerais State, which had at one time overflowed with gold and diamonds. Niemeyer had promised to send us a station wagon and driver from Brasília. No one was to be seen; our trip was beginning badly. Finally the car arrived, driven by a man with moustachios. We saw a Niemeyer-designed chapel beside a blue lake, and then, in the town, another sample of his work, a very beautiful apartment building that seems to move as you go around it.

We spent the afternoon at Sabará, once inhabited by gold prospectors; in the Gold Museum, an old colonial-style house where the gold was once weighed and stored, there were samples, nuggets, tools, models and panoramas re-creating the town's past. With its narrow streets, its tiled roofs, Sabará looked like a little town in Europe. In the churches, with their gaily painted mouldings, their red and blue walls, we observed with surprise that in the frescoes, God, the angels and the saints all had slanting eyes: the Portuguese artists who painted them had once lived in Macao.

We had already seen some minor works of Aleijadinho,[1] the slave with hands gnawed by leprosy, who ranks as the greatest sculptor and architect of colonial Brazil. We went up the central street of Congonhas, very straight, narrow, full of rubbish, cripples, and hungry-eyed children, as far as the great terrace above which rises the church he erected there, together with the twelve soap-stone statues of the prophets; several of them, roughhewn and inspired, are very beautiful and the group as a whole is striking. From the porch down to the foot of the hill, there are over-life-size figures inside glass kiosks representing scenes from the Passion; garishly coloured, naturalistic, theatrical, they prove that Aleija-dinho was prolific, but also that he sometimes lacked discrimination. At Ouro Prêto we sensed his genius: it was he who had conceived those admirable façades, the cunning balance of their curves that catch and hold the light, the diversity of their designs.

We arrived in the capital of black gold as night fell. The hotel where we spent the night was an early work of Niemeyer's; he was so fond of staircases at the time that he had put one in every room. Next morning, I looked down from my balcony onto faded red roofs, tortuous streets, gardens, terraces, here and there yellow or blue windows making a bright splash of colour, all around, hills covered with glossy greenery; there were steps leading up to dis-tant churches; a light, gentle air with a smell of the country caressed my lungs. We set out on foot. From church to church, from square to square, we went up and down streets and steps, across old bridges. One of the old painted houses was pointed out to us as being the one where they arrested Tiradentes – the teeth puller – who plotted against Portuguese domination in 1788; a statue has been put up in Rio, in the square where he was hanged and quartered. On the main square of Ouro Prêto there is a mu-seum devoted to the *Inconfidentes* of which he was the leader. I left Ouro Prêto regretfully; it was a place where I should have liked to stay longer.

The next morning in Belo Horizonte we had another long wait for our driver. During the journey we understood why he was

1. 'The little cripple.' His name was Antonio Francisco Lisboa and he lived from 1739 to 1814.

always late: all the dashboard compartments were packed with watches and jewellery he was hoping to sell in the towns where we stopped. He explained to Amado that he was combining the functions of chauffeur and cop and that this double function provided many fruitful contacts with a professional body very important in Brazil – the smugglers. He confiscated their merchandise from them or bought it at low prices, then took it on to Brasília, where the people were cut off from the rest of the world and willing to pay very high prices. He described his various ruses with typically Brazilian innocence, we were told by a delighted Amado.

We drove all morning across the *cerrado* along an infinitely straight road: brush, thorny shrubs, stunted trees without a single green leaf or a flower, except, at rare intervals, unexpectedly, great purple clusters swaying amid the bare branches. For hours we didn't see so much as a hamlet, not even a house, only, two or three times, one of those 'sullen animals' La Bruyère described: a barefooted, ragged, emaciated peasant. Despite the opposition of our cop-driver, who didn't consider the place a suitable one for his particular commerce, we stopped for lunch in the middle of the desert, in the artificial town that has been created on the bank of the San Francisco during the construction of a large dam. Labourers, engineers, technicians with their families, about fifteen thousand people live there in huts set directly on the gravel and surrounded by barbed wire. To get in, we had to show our identification papers. An official escorted us around and showed us the colossal dam, still unfinished, which was to make irrigation of the region possible. After lunching in the restaurant hut, we set off again on our dismal way. The town where we spent the night had an airport, but no electricity; we went out walking after dinner along dark streets full of people coming home after an election meeting, all bumping into each other in the dark; every so often there were acetylene lamps or candles in a bistro; we drank *cachaça* as a few fireworks were set off, rather desultorily. Then the same brush, the same solitude for another whole day; that evening, at last, we reached Brasília.

'A life-size model,' I noted down. I learned with regret later that I had overlapped Lacerda's phrase: 'An architectural exhibition, life-size.' This inhumanity is the first thing that strikes one. The main avenue, 400 feet wide and 16 miles long, is curved, but so slightly that it seems quite straight; all the other main roads are parallel to it or cross it at right angles, all danger of collision being removed by the use of cloverleaf crossovers. The only way to get around is by car. In any case, what possible interest could there be in wandering about among the six- or eight-storey *quadra* and *super quadra*, raised on stilts and all, despite superficial variations, exuding the same air of elegant monotony? They intend to build a section for pedestrians only, on the model of Venice and its network of *calle*; so you'll have to get in a car and drive six miles just to be able to walk. But the street, that meeting-ground of riverside dwellers and passers-by, of stores and houses, of vehicles and pedestrians – thanks to the capricious, always unexpectedly changing mixture – the street, as fascinating in Chicago as in Rome, in London as in Peking, in Bahia as in Rio, sometimes deserted and dreaming, but alive even in its silence, the street does not exist in Brasília and never will. Each section of housing, designed for fifteen thousand people, has its own church, its own school, stores and playground. While he was with us, Niemeyer sadly wondered out loud: 'Is it possible to create Socialist architecture in a non-Socialist country?'; he answered his own question: 'Obviously not.' Social segregation here is more radical than in any other city, since there are luxury blocks, middle-income blocks and low-income blocks. The people who live in them do not mix; rich children do not rub elbows with poor children on the school benches; nor does the wife of the highly placed civil servant brush against the clerk's wife at the market or in the church. As in American suburbia, these communities allow their members only the absolute minimum of privacy; since they are all the same, they have nothing to hide from each other. Brasília is like the crystal city Zamiatin envisaged in *Nous autres*: great glass windows take up the whole façade of the buildings and people feel no need to draw their curtains; in the evening, the avenues are so wide that you can see all the families from top to bottom of the buildings living inside their brightly lighted rooms. There are certain residential streets lined with low houses that are referred to as 'the *catingo*'s television';[1] through the large windows on the ground floor the workers can watch the rich dine, read the newspaper, and watch their own television. Apparently there are clerks and secretaries who are mad about Brasília. But the ministers themselves are still

[1]. The '*catingos*' are the workers brought in from the country districts to build Brasília.

[565]

nostalgic for Rio, and Kubitschek had to threaten to ask for their resignations in order to make them settle in the new capital. Tiny jet planes allow them to hop from one city to the other in an hour.

However, each of the public buildings Niemeyer has designed is individually very fine: the Palace of Government, the High Court building, the two skyscrapers of offices, the inverted hemispheres containing the House of Representatives and the Senate, the cathedral in the form of a crown of thorns. They are made to balance and harmonize with each other by a series of subtle asymmetries and bold contrasts that is completely satisfying to the eye. Niemeyer pointed out how the sun-screens, such an important element of modern Brazilian architecture, fulfil the same role as the volutes of baroque art: they give protection from the sun while at the same time avoiding straight lines. He explained the problems he had to solve in order to achieve certain feats; the horizontal sweep of one sun-screen, apparently without support, never fails to astonish visitors. Thanks to his measured extravagance, in this palace of functionaries one escapes – at last! – from the functional.

A long way off, at least six miles, rises the Dawn Palace, the residence of the President, flanked by a spiral chapel which is perfection. It is reflected in a pool in which two bronze nymphs are arranging their hairdos; the story runs that they represent Kubitschek's daughters, tearing out their hair in despair over their exile in Brasília. As we were driving along a track through the brush, the mayor, who was escorting us around that day, suddenly cried eagerly: 'Ah, there's the French Embassy!' I looked back; there was a big placard that read FRENCH EMBASSY; there were other placards indicating the sites of other embassies.

The Brasília Palace, half a mile from the Dawn Palace, is also a Niemeyer building and very lovely, but suffocating inside; and what a long way to go! Even by car, buying a bottle of ink or a lipstick was an arduous expedition because of the heat and the dust. The wind and the soil have not proved amenable to the planners' decisions, which are flouted everywhere by incandescent whirlwinds of dust. On the Plaza of the Three Powers it would take fortunes to cover the red laterite with asphalt. Man wrested this most arbitrary of cities from the desert, and the desert will take it back from him if ever his determination begins to weaken; it lies there on every side, menacing. The artificial lake is no refreshment to the eye; the sheet of blue water seems no more than an earthly reflection of the burning sky.

Amado and Niemeyer took us in to meet Kubitschek; we had a brief, very formal talk with him in his office. He considers Brasília as his personal accomplishment. On the Plaza of the Three Powers there is a museum, designed by Niemeyer, devoted to the history of the new capital. It looks like an abstract sculpture, simple, unexpected and very beautiful; unfortunately, from one of the walls, larger than life and green, protrudes the head of Juscelino; underneath are carved the tremendous eulogies he inspired. On Sunday, people go on pilgrimages – where else would they go? Outside Brasília there is literally *nothing* – to the wooden house where he would come for short periods when work was just beginning on the city; they look around it, have a drink in the café in the shade of the few trees and contemplate his statue which has inscribed on its base the words: THE FOUNDER, and an account of his exploits.

If you need an airplane ticket, medicine, or anything at all, you go about twelve miles out to the 'free city' where building is not officially regulated. As soon as the plan of Brasília had been laid out, the workmen hurriedly threw up a lot of wooden huts which were made into stores, hotels, restaurants, agencies and homes. It looks almost like a frontier town, except that instead of horses and carts there is a deafening stream of automobiles, vans, and trucks ploughing up the red roads; stores belch out ear-shattering music, the advertising vans shriek slogans at you. The sidewalks are a madhouse; your feet get trampled, the dust turns your shoes red, gets in your ears, irritates your nostrils, and makes your eyes smart, while the sun bludgeons the top of your head; yet you are happy here, simply because you are back in the land of men. Fires are frequent; in the dry heat, the wood ignites quickly; just before we got there, a whole neighbourhood had burned down; no victims, but charred remnants, twisted wood, blackened furniture, ironwork, disembowelled mattresses. The gloom of these sights was dispelled, however, as we watched the *catingos* slapping each other on the shoulder in the street and laughing. No one laughs in Brasília. During the day, people worked; sometimes in the evening they would wander dismally around this world they were building and that was not for them.

To understand them, I had to remind myself of the human animals we had passed on our way here, of the hovels of Recife, and all I knew of the north-east. I had just read Amado's *Hunger Road* in which he tells the story of an exodus long ago through the *catinga*; at that time the peasants scourged by hunger – the *flagelados* – set off on foot towards the south, and very few survived. Now they all huddle into old dilapidated trucks which are referred to as 'parrot perches'. Overloaded, with the drivers keeping themselves going on *cachaça*, they often end up down in the ditch; the newspapers tuck away the announcement of the twenty or perhaps fifty deaths on a back page. Sometimes – and I was told this happened in Brasília – when a contractor needs an unskilled labour force, he pays a conveyor a small sum per head to bring in recruits. Once on the site, the men are obliged to accept the wages and living conditions that are offered them. The labourers working on Brasília were all squashed together in 'satellite towns', gigantic *favelas* ten or fifteen miles away from their work. I observed that the drivers of the trucks that take them across the city treat them with incredible brutality; they wouldn't slow down at the stops, and the *catingos* had to jump off while the truck was moving, often falling head over heels on the ground. I was told that they were sometimes injured, or even killed.[1]

I heard a great many discussions about Brasília. The rulers of Brazil had been thinking of transferring the capital of the country inland for nearly a hundred years, and the scheme has always been popular. But the site of Brasília isn't in the real centre of the country; rising as it does on the fringe of vast tracts of unexplored territory, is more like a 'last frontier outpost'. And the scrub around it will not be reclaimed by civilization for a long time to come. A German agronomist who was approached on the subject of getting it under cultivation replied: 'All right. But it means importing thousands of bulldozers, trucks, tractors. And then tons of fertilizer . . . and also soil.' There are no agricultural, mineral, or industrial resources whatsoever around Brasília. It risks remaining for a long time to come nothing but a very distant suburb of São Paulo and Rio, linked to them by a single road – the one we came by – and by air. But that is exactly the reason, Kubitschek told us, why Brasília, by its very existence, will force into being a network of roads that will help unify the country; the highway through the

1. The satellite towns were scheduled for demolition once the capital was finished. But the labourers preferred to stay and try their luck in Brasília rather than go back to the country, so the towns are still there.

virgin forest that is to link Belém to Brasília is already under construction. His opponents reply that the work has already cost a sum, in human lives as well as in cruzeiros, that no practical advantage can ever repay, unless it be the creation of a smuggling route – American automobiles, scent etc. – from Belém down to São Paulo and Rio. The fact is that the north-east doesn't need any outlets, because it has almost no products; on the other hand, its poor artisan class – the cobblers for example – risk being ruined by an influx of manufactured goods from São Paulo. The capital that has been sunk into Brasília should have been used to give the north-east a network of local roads, to irrigate it and set up industries there. Amado admitted that Brasília was a myth but, he added, Kubitschek was able to obtain support, credit and sacrifices from the people only because it was a myth he was selling; any more rational, less fascinating project the nation would have rejected outright. Perhaps I still retain the impression of having seen the birth of a monster whose heart and lungs are made to function artificially by methods devised at breathtaking cost. In any case, if Brasília survives it will fall prey to speculators. The lands along the lake, which in Lucio Costa's original plan were to remain public property, are already being sold off by the municipality to private buyers. Yet another example of the contradictions prevalent in Brazil: the number-one city of this capitalist country was built by architects who were also adherents of the Socialist cause. They have accomplished beautiful work and built a great dream, but it was never possible for them to win out.

I wanted to see some Indians. Amado told us that there were some to be found about 500 miles away, on an enormous and almost deserted river island where Kubitschek had just founded a new town, the farthest west in all Brazil. The governor of the island invited us there. Amado, who really did dislike airplanes, stayed in Brasília. His brother and Zelia climbed with us into the little aircraft that had been put at our disposal; there were just the four of us plus the pilot and a steward. We flew over still-virgin savannas of dark, changing green. After two hours, the river appeared, clasping between its giant arms an island so long we couldn't see the other end. 'The Indians will be at the airfield,' the pilot said with a laugh. He wasn't joking. We could see them from a long way off, almost naked, feathers on their heads, bows in hand, their long straight hair framing their red and black painted faces. 'Do you want to go up to them, or would you rather they came to you?' we were asked as we climbed out of the cockpit. We went to them. They shouted greetings at us with utter lack of conviction. There were women hanging back behind them dressed in their usual rags, babies in their arms, looking worn out. We felt appallingly embarrassed by this masquerade and our idiotic role in it. Exchange of smiles, handshakes; they gave us – as they had been told to do – weapons, arrows, feather headdresses which they had to put on our heads themselves. Then, although it was like walking through a furnace, we were taken around their village: along a bamboo hedge, huge tents full of women and children lying on the ground or sleeping in hammocks. Protected by the government, they fish, cultivate a few plots of ground, make clay dolls and pots which are sold on their behalf or which they give as presents to visitors – who in exchange hand over a sum of money to the foundation. We left with some baked-clay drinking vessels decorated with black and red patterns, and some figurines; sitting and standing women, some cradling infants, some working. Inside the dark tents I noticed some wretched featherless parrots; they had been stripped of their plumage to provide the headdresses we had been given. With their ceremonial paint washed off, some of the men looked quite robust and contented; the women, although we had been told they had a great deal of influence within the community, seemed degenerate. Removed from their natural way of life, without having been assimilated like the Indians in the reservations of New Mexico, their existences were as artificial as those of wild animals in a zoo. The pilot had suggested that another hour's flight would allow us to see another less domesticated tribe. I was hoping we'd be able to snatch a quick lunch and then set off again.

A jeep took us into the centre – canteen, dormitory, dispensary – where the people working for the foundation lived. There was a young doctor full of blind contempt for the Indians and two bearded men who loved them and hence quite deliberately scorned the other white people. They had recently just missed being massacred by a tribe on the Mato Grosso, but that hadn't made them feel any differently. They could have given us the information we would have liked about the village, but despising as they did all tourists who came looking at other men as though they were strange beasts, they turned their backs on us with admirable discourtesy. We stayed sitting on the veranda, looking out across the vast river flowing beneath us towards the danger-filled Mato Grosso on the other side. At last we heard the thrumming of an airplane: the governor and supplies. The governor greeted us, emptied a bottle of beer without offering any to anyone else, and lay down in a hammock. People began piling tables, chairs, crates of dishes and food into jeeps and an amphibian truck: we were going to eat in the new town Kubitschek had founded, a few miles away. When? I was hungry, I was thirsty, I was hot, the whole expedition seemed to me an idiotic mistake. An old ex-*cacique* came and smoked his pipe near us, delivering a monologue in Portuguese. Someone told us that when he was named *cacique*, one of his cousins had disputed his claim and lodged a complaint with Vargas, when he came to visit the village. 'Let the best man win,' the President said, and invited them to settle the dispute in single combat. The cousin won. Vargas was strongly criticized for having allowed the tribe's decision to be questioned. At about three we got into a boat. The sun felt like a sledgehammer on my head, the river seemed to be giving off blinding flames. One of the bearded men was bathing near the wharf, cautiously, because the water is full of tiny carnivorous fish with very sharp teeth. He didn't join our party. 'Where is the town?' I asked. They pointed to a hotel eventually intended for tourists but not yet completed. A fine example of Brazilian bluff! The site had its grandeur: beaches of white sand, the steel-coloured river, and the brush-covered plateaux stretching away to infinity under the metallic sky. But so hot, so stark! We took refuge under the house, between the piles – the only place where there was any shade – and while the women set the table, the doctor put on some Carlos Gardel records. Zelia managed to snatch a bottle of beer out of the governor's hand, and we drank it. At last we were served rice and shrimps; I was so hungry by then I couldn't eat. Sartre made an effort to start a conversation. 'Veeery interesting,' he kept saying to whatever the governor said. 'The hotel will certainly attract young honeymoon couples.' 'Veeery interesting.' He even asked some questions: 'Will there be planes to bring them here?' These excessive demonstrations of goodwill were too much for Zelia, who exploded in a fit of hysterical laughter and had to leave the table and pretend to be admiring a shrub covered with cottony flowers; one of the guests leaped up to show her the way to the rest rooms.

No question of going to see the other village; in any case, that too was administered by white people and wouldn't have taught us anything new. The only interesting tribes are both inaccessible and dangerous. There are a great many outlaws hiding out in the district who have guns and amuse themselves by killing the 'savages'. The authorities have had one of these murderers executed in front of the Indians, but even that wasn't sufficient to reassure them; when they see a white man they attack.

It was six when the boat took us back to the centre. The doctor had stayed behind at the hotel with the jeep. 'If we don't leave immediately, we'll have to spend the night here,' the pilot said. The Brasília airfield isn't lighted at night, and landing is forbidden after sundown. Sartre leaped to his feet. 'Let's walk!' Despite our burden of pottery, we covered the half mile out to the airfield on foot. We were all settled in, the propellers turning, when the doctor appeared, completely drunk and waving his arms. We hauled him up. He sank down at full length on the floor and went to sleep. We all four sighed with relief at finding ourselves alone again.

A few days later, the Amados flew off to Rio. I was upset at saying good-bye to them. We were continuing north, and then going on from Manaus to Havana. We had been invited back there, and our plane tickets were supposed to be waiting for us at an agency; otherwise we would go back to Recife and get a plane to Paris. After being so very close for six weeks, it was difficult to believe we wouldn't see them again for many years; or even, perhaps, forever.

The rector of Fortaleza, introduced to us in Recife, had invited us there. The coolness of the wind was astonishing so close to the equator; what a pleasure to see the sea leaping once more, and a real live town! There were the white-sailed *jangadas* again, a covered market full of strong smells, narrow shopping streets – cloth, shoes, clothing, drugstores – wonderfully casual squares, little parks, kiosks, and human bustle. Sartre gave a lecture, there was an official lunch in a club at the edge of the sea, and a cocktail party in the rectory gardens with the students' choral society singing folk songs. But we had a great deal of time to ourselves. In the evenings, we sat beneath the glossy fronds of a big square, on the terrace of a café-restaurant where soldiers brought young prostitutes for a drink; they picked them up in the nearby brothel district, a section of the teeming *favela* squashed down along the sea.

In its bistros, open wide to the night, along its alleys, men and women were laughing and talking, united beyond the venality of their commerce by their common poverty. One evening, at sunset, I crossed through another section of the *favela*. There was something disturbingly beautiful about the swiftness of the dusks there; no sooner had the afternoon light begun to fade than the horizon was already flaming and it was night. The *jangadas* beached on the sand looked like great dying birds; men and women, coming on foot or riding donkeys, were buying the catch the fisherman had just brought in; they scarcely spoke in the gentle light of the dying day, and this silent exchange between equally dispossessed buyers and sellers had all the simplicity of primitive barter. As I retraced my steps, there were faint lights glowing in the shanties of the *favela*.

In the little café on the square they were always playing one record over and over again, a song in praise of Jânio Quadros. One evening he arrived at our hotel with his entourage. The night broke into bedlam. There were groups of young people running through the streets yelling and dancing with brooms in their hands. An hour before his speech the place was covered with people carrying brooms. Loudspeakers, fireworks, yells and laughter. Jânio's victory seemed to be assured and Sartre would have liked to meet him; but our friends, grimly preparing to vote for Lott, would have been put in a difficult position if he had.

After having heard so much about it, we wanted to have a look at the *catinga* – the white forest. A professor procured for us the good offices of the local chief of police, who spoke French and owned land in that district. Between fifty and sixty, bald, he treated us to a series of admiring comments on Rostand's *Cyrano* as we drove out of the town. At first the landscape was dominated by tall, spiky palm trees, the *carnaúba*; their trunks are used to make fences and walls, their fibres to cover roofs, and their pith and their fruit as food; and above all, the wax that protects the leaves against the drought by preventing transpiration is collected and exported to make films, records, candles, matches. They belong to the great landowners who are opposed, or so I heard, to irrigation plans for the region. Soon they disappeared behind us; there was nothing to be seen but stunted bushes, woody and spiky, with dismal greyish leaves; and cactuses – cactuses like candles, like many-branched candelabra, like giant artichokes, like shuttle cocks, like octopuses, like rosettes, like sea urchins. It was in this ungrateful land that the mystics flourished and the *cangaceiros* who put their hope in God or their confidence in their weapons to change their interminable agony into a human life. Saints and brigands are now both extinct. In the fight against hunger one can no longer count on anything but the *açudes* which store up the water of the rainy season; most of them are dry. We saw one, the size of a lake, to which men were coming with donkeys and filling little barrels to take away with them, often for great distances; it would have been possible to use this natural reservoir for the irrigation of a great tract of this land, which produces as soon as it is moistened, but no system of canalization had at that time been even begun. Some economists claim that any programme of irrigation for the 'polygon' is utopian; the only solution would be to transport the entire population to the south. Others are of the opinion that if enough money were put into it, this zone could be made to yield crops; still others think that for the moment the lot of the peasants would be made more tolerable if they could use the land for their own profit and according to their own needs; but it would take a revolution to bring about any real agrarian reform, and that is highly unlikely.[1] There is no doubt that for a long time to come the children of the polygon will go on eating, for lack of other food, the earth that nourishes and kills them at the same time. Our policeman, however, was complaining that in Brazil everything moves too fast; 'they' had abolished slavery prematurely, and were now intending to arouse and educate the peasants prematurely. Engine trouble finally brought these lucubrations to a halt. We walked a few steps along the road in the hope of finding shelter in the shade of some house; the sun was flaying me alive.

The car repaired, we passed a couple leading by the hand a little boy dressed up as a Franciscan; farther on, there was a family resting in the ditch under a tarpaulin. The feast of Saint Francis was approaching, and on that day the little town we were going to was invaded by an enormous pilgrimage. The pickpockets become very active during the celebrations, and our chief of police was coming to see that the streets were properly patrolled. We lunched in a shady inn; our hostess wouldn't accept a cent from us – nor would the café owner, in whose place we had a drink on the way back.

1. Since 1960, the peasant leagues have developed considerably; the peasants have appopriated land for themselves, they are beginning to be organized.

The friendship of the chief of police was well worth a few little concessions of this sort.

In the street, they were selling hideous pictures of the sanctuary dedicated to Saint Francis; it was as ugly as they were. But the shed containing the ex-votos was even more extraordinary than the sacristy of Senhor do Bonfim. In the middle were piled up all the wooden objects that are burned on a bonfire every year: effigies of witches, arms, legs, feet, hands, head, sexual organs, crutches; the pile almost reached up to the ceiling. On the walls were photographs, drawings, paintings representing the accidents from which the true believer had escaped or the diseases Saint Francis had cured: ulcers, wounds, tumours, wens, goitres, pustules, eczemas, chronic ailments, deformities. Modelled out of plaster and wax were facsimiles of offending organs and limbs: livers, kidneys, and innumerable sexual organs; with the passage of time these simulacra had become mouldy and rotten. It was enough to make the idea of having a body at all quite disgusting.

On the way back, in the gentle evening air, the *catinga* appeared less implacable. We drove through a village full of banners, garlands and vendors' booths giving promise of an approaching celebration; we passed some old jalopies full of youngsters, while others walked along in groups; the boys were wearing brilliant green shirts, the girls brightly coloured dresses; they were holding their shoes in their hands in order not to spoil them, and to give their feet a rest.

Sartre didn't much want to go to Amazonia, and no one had invited us to. But Bost had once written a description of Manaus for *Les Temps Modernes* that had inflamed my curiosity; Alejo Carpentier and Lévi-Strauss had kept it alive. 'Yes, you must go to Amazonia,' Christina T. said, 'the people there are completely different from the ones here.' And so, one evening, we landed at Belém. It was a pleasant change not being expected, but there were no taxis, and we felt a bit lost as we wandered about through the suffocating damp of the airport. At last we got a cab to take us to our hotel. Our rooms were like Turkish baths; in the air-conditioned bar we sat and shivered. As soon as we went out, the humid heat enveloped us, making it impossible to breathe. We had only French money left; the hotel refused to accept it, as did the bank I went to; they told me to try another, the only one which would change foreign currency – American dollars exclusively. What was I to do? I argued in English with the clerk, who finally called up one of his acquaintances. The acquaintance turned out to be a curio dealer – stuffed snakes, feather headdresses, Indian pottery – who bought my francs for half their value. I inquired if there was a plane for Manaus: no seats for the next three days. Three days seems a long time when the climate and the circumstances preclude all activity. Yet I have pleasant memories of Belém. On the wharves along the Amazon, in the market, between the stalls piled one against the other, wandered Negroes, foreigners, smugglers, adventurers, all sorts of people on the loose who also packed the taverns. The mouth of the river, 200 miles wide, contained an island bigger than Switzerland, and one could make out the damp verdure of its banks, across the swollen waters. The old Portuguese town had remained almost intact: churches, colonial-style houses, squares planted with sombre trees and decorated with *azuléjos*. Far out of town, along vast avenues cutting through empty lots, straw huts bathed in the luxuriance of the banana trees; superb palms exploded into the troubled sky; from the yellowish alluvial soil rose a smell of greenhouses, of dying plants and freshly ploughed land. There were gardens stretching out in front of our hotel; we used to eat exotic ices in an exotically decorated kiosk and watch the flamboyant parade of American cars, smuggled into Belém and almost never seen in Rio or São Paulo. Belém's reputation is such that perfumes sent from São Paulo are sold there as being illegally imported from Paris. All day long, the loudspeakers never stopped urging the electors to vote for Jânio, and at night a thousand fireworks were set off. Election day itself, on the other hand, was very calm.

One morning in the hotel bar, a journalist came up to Sartre. 'I was the first person to announce your death,' he told him. A few years earlier, during the course of a fairly high-powered drinking bout, he had sent a telegram to his paper saying that Sartre had just been killed in a car accident outside Belém. A Parisian journalist had called at Rue Bonaparte and asked Sartre's mother if he was in Brazil at the time. 'No, of course not,' she said, 'he's here.' 'Oh! Good! Because there's been an announcement that he's just had a car accident over there. . . .' She thought she was going to faint; she opened the door of his study to make sure Sartre was really inside. This fantasy gained its originator a certain notoriety. 'Don't go and get killed in a plane crash,' he said finally, 'because this time no one would believe me. . . .'

I flew over the Amazon, the infinite network of its tributaries, the infinite green expanses of its forests, delighted yet at the same time disappointed, because I knew that was all I was going to get to see. Every month a plane leaves Manaus taking fresh supplies to the distant trading stations where the Indians come to get their provisions; but we wouldn't have been able to visit their villages and, in any case, there could be no question of staying in Manaus more than three or four days. I had been told that it was an astonishing place. Having become a wealthy capital at the end of the nineteenth century, thanks to the discovery of rubber and Brazilian *hevea*, it was ruined in the course of a few months when the seeds stolen by the Englishman Wickham gave rise in 1913 to *hevea* plantations in Ceylon and Java with which Manaus was unable to compete. It was abandoned by almost all its inhabitants, who left a carcass that soon began to decompose; the introduction of some light industries drew back a population of about 170,000 which now languishes there amid the vestiges of the town's past splendour, between the impenetrable jungle and the Rio Negro, which apart from the air route is the only means of access to the place.

On the walls of the Amazonas Hotel, a handsome, prismatic edifice built only a few years ago, are murals of narrow rivers overhung by low vaults of thick foliage, with tourists, guns in hand, gliding laughingly along in boats. About ten years before, these pictures, reproduced in tourist leaflets, had attracted the attention of a lot of rich, young people in São Paulo who then arrived eager to sample the hunting, the fishing, the mysterious glamour. They left again without having seen anything or fired a single shot, and they didn't keep their disappointment to themselves. The hotel was almost deserted. It was the reverse of Belém in that you froze in your room and sweated in the bar and the restaurant. Outside, you turned into a sticky rag. At six in the evening, when the sun was snuffed out like a candle, a new wave of heat rose up from the ground, as dense as the night without a single light to pierce its gloom: there is no electricity in Manaus (though the hotel did have its own generator). The saliva dried inside our mouths, it was impossible to eat. The rich mansions of the city's golden age – marble brought from Italy, carved masonry

– had grown old without grace, the weeds were devouring them; only the port was alive, with its boats packed with passengers and cargoes, its floating docks, its little houses projecting out over the water and the black, heavy flow of the river.

As in Belém there was no bank that would risk such a perilous speculation as changing French francs; but an old jeweller from Alsace provided us with some cruzeiros at the normal rate of exchange and without any fuss. His friend the consular agent, another old Frenchman, who had been living in Amazonia for fifty years, made us very welcome and took us out by car along the road that cuts into the jungle for several miles. Tijuca had been much more attractive; here, we *knew* that we were surrounded by an ocean of chlorophyll, but all we could see was two curtains of trees; we could have been anywhere. The following day's excursion left us feeling even more bewildered. Amazonia is still putting all its hopes on oil, and Petrobraz is having it prospected. We went down the river on one of the company's boats with the consul and a Swiss technician. Its bronze-tinted waters are separated from the White Amazon by a line so clear-cut that it seems to have been drawn by hand across solid land. Fishermen were sitting in their boats throwing nets into the piranha-infested water. We turned into a tributary and went up it till we reached a group of floating huts, the refectories and dormitories of the oil workers and technicians; we shared their meal with them; then we drove in an uncovered truck, viciously hammered by the sun, out to a derrick; on either side of the road and all around the clearing, the jungle's hermetic density shut off our gaze. We were far from the translucent mysteries evoked in the pages of Alejo Carpentier. I came back completely exhausted. Next morning, the consul took us to admire the town's crowning and most ludicrous glory: the theatre, all marble, topped with a polychrome cupola, in which the most famous artists of the world had danced and sung. By this time I could scarcely stand; the earth was in a fever, I was dripping with its sweat, feverish and sweating myself. I went to bed. 'Do you want to leave anyway?' Sartre asked. Yes, oh yes! Apart from the sinister atmosphere of the town, apart from my fatigue, there was the feeling of panic at being cut off from the world. There had been no tickets to Cuba waiting for us, and we hadn't been able to get through to Rio by telephone. Our attempts to exchange telegrams with the Amados proved futile. In Brazil, only the American telegraphic service works properly, and their lines don't come up to Manaus; a wire takes a week to get through from Rio, the consul told us – if it does get through. There were things happening in Paris; the telephone company announced the connexion I'd been waiting two hours for: Lanzmann's voice crackled a long way away, he was telling me not to come back to France before I'd received a letter, he couldn't hear me, and his voice suddenly faded away in the middle of a word. I was in a hurry to get back to Recife, to Paris. The consul took us out to the airport during the night, telling us about the elections on the way. It takes weeks to count all the votes because the country is so vast and communications so bad; but Jânio was so far ahead that his victory was already certain. The governor of Manaus had voted for Lott, however; he was a member of the Left, and honest. 'There are two kinds of governors,' the consul explained, 'the bad ones, who put all the money in their own pockets and do nothing; and the good ones, who put some of the money in their own pockets and do something.'

It was an eighteen-hour journey; every two hours we landed and almost suffocated in the little airports. When we arrived at about eight in the evening, the customs officer tried to search our luggage: everyone coming from Amazonia is suspected of smuggling. Sartre's anger, and the intervention of Christina T. who had come to meet us, made him change his mind. I went with them to a restaurant despite my fatigue, since it is improper in the north-east for a man to go out alone in the evening with a young woman. For the same reason I took part in the excursion Christina had planned for us next day. We were glad to see her again. Her rebellions had as much real depth as impetuosity and drew on a great fund of natural generosity; they were not directed at the conformism of her immediate circle – which she found restricting – but against injustice. The word Communist frightened her; she had arrived at her present position only by cutting through a number of prejudices, which was a guarantee of its sincerity and its solidity. And then she was always bursting with life, she had gaiety and humour, though underneath lay a basic melancholy, for she felt very much alone. But I really was in very bad shape. I dragged myself along through the dreary market-places of the dreary villages whose poverty-stricken state she wanted us to see. For two months I had loved Brazil; I love it now when I look back on it; but at that moment I was suddenly sick to death of all the dryness, all the hunger, all the misery of the place.

That night I was burning hot, and the next morning I committed the imprudence of asking for a doctor. A friend of Doctor T. – the brother of Lucia and Christina – diagnosed typhoid; but the Brazilian kind lasts only a few days. A penicillin injection brought down my fever. Nevertheless, he still had me removed to the hospital for tropical diseases.

I shall never forget those few days, the feeling of being in hell, eternally. I had a private room with a bathroom, and very nice nurses. But I was just strong enough and just weak enough to find this enforced retreat intolerable. The patients and the staff kept chattering on late into the night; every quarter of an hour a great clock chimed; I almost became hysterical the first morning, when they woke me up at dawn just as I had at long last closed my eyes. After that I got used to the noise; at five in the morning I would haul myself up in bed and feel my heart sink at the thought of the long day stretching ahead, waiting to be filled. I had things on my mind as well. In the evening, Sartre would down one or two melancholy Scotches in the hotel bar, then go upstairs to bed at ten; he was stuffing himself with gardénal so he could sleep. The Brazilian pharmacist didn't even ask for a prescription. 'Orally, or for an injection?' was his only question. (The Brazilians are amazing the way they're prepared to give themselves injections – of penicillin, of practically anything – at the drop of a hat.) All the same, Sartre sometimes woke up again at two in the morning and was so bored he'd get up and shave. When he got out of bed in the morning he'd stagger around to visit me, and once when I was having an intravenous feeding, he nearly sent the whole apparatus flying. Since the fall of 1958, death takes me by the throat at the slightest alert. I waited for him and said good-bye to him with fear in my heart; and the English detective novels he bought me in the town's only bookstore were not entirely successful as a means of distraction since I'd read almost every one of them before.

Besides, the letter Lanzmann had told me about still hadn't arrived; and we couldn't get any French newspapers. The Embassy in Rio was plugging ever more insistently the rumour that Sartre would be thrown into jail as soon as he got back. The French colony in Recife was saying that my illness was a diplomatic manoeuvre and that we were afraid to return to France. In fact, we couldn't wait to be arraigned like all our friends. I loathed the feeling of being imprisoned in that hospital, of eating the inevitable rice and chicken soup every morning and every night. From my bed I could look out and see coconut palms stretching up into a washed-out blue sky, reeds, bamboo, some rather insipid foliage and, on the horizon, the town itself; I would lean out of the window and stare at the straw huts and the women bustling around their little fires. There were a few showers of rain, violent and quickly over, often a slow, heavy wind. Hypnotized by the excessive calm of this landscape, by its humid silence, I felt I had been put under a curse: I was never going to get away from here. In the suspicious calm of one early morning, while the world was still asleep, I saw a young Negro climbing barefoot up the trunk of a coconut palm; he tossed the nuts down on to the ground. Agile, graceful, so near, so far from me, his presence – and mine – brought tears to my eyes. The evenings were beautiful, with the green and red lights of Recife in the distance, but my throat was always tight with the thought of the night still to be got through, the nightmares to be fought off, the next day to be faced.

This eternity lasted seven days. I received Lanzmann's letter. The Jeanson trial had been brought to an end on 4 October by a despicable verdict. Charges against the '121' – of whom by now there were considerably more – continued to multiply. Those who had signed the manifesto were no longer allowed to appear on the radio or on television, nor even to have their names mentioned on any programme. Vidal-Naquet had been suspended, Barrat arrested. In Metz, Debré had denounced the '121' and their 'appalling and at the same time laughable attempts to cause trouble'. On 1 October there had been searches and arrests on the premises of *Les Temps Modernes, Esprit, Vérité et liberté*; Domenach, Péju and several others had been held for some hours by the police. The October issue of *Les Temps Modernes* had been seized. In the course of a demonstration which had been given a great deal of publicity by the press, five thousand veterans had paraded down the Champs-Élysées shouting: 'Shoot Sartre.' On behalf of all our friends, Lanzmann asked us to come back no closer than Barcelona, where they would keep us informed of the situation.

I told the doctor I wanted to leave. I had typhoid, he objected – the hotel would turn me away. The T. sisters, who were at that moment staying with their family at a villa down on the beach, offered me the use of their house in Recife. I spent three days in a room full of antique furniture and scarcely cooled at all by its primitive and noisy air conditioner; summer was beginning, and beyond the windows the heat was settling down for a siege. Early every morning, some cousins of the T. family who lived opposite would have breakfast sent over to me. Once, at about six in the morning, I was astonished to hear Sartre's voice floating up from the garden; furious at not being able to sleep, he'd got up and come around. One evening the young Doctor T. came to examine me; he took rather a long time, so I told his sisters and Sartre to go off and eat without waiting for him. They refused; it was not permitted to leave a man alone in a house with a woman, even one of my age. They didn't subscribe to these prejudices themselves, but the street was full of cousins who were keeping an eye on them. The doctor gave me permission to go out for a bit. After a quarter of an hour walking along streets full of air that felt like treacle, with Sartre staggering along beside me, I collapsed into a chair on a café terrace, feeling more dead than alive; two days later, during our first lunch with the Amados, in a familiar *churrascaria*, I fainted completely.

The Cuban *chargé d'affaires*, despairing of ever getting through to us by phone, had come to Recife. Havana was insisting that we spend a few days there; the only way of getting there was to go back down to Rio, 1,000 miles away. The pleasure of seeing the Amados and Copacabana again was spoiled for me by my fatigue; and I was homesick, even though Lanzmann had told me again by phone that the ultras were after Sartre's head.

The evening we were due to leave for Cuba, a tornado swept the airfield; it ruffled the potted palms in the waiting room and filled it with whirling bits of paper. We sat for hours, dozing, stupefied, waiting for it to pass. Finally we got into the plane. The engines were spitting out too much flame; it was one of those nights when the worst seems certain to happen; when we landed into the grimy darkness at Belém, the absurdity of being back there at all confirmed my presentiment: this continent was a great net from which we were never going to escape. I recovered my calm only the next morning when I looked out and saw a plateau crushed between a cliff and the turquoise sea; Caracas was below us. We landed. As we drank a coffee in the buffet, I gazed out at the glittering aircraft, all its windows spitting back the sun, which in an hour or two was going to tear us away from these poverty-stricken lands; an old woman was going among the tables, picking up bread crusts, chop bones, remains of egg white, which she then wrapped up in a piece of paper to feast her family on later. Some students came and asked Sartre to stop for a few days in Caracas. We felt sympathetic towards them; Venezuela was on the move. (There was a student demonstration that very afternoon, and a few days later the police killed several of the participants.) But we were expected in Cuba, and we were frantically eager to get back there.

An airport official came up. 'Have you a return ticket? Your ticket on to Paris? No? Then you can't leave: orders from Havana.' 'But we've been invited there,' Sartre said. 'Prove it.' We hadn't a cent between us to pay for return tickets, and no official papers. The glittering plane was going to fly off without us! Sartre telephoned the Cuban Embassy and opposed the airport officials with a rage that finally carried the day. At the last moment, we were allowed on board. We were never to discover the reasons for this contretemps; the Cubans had absolutely no immigration restrictions.

At last the coast was behind us! At last! We flew over Jamaica, and it was as though with a single beat of our wings we had reached England: glowing green lawns, cottages flanked by swimming pools. Sartre, who had been there, told me that there is no more baleful colony in the world. And soon we were in Havana with our friends waiting for us – except Franqui and Arcocha, who were in Moscow at the time – and a group of musicians in costume plucking their guitars.

Havana had changed; no more nightclubs, no more gambling, no more American tourists; in the half-empty Nacional Hotel, some very young members of the militia, boys and girls, were holding a conference. On every side, in the streets, on the roofs, the militia was drilling. It was known, through Guatemalan diplomats, that an army of Cuban émigrés and American mercenaries was being trained in Guatemala. They were going to try to gain a foothold on the island and then, in the name of an imaginary government, call for help from the United States. Faced with these threats, Cuba was toughening up; the 'honeymoon of the revolution' was over.

Oltuski was no longer a minister. He was working at the Institute which Guevara had just founded for the country's industrialization and which he took us to see. The leaders didn't hide their difficulties from us. There was a shortage of trained men; certain engineers were each working on the planning of three or four different industries; and yet it had still not been possible to utilize the whole of the capital allotted for the creation or renovation of the industrial plant.

We visited a cloth mill near Havana: an already outmoded plant, with well-designed workrooms, surrounded by trees and lawn, with comfortable housing for the executives and workers. There was a celebration going on in the park: the workers and their wives, in their best clothes and low-cut dresses, their children, ice-cream and candy vendors. Standing in a kiosk in the middle of the lawn, Sartre spoke of his friendship for Cuba. He was asked about France, and then he asked questions in his turn: What advantages had the mill workers gained from the change of regime? Some of the workers were about to reply when a union leader stopped them and answered for them instead.

During our conversation with the intellectuals, Rafael and Guillen, who hadn't opened their mouths in April, had a great deal to say. Talking about poetry, Guillen declared: 'I consider all research into technique and form counter-revolutionary.' They were insistent that writers should comply with the rules of socialist realism. Some writers told us in private that they were beginning, against their will, to censor their own work, each asking himself the question: 'Am I really a revolutionary?'

Less gaiety, less freedom; but much progress on certain fronts. The cooperative we visited was a great deal more advanced than any of the old ones we had seen before. It was growing mostly rice, but using intensive methods of cultivation to such good effect that it had reclaimed more land, on which tomatoes and various vegetables were now being grown. With the help of masons from town, the peasants had just finished building a village: comfortable houses, a movie theatre, schools, playgrounds. There was a State store selling the products of prime necessity to life at almost cost price. There was a shoe factory and also a tomato-canning factory working directly for the cooperative; in this way they were realizing on a modest scale what the Chinese communes had aimed at: direct contact between industry and agriculture. The peasants seemed even more attached to the regime than before, but feverish. The village was near the spot where the landing was expected. The head of the cooperative was over-excited; he had a revolver stuck in his belt and told us he was waiting impatiently for his opportunity to fight.

The evening before our departure, Sartre gave a press conference; just as it was about to begin, one of our journalist friends whispered in his ear that troops were landing at that moment along the Santiago coast. Sartre nonetheless declared before the press, the radio microphones and the television cameras that he did not believe there would be any intervention by the United States in the immediate future; America was in the middle of a Presidential election, and the Republican Party wasn't going to spoil Nixon's chances by assuming the responsibility of any such risky adventure. We had supper with the reporters from *Revolución* at the bar-restaurant of the old Hilton, now the Habana-Libre. It was a dismal sight, that vast room with its pseudo-Polynesian décor. Our friends kept leaving the table to go and phone; the invasion rumour was apparently true. 'We'll throw them back,' they said darkly. The next day, the rumour was denied, but to the Cubans this only meant that the battle had been postponed.

We hadn't seen Castro. We went to visit Dorticós the day we were due to leave; it was the anniversary of the death of Camillo Cenfuegos, who had been idolized almost as much as Castro and whose plane had crashed into the sea a year before. There were processions of students, labourers, clerks, women and children filing through the streets carrying sheaves of flowers and crowns which they were throwing into the ocean. While we were talking to the President, Jiménez was talking to Castro's secretary on the telephone: he happened to be in the neighbourhood of Havana and was asking us to wait so that he could see us. Impossible, it was six already, the plane was due to take off at eight. Jiménez took us to our hotel and we went up to collect our luggage; we pressed the button for the elevator; it came up, the door opened, and out burst Castro followed by four bearded men and Edith Depestre. He had lost none of his gaiety and his warmth. He put us into his car. What had we seen? What hadn't we seen? It was difficult to make much progress; there were processions blocking the streets and the crowd kept stopping the car with cries of 'Fidel! Fidel!' 'I'll take you to see the Students' Quarters at the University,' Castro said as we finally drove out of Havana. 'But the plane leaves at eight ...' I murmured. 'It will wait!' The largest of the barracks in Havana had been transformed into a group of pavilions, buildings and sports grounds. We had a quick look at it, then, on the pretext that it was a shortcut, the driver plunged into a series of deserted byroads punctuated by great puddles. The plane has left without us, I said to myself. At the airport, the barriers were raised and the car took us out on to the airfield and put us down right beside our plane, which the mechanics were still checking; they would be a long time yet. Oblivious of all the signs forbidding it, Castro stood chewing his huge cigar a few yards away from the engines. 'The landing is a certainty,' he told us. 'But it is also a certainty that we'll repulse it. And if you hear I've been killed, just don't believe it.'

He left. Jiménez, Edith, Otero, Oltuski and some other friends took us to have dinner in the buffet. The airport was full of people giving us very unfriendly looks. 'They're waiting for the plane to Miami, and they won't be coming back.' You could tell their class from their clothes. When the loudspeakers announced: 'All passengers for Miami,' they rushed in a body to the boarding gates.

We took off. There was a landing in Bermuda. I was expecting another on the Azores; we seemed to be up a long time. Here we are! I thought as I saw land appear. But there didn't seem to be any other side to these islands. And I thought I recognized the colour of the earth, its contours, the indentations of the coast, the green of that river—the Tagus; it was Spain, the snowy crest of the Sierras, Madrid, reached in fourteen hours, but already clothed in dusk. Another plane took us on to Barcelona.

We'd arranged to meet our friends at the Colón Hotel; the one I knew no longer existed, we were told by the reporters who nabbed us as we arrived. But another with the same name had opened near the cathedral and was very pleasant. We met Bost and Pouillon there the next morning. They gave us a detailed account of all that had happened since September. The Jeanson trial and the manifesto of the '121' had been instrumental in causing the Communist and Socialist youth groups, the trade unions, the Communist Party and the Socialist Party to take various forms of action against the war. The trade unionists and university teachers had launched an appeal for 'a negotiated peace'. The unions had supported the demonstration organized by the U.N.E.F. on 27 October, which had been an enormous success, despite the scuffles and truncheon charges. The measures taken against the '121' had raised a good deal of protest. All the actors engaged on television work had gone on strike as an expression of solidarity with Evelyne when she was fired from a programme. Meanwhile, Laurent Schwartz had been dismissed from his chair at the École Polytechnique, the professors had been suspended, and so had Pouillon and Pingaud, recording secretaries in the Assembly. Marshal Juin had signed a manifesto against 'the professors of treason'. The National Union of Armed Services was asking for 'the sternest possible measures against irresponsible persons, and above all against traitors'. The central committee of the U.N.R. stigmatized the actions of 'so-called intellectuals'. The National Union of Reserve Officers was demanding that action be taken against them; the list of the '121' had been posted in all messes, etc. Sartre was the one most attacked. His statement to the court had caused many people to hate him passionately. By telephone, Lanzmann, who had been detained in Paris, asked us, as did his comrades, to come back by car; if we took the plane, Sartre would get a very stormy reception at the airport, there would be brawls, he would be forced to answer the reporters' questions in such a way that the police would haul him in. I think now that it would have been better to create as much publicity for the '121' as possible; but we listened to the advice of our friends, whose solicitude I can sympathize with, for there is a certain frivolity in worrying too little about others. We went out and strolled around Barcelona, which Sartre found no more pleasant to revisit than Madrid; I, on the other hand, was quite happy just being on the Ramblas. We looked at Gaudi's fantastic and never-to-be-finished cathedral; we went up to Tibidabo, looked around the Museum of Catalan Art, and the following afternoon we set off for the frontier.

The press had been insulting Sartre so copiously for the past two months – traitor, enemy of France, etc. – that we expected to get a pretty rough reception when we got back. Night had already fallen when we reached the frontier post. Bost took the four passports in to the police and came back. The commissioner wanted to see us. He had orders to advise Paris when we crossed the frontier, he told us apologetically. He sent one of his subordinates to buy us newspapers, offered us cartons of cigars and cigarettes – no doubt confiscated from returning tourists – and as we were saying good-bye asked us to sign his visitors' book. He advised us to get in touch with the police when we got back to Paris. We spent the night at Béziers. After so many foreign splendours, I was very moved next morning as we drove along under a pale sky and I found myself looking out at the pale gilt of the plane trees, the vineyards flaming in the autumn sun and, instead of hovels scattered about over wasteland, real villages. Would I be permitted, one day, to love this country again?

In Paris, our first concern was to get ourselves officially charged; we hired Roland Dumas, who had been counsel for the defence in the Jeanson trial, as our lawyer and he undertook all the necessary arrangements. The police pushed politeness to the point of coming around themselves to my apartment for the official interview; the youngest officer, stiff with embarrassment, hurt his finger typing out our statements and bled all over the keys. Commissioner M. helped us phrase our statements and vary them a bit. He had been astonished at first by the determination of the '121' to inculpate themselves as much as possible; now he just smiled. 'Well then, you can set your minds at rest now, you've been quite properly charged,' he concluded encouragingly. But no. The night before the day set for our hearing, the examining magistrate reported sick. A new date was set; at the last moment it was postponed *sine die* on the absurd pretext that our files were still in the office of the Public Prosecutor. Then they announced that no more charges were to be made. Obsessed as ever with its greatness, the seat of power had seen fit to deprive civil servants of their daily bread but not to appear in the eyes of the world as the persecutor of famous writers. It also hoped to shatter the unity of the '121' by sparing some and keeping a permanent threat hanging over the heads of the others.

To counter this ploy, Sartre called a press conference; before some thirty French and foreign journalists gathered in my apartment, he explained his part in the manifesto and gave an exposition of the present situation. Thierry Maulnier, sitting cross-legged on the carpet, wanted to ask him a question: 'I wouldn't like to misrepresent what you've said . . .' 'Then it would be the first time such a thing has worried you,' Sartre answered. The press printed only summary accounts of what he had said. And the incident was closed.

CHAPTER ELEVEN

By the shabby expedient of barricades, the government was encouraging a Fascist revival; but the youth of the country had begun to move, we thought that they were going to act. In December, the green and white flag waved over the Casbah, crowds acclaimed Abbas[1] and the truth became apparent to the whole world: behind the wall of silence and the masquerades imposed on them by force, the Algerian masses were unanimously demanding their independence; it was a political triumph for the F.L.N. that brought its hour of victory nearer.

The Prime of Life came out, with a success that would have satisfied me completely when I was a beginner. In fact, when I visited Gallimard in November and was told that forty thousand had been sold before publication, I was rather unpleasantly affected by the news. Had I become one of those best-seller manufacturers with a recognized public, the value of whose works no longer has anything to do with their sales? Many critics assured me that I had just written my best book; there was something disquieting about this verdict. Should I, as some of them suggested, burn everything I had written up till now? Above all, I converted such praise into demands; when I received letters that moved me, I felt I still had to deserve them. This final volume of memoirs was giving me trouble, and I said to myself sadly that at best it would turn out as good as the preceding one, without having the same freshness. On the whole, however, my satisfaction prevailed over my doubts. I had feared misrepresenting the things dearest to my heart; but my readers had understood. The *Memoirs of a Dutiful Daughter* had appealed to a great many people, but in a somewhat ambiguous way; I took it that those who liked *The Prime of Life* were really on my side.

I accommodated myself without regret to the austerity of my everyday life. We had been living in semi-retirement for a long time; now we stopped going out altogether. The usual sort of restaurant customers often showed hostility towards us, and we

1. At a terrible price: the F.L.N. announced thousands of victims to the U.N.

could no longer bear sitting next to them. We spent our evenings together in my studio, dining on a slice of ham, talking and listening to records; when I was alone, I would listen to them for hours on end. I never put my nose outside the door at night, except with Lanzmann or Olga. This life of seclusion strengthened our ties with our little group of friends. The *Temps Modernes* team, enlarged by two new members, Gorz and Pingaud, used to meet at my place two mornings a month. Gorz would arrive first. 'I just can't help being on time,' he used to say. There were fewer of us than in the bagpipe days, so our discussions were more closely argued. My taste for it reawakened by an evening Sartre and I had spent at Monique Lange's with Florence Malraux, Goytisolo and Serge Lafaurie, I gave an all-night party. I didn't arrange it deliberately, but all our friends naturally tended to be 'committed'; at least one member of all the couples I invited had signed the '121' manifesto. I'd prepared a sequence of jazz records, but they weren't needed: we talked.

There was another dinner at the Soviet Embassy. I was placed next to Mauriac, whom I was meeting for the first time; Sartre had told me he had a sharp tongue and a comic gift; was it age that had extinguished him, or his De Gaulle worship that had worn him out? I looked for him, but there was no one there. Sartre talked to Aragon, whom he advised to visit Cuba. 'We're too old,' Aragon said. 'Bah!' Sartre replied. 'You're not so much older than I am.' 'How old are you?' 'Fifty-Five.' '*It* begins at fifty-five,' Aragon said, with a knowing look. Elsa gave us a graceful account of the troubles that had forced her to start putting artificial tears in her eyes and then, in her knees, 'parallel hearts'. The occasion was in honour of Galina Nikolaeva, the author of *The Engineer Bakhirev*; in her book she had written in a very lively and even romantic way about a subject that is rarely and badly treated in the West: work. I only caught a glimpse of her but we invited her and her husband around to my apartment. She was suffering from a serious heart disease and had an attack that day, so he came alone with an interpreter. He greeted us with formality and behaved during the entire conversation as though he had a whole delegation standing behind him. He told us that the writers of Russia would be very happy to see us in Moscow. We would very much like to go, Sartre answered.

André Masson had signed the '121' manifesto. We admired his

work and found his face and his slyly ingenuous remarks full of charm. He was an old anarchist, and we had been alienated by his excessively a-political attitude. Diego's arrest had opened his eyes. Rose was spending all her time helping the Algerian prisoners and their families. I saw her on various occasions, and we had dinner at their apartment in the Rue Sainte-Anne, once with just the two of them, once with Boulez, who had also signed the manifesto. Masson, who wore a beard now, told us delightful stories about the golden age of Surrealism. Of Boulez's work we already knew and liked *Le Marteau sans maître* and the first *Structure*; we had not gone to the performance of *Pli selon pli*, fearing we wouldn't be able to make head or tail of it on just one hearing. The image of him we had formed from Goléa's book and Masson's stories pleased us greatly. A young German composer performing one of his works during a concert conducted by Boulez was hissed and fled at the end of the piece, completely crushed. Boulez dragged him back onto the stage. 'Your booing proves you haven't understood anything; he will now play it again.' The composer did play it again, and the audience listened in silence. Boulez's appearance matched what I had heard of him. He was working in Baden-Baden because he found that the standard of playing in Germany was much higher than in France. I asked him some questions. He explained how old music is reconstructed, and how works are recorded: not, as I had thought, all in one piece but in small fragments; the bits of tape are then spliced together rather the way a film is edited. It takes several hours to perfect five to ten minutes of music; the slightest error or extraneous noise, which would pass unnoticed in a concert, becomes intolerable when repeated every time the record is played. That's why records are so expensive; it takes a considerable amount of work to produce them. The methods used permit certain tricks. One virtuoso performer was able to play both the piano part and the violin part in a recording of some Bach sonatas. Boulez talked about his work as a conductor. The instrumentalists, he told us, each know only a particular profile of a piece, determined by their place, the instrument they play, and the instruments around them; the triangle doesn't hear the same symphony as the first violin. If you change their usual seating arrangements, they get completely bewildered.

Shortly after the referendum in January 1961 there was a meeting of the Boupacha committee. I noticed Anne Philipe, very serious and touching, and the bizarre close-cropped head of Françoise Mallet-Joris; Laurent Schwartz seemed much younger than I had imagined him. Being able to regard all these people with sympathy was a great comfort to me; sympathy had become such a rare thing. Suddenly, there were noises and shouts, and all the people attending our meeting rushed to the windows; some P.S.U. members were holding a meeting in a room on the ground floor to decide how to reply to the referendum; two of them rushed in: 'The Fascists are attacking us, come and help.' Schwartz rose to his feet, determined hands restrained him, and some of the young people went downstairs. There was a lot of running up and down the stairs, then two cops opened the door and asked for the chairlady. 'You must give her back to us,' someone said politely. They wanted to know if two militant P.S.U. members, picked up after a brawl, belonged to our committee; I didn't destroy their alibi. Exchange of courtesies; on the way out, some members of the P.S.U. escorted Claudine Chonez and me to her car.

Some students asked me to go out to the Antony Cité Universitaire to discuss why one should answer No to the referendum. I had never seen those vast buildings before; I believe they accommodate four thousand young people who can live there for weeks, as though they were on an ocean liner, without having to go outside for anything. The entrance hall was hung with slogans – VOTE NO PEACE IN ALGERIA – and photographs depicting French atrocities; the committee was entirely leftist; the right-wing students were not very numerous and kept very quiet. I took my place with Arnault, a Communist, and Chéramy, an ex-Trotskyite, in a big hall packed with students and decorated with banners: VOTE NO. There was lively applause for the position taken by the '121', whom I was considered to represent. I emphasized the absence of a Third Force in Algeria and also De Gaulle's repugnance at having to come to terms with mere peasants. On the question of disobedience, Arnault and I defended different points of view, but without making our dissensions too obvious, even though I was very much irritated by his official optimism: he knew perfectly well that the 'French people' weren't fraternizing with the Algerians either in the army or in the factories. On the way out I talked with the students; we were in agreement on everything.

A little later, some Belgian students belonging to *La Gauche* –

the extreme left wing of the Belgian Socialist Party – reminded me of the promise they had extracted from me a year earlier to give a lecture in Brussels. Their newspaper had opposed the Algerian war; many of them were secretly helping the Algerians, taking them in and getting them over the border; they had no objections when I warned them that under the title 'The Intellectual and the Government', I should in fact be talking about Algeria.

I am always nervous when I appear before an audience; I am afraid I may not measure up to their expectations or to my own intentions. I talk too fast, terrified by the length of the silence I must fill and by the quantity of things to be said in such a short time. On this occasion my anxiety was worse than usual. My talk was what is called 'an open lecture' which meant it had attracted, from motives of snobbery, idleness or curiosity, people who had nothing whatever in common with myself: big businessmen and even government ministers. And as soon as I started, I had the feeling that in one way or another they'd all made up their minds in advance. On the way out, a Communist criticized me for not being Communist, a rebel for not castigating those who conformed. Several people thought it regrettable that I hadn't tackled the problems of the Congo: I had alluded to them, but didn't feel I was qualified to discuss them at length. I was depressed even more by the reception that followed my lecture than by these criticisms as I left. People would come up to me with beaming smiles and say: 'I don't agree with you politically; but I liked your book so much!' 'Let's hope you don't like the next one,' I replied to one of them. It is true that in *The Prime of Life* I had taken a very objective attitude towards my past beliefs; all the same, I did make it perfectly clear how distasteful I find bourgeois institutions and ideologies; I shouldn't have been receiving the approval of people who were attached to them. Lallemand, a lawyer forbidden to practise in France because he had supported the Algerians, consoled me: 'It's the paradox of their position; they lump all culture together. They swallow Sartre, they swallow you; but it means they have to swallow your attacks as well; it all helps their ideological breakdown.'

I spent three interesting days. I visited the museum again, alone and at length; Lallemand drove me around Brussels. I had dinner with the *La Gauche* team, who told me a lot about the Congo; I gave a lecture on Cuba to a small and politically minded audience.

Then Lallemand drove me out to Mons and arranged for me to meet fifteen or so trade unionists who explained the reasons behind the thirty-two-day strikes involving a million workers. The Belgian workers' standard of living was relatively high; many arrived at the meetings in automobiles. They had been fighting to consolidate their position, to make sure they wouldn't have to meet the expenses of decolonization, and above all to bring a new economic policy into being; it had been the first general strike in Europe intended to reorganize a country's economy on a socialist basis. They all expressed different opinions on the personality of Renard, who had both fermented the strike and held it in check; but they all agreed in accusing the parliamentary Socialists of robbing them of their victory; it was in part against the conservatism of their leaders that their struggle had been directed.

Invited by these same members of Parliament whom the strikers considered traitors, I gave the same lecture in the Mons Hôtel-de-Ville that I had given in Brussels, though with less distress, since the audience was quite obviously all left-wing. Afterwards, I had dinner with my hosts. 'Those are your real enemies,' Lallemand had told me, 'the ones who don't integrate: they don't read your books. Culture's just a joke to them; that's their strength.' Over the duck with peaches, we asked them some embarrassing questions: 'Why had the strike been called off in mid-career?' 'Because it would have ended in a revolution, and we are reformists.' 'And how does the rank and file feel about it?' 'Very badly indeed,' M. replied placidly; his fellow politicians then told us with a great deal of accompanying laughter how he had got himself booed by twenty thousand strikers. One of them rallied to his support: 'You know what the masses are; you have to know how to manage them. . . .' 'Do you mean to say,' I said, 'that you, a Socialist, despise the masses?' People looked at him, scandalized: 'Did you say you despised the masses?' C. spoke in a hurt tone about the French Left: 'I realized that the union of left-wing parties didn't stand a chance when I heard Daniel Mayer talking with such hate about . . .' I was afraid he was going to say: 'the Communists', but what he said in fact was: 'Guy Mollet.' 'But he was quite right,' I said. 'Guy Mollet is an honest man,' C. said. There were murmurs from some of the guests. 'He is honest. He's never taken a sou for himself,' C. said in a tone of reverence. I had never frequented professional politicians, and the fatuity of this particular tableful stupefied me. 'The only thing they're interested in is getting re-elected,' Lallemand told me next day, when he came around to my hotel at dawn to show me the rest of Mons and its outskirts before taking me to my train. In the town, with its closed shutters, the light turned all the stone buildings pink, like the cathedral at Strasbourg. I saw Verlaine's prison, the Borinage, where Van Gogh had lived, the slag heaps of abandoned mines, already covered by thick vegetation: in the middle of the plain, an abrupt landscape of artificial hills. The closing of the mines could not be avoided; what was so revolting was that the operation should have been carried out at the miners' expense; the only inhabitants left in the mining villages were old-age pensioners. Though even normally, Lallemand told me, no one tended to go on working here after the age of forty. The prevalent silicosis had been aggravated by the use of the pneumatic drill; he described the strange faces of the men with silica-encrusted eyelids.

I took part in the C.N.E. sale. The Communists had criticized the action of the '121'; by going together to the Palais des Sports in one bloc, we would be demonstrating the solidarity that still existed between us; it was a way of getting them, willy-nilly, into the soup with us. As it turned out, we found ourselves scattered all over the place, each one squeezed behind his or her counter. There were loudspeakers braying Bach at us rather too emphatically. I felt closer to the public there than I had to the people who came to hear me in Brussels, though I was too busy signing my name to be able to establish much contact with them. I was still disturbed about my success. The book had been so well received because of an optimism which I was far from feeling at present. The various resistance movements had not proved so strong as we had expected. We were falling back into our previous state of isolation.

I went with Sartre to the Dubuffet exhibition, whose work we had rather misjudged in 1947. The pictures of his latest period wrenched us out of our everyday routines of perception, replaced them with a science-fiction vision of the world. A Martian would see our landscapes and our faces thus, in their naked materiality, capable of indefinite and minute variations, but stripped of all human meaning. When I came out, I couldn't look at people's faces in any other way: an opaque mass covered by a superficial network of lines.

I met Christiane Rochefort several times, always with great pleasure. I liked *The Gallery Gods* very much. To convey with appropriate savagery the world of the psychotic, she had invented a voice, a tone, that – even more than her assiduous re-creation of a Communist family – suggested the possibility of a quite different world. This book had caused less of a scandal than her first, but she'd had another cartload of self-righteous filth emptied on top of her all the same. 'It's happened to me too,' I told her. 'It must have been worse for you, though,' she said sympathetically, 'because I'm a tramp anyway, you know.' And indeed, I was always conscious of my middle-class origins when I was with her; she was a real working-class girl, and there wasn't much she hadn't seen: I envied her daring, her fire, her inner freedom. For the time being, she wasn't writing. 'I can't get interested in my piddling little stories, not at the moment!'

I understood how she felt. The assassination of Lumumba, the last pictures of him, the photographs of his wife leading his mourners, head shaved, breast bared – what novel could compete with that? This murder was a stain on the good name not only of Kasavubu and Tshombe, but of America, the U.N., Belgium, the entire Western world and Lumumba's immediate circle of followers. 'Everyone was betraying him, even his relations,' Lanzmann was told by Serge Michel, who had been Lumumba's press attaché. 'He didn't want to believe it. And he thought all he had to do was go down into the street and talk to the people, and all the plots would just vanish into thin air.' He also said: 'He hated violence; that's what killed him.' Lanzmann had this conversation in Tunis, where he had gone with Péju to represent *Les Temps Modernes* at the anti-colonialist conference there. They had a talk with Ferhat Abbas, who bounced his little niece up and down on his knees during the entire conversation. 'He thought we were from *Esprit*,' Lanzmann told me. 'What can you expect,' Abbas told them, 'these Communists give people bread to eat, and that's good; but man does not live by bread alone. We're Moslems, you see, we believe in God, we want to elevate their minds; the mind must be nourished too.' It was evident that his role in the revolution was no longer more than a decorative one. Which is what we were also told by an F.L.N. leader. 'Abbas is old, sixty. There's the generation in its sixties, then the one in its forties, and one in its twenties. It's good for the revolution to have a figurehead. But he isn't the man who's giving the orders, and he won't be giving orders in the future.' There were two generally recognized tendencies among the leaders, he said: the classic politician, prepared to accept collaboration with France, in other words to call a halt to the revolution; and the other type, supported by the guerrillas and the rank and file, who demanded agrarian reform and socialism. 'And if the revolution is sabotaged, we'll take to the hills,' was the attitude of certain leaders, the ones who wanted to wage war to the bitter end, with the help of the Chinese if necessary.

Fanon, the author of *Peaux noires, masques blancs* and *L'An V de la révolution algérienne*, was among those opposed to a compromise peace. A psychiatrist born in Martinique, he had won great applause in Accra by opposing Nkrumah's pacifist theories with a speech on the necessity and value of violence. *Les Temps Modernes* had published a striking article by him on the same subject. From his books and all we had heard of him, we had the impression that he must be one of the most remarkable personalities of our time. Lanzmann had a great shock when he discovered him sick in bed and his wife, as soon as she came out of his room, in tears. He had developed leukemia; according to the doctors, he had less than a year to live. 'Let's talk about something else,' he said immediately. He asked some questions about Sartre, whose philosophy had influenced him; he had been passionately interested by *La Critique de la raison dialectique*, especially by the analyses of terror and brotherhood. He was being torn apart by events in Black Africa. Like so many African revolutionaries, he had dreamed of a united Africa freed from all foreign exploitation. And then, in Accra, he had realized that before achieving brotherhood, the Negroes of Africa were going to go through a stage of killing each other. Lumumba's assassination had completely shattered him. He himself, during one of his trips through Africa, had only just escaped a similar attack on his life.

Everyone was very uncertain at that particular time – De Gaulle having abandoned the 'preliminary talks at Melun' – as to what concessions the Algerians were prepared to make. We knew they wouldn't compromise on the question of Algeria's independence and their refusal to alter the present frontiers. But would their victory lead to socialism? We thought it would.

Six women prisoners in the La Roquette prison escaped; a pretty feat, well organized, and one that should have been a help to all women in getting rid of their inferiority complexes. I went with Sartre to the Lapoujade exhibition. Sartre had written a study of 'committed' painting with reference to his work; I liked his paintings. Spring appeared, unbelievably mild: 70° in March, the first time since 1880, according to the newspapers. The sky was so blue that as I sat facing my open window I wanted to write just for the sake of writing, as I would have sung just to sing, if I'd had any voice. 'I've got some things to show you,' Lanzmann said one evening. He took me to dinner just outside Paris in a sleepy village full of country smells, and suddenly, hell was back on earth. Marie-Claude Radziewski had given him a file which contained accounts of the treatment inflicted by the *harkis*, in the cellars of the Goutte d'Or, on Moslems handed over to them by the D.S.T.: electrodes, burning, impaling on bottles, hangings, stranglings. The physical tortures were interspersed with psychological treatments. Lanzmann wrote an article on the subject for *Les Temps Modernes* and published the dossier of complaints. A girl student told me that she had been in the street near the Goutte d'Or and seen bleeding men being dragged from one house to another by the *harkis*. The people living in the neighbourhood heard their screams every night. 'Why? Why? Why?' The unendingly repeated cry of a fifteen-year-old Algerian boy who had watched his whole family being tortured[1] kept tearing at my eardrums and my throat. Oh, how mild they had been in comparison, those abstract storms of revolt I had once felt against the human condition and the idea of death! One can engage in convulsive struggles against fatality, but it discourages anger. And at least my horror had been directed at something outside myself. Now, I had become an object of horror in my own eyes. Why? Why? Why must I wake up every morning filled with pain and rage, infected to the very marrow of my bones with a disease I could neither accept nor exorcise? Old age is, in any case, an ordeal, the least deserved, according to Kant, and the most unexpected according to Trotsky; but I could not bear its driving the existence which until then had contented me into this abyss of shame. 'My old age is being made a living horror!' I told myself. And when there is no pride left in life, death becomes even more unacceptable; I never stopped thinking about it now: about mine, about Sartre's.

1. Reported by Benoît Rey in an excellent and appalling book: *Les Égorgeurs*.

Opening my eyes each morning, I would say to myself: 'We're going to die.' And: 'Life is a hell.' I had nightmares every night. There was one that came quite often, and I noted down one version of it.

Last night, a dream of extreme violence. I am with Sartre in this studio; the phonograph is motionless beneath its cloth cover. Suddenly, music, without my having moved. There is a record on the turntable, it revolves. I twist the control to stop it; impossible to do so, it turns faster and faster, the needle can't keep up, the tone arm gets into the most amazing positions, the inside of the phonograph is roaring like a furnace, there seem to be flames, and the black surface of the record is becoming insanely shiny. At first, the notion that the phonograph is going to collapse under the strain, mild panic which then becomes all-devouring: *everything* is going to explode; a supernatural rebellion, incomprehensible, the collapse of all that exists. I am afraid, I am at the end of my rope; I think of calling a specialist. I seem to think he's been here, but then I'm the one who thought of disconnecting the phonograph, and I was afraid when I touched the plug; it stopped. What a mess! The tone arm reduced to a twisted little stick, the needle in shreds, the record shattered, the turntable already ruined, the accessories blasted out of existence, and the disease still lurking inside the machine.

At the moment when I awoke and went back over it in my mind, this dream seemed to me to have an obvious meaning: the mysterious and untamable force was that of time and circumstance, it was laying waste my body (that pitiful, blasted twig that had once been an arm), it was hacking away, threatening my past, my life, all that makes me what I am, with total destruction.

'Man is elastic'[1]; that is his good fortune and his shame. Against the background of my revolt and my disgust, I went on with my other occupations, experienced pleasures – rarely unalloyed. The Berlin Opera presented Schoenberg's *Moses und Aaron*; I went to hear it twice, once with Olga, once with Sartre. I found it painful, before the overture, to see Malraux enthroned up there in his flower-decked box and hear them play the *Marseillaise*. In the circumstances it seemed to fit in too well with the *Deutschland über Alles* they launched into immediately afterwards, and much as I tried, I couldn't forget that enemy audience sitting all around me; I couldn't forget that I was making myself their accomplice yet again.

1. Sartre, *Saint Genet*.

Sartre left for Milan to receive the Omonia prize, which the Italians had awarded him for his struggle against the Algerian war; they had given it to Alleg the year before, and that was why, despite his aversion to ceremonies, he had accepted it. As soon as he left, I moved to a hotel just outside Paris with my work, some books, my record player and a transistor radio. In this mournful period, the happy days stand out. I was the only person staying there. I used to sit in the sun in the park where a few trees were beginning to turn green; most of them were still just black lace against the sky, with white pompons ornamenting the tips of their branches; there were ducks gliding across the waters of the pond, or copulating violently on its edges. For the first time in my life I heard nightingales singing in the darkness, as deliciously as they do in Handel and Scarlatti. Above this peaceful scene, great white bellies would pass by, screaming thunderously. The lights of Paris shone on the horizon. The jets and the birds, the neon and the scent of grass: there were moments when it did seem important again to put down on paper what this earth had been like in our time (this earth, where, in the cellars of the Goutte d'Or . . .).

I had suggested to Sartre, who found Paris tiring, that we should leave for Antibes. We went there, with Bost, by way of Vaison, so gay, and the summit of Mont Ventoux, swept by a great wind, lunching in a garden above Manosque; whenever we stopped I applied myself stubbornly to the match game, made fashionable by *Last Year at Marienbad*, until I had worked out the secret. On arriving, we learned about the attempt to invade Cuba. The accounts we heard, disquieting enough in themselves, conformed so exactly to the plans of the émigré forces – as they had been explained to us by the Cubans – that they sounded more like wishful thinking on their part than like descriptions of actual events. And it turned out in fact that they hadn't so much as set foot on the Isle of Pines, and that their leader had been completely unable to land. Soon they began to accuse each other and then all turned and attacked the Americans, who began to have doubts about the efficiency of their intelligence service. Anybody who wanted to was free to go to Cuba and see the situation for himself. It took an Allan Dulles to imagine that the peasants there would fall into the arms of the mercenaries and landowners' sons who were coming to take their lands away from them again. The ludicrousness of this escapade disposed of the danger of an American intervention for a long time to come. So our stay started off well. From the hotel terrace we looked out over the sea, the ramparts, the mountains; every evening we made the trip around the headland to see the lights shining along the coast; we went on a pilgrimage to the villa of Mme Lemaire, now surrounded by tall buildings and transformed into a clinic. We visited the Léger museum at Biot.

As soon as the new negotiations were announced, the ultras had exploded a series of plastic bombs in public places; they set two in the home of the mayor of Évian, who was killed: the Secret Army Organization had just come into being. Generals Salan, Challe, Jouhaud and Zeller seized power in Algiers; most of the high-ranking officers throughout Algeria rallied to their cause. Their only hope of maintaining their position was to bring off a *putsch* in France with the minimum possible delay.

One Sunday night, I was asleep in bed, having listened to Tebaldi sing Turandot on my transistor radio, when the telephone rang. It was Sartre: 'I'm coming up to your room.' He'd just had a call from Paris saying the paras were expected any moment. Debré was begging the people of Paris to stop them with their bare hands; they had put buses across all the bridges to block them. This detail, because of its very incongruity, seemed to us particularly disquieting. We tried to get more news on my radio, but without success. I finally got to sleep again. Next morning, the paras still hadn't arrived; that afternoon, twelve million workers throughout France went on strike. By the following evening, the generals and their faction were all in flight or arrested. The attempt to seize power in France had failed, largely because of the attitude of the ranks; urged to disobey their superiors by De Gaulle's speech on the evening of the 23rd, fearing to find themselves cut off from France and doomed to continue their military service indefinitely – some of them because of their political convictions as well – the soldiers had opposed the officers' sedition either by passive disobedience or by violence.

At the beginning of the winter, Richard Wright had suddenly succumbed to a heart attack. I had discovered New York with him, I had kept a whole store of precious images of him that were suddenly snatched from me into the void. In Antibes, a telephone call informed me of the death of Merleau-Ponty; in his case too, quite suddenly, the heart had stopped. This life I'm living isn't mine any more, I thought. Certainly I no longer imagined I could manoeuvre it the way I wanted, but I still believed I had some contribution to make towards its construction; in fact, I had no control over it at all. I was merely an impotent onlooker watching the play of alien forces: history, time and death. This inevitability did not even leave me the consolation of tears. I had exhausted all my capacities for revolt, for regret, I was vanquished, I let go. Hostile to the society to which I belonged, banished by my age from the future, stripped fibre by fibre of my past, I was reduced to facing each moment with nothing but my naked existence. Oh, the cold!

Giacometti exhibited his great walking figures and some paintings at the Maeght gallery. I am always very happy and yet slightly horrified when I see his works torn from the chalky gloom of his studio and arranged between well-dusted walls with plenty of space around them. I went to a private showing of *Last Year at Marienbad*, which didn't live up to its ambitions, and Buñuel's *Viridiana* which burns with such genuine fire that I was willing to accept its excesses and its occasional old-fashionedness. I saw several other films; I read, I wrote. Sartre was taking refuge in work, so frenetically that he had no control over it any more; he wrote a second version of his essay on Tintoretto without even taking the time to re-read the first.

Whipped into a fury by the opening of the Évian negotiations – in any case doomed to failure by the French claims to the Sahara – the activists began setting plastic bombs in the homes of prominent left-wingers and members of the U.N.R. One such attack having devastated the headquarters of *L'Observateur*, Sartre commented on the incident in an interview and began receiving threatening letters. Bourdet showed us one advising him of the imminent liquidation of the '121'; it was likely they would start with Sartre's apartment. He put his mother in a hotel and came and camped out in my place.

Lanzmann came back from Tunisia, where he had spent several days on the frontiers, with A.L.N. units and at Boumedienne's headquarters. Finding himself transported, in three hours, from Paris to the *maquis*, sleeping on the ground beside Algerian fighters, sharing their life, had been a striking experience for him which he described to me at length. He had also visited a village of evacuated peasants whom the army had managed to get out of a camp near the frontier and across the border. There was nothing new in what he told me;

but he had seen with his own eyes the old man with his shoulders torn to shreds by the dogs, the women's faces haggard with hate, the children. . . .

In July, the Massons passed on an invitation to us from Aït Ahmed, who was in the prison hospital at Fresnes. We drove in along an avenue flanked by little houses with automobiles parked in front of them. The wives of the *putsch* leaders were visiting their husbands; they were allowed in at once, whereas the Algerian wives were forced to wait outside for hours. Michelle Beauvilard, the lawyer, took us through a first door; cops, I.D.s; a little farther on, more cops, another checkpoint. Because he was a cabinet minister, Aït Ahmed had the right to a decently kept cell and a special diet. He preferred Fresnes to Turquant because he came into contact with his compatriots there and could be of service to them. As he was telling us about the exterminations of entire populations, about the slaughtered flocks, about the scorched earth, two men came in, one of them a frail old man with gentle glowing eyes set in a face carved with scars – Boumaza, thirty-one years old: 'Prison and maltreatment have turned him into an old man.' The cliché could be a fact, then; the tortures, the hunger strikes – the water cut off by the thoughtful M. Michelet – had destroyed him. He spoke to us in a tone of friendship that filled me with shame. 'After all, it's not as though it's my fault,' I said to myself. But then the same old refrain was there in my head: I'm French.

On 3 July a general strike cost the Algerians 18 dead and 91 wounded, according to the French press. The French admitted that 80 Moslems were killed and 266 wounded during the evening of the 'National Day' on 5 July[1]; according to Yazid, the number of victims ran to several hundred. In Lyons, despite the overwhelming weight of the evidence against him, they acquitted the activist Thomas, accused of having deliberately brutalized an Arab prisoner. In Algiers, every day brought more news of Moslem stores devastated by plastic bombs.

Towards the middle of July, we had lunch at the Coupole with C. Wright Mills and one of his friends. Mills' book *White Collar* had opened the way for all the subsequent studies of American society today. *Les Temps Modernes* had published long extracts from another of his books, *The Power Elite*. Bright-eyed, bearded, he said

1. Organized as a protest against the partition of Algeria which France had been considering since the failure of the Évian talks.

to me gaily: 'We have the same enemies,' reeling off the names of certain American critics who didn't have much use for me. He had become so disgusted with America that he was settling in England. His friend, married, with children, was not allowed back in the United States because he had stayed on in Cuba after diplomatic relations between Havana and Washington had been broken off; his wife was not allowed a passport because she had visited China; they could only meet in Mexico or Canada.

C. Wright Mills was popular in Cuba; he had lived there for some time and then written a book about it in an attempt to share his experiences with his fellow Americans. Like us, he was wondering what was happening there at the moment. The Communist Party was providing the regime with an administrative framework that it had lacked, true enough; unfortunately, it contained within its ranks a clique, led by Aníbal Escalante – whom we had thought a pompous imbecile in February 1960 – whose sectarianism and opportunism were threatening to force the Castroist revolution into a blind alley. Rafael's newspaper *Hoy* was gaining ground from *Revolución*, which was now threatened with either collapse or reversion to another group.

We were going to spend the summer in Rome once more; it would give us a rest from France, and I was hoping that Sartre would work less there. He was writing an article on Merleau-Ponty and taking so much corydrame that he was quite deaf by evening. One afternoon when I came as usual to join him in his apartment, I rang his doorbell for five minutes without getting an answer. As I sat on the stairs waiting for his mother to come back, it occurred to me that he'd had an attack. When I finally made my way into his study I saw that he was perfectly well; he just hadn't heard the bell ringing.

The morning of our departure, we were just putting the finishing touches to our packing when, at half past seven, the telephone rang. It was Sartre's mother. A plastic bomb had exploded in the entrance hall of 42 Rue Bonaparte; the damage was not serious.

Sartre having been won over by the artificial coolness of the Nacional in Havana, we booked communicating rooms in Rome equipped with air conditioning. The machinery didn't work very well, but luckily the hotel was up on a plateau at the edge of the city, and the temperature was a little less savage than in the downtown area. As I sat working in front of my big plate-glass window, I looked out at *The Tiber near the Milvio Bridge, about 1960*. The landscape was still half rustic: the green river with canoes gliding over it, yellowish grass scarred by wide paths, pine woods, and the Alban hills in the distance; but they were already beginning to build there, and it was easy to think back to old engravings of Paris or Amsterdam or Saragossa and imagine what it would be like with those houses, those avenues and wharves and parapets and bridges. Below me, the little train to Viterbo would go by between the pale blue reservoirs. Just under my window, on the other side of the street, was a shooting booth. I couldn't see the marksmen, but occasionally one of the clay pigeons would come flying out of the trap, and there would be the bang of a gun. Next door there was a family who ran a market garden; I would wake up in the morning to the smell of burning weeds.

Up late, we'd listen to some *bel canto* on my transistor, then go down for coffee and read the newspapers. We worked, then spent a few minutes getting into the centre of Rome by car and went for a walk. A few more hours of work, then we'd eat dinner in one of our favourite places, often the Piazza Santa Maria del Trastevere where we'd sit absorbed in the fountains and the faded gold of the mosaics; an orange flame flickered under the greenery of a terrace roof; a Vespa rushed in from a side street, tied on the handlebars a giant bunch of multicoloured balloons. Then a last drink near our hotel on the tree-planted terrace overlooking the plain. Below us, luminous serpents wreathed around dark pits of shadow, their blackness occasionally broken by a passing flicker of red light; headlights sliced brilliant furrows of light through the sombre hills; the hum of the cicadas kept up its stubborn earthly answer to the stars glittering in the cold velvet sky. The sight of artifice and nature glorifying and denouncing each other made me feel that I was somewhere that didn't exist, or perhaps on an interplanetary space station.

I wasn't getting on very well with my book; we were being hounded by the present. The Lugrin talks ended in failure. In Metz, amid general indifference, the paras were hunting down Arabs: 4 killed, 18 wounded. And then the slaughter in Bizerte. I found it difficult to get interested in myself and in my past. Sartre had stopped work altogether. We read books that taught us more about the world, and a lot of detective novels.

Fanon had asked Sartre to write a preface for *Les Damnés de la terre* and had sent him the manuscript via Lanzmann. While in

Cuba, Sartre had realized the truth of what Fanon was saying: it is only in violence that the oppressed can attain their human status. He was in agreement with Fanon's book – an extreme, total, incendiary, but at the same time complex and subtle manifesto of the 'Rest of the World'; he agreed gladly to do a preface for it. We were very pleased when Fanon, who was going to the north of Italy to be treated for his rheumatism, said he would pay us a visit. I went with Lanzmann, who had arrived the evening before, to meet him at the airport. Two years earlier, having been wounded on the Moroccan border, he had been sent to Rome for treatment; an assassin had managed to get into the hospital and made his way to Fanon's room; by chance, the intended victim had read in a newspaper that morning that his presence there had been disclosed, and had had himself moved, as secretly as possible, to another floor. This memory was obviously very much on his mind on landing. We saw him before he noticed us. He was sitting down, getting up, sitting down again, changing his money, collecting his baggage, all with abrupt gestures, agitated facial movements, suspiciously flickering eyes. In the car, he talked feverishly: in forty-eight hours time, the French Army would be invading Tunisia, blood would be flowing in torrents. We joined Sartre for lunch; the conversation lasted until two in the morning; I finally broke it off as politely as possible by explaining that Sartre needed sleep. Fanon was outraged. 'I don't like people who hoard their resources,' he commented to Lanzmann, whom he kept up till eight the next morning. Like the Cubans, the Algerian revolutionaries never slept more than four hours a night. Fanon had an enormous quantity of things to tell Sartre and questions to ask him. 'I'd give twenty thousand francs a day to be able to talk to Sartre from morning to night for two weeks,' he told Lanzmann, laughing. Friday, Saturday, all Sunday until he caught his train to Abano, we talked without stopping. And again when he came back through Rome ten days later before flying on to Tunis. With a razor-sharp intelligence, intensely alive, endowed with a grim sense of humour, he explained things, made jokes, questioned us, gave imitations, told stories; everything he talked about seemed to live again before our eyes.

In his youth he had thought it possible to break the colour barrier on the strength of his education and personal merit; he wanted to be French. During the war he had left Martinique to join up and fight. While he was pursuing his medical studies in Lyons, he realized that in the eyes of the French a Negro was always a Negro, and he had aggressively accepted the conditions forced on him by the colour of his skin. One of his best friends, when they were cramming for their finals, exclaimed: 'We've really worked like nig –'. 'For goodness sake, say it,' Fanon said. 'Like niggers.' And they didn't speak to each other for months. An examiner asked him: 'And where are you from, *boy*? . . . Ah, Martinique, a beautiful country. . . .' Then, paternally: 'What would you like me to ask you about, *boy*?' 'I plunged my hand into the basket and took out a question,' said Fanon. 'He gave me five out of ten when I deserved nine. But he stopped calling me *boy*.' Fanon had attended Merleau-Ponty's philosophy classes without ever speaking to him; he found him distant.

He married a Frenchwoman and was appointed director of the psychiatric hospital at Blida: this was the integration he had dreamed of in his youth. When the Algerian war broke out, he was torn in all directions at once; he hated to give up a status it had cost so much to attain, yet all colonized peoples were his brothers; he recognized the Algerian cause as identical with his own. For a year he helped the revolution without relinquishing his post. He harboured guerrilla leaders both in his own home and in the hospital, gave them drugs, taught the freedom fighters how to care for their wounded, trained teams of Moslem nurses. Eight assassination attempts out of ten were failing because the 'terrorists', completely terrorized, were either getting discovered straight off or else bungling the actual attack. 'This just can't go on,' Fanon said. They would have to train the *Fidayines*. With the consent of the leaders, he took the job on; he taught them to control their reactions when they were setting a bomb or throwing a grenade; and also what psychological and physical attitudes would enable them to resist torture best. He would then leave these lessons to attend to a French police commissioner suffering from nervous exhaustion brought on by too many 'interrogations'. This contradiction became intolerable. At the height of the battle of Algiers, this French civil servant sent Lacoste a letter of resignation in which he broke completely with France and openly declared himself an Algerian.

After a short stay in France with Francis Jeanson, he went to Tunis, where he became political editor of *El Moujahid*; he wrote the article attacking the French Left that so upset them. Two years later the G.P.R.A. sent him as their ambassador to Accra; he made many trips through Africa, assuring Algerian support to all those who rose in revolt against colonialist domination. He maintained very close ties with Roberto Holden, leader of the U.P.A., and persuaded the G.P.R.A. to train Angolan freedom fighters in the A.L.N. *maquis*. His principal objective was to bring the African peoples to awareness of their solidarity; but he knew they would not find it easy to overcome their various cultural antagonisms and idiosyncrasies. In Tunis, the eyes that turned to watch him in the street never let him forget the colour of his skin. He went with some delegates from a Negro country – Mali or Guinea – to see a film they'd been invited to by the Minister of Information. During the intermission there was a commercial: some cannibals dancing around a white man tied to a stake who saved his skin by giving them all Eskimo Pies. 'It's too hot in here,' the delegates said, and left. Fanon complained to the Tunisian minister. 'Oh, you *Africans*, you're all so sensitive,' came the answer. In Guinea, on the other hand, his friends couldn't bring themselves to hold important conversations in the presence of his wife, a white woman. He also described his embarrassment one evening when he took a delegation of Algerians to a theatrical performance mounted by the government of Guinea in their honour; some beautiful Negro women came on and danced. 'Breasts flying; they've got breasts so they show them,' Fanon said; but the austere Algerian peasants were deeply shocked. 'Are these women respectable?' they asked him. 'Is this a Socialist country?'

It was while Fanon was in Ghana that he fell ill and that the doctor discovered an excess of white corpuscles. He went on working and travelling. When he got back to Tunis, his wife was so terrified by the amount of weight he'd lost that she forced him to see a specialist: he had leukemia. On several occasions after that he thought his last hour had come; for a week or two he had lost his sight; he felt sometimes that he had become a dead weight and was 'sinking into the mattress'. He'd been sent to the U.S.S.R., where more specialists confirmed the diagnosis. They advised him to go to the United States for treatment; but he found the idea of being in a hospital in that country of lynchers repugnant, he told us. There were moments when he refused to recognize his illness; he would make plans as though he still had years and years ahead of him. But death always haunted him. This was to a large extent the explanation of his impatience, his talkativeness, and also of the obsession with disaster which so struck me from the moment he began to speak. He was satisfied with the decisions taken by the C.N.R.A. at

Tripoli and by the nomination of Ben Khedda; he believed victory to be at hand, but at what a price! 'The towns will rise in revolt; there will be five hundred thousand people killed,' he said once; and on another occasion: 'a million'. He added that the aftermath would be 'frightful'.

The complacent way in which he always accepted the worse possible outcome as being the most likely also betrayed serious inner difficulties. Though an advocate of violence, he was horrified by it; when he described the mutilations inflicted on the Congolese by the Belgians or by the Portuguese on the Angolans – lips pierced and padlocked, faces flattened by *palmatorio* blows – his expression would betray his anguish; but it did so no less when he talked about the 'counter-violence' of the Negroes and the terrible reckonings implied by the Algerian revolution. He attributed this repugnance to his intellectual conditioning; everything he had written against the intellectuals had been written against himself as well. His origin made this inner conflict even worse; Martinique was not yet ready for a rising. Anything gained in Africa serves to advance the cause of the Antilles as well, yet it was evident that he found it distressing not to be fighting the battle on his native soil, and even more so not to be an Algerian-born. 'Above all, I don't want to become a professional revolutionary,' he told us anxiously; theoretically there was no reason why he shouldn't work for the revolution in one place rather than in another, but – and this is what made his situation so pathetic – he had a passionate desire to send down roots. He was constantly reaffirming his commitment: the Algerian people was his people; but the difficulty was that no one person or group among the leaders could really be said to represent that people completely. About the dissensions, the intrigues, the liquidations, the antagonisms that were destined to break out into such open and violent conflict later on, Fanon already knew much more than he was able to tell us at the time. These dark secrets, and perhaps his personal hesitations, too, invested his remarks with an enigmatic quality, as though they contained obscure, disturbing prophecies.

He defended himself against the future and the present by exaggerating his past feats in a way that astonished us, since their undoubted importance made such inflation unnecessary. 'I have two deaths on my conscience for which I can never forgive myself: Abbane's and Lumumba's,' he said; if he had forced them to follow his advice they would have escaped with their lives. Often he spoke as though he were the G.P.R.A. all by himself. 'Perhaps I'm a para-phrenic,' he admitted once without prompting. And once, when Sartre had made some comment, he gave an explanation of his ego-centricity: a member of a colonized people must be constantly aware of his position, of his image; he is being threatened from all sides; impossible to forget for an instant the need to keep up one's de-fences. In Italy, for example, it was always his wife who booked the hotel rooms; he would be asked to leave, for fear his presence might upset the American customers or, less specifically, cause some sort of scene. On his way back from Abano he told us how a chambermaid there had watched him for several days and then asked: 'Is it true what they say? That you hate white people?' And he concluded angrily: 'The heart of the matter is that you white people have a physiological horror of Negroes.'

This conviction did not simplify relations with him in certain difficult respects. When Fanon was discussing questions of philoso-phy or his own problems with Sartre, he was open and relaxed. I recall a conversation in a *trattoria* on the Appian Way. He couldn't understand why we had taken him there, since the European tradi-tion had no value in his eyes; but then Sartre began asking him about his psychiatric experiences and he came to life. He had been very dis-appointed by Russian psychiatry; he disapproved very strongly of confinement and wanted mental patients to be treated without re-moval from their home environment; he attributed great importance to economic and social factors in the formations of the psychoses and dreamed of supplementing psychotherapy with civic education for the patients. 'All political leaders should be psychiatrists as well,' he said. He described several curious cases, among others that of a homosexual who, at every successive stage in his psychological deterioration, took refuge in a lower social stratum, as though he were aware that anomalies of behaviour visible at the top of the social scale may be easily confused, lower down on it, with irregu-larities due to extreme poverty; his psychosis progressed in this way until finally he was living in a state of semi-dementia in the colonies, just one bum among all the others. By then his social dis-integration was so complete that his mental deterioration was scarcely noticeable.

Yet Fanon could not forget that Sartre was French, and he blamed him for not having expiated that crime sufficiently. 'We have claims on you. How can you continue to live normally, to write?' Sometimes he would demand expiation, through the discovery of some effective means of action, sometimes by martyrdom. He lived in a different world from ours; he imagined that Sartre would shake public opinion to its foundations by announcing he would not write another word until the war was over. Or let him get himself thrown into jail: that would provoke nationwide horror. We couldn't manage to persuade him that this wasn't so. He quoted us the example of Yveton who, with his dying breath, had declared: 'I am Algerian.' Sartre, for his part, asserted his entire solidarity with the Algerian people – as a Frenchman.

Our conversations were always extremely interesting, thanks to the wealth of his knowledge, his powers of description and the rapidity and daring of his thought. Because of the friendship we felt for him, and also because of what he could do for the future of Algeria and Africa, we hoped that his illness would allow him a long reprieve. He was an exceptional man. When I shook his feverish hand in farewell, I seemed to be touching the very passion that was consuming him. He communicated this fire to others; when one was with him, life seemed to be a tragic adventure, often horrible, but of infinite worth.

After his departure, Sartre settled down to write a preface for *Les Damnés de la terre*, but without haste; he had finally sickened of the struggle he had been waging blindly all these months against the clock, against death. 'I am re-composing myself,' he told me. Calm was winning me over again, too, more or less. I could get interested in news that wasn't about Algeria. As we sat having breakfast in the Square of the Muses, we saw that the front page of the newspaper our neighbour was reading contained nothing but an enormous picture of a face: Titov was circling the earth. A little later on, we followed events in Brazil. It was a country that existed for us now; Quadros, Lacerda, Jango, were real live people; the names Brasília and Rio conjured up definite pictures. We asked ourselves: 'What are the Amados thinking? What are Lucia and Christina doing?' Jânio was confirming the judgement of our friends: 'A fine programme, but he won't have the nerve to put it through.' We were glad that the army's attempt to seize power failed, both for Brazil and for France; a success there might have encouraged our own generals back home.

The Viareggio prize, increased that year by the Olivetti firm to four million lire, was awarded to Moravia, a decision that produced a lot of malicious comment in the Italian press, which we found un-just but entertaining; Moravia himself wasn't in Rome, we didn't see him. We encountered Carlo Levi. We had dinner in Trastevere with the Alicatas and Bandinelli, whom we got on with just as well as in 1946. There was talk of a discussion the Istituto Gramsci wanted to organize in the spring between the Italian Marxists and Sartre, on the subject of subjectivity and the problems the latest capitalist tactics were producing in Italy and France.

We had several expeditions into the countryside around Rome. I hadn't been back to Hadrian's Villa since 1933. I could remember being greatly moved by brick walls and cypress trees; and it was in fact very moving when I did see it again, the ruins faded by the sun, the dark green of the pines and cypresses spilling their colour onto the blue sky. Taking a road that had just been opened, we climbed up to Cervera, a black and haughty village that dominates the plain of Latium from a height of three thousand feet. We saw Nettuno again, and Anzio, where we were intrigued by the sight of a red galley floating on the blue sea: Cleopatra's galley from Liz Taylor's film they were having such trouble shooting. From Frascati we went up to Tusculum; the view could scarcely have changed at all since ancient times: the Alban hills and their villages, Latium, the site of Rome in the distance. Sitting beside Sartre in the ruins of the little theatre, for an instant I caught once more the taste of past happiness. Little by little, Rome had lulled me back into a state of calm; my dreams at night were peaceful ones. I said to myself, I said to Sartre: 'If we've got another twenty years to live, let's try to enjoy them.' Isn't it possible to stay alive in the world and not tear oneself to pieces all the time with emotions that don't do anyone a scrap of good?

Evidently not. The answer of the O.A.S. to the new policy of 'disengagement' was an attempt to assassinate De Gaulle[1] – which didn't upset me particularly – and a general incitement to murder. The Arab-hunts in Oran, the Moslems stoned to death, burned alive in their automobiles – how could one think of these things and stay calm? Our Roman holiday had been only a truce; I was to find Paris and my life there completely unchanged when I got back.

Sartre, who gets bored on long car trips, was going to return by

1. On 5 September, De Gaulle had finally recognized the 'Algerian charac-ter' of the Sahara.

plane, so I left him behind and started on the journey north with Lanzmann, who had come down to drive with me. Lanzmann was making frequent visits to Fresnes. The Algerian prisoners there were convinced that an agreement would soon be reached. He told me all about Boumaza's plan to escape. Every day, an electrician – a common-law prisoner – came to work on a ladder resting against the inside surface of the prison wall; there was always a warden keeping an eye on him; one of these mornings the electrician would be sick; when that happened his place would be taken by Boumaza, and that of the warden by a common-law prisoner. The *garde mobile*, accustomed to the two figures, would see nothing amiss; at a suitable moment the two accomplices would leap over the wall, where an automobile would be awaiting them on the other side.

I left Lanzmann in Zürich and went to visit my sister, who lives in a village near Strasbourg. The house smelt of woodsmoke; Lionel, who has to travel a lot in his profession, had brought back some hangings from Dahomey that made a pleasant decoration for the studio. More daring and more inspired than in the old days, my sister's latest pictures left everything she had done till then far behind; I spent a long time looking at them, we chatted, and spent a carefree day together. I set out with her next morning for a drive through the Black Forest and stopped at Strasbourg to telephone to Lanzmann; he raged to me about the clubbings at the Arc de Triomphe. The police waited for the Algerians to come up out of the métro stations, made them stand still with their hands above their heads, then hit them with their truncheons. He'd seen teeth smashed in and skulls fractured with his own eyes; to protect themselves, the Algerians had covered their heads with their hands; the police just smashed their fingers. Corpses were being found hanging in the Bois de Boulogne, and others, disfigured and mutilated, in the Seine. Lanzmann and Péju had immediately taken the initiative in launching an appeal urging the whole of the French people to show that they could no longer be satisfied by moral protests and to 'demonstrate their opposition on the spot to the renewal of such acts of violence'. There were only 160 of us who signed it[1]; respectively, the *Express* team, with two exceptions, and nearly all the staff of *L'Observateur*, took part in a protest march. A fine welcome home to my mother country! I thought to myself as I drove through the pine trees along the roads edged

1. At the end of a week there were 229 of us.

with snow. It was impossible to get to sleep that night; I stayed up alone for a long time next to the fire, the old horror, the old despair burning at the backs of my eyes, welling up like the refrain of some too-familiar old song. The next day, I went with my sister and Lionel to see Riquewihr and Ribeauvillé again; the villages and vineyards were as pretty as they'd always been, we ate pheasant cooked with grapes, but I couldn't bear any more of the prettiness, the gastronomy, the old traditions that had brought us to this pass. In the evening I listened to the radio. Keeping to his plan, step by step, Boumaza had escaped. But then I listened to the interview with Frey and all his calm lies: two deaths, when fifty corpses had been discovered already. Ten thousand Algerians had been herded into the Vel' d'Hiv', like the Jews at Drancy once before. Again I loathed it all – this country, myself, the whole world. And I told myself that even the most beautiful things in it – much as I have loved them, well as I've known them – are not really so beautiful after all; you reach the bottom pretty soon; only the evil in the world is bottomless; they could have blown up the Acropolis then, and Rome, and the whole earth, and I wouldn't have lifted a finger to stop them.

The following Sunday, early in the afternoon, I arrived in a deserted, dismal Paris crawling with cops. My friends told me that more than fifteen people had been found hanged in the Bois de Boulogne and that more corpses were being fished out of the Seine every day. They would have liked to be able to do something; but what? We were living through days of police dictatorship: newspapers seized, meetings forbidden. Neither the political parties nor the trade unions had as yet been able to get into action. On 18 October, several small groups and a few people on their own had decided to make some protest, whatever the cost. The Committee of the 6th Arrondissement's section of the Communist Party had asked its members to demonstrate. Only a few of them had appeared. Lanzmann and Pouillon had provoked the cops and got themselves arrested. Evelyne had tried in vain to follow their example. The cops had knocked them about a bit: 'Ah! You cocksuckers! The cops can go out and get themselves killed and you don't give a shit, but if it's those Algerian bastards who get it, then you start screaming.' I talked through the whole night, first with one group, then with another. At five in the morning, I was in the Falstaff with Olga and Bost when a brawl started between the customers and the waiters; the waiters got hold of a man who'd been knocked senseless and were dragging him outside while his wife was screaming: 'We'll blow up this dump of yours; we're *pieds noirs*. . . .'

Sartre came back the next day and I began to get a foothold once more in this Paris full of autumn leaves and blood. Lanzmann spent a day at Nanterre: wounds, disfigurements, mutilations – they had to amputate the hands of the ones with shattered wrists; women mourning the husbands who had not come back. . . . To our surprise, several newspapers denounced the 'police brutalities'; it almost looked as though certain members of the government were hostile to Papon and were encouraging the publication of these truths. Then too, a great many readers, outraged by what they'd seen, had written letters to *Le Monde* and *Figaro*; apparently if they actually had their noses rubbed in blood, people could still react. Pouillon told us about a session in the Chamber during which Claudius Petit said to Frey: 'Now we know what it meant to be a German when the Nazis were in power!'; his words were greeted by a dead silence. It was five years since Marrou had reminded them of Buchenwald and the Gestapo; for years now, the French people had been just as much accomplices to what was going on as the Germans under Nazi rule; the belated uneasiness some of them were feeling about this fact did nothing to reconcile me with them.

On 1 November, the Federation of France forbade the Algerians to stage any more demonstrations that would provide pretexts for fresh massacres. In the police state that France had now become, there was almost no possibility for action on the part of the Left. Schwartz and Sartre summoned the intellectuals to a silent demonstration in the Place Maubert. We all met, one cool and sunny morning, in the Square Cluny. Rose and André Masson were there, agonized because the Algerian prisoners and their French 'brothers' in all the prisons throughout France were just beginning a hunger strike. I recognized a great many other faces as we walked off towards the statue of Étienne Dolet, near which about twelve hundred people were assembled.

A police cordon halted us near the entrance to the métro. Schwartz talked to the commissioner, who had evidently been given orders to avoid any sort of trouble, and he allowed us to stand there for ten minutes in silence. There was one short speech:

Sartre explained the reason for the demonstration. Some photographers took photographs; Schwartz and Sartre murmured a few words into a microphone. After five minutes, the commissioner gave the order: 'Move on.' There were protests. Chauvin, a P.S.U. member used to trouble, shouted: 'Shoot then. Go on, shoot!' The cop (in plain clothes) shrugged his shoulders, as if no cop within living memory had ever shot at anybody. Someone suggested: 'Let's sit down,' and the commissioner raised his eyes to heaven in exasperation. Since the boulevard had been blocked and the press alerted, there was nothing more to be gained by our all languishing in jail for several hours, so we broke up. I went off towards the Rue Lagrange with Pouillon, Pontalis, Bost, Lanzmann and Evelyne. 'Thank you for coming,' a woman said to me as I went by, which gave me something to think about. Suddenly I heard the noise of an explosion behind me, someone shouted: 'Oh, the bastards!' and I glimpsed some blackish smoke trails curving down towards the crowd in the Place Maubert. We rushed back the way we'd come. But a plastic bomb is scarcely more dangerous than fireworks in the open air; some windows had been blown in, and two people had been grazed by flying splinters (one of them the son of my cousin Jacques who happened to be going by just then). I bumped into Olga, who had arrived late and hadn't been able to get into the Place Maubert; in the corner where she was, and in the Place Médicis, people had started a sit-down on the sidewalk, and some of them had been pulled in. Afterwards, I went with Sartre and a group I met up with at the Balzar to have lunch in a restaurant on the Boulevard Saint-Michel. The radio was giving our demonstration a lot of publicity; during the course of the meal they broadcast three separate accounts of it.

That afternoon, about twelve hundred P.S.U. members had cleverly arranged to meet in a movie queue in the Place Clichy; they were able to form a procession without being disturbed. Then, carrying banners and chanting slogans, they marched down as far as Rex et Depreux to lay bunches of flowers on the spot where two Moslems had been shot.

At noon, however, while declaring that 'everything is calm in Algeria,' the radio announced that forty people had been killed. That evening, on Europe No. 1, the French Government delegate came out with the story that the Algerian people had not been involved, that *agents provocateurs* had fired on a police patrol while on duty and killed three of them – and that seventy-six Moslems had been killed! Some reporters then added that they had heard bursts of gunfire, but that they had not been allowed to go and investigate: another massacre. In Oran, all had remained quiet. And in some Moslem districts, the anniversary had been a real day of celebration; the radio re-broadcast recordings of joyful cries, chants, and songs.

No one was in much doubt that independence was just around the corner. Negotiations were in progress, and the entire press was giving them coverage. De Gaulle was being forced into making peace – by the F.L.N., by public opinion, and by the harm the war was doing to his policy of *grandeur*. When he announced at Bastia that 'the last quarter of an hour' had come, we felt that his words corresponded, for the very first time, to some sort of reality. But until Ben Khedda was finally established in Algiers, the Fascists would go on making life difficult for us. We needed to organize.

In the U.S.S.R., with the report of the 22nd Congress, de-Stalinization had moved into its second phase.[1] In the French Communist Party, there were several intellectuals, Vigier among others, who were in favour of a rapprochement with the non-Communist Left; he suggested that Sartre sign, and get others to sign, a pamphlet directed against the present regime and against racism. This was to form the jumping-off point for a demonstration and the basis for an anti-Fascist organization. But difficulties began to arise immediately. Sartre and our friends wanted to express their solidarity with the Algerian revolution in acts; to destroy the O.A.S. it was imperative, in their opinion, to attack the government which was the organization's objective accomplice. The Communists, being concerned to 'retain what unites and reject what divides', wanted to limit the movement to fighting the O.A.S. Sartre decided that an attempt should be made to overcome these differences; without the Communists we could do nothing. We won't be able to do anything with them, predicted Lanzmann, Péju, Pouillon. Finally, for want of anything better,

1. Khrushchev had expressed antagonism to Albania and China; he had delivered another attack on Stalin, whose remains had been removed from their resting place in the Red Square, together with the wreaths and garlands around them (including the one Chou En-lai had placed there eight days earlier). He had been buried in the group of tombs backed up against the Kremlin wall, and Khrushchev had suggested that a memorial be erected to 'the despot's victims'.

they decided to make an attempt, and supported Sartre when he joined Schwartz and Vigier in the creation of a 'League for Anti-Fascist Movements'.

The assassination attempts had begun again, and were even more serious than before the summer vacation. Sartre wanted to take a room in a hotel, but the manager turned him away; he had just had the outside of his place repainted. We were forced to resort to trickery. Claude Faux – who had taken over Cau's job as Sartre's secretary some years before – rented a furnished apartment on the Boulevard Saint-Germain in his name, and we moved there; the building was still not finished, there was no light in the rubble-filled staircase, and from eight in the morning till six at night there were workmen banging in nails; there was no sun from the windows overlooking the narrow little Rue Saint-Guillaume, and we were forced to keep the electric lights on all day. I have lived in more squalid places, but never in one so depressing.

I wrote a preface to Gisèle Halimi's book on Djamila Boupacha; General Ailleret and Cabinet Minister Mesmer had been reduced to openly obstructing the course of justice; we wanted to show all the traps we had to spring before they were finally forced into the open. Gisèle Halimi also had the idea, approved by experts like Hauriou and Duverger, of instituting legal proceedings against Ailleret and Mesmer; we obviously wouldn't succeed in getting them inculpated, but it seemed to us a good thing in the circumstances to make it perfectly clear what they had done. We did not then foresee the quiet explosion the military courts were about to cause by suddenly joining in our attack, nor the series of revelations that were later to confirm their verdicts, amid public indifference. The Committee contained a certain number of left-wing Gaullists who were hoping to combat the use of torture while keeping the fight within a purely moral sphere. They hung back, a section of the board resigned and another was elected.

A surprise demonstration against Fascism and racism was planned for 18 November; it was essentially the young Communists who organized it. Such a demonstration stood no chance of success unless it could be started without the police hearing of it; the meeting-place was kept so secret that when the League assembled in front of the Paramount no one knew where to go. There were scores of police cars parked in the Place Saint-Germain-des-Prés; the Left Bank was in a state of siege. Vigier gave us the order: Strasbourg-Saint-Denis. 'Go there by métro,' he advised us; I went with Sartre, Lanzmann, Adamov and Masson, the latter saying sheepishly: 'I know it's bad and undemocratic, but I've never been able to take a subway.' (In New York, he had a label with his address on it sewn inside his jacket which he showed to cab drivers. . . .) With his cap, his black leather jacket, his pale eyes, he looked as though he'd just popped up, green and astonished, from some bygone anarchist era. There were a lot of young people in the métro. A few yards in front of me, in the exit corridor, three fifteen-year-old boys were having a discussion. 'I feel very nervous; I'm keeping myself under control all right, but I'm nervous,' one of them was saying. The Saturday night crowd was packing the sidewalks; it looked to me as though our scattered groups waiting in different places would be submerged by them. 'You'll see,' Lanzmann said, 'in a minute, all of a sudden, it'll begin to *take*.' And at that moment a procession appeared carrying a placard: PEACE IN ALGERIA, which soon had hundreds of people clustering behind it; others began coming from all sides; we ran to get a place just behind the placard, in the front of the procession. I took hold of Sartre's arm on one side and that of someone I didn't know on the other, noticing with surprise that the boulevard suddenly stretched as far as the eye could see in front of us, quite empty. (It was a one-way street; the procession was blocking the traffic behind us; in all the side streets, cars were suffering from very opportune breakdowns in the middle of the pavement and preventing the police cars from getting through.) We had spread onto the sidewalks too by this time; it was as though all Paris belonged to us. At the windows – except those of *Humanité*, noisy and triumphant – a row of expressionless faces; lots of reporters and photographers along the whole route. As we marched we chanted: 'Peace in Algeria – Solidarity with the Algerians – Free Ben Bella – O.A.S. murderers'; less frequently: 'United action – Hang Salan.' As we went past the Musée Grévin, some people shouted: 'The Museum for Charlie', and at the sight of a para: 'Put the paras in the factories'; I also heard one or two shouts of: 'Hang Charlie.' But the slogan 'Peace in Algeria' was far and away the most popular. Astonished to find itself walking along like this unmolested, the crowd became infected with tremendous gaiety. And how good I felt! Solitude is a form of death, and as I felt the warmth of human contact flow through me again,

I came back to life. We reached Richelieu-Drouot; as we moved on into the Boulevard Haussmann, there was a movement in the crowd and a stampede. The cops had started using their truncheons; a lot of people disappeared down a street to the right; Lanzmann, Sartre and I followed them, then turned left and went into a bistro, whose doors were promptly slammed shut behind us. 'You're afraid!' Lanzmann said. 'I don't want my place busted up,' the owner said. 'The tobacco shop on the corner stayed open the other day, trying to be smart; the cops turned up – two million francs' worth of damage.' Then, addressing Sartre with a half smile, he added: 'You can write a novel about it and put me in it, but that won't do *me* any good. . . . I've got three kids, I don't want anything to do with politics; politics, that's for the big time.' He mimed vast piles of gold with his hand. 'The real big time; we're not in that class.' After a short while we went back to the main intersection; there were big splashes of blood on the street corner and police cars along the boulevard; the demonstrators had just finished dispersing. We went home in a taxi, and the telephone rang as soon as we got back; Gisèle Halimi and Faux, who were just beside us at Richelieu-Drouot, had been caught in the police charge; they had seen one demonstrator with the flesh hanging away from his face, another knocked senseless and his skull fractured. The cops had been using special truncheons, jumbo size; they had been hitting out just for the fun of it, since the crowd was quite satisfied with the run it had had, and would have dispersed as soon as it was ordered to. Yet Evelyne, Péju, Adamov, Olga and Bost, only a few rows behind us, had known nothing about this incident; they had gone on to the Gare Saint-Lazare, via the Boulevard des Italiens and the Rue Tronchet, without meeting any police at all; the demonstrators – of whom there were by then about eight thousand – disbanded at the request of the organizers. When I went down to buy something for dinner, I heard distant noises, the traffic was jammed along the Boulevard Saint-Germain; demonstrations were still going on near the Odéon, and we heard later that there had been some fighting in the Latin Quarter. It had been a marvellous day, and one that encouraged us to hope.

A flash in the pan. This already dark autumn turned finally to utter blackness in a drama enacted on the other side of the Atlantic. At the beginning of October Fanon had suffered a relapse and his friends had sent him to the United States for treatment; despite his repugnance he had accepted. He had stopped over in Rome, and Sartre spent a few hours in his hotel room along with Boulahrouf, the G.P.R.A. representative in Italy. Fanon lay flat on his bed, so exhausted that he didn't open his mouth during the whole interview; his face tense, he kept shifting his position the whole time, the only way he could express revolt against the passivity to which his body had been reduced.

On my return to Paris, Lanzmann had shown me some letters and cables from Fanon's wife. As a member of the G.P.R.A., Fanon had supposed that he would be warmly welcomed in Washington; he had been left to rot in his hotel room for ten days, alone and without medical attention. She had gone over to join him with their six-year-old son. Finally admitted to a hospital, Fanon had just been operated on; they had changed all his blood, in the hope that the shock to his system would start his marrow functioning again, but there was no hope of recovery; at the most, he would live another year. She wrote again, she telephoned; at a distance of 4,000 miles we followed his death agony day by day. Fanon's book came out, there were articles loading him with praise; his wife read him the ones in *L'Express* and *L'Observateur*. 'That's not going to get me my marrow back,' he said. One night, at about two, she telephoned through to Lanzmann: 'Franz is dead.' He had caught double pneumonia. Beneath the restrained tone of her letters, one could detect her real despair, and Lanzmann, though not knowing her very well, flew over to Washington. He returned after a few days, appalled and shaken. Fanon had lived every moment of his death and savagely refused to accept it; his aggressive sensitivity had cast off all restraint in his deathbed fantasies; he loathed the Americans, all racists in his eyes, and distrusted the entire hospital staff; the last morning, as he woke up, he betrayed obsessions by saying to his wife: 'Last night they put me in the washing machine. . . .' His son had gone into his room one day when they were giving him a transfusion; he was lying there with tubes connecting him to a series of plastic bags, some full of red corpuscles, some of white corpuscles and blood platelets; the child rushed out screaming: 'The bad men have cut Daddy up with knives!' He went through the streets of Washington waving the green and white flag defiantly. The Algerians sent a special airplane to take Fanon's body back to Tunis. He was buried in Algeria in an A.L.N. cemetery; for the first time, and in the middle of the war, the Algerians gave one of their people a national funeral. For a week or two I kept seeing Fanon's photograph all over the place in Paris: in the kiosks on the cover of *Jeune Afrique*, in the window of the Maspero bookstore, younger, calmer than I had ever seen him, and very handsome. His death lay heavy on us because he had weighted it with all the intensity of his life.

Sartre received the invitation from the Istituto Gramsci that we had talked about in September; he stayed a few days in Rome and held a press conference about Algeria, at which Boulahrouf was present. The Italians, no longer having any colonies, are all anti-colonialist and applauded him wildly. There were a few Fascists there nevertheless – heroes according to Sartre – to throw hand-bills – SARTRE IS NOTHINGNESS, NOT BEING – and to boo. Everyone turned around, ready to rush at them, and the president said calmly: 'Let their neighbours see to them.' Guttuso tried to get at them all the same, but the wretches were already halfway down the stairs, head first; some of them were taken to the hospital, the rest to jail. The French press reported that Sartre had been bombarded with rotten eggs and published a photograph of him side by side with Boulahrouf. When he got back he began receiving threatening letters from Oran.

On 19 December there was yet another anti-O.A.S. demonstration, forbidden at the last moment. All the same, we went to our meeting point in front of the Musset statue; all the same faces as at the Balzar on 1 November and in front of the Paramount on 18 November, everyone knew everybody else, it was like being at a literary cocktail party. This time the procession was supposed to start on the Boulevard Henri-IV; I took the métro with Sartre, Lanzmann and Godemant, whose apartment had been blown up a few days earlier. His wife had been inside and was still in a state of shock. The boulevard was black with people but blocked by a police cordon in the direction of the Bastille. I don't know exactly what happened – it's all a bit like Stendhal's battle of Waterloo, a demonstration; one only sees such tiny fragments – we came out of the Rue Saint-Antoine on the other side of the barrier; Bourdet, who looked radiant underneath his stunning pointed hat, came and took Sartre by the arm before disappearing into the vast procession that was moving in orderly fashion along the street and both side-walks; at the head of it, a few rows in front of us, were municipal and national councillors carrying placards; the police cars and policemen stationed along the sidewalks watched us go by without moving a muscle. Suddenly, at the Saint-Paul métro, we were caught up as the crowd began to eddy; the people in front were moving back. Behind, they were still advancing with cries of: 'Don't turn back!' I was being suffocated, I was swaying, and so many people had stamped on my feet that my right shoe had come off; afraid of falling and being trampled on, hanging on to Sartre's arm which I didn't want to let go, though it hampered my movements, I felt myself turning pale. Lanzmann, who is taller than either of us, could breathe better; he helped us reach a side street, where even so it was impossible to move because so many other people had taken refuge there too. I sat down with Sartre in a little café on the Place des Vosges, and Bianca brought me a woollen sock, fortunately, because I had to hobble about for an hour before we got a taxi. Then the driver said to us angrily: 'They're blocking all the streets.' The telephone calls that evening were less gay than the month before. Some of our friends had walked in circles around the Place de la Bastille and then choked with tear gas; there had been fighting at Réaumur-Sébastopol; Pouillon's son, a believer in non-violence, had helped some friends turn over a police car and then beaten a policeman with a stick. Bianca had gone down to take the métro at Saint-Paul; there was a young man on the platform at the next station fighting off a C.R.S. man who was pushing him into a car: 'I've lost my glasses! Let me find my glasses.' The C.R.S. man began hitting him; some fifteen men rushed out of the train yelling: 'Murderer'; the policeman threw himself down on a bench with his heavy boots out towards them, and then some more C.R.S. came to his rescue. Several more passengers wanted to get off and join the fight, but the guard had closed the doors. As Bianca was trying to open them, a man with skis on his shoulder stopped her. 'What good would it have done?' he said to her in a voice from another world. The next day we learned that the police had suddenly charged the head of the procession and beaten up the dignitaries carrying the placards. Some people had been badly wounded, women were trampled on, and yet this peaceful procession had been a demonstration against enemies of the government. 'Next time, we must be armed,' was the conclusion drawn by Bourdet in his article.

The government was playing the game of the O.A.S., and except for a small minority the country accepted the government.

Negotiations were under way, but the massacres and the tortures still went on. 'My first reaction is no longer to fight these things, as it once was, nor even to protest, for they are taking place under the presidency of General De Gaulle,' wrote Mauriac.

All we could do was work. Sartre had gone back to the Flaubert study he had sketched out a few years earlier and was writing away with desperate concentration. He took part, with Vigier, Garaudy and Hippolyte, in a debate at the Mutualité on the dialectics of nature which a public of six thousand seemed to find passionately interesting. But he couldn't really give more than a summary account of his thought in a mere twenty minutes, and I would rather he hadn't made the attempt. I had reached the years between 1957 and 1960, and the story of that abominable time seemed to suit only too well the abominable winter we were living through. I wasn't in the mood for all the New Year's festivities. I stayed in my dismal apartment. De Gaulle spoke on New Year's Eve, and I turned the radio off after two minutes, sick to my stomach with all that neurotic narcissism and empty grandiloquence. At about midnight, I heard a chorus of car horns: hundreds of cars moving in noisy procession along the Boulevard Saint-Germain. I thought something was happening; but no, it was just a sudden outburst of joy, without rhyme or reason, just because it was New Year's Eve and they all owned cars. I took some belladénal to escape all that hateful gaiety, the gaiety of the French people, of murderers, of butchers. *How I loved those nights, on the Boulevard Montparnasse, in the bright glare of the lights, surrounded by laughter and shouts, how I loved the crowds and their gay festivity, when I was twenty, when I was thirty.*

At the beginning of January we arranged to have dinner with the Giacomettis and went to their place to fetch them. He was sitting down, glasses on his nose, in front of an easel, working at a very beautiful portrait of Annette in grey and black; against the walls there were more portraits, also grey and black. I expressed astonishment at seeing a splash of red on his pallette; Giacometti laughed and pointed at the floor: there were four red marks indicating the exact spot for the model's chair. As usual, I was intrigued by the statues swathed in their wet cloths. At one time, Giacometti had modelled the human form in its general aspect; for the past ten years he had been seeking to individualize it, and was never satisfied with the result. He uncovered one of his busts and there before my eyes, as dense, as inevitable as any of his earlier works, was the head of Annette. It was so obviously a success and therefore of course so apparently simple that one wondered: 'Why has it taken him ten years?' He admitted that he wasn't displeased with it himself. For an instant it seemed to me important again to take plaster, or words, and create something.

I read *The Letters to Madame Z* by the Polish writer Brandys; and also, in manuscript, Colette Audry's *Derrière la baignoire* and Gorz's *Le Vieillissement.* Very different works, but all three free and direct; they hurled me into the heart of an experience different from my own, and so took me out of myself, while still talking about things that I found interesting.

One night, at about two in the morning, I was awakened by a very loud but dull noise; I found Sartre out on the balcony. 'Well, they've nosed us out,' he said. There was smoke floating up from the Rue Saint-Guillaume, some planks had been blasted out into the roadway, and in the silence we could hear the faint tinkling of a xylophone: shards of glass still falling into the street. No one stirred. After ten minutes, the windows in the house opposite lit up; men and women appeared in bathrobes, carrying brooms, each one alone, and began sweeping up the debris piled up on their balconies; not a word spoken; side by side, one above the other, they all went through the same gestures unaware of each other's presence. Concierges appeared, wearing pyjamas under their topcoats. Finally, police cars and firemen appeared. I threw on some clothes and went down. The shirt shop on the corner was blown to bits. A policeman questioned me and followed me to the door of the apartment; seeing me open it, he didn't ask for identification, but it was a near thing. Was it the shirt shop they'd been trying for? Too odd a coincidence; no, we were the one they were after; but in that case the O.A.S. was curiously well informed. At ten next morning, Claude Faux came to see us in a state of consternation: there could be no doubt that the plastic bomb had been meant for us. Lanzmann telephoned: the same story. We thought we were going to be forced to move again; we were shivering where we were because the heating had been cut off, and felt pretty gloomy. It was a relief to discover that the bomb had been intended for Romoli, a *pied noir* who had refused to collect funds for the O.A.S. In his window there was an enormous placard with the announcement: STORE BOMBED, BUSINESS AS USUAL. There were glaziers working on every floor of the building opposite, and we could see the tenants wandering about their apartments, still as isolated as ever in the midst of their collective adventure.

Three days passed; towards eleven one evening Faux telephoned. *Libération* had just called him to say that 42 Rue Bonaparte had been blown up. It occurred to us that there was a faintly amusing irony in the coincidence; but when Faux called again an hour later he wasn't laughing any more. 'They were really after your blood this time.' He had told the policeman standing guard on the house: 'I'm the owner's secretary, I've got keys.' 'Oh you won't need keys!' was the reply. The plastic bomb had been left on the floor above Sartre's; the two fifth-floor apartments had been blown up, as well as the bedrooms on the sixth; Sartre's place hadn't suffered much, but the door had been torn off and the Norman cupboard standing on the landing smashed into oblivion; from the third storey up, the staircase was hanging out over a void, the wall having collapsed. Evelyne telephoned to say that she had been passing nearby in a car and heard the explosion; she had mingled with the crowd of onlookers around the door of the building, who didn't seem at all curious. 'If he had any sense of publicity he'd come down and give autographs,' one young man said. The bomb had been a reprisal for the press conference Sartre had called in Rome. I went next day with Bost to see how much damage had been done; one of the tenants in the building, a well-to-do man in his fifties, shouted after me as I picked my way across the rubble in the courtyard: 'This is what happens because of all your politics, making trouble for everyone!'

We went up the service stairs, passing tenants coming down with suitcases in their hands. The vanished cupboard, the staircase open to the sky – even though I'd been told, I couldn't believe my eyes; inside the apartment, there were papers all over the floor, doors torn off, walls, ceilings and floors covered with a sort of soot. Sartre would never be able to move back into it – another piece of my past disappearing into the blue. Sartre received a great many letters and telegrams expressing sympathy, and phone calls too, taken by Faux. Some of his friends demonstrated under his windows: 'O.A.S. murderers'. In a restaurant, a customer came up to him, hand outstretched: 'Bravo, Monsieur Sartre!'

A few days afterwards, when Sartre had gone down to fetch the newspapers one morning, there was a knock at the door. 'Precinct police,' said a big fat man, showing me his card. 'I'm looking for a well-known person . . . a writer . . .' 'Who?' 'I may be able to tell you later . . . he lives in this building, but there doesn't seem to be a concierge. . . . Do you live alone?' 'Yes.' He couldn't make up his mind to leave. I heard steps on the landing. 'Which writer is it you're looking for?' 'M. Jean-Paul Sartre.' 'Well, here he is!' I said as Sartre walked through the door. 'We've received a request for protection on behalf of M. Jean-Paul Sartre,' our policeman explained. Apparently the initiative for this move had come from M. Papon; this was his odd way of assuring that certain 'well-known persons' were protected; there would be a policeman keeping watch in front of the building all day; and Sartre was to let him know in the evening when he came home for good, whereupon the policeman would go away. 'But that will simply advertise the fact that I live here,' Sartre said. 'Quite true,' replied M. Papon's envoy, 'the *plastiqueurs* work at night. And in any case,' he added jovially, 'they don't arrive carrying a trunk: a little parcel in their pocket, no way of seeing, no way of knowing.' His parting words as he took his leave were: 'If you should move, tell the fellow on duty outside'; then, with an air of complicity: 'But you don't need to tell him where you're going.' So from then on, there were two policemen in front of our door; they stood and chatted with another couple who were stationed twenty yards up the street looking after Frédéric Dupont.

There was nothing surprising about the police knowing our address. The house painters, the architects, the labourers working in the staircase and also the house agent all knew who we were; when they found out, the owners tried to throw us out. That didn't worry us; the police were really becoming far too solicitous of our welfare. The morning after the night there had been eighteen bomb attacks, we received a further visit from two plain-clothes policemen. They addressed Sartre as 'Maître' and gave him the telephone number of the police precinct he should phone for help if he was in danger. They commented on the arrest of two Saint-Cyr students who had been caught red-handed setting some plastic bombs: 'Boys from good families! It's all got beyond us!'

They were really putting their backs into it, the boys from good families. In Algeria there was a reign of terror: thefts of arms, rackets, bank hold-ups, Sten-gun attacks, assassinations, plastic bombs. At Bône, a Moslem tenement was blown sky high. In Paris, the sound of explosions was heard almost daily. A bomb left in the Quai d'Orsay killed one man and injured fifty-five others. Yet a military court at Reuilly acquitted three officers who admitted having tortured a Moslem woman to death; the effrontery of this caused a certain uneasiness among the press.

We lunched at the Massons' with Diégo and the Abbé Corre who had just come out of prison. They were not finding it too easy readapting to the solitude of middle-class life; at one stroke they had lost six hundred friends. 'It's so complicated to see people,' said Diégo. 'You have to write, telephone, arrange to meet. Back there, all you did was open a door.'

The very same day we left the Boulevard Saint-Germain, Romoli was given a second dose of plastic; the tenants of the building opposite had their windows all broken again, and some were on the verge of hysteria. Our house agent had found us an apartment on the Quai Blériot in an immense barracks of a place (in which two O.A.S. killers were hiding, it was later discovered); it was expensive, huge, with great big windows overlooking the Seine. When I woke up, there was bright, pale sunlight flooding across the wooden floor; a smell of the countryside wafted in through the window, and I had something to look at while I worked. Through the black trelliswork of the plane trees the geometric façades on the opposite bank showed through just like a Buffet painting; at night, the water glittered, very black, stretching, spreading, breaking, re-forming the rippling reflections on its surface. The snow came, immaculate on the motionless barges and the abandoned river banks; at noon, it shone resplendent in the sun, and the grey surface of the river sparkled as the gulls caressed it with their wings. From the kitchen, which we usually ate in, there was a view over a big protected 'green space' that was also used as a parking lot. The whole life of the 'Organization Man' and his wife was on display there – the French product copied from the American model. He left for work, she went out shopping; in the morning she took the dog out (the husband walked it in the evening), in the afternoon her children. On Sunday, he would clean the car, then the family would go off to church or on a picnic.

Most of the left-wing journalists, political figures, writers and university teachers had by now been the target of a bomb attack. The day after the book about Djamila Boupacha came out – I had finally accepted co-authorship with Gisèle Halimi in order to share the responsibility – I went back to my apartment to collect my mail; the super and his wife hadn't slept a wink all night; they had received a telephone call: 'Watch out! Simone de Beauvoir is getting blown up tonight!' The husband was an ex-F.T.P. member and a left-winger, his wife too, and I knew they would do all they could to protect me, but I didn't like to think of their not being able to sleep for the next few nights. The police refused to help them; the private protection agencies did little more than make very infrequent visits. For five days I could get no one to do anything; finally the F.U.A. sent a few students to spend the nights in my place; among them was Benoît Rey, to whom the caretaker lent a big monkey wrench on one occasion; as he was walking up and down keeping guard outside, some policemen came by and whipped him off to jail on a charge of possessing illegal weapons; his publisher, Lindon, had him released after five hours, but they still maintained the charge against him.[1]

My young lookouts, leaning out of the windows, spying through the door, often saw suspicious cars draw up in the night; we certainly owed it to them that the house was left untouched. One night, Evelyne was sleeping in her apartment on the Rue Jacob when she heard a bang. Oh hell, I've got plastic bombs on the brain, she thought to herself. There were shouts of 'O.A.S. murderers' in the street. Throwing a topcoat over her pyjamas, she rushed down to join the handful of people – several of them antique dealers in the Rue Jacob – who were demonstrating in front of the damaged *Seuil* offices. The district commissaire came up: 'Keep quiet, there are people asleep; there are sick people, you'll wake them up.' Several days after that, Pozner was seriously wounded; skull fractures, loss of memory; they had to operate several times and he took months to recover.

Sartre and Lanzmann were devoting a lot of their time to organizing preliminary meetings for the League. With Schwartz and many others, they had set themselves the task of fighting the country's indifference and its gradual slide to the Right by radical action among the masses. The Communists didn't agree with this. They stubbornly insisted that the offensive should be directed exclusively against the O.A.S. They were afraid that the League might become involved with the Party district committees and assume political importance; they wanted to limit the membership to intellectuals only. Sartre refused to be shut up in a ghetto like this. He wasn't

1. Nevertheless in June the court acquitted him.

finding the support among the 'open' Communists that he had been counting on. 'You'll get us in trouble with the Party,' they told him; thus they were keeping the whole enterprise up in the air. Sartre was thinking of handing in his resignation.

On 8 February he lunched with Schwartz and Panigel to discuss these problems; I joined them for coffee. There was an anti-O.A.S. demonstration planned for that afternoon as a protest against the bomb attack that had cost little Delphine Renard an eye. It had been arranged only the evening before, and none of us was going. The following morning there was a call from Lanzmann: five dead at the Bastille, one a child of sixteen, and many seriously injured. During the day we heard about it from people who'd been there. 'There's only Communists left now, go get them,' a sergeant had shouted as the demonstrators were beginning to disband; the police charged; people hurried down into the Charonne métro station; the cops tore up the metal tree guards and hurled them down the steps after them. The child had been *strangled*. One of the cops was crying, and another one said to him: 'Well, he's had it; what's it to do with you?' Many newspapers published detailed accounts of this butchery; the Right, however, quickly took up the slogan provided for them by the government: 'The crowd crushed itself.'

The trade unions decided to make the funeral into a mass demonstration and the government was obliged to give its consent. A few members of the League, ourselves included, arranged to meet at nine near the Bourse du Travail where the caskets were on view. There would be very few taxis. (I had spoken to a woman cab driver the day before who said: 'Tomorrow I'll stay home.' 'Aren't you going to the funeral?' 'Oh no! I can't take crowds. My husband took me to the Kermesse aux Étoiles once; I found out what it's like!') Lanzmann was to call for us at half past eight. From the kitchen, beginning at eight, we could see enormous red sheaves and wreaths of flowers on the top of cars moving bumper to bumper down the Avenue de Versailles. Lanzmann arrived late, in a taxi, his car having broken down. The jams were so bad that the driver let us out at the entrance to a métro station. It was ten by the time we arrived at the Place de la République. From then on, there was just no means of transport available; all the workers of Paris were on strike. There was an immense crowd on the side-walks, behind the police barriers; many groups, laden with red wreaths, were moving in the direction of the Bourse du Travail. We went into the hall where the delegations were waiting; then they were called; a lot of Communists and a proportionate number of P.S.U. members; no Socialist delegation. We took our place in the procession, behind the hearses. Out in the square there were thousands of people gravely, patiently waiting to take their places in the cortège. On the Boulevard du Temple I got up on to a traffic island. I could see the hearses covered with red flowers, the black and red boulevard, the slow-moving clumps of men and flowers solemnly punctuated by dark gaps of asphalt; behind me, stretching to infinity, the crowd; vaster than in Peking on 1 October – at least seven hundred thousand people. When the unions get together, then the people march.

The government had shed blood in order to disperse fifty thousand demonstrators; it was now obliged to allow seven hundred thousand of them to march through the heart of a Paris on strike. Silent, disciplined, this mass of people was proving that if left to themselves they had no desire to turn their city into a bloody chaos, and that if the police could refrain from attacking them, no one would be smothered, no one trampled on. There were militants posted along the whole route maintaining impeccable order. In the stormy light, a great wind lashed the black trees into motion against the black sky; melting snow fell and froze our feet; we walked on, numbed, our hearts warmed by the vast presence of all the fellow beings around us. I hoped that it would be of some comfort to the victims' families, that it would give some meaning to their grief. For the dead, this apotheosis was as unexpected as their deaths had been. A 'good funeral': usually a whole life has gone into the preparation of it, so much so that the deceased is in a way present for it. In this case, they were not. Even from this reverse of their absence, they were still absent.

As we reached the gates of Père-Lachaise, the sky turned blue. There were men perched upon the wall of the cemetery, others on the graves. Quite still, we listened to Beethoven's *Marche Funèbre*. The wind played amid the black branches as if to make the moment more dramatic. My God! How I had hated the French! I was overwhelmed by this suddenly recovered sense of brotherhood. Why so long? First Dominique Wallon, on behalf of the U.N.E.F., then a secretary of the C.F.T.C. made speeches, recalling the massacres of 17 October, laying the murders of 8 February to the charge of the government. Everyone seemed to approve of these speeches and I asked myself: 'If the Communist Party, if the unions, had called their ranks to action against the Algerian war, wouldn't they have obeyed?' Doubtless one couldn't lay all the blame on circumstances, on party structures, on the complications and cleavages of party machines; but there was also no doubt that there was an enormous fund of goodwill being demonstrated that morning that had been allowed to go to waste. I didn't know whether this discovery was comforting or distressing.

We went on across the cemetery. Victor Leduc had his forehead crisscrossed with Band-Aid; he had been truncheoned on 8 February. Our way lay between marble slabs carved with the names of great bourgeois families; half-naked women were playing lutes or stretching their arms to heaven in dire lament. Near the Mur des Fédérés we came to a halt at the edge of a vast carpet of red and white flowers. There were people still filing past when the cemetery closed, late in the afternoon. Being unable to minimize the event, the newspapers chose to recognize its importance but to attribute all the credit for it to the government, as though the murderers at Charonne had been O.A.S. killers and not loyal partisans of those in power.

The preliminary League meetings took place that Sunday at Grange-aux-Belles. The afternoon session proved rather stormy. On one point Sartre and his friends had yielded to the Communists; the result of their appeasement was that the movement was now called 'Front for Action and Coordination among University Teachers and Intellectuals for an Anti-Fascist Movement'.[1] But they convinced the meeting that in the text to be published as a result of the day's discussion the F.A.C. should proclaim its solidarity with the Algerians and declare its determination to fight both the present regime and the O.A.S. at the same time. There was a meeting several days later which I attended. There were eighty people packed into a smoky, overheated room intended for thirty, who spent three hours discussing the definition of the Front all over again. Nothing concrete was decided about the action to be taken. Not that day, nor on any subsequent day.

Peace was being negotiated. 'The peace at all costs, on which we spit,' Lanzmann wrote to one of his Algerian friends. On the evening of Sunday the 18th, down in one corner of a newspaper,

1. F.A.C. for short.

we read that it had been signed; we felt not the slightest surge of joy. There were still the army and the *pieds noirs* to be reckoned with. And the Algerians' victory didn't just wipe out the seven years of French atrocities, suddenly brought out into the light of day. One of the torturers acquitted by the Reuilly court, Sanchez, was outraged when his teaching post was taken away from him and said angrily: 'It's the use of torture itself they're trying to condemn, through me!' All the people in the village supported him. 'Well, what do you expect? There's always torture in war-time. . . .' Now the French people knew at last, and it made not an atom of difference, because they'd always known. They were told: 'You're like the Germans under the Nazis!' And they answered – I heard it with my own ears, and it was the prevailing sentiment – 'Yes, the poor Germans; one realizes now it wasn't their fault.' But what about that funeral, then? The answer is that collective egoism is a matter of politics, not of psychology. In the victims of 8 February the people of Paris were recognizing *their own*.

Sartre had agreed to give a lecture in Brussels on Algeria and Fascism. Bost took us up in his car. Since there are a great many French Fascists in Belgium over and beyond the actual Belgian right-wing groups, it was just as well to take certain precautions. The principle organizer, a man of thirty-five called Jean, had spent years getting Algerians over the border; accustomed to the strict security measures entailed in this work, he applied them to Sartre's visit. It was not until the moment we were due to leave, and then only in prearranged terms, that he gave us our itinerary over the phone. At Rocroi, Sartre joined Lallemand and L., a young, dark-haired Communist, in a Belgian car escorted by vehicles full of armed militants. A young blond Communist took Sartre's place between Bost and myself. 'The situation is very unpleasant at the moment,' he told us. 'It's the unity-of-action business we're having; it causes all sorts of squabbles.' We stopped off at Jean's house for a short television interview, and then zigzagged for half an hour through the town before arriving at L.'s place for dinner. He had invited various representatives of the Belgian Left and the burgo-master who had agreed, despite certain pressures, to let the lecture be given in his district. During the meal, Jean left the table; after a moment, a distraught maid rushed in. 'The gentleman has fallen down in the bathroom!' He had fainted and split his head open against the tub. 'I behaved like some green girl,' he told us the next day with embarrassment. In fact, his friends looked upon him as a hero; the risks he'd been running – all the Algerians he helped had been determined to sell themselves dear if the need arose – and the responsibilities he assumed had worn him out. We slept at Lallemand's place; when we came down for breakfast, we discovered that our young bodyguards had spent the night in the hall – their revolvers within reach in a nearby plant stand.

The lecture was given that evening up on the sixth floor of a factory building in a room containing an audience of six thousand. There were a great many police deployed all around the block, in the garages, and on every side of the platform; the chief of police claimed that he was completely gripped by Sartre's logic. Sartre gave a full, but austere account of his subject; he found it difficult talking to the Belgian audience because they were too well-informed for him merely to feed them the facts, and yet there was not that fund of shared experience and things unsaid which he could count on with his French public; many there criticized him – as they had me the year before – for not dealing with *their* problems. Lallemand was situated to the left of the P.S.B.; we had to keep the balance even; after a thousand and one twists and turns, a thousand and one cunning manoeuvres, we got to the house of the militant Communist where we were to spend the night. During supper, we talked about the numerous attacks that had been made on the lives of Belgian left-wing leaders. Professor G. told us how his wife had received a package similar to one that had killed one of his colleagues – a doctored copy of *La Pacification*; smelling a suspicious odour, she had put it out in the middle of the garden.

The following day, our friends escorted us to the border, down through the Meuse valley full of the scent of spring. As we said good-bye, young L. asked Bost: 'What have you got in the way of weapons?' 'Nothing,' Bost said. 'But you must have thought we were all crazy. . . .' L. said, stunned by this piece of French frivolity, but a bit worried. In fact, we had been very touched to see how concerned they were for our safety.

I locked myself up once more. Through Bost, we heard saddening rumours about the old Saint-Germain-des-Prés we used to know. Rolland had inherited money and become a Gaullist; he had his estate to think of. Scipion had followed him. Anne-Marie Cazalis had amused herself for a long time flitting between Left and Right; her marriage had finally forced her to make a choice, which in the circumstances could not be taken lightly; her left-wing friends didn't see her any more. The dissolution of our past was almost complete. When Pouillon and Pingaud lost their salaries because they had signed the '121' manifesto, their colleagues made a collection on their behalf; Pagniez didn't give anything. Mme Lemaire, whom we hadn't seen for some time, telephoned Sartre's mother just after the apartment in the Rue Bonaparte was blown up; she made no reference to the incident. 'Of course, you know, I'm for Algeria staying French,' she said. She came to dinner with us in our apartment on the Quai Blériot all the same. 'I hope there's no plastic bomb here,' she said with a laugh. It was her only allusion to such things. We didn't seem to have much to talk about.

I loathed the district where we were living, and sometimes didn't put my nose outside the door for three days on end. I no longer listened to music; I was too tense. I read, but hardly any novels. All writing, my own as well as that of others, seemed so meaningless I couldn't bring myself to bother with it. So many things have happened since 1945, and hardly any of them have really been expressed in books. Future generations will have to look to sociological works, statistics, or simply the newspapers, if they want to find out about us. I find the preconceptions involved in what's called the *nouveau roman* particularly distressing. Sartre had predicted the return of what he called 'consumer literature': the writing of a society that has lost its grip on the future. In 1947, he was writing:

The producer's literature now coming into being[1] will not force consumer's literature, its antithesis, into oblivion. . . . Perhaps it may even disappear itself: the generation coming after us seems hesitant. And even if this literature of *praxis* does succeed in establishing itself, it will pass one day, like the literature of *exis*, and perhaps the history of these next decades will see them alternate continually. If so, it will mean that mankind has failed once and for all to bring about a Revolution of infinitely greater importance.

In consumer's literature he went on to say: 'One does not come into contact with the world; one swallows it raw with one's eyes.'[2] The literature of *exis* is that of Nathalie Sarraute; remodelling the old French psychologism to her own purposes, she uses her talent to describe the paranoiac attitude of the lower middle classes as if it constituted the immutable nature of mankind. The 'objective'

1. What has been called 'committed literature'.   2. *What is Literature?*

school, on the other hand, aims at swallowing the world raw with its eyes; and it expels man from that world even more completely than nineteenth-century naturalism did. The work of art should be able to stand on its own, surrounded by a collection of objects all completely devoid of meaning. The idea of the work – thing haunted the generation of poets, sculptors and painters which preceded my own; Marcel Duchamp carried it to extreme lengths; the great creators – Picasso, Giacometti – moved beyond it. As for the 'objective' theories, the metaphysic they imply represents such a regression in relation to modern ideologies that the writers who advance them cannot possibly believe in them. Not that the weaknesses of a system are of great importance if the researches they inspire are fruitful in themselves; both the Impressionists and the Cubists entertained false theories about perception. But in the 'objective' school the justifications and the discoveries coincide: the Revolution has failed, the future is slipping from our grasp, the country is sinking into political apathy, man's progress has come to a halt; if he is written about, it will be as an object; or we may even follow the example of the economists and technocrats who put objects in his place; in any event, he will be stripped of his historical dimension. That is the common ground shared by Sarraute and Robbe-Grillet; she confuses truth and psychology, while he refuses to admit interiority; she reduces exteriority to appearances, in other words, a false show; for him, appearances are everything, it is forbidden to go beyond them; in both cases, the world of enterprises, struggles, need, work, the whole real world, disappears into thin air. This vanishing act is common to all the different varieties of the *nouveau roman*. Sometimes, with the intention of saying nothing, they mask the absence of content with formal convolutions in a pastiche of Faulkner and Joyce, who both invented hitherto unheard-of ways to say something new. Sometimes they put their money on the eternal: an exploration of the human heart or the space – time complex. Or literature becomes its own object: Butor insists on the spatial and temporal inadequacy of the narrative. Or things are described – or so the writer supposes – in their immediate being.[1] In any case, man is kept resolutely out

1. This prejudice leads to a great deal of very ugly writing among Robbe-Grillet's acolytes; for want of a subject, they are forced into making objects animate and so fall into the stereotyped phraseology characteristic of a worn-out academicism: the bridge *straddles*, the bushes *part*. Etc.

of the picture. Robbe-Grillet, Sarraute, Butor, interest us insofar as they are unable to keep themselves, their schizophrenia, their obsessions, their manias, their personal relations to things, people and the age out of their writing. But on the whole, one of the constant factors of this whole school of writing is boredom; it takes all the savour, all the fire out of life, its impulse towards the future. Sartre defined literature as a celebration: joyful or tragic, but a celebration; we're a far cry from that! It is a dead world they are building, these disciples of the new school. (There is no connexion with Beckett, who makes the world of the living decompose itself before our eyes.) And it is an artificial world in which they themselves can find no place, since they are living beings. As a consequence, the man in them becomes dissociated from the writer; they vote, they sign manifestoes, they take sides – usually against exploitation, the privileged classes and injustice. Then they go back into their old ivory tower. 'When I sit down at my desk,' Nathalie Sarraute said in Moscow, 'I leave politics, current events, the world, outside the door; I become a different person.' How is it possible not to put the whole of oneself into the act that for a writer is the most important one of all – writing? This deliberate maiming of oneself and of one's work, this escape into fantasies about the absolute, are evidence of a defeatism justified by the depths to which our country has sunk. France, once the subject, is now no more than the object of history; her novelists reflect this degradation.

In Algiers, there were a hundred and four explosions in one night. People began to wonder if the army was going to go over to the *pieds noirs*. One morning, taking a taxi, I heard over the radio that an automobile with a bomb secreted in it had exploded in front of the hall in Issy-les-Moulineaux where the Peace Movement Congress was about to take place; there had been deaths and injuries. Witnesses described the incident. Not a day that was not poisoned somehow.

The F.A.C. held a meeting at the Mutualité. At the beginning of the meeting the organizers received a telephone call warning them that a bomb was going to explode – a classic manoeuvre. Sartre spoke in a much warmer and more human way than at Brussels. But not many people came: two thousand when we should have been able to count on six. The conclusion of the cease-fire negotiations had speeded the decline of the French people towards complete political apathy; also the F.A.C. was still not really in favour with the Communist Party, and the Communist members helping to organize the meeting had not made as much of an effort as they might. In the end, Sartre and Lanzmann were both right; they couldn't have done anything without the Communists, and they hadn't been able to do anything with them. This failure saddened them both.

The referendum on 8 April showed that almost everyone in France was now in favour of the liquidation of the war in Algeria; but it was being carried out in the worst possible conditions. After the shooting at Isly and the round-up at Bab el-Oued, the *pieds noirs* knew they had lost; they started systematically sabotaging the already devastated country and launched into a series of massacres even more horrible than the war itself; the O.A.S. bombarded the Moslem districts with mortars, drove flaming trucks into them, mowed down unemployed men with Sten guns in front of the Labour Exchange, and murdered their Moslem charwomen. I opened the newspaper every morning in a state of dread: what was there worse to come? At first, the press honoured these crimes with a place on the front page; the Moslems would soon strike back; people were frightened. And then, with great relief, they began expressing admiration for their discipline; they were really behaving very well! Whereupon the twenty or thirty (official figures) Moslems shot every day in Algiers or Oran were promptly relegated to a little corner on the back page, among the automobile accidents. The prisoners murdered in the jails, the wounded finished off in the hospitals, merely provoked mild, hypocritical expressions of indignation. It was only when the *pieds noirs* rushed into France, competing with the French for work and housing, that they finally became unpopular; just in time to replace the old one, we watched the rise of a new sort of racism between members of the same race, as if we always needed the Other to hate, in order to be assured of our own innocence. As if the army, as if the governments that had conducted this war had not been composed of Frenchmen from France, as if the entire country had not been behind them! Every day brought fresh evidence of hidden complicities: torturers received an amnesty, but not deserters, those who had disobeyed or the members of the assistance organization. Jouhaud, condemned to death, was not executed; Salan was saving his neck. Only the hangers-on were shot; in the course of the trials, the only thing people were worried about was the loyalism of the defendants and the sincerity of their chauvinism; the murdered Algerians didn't count. Never had the Algerian war been more hateful to me than during those weeks when in its last agony it proclaimed the final truth.

We had been very much concerned the whole year by what was happening in Cuba. Apparently Aníbal Escalante was becoming a law unto himself. Even though the blockade and a succession of serious errors had lowered the standard of living, there was no serious opposition in existence; nevertheless the police had established a preventive reign of terror. Small landowners had been forced to join cooperatives. Most of our friends were being harmed by these changes. Oltuski had lost his post. *Revolución* was in its death agony; the price of the subscription to *Hoy* was being deducted from the workers' wages, and they were not buying any other newspaper. A homosexual writer of our acquaintance had been marched through the streets of Havana with a whole group of pederasts; they were made to wear a big P on their backs and then thrown into jail. All this information reached us in snatches and without commentary. There seemed no explanation for the Cuban Communist Party's condemnation of 'Polish deviationism', or its alignment with China and Albania and adoption of Stalinist methods. And above all, it was stupefying that Castro was letting it happen. No doubt he had been severely shaken by certain setbacks; the I.N.R.A. had suffered a great many. He had felt the need for an administrative framework and decided to put his faith in the only one already existing, the Communist Party. But faced by the errors that had been committed, how was it that he had not taken things back into his own hands?

He did so. On 26 March he delivered a speech attacking Escalante and all the little Escalantes who had begun swarming all over the place. He expelled him from Cuba. He set himself the task of repairing all the mistakes of recent months. He destroyed the cooperatives created by force. He called back Oltuski and his team. *Revolución* regained its importance. During our trip to Moscow we met Oltuski and Arcocha; no more police rule, no more sectarianism, they told us. There were Communists sharing in the task of government, relations between Cuba and the U.S.S.R. were excellent; but Castro was master of the ship once more. Despite the difficulties caused by the blockade and the absence of administrators, there was a feeling that the revolution had come alive again.

The Union of Soviet Writers had invited us to Moscow. In the field that particularly interested us, that of culture, the 20th and 22nd Congresses had borne fruit; the trips made by Yevtushenko confirmed this, as did the presence in Paris of students from Russian universities. I had met a girl from Georgia who had been working for a whole year in complete freedom on a thesis on Sartre; there was really something new under the Soviet sun.

Three hours in the air and on 1 June we touched down on an airfield encircled by birches and pines. Soon I was seeing Red Square again, the Kremlin, the Moskova, Gorki Street, old Moscow, with the lace of its *isbas*, its labyrinth of courtyards and gardens, its peaceful squares full of men playing chess. The women were dressed more gaily than in 1955, the store displays – despite fairly strong evidence of shortages – more attractive. Their information advertising had made great progress; there were posters on the walls, often inspired by the drawings of Mayakovsky, and amusing; also still photographs from the movies being shown. The evening was bright with neon signs. The streets were pleasant; very animated, but without any jostling or undue haste; bustle, but leisure as well, young people and laughter; fairly heavy traffic on the roads, mostly trucks and vans. The new residential districts however are as boring as our own H.L.M., despite the abundance of trees; they form a ring right around the city, which now has a population of eight million.

We saw some of our old acquaintances again – Simonov, Fedin, Surkov, Olga P., Korneychuk, Ehrenburg's wife (he wasn't in Russia at the time) – and met some new people. Lena Zonina, secretary to the French section of the Union of Writers and Critics, acted as our interpreter; she knew our books well and had written articles on *The Mandarins* and *Altona*; she quickly became a friend. The secretary of the Italian section, George Breitbourd, who spoke French well, sometimes stood in for her. We were amazed to find ourselves getting on so well with them.

We had decided to limit ourselves to meetings with intellectuals: writers, critics, movie makers, theatre people, architects. And we had the impression that we were present, after the austerity of the Dark Ages, at the dawn of a Renaissance.

An ardent and stormy dawn; a struggle was in progress between innovators and conformists. Most of the young people were in the former camp; but it also contained older men, Paustovsky, Ehrenburg, whose *Memoirs* were being devoured by the students; some of the young ones on the other hand were opportunist and sectarian. But despite these anomalies, it was without doubt largely a conflict between the generations. 'The most remarkable thing in our country today is the young people,' all our friends told us; but there were a lot of people who wanted to keep them on a leash. 'Everything seems so easy to these young people!' said one fifty-year-old, who was nevertheless quite friendly towards them. We understood this bitterness. The sons were covertly blaming their fathers for having supported Stalinism; what would they have done in their place? They had had to live; they lived. A life that involved contradictions, compromises, lacerations, sometimes cowardice; but examples of loyalty too, of generosity, of daring that had taken more courage than any Soviet citizen of twenty-five had ever had the opportunity to show. To take a superior attitude to people whose difficulties one hasn't shared is never just. And yet, these young people were right in wanting de-Stalinization not to remain merely negative, in wanting to be allowed to blaze new trails into the future. There was no hint of their returning to bourgeois values; they were fighting against the remnants of Stalinism; after so many lies they were demanding the truth; it was their belief that revolutionary art and thought need freedom.

In one field they had won their victory: poetry. We only caught a glimpse of Yevtushenko, but we often saw his younger colleague Voznesensky, who is almost as popular, though his work is more difficult. We met him by chance on the railway platform, the evening we were leaving for Kiev; very young, very pink, with a laughing mouth, liquid eyes, wearing an odd little blue skullcap, he spoke to me in English with a pleasant spontaneity. When we got back, he suggested we might like to attend a discussion of his poems in the library near his home; he was already quite used to the recitals that are traditional in Russia, and which often attract audiences of thousands, either in halls or in the open air; on this occasion it was a rather smaller meeting – four or five hundred – at which he was asked to reply to a severely critical article in the *Literary Gazette*. He was nervous. 'They're enemies out there,' he whispered to us as he took his place facing the audience. Standing up, eyes half-closed, he declaimed some poems, of which Lena Zonina gave us a murmured translation. The applause nearly brought the place down around our ears. A young girl got up. She had heard some of Voznesensky's poems for the first time in Mayakovsky Square; the boy who was reciting them, the people who were listening, seemed to her rather shady, and there were terrible things in the poems about women; she had gone home quite upset, cried, couldn't eat her dinner, her parents were worried. There were hostile murmurs and laughs during this complacent description of her virtuous horror. Today, she ended by saying, it was different; what she had just heard had pleased her. Teachers and students spoke of their admiration for Voznesensky. 'Is it good poetry? Poetry that will last? We don't care; it's our poetry, the poetry of our generation,' one of them said.

The first time I read his poems [said a woman doctor] I didn't understand them at all, they were too hermetic. And then I realized that it was precisely for that reason that some of the images, some of the lines had stayed in my head; I found I was saying them over to myself quite often. I read Voznesensky again several times, each time I enjoyed him more. So the question I'd like answered is this: Poets like Voznesensky, and painters like Picasso – are they right in not wanting us to understand them straight off? They force us to make an effort that enriches us. But on the other hand, it takes up quite a bit of time; and when one works ten hours a day, time is precious.

The general opinion was that one had no right to criticize a poet for being difficult. 'When I read an article on my own subject, I expect to go back over it more than once,' said an engineer, 'why shouldn't poets ask us to do the same for them?' A woman teacher, about forty, got up and began to read out a long essay – a criticism of Voznesensky's obscurity; her class of twelve-year-olds couldn't make head nor tail of him. (Shouts of protest, laughter.) He used hermetic words, such as chimera (laughter, boos). He talked about 'The colour of blotting paper' when blotting paper can be any colour. Undeterred by the angry and sarcastic storm of protest raging around her, she ploughed on calmly to the end of her indictment. 'And she teaches literature to *our children*! It's shameful!' the teenagers shouted. When she had finished, a young Oriental stood up; he was taking a correspondence course in creative writing from the Gorki Institute, and knew Voznesensky by heart. 'You are wrong to insult this woman,' he said gently, 'she deserves all our pity.' All the young people we met subsequently were devotees of the Voznesensky cult. 'We are specialists, you see,' the physicists and technicians would explain to us. 'He speaks for us, and when we read him we feel like complete men again.' He himself said to us: 'Poetry is the form prayer takes in socialist countries.' There are critics who attack the young poets, and bureaucrats who make things difficult for them, but to prevent their expressing themselves as they please there would have to be a complete return to Stalinist methods; to begin with, the suppression of the meetings that Voznesensky refers to as 'my concerts'. In fact, they suffer from very few restrictions.[1] They can travel. A group of them went to the United States, where they got on very well with the beat poets. Their books are published in printings of hundreds of thousands.

The prose writers, not having any direct contact with their readers, are dependent on the publishing houses and magazines, whose freedom is restricted by their fear of displeasing the public on the one hand and the authorities on the other. The *Novy Mir* team is the most daring; among the others, caution has the upper hand. No short story or novel of any originality can be got into print without a struggle from scratch every time. Certain critics have trouble finding someone to print the articles that really express their thought. They are asked to dilute them, to disguise them, to cut bits out; they agree or they refuse, they manoeuvre, forcing themselves to be content with wearing away the resistances little by little; in the long run, this policy gets results. There are articles and essays being published today that would never have seen the light of day a few years before.

The public is avid for novelty; at the time we were there, translations had just appeared of the complete works of Remarque – why? – and Saint-Exupéry; they were selling like hot cakes. 'Translate Camus, Sagan, Sartre, everything,' the young people were crying. In a discussion with the *Foreign Literature* team, Sartre produced a shiver of pleasure by suddenly bringing out the name of Kafka; the other faction got very spiky: 'He has been taken over by the bourgeois intellectuals.' 'Then it's up to you to take him back,' said Sartre. The magazine was about to publish a Kafka short story, all the same. Brecht, who was regarded for a long time with suspicion in the U.S.S.R., as I have said, was beginning

1. Things have changed a great deal since our trip, as everyone knows.

to make an appearance. In Leningrad, we saw a version of *The Good Woman of Setzuan* put on in realistic Stanislavski style. The result was deplorable; the text disconcerted the general public, and the Brechtians were shocked by the production. But Yushkevitch was going to put the play on in Moscow. Was it thanks to Brecht's influence that Schwarz's *Dragon* was put on with such freedom and wealth of invention? Written as an attack on Fascism, but withdrawn after its first performance in 1944 because the dragon made people think of Stalin as much as of Hitler, this comedy had just been revived in Leningrad with great success.

The public is also very much attracted by the Italian cinema.[1] The conformists are afraid that its influence may lead the young directors to break with their own national tradition. But no film has made me feel what the war was like for the people of the U.S.S.R. as much as *My Name is Ivan*. 'It's more than just the story of a child,' George Breitbourd told us, 'it's the story of a whole genera-tion of children.' His mother killed before his eyes, his village burned to the ground, Ivan goes half mad; his dreams are the inno-cent dreams of a ten-year-old; awake, he is possessed by hatred and the desire to kill; he is charming, pathetic, touching and heroic, but a monster. He is entrusted with a mission by some officers against their better judgement, and never comes back. In Berlin, amid the tumult of victory, one of the officers comes across a filing card with Ivan's name and photograph: hanged. The beauty and the novelty of this film is that Tarkovski shows at the same time the greatness of the triumph won by the U.S.S.R. and the irreparable nature of this shocking event: the murder of a child. Tarkovski is twenty-six. His film aroused violent hostility; but it was sent to Venice and won the Golden Lion in the festival there. There have also been a great many attacks on Yushkevitch's film, inspired by Mayakov-sky's *The Bath-house*, in which he made use of a mixture of anima-tion, puppets and documentaries; and yet the daring originality of this film marks it as a work that could have been conceived no-where but in the U.S.S.R. In a local movie house we saw *And if it were Love?*, a film directed against the '*petit-bourgeois* attitude' prevalent in the apartment blocks. Two young people reminiscent of Christiane Rochefort's *Gallery Gods*, a girl and a boy, both stu-dents, innocently fall in love; the persecutions of their parents and their neighbours, the gossip and the lies told about them, drive

1. *Cabiria, Rocco and His Brothers.*

them into such a state of bewilderment and unhappiness that they end up going to bed together and making a terrible mess of it, one infers, since the girl tries to kill herself and then goes a long way away. A mediocre film, but speaking with a new voice: harshly critical, without a positive hero, without a happy end.

'In sculpture and painting, we're mere provincials,' a friend told us. Though this was not intended to include Neizvestny, whose studio we visited with him: a high-ceilinged, narrow room, so packed with sculptures that there was hardly room to move; a steep little staircase leading up to a tiny bedroom. Neizvestny is trying to express the 'automated man' of our times, which has led him to invent some pretty daring forms. The State has commissioned several things from him. The young painters are seriously handicapped; they have seen scarcely any Western art, they are having to start practically from scratch, and their attempts to find their own direction are looked on with a rather bilious eye, since Khrushchev doesn't like abstract art or modern art in general.[1] The nonconformists work in semi-secrecy and only show to a closed circle of friends. They sell their work, but life is a struggle for them. We went to visit two of them; they both had rather small single rooms in a communal apartment that had to serve as both studio and bedroom. Yet for some years now there have been splendid collections of the Impressionists on show in Moscow and Leningrad, paintings by Van Gogh, Gauguin, Matisse. Picasso was awarded the Lenin prize; there is a book available about him with reproductions of his pictures; in the Hermitage there is a whole room devoted to him.[2] The crowds are much more shocked by the 'woman with the fan', in which the human body is treated as an object, than by the Cubist canvases which suggest still-lifes. I had repeated to me the commentary of a guide who was taking a group around and lecturing them on the paintings; he spoke with respect of the Blue Period Picassos, then, with a gesture around the rest of the room: 'Here we have a painter who instead of continuing to make progress simply retrogressed.' Faced with the Gauguins, he said: 'Unfortunately all the colours are false.' On the other hand, the woman director of the French section of the

1. The incident in December was evidence of this: Neizvestny was forced to criticize himself publicly. I saw a programme on Moscow television ridiculing his work.
2. By January 1963 there were two.

Hermitage showed us a quantity of modern works acquired by the Museum which she discussed in the most enlightened terms.

Because they hate any 'distortion' of the human figure, the Russians – who are so anxious to lay claim to their past in every other field – don't do justice to their primitives. Rublov is the equal of Giotto and Duccio; when he saw the icons, Matisse – who drew inspiration from them – wept with admiration. There are only a hundred or so on exhibition, though they have immense quantities hidden away in storage. It took quite a fight to found the Rublov Museum, where a collection of original works and reproductions by the master and his followers is on show. Tarkovski would like to make a film about him; he is faced with lively opposition. Obviously it is difficult to boost Rublov and Repin at the same time; officialdom has opted for Repin.

The public is also passionate about painting. The morning we went to the Hermitage, it was a public holiday; people were fighting to get near the doors, and a young girl had all the buttons of her topcoat torn off. Lena Zonina asked one of the administrators to get us in through a private entrance. There are such stampedes at the entrances to exhibitions that they have to call the police in to keep order. When a bookshop announces the arrival of a book on Impressionism or on Miró, there is a queue in front of the door as early as five in the morning; every copy has been snatched up an hour after they open. Will this pressure be powerful enough to force further concessions?[1]

For the architects, the situation is much better. Khrushchev is interested in architecture and likes simplicity. He gave his approval to the Memorial for the Unknown Soldier in Kiev, even though most of the city's notables were horrified by its starkness. The Palace of the Pioneers, which has just been built, looks almost as if it could have been designed by Niemeyer; the pensioners in a home for old people on the other side of the valley have written letters of protest: this horror is ruining their view. But Khrushchev likes the Palace; the letters were sent on to the architects, and that was the end of it. When we met them, they said to us: 'We've got bad consciences too: all those rows of pillars upon those fourth floors.'

1. Since December 1962 one is tempted to give a pessimistic reply. However, the toughening attitude of the official camp seems to imply that despite the retractions wrung from some of its members, the resistance in the innovators' camp is very strong.

But that style of ugly ostentation so dear to Stalin is now a thing of the past; the new apartment blocks are dismal, but built with some care for economy. The finest of the new buildings is the Palace of Congress. 'They shouldn't have put it inside the Kremlin,' some of our friends said; but the Middle Ages, the eighteenth century and the nineteenth century all seem to have got on very well in there so far, why shouldn't there be a place for the twentieth century as well? answer the others. The Russians have discussed the subject a lot, among themselves and in the newspapers. I must say I found the sight of the old gilded onion domes reflected in the glittering glass of the new Palace very beautiful. Another modern building, of an ingenious and sober elegance, is the Palace of Youth; as we were having tea in the main hall with Simonov's wife[1], who works in an Institute of Applied Art and is an art critic herself, she pointed out that the furniture and the china were completely out of keeping with the room itself. There is nothing more difficult in Moscow than to find a really good plate or cup or chair; it will not be easy to dissuade the Muscovites from their predilection for baubles, ruching, chasing, moulding, embossing and over-decoration in general; but a big effort was being made, she said; they are trying to design and produce good things and to teach people to like them.

When Sartre visited a class of students in 1954, he had mentioned Dostoyevsky. 'Why do you bother with him?' a girl of twelve had asked rather aggressively. Now they were reading him, and liking him. We had been struck by the way in which Pasternak was being spoken of. When Yevtushenko was in England and said: 'In my opinion he is a very good poet,' many people criticized him for this understatement; everyone in Russia, they said, believes him to be one of the very greatest Russian poets. 'His death has forced us to write,' said Voznesensky. 'Before, there was no point; he *was* poetry.' When we were driven in a car lent by the Writers' Union to visit Fedin, the driver stopped in front of a house surrounded by trees. 'Pasternak's *dacha*!' he said with reverence. Even officialdom does not attack him any more. If his erstwhile mistress was sent to a camp,[2] it was because she had engaged in illegal currency transactions.

The camps: the subject was approached without reticence.

1. His second wife. He divorced the first and remarried.
2. Only non-political prisoners are interned in them now.

'Every night for a whole year my father used to sit down in his armchair, gazing straight in front of him, waiting for them to come and arrest him; all his comrades had been shot; he never knew how he came to escape,' a young woman told me. 'My father was in a camp for six years,' a woman teacher said, 'and yet, the night Stalin died, I wept.' 'I was sent to a camp in 1942 for humanitarianism,' a professor told us, 'because I was against shooting prisoners of war. I was there five years.' Many of the internees, went one story, approved of the camps in principle; they found the incarceration of their fellow prisoners quite reasonable; they themselves had been the victims of an error which did not invalidate the system in general. Until 1936, apparently, the camps really were rehabilitation centres: moderate work hours, liberal regime, theatres, libraries, discussion groups, familiar, almost friendly relations between inmates and those in charge. In 1936 there were changes; the maximum penalty was still ten years, as it had been before, but the prisoner either had the right to correspond with his family or not. Accurately construed, this meant that those in the second category were shot; conditions in the penal camps became so bad that many inmates died; after 1944 as well, but the shooting was stopped. Whether from simple repugnance, ignorance, or because it was an officially forbidden subject, no one gave us any details about life in the concentration camps. All we heard were anecdotes: a Pushkin specialist who was deported to one let it be known that he had discovered the last cantos of *Eugene Onegin* just before the event; his papers had been lost, but he had an excellent memory and would be able, given the leisure, to reconstruct the text; he began the attempt and was encouraged to continue, for Pushkin seemed almost to have anticipated the Jadnovian aesthetic: nationalism, heroism, optimism, everything was there. He finished the work and continued to enjoy preferential treatment, so delighted were the Stalinists to have discovered a Pushkin exactly after their own heart. Other specialists began saying it was a forgery; but they were forced to recant until the day the prisoners were released and the critic admitted he had made up the whole thing. The return of the prisoners had given rise to many practical, moral and emotional complications. Victor Nekrasov produced a novel about the difficulty one of these ghostly figures had in readjusting to reality. Ex-prisoners in concentration camps had written or were writing their reminiscences, in the hope of getting them into print one day.

We were not entertained at all in the same way as Sartre had been in 1954. No more banquets or solemn toasts, no more propaganda. People invited us to their homes with just a few other people; sometimes agreeing with them, sometimes disagreeing, we discussed things on our own ground. We had dinner at Simonov's *dacha* with Dorosh, a writer of about fifty who lives in Moscow but spends long periods out in the country at Great-Rostov; he has rented a little room in an *isba*; he loves the peasants, takes an interest in their life and describes it in his books, without hiding its difficulties or its harshness, and without glossing over the mistakes made by the people in charge of agriculture. The Writers' Union lent us a car, and he took us to spend two days in Rostov. His wife went with us; a physics professor and a very good cook, she had packed the trunk of the car with everything necessary to feed us for two days. Rostov, 120 miles from Moscow, is the cradle of Russia; today it is a large village with a population of 25,000, on the edge of a lake, dominated by a Kremlin older than the one in Moscow, more rustic and on the whole more beautiful. The architect who is restoring it was camping out in one of the round towers on the walls; we were expecting to be able to eat our meals in his quarters; he was to show us all the places of interest, and Dorosh was to introduce us to a few of the peasants he knew. But on the way there he warned us: 'The gentlemen of Yaroslavl[1] have their own ideas about what French writers find interesting.' We went in through one of the gates of the Kremlin, we got out of the car. Three men in straw hats advanced towards us and greeted us stiffly; two of them were leading members of the local Soviet, the third was Head of Propaganda. They came up with us into the tower and shared our meal. Through the narrow windows, there were glimpses of the silken water and the plain; the round room was charming, so was the architect, but the presence of the three officials got on our nerves. They followed us as we went on a tour of the churches with their azure-coloured, golden, slaty onion domes, some smooth, some with scales. The frescoes decorating the chapels are more serene than ours, there are hardly any scenes of hell at all. After that we were supposed to visit a *kolkhoz*; they postponed our departure until late afternoon. When we arrived the peasants had almost all gone home, except for one woman who

1. The centre of local government for the area, a large town on the Volga thirty miles from Rostov.

lingered behind in the barn and turned out to be the best milker in the district. Could we visit her *isba*? No, it just happened that she'd washed all her linen that day. We were taken for a walk around a field of kidney beans; Khrushchev had just officially recommended that they be grown, and the head of the *kolkhoz* had come to the same decision two years before! Dorosh had wandered off and was kicking at lumps of earth. Our guides then led us off to see the home of one of the section heads. The inside looked more like the house of a poor lower-middle-class family than a French farm. Although the owner was a Party member, there was a lamp burning in front of an icon. As we left I asked: 'Are there a lot of peasants who are practising Christians?' 'They can all decide for themselves,' was the propagandist's answer. He evaded all our questions. To explain the 'peasant mentality' to us, he quoted a famous phrase from Lenin followed by a string of platitudes. During dinner Sartre advanced to the attack. Tomorrow, we wanted to see some peasants, alone with Dorosh. Writers understand each other, he would be able to make them talk in a way that would interest us. The officials did not reply. They took us off, Lena Zonina, Sartre and myself, to Yaroslavl where they had booked rooms for us, and next morning they tried to take us on a visit to a shoe factory. We refused. The Head of Propaganda showed us the banks of the Volga, the house where Natasha found Prince André dying, some old churches. It was a very pleasant outing, but he got us back to Rostov two hours later than the time we had agreed upon with Dorosh; and he was quite determined to stay with us the rest of the day. We gave up. After lunch we went back to Moscow. During the return journey, and later in Moscow when we saw him again, Dorosh talked to us at length about the human problems that arise in the country: the condition of women, the ambitions of the young people, the relations between workers and peasants, the attraction of the towns, what ought to be done and what had been done to keep the new generation in the villages when even mechanization had proved insufficient to attach them to the land, the conflict between those who want a radical transformation of rural conditions and those who wish to see certain traditions maintained.

One night by train took us to Leningrad, one of the most beautiful cities in the world. It was a stroke of genius on the part of Catherine II to order Rastrelli to bring the Italian Baroque to the banks of the Neva, where it has made a perfect marriage with the pinks and blues and greens that clothe it here in the pale nordic light. Like Rome, Leningrad is an enchantress; above all in the immense square glittering with the windows of the Winter Palace. Superimposed by my memory on its mysterious majesty lay black and white scenes from the 'ten days that shook the world' and from the revolts that heralded them. A bustling crowd hurried up and down the Nevsky Prospect: I recalled a photograph showing the roadway and the sidewalks piled with dead and dying. In the middle of the Neva Bridge, I saw a horse-drawn cab: the bridge rose; horse and vehicle went tumbling down, caught in the deep silence of those old films. Smolny. The Admiralty. The Fortress of Peter and Paul. Oh, the reverberation of those words inside me as I read them for the first time when I was twenty. During the day, it was Lenin's city I was walking in (and that other's, who is never named).

And then, in all its brightness, came the night. 'The White Nights of St Petersburg'; in Norway, in Finland, I had thought I knew what they were like; but the magic of the night-time sun needs this ghost-haunted, petrified décor from the past to complete its spell.

We had dinner at the home of the writer Guerman, his family, and also Heifitz, the director of *The Lady with a Dog*. We knew that he had escaped deportation to Siberia only by going into hiding and also, in part, thanks to Ehrenburg. 'Not once did I write the name of Stalin,' he told us, piling our plates with Siberian ravioli. We talked about the cinema and about theatre; he told us some of the things he remembered about Meyerhold. Heifitz's wife and twenty-year-old son arrived in time for coffee. They had been to see *Rocco and His Brothers*; she was very stirred and delighted. Young Heifitz and Guerman's children compared the merits of Voznesensky and Yevtushenko; he preferred the former, they the latter. Sartre had a long discussion with Mme Heifitz on the relations of children with their parents; he based some of his remarks on Freudian theories that she opposed passionately. At midnight we all went down together to the Campus Martius. There were lovers kissing on the benches in the fresh smell of early morning, young people playing the guitar and groups of boys and girls walking along laughing.

Two days later, we met them again in a restaurant at about eleven, after the theatre. They took us by car to see the Dostoyevsky neighbourhood by the light of the pale sky: his house, the place where Rogojine had lived, the courtyard of the old woman moneylender killed by Raskolnikov, the canal where he disposed of the axe. On the way we glimpsed the window of the room where Essenin killed himself. They showed us the very first place where Peter the Great had lived, and the first canals. On the outskirts of the town, at the spot where Pushkin came to fight the duel in which he was mortally wounded, we drank vodka to his memory.

There are now four million people living in Leningrad, the same figure as before the war, but almost all of them are new arrivals; during the siege, three and a half million people succumbed to famine, the food warehouses having been burned down in the first few days. An old professor described to Sartre the ice-covered roads piled high with corpses that the passers-by no longer even noticed; all anyone could think of was getting his bowl of soup home without collapsing from weakness. If you did, you wouldn't have the strength to get up again; and even if someone had stretched out his hand to help you, it would have done no good; he would have fallen over too.

The Russians still boast about the beauty of Kiev; Sancta Sofia, which we were taken to see by the Ukrainian poet Bajan, deserves its fame. But all the mid-town neighbourhoods – half the city – were pounded into dust by the Germans; Stalin had one of the city's most famous churches demolished, and rebuilt Kiev in the style he loved so much; arcades and colonnades, the main avenue is a colossal nightmare. In the Ukraine, too, the people are all obsessed by their memories of the war. Kiev was a mound of ashes when Bajan got back to it, the rare passers-by seemed to him like ghosts; he recognized the face of a friend; they stayed looking into each other's eyes for a long time without a word, unable to believe their eyes. The Nazis, who had made the total annihilation of Slav culture one of their aims, had deliberately set fire to the Avra monastery, a famous pilgrimage site; on a hill above the Dnieper, there is a stretch of painted wall, an onion dome, its gold roofs blackened by the flames, and a few charred remnants. The shots from *My Name is Ivan* were still in my mind's eye, and beneath the strawberry fields where the peasants from a nearby *kolk-hoz* were gathering their baskets of fruit, huge and succulent, I could see those tracts of devastated land.

We had lunch with Korneychuk and his wife, Wanda Wassileska, in their *dacha* just outside Kiev; they had a garden full of tulips sloping down to the edge of a lake. He wanted very much for Sartre to attend the Peace Congress that was going to be held in Moscow, and to speak there on the subject of culture. Ehrenburg, through his wife, Surkov and Fedin were also insisting that Sartre take part in the Congress; they wanted him to cooperate with them in organizing a discussion between intellectuals from all over the world. *Hyena with a fountain pen, enemy of mankind, filth pedlar, tool of the bourgeoisie, gravedigger* – as he came out of these conversations, Sartre remembered these things and laughed.

In Moscow, we stayed at the Peking Hotel, one of the buildings that have been put up here and there throughout the town in the belief that they harmonize with the towers of the Kremlin. But we were in it as little as possible. We preferred queuing up with the people of Moscow outside the restaurants and cafés. Sometimes we ate dinner at the writers' club or the theatre club. All the public places close at eleven in the evening, except the restaurants of a few big hotels, where one can eat, drink and dance until half past twelve; yet the streets remain full of life until quite late; people pay each other visits. Housing conditions are still bad; eighty per cent still live in communal apartments; but there has been no relaxation in efforts to construct more living space, and the new buildings are very pleasant inside. George Breitbourd was living in a block reserved exclusively for intellectuals and had quite a big, light studio, with bathroom and kitchen that many a French bachelor of about the same professional status as himself might well have envied. In old Moscow, you have to go through more or less squalid courtyards, climb up dilapidated staircases or take elevators that are really more like builders' hoists; but the apartments of the writers and directors who invited us – of course they're a privileged class – were quite large and often elegant. The public transport system is very convenient. Not many taxis, but a great many buses, and a considerable subway system with escalators in most of the stations. However, the day of the housewife in Moscow is made rather wearing by the paucity of goods to be had; she must run from store to store and stand in lines all the time; and even then she doesn't always get everything she's looking for.

This is because the U.S.S.R., as its leaders openly admit, is in the grip of serious economic difficulties; its agriculture has never gone well; there have been numerous denunciations recently of officials who have accepted bribes and generally used their powers for their own ends – the socialist equivalents of the frauds and swindles and financial scandals that we get back home. Such things are severely punished, the death penalty even being applied in really serious cases. And there is little doubt that this poverty is the price the Russians must pay for their successes in the exploration of space. Will it decrease or get worse? The articles of the economists and the statisticians' figures will be of more help in answering such questions than our three-week trip. But for us they were a profitable three weeks. When the Cold War began, we backed the U.S.S.R.; since it began to change over to a peace policy and become de-Stalinized, our doubts about this choice had ceased; its cause and its opportunities are ours too. Our stay this time turned this bond into a living friendship. A truth is rich insofar as it has *become*; it would be wrong to think of the conquests of the Russian intellectuals as small: those conquests include all the obstacles they have vanquished. The contradictions in their past experience – among others the rejected heritage of their Stalinist past – are forcing them to think for themselves, and this is what gives their thought a depth that is quite exceptional in our age of *other-conditioning*. One senses in the people, especially among the young, a passionate desire to know and to understand: cinema, theatre, ballet, poetry, concerts – every seat is always taken in advance; the museums and exhibitions have to turn people away; books are sold as soon as they come off the press. Everywhere, discussion and argument. In the technocratic world that the West is attempting to impose on us, the only things that count are tools and organization, the means of attaining other means with no end ever in sight. In the U.S.S.R. man is in the process of making himself, and even if he is encountering difficulties on the way, even if there are hard knocks to be taken, relapses, mistakes, all the things surrounding him, all the things that happen, are heavy with meanings.

On the way back we stopped in Poland. Warsaw, the ghetto: ruins, mass graves, a desert of ashes. And I saw a great new city, with wide avenues, parks, workshops and here and there, for no reason, a house half collapsing. Of the ghetto, there remains only a stretch of wall and a tower set in the midst of empty lots disguised as green lawns and elegant apartment blocks. The old town has been reconstructed very well: the market-place, the cathedral, the little streets with their low, bright-coloured houses. The rest of the town – ugly in some places, pretty in others, according to the year in which it was rebuilt – lacks cohesion, personality, soul; it is a magnificent victory over death, but it is as though life has still not made up its mind to come back again. Praga on the other side of the Vistula, industrial, populous, old and dirty – the Russian armies halted there so it escaped destruction – I found reassuring because here time had never stopped.

Lissowski, a Communist, who speaks French as well as he does Polish, took us around in a little automobile. We were struck by how empty the roads were. But the streets were full of life and, at least in the centre, gay: slim, well made-up women; elegant window displays; all the objects in everyday use – the furniture, the restaurant and café décors – were pleasant to look at. At ten in the evening, all the public places close, so the heavy drinkers get to work earlier; there are already quite a few drunks on the street by nine. There is less inequality in the matter of wages than in the U.S.S.R., but the standard of living is very low. Food costs almost nothing, but on the other hand clothing is fabulously expensive; a pair of shoes costs as much as a quarter of the average monthly salary. Housing is free, but very difficult to come by; Warsaw is a closed city, no one is allowed to move into it simply because a large proportion of its present population is still living piled on top of each other in hovels. The architects are not quite sure what to do. They have designed all their apartments with bathrooms; because they're not used to such things, the tenants don't use them; wouldn't it be better to leave them out and increase the number of available apartments? But that just means trouble in the future; the people of Warsaw aren't going to learn to be hygienic if the means of being so aren't available. Should they put the immediate need for accommodation first, or the welfare of the rising generation? It is the second consideration that has prevailed.

We saw Cracow, a charming, old-fashioned, provincial town: the University, Doktor Faust's study, his alembics, and the mark of Mephistopheles' foot; the cathedral standing in the market, its beautiful tall tower with a trumpet that sounds to the four corners of the horizon every hour on the hour; the royal castle, the study and private projection room that Frank, the butcher of Poland, had installed for him. We caught glimpses of Nowa Huta, the immense *combinat*, the Workers' City, a fine Cistercian monastery and a wooden church set in the middle of a meadow. We returned to Warsaw by car. For nearly two hundred miles the road winds through meadows, fields of tender green crops and thatched peasant houses with walls washed yellow or blue. Nothing but private property; the 'Polish October' set the seal on the failure of collectivization. Frequently we passed groups of peasant women dressed in traditional costume: brightly coloured capes and skirts, kerchiefs tied under the chin; there were children with them holding candles, showing that they were on the way back from some religious ceremony. In the country, religion still weighs on the peasants as heavily as ever. We were shown an astonishing documentary film which the clergy had allowed to be made only on condition that no commentary be added to it: a re-enactment of the Stations of the Cross that takes place every year in a certain village and is attended by a vast audience that flows in from every corner of the surrounding district. Christ, bearing his cross, climbs a hill, struggling, gasping, sweating, stumbling; he falls with such extraordinary conviction and art that the moment becomes an event that is really happening; there are men following him, staggering under the weight of the stones biting into their shoulders; the women look on, lost in ecstasy, weeping, ready to break out into lamentation; and with its beautiful, disciplined chants, the clergy provides an austere framework for this frenzy of masochism. Moving because of the question it asks, revolting because of the answer it gives, this film has not been publicly shown. In the towns, sixty per cent are believers, one of our friends told us; others consider this figure to be completely false. Warsaw Cathedral was full on Sunday morning, but the population of the old neighbourhoods are of bourgeois origin; the workers don't go to church, at least not the men. What is still very much alive and kicking is Polish anti-Semitism: in one of the mouths of the admittedly hideous memorial erected to the memory of the ghetto Jews, someone had stuck the butt end of a cigarette.

Through the newspaper *Politica*, we met some journalists who had recently taken part in an inquiry into the workers' councils, and also the president of the councils himself. They are slowly dying; they take up a great deal of time, and the workers, feeling they don't know much about such things, generally leave all the decisions to the engineers and executives. So the councils will probably disappear altogether.

I was already quite familiar with post-war Polish culture; I had seen most of the Polish films shown in France, including *Ashes and Diamonds*, which has all the freshness and sincerity sought by the 'New Wave' and also means something as well. Since 1956, we had read and published in *Les Temps Modernes* a great many pieces of Polish writing. The Poles had reciprocated by putting on most of Sartre's plays and by translating both his works and mine. Almost all their writers spoke French. We had met several in Paris; we always got on very well with them. But we'd never met Brandys before, though we'd published *The Defence of Granada*, *The Mother of the Kings*, and *The Letters of Mme Z*. Warm beneath his aloof exterior, as sensitive as he is intelligent, his conception of writing coincided exactly with ours. We spent a long time with the Polish translator of Sartre's plays, Jan Kott, whose remarkable book *Shakespeare, Our Contemporary* was about to be published in the *Temps Modernes* series. The intellectuals in Poland are spared the perpetual struggle that goes on in the U.S.S.R. between those who are for and those who are against cultural freedom. They know all that's going on in the West, they write and paint more or less as they choose. But they have their own troubles; they belong to a country less advanced than the U.S.S.R. on the path of socialism, a country in which many reactionary forces still subsist – religion, anti-Semitism, a peasantry clinging to the idea of private property; they are opposed to the idea of removing these concepts by main force, but suffer from the knowledge of their country's backwardness. Since they are relatively few in number and not very industrialized, the fate of the Polish people is bound up with that of Russia; but though they are ideologically and politically in agreement with her, they have many reasons, some old, some new, for not losing much love over their great neighbour. The writers are very sensitive to this feeling of dissatisfaction, and it is admirably expressed in the works of some of them.

While in Moscow, we learned of the agreements reached between the G.P.R.A. and the O.A.S. Their safety once assured by the amnesty, the secret army had ceased its attacks; in fact, it was capitulating. A complete reversal of attitude had immediately appeared among the *pieds noirs*; all those who stayed in Algeria voted Yes on the day of self-determination.

On 5 July, the Algerians celebrated their independence; they invited their French friends and the officials of various countries to a reception at the Continental Hotel in the late afternoon. We asked the door-man where it was being held. 'The Algerian meeting? It didn't come off,' he replied in a triumphant tone. In an adjacent street, there were about a hundred or so people – the ones we always saw at the demonstrations – stamping their feet beneath an icy sky; some ambassadors had come and left again. There was talk of the hotel having been threatened by the O.A.S., or else the local authorities had refused to provide the protection the manager had deemed necessary. Whatever the pretext, we were completely sickened by this final piece of French boorishness. We stood there, bewildered, chatting to each other, while a group of helmeted cops stood at the end of the street muttering: 'What's up? Why don't we clear them out?' Sartre and I joined up with a little group and went off to the North African students' head-quarters on the Boulevard Saint-Michel. There was an enormous crowd of people there, and a lot of smoke; we almost suffocated in the little overcrowded room; up on a platform, some beautiful Algerian girls dressed in white and green were singing to the accompaniment of a small orchestra. This gaiety was not un-clouded; serious differences of opinion had broken out among the Algerian leaders. Eventually they would be settled. But for us, the French, the situation in which we were leaving Algeria left no room for joy. For seven years we had desired this victory; it came too late to console us for the price it had cost.

I went off on vacation, I came back; I am settled once more in my own apartment, a cold, blue autumn streaming into my studio. For the first time in years, I have walked through the Paris streets and seen Algerian labourers who were smiling. The sky is not so heavy any more. A page has been turned and I can attempt to sum up.

THERE has been one undoubted success in my life: my relationship with Sartre. In more than thirty years, we have only once gone to sleep at night disunited. These years spent side by side have not decreased the interest we find in each other's conversation: a woman friend[1] has observed that we always listen to each other with the closest attention. Yet so assiduously have we always criticized, corrected or ratified each other's thought that we might almost be said to think in common. We have a common store of memories, knowledge and images behind us; our attempts to grasp the world are undertaken with the same tools, set within the same framework, guided by the same touchstones. Very often one of us begins a sentence and the other finishes it; if someone asks us a question, we have been known to produce identical answers. The stimulus of a word, a sensation, a shadow, sends us both travelling along the same inner path, and we arrive simultaneously at a conclusion – a memory, an association – completely inexplicable to a third person. We are no longer astonished when we run into each other even in our work; I recently read some reflections noted down by Sartre in 1952 which I had not known about till now; there were passages in them which occur again, almost word for word, in my *Memoirs*, written ten years later. Our temperaments, our directions, our previous decisions, remain different, and our writings are on the whole almost totally dissimilar. But they have sprung from the same plot of ground.

This relationship has been stigmatized by some as a contradiction of the views on morality expressed in *The Second Sex*: I insist that women be independent, yet I have never been alone. The two words are not synonymous; but before I explain myself further on that point, there are a few stupid misconceptions I should like to dispose of.

It has been said by some people that Sartre writes my books. The day after I was awarded the Goncourt, someone advised me with no malicious intention whatever: 'If you give any interviews, make it quite clear that you did write *Les Mandarins*; you know

1. Maria-Rosa Oliver in an interview she gave to an Argentine newspaper.

what people are saying: that Sartre stands behind you . . .' It has also been said that he made me as a writer. The only thing he ever did in this line was to pass two of my manuscripts on to Brice Parrain, one of which was in any case rejected. Let it pass. Long before I came on the scene they were saying that Colette 'slept her way' to fame; so anxious is our society to maintain the accepted status of members of my sex as secondary beings, reflections, toys or parasites of the all-important male.

Even more strongly held is the belief that all my convictions were put into my head by Sartre. 'With someone else, she would have been a mystic,' wrote Jean Guitton; and quite recently a critic, Belgian if I remember rightly, mused in print: 'If it had been Brasillach she had met up with!' In a broadsheet called the *Tribune des assurances*, I read: 'If instead of being a pupil of Sartre, she had come under the influence of a theologian, she would have been a passionate theist.' Fifty years have gone by, but this is still the same old idea my father held: 'A woman is what her husband makes her.' He was deceiving himself; he never altered by so much as a hairsbreadth the beliefs of the pious young lady formed by the Couvent des Oiseaux. Even the gigantic personality of Jaurès shattered against the stubborn piety of his wife. Youth has its own specific gravity, its own resilience; how could the girl I was at twenty possibly have succumbed to the influence of a believer or a Fascist? But people in our society really do believe that a woman thinks with her uterus – what low-mindedness, really! I did come across Brasillach and his clique; they filled me with horror. I could only have become attached to a man who was hostile to all that I loathed: the Right, conventional thinking, religion. It was no matter of chance that I chose Sartre; for after all I did choose him. I followed him joyfully because he led me along the paths I wanted to take; later, we always discussed our itinerary together. I remember that, in 1940, receiving his last letter from Brumath, written hurriedly, slightly obscure, there was one sentence as I read it through for the first time that filled me with terror: was Sartre about to compromise? During the instant that the fear gripped me, I knew from the way I stiffened, from the pain I felt, that if I could not dissuade him we were doomed to spend the rest of our lives in opposite camps.

This does not alter the fact that philosophically and politically the initiative has always come from him. Apparently some young women have felt let down by this fact; they took it to mean that I was accepting the 'relative' role I was advising them to escape from. No. Sartre is ideologically creative, I am not; this bent forced him into making political choices and going much more profoundly into the reasons for them than I was interested in doing. The real betrayal of my liberty would have been a refusal to recognize this particular superiority on his part; I would then have ended up a prisoner of the deliberately challenging attitude and the bad faith which are at once an inevitable result of the battle of the sexes and the complete opposite of intellectual honesty. My independence has never been in danger because I have never unloaded any of my own responsibilities onto Sartre. I have never given my support to any idea, any decision, without first having analysed it and accepted it on my own account. My emotions have been the product of a direct contact with the world. My own work has demanded from me a great many decisions and struggles, a great deal of research, perseverance and hard work. He has helped me, as I have helped him. I have not lived through him.

As a matter of fact, this accusation is just one of the weapons in my adversaries' well-stocked arsenal. For the story of my public life is that of my books, my successes, my failures; and also of the attacks that have been launched against me.

In France, if you are a writer, to be a woman is simply to provide a stick to be beaten with. Especially at the age I was when my first books were published. If you are a very young woman they indulge you, with an amused wink. If you are old, they bow respectfully. But lose the first bloom of youth and dare to speak before acquiring the respectable patina of age: the whole pack is at your heels! If you are conservative, if you yield with grace before the accepted superiority of the male, if you seem insolent and in fact say nothing, then they'll leave you unscathed. I am of the Left, I had things I was trying to say; among others, that women are not just a tribe of moral cripples from birth.

'You've won. You've made all the right enemies,' Nelson Algren said to me in the spring of 1960. Yes; the insults I received from *Rivarol*, from *Preuves*, from *Carrefour*, from Jacques Laurent, delighted me. The snag is that ill will spreads like oil in water. Slanders are quick to produce answering echoes, if not in people's hearts at least in their mouths! No doubt this is just one of the forms of the dissatisfaction we all feel to some extent at being no more than we are. We are capable of understanding, but we prefer to belittle. Writers are a favourite target of this sort of spite; the public treats them with reverence, knowing full well that they are people just like anybody else, and then feels resentful towards them because of this contradiction; all the outward signs of their common humanity are entered on the debit side of the ledger drawn up against them. An American critic, and one quite well disposed towards me, in his review of *The Prime of Life* said that despite all my efforts I had brought Sartre down off his pedestal: what pedestal? He ended by adding that even if Sartre had lost a bit of his prestige, at least he had been made more lovable. Generally speaking, if the public finds out that you are not super-human then it classes you down among the lowest of the low – a monster. Between 1945 and 1952, we were particularly subject to such distortions because we were so difficult to classify. Left-wing but not Communists, in fact in very bad odour with the Communist Party, we were also not 'bohemians'; I was criticized for living in a hotel, and Sartre for living with his mother; at the same time we rejected middle-class life, we were not part of 'society', we had money but we didn't live in style; our lives were intimately linked without either of us being in any way subjected to the other. This complete bypassing of all their touchstones disconcerted and irritated people. I was struck for example by the fact that *Samedi-Soir* should have waxed so indignant over the price we had paid for a taxi from Bou Saâda to Djelfa: to hire a car for a thirty-mile journey is less of a luxury than to own an automobile of one's own. Yet no one criticized me later on when I bought my Aronde; the price of buying a car is a classic expense perfectly acceptable by bourgeois standards.

One of the factors that contributes most to distorting writers' public images is the number of people who include us in their fantasy lives. At one time my sister moved about a great deal in society, where she was always introduced by her husband's name. She used to be stunned by the things that were said when the conversation got onto the subject of me and my work. 'I know her very well . . . she's a great friend of mine . . . I happened to have dinner with her only last week'; this from people I had never set eyes on. There was a wealth of comments too. With a smile, she stood and listened to a lady who assured her: 'She's a fishwife!

Swears like a trooper, you know.' One year, in New York, Fernand and Stépha asked me reproachfully: 'Why have you hidden your marriage to Sartre from us!' I denied that we were married; they laughed. 'Oh come now! Our friend Sauvage was a witness at the ceremony; he told us all about it himself.' I had to show them my passport to convince them. In about 1949, France Roche featured us in the *France-Dimanche* gossip column: Sartre and I had bought a country house called La Berle and carved two hearts on a tree there. Sartre sent a letter denying it, which was not published, and she told a friend: 'But I know it's a fact because it was passed on to me by Z., who had tea with them in their garden.' I also remember the young woman who came up to me timidly once in the Deux Magots. 'Excuse me for disturbing you, but I'm a very good friend of Bertrand G.' I looked at her questioningly and she seemed astonished. 'Bertrand G., who has lunch with you every week.' I felt awful for her and said hastily: 'I expect you've got the names mixed up. My sister's a painter, she's called Hélène de Beauvoir, I expect he's one of her friends . . .' – 'No,' she said, 'it wasn't your sister he meant. I understand now. Excuse me . . .' She left in complete confusion, and the suddenness with which her eyes had been opened was obviously so painful to her that I felt almost guilty. Obviously such people's fantasies are only interesting if they've got some pretty worthwhile facts – such as a secret marriage, or else a spicy detail or two – to divulge. It's not difficult for them to find an audience; the public likes gossip. There are some maniacs for whom no fact is really true unless it has been seen through a keyhole. I recognize that there is some excuse for this peculiarity; official accounts and portraits are always patently full of lies, so people imagine that truth must have its mysteries, its initiates, its hidden channels. Our enemies exploit this credulity.

Two images of me are current: I am a madwoman, an eccentric. (The newspapers in Rio reported in a tone of surprise: 'We were expecting an eccentric; we were rather let down to be introduced to a woman dressed like anyone else.') My morals are extremely dissolute; in 1945, a Communist woman told the story that during my youth in Rouen I had been seen dancing naked on the tops of barrels; I have assiduously practised every vice, my life is a perpetual orgy, etc.

Or, flat heels, tight bun, I am a chieftainess, a lady manager, a schoolmistress (in the pejorative sense given to this word by the Right). I spend my existence with books and sitting at my work-table, pure intellect. 'She doesn't live,' I've heard a young woman journalist say. 'If I were invited to Mme T.'s Mondays I'd be there like a shot.' The magazine *Elle*, depicting various categories of women for the benefit of its readers, gave my photograph the caption: 'Exclusively intellectual life'.

Apparently a combination of these two portraits involves no contradiction. I can also be an egg-headed whore or a lubricious manageress; the essential is that the figure I cut should be abnormal. If my censors are trying to say that I am different from them, then I take it as a compliment. The fact is that I am a writer – a woman writer, which doesn't mean a housewife who writes but someone whose whole existence is governed by her writing. It's as good a life as any other. It has its reasons, its order and its ends, which one must misunderstand completely in order to think of it as extravagant. Was mine really ascetic, purely cerebral? God knows I don't get the impression that my contemporaries are getting all that much more amusement out of this world of ours than I, or that their experience is any larger. In any case, looking back over my past, there is no one I envy.

I trained myself when young not to care for public opinion. Since then, I have had Sartre and solid friendships to protect me. All the same, there have been certain whispers, certain looks that I have found it hard to bear: the sneering laughter of Mauriac and the young people with him in the Deux Magots. For several years I loathed showing myself in public; I stopped going to cafés, I avoided theatre openings and all 'Parisian' entertainments. This reserve was in accordance with my distaste for publicity: I have never appeared on television, never talked about myself on the radio, almost never given an interview. I have already explained my reasons for accepting the Goncourt and nevertheless refused even then to exhibit myself in any way. I wished to owe any success I might have to my own efforts and not to outside influences. And I knew that the more the press talked about me, the more I should be misrepresented. It was my desire to establish the truth of these matters that was largely responsible for my writing these memoirs, and many readers have in fact said that the ideas they entertained of me beforehand could scarcely have been more false. I still have my enemies; I should be very worried if I hadn't. But with time my books have lost their flavour of scandal; age, alas! has conferred on me a certain respectability; and above all I have won for myself a public that listens when I talk to them. At this stage, I am largely spared the unpleasant aspects of notoriety.

As a beginner, I experienced only the pleasures it brings, and even in the years since then they have always come in far fuller measure than the disadvantages. Fame gave me what I desired: that people should like my books, and through them me; that they should listen to me and let me serve them by showing them the world as I saw it. I have known these joys since the day *L'Invitée* was published. I have not avoided being deceived by false illusions, I have experienced vanity: it flowers as soon as one smiles at one's own image, as soon as one shivers at the sound of one's name. At least I have never become self-important.

I have always taken my failures well; they were nothing but shots off target, never obstacles in my path. My successes, until recent years, have given me pleasures without reserve; for me, the approval of my readers always carried more weight than the praises of the professional critics: letters received, sentences overheard, the traces of an influence, in a book, in someone's life. Since the publication of the *Memoirs of a Dutiful Daughter*, and even more so since that of *The Prime of Life*, my relationship to the public has become ambiguous because the horror my class inspires in me has been brought to white heat by the Algerian war. There is no hope of reaching the wider reading public if one's books are not the sort they like; one is only printed in a cheap edition if the normal first-run edition has sold well. So, willy-nilly, it is the middle classes one is writing for. And among them there are some of course who have torn themselves away from their class, or are at least trying to – intellectuals, young people; with them I am on the same wavelength. But I feel ill at ease if the middle class as a whole gives me a good reception. There were too many women who read the *Memoirs of a Dutiful Daughter* because they enjoyed the accuracy with which I had depicted a milieu they recognized, but without being at all interested in the effort I had made to escape from it. As for *The Prime of Life*, many's the time I've stood gritting my teeth as people congratulated me: 'It's bracing, it's dynamic, it's optimistic,' when I was so sickened by everything that I would rather have been dead than alive.

I am by no means insensitive to praise or blame. Yet, if I dig down into myself, it is not long before I reach a bed-rock of almost total indifference to the extent of my success. There was a time, as I have said, when pride and caution prevented me from making an estimate of my powers; today, I no longer have any idea of what standard of measurement I should use. Should it be with reference to the public, to the critics, to a few selected judges, to my deep personal convictions, to my publicity, to the lack of it? And what would this estimate be *of*? Fame or quality, influence or talent? And then again: what do those words mean? Not only the possible answers to them, but these questions themselves now strike me as inane. My detachment goes deeper than that; it has its roots in a childhood devoted to the absolute: I have remained convinced of the vanity of earthly successes. My apprenticeship to the world strengthened this disdain; I discovered in the world an amount of misery too immense for me to disturb myself unduly over the place I hold in it or over the rights I may or may not have to occupy a place in it.

Despite this undertow of disenchantment, though all idea of duty, of mission, of salvation has collapsed, no longer sure for whom or for what I write, the activity itself is now more necessary to me than ever. I no longer believe it to be a 'justification', but without it I should feel mortally unjustified. There are days so beautiful that you want to shine like the sun, I mean to splash bright words over all the world; there are hours so black that no other hope is left but the cry that you would like to vent. Whence does it come, no less urgent now at fifty-five than it was when I was twenty, this extraordinary power of the Word? I say: 'Nothing takes place but the place,' or 'One and one make one: what a misunderstanding!' and in my throat rises a flame that as it burns exalts me. Words without doubt, universal, eternal, presence of all in each, are the only transcendent power I recognize and am affected by; they vibrate in my mouth, and with them I can communicate with humanity. They wrench tears, night, death itself from the moment, from contingency, and then transfigure them. Perhaps the most profound desire I entertain today is that people should repeat in silence certain words that I have been the first to link together.

There are obvious advantages in being a well-known writer; no more bread-and-butter jobs, but work you are doing because you want to, meeting people, travel, a more direct grip on events than before. The support of the French intellectuals is sought by a great many foreigners at variance with their own governments; we are often asked as well to demonstrate our solidarity with friendly nations. We are all a bit crushed by the weight of the manifestoes, protests, resolutions, declarations, appeals and messages that we have to draw up or sign. It is impossible to take part in all the committees, conferences, discussions and meetings to which we are invited. But in exchange for the time we do give them, the people who ask for our support keep us informed in a much more detailed, more exact and above all more living way than any newspaper about what is happening in their country: in Cuba, in Guinea, in the Antilles, in Venezuela, in Peru, in the Cameroons, in Angola, in South Africa. However modest my contribution to their struggles is, it gives me the feeling that I do have some little effect on history. Instead of being 'well-connected' in the usual sense, I have connexions with the world as a whole. An old friend once said reproachfully: 'You live in a convent.' Perhaps I do; but I spend a great deal of time in the parlour talking to my visitors.

Yet it was with nostalgia and with anxiety that I discovered the full bloom of Sartre's celebrity and my own budding fame. The carefree days were over the moment we became public persons and were always forced to take this new objectivity into account; the adventurous side of our earlier trips was lost forever; we had to give up all sudden whims, all wanderings where we chose. To protect our private lives we had to erect barriers – leave hotel and café life behind – and I found it weighed on me to be cut off like that, I had so loved living mixed up together with everyone else. I see a great many people; but most of them no longer talk to me as they would to just anyone, my relations with them have been falsified. 'Sartre is never to be seen with anyone except the people who are to be seen with Sartre,' Claude Roy wrote once. The same is true of me. I run the risk of understanding them less well simply because I no longer entirely share their lot with them. This difference between us is simply a product of celebrity and of the material ease that follows in its train.

Economically I belong to a privileged class. Since 1954, my books earn me a great deal of money; in 1952 I bought myself an automobile, and in 1955 an apartment. I don't go out, I don't entertain; I still retain the repugnance to glamorous luxury places that I felt when I was twenty; I dress without ostentation, I eat sometimes very well, usually very little; but all such things I leave to the caprice of the moment – I never deliberately deprive myself. There are censorious critics who reproach me for the comfort of my life: right-wingers, it goes without saying; on the Left, no one ever condemns another left-wing member on the score of wealth, even if he be a millionaire;[1] they are simply grateful to him for being on the Left. Marxist ideology has nothing to do with Evangelical morality, it demands neither asceticism nor poverty of any individual; to tell the truth, it is not concerned with your private life. The Right is so persuaded of the legitimacy of its claims that its adversaries can justify themselves in its eyes only by making martyrs of themselves; then too, its choices are all dictated by economic interests and it has difficulty in conceiving that the two could possibly be dissociated: a Communist with money, in their estimation, could not possibly be sincere. Finally, and most important, as far as the Right is concerned any stick will do to beat a dog, when it comes to attacking their leftish enemies. One critic, who was doing his best to be impartial moreover, wrote after reading *The Prime of Life* that I had a taste for 'low life' because at a time when I was very poor during the war I lived in several sordid hotels; what wouldn't they find to say now if I elected to move into some cheap tavern! A warm topcoat is a concession to the middle class; a neglected appearance would be construed as affectation or as unseemly behaviour. You are accused either of throwing money down every drain or of being a miser. And don't think you can escape by trying to stick to some happy medium or other: they'd soon have a name for that too – petty-mindedness, for example. The only solution is to follow your own conscience and let them say what they will.

Which doesn't mean that I accept my situation with a light heart. The uneasiness it caused me around 1946 still persists. I know that I am a profiteer, and that I am one primarily because of the education I received and the possibilities it opened up for me. I exploit no one directly; but the people who buy my books are all beneficiaries of an economy founded upon exploitation. I am an accomplice of the privileged classes and compromised by this connexion; that is the reason why living through the Algerian war was like experiencing a personal tragedy. When one lives in an unjust world there is no use hoping by some means to purify

1. There are left-wing millionaires in South America.

oneself of that injustice; the only solution would be to change the whole world, and I don't have that power. To suffer from these contradictions serves no good purpose; to blind oneself to them is mere self-deception. On this point too, since I have no solution, I trust to my mood of the moment. But the consequence of my attitude is that I live in what approaches isolation; my objective condition cuts me off from the proletariat, and the way in which I experience it subjectively makes me an enemy of the middle classes. This relatively monastic life suits me quite well because I am always short of time; but it does deprive me of a certain warmth – which I was able to re-experience with such joy during the demonstrations of the past few years – and also, a more serious matter for me, it sets limits to my experience.

To these mutilations of my life, which are only the reverse aspect of my good fortune, must be added another for which I can discern no compensation. Since 1944, the most important, the most irreparable thing that has happened to me is that – like Zazie – I have grown old. That means a great many things. To begin with, that the world around me has changed: it has become smaller and narrower. I can no longer forget that the surface of the earth is finite, finite the number of its inhabitants, of its different plants and animal species, finite too the books, the pictures and the monuments set there. Each element of it can be explained with relation to that whole and refers back only to it; its richness too is limited. When young, Sartre and I often used to meet 'personalities on a higher level than our own', which meant that they were impervious to our powers of analysis and so were still endowed in our eyes with some of the magical prestige of childhood. This core of mystery is now dissolved. There are no more oddities, madness is no longer holy, crowds have lost the power to intoxicate me; youth, which once fascinated me, seems now no more than a prelude to maturity. Reality still interests me, but it no longer reveals itself like an awful lightning flash. Beauty yes, beauty remains; even though it no longer stuns me with its revelations, even though most of its secrets have gone flat, there are still moments when it can make time stop. But often I loathe it too. The evening after a massacre, I was listening to a Beethoven *andante* and stopped the record halfway through in anger: all the pain of the world was there, but so magnificently sublimated and controlled that it seemed justified. Almost all beautiful works have been created for the privileged and by privileged people who, even if they have suffered, have always had the possibility of expressing their sufferings; they are disguising the horror of misery in its nakedness.[1] Another evening, after another massacre – there have been so many – I longed for all such lying beauty to be utterly destroyed. Today, that feeling of horror has died down. I can listen to Beethoven. But neither he nor anyone else will ever again be able to give me that feeling I used to have of having reached some absolute.

For now I know the truth of the human condition: two thirds of mankind are hungry. My species is two thirds composed of worms, too weak ever to rebel, who drag their way from birth to death through a perpetual dusk of despair. In my dreams, ever since my youth, there are objects that have always recurred, in appearance inert, but receptacles of suffering: the hands of a watch that begin to race, no longer moved by a mechanism but by a secret and appalling organic disorder; a piece of wood bleeds beneath the blow of the axe, in a moment a disgustingly mutilated being will be discovered beneath the woody carapace. I feel the terror of these nightmares in my waking hours, if I call to mind the walking skeletons of Calcutta or those little gourds with human faces – children suffering from malnutrition. That is the only point at which I touch infinity: it is the absence of everything, with consciousness. They will die, and that is all that will have happened. The void frightens me less than misery made absolute.

I no longer have much desire to go travelling over this earth emptied of its marvels; there is nothing to expect if one does not expect everything. But I should very much like to know the sequel to our story. The young of today are simply future adults, but I am interested in them; the future is in their hands, and if in their schemes I recognize my own, then I feel that my life will be prolonged after I am in the grave: I enjoy being with them; and yet the comfort they bring me is equivocal: they perpetuate our world, and in doing so they steal it from me. Mycenae will be

1. Popular art and certain works that I should qualify as 'untamed' constitute exceptions to this rule; for example, I have heard the chant of a rabbi for the dead at Auschwitz, and another sung by a Jewish child telling the story of a pogrom. And yet, even in these cases, the very fact that relief has been sought in communication already tends to place one at a remove from the horror, which is, by definition, evil's absolute irrecoverability.

theirs, Provence and Rembrandt, and all the *piazze* of Rome. Oh, the superiority of being alive! All the eyes that rested before mine on the Acropolis seem to me already to have sunk into the abyss. In the eyes of those twenty-year-olds, I see myself already dead and mummified.

But whom do I see thus? To grow old is to set limits on oneself, to shrink. I have fought always not to let them label me; but I have not been able to prevent the years from enmeshing me. I shall live for a long time in this little landscape where my life has come to rest. I shall remain faithful to the old friendships; my stock of memories, even if there are some additions still to come, will stay as it is now. I have written certain books, not others. And at this point, suddenly, I feel strangely disconcerted. I have lived stretched out towards the future, and now I am recapitulating, looking back over the past. It's as though the present somehow got left out. For years I thought my work still lay ahead, and now I find it is behind me: there was no moment when it took place. It's a bit like the number in mathematics which has no place in either of the two series it separates. I was learning all the time so that one day I could put my store of knowledge to good use. I have forgotten an enormous amount, and for all that still floats on the surface of my memory I can see no possible use. As I retrace the story of my past, it seems as though I was always just approaching or just beyond something that never actually was accomplished. Only my emotions seem to have given me the experience of fulfilment.

The writer nevertheless has the good fortune to be able to escape his own petrifaction at the moments when he is writing. Every time I start on a new book, I am a beginner again. I doubt myself, I grow discouraged, all the work accomplished in the past is as though it never was, my first drafts are so shapeless that it seems impossible to go on with the attempt at all, right up until the moment – always imperceptible, there, too, there is a break – when it has become impossible not to finish it. Each page, each sentence, makes a fresh demand on the powers of invention and requires an unprecedented choice. Creation is adventure, it is youth and liberty.

But then, once my worktable is left behind, time past closes its ranks behind me. I have other things that I must think; suddenly I collide again with my age. That ultra-mature woman is my contemporary. I recognize that young girl's face belatedly lingering amid the withered features. That hoary-headed gentleman, who looks like one of my great-uncles, tells me with a smile that we used to play together in the gardens of the Luxembourg. 'You remind me of my mother,' I am told by a woman of about thirty or so. At every turn the truth jumps out at me, and I find it hard to understand by what trick it manages to attack me thus from the outside when it lives inside me all the time.

Old age. From a distance you take it to be an institution; but they are all young, these people who suddenly find that they are old. One day I said to myself: 'I'm forty!' By the time I recovered from the shock of that discovery I had reached fifty. The stupor that seized me then has not left me yet.

I can't get around to believing it. When I read in print Simone de Beauvoir, it is a young woman they are telling me about, and who happens to be me. Often in my sleep I dream that in a dream I'm fifty-four, I wake and find I'm only thirty. 'What a terrible nightmare I had!' says the young woman who thinks she's awake. Sometimes, too, just before I come back to reality, a giant beast settles on my breast: 'It's true! It's my nightmare of being more than fifty that's come true!' How is it that time, which has no form nor substance, can crush me with so huge a weight that I can no longer breathe? How can something that doesn't exist, the future, so implacably calculated its course? My seventy-second birthday is now as close as the Liberation Day that happened yesterday.

To convince myself of this, I have but to stand and face my mirror. I thought, one day when I was forty: 'Deep in that looking glass, old age is watching and waiting for me; and it's inevitable, one day she'll get me.' She's got me now. I often stop, flabbergasted, at the sight of this incredible thing that serves me as a face. I understand La Castiglione, who had every mirror smashed. I had the impression once of caring very little what sort of figure I cut. In much the same way, people who enjoy good health and always have enough to eat never give their stomachs a thought. While I was able to look at my face without displeasure I gave it no thought, it could look after itself. The wheel eventually stops. I loathe my appearance now: the eyebrows slipping down towards the eyes, the bags underneath, the excessive fullness of the cheeks, and that air of sadness around the mouth that wrinkles always bring. Perhaps the people I pass in the street see merely a woman in her fifties who simply looks her age, no more, no less. But when I look, I see my face as it was, attacked by the pox of time for which there is no cure.

My heart too has been infected by it. I have lost my old power to separate the shadows from the light, to pay the price of the tornadoes and still make sure I had the radiance of clear skies between. My powers of revolt are dimmed now by the imminence of my end and the fatality of the deteriorations that troop before it; but my joys have paled as well. Death is no longer a brutal event in the far distance; it haunts my sleep. Awake, I sense its shadow between the world and me: it has already begun. That is what I had never foreseen: it begins early and it erodes. Perhaps it will finish its task without much pain, everything having been stripped from me so completely that this presence I have so longed to retain, my own, will one day not be present anywhere, not be, and allow itself to be swept away with indifference. One after the other, thread by thread, they have been worn through, the bonds that hold me to this earth, and they are giving way now, or soon will.

Yes, the moment has come to say: Never again! It is not I who am saying good-bye to all those things I once enjoyed, it is they who are leaving me; the mountain paths disdain my feet. Never again shall I collapse, drunk with fatigue, into the smell of hay. Never again shall I slide down through the solitary morning snows. Never again a man. Now, not my body alone but my imagination too has accepted that. In spite of everything, it's strange not to be a body any more. There are moments when the oddness of it, because it's so definitive, chills my blood. But what hurts more than all these deprivations is never feeling any new desires: they wither before they can be born in this rarefied climate I inhabit now. Once, the days slipped by with no sense of haste. I was going even faster than they, drawn into the future by all my plans. Now, the hours are all too short as they whirl me on in the last furious gallop to the tomb. I try not to think: In ten years, in a year. Memories grow thin, myths crack and peel, projects rot in the bud; I am here, and around me circumstances. If this silence is to last, how long it seems, my short future!

And what threats it includes! The only thing that can happen now at the same time new and important is misfortune. Either I shall see Sartre dead, or I shall die before him. It is appalling not to be there to console someone for the pain you cause by leaving him. It is appalling that he should abandon you and then not speak to you again. Unless I am blessed by a most improbable piece of good fortune, one of these fates is to be mine. Sometimes I want to finish it al¹ quickly so as to shorten the dread of waiting.

Yet I loathe the thought of annihilating myself quite as much now as I ever did. I think with sadness of all the books I've read, all the places I've seen, all the knowledge I've amassed and that will be no more. All the music, all the paintings, all the culture, so many places: and suddenly nothing. They made no honey, those things, they can provide no one with any nourishment. At the most, if my books are still read, the reader will think: There wasn't much she didn't see! But that unique sum of things, the experience that I lived, with all its order and its randomness – the Opera of Peking, the arena of Huelva, the *candomblé* in Bahía, the dunes of El-Oued, Wabansia Avenue, the dawns in Provence, Tiryns, Castro talking to five hundred thousand Cubans, a sulphur sky over a sea of clouds, the purple holly, the white nights of Leningrad, the bells of the Liberation, an orange moon over the Piraeus, a red sun rising over the desert, Torcello, Rome, all the things I've talked about, others I have left unspoken – there is no place where it will all live again. If it had at least enriched the earth; if it had given birth to . . . what? A hill? A rocket? But no. Nothing will have taken place, I can still see the hedge of hazel trees flurried by the wind and the promises with which I fed my beating heart while I stood gazing at the gold-mine at my feet: a whole life to live. The promises have all been kept. And yet, turning an incredulous gaze towards that young and credulous girl, I realize with stupor how much I was gypped.

June 1960 – March 1963

Abbane, 609

Abbas, Ferhat, 353, 589, 596

Acheson, Dean, 264

Action, 16, 37, 51, 52, 59, 79, 140, 160, 201

Adamov, 82, 91, 335, 405, 413, 450–51, 619–20

Adenauer, Konrad, 310

Adhemar, 538

Africa, visits to, 63–8, 173–5, 192–4, 215–35, 311–14

Ahmed, Aït, 603

Ailleret, General, 618

Alain, 12

Algeria, visits to, 68, 173–5, 194, 215–19

Algren, Nelson, 133–5, 144–6, 164–71, 173, 175–7, 188–95, 197–8, 207, 236–41, 244, 256–7, 261–2, 266, 386, 505–10, 513, 520–22, 661

Alicata, 368, 612

Aliquié, 52, 92

Alleg, Henri, 396

All Men are Mortal, 21, 62, 70–75, 130, 166, 266, 274, 277, 494

Altmann, 81, 156–7, 182, 185–6, 187

Amado, Jorge, 337, 499, 524, 527–31, 533–6, 543–52, 556, 562, 564, 567–9, 572, 582

Amado, Zelia, 527, 532, 543–6, 550–51, 562, 569, 571–2, 582

Amazonia, visit to, 575–9

America, visits to, 131–7, 144–6, 164–7, 169–71, 237–41, 261–2, 311–14, 504–5

America Day by Day, 132, 134, 145n., 172, 196, 338, 359, 430, 490

Ansermet, Ernst, 86, 100

Antelme, 562

Apteckman, 407–8, 414

Aragon, 17, 19, 26, 81, 90, 182, 213–14, 302, 375, 477, 492, 590

Araraquara, visit to, 556–8

Arbenz, 316

Arcocha, 501, 583, 639

Arnaud, George, 513–15

Arnault, 592

Aron, Raymond, 17, 18, 22, 45, 55, 77, 82, 86, 92, 102, 116, 147, 211

Assailly, Gisèle d', 247

Astier, d', 318, 351, 458

Astruc, Gabriel, 17, 69–70, 152

Audin, 392, 481, 483, 513, 514

Audry, Colette, 28, 178, 201, 246, 361, 512, 625

Audry, Jacqueline, 318

Auriol, 408

Badel, 23

Badiou, 156, 456

Bahia, visit to, 527–36

Baker, Josephine, 479

Balachova, 99

Bamako, visit to, 230–33

Bandinelli, 110, 612

Baragagno, 502

Barbezat, Olga, 38, 86

Bardèche, 162

Barrault, Jean-Louis, 122, 159, 187, 249

Barron, Marie-Louise, 200

Bastide, Roger, 529

Bataille, Georges, 70

Bataille, Laurence, 519

Batista, 265, 391, 474, 555

Battesi, M., 561

Baudin, Lucienne, 255–6, 268

Beaufret, 52

Beaumont, Pastor, 481n.

Beauvilard, Michelle, 603

Beckett, Samuel, 310

Beer, 122

Behan, Brendan, 506
Belden, 336
Belém, visit to, 575–6, 582
Belgium, visit to, 593–5
Belgrade, visit to, 306–7, 363
Belhadj, 471
Bellon, Loleh, 39, 208
Bellounis, 442
Beloeil, Commissioner, 471
Ben Bella, 371, 377
Benda, Julien, 63
Bénichou, 411
Ben Kheddah, 552, 609, 617
Ben Mihidi, Larbi, 380
Bénouville, 147
Benson, Nelly, 134
Bérard, Christian, 79, 187, 245
Beria, 310
Berlin, visit to, 153–5
Bernard, Tristan, 409
Berriau, Simone, 122, 129, 160, 163,
    247–8, 249, 251–3, 263, 333,
    437, 462, 464–5, 484
Berthoin, 451
Besse, Guy, 354
Beuve-Méry, 185, 242, 417, 514
Bidault, Georges, 36, 139, 315, 399
Bienvenuda, 344
Billoux, 355
Billy, André, 94, 327
Blanchot, 52n.
Blin, Roger, 38
Blood of Others, The, 20, 44–5, 71,
    91, 130, 201, 266, 278, 282
Blum, Suzanne, 208, 327
Bobo-Dioulasso, visit to, 227–9
Boegner, Pastor, 469
Boideffre, 198
Bonafé, 147
Boniface, M., 303
Borg, Ariane, 37, 208
Bost, 24, 25, 26, 40, 59, 61, 62, 68,
    79, 80, 81, 83–4, 86, 87, 89,
    90–95, 116, 141, 161, 163, 174,
    178, 189, 190, 194, 200n., 246,
    250, 253, 263, 265, 266, 269, 291,
    298, 299, 318, 327, 378, 400, 403,
    407, 409, 413–14, 452, 478, 483,
    487, 491, 496, 505–8, 518, 575,

586, 600, 614, 616, 620, 634
Bost, Olga, 23, 25, 38, 61, 62,
    68–70, 81, 84, 85, 89, 92, 95–6,
    131, 141, 163, 189, 194, 208, 246,
    249–50, 253, 256, 262, 265, 266,
    298, 318, 327, 407, 409, 413, 491,
    505–8, 590, 599, 614, 616, 620
Boubal, 79, 82, 191, 460
Bouches Inutiles, Les, 23, 26, 46,
    56–59, 70, 136
Boudot, 379
Bouhired, Djamila, see Boupacha,
    Djamila
Bouissounouse, Jeanine, 110
Boulahrouf, 622
Boulez, Pierre, 591
Boumaza, 471, 603, 613, 614
Boumendjel, 340, 380
Bounoumi, Mme, 333
Boupacha, Djamila, 381, 513–18,
    591, 618, 628
Bourdet, 148, 157, 162, 179–81,
    185, 187, 214, 235, 330, 351, 401,
    420, 458–9, 602, 622–3
Bourguiba, 303, 341
Boutang, 51, 162
Boutbien, 156
Boyer, Charles, 179
Bradley, General, 214
Braga, Rubem, 530, 546, 552
Brandel, 249
Brandys, 625, 657
Brasília, visit to, 564–72
Brasillach, 28–30, 163, 660
Brasseur, Lina, 251–2
Brasseur, Pierre, 249–52, 298–9,
    310, 361
Brazil, visit to, 522–59, 562–82
Brecht, Berthold, 316, 335, 347n.,
    400, 643
Breitbourd, 640, 644, 653
Bresson, Robert, 17, 246, 487
Breton, 42, 90, 126, 148, 180, 214
Brianchon, 247
Brinon, 163
Brisson, 26, 242
Bruckberger, Father, 17
Bruguier, Maître, 395
Bruneval, 139

Bulganin, Nikolai, 332–3
Butor, 636–7

Calder, 127
Caldwell, Erskine, 20, 189
Camus, Albert, 12, 16, 17, 22,
    24–30, 37, 39, 45, 53, 56, 60–61,
    68, 75, 93, 115–21, 138, 141,
    148–50, 162, 180, 181, 187, 200,
    207, 214, 243, 252–3, 264,
    271–2, 280, 281, 328, 354, 362,
    377, 396, 470, 492, 496–7, 643
Camus, Francine, 25, 118, 149, 243
Capitant, 340, 380
Capote, Truman, 387
Capri, Agnès, 151, 206
Capri, visit to, 389–90, 445–7
Carbillet, Colonel, 67
Caron, Leslie, 187
Carpentier, Alejo, 575
Carral, Evelyne, 25
Cartier-Bresson, 316, 336
Casarès, Maria, 60, 249, 252–3
Cassou, 235
Castille, 378
Castries, Colonel de, 315
Castro, Fidel, 391, 474, 499–503,
    585–6, 639
Castro, Josué de, 358, 547
Catroux, 350
Cau, Jean, 101–2, 178, 190, 197,
    251–2, 263, 291, 318, 326, 618
Cavalcade, 94
Cayatte, André, 486–7, 497
Cazalis, Anne-Marie, 138, 151–2,
    189, 191, 634
Chabrol, Claude, 478
Chamaco, 342
Chambure, 263
Chamson, 85
Chanderli, 504
Chaplin, Charles, 22, 298, 361
Chapsal, 405, 417
Charbonnier, Captain, 513
Chauffard, 38, 39, 99–100, 121, 208,
    252, 335, 405
Chauvin, 616
Chazot, Jacques, 477
Che Guevara, 502, 520, 583

Chehkal, Ali, 392–5
Chevalier, Maurice, 247
Cheyney, Peter, 20, 30
Chiang Kai-shek, 209, 265
Chicago, visits to, 134–5, 145, 165
    237–41
China, visit to, 389–90, 445–7
Chonez, Claudine, 154, 196, 458,
    592
Clavel, 423
Clo, Mme, 299
Clouzot, Georges, 208, 244, 445
Clouzot, Vera, 244, 445
Cocteau, Jean, 100, 161, 187, 206,
    247–8, 410, 493
Colette, 247–8, 660
Combat, 12, 16, 24, 28, 37, 39, 46,
    60, 81, 82, 87, 116, 138, 157, 185,
    201, 214, 242, 281, 423
Connolly, Cyril, 26
Copacabana, visit to, 539, 542
Corniglion-Molinier, 17
Corre, Abbé, 628
Costa, Lucio, 523, 540, 546, 569
Coste-Floret, 139
Coty, 404–405, 407, 408
Courtade, 52, 355–6
Crete, visit to, 522
Cuba, visits to, 500–504, 582–6
Cuny, 121

Daix, 213
Dakar, visit to, 233–4
Dalmas, 235
Daniel, Jean, 391, 417
Darfeuil, Colette, 246
David, Jean-Paul, 264
Davis, Gary, 180, 186, 209, 271, 417
Davos, visit to, 387
Debré, 510
Deharme, Lise, 18, 60, 68, 131,
    239–41, 257
Delannoy, 434
Delorme, Danièle, 457
Delouvrier, M., 468–9
Denner, 208
Depestre, Edith, 585–6
Derogy, 512
Dery, Tibor, 356, 391

Desanti, 339
Desmarets, Sophie, 90
Desnos, Robert, 41
Diaz, M., 523
Di Cavalcanti, 523, 546
Dimitrov, 184
Domarchi, 236
Domenach, 197, 235, 581
Donnini, 110
Dorosh, 649–50
Dorticós, 474
Dos Passos, 386
Douking, 23
Duchamp, Marcel, 93, 636
Duclos, 273
Duhamel, Marcel, 20, 25
Dulles, Allen, 358, 600
Dulles, John Foster, 474
Dullin, 20, 25, 37, 70, 88, 159,
    207–8, 266
Dullin, Camille, 25, 207–8, 266
Dumas, Roland, 588
Dumont, René, 358
Dunham, Katherine, 187
Dupont, Frédéric, 627
Duras, Marguerite, 562
Dutourd, 492

Eaubonne, Francoise d', 455, 458
Eden, Anthony, 372
Edinburgh, visit to, 260
Ehrenburg, Ilya, 123, 310, 317–18,
    338, 339, 377, 478, 640, 641, 651,
    653
Eisenhower, Dwight D., 242, 264,
    273n., 478, 484, 511
Eluard, Paul, 105, 363
Erval, 178
Escalante, Aníbal, 639
Ethics of Ambiguity, The, 75–6, 80
Expérience vécue, L', see *Second
    Sex, The*

Fadeev, 182
Fancis, 471
Fanon, 597, 605–11, 620–22
Farrugia, 482
Fauchery, 84
Faulkner, William, 386

Faure, Edgar, 247, 329, 349
Faux, Claude, 618, 620, 625–6
Fechoz, 378
Fedin, 316, 337, 647, 653
Fejto, 374
Fellini, Federico, 334, 388, 438
Feltin, Mgr, 469
Femme et les mythes, La, 177
Ferry, Jean, 86
Figaro littéraire, Le, 94, 197
Fischer, Louis, 182
Flandin, 162
Flon, Suzanne, 416, 423
Forrestal, 179
Fortaleza, visit to, 572
Fortini, 104
Fougeron, 183
Franck, Bernard, 494
Franco, Francisco, 32–3, 36, 209,
    265, 321, 331
Francotte, Senator, 454
Frank, Waldo, 505
Franqui, 499, 583
Freud, Lucien, 260
Freud, Sigmund, 441–3
Frey, 614–15
Freyre, 523, 525
Frogier, 378

Gaillard, 399
Galard, Geneviève de, 315
Gallimard family, 20, 24, 43, 57, 60,
    69–70, 85, 87, 89, 125, 130, 177,
    178, 189, 195, 204, 207, 247, 311,
    327, 336, 402, 424, 459, 492, 511,
    589
Gao, visit to, 225–6
Garaudy, 51, 140, 359, 624
Garfield, John, 236
Gary, Romain, 17
Gasperi, 157
Gatti, 440
Gau, Abbé, 340
Gaulle, Charles de, 52, 115, 139,
    146–7, 150, 172, 399–411,
    416–22, 425, 434–5, 437–8, 440,
    448–9, 453–4, 464, 468, 470, 481,
    483, 515, 592, 597, 601, 612, 617,
    624

Gauthier, M., 513–14
Gazier, 148
Gégé, 405
Genet, 11, 27, 59, 83, 85, 87, 103, 129, 138, 141, 187, 204, 207, 209–10, 242, 248, 253, 263, 328n., 450, 455
Geneva, visit to, 96–7
Gengenbach, Abbé, 126
Gennari, 425
Gérard, Rosemonde, 207
Gerher, Cardinal, 470
Giacometti, 79, 80, 82, 84, 90, 94–5, 100, 175, 196, 245, 602, 624, 636
Gijon, 342
Gillois, André, 244
Gilson, 185, 242
Giroud, Françoise, 333, 417
Godemant, 622
Gomulka, 369–70, 376
Gorz, 100, 389, 420, 590
Goytisolo, 507–10, 590
Gracq, Julien, 196
Gramsci, 112
Greco, Juliette, 189, 194, 381
Greece, visits to, 363–4, 520, 522
Greene, Graham, 20, 30
Grenier, Roger, 89
Grimaud, 84
Grosjean, Abbé, 103
Guérin, Daniel, 182, 562
Guerman, 651
Guerroudi, Jacqueline, 395
Guevara, 502, 520, 583
Guillemin, 273, 404
Guillen, Catherine Varlin, 339
Guillen, Nicolas, 337, 545, 584
Guitton, Jean, 198, 660
Guitry, Sacha, 162, 171–2
Gurvitch, 331
Guth, Paul, 94
Guttoso, 110, 368, 371, 492
Guyonnet, 178, 190
Guyot, Raymond, 400

Hached, Ferhat, 303
Haedens, Kléber, 326

Halimi, Gisèle, 457, 459, 462, 471, 513, 515–18, 618, 620, 628
Hassine, Amour, 192–3
Hébertot, 122
Heidegger, 13, 16, 301
Heifitz, 651
Helsinki, visit to, 336–40
Hemingway, Ernest, 20, 23–4, 310, 342, 386–7, 502
Herbart, Pierre, 46, 416
Herbaud, 152, 266, 466
Hériat, Philippe, 59
Hermantier, 249–50
Hervé, 16, 52, 148, 302, 354
Hikmet, Hazim, 403
Hillary, Richard, 20
Hippolyte, 624
Hitler, Adolf, 11, 35, 310
Hlasko, 426
Ho Chi-minh, 139, 214, 309, 314
Holden, Roberto, 608
Holland, visits to, 126–7, 296, 308
Hoog, Armand, 198
Hook, Sydney, 186
Huston, John, 334, 416, 423, 486

Iceland, visit to, 258–9
Idir, Aïssat, 481
Invitée, L', 45, 70, 71, 74n., 199, 266, 275, 283, 428, 665
Istanbul, visit to, 520–21
Italy, visits to, 104–13, 191–2, 291–4, 304–5, 360, 364–70, 388–90, 425–48, 479–80, 604–12
Izard, 148, 156

Jaeger, 361–2
Jango, 611
Jaurès, 30, 660
Jausion, 18
Jeanson, Colette, 330
Jeanson, Francis, 202, 271, 330, 382–3, 472, 504, 513, 559–62, 581, 588, 607
Jeanson, Henri, 123, 178, 251–2
Jiménez, 502, 585–6
Joliot-Curie, 157, 185
Jouhandeau, 27
Jouvet, Louis, 138, 249, 252

Juin, Marshal, 341, 587
Julien, Claude, 424
Julliard, René, 178, 492
Jusquin, 455, 457

Kaan, Pierre, 41
Kádár, 371
Kaganovitch, 369
Kahn, Émile, 393
Kanapa, 51, 115, 160, 183, 211, 213
Kanters, Robert, 23
Kasavubu, 596
Kemp, 253
Kennedy, John F., 331
Khebaïli, 471
Khrushchev, Nikita, 333, 355–6, 369, 373, 484, 492, 510–11, 617n., 645, 646, 650
Khrushchev, Nina, 510
Klossovski, 477
Knout, Betty, 156
Kochno, Boris, 187
Koestler, Arthur, 26, 81, 97, 115, 118–20, 149–51, 236
Koestler, Mamaine, 118–19, 138, 149–50, 260
Koethly, A., 371
Korène, Vera, 484–5
Korneychuk, 640, 652
Kott, Jan, 377, 657
Kravchenko, 183, 210
Kubitschek, 538, 549, 555, 566–9, 571

Laage, Barbara, 206
Labarthe, André, 17
Labisse, 252
La Bollardière, General de, 381
Lacheroy, Colonel, 215n.
Lacoste, 350, 372, 391
Lacour, Doctor, 514
Laffont, 178
Lafaurie, Serge, 590
Lagaillarde, 400, 419
Lainier, Christiane, 38
Lallemande, 593–4, 633–4
Lange, Monique, 507–9
Lanzmann, Claude, 263–4, 291, 294–314, 316, 318, 321–2,

325–7, 330, 332, 334, 341–4, 356, 359, 362, 364, 371, 373–5, 378, 381–2, 387, 390, 394, 398, 400–4, 410, 412, 428, 434, 436–7, 440, 444, 447, 448–52, 454–6, 460, 473, 479–80, 487, 491, 493, 496, 505, 507, 511, 514, 559, 562, 579–81, 587, 590, 596–8, 602, 606, 613–17, 619–23, 625, 629–33
Lanzmann, Jacques, 334, 411, 415, 424–5, 507
Lapland, visit to, 143
La Pouèze, 23, 44, 153
Laurent, Jacques, 331, 378
Lausanne, visit to, 100
Lazareff, 152, 252
Leclerc, Guy, 140
Leduc, Victor, 632, 638
Leduc, Violette, 27, 150, 335–6
Lefèvre-Pontalis, 61, 79, 81, 83, 88, 89, 147, 178, 405, 417–18, 498, 616
Lefort, 178, 301
Léger, 42, 207
Le Hardouin, Marie, 519
Leibowitz, René, 42, 100
Leiris, Michel, 22, 42, 52n., 55, 79, 87, 88, 94, 103, 130, 177, 196, 215, 404, 465
Lejeune. Max, 372
Lemaire, Mme, 22, 38, 153, 204, 266, 635
Lemarchand, Jacques, 59, 141
Le Meur, Jean, 519
Leningrad, visit to, 650–53
Leonov, Leonid, 492–6
Lestienne, 411, 415
Lettres françaises, Les, 16, 17, 140, 183, 200, 326
Leuliette, 379
Levi, Carlo, 107–8, 181, 192, 316, 347, 368, 446, 612
Lévi-Strauss, 177, 203, 358, 408–9, 575
Lhote, Henri, 220–21
Limbour, 87
Lissowski, 377, 384, 655
Litri, 343

Littéraire (*Le Figaro littéraire*), 94
London, visits to, 260, 360
Long March, The, 202, 344n.,
  358–9, 490
Lott, Marshal, 538, 549, 555, 579
Luguet, 160–61
Lukács, 183, 337
Lumumba, 596, 609
Luter, Claude, 137n., 194
Lysenko, 182

Mabille, Pierre, 456
Macaigne, Pierre, 469
MacArthur, General, 242, 244, 256,
  264
McCullers, Carson, 387
Madaule, 457
Madrid, visits to, 31–2, 344, 500
Magnane, 160
Magnani, Anna, 371
Maillot, Lieutenant, 350–51
Malenkov, 302, 310, 332–3
Malester, 371, 428–30
Mallet, 467
Mallet-Joris, Françoise, 592
Malraux, 20, 22, 39, 51, 82–3, 87,
  103, 178, 330, 331, 333, 373, 405,
  416, 422, 425, 438, 440, 449, 470,
  472, 480–81, 522
Malraux, Florence, 590
Mandarins, The, 74, 133, 135, 167,
  213n., 237, 268, 274–86, 301, 311,
  314, 326, 329, 332, 338, 339, 361,
  383, 429, 432, 435, 454, 455, 458,
  459, 488, 505, 511–12, 640, 659
Mandouze, 351
Mao Tse-tung, 179, 189, 214, 362
Marceau-Pivert, 148
Marcel, Gabriel, 45, 75, 242n., 301
Marco, 153
Marr, Dora, 42
Marrou, 351
Martin, Claude, 208
Martin, Henri, 272, 301
Martin-Chauffier, 392
Martinet, 300, 373–4
Marty, 302
Marzoli, Mme, 104, 106
Mascolo, 87

Maspero, 515
Massignon, 394
Massin, Jean, 247
Massini, Paula, 368
Masson, André, 590–91, 602, 615,
  619, 628
Masson, Diégo, 519, 591, 628
Masson, Rose, 519, 591, 602, 615,
  628
Massu, 396
Mathiot, 454
Maublanc, 51
Maulnier, Thierry, 588
Mauriac, 16, 28, 162, 197, 200, 242,
  253, 302, 329n., 333, 400, 420,
  455, 590, 624, 664
Maurois, 492–3
Maurras, 162
Mayakovsky, 347
Memoirs of a Dutiful Daughter, The,
  285, 385, 402, 416, 425, 444, 456,
  475, 589, 659
Mende, Tibor, 358
Mendès-France, 39, 315, 323, 329,
  330, 407, 410, 415, 417, 454
Mènegos, 361–2
Meray, Tibor, 356
Merle, 206
Merleau-Ponty, 22, 52, 70, 79, 82,
  85, 94, 97, 115, 120, 140, 147,
  148, 156, 159, 178, 186, 196, 209,
  212–13, 242, 244, 247, 253, 264,
  270, 298, 300, 331–2, 441, 498,
  601, 604, 607
Mérode, Cléo de, 207–8
Merriam, Eve, 133
Messemer, 253, 361
Mexico, visit to, 168–9
Meyer, Jean, 33
Michel, Serge, 596
Mikoyan, 369, 371, 500
Milan, visits to, 104–6, 371–2,
  425–7
Mills, C. Wright, 603–4
Mindszenty, Cardinal, 184, 209, 371
Mirande, Yves, 163–4, 249, 484
Misrahi, 75, 155–6
Mitterand, 415
Moch, Jules, 179, 425

Mollet, Guy, 350, 351–3, 355, 372, 382, 401, 411, 434–5
Molotov, 139, 369
Mondadori, Arnaldo, 106, 107
Monnerot, 94
Montandon, 85, 90, 97
Montherlant, 162
Morane, Jacqueline, 56
Morante, Elsa, 446
Moravia, Alberto, 109, 368, 445, 611–12
Moreau, Yves, 208, 373
Morgan, Claude, 14, 375
Morihien, Paul, 92
Morocco, visit to, 234–5
Moscow, visits to, 346, 347–8, 640–650, 653–4, 657
Mougin, 51, 140
Mouloudji, 25, 38, 42, 104, 123, 151, 174, 191
Mounier, 180, 202, 235
Mounin, 94
Mourre, Michel, 235
Müller, 379
Munich, visit to, 323
Mussolini, Benito, 11, 105

Nabokov, Vladimir, 477
Nadeau, 202
Nagel, 87, 123, 130, 179, 291, 324
Nagy, Imre, 309, 333, 356, 370–72, 375, 376, 428–9, 443
Naples, visits to, 111, 192
Navarre, General, 314
Naville, 52, 354
Neizvestny, 645
Nekrasov, Victor, 648
Nenno, 113
Nero, 57–8, 94
Neruda, Pablo, 545
Newman, Mme Beuber, 184
New York, visits to, 131, 135, 165, 169–71, 504–5
Nezval, 324–5
Niemeyer, 540, 546–7, 562–3, 565–7
Nikolaeva, Galina, 590
Nimier, Roger, 183, 198

Nizan, Rirette, 41, 86, 213–14, 501, 511
Nkrumah, 597
Nocher, Jean, 103, 434
Norway, visit to, 257–8

Observateur, L', 214, 242, 302, 354, 420, 434, 438, 462, 482, 494, 602, 613, 621
Oliver, Maria Rosa, 337, 659n.
Olivier, Marie (Wanda), 62, 99n., 122, 160, 246, 249, 252, 253, 298
Ollivier, Albert, 22, 81, 82, 86, 116, 148
Oltuski, 503, 583, 586, 639
Oppenheimer, 316, 416
Orlova, 492
Ortega, 344
Orwell, Sonia, 260
Otero, 586

Pagliero, 141
Pagniez, 94, 142, 153, 204, 635
Paillat, 468n.
Palle, Albert, 17, 84, 415
Panigel, 630
Papon, M., 627
Parinaud, 494
Parlange, General, 468n.
Parmelin, Hélène, 376, 458
Parrain, Brice, 13, 660
Passeur, Mme Stève, 122
Pasternak, Boris, 473, 647
Patin, M., 516–18
Paulhan, Jean, 22, 82, 89, 125, 180, 248
Paustovsky, 641
Pauvert, 255
Pavese, 293, 335
Péju, 263, 302, 404, 408, 460, 514, 519, 559, 581, 596, 613, 617, 620
Péron, Alfred, 27, 41
Perrault, 354n.
Perrier, 161
Petit, Claudius, 615
Pevsner, Antoine, 435
Pflimlin, 399–400, 404–5
Philipe, Anne, 405, 591
Philipe, Gérard, 56, 159

Pia, 102
Picard, Yvonne, 41
Picasso, Pablo, 19, 22, 95, 99, 298, 636, 645
Pierre, Abbé, 311
Pignon, 458
Pineau, 351
Pingaud, 587, 635
Pleven, 242, 315
Plievier, 181, 187
Poland, visit to, 654–7
Politzer, 273
Ponge, Francis, 16, 17, 37, 79
Portugal, visit to, 33–6
Postel-Vinay, Anise, 515–18
Pouillon, 83, 92, 178, 197, 400, 408, 475–6, 586–7, 614–17, 635
Poujade, 352
Poulenc, 247
Pozner, 405
Prague, visit to, 324
Presle, Micheline, 141, 159
Prestes, 548
Prime of Life, The, 14n., 57n., 133, 134, 589, 593, 662, 665, 668
Pyrrhus et Cinéas, 20, 71, 75

Quadros, Jânio, 538, 573, 576, 579
Queneau, Raymond, 43, 68–9, 87, 88, 94–5, 103, 130, 187, 190, 206, 477

Radziewski, Marie-Claude, 598
Rafael, 584
Rajk, 355, 376
Rajk, Mme, 356
Rakosi, 309, 333, 370
Ramadier, 148
Recife, visits to, 526, 551, 582
Reggiani, 420, 430, 484–5
Reinhart, Max, 175, 486
Renard, Delphine, 630
Renoir, Jean, 261
Repacci, 368
Rey, Benoît, 598n., 629
Rey, Evelyne, 334–5, 361, 409, 413–15, 450, 514, 614, 616, 620
Rhee, Synghman, 265, 520
Ridgeway, Colonel, 273

Rigaud, Jean, 162
Rio de Janeiro, visit to, 539–52, 558, 562–3
Robbe-Grillet, Alain, 636–7
Robert, Marthe, 82
Robert, Yves, 457
Robichon, 241
Rochefort, Christiane, 198n., 478, 596, 644
Rodhain, Mgr, 468, 470n.
Rodriguez, Amalia, 508
Rogier, Senator, 396
Rokossovsky, 369
Rolland, G.-F., 17, 52, 80, 327, 375, 413, 416, 634
Romains, Jules, 208
Rome, visits to, 107–110, 191, 364–70, 388–9, 437–44, 479–80, 604–12
Roosevelt, Eleanor, 185, 186
Roosevelt, Franklin D., 41
Rops, Daniel, 253
Rosenberg, Harold, 505
Rosenfeld, 350
Rosenthal, 156
Rougemont, de, 477
Rouleau, Raymond, 23, 335, 359
Rous, Jean, 156
Rousset, David, 148, 156–7, 181, 185–6, 212–14
Roy, Claude, 52, 161, 375, 405, 411, 412, 562, 667
Roy, Jules, 91, 178
Rublov, 646

Sachs, Maurice, 28
Saddok, Ben, 392–5
Sagan, Françoise, 318, 476–7, 514, 643
Saint-Exupéry, 13, 643
Saint-Just, de, 477
Salacrou, 62, 78, 90, 122, 123n., 159, 208
Salan, 331, 400
Salazar, 12, 36, 265
Salengro, 30
Salinger, J. D., 387
Salzburg, visit to, 324
São Paolo, visit to, 552–6, 558

Sarraute, Nathalie, 27–8, 88, 283, 480, 635–7

Sartre, Jean-Paul, 12–16, 19, 20–27, 38, 41–4, 45–58, 60, 68, 70, 77–104, 106–7, 109, 113, 114, 116, 117, 119–24, 127, 129, 131, 134–8, 140–44, 147, 149–57, 159–62, 164, 171–4, 178–9, 181–4, 190, 195, 196, 203–12, 214–37, 241–6, 248–54, 257–61, 263–4, 267–74, 281, 286–8, 291–3, 296–303, 309, 314, 316–21, 323–9, 331–4, 336–40, 346–8, 351–2, 354, 358–9, 362–77, 380–82, 384, 389–90, 392–4, 396–9, 402–4, 409–20, 422, 425–48, 452, 455, 459–67 474–5, 479–81, 484–7, 492–3, 496, 498–504, 507, 510–11, 514–15, 518–19, 522–88, 590, 595, 597–602, 604–6, 610–12, 615–30, 633–5, 637–8, 640, 643–4, 647, 649–51, 653, 657–8, 659–64, 667, 669, 673

  Age of Reason, The, 20, 46, 201; Altona, 48, 484, 486–7, 640; Bariona, 14, 49; Being and Nothingness, 12, 15, 50, 51, 93, 101, 331; Communistes et la paix, Les, 293, 300, 301, 359; Critique de la raison dialectique, 384, 397, 487, 597; Dernier Touriste, Le, 389; Fantôme de Staline, Le, 210–11, 374, 375; Flies, The, 49, 70, 154, 208, 249, 254; Huis clos, 20, 56, 87, 98, 101, 114, 334; Last Chance, The, 184, 205; Lucifer and the Lord, 250–54, 263, 272; Mains sales, Les, 159–61, 179, 205; Morale, La, 86; Nausea, 48; Nékrassov, 333–4, 484; Presentation, 48; Reprieve, The, 20, 46; Respectful Prostitute, The, 122–4, 141, 165, 206, 377, 492; Roads of Freedom, The, 204; Sorcières de Salem, Les, 359; Troubled Sleep, 172, 184, 204–5; Victors, The, 121–3, 141, 160; What is Literature?, 140, 157, 635

Saurel, Renée, 88, 178, 334, 458

Sauvage, 505

Schumann, Robert, 148, 180

Schwartz, Laurent, 587, 592, 615–16, 618, 629–30

Schwartz-Bart, 493–6

Scipion, 17, 81, 110, 189–91, 253, 257, 327, 451, 634

Second Sex, The, 178, 184, 195–203, 207–8, 213, 266, 274, 298, 326, 332, 429, 488, 659

Seghers, Anna, 155, 316, 337

Sérant, 214

Servan-Schreiber, 380, 448, 492, 519

Sézenac, 329

Sicard, Solange, 84

Sicily, visit to, 388

Signoret, Simone, 246, 562

Silone, 109, 192, 236

Simon, Pierre-Henri, 380, 561

Simonov, 317, 320, 346, 348, 640, 649

Skira, Albert, 96–7, 99, 100

Slansky, 376

Smadja, 214

Sorbets, Mme, 201

Soro, 204

Souami, 471

Soupault, 94, 114

Soustelle, 22, 341n., 350, 399, 438, 471

Spain, visits to, 31–4, 321–3, 341–4, 500, 509–10, 586–7

Sperber, Manès, 119, 153

Spoleto, visit to, 436–7

Staël, Nicolas de, 361

Stalin, Josef, 112, 133, 149, 209, 213n., 235, 302, 338, 355, 478, 617n., 648

Stéphane, Roger, 82, 162, 178, 210, 214, 235, 244, 300, 351

Stern, Betty, 175, 507

Stern, Nora, 507

Stibbe, Ali, 392, 394, 457–9

Stil, André, 273, 351, 355, 373, 375

Sullivan, Vernon, 120

Surkov, 337, 640, 653

Suslov, 371

Suyin, Han, 461–2

Sweden, visit to, 143–4

Switzerland, visits to, 95–101, 387
Sybille, Mme, 368
Sylvia, Gaby, 23

Taleb, 395
Tarkovski, 644, 646
Temps Modernes, Les, 22, 26, 46,
  48, 51–3, 55–7, 60, 70, 76, 79,
  94, 102, 107, 109n., 120, 125, 140,
  147, 148, 154, 157, 177, 178, 179,
  185, 187, 195–7, 201, 203, 205,
  209, 210, 212, 242, 247, 255, 263,
  271–2, 274, 281, 294, 300, 301,
  303, 330, 334, 348n., 349, 352,
  354, 355, 375, 377, 380, 391, 398,
  467, 475, 481, 496, 505, 511, 519,
  575, 581, 596, 598, 603, 657
Terre des hommes, 46
Terrenoire, M., 562
Thao, Tran Duc, 210, 236
Thomas, Henri, 82
Thorez, 16, 52, 92, 115, 140, 355,
  519
Till, Emmet, 385
Tillon, Germaine, 394, 452, 515–16
Timbuktu, visit to, 226
Tito, Marshal, 104, 172, 189, 209,
  235, 305
Todd, 178
Togliatti, 109n., 321
Torrès, 147
Traven, B., 334–5
Trépel, Mireille, 187, 253
Triolet, Elsa, 17, 140, 160, 214, 316,
  347, 492–3
Trotsky, 178, 598
Truffaut, François, 479
Truman, Harry S., 214, 243
Tshombe, 596
Tubert, General, 394
Tunisia, visits to, 63–8, 192–4
Tzara, 82, 97, 405

Ulanova, 315
United States, *see* America
Union of Soviet Socialist Republics,
  visits to, 346, 347–8, 640–54
Urrutia, 474

Vailland, 375
Valde, 161
Valéra, 333
Vallentin, Antonina, 182, 247, 310
Vallès, Jules, 95
Vallon, Louis, 130, 187, 246, 340
Van Chi, 179, 181, 187, 351
Van Lennep, 127
Vargas, 537, 548, 556, 571
Vedrès, Nicole, 159
Veneziani, 104
Venice, visits to, 304, 363, 428–36
Vercors, 180, 339, 375, 377, 391
Verger, Pierre, 530, 533
Vergés, 481
Vermesch, Jeannette, 512
Vian, Boris, 68–9, 89, 93, 103, 120
  137–8, 151, 189–91, 235, 246, 270,
  479, 497
Vian, Michelle, 69, 190–91, 246, 250,
  270, 298, 311, 316, 321, 327, 362,
  364, 381, 507
Vibert, 121
Victor, Paul-Émile, 259
Vidal-Naquet, 518
Vigier, 617–18, 624
Vigorelli, 104–5
Vilar, 249, 252
Villefosse, Louis de, 110, 375
Vinogradov, 492
Vintenon, Francis, 84, 114, 329
Visconti, Luchino, 368
Vitold, 23, 38, 39, 43–4, 56, 60, 87,
  121–2, 249, 333
Vitrac, 151
Vittorini family, 104, 106
Vivaldo, 530–31, 537
Vivet, 89
Voiturin, M., 263
Voznesensky, 641–3, 647, 651
Vuillaume, 340n.

Wahl, 82, 498
Walberg, Patrick, 11, 19
Wassileska, Wanda, 652–3
Weil-Hallé, Doctor, 512–13
Weiss, Louise, 86
Welles, Orson, 20, 103
Wols, 248, 435

Wright, Richard, 20, 90, 131, 133,
    180, 181–2, 186, 361, 386, 601
Wurmser, 213, 355
Wybot, M., 471
Wylie, Philip, 198n.

Yevtushenko, 640, 641, 647, 651
Yucatan, visit to, 167
Yugoslavia, visits to, 305–7, 363

Yushkevitch, 644
Yveton, 380, 395

Zavrian, 481
Zette, 87, 130
Zonina, Lena, 640, 641, 646, 650
Zukov, 369
Zurich, visit to, 98–100